the SORROW of BELGIUM

To Jacques who may remember
Those years & his growing up.

with love from
Maman

Easter 1992

the

SORROW
of
BELGIUM

hugo claus

Translated from the Dutch by Arnold J. Pomerans

pantheon books • new york

Translation Copyright © 1990 by Random House, Inc.

Library of Congress Cataloging-in-Publication Data

Claus, Hugo, 1929–
[Verdriet van België. English]
The sorrow of Belgium / Hugo Claus : translated from the Dutch by
Arnold J. Pomerans.
p.   cm.
Translation of: Het verdriet van België.
ISBN 0-394-56263-1
1. World War, 1939–1945—Fiction. 2. Belgium—History—1914–
—Fiction. I. Title.
PT6410.C553V3613   1990
839.3' 1364—dc20   89-16177

This translation has been made possible in part through a grant
from the Wheatland Foundation.

Book Design by Anne Scatto

Manufactured in the United States of America

_____ *contents*

v

part two

OF BELGIUM
233

translator's note

The events in this book take place between 1939 and 1947, and cover the adolescent years of a young Flemish boy in Belgium. His hometown, called Walle in the book, is based on Kortrijk, or Courtrai, in the province of West Flanders. The two names, one Flemish, one French, illustrate the dichotomy that is Belgium.

Belgium is a country not much larger than Wales or Massachusetts, and has only been independent since 1830. It lies at the divide of the Germanic and Romance languages, the boundary between French-speaking Walloons in the south of the country and Flemish-speaking Flemings in the north having remained virtually unchanged since the Middle Ages. The land that became Belgium in 1830—known variously through the centuries as the Low Countries, Flanders, or Belgica—was first divided in this way in Frankish times, fifteen hundred years ago. The linguistic separation is now official and institutionalized and is reflected in all sectors of public life, including education, local government, and the law.

The French influence in Flanders, which had been present since medieval times, increased dramatically in the eighteenth century, and even more so after the French Revolution. By the time Belgium gained her independence from the Netherlands, following the revolution of 1830, Flemings had been made to feel second-class citizens in their own country. Power was concentrated in the hands of the upper classes, who spoke French whether they lived in Flemish or Walloon provinces. It was not surprising, therefore, that the nineteenth century saw the birth of the Flemish Movement, whose aim, after centuries of domination by the Romans, the Dukes of Burgundy, the Spanish, the Hapsburgs, and Napoleon, was to place Flemish on an equal footing with French in Belgium. Guido Gezelle, the Flemish priest and poet, was one of the founding fathers of this movement. By the early twentieth century it was being suggested that in order to bring about radical change it would be necessary to establish a Flemish-speaking élite.

The Catholic Church, to which over eighty percent of Belgians belong, was divided over the Flemish question, the hierarchy generally supporting Belgian unity, and the lower Flemish clergy supporting Flemish nationalism, or even the Great-Netherlands movement which considered Flanders to be part of a greater Dutch-speaking nation that included the Netherlands.

Between the two world wars the Flemish movement gained strength, as well as a certain mystical and religious appeal. The 1930s also saw the emergence of several fascist groups in Belgium—as elsewhere in Europe—which drew for support on social discontent and primitive chauvinism, not least among Flemish speakers. These groups included Rex, the Belgian Fascist Party, representing French-speaking fascists, and the Flemish VNV, Dinaso, and DEVLag parties. At the start of the Second World War, the Catholic Church, in general, supported a united Belgium, viewing the separatist Flemish movement with disfavor. During the German occupation of Belgium, the relatively few supporters of the various fascist groups, the most prominent of which came to be known as the Black Brigades, collaborated with the Germans, and were opposed by a strong Belgian Underground and Resistance movement which included the so-called White Brigades.

Today we use the term Flanders to mean the whole of Flemish-speaking Belgium (the provinces of West and East Flanders, Antwerp, Limburg, and part of Brabant). The people of Flanders speak Flemish, a variant of Dutch which is distinguished from the version spoken in the Netherlands by minor differences in accent and vocabulary only.

The strands of these linguistic differences, together with those of the various religious, cultural, and political differences, are woven into Hugo Claus's long novel. The speech of his Flemish characters is sprinkled with old-fashioned, sometimes archaic, words (which makes it High Flemish), with dialect (Low Flemish), and with a great many gallicisms. The irony in the use of so many French words and phrases by Flemish nationalists (the "Flamingants")—in direct contradiction to the scorn they express for the French-speaking Flemish élite (known as the "Franskiljons")—is pointed.

The task of the English translator in conveying the multilayered complexity of Hugo Claus's work has not been made easier by differences in current American and British usage. Settling on slang and idiomatic expressions acceptable and intelligible to both cultures has proved a hurdle too great to cross in some cases. The decision, in many instances, to adhere to British rather than American usage was taken in the belief that in this way the writing would retain a more European flavor. At the author's suggestion, moreover, a few words or short passages which might be obscure or confusing for English-speaking readers have been either omitted or clarified.

Arnold J. Pomerans

———————————————————*part one*

THE
SORROW

the visit

Dondeyne had hidden one of the seven Forbidden Books under his tunic and then coaxed Louis into coming along. They were sitting under the creepers in Bernadette Soubirous's grotto.

Dondeyne's Book was _ABC,_ a Socialist weekly that was sure to be on the Vatican Index, and which his brother had given him in the hospital. Dondeyne had been discharged with a bright-red ear, which he kept pulling on all the time. During the day the Book lay at the bottom of his wardrobe, behind his boots.

The four missing pages, glossy and smooth, though a little frayed at the edges, lay under the blue wrapping paper that lined the drawer of Dondeyne's desk. To make doubly sure, he had pinned the paper down with what they called _punaises,_ thumbtacks. ("Do you have to call them _punaises,_ " said Louis's Grandpa, "when we have a perfectly good Flemish word for them?" But Louis would never have used it, everybody already laughed enough at the way he spoke.)

The opened-out pages gleamed in the sunlight, unfortunately split down the middle by a shadow and a jagged tear. Louis would never have torn up any of his own Forbidden Books, not even under the most imminent threat of being found out. But Dondeyne was a Hottentot.

The four Apostles had seven Forbidden Books between them. Vlieghe had three: *Love in the Mist,* a program for the operetta *Rose Marie,* and, most dangerous of all, a biography of George Bernard Shaw, the heretic and Freemason. Byttebier had *Tales of the South Pacific* and a photograph of Deanna Durbin in a slip, shocking enough to be treated as a Book. Louis's Book might not have landed him in trouble even if it had been discovered by the Sisters, he could easily have kept it in the open among the well-thumbed, sweet-smelling books from the Davidsfonds, the Catholic book club, that he had brought back with him after the Easter holidays, but it had been a good feeling, hadn't it?, to smuggle a Forbidden Book wrapped in a nightshirt through the high walls of the Institute. It was called *The Flemish Banner,* Papa himself had bound it in reddish-brown cardboard. You could easily recognize Papa's binding by the way he sliced the edges perilously close to the text with the paper cutter. *The Flemish Banner* was about rebellious students in a seminary at the end of the last century who, spurred on by long-haired priests wearing pince-nez, had formed a secret society called The Silent Oath and had plotted together in the dead of night against the Belgian, that is anti-Flemish, ministers and bishops. Louis had stolen the book from the family bookcase because he had heard Papa say that when priests found this text in the possession of any parishioner, they threatened him then and there with excommunication from the Holy Church. When the other three Apostles had first set eyes on the unimportant-looking book with its faint, grayish print and lack of illustrations, they had not been very impressed. Only when Louis had, with wild exaggeration, evoked its origins, contents, and dangers did they acknowledge the wretched thing that night as a Forbidden Book, placing it beside the others on Byttebier's pillow, crossing themselves three times, and whispering, "Seek ye and look—in each black book—lest ye defame—the Virgin's name." No Forbidden Book could ever be read unless at least one other Apostle was present.

Dondeyne and Louis examined the blurred photographs of the radio operator's trial at the Bruges Court of Assizes. The victim's father, a broken figure with a white goatee and a forage cap, looked like the Russian Czar imploring Rasputin to save his hemophiliac son. The mother, an old crone challenging the murderer, who was out of the picture, with a myopic stare, had her black handbag raised as if about to either strike out with it or throw it, the lawyer's robe was the same sepia color as his curly hair, a photographer in a checked cap wielded his camera like an accordion with a gaping square hole, and then, and then, there was the radio operator himself, the criminal, who, according to the indictment, had buried his girlfriend alive in the dunes. He stood there smiling under a thick mustache, hands behind his back, stomach stuck out, because the photograph had, of course, been taken earlier, not at the moment of fear and trembling on the beach or later when it was time for remorse and nightmares.

"Alive in the sand," said Dondeyne. "And such a gorgeous girl, too!"

"How do you know?" asked Louis. "Maybe she was ugly or blind in one eye."

"Didn't you see her, then?" Dondeyne closed the paper, turned it over, and pointed to the front page, where a beautiful, smooth-skinned woman wrapped in silk or satin smiled out at the reader. Her pupils were the same pale orange as her indistinct lips. There was a vicious tear in the paper through the middle of her forehead.

"You Hottentot," Louis said wearily "That's a film star. There's her name there in big, fat letters, Wynne Gibson. The Socialists always put a film star on their front page."

"Oh, yes," said Dondeyne, but he did not believe a word. He caressed his translucent red ear.

"She was a monster," said Louis, "the radio operator's girlfriend. They didn't put it in the paper, but she asked for it. She ruined his life."

"*His* life?"

"Of course," said Louis.

"Girlfriend," said Dondeyne, "does that mean . . . ?"

"That they weren't married." Scooping out a hole in the sand and shoving the squirming, innocent woman into it had seemed right to him. Effective. Although "girlfriend"? That could just mean that the girl had been an acquaintance, a neighbor. Otherwise, why didn't they use "fiancée" or "lover" or that slippery, smutty, furtive word "mistress"?

Across Wynne Gibson's amber curls Louis read: March 31, 1935, Vol. 4, 1F.25.

"This *ABC* is four years old," he said.

"So what?"

"Wynne Gibson could have died in the meantime."

"No, we would have heard about it."

Who? Us? Dondeyne, you Hottentot! How could we have heard? In any case, who ever heard of Wynne Gibson?

In the music room the little ones were singing "Bayard the Steed" for the twelfth time.

Just as Louis was thinking fiercely, Apostle or no Apostle, I'm going to break all the rules and just grab the book from him and run off to the kitchen garden, Dondeyne passed him the *ABC*. "Look," he said, "just like Dobbelaere with his filthy pimples." A clumsily drawn girl was gazing in despair at a black dagger, or a sword, or an ebony ninepin. Then Louis realized that it must be a mirror, seen from the side. There were speckles and spots of black all over the girl's face. A woman with incredibly long fingers was poking at one of them on the girl's cheek. "A mother's advice," it read across the top.

"She knew that her mother had guessed her shameful secret. Open pores, blackheads, and a dirty, sallow complexion made her feel like an outcast. But she did not know what most mothers know, that a simple remedy can bring undreamed-of relief to many a young girl."

He handed the paper back to Dondeyne, who let it fall open across his grazed knees. What most mothers know! Nothing, that's what.

Then, while Dondeyne was reading aloud in the stilted High Flemish used on the Radio Walle news but with a touch of the singsong chant used for psalms at vespers: "A jar of our invigorating and invaluable, cleansing and astringent essences works like magic on the plainest-looking complexion. You will marvel at your newly discovered beauty," Sister Adam materialized from behind the thorn hedge. Louis was certain that in the instant before she had appeared he had heard her skirt rustle as it brushed against the thorns. She stopped briefly, arms folded so that the full sleeves fell across her stomach in the shape of a small black altar. Dondeyne saw her, too.

"Ow, ow, ow," he said. "There she is, I knew it." And then, in a squeaky voice, "I took two helpings of rice pudding, she saw me do it."

"When?"

"At supper, last night. And two helpings of brown sugar, she saw me do that too."

"You fathead," said Louis. "She's come for me." For he had seen Sister Adam's lips, lips that did not curve upward and laugh, no, indeed, but that *could* laugh whenever she was reminded that for tactical reasons she ought to laugh, to entice, to cajole, unctuously and shamelessly, and he saw that her face, that pale blob seared by the intense whiteness of her coif, that helmet of light, was turned toward him and him alone. The face took on color, drew near with its washed-out eyes and its square teeth.

"Louis," said Sister Adam, and stretched her long arm out of its black woolen sleeve, and the smell of the newly mown grass from the meadow behind Bernadette Soubirous's grotto wafted away, dispelled by something sweet, gingerbread, warm sugared dough, as she said "Louis" again.

"Yes," said Dondeyne, who was openly holding the fatal book in front of him. But Sister Adam only had eyes for her immediate prey and laid her hand on Louis's shoulder, near his neck, he could feel her thumb. He followed in her shadow, almost gratefully yielding himself up to her; the sun's radiance was more sumptuous than the golden brocade of a doge, softer than the velvet worn by the Count of Flanders when he set off to submit to the King of France. As he followed her past the avenue of yews, the thorn hedges, the poison-trees, she said that there were visitors and he did not ask who, as expected, and she said, "Come along, now," and he mouthed silently, "Come-aling-along." The dormitory was deserted, and in the washroom she rubbed his face with a wash-mitt, not his own but Den Dooven's, which had been put out to dry on a windowsill. Distantly, not hurriedly but not slowly either, she rubbed away as if she were scouring a pan, and his face tingled. Then she threw a handful of water over his hair—a baptism—and combed it too hard.

"Bayard the Steed goes on his rounds, as through Dendermonde he pounds!"

They crossed the playground. She stopped suddenly so that he, absorbed in her moving darkness, collided with her, which made her smile though she was still frowning—a two-faced goddess of vengeance or worse—and she spat into the palm of her hand and flattened a tuft of hair over his left ear. Then, on the other side of the playground, by the motionless cast-iron merry-go-round on which one of the little ones sat dangling his legs, he spotted Vlieghe. Who saw him, too, but did not move, a figure of pastel-colored porcelain between the white poles of the merry-go-round.

Louis mewed, knocked Sister Adam's hand away from his ear, and continued walking six feet away from her.

Her fiddling with his hair must have looked like a caress, that's what Vlieghe is certain to have taken it for, he will never mention it, of course, not Vlieghe, but it must have looked like treachery to his slanting hazel eyes, something that can never be put right now, no matter how hard I try to conjure it away, later, tonight. He pushed a little piece of licorice into his mouth and chewed furiously. He was getting hot, and moved farther away, toward the outside wall, and saw his father's saffron-yellow DKW through the open gate. A gigantic man sat sleeping behind the wheel, someone he had never seen before. And yet I know him.

Sister Adam stopped, crucifix dangling against her side, she beckoned, called, "Come along, they're waiting."

They? So both his parents had come after all? That was something new. He looked back quickly at the DKW, to take in all the details he would be reporting later, that night, to Vlieghe, who was mad about cars and airplanes. But all he could see was that the car was astonishingly clean and that there was a round sticker in the rear window.

Still burning with shame (Vlieghe! Vlieghe! It wasn't what you thought

7

it was!), he stepped into the cool, broad corridor. Sister Adam rushed ahead as if she, messenger angel, were determined to be the first to announce his arrival. Just like St. Anne running along a low brick wall to convey the Message, the Glad Tidings. She could run all night, Anne. And her imagination could run riot. Louis spat out the lukewarm licorice into his hand, a stringy, golden-ocher lump the color of Vlieghe's eyebrows. He put it in the pocket of his tunic, together with the shoelaces, the marbles, the quarter-francs.

The corridor smelled of ammonia. Not so long ago, during Sunday visiting hours, little Sister Angel had done something that was recorded in their dormitory that same night in the square exercise book with the label "Acts of the Apostles." Vlieghe, the Apostle with the best handwriting, had written: "Sister Marie-Ange, HUMILITY, 8 out of 10." A very high mark for an ordinary nun.

For, without any warning, quite unexpectedly, Sister Angel had knelt down in the corridor at Dobbelaere's feet, and as the Sunday visitors gaped she had used both her hands to pull Dobbelaere's black socks up to his knees. Whereupon Dobbelaere's mother, a peasant woman from Anzegem, had turned purple and snarled at her son, "Aren't you ashamed of yourself, Omer?" Mother Superior had hissed, "Sister Marie-Ange, that will do, thank you very much, you can go now." And Sister Angel had trotted off, meek but unbowed.

Ever since, whenever Dobbelaere said something stupid or came in last when they played prisoner's base, collapsing breathlessly against the ivy on the outside wall, the Apostles would say, "Aren't you ashamed of yourself, Omer?"

Louis's father was standing, legs apart, at the front door of the Institute, the sounds of the village street audible beyond him. He beckoned with a crooked index finger.

"Here he is, Mijnheer Seynaeve, that good-for-nothing son of yours," said Sister Adam, her words reverberating between the dwarf palms and the painted imitation-marble walls.

"Good-for-nothing. You may well say so, Sister," said the balding, pink head.

"Come along, Louis, shake hands," said Sister Adam. After the handshake, his father wiped his hand down his gray-and-blue checked jacket.

Sister Adam rubbed my face too hard, that's why it's burning. That's why. There's no other reason. Her bony fingertips scrubbed right through Den Dooven's worn-out old wash-mitt. There's no other reason. Vlieghe is still waiting for me next to the white-painted merry-go-round.

"Well, how are things with you, my boy?"

"Fine."

"Fine, who?" said the nun.

"Fine, Papa."

"That's fine," said Papa and nodded four times. Now he'll say something about his wife, about my mother. Why hasn't she come? It was true she had said on her last visit, "It'll be some time, sweetie, before I can come again, because I've been a bit unsteady on my legs lately," but Louis had taken it for a ruse, an obvious precaution just in case she wouldn't be able to come. But now?

Sister Adam reached between the tails of his tunic and tugged at one of his suspenders so that the seat of his shorts jerked upward. Papa was watching the oak door of Sister Econome's office, which had silently swung open. Sister Econome stayed out of sight, hidden behind a doorjamb. Grandpa stepped out, Louis's godfather who was also his grandfather, dressed in his usual black suit with his usual dove-gray silk tie. As usual there is not a speck of dust on his shoes with their rounded toecaps and round copper eyelets. The shoes halt, the heels almost touching, the toes pointing upward, as if the shoes are about to leave the ground at any moment.

"He has grown," said Grandpa. He said that every time.

Set a rat loose in this corridor and it wouldn't stand a chance. Every joint between the walls, the tiles, the skirting boards, is perfectly sealed. Grandpa's shoes would do their work easily, trampling, crushing.

Grandpa's head was screwed into a celluloid collar, a shriveled, tanned little apple with a small smudge of newly trimmed stubble under the snub nose. A squashed apple with a mustache. Obviously of far less importance than the man with the plump, round face on the painting behind him, the late Achille Ratti, until a few months ago Pope and leader of the Christian world.

"Two inches at least," said Grandpa in an accent that would have made peasants and Hottentots sneer.

"That's because it's spring," said Papa.

Through the tall, narrow window you could see the pear tree in the middle of the playground. Why hadn't Vlieghe come to spy? Louis smirked. Vlieghe never spied. Others spied on him.

"You look amused," said Grandpa. "I can see that."

"Yes, Grandpa."

"Time enough to be sad when you're old, eh, Father?" said Papa, and Grandpa nodded obligingly.

Louis saw himself running away, right across that endless paved prairie, the playground, ducking under the music room windows—"All in Aalst are praying ha-ard, for they fear the Steed Baya-ard"—and making for the kitchen garden where a Sister who was hoeing looked startled and shouted, "Seynaeve!" and then he saw himself racing past the rain barrel and the stone cliffs and the sandbanks, the wind in his jug ears, those ears Papa had said he ought to pin back to his head at night with *punaises*. And Grandpa had said, "Why do you have to use French words all the time, Staf, why don't you speak plain Flemish! Anyway, if you tied an elastic band around the boy's head at night, it would hurt less, eh, Louis?" And then Papa had said in a pained but (for once) triumphant voice, "Elastic band? Elastic, that isn't good Flemish either, Father, you ought to say *rubber* band." And Grandpa had turned away, like a cat that had caught a rat in a convent corridor, and said, "What's good enough for Guido Gezelle and Herman Teirlinck is good enough for their pupil, yours truly, Hubert Seynaeve."

"Come on, Louis, let's go and get some fresh air," said Grandpa.

In the playground the merry-go-round was rotating with soft little squeaks. Vlieghe had given it a violent turn before making off.

Papa held his hand over his sparse eyebrows as if looking out to sea at Blankenberge (last summer, hundreds of people with bare shoulders shouting in the waves) and not straight at the bell tower of the chapel (where Vlieghe was at this moment on his knees praying to the Holy Virgin to forgive him his evil thoughts and fits of rage).

Grandpa put one hand on a low branch of the pear tree. Some of the little ones were hanging around the basement kitchen. Not so very long ago Louis had lined up there himself, kitchen smells wafting around him, four inches shorter and holding Vlieghe's wet hand in his own.

"We are very satisfied with our Louis," said Sister Adam. "He was first in Religious Instruction and in Geography."

"And Arithmetic?"

"That's still a problem," said the nun.

"He got that from his father," said Grandpa.

"That's a fact," said Papa. "But then we can't all be as clever as you."

Grandpa took out a white handkerchief and patted his forehead, his thin hair. Then he wiped the crumpled handkerchief between his creased neck and the celluloid collar. Light glinted from the pearl in his gray tie.

"Louis," he said, "I'm not dissatisfied, but that arithmetic of yours, well, you're just going to have to work harder. And your general conduct isn't up to much either, or so I've been told."

"By well-informed circles," said Louis.

Grandpa stuck the tip of his beringed finger into his nostril and shook it vigorously. Then he released the rubbery nose. "You cheeky little devil," he said.

Papa was alarmed. He screwed up his eyes. Nearsighted? No, that was the way William Tell had looked at his son under the apple tree as he drew his crossbow.

"Don't forget," said Grandpa, tapping Louis on the arm, "that I'll be examining your report when you come home next holidays. And, my boy, always remember the Seynaeve name." He moved away. For the first time Louis noticed that his legs were bowed like a horseman's. "By the way," said Papa, "this is for you." Louis recognized the smell at once, he took the familiar paper bag with its flowing, silvery, ornate lettering, chocolates from the bakery around the corner. The paper bag was crumpled, Papa must have had a go at it himself. To make quite sure, he looked inside. Some of the dark- and light-brown lumps had stuck to each other. He put the paper bag in Sister Adam's outstretched hand.

"You may have two tonight," said the nun. "There's no alcohol in them, I trust, Mijnheer Seynaeve?"

Papa whinnied. "What an idea, Sister," he said, and suddenly he was the modest, almost pious citizen. "I never take strong drink, Sister. An occasional beer, when it's hot or to be sociable. But drink?" He looked hard into Louis's face. "I'd cut off his hands right now if I knew he was going to take to drink."

"Quite so," said the nun. "Once, by mistake, Mother Superior ate two chocolates filled with Élixir d'Anvers at a funeral. It went straight to her head."

She was lying. That had happened to her, Sister Adam. And it had been five, maybe seven, chocolates. Louis sought for signs of the lie in that immaculate oval framed by the coif.

"Right," said Papa and coughed.

"Don't leave yet," said Louis. "Not just yet."

"No," said Papa and paused. "Oh, yes," he added, "Mama is well. That is, well and not well. You probably expected her to come this time, but it just wasn't possible. What I wanted to tell you is that Mama sends you lots and lots of love."

"She doesn't *want* to come," said Louis. Despite himself, he made it sound like a question. (Forty-one days ago, when she had come on her last visit, Mama had said, "What on earth am I doing here? I drop everything at home and when I'm here you don't have anything to say to me. I ask you something and it's just 'Yes' or 'No,' and the rest of the time you stand and stare at me as if I were some sort of prize idiot. If you'd rather I didn't come again, Louis, just say so. But you never come straight out with anything, do you?")

"Of course she wants to come," said Papa, "but . . . how can I put it?" He turned his rosy, blooming face helplessly toward Sister Adam and then said bitterly to the pear tree, "If she can't, she can't, and that's all there is to it."

"Louis is a bit on edge today," said the nun. "It's partly the weather. The sudden heat."

"Yes. There's going to be a thunderstorm," said Papa.

She's on edge herself. Why? Don't ask yourself. Don't even ask why you mustn't ask yourself.

"The chocolates are from the bakery around the corner," he said.

"That's right," said Papa.

"And they got melted in the heat."

"What difference does that make?" said the nun. "It's the taste that counts."

Hanging on the wall in Sister Econome's office was a hand-colored photograph of Henricus Lamiroy, Bishop of Bruges, whom Grandpa claimed as a distant relative of the Seynaeves', on Aunt Margo's side. The Bishop had his head tilted to one side, his elbows resting on a medieval desk on which stood a bronze inkwell, a telephone, and an empty ashtray.

Through the window with its thick, round, dust-covered bars you could see the DKW. Grandpa was sitting diagonally opposite the fireplace, his legs crossed, jiggling his round-toed shoe up and down and smoking a cigar. Sister Econome's severe expression barely altered when she saw Louis.

"Lou, dear," she said, and one day Louis will pick up, raise high the paper knife with the Congolese-ivory handle that lies there on the moss-green blotter. She will squawk, Sister Econome, squeal until she wets herself.

He stood by the window and said, "Why does it say 'Rex' on our car?"

"Yes," said Papa, but you could hardly hear him as Grandpa leaped to his feet, babbling, "What? Rex? Where?" Cigar smoke blew into Louis's face. Next to him Grandpa was muttering, "It can't be!" Papa joined them at the window. Interested regulars in the tap room of the White Horse across the road could now observe three generations of Seynaeves behind bars.

"Now that you mention it," said Papa. "On the rear window."

Grandpa's words crackled, the pronunciation was refined, aloof, the breath between the sounds fire and brimstone: "Staf, you will do me the great kindness of immediately, and I mean immediately, removing that sticker."

"Immediately," Louis said to himself.

"Staf!" snarled Grandpa.

"It must have been Holst," said Papa and went to the door.

"Yes," said Grandpa. "I cannot imagine who else it could have been."

"Is that Holst?" asked Louis. On an unheard command from Papa, the gigantic man was extricating himself laboriously from behind the steering wheel. When he stepped into the street, Louis saw, with irrational joy, that the man was a whole head taller than his father.

"What scum," said Grandpa. "Sister Econome, the times we live in . . ."

"The archbishop warned us on the radio against the Rexists in so many words," said Sister Econome. "But by all accounts King Leopold is not totally opposed to them. Although, of course, he can't say so officially." She smiled. Louis had never seen her do that before. Suddenly there she sat, a woman with a childish, peasant-like expression. Even her hands, twirling an emerald-green fountain pen, had something girlish about them.

"Rex on our car," said Grandpa bitterly.

"At least it's better than a Socialist sticker," said Sister Econome.

"That's all we need," said Grandpa. He stepped abruptly up to the desk and rapped on it with his signet ring. "That's not the end of the matter," he said, and left without a look or a word of farewell. Sister Econome rose.

"That grandfather of yours is going to get apoplexy one of these days, the way he works himself up," she said.

In the sunny street outside, the giant Holst was trying to scrape the sticker off with a pocketknife, but Papa pulled him away and, sweating, began picking cautiously with his fingernails at the glass and the paper. Grandpa appeared beside the car, roared something unintelligible, and flung his cigar onto the cobblestones.

Sister Econome stepped outside, having first stuck the coconut matting between the door and the doorjamb.

Although it was forbidden, absolutely forbidden, Louis suddenly found himself unattended, unshadowed, outside in the street, under the plane tree with its buzzing midges. Papa had put the odious round sticker, apparently intact, into his pocket. Grandpa had sat down in the car, next to the driver's seat. He was wearing a dark-gray trilby hat. The giant Holst was stroking the bonnet of the car.

"Now then, my boy," said Papa cheerfully. Outside he looked stronger and bigger than he had while kept on Grandpa's leash inside the school. "Next time things will be different and better. Don't eat your heart out for your mother. Everything will be just fine."

"Does Mama have galloping consumption, then?" asked Louis.

"For goodness' sake, Lou!" said Sister Econome.

Papa looked at his son as if he were an orphan come to sing outside the door on Twelfth Night. Then he pretended to be overcome with giggles, drumming on his stomach as if to suppress an irresistible outburst of laughter.

"What an extraordinary idea!" he gasped. "Eh, Sister? You're a strange one, my boy. There hasn't been any consumption among us Seynaeves these past fifty years. Eh, Sister?" She did not know whether she was expected to agree. Papa cleared his throat and leaned forward. "What happened is nothing really, it's just that Mama fell down the stairs, that's all, she's going to have to lie down for a while."

"On the stairs?"

Haggard, Papa sought support from Sister Econome, who looked down the street as if expecting someone. The giant Holst held the door of the DKW open.

"She has to stay in bed for a while, but not much longer," said Sister Econome.

"Now then, my boy," said Papa. "When you see Mama next time she'll have a nice present for you."

"Definitely," said Sister Econome.

"What present?"

"That's a surprise," said Papa.

"You'll be bowled over by it," said Sister Econome. In the car Grandpa reached across and blew the horn. The dog from the White Horse immediately started to bark.

"Now then, my boy," said Papa.

"Now then, Papa," said Louis, but it did not sound as scornful as he would have liked.

"Next time I'll . . . ," said Papa, sidling over to the DKW. When he had sat down in the back, Grandpa started to harangue him. There was a lot of room left next to Papa. Louis could easily have fitted in as well. All the way home he would have kept his hand on Papa's knee. He was still waving when the car disappeared around the corner and the cloud of dust over the village street had begun to drift away.

The playground was deserted, hazy. The chatter of the little ones rose from the basement kitchen.

Vandezijpe came up to him. He was eating a carrot.

"Ugh, paleface," he said.

"Ugh, Hottentot," said Louis. And although he didn't want to in the least, he said to Vandezijpe, who was crunching little orange-colored pieces with his mouth open, "My mother fell down the stairs."

"There's always something the matter with you," said Vandezijpe.

*C*hugging, the DKW drives through the center of the village, past houses with shiny yellow bricks and balconies painted lilac and beige, past shoe shops, a blacksmith's, a churchyard where a woman in mourning is sucking her thumb.

Purring, the car drives along a deserted asphalt road, past the clay pits with sides as tall as houses, but what is Grandpa barking about? You can lip-read it. Grandpa is furious, he who at Louis's baptism in St. Mark's Hospital snatched the sprinkler from the priest's hand and brandished it over the frightened little mite with the crumpled, long-vanished little head that you can still see in a photograph in the living room at 10 Oudenaarde Road. The photograph is pushed in at an angle at the bottom of the frame of *The Good Shepherd.* Grandpa, who, every time Louis stoutly recited his New Year's greeting (ending with a bow and a relieved and triumphant "To his Grandpa ever dear from his godchild most sincere"), seized Louis's wrist, peeled open the boy's clenched fist, and, turning his back on him, pressed five francs into it, filthy lucre. Grandpa, who used to call himself "Professor Seynaeve." "I thought you were a teacher. What subject are you professor of?"—"Of the art of living, dear lady!" This same Grandpa is now berating his son, who cringes, appalled, in the rear seat of the cramped, hot car. After the clay pits come the fields of rye, then the landscape grows less hilly and signposts to Kuurne, Lauwe, and Verdegem appear.

Grandpa is still talking, no more calmly but more wearily. His words come out loud and clear. "Staf," he says, "I can understand your having opinions, a man without opinions should be thrown in the dustbin, but after all, Staf, *il y a la manière.*"

"In Flanders, Flemish!" Papa shouts. You can see the man behind the wheel snicker, though the other two don't notice. No, Grandpa sees the man's shoulders shake.

"Holst, look where you're going," Grandpa hisses.

A funeral goes by. A drunken nun is being supported by two officers, each with a wreath around his neck. A brass band. The people in the shuffling cortège look as if they have been cut out of cardboard one by one, painted, and then manipulated by a clumsy boy pulling invisible strings. The boy makes them hop, skip, and caper about. *Dies irae,* crash bang, *dies illa,* boom boom!

"Staf," says Grandpa resignedly, "you are a good fellow, but no *commerçant,* no businessman." That is the worst possible insult, and Papa sinks even further back into his seat.

"Staf, talking to you is like talking to a brick wall."

Having reached the churchyard, the black cortège with its sobbing women disperses amongst the crosses, then reassembles in front of the freshly dug grave, where the woman in mourning sets up such a terrible din from inside her black veil that the bystanders go red and nudge one another.

"Staf, that was a really bad lapse, that Rex sticker of yours. Is that what I brought you up for?"

You didn't bring me up, it was Grandma. Papa would never dare say anything like that. Nor would he call his own mother Grandma. And Papa would never interrupt Grandpa, his own father.

". . . what I specially built up a business for, for you, my heir, a business the likes of which you won't find anywhere else in West Flanders?"

"Father, you are the only wholesaler in school supplies in all of West Flanders."

"Exactly what I've been saying. We have no equal."

Flocks of crows alight in the churchyard, flapping, scratching in the turned-over earth. A man in black chases them away with an umbrella.

"Staf, why have you made me the laughingstock of every religious order in West Flanders? Because you may rest assured that Sister Econome is on the telephone this very minute. By now, even the Maricole Sisters in Deinze will have heard how ridiculous . . .''

"Rex is not ridiculous."

"Rex will win," says the man who turns the wheel with huge, swollen red hands as if it were as light as a feather.

"Holst, look where you're going."

"Belgium will be Rexist or die."

"Holst, that's enough."

Grandpa takes out a little tube that smells of mint, unscrews the cap, and pushes it into his nose. His eyes water. He moans, "Where have I gone wrong? You, up there in Heaven, please tell me. I have always done the best for my family and my grandchildren and for Louis in particular."

Did Papa hear that last remark? He doesn't let on. Holst whistles "The Beautiful Blue Danube," taps his foot in waltz time on the accelerator. Would that make the DKW judder and shake? Must ask Vlieghe.

"Staf."

"Yes, Father."

"The fact that I've done well in life, that I am widely respected, not just in Philip of Alsace Avenue but far beyond Walle, even in the smallest village, anywhere there's a school or a convent, I owe to my nose. I can *smell* where there is business to be done, and then I do it. And for that I am esteemed as a *commerçant* and as a man. Actually, *more* than just a man, since in a sense I am like a priest, having a special licence from the diocese to dispose of my goods to the private schools. Am I right or am I not? And now my future and yours and Louis's have been jeopardized because you, Staf, see fit to fool around with that political propaganda of yours. And for Rex, of all things. My boy, I only hope Leon Degrelle is paying you well, how much, fifteen thousand francs? More? Thirty thousand pieces of silver to humiliate me *en plein public?*"

"Hardly anyone noticed."

"*Tiens, tiens.* You call your own child 'hardly anyone'? Oh, that's very good. I'll mention it to Louis's mother. She'll sit up when she hears that what she whelped is 'hardly anyone.' "

"Whelped?"

"Gave birth to, is that better? Answer me, Staf. Don't play the innocent with me!"

Now that he is no longer at the Institute, Grandpa is speaking broad Flemish. Grandpa holds a teacher's diploma; for years he insisted on talking High Flemish under all circumstances, even, to her annoyance, with Grandma, who had long since forgotten that his refined language had been one of her reasons for marrying him. Then, one fine afternoon, "one of the turning points in my life," Grandpa and some friends had paid a visit to Herman Teirlinck, the prince of Flemish letters, in his villa in Oostduinkerke. That's where Grandpa had acquired the burred *r*, the long-drawn-out, high-pitched *aa*, which Louis had made his own as well and which had earned him the scorn of the Sisters and pupils at the Institute of St. Joseph. Ever since that afternoon's chat about culture and science in Oostduinkerke, Grandpa, to many people's surprise, had begun to come out with Walle expressions in the Walle dialect, at home no less than in his local café, the Groeninghe. Not regularly, because he did not, of course, want to be taken for a clown, but unexpectedly, at cards, or when some ready wit was called for. He had explained it all a year ago, over Christmas dinner. "Herman Teirlinck went to fetch some cider from the cellar, and while he was pouring it, his wife came into the drawing room, and do you know what that great, refined, not to say decadent genius did then? He went up to her, gave her a resounding kiss on the cheek, and said: 'Ere, me ol' dear, come and 'ave a drink. Them gents are from the Free Schools. But gi' us a kiss first.' We were dumbfounded. Later when we talked about it, we all agreed that this man, whom our circles attack so savagely, had just given us clear proof of his humblest ties with our people, of his respect for the language of our people in its original form."

What has happened to the widow who lost her husband and child through her own fault? The brass band plays a subdued accompaniment to the singing of *"Quantus tremor est futurus, quanto-o ju-udex est venturus, cuncta-a stricte discussurus."* The grave gapes, the earth reeks. Inside its coffin the child is still warm, while his father in the coffin below has long since turned to concrete cold as ice. A gold coin has been pressed between the child's lips, a Louis d'Or.

Grandpa gestures to Holst to stop the car near the grave. In his shiny, round-toed shoes Grandpa walks up to the edge of the pit. Papa sneaks up behind him and, just as he comes within reach of his father's back, puts out two gloved hands, fingers extended, and seizes his father around the hips. Grandpa totters.

Papa does not push the school supplies tycoon into the pit but tickles him instead. Grandpa's shoulders and hips writhe. The two Seynaeves giggle like two brothers. Will they start throwing loose earth at each other next?

Holst stays by the car and rubs under the bonnet with a chamois. Although he pretends not to see Louis, he is sending the signal: "Look, I am much too big and too strong to hurt anybody, even you. Do you know who I am? I have been sent to you, Louis, to protect you."

Grandpa lights up a clay pipe, brought from Bavaria by Aunt Mona, his favorite daughter.

"Holst!"

"Yes, Professor?"

"Why did you put that Rex sticker on our car?" (*Our* car, because Grandpa paid for it.)

The man does not reply. He doesn't think it's worth the trouble. He has been sent on a different mission.

"It must have been a boy, one of those snotty day pupils," Papa says.

"A boy five foot tall, then," muses Grandpa, "otherwise he couldn't have reached the back window."

"Or a criminal," says Papa.

Grandpa turns up his nose disdainfully, like the King of France the year before the Battle of the Golden Spurs, when he faced the delegation of Flemish nobles decked out in their sumptuous robes, with their upright bearing, their unmistakable nobility.

"Criminals," says Grandpa, referring to the crowd around the open grave, because they do not wail, do not tear their hair or their mourning clothes, do not even sigh, just stand about, cold and bowed like the white marble pietàs throughout the churchyard. "Enough," says Grandpa, and two moths fly out of his mouth. "Enough," says Grandpa and leans forward and says "enough" to the still lukewarm child in the coffin, which is already soaked with moisture from the soil. And the car drives into Oudenaarde Road and sputters and falls silent outside the door where Mama stands shivering on the threshold,

no,

she can't be, because Mama is lying in bed under the eiderdown quilt in that pigsty of a room of hers, she can't get up because either her legs or her ribs have been bruised or broken.

Louis caught his breath. Two Sisters were walking by behind the bushes, you could recognize Sister Kris by her step. The shouts of the Hottentots, returning from football, could be heard in the distance. Louis slid farther, deeper into the bushes on wet knees, then sat back on his heels, his face against the bitter leaves.

Mama's getting hurt had been his fault and nobody else's. It would never have happened if he had been at home, because then he could have stopped her at that split second when, sleepwalking through the passage outside her bedroom, she fell and broke both her elbows.

It would never have happened if he had been thinking of her, here in the Institute. (Not fleetingly but with a precisely focused, deliberate, concentrated thought that reached her just as she, a figure crying out for protection, was fumbling along the passage on white, faltering feet, to the head of the stairs.) If only his thought, his prayer, had enfolded her while she was still asleep. If only she had caught his thought, breathed it in. She would have woken up and whispered, "Yes, my own little Louis, tell it to Mama," and would have stroked the back of his neck. None of it would ever have happened if he had never existed. For if he hadn't been born, then she would never have been overtaken by giddiness next to the stairs. Because when he was born something had got into her blood, as she had told Aunt Nora. If he had never existed, then she would never have found it in her soul, disabled and weakened by his birth, to pack him off—her dangerous offspring, her problem child—to boarding school, bag and baggage, that fatal moment.

Being born also hurts. Louis could not imagine it, but at the same time he believed it. Actually, he did not really want to imagine it, it all had to do with sheets full of shit, with moaning that brought the neighbors crowding in, and with straining and compulsion and "forcing."

"You must never, never force yourself, Constance," said Aunt Nora.

"But if the Professor keeps shouting, 'Push, push,' what do you do?" (Mama, chuckling.)

"I'd say, 'Professor, push yourself, leave me alone, you push with your own behind,'" Mama laughed. It was about four o'clock, she was eating bread and butter and quince jam with Aunt Nora, who said there was too much chicory in the coffee. He heard Mama laughing in the front room, and he went on playing at the kitchen table with the cut-out figures of knights and fair ladies.

"I can't remember any longer," said Mama, "I know it hurt terribly, that I do know, I wanted to jump out of the window, I was being torn, but a woman must have some sort of mechanism that wipes it out once it's all over."

"But they say that being born hurts, too. And that once it's all over, the newborn baby forgets as well. That's the way Our Lord has arranged it."

"It's just as well you forget."

"Yes, or no one would want any more children."

"If it was only a question of wanting."

"Anyway, with me, it's all healed up beautifully."

That had been during the last holidays, so long ago now. A flood of light voices, drenched by the sun. Women heal. Or are stitched back together.

"My hemorrhoids still need a bit of attention," Mama said.

"Ah, that'll pass as well."

"With Tremazin. Or Premazin. The little blue tube."

"I use White Cross ointment."

"All those ointments come out of the same factory. They just give them different names and different tubes. For marketing them."

"Our mother always went to Jules Verdonck for that sort of thing."

"To that healer?"

"If you like. Herbs and nettles from the woods. He made a kind of broth out of them. Two francs. It was good for everything, he said, for animals as well as people. It was good for the stomach, for cramps, for headaches, for constipation. You couldn't have too much of it, he said, it was life itself, that broth was."

"Little Madame Vandenbussche tried a healer too, and didn't she suffer for it."

"Yes, but, Constance, he was a charlatan. And in any case it was too late to do anything."

"Apparently it was a little boy."

"How many months?"

"Six."

"To think that she was running about all that time with that, with that thing rotting away inside her."

"Yes, I did wonder why she let it drag on so long. She could be a bit flighty, that little Madame Vandenbussche, her hair in her eyes all the time, still you can't help but notice if something's gone amiss. Especially as she had diabetes."

"And something wrong with her thyroid."

"That, too."

"On the other hand, Constance, you can't always feel it. I didn't feel anything with our Alfons, not a thing. I went out to the privy, sat on the bowl, said, 'Tiens, what have we got here?' and out he slipped."

"You'd wanted to call him Alfons."

"Yes, that was the curate's idea. Call him after me, he said, Alfons."

"Little Madame Vandenbussche's . . . ," Mama said, and lowered her voice. Louis could hardly hear her. "I'm only telling you what she told me herself, but it seems it wasn't Mr. V.'s."

"Really, Constance!"

"I'm not going to let on whose it was, all I'll say is that he's a terrible drunk. Pernod, if you really want to know. I'll say no more."

"A Pernod drinker," said Aunt Nora. "Well, well. I can guess who that is."

A chair scraped across tiles. The kettle was picked up.

"Not too much chicory, please, Constance. It's far too bitter."

"The chicory's from the Sarma. I've heard that people are lining up for it. And coffee's going up and up."

"I know for a fact there are people on this very street who have bought up hundreds of packets of coffee. And bags of salt. In case something happens."

"Yes, what with the trouble in Czechoslovakia."

"Things aren't going to improve, that's for sure."

"Better not go on about it."

But they did go on. They went on talking about Nicole, Aunt Nora's daughter, and her thyroid. Louis came out of the kitchen, and Aunt Nora said, "My word, young man, how you've grown!"

What else could she have said? All of them, the Seynaeves on Papa's side and the Bossuyts on Mama's, all these aliens more than five feet tall worry about how the wheat, how the dogs, how Louis grows. But what about you yourself, Louis? Admit that you liked it when you heard Aunt Nora call you "man," even though you know that "man" does not just refer to you but embraces all mankind, including Sisters, Apostles, Hottentots (and even Mizzlers, who aren't men at all but droppings of pagan gods that may turn into men at any time).

"Man," said Louis and stood up because the bushes, which had been absorbing and giving off his sweat, were now invaded by sweat midges. He thought of going across to the chapel and praying. It was a sinful notion. It wasn't the sudden welling up of the fear of God, such as had often seized the sainted Jan Berchmans, that lucky fellow, but merely a ruse to explain his absence from the refectory. Or did a prayer inspired by base motives also count? Christ our Savior—Meerke always said, 'Christ our Saver': was that because she was such a penny-pincher?—accepts every prayer. After all, He came not to save the just but for the sake of sinners. In His all-knowing, all-seeing surveillance of every soul, He had, in any case, long since caught on to Louis's evil intentions, and once more in His charitableness had converted them into true prayer.

Was it to be the chapel, then, or not?

Before he could make up his mind, something occurred to him with such exquisite clarity that he sank back on his haunches among the sweat midges in the bushes. Holst was an angel. In the shape of a friend of Mama's. Someone from Mama's part of the country, anyway. For when Louis had heard Holst's voice just now, when he had filled in the lipreading of the road signs with tones, sounds, and words, Louis had clearly made out the Bastegem dialect, the dialect spoken where Mama and Meerke and the multitudinous Bossuyt clan came from.

That meant that the angel Holst was Mama's secret messenger. That the menfolk, the Seynaeves, had forced Holst to stay in the car or by the car to stop him from passing on Mama's message. Holst had been given no chance of coming anywhere near Louis and whispering rapidly out of the corner of his mouth, "Your mother has had a fall, but she is still alive," or "Both your mother's knees are broken, but she is thinking of you," or "Your mother is bleeding, but she hasn't forgotten you."

Of course! Why hadn't he thought of it before? Holst, like Mama, was a prisoner of those jailers, Grandfather and Father Seynaeve, just as women, chauffeurs, and children are held in thrall at all times by men and by Sisters. But if Holst was an angel in human form, wasn't he more powerful than they?

Unobserved—unless by Sisters behind the windows on the second floor of the Keep—he stood up and rubbed his dark-green knees. He trudged past the infirmary, where a Hottentot was bleating for his Hottentot mother, dozens of villages away.

But perhaps Holst had signaled to him after all. And he hadn't realized, as usual. Perhaps the signal in all its blinding clarity would not reach him until late tonight or tomorrow. What could the sign of the angel be?

As he tried to conjure up Holst's large figure, beside and behind the backs of the Seynaeves, a warmth came stealing and creeping over his skin, and became a smell and a noise and a vivid red darkness.

Louis felt the arms of someone like Holst around his ribs. They were Holst's fat, flabby arms, blown up as with a bicycle pump. They slid across his chest, wrapped around his throat. Holst it was who had lifted him up, long ago when he had been the littlest of the little ones, and handed him over, light as a string bag of tomatoes, to another giant, just as big, standing close by. Holst it was who, all these long years, had been Mama's minion. All that time Mama had banished the angel and kept him hidden in Deinze, in her part of the country, amid the scattered members of her Bossuyt clan, against the day when she would need him.

That other giant, bigger than Holst, had taken hold of Louis with hands that stuck out of scarlet sleeves edged with gold brocade, his signet ring scraping the skin of Louis's neck. A huge face with a potato nose, crisscrossed by wine-red veins, a smudge in the middle of a cloud of cotton fibers, spun sugar and snow, under a sparkling miter. The lips opened, a furred tongue and ocher teeth appeared, the giant breathed vinegar and tobacco, inquiring, "What is your name, little man?" Mama, invisible, far away, said, "My Louis is a good boy," and Louis had screamed and squirmed, struck out at the always out-of-reach face. "It's St. Nicholas, Louis, look." He was clamped tight against the rustling coat, placed on a knee. Years later Holst, Mama's spy and minion, had probably come to the Institute as well. Been seen and greeted by everyone except

Louis. Holst, twin brother of a man hidden behind foaming white locks who for years had passed himself off as a saint, as a bishop, as the patron of sailors, publicans, and children, and who pretended he had rescued those three children who had been chopped into little pieces and stuffed in a barrel full of brine. Minced children brought back to life.

Thus the angel Holst must also have been prowling, long ago, through the dormitory during those sleepless, dense, dark nights full of squalling little ones, squeaking Hottentots, barking Sisters.

Perhaps it was Holst who had brought him to the Institute on Mama's orders. No, Mama had brought Louis herself. Mama runs in her floating lace negligée, pursued by strangers. She rocks Louis joltingly in her arms as she careers through the empty streets in Haarbeke. She reaches the wide-open front door of the Institute and throws down the bundle inside which Louis, soaking wet, has been tightly swaddled, makes the sign of the Cross nervously over my curls. Giggling, she vanishes and leaves me lying on the tiles. The mouth-flies drop on my wet lips. The eye-moths, in pairs as always, settle on my eyelids. I can hear their warm wings quivering in my sleep.

_____*mary the cow*

*B*aekelandt was busy with a rake behind the low wall and the evergreen shrubs. His name was Baekelmans, but the Apostles called him Baekelandt after the robber chief beheaded in the market square at Bruges for stealing gold from the rich and giving it to the poor. According to Papa, however, the real reason why the French had decapitated him and his twenty-two comrades, to the cowardly cheers of the Franskiljons, the Flemish but French-speaking citizens and nobles, was that Baekelandt had been a Flamingant, a Flemish patriot.

This Baekelandt, the gardener, was anything but a rebel. Dwarf that he was, he went in fear and trembling of the Sisters. He suffered from asthma, a condition allegedly brought on by gas in the trenches in '14–'18. But he was a liar.

Baekelandt's head, bent forward, showed just above the little wall as if it were floating detached over the tiles along the top. Raking, Baekelandt came into full view at the point where the wall had collapsed (tradition had it that one of the Sisters, pursued by Napoleon's soldiers, had witnessed the wall give way right in front of her imploring eyes, much as the Red Sea had opened up for Moses). (But that wasn't true. Everyone makes things up. We are apparitions. We are never what others think we are. I live but I do not live, Jesus lives in me.)

Bernadette Soubirous, who stood in front of Louis and Dondeyne in her gown of concrete painted cornflower-blue, with her round, rosy face and carmine lips, must also have been quite different from the way Louis now saw her.

Bernadette said to the other Sisters, "I shall continue my work."

"What work, Bernadette?"

"Being ill."

Thus Sister Angel recounted it three or four times a year. Bernadette had been canonized six years ago, not because she had seen the Holy Virgin, or because miracles surfaced in her vicinity, but because she had sacrificed herself. Though horribly martyred by the world with its lack of understanding, its distrust, and its insinuations, she was still not recognized as a martyr.

"My mother fell down the stairs," said Louis. "Onto her neck. She's completely disfigured."

"Come, come," said Dondeyne as if calling a cat, and he grinned. Louis could not imagine why. But it was beneath his dignity as founder and leader of the Apostles to pursue the matter. He called across to the raking gardener, "Baekelandt, have you got anything for us?"

The man stood up. "That I have, that I have, for the both of you!"

"What is it?" called Louis eagerly.

"A hiding, my boy, a mighty good hiding!"

The two Apostles exploded with laughter, nudging each other. You could get Baekelandt to make threatening noises anytime you wanted, always the same, and always just as bad-tempered and violent as the first time. His wife, Trees, as skinny as he was, with even more crooked legs, had adopted his ways after all their years together, and she, too, would often scream abuse at you. Two turkeys.

Baekelandt had never served in the army, he had been too thin and scrawny. Even though they had used dwarves as well as children in '14–'18 for slipping under the barbed wire that kept the Germans out of the Belgian trenches. If Baekelandt had ever been a soldier, it must have been in some past life, in the shape of one of the mocking mercenaries who threw dice on Golgotha for Christ's clothes.

Sister Adam had once turned up her nose at Den Dooven and told him that he smelled as bad as Baekelandt, who never washed.

"Of course Baekelandt doesn't wash," Louis said. "Why should he? He only gets filthy again as soon as he starts working."

"My mother sometimes washes twice a day," said Dondeyne. (Come, come. *My* mother fell down the stairs. *His* mother washes.)

"Where?"

"In the kitchen. At the pump in the sink."

"No, where does she wash herself? Her face?"

"Yes. And her hands."

"And her feet?"

"I've never seen her do that," said Dondeyne. "Women wash more than men. Because they need to more. They start to stink more quickly."

Where had Dondeyne come by that piece of information? His uncle was a pharmacist.

Baekelandt stood at the crumbling gap in the wall. He had pushed his cap back, and above his eyebrows ran a blood-red weal, one finger wide. He held the rake against his shoulder like a rifle. According to Sister Angel, war could break out over the entire planet at any moment.

"You are two strapping boys," said Baekelandt. "Our Leon has gone up to town and I've been left on my own with my Trees, you could give me a hand with Mary, she's about to calve. All you have to do is pull. Help to pull. If it were my cow I'd say I'd do it on my own, but it belongs to the convent after all . . ."

"Drop dead," Louis said.

"Drop dead," said Dondeyne.

"You're chicken." Baekelandt brought the rake down from his shoulder and leaned on it. He smelled of beets.

"We aren't allowed in the cowshed," said Louis. "If a Sister ever caught us . . ."

"Chicken."

"How many calves are there inside her?" Dondeyne asked.

"By God," said Baekelandt. "What a comedian. You think a cow is some kind of factory? Wait till I tell Trees. By God!"

"Sister Imelda could help you," said Louis.

"Oh, her. She'd only get in my way. She's all thumbs, that one."

"She studied agriculture," Louis said.

"That's why," said Baekelandt, giving his crotch a leisurely scratch.

"You're scared shitless, the both of you," he said finally. "And that's what we've got to defend our fatherland with. If we'd had to count on the likes of you in '14–'18!"

He stuck a crumpled, brown, wet cigarette stub into the corner of his mouth. In Cairo and Aswan, people in rags wait lynx-eyed for a stranger to throw his cigarette away, then pounce like lightning on the prize. But if the police catch them, they can be fined twenty-five Turkish pounds.

At home, in Walle, Louis once took five pulls from Grandpa's cigar when Grandpa had gone out to the privy, and had been as sick as a dog. Scolding, Mama had washed his face. Papa never smokes. Men without pipes are unmanly types.

"If anything goes wrong with Mary, it'll be your fault," Baekelandt said.

"What can go wrong?" Louis went cold all over. St. Francis would never knowingly have let any animal die.

"Maybe we could get away after supper, Dondeyne and I. But you know the rules."

Baekelandt pulled his cap down, as far as the blood-red weal. Louis had a sudden pang of longing for the chocolates lying in the ceiling-high cupboard of the refectory, all moldy by now, or all shriveled up, no good anymore, anyway.

"The rules! If we'd kept to the rules in '14–'18, our whole regiment would be pushing up daisies now. Animals come before rules, just like people, if need be. You all, you've got no respect for animals. And I'm sorry to say you're worse than that German crown prince who fed his horses on the best oats right up to the end of the war while his men had to make do with sugar beets and dry bread mixed with chopped straw. And that wasn't all. While his men were losing arms and legs and dying because there were no tires and no fuel to get them away, the crown prince was sending cars and chauffeurs all over Europe to track down a she-ape to marry the ape that Enver Pasha the Turk had given him. They got married, those two apes, in the middle of the war, with an orchestra and a whole crowd of princes and ambassadors there to see it."

Mary the cow died that night at half past nine. The sound of her bellowing and the shouts of Baekelandt and Trees penetrated to the dormitory, where they drowned out the whimpers of the little ones and the snores of Sister Kris. Toward morning a fat, bloated white cow charged at Louis. He ran for the barbed wire, but it wouldn't give way, refused to yield. The cow lowered her head, her accusing, bloodshot eyes wreathed with white lashes, then jumped weightless into the air and landed on Louis's stomach with hooves of marble and iron. For three days Louis wore a black wool mourning thread around his wrist, and all week he prayed to St. Francis for forgiveness.

*T*he Book of Rules with its dizzying ramifications of subsidiary regulations never became known to any pupil in its entirety, because no pupil had ever been allowed to see the rules in their written form in the bulky volume bound in calf with brass corners, which the Sisters kept hidden in their Keep and consulted on any controversial issue, however trivial. The Sisters themselves had few arguments, because they had turned their backs on the world not least in order to keep their solemn vow of peaceful coexistence.

In this Book of Rules, which Sister Econome, or, if she was ill, Sister Sapristi, would update on Saturday nights, you can read at what hour the Sisters and their prisoners, the pupils, have to rise, how much time may be wasted between getting up, washing, and the first bite of bread and butter, on what days there is hot chocolate, buttermilk porridge, blood sausage, what kind of meat you might eat as a last resort on a Friday if you were in an oasis starving to death, how far above the knee a pair of shorts may end, must end, in the winter, whether during break you are allowed to laugh and if so how loudly two weeks after the death of a relative, on what day and at what hour you must don a celluloid collar and how deep a blue your lavaliere should be, since if it were nearly black you would be in unwarranted mourning and that would displease the Eye of the Lord, what time of the year boaters may first be worn, which is not necessarily at Easter, what sanctions should be used against a pupil who, though no longer a little one, has nevertheless wet his bed, if you may swap three clay marbles for one of colored glass, if you may put more than three pieces of chewing gum in your mouth at the same time, at precisely what hour vespers starts and why, and so on and so forth.

The rules are written in different colors depending on the subject. God's teaching, for instance, is naturally recorded in red because of the blood of the Sacred Heart. In this section are to be found the articles of faith and the liturgy, what, when, why, and how to sing and to pray, how to subdue the ever vigilant foe with song, or how to ward him off with prayer, whether you may lead him to believe that you are his friend and then take advantage of his credulity and destroy him, first with fervent invocation and then with a litany, later still with mortification of the flesh, and finally with martyrdom. If you are a doubting or a wavering Sister, you can look up who the Savior's true friends are—in the list of saints and the beatified—and who the heretics, the renegades, the apostates; who has disregarded the laws of God and of Belgium, for instance by slandering His Majesty King Leopold as the Socialists and the Liberals do; who has vowed publicly or in secret never to fight for Christ the King; who, for instance, has been scoffing (as that dimwit Byttebier did last week) at the Spanish Catholic Youth dressed in short pants, who, armed only with shotguns, are taking on the international Communists, men challenging the reign of Christ's paladins in Spain; who has been so cowardly as to put his hands up in the face of evil; who does not resist the daily provocations of evil—and on that subject a special rule lays it down that in exceptional cases you may accept evil and even yield to it, to repent of it all the more fervently afterward rather than pretend that evil does not exist, and that in the fight against evil even the smallest among us can play his part, for the little ones look innocent at first sight and hence can all the more skillfully insinuate themselves into evil, as under the barbed wire in the trenches of '14–'18.

The devils, too, are listed in the book, with descriptions of their features, lest you be unable to tell them apart, those fallen angels who since their insurrection may no longer appear before the eyes of God, or rather may no longer behold God with their own eyes, they who were created light and white like angels on the second day of Creation, but who frittered their chances away. The devils are listed in alphabetical order, with appended terrestrial and celestial maps showing where you may chance—

or mischance—to meet them, for most of them dwell in the mists. Some are found in the sun, or in the bowels of the earth, but all have been numbered and listed in sequence, those six thousand, six hundred and sixty-six legions with their princes, dukes, prelates, and counts commanding the forty-five million conscripts of evil. For there are devils of the fire who live far away, those of the air who swarm about us like flies and cause thunderstorms, those of the earth who mingle with us in human form leading us astray, those of the water, those of the underground who fan the flames of Etna and Stromboli and torment the miners of Limburg, devils in women's bodies, and sometimes the age of a devil is known and is listed as well, and all this information has been kept meticulously up to date by hundreds of Sisters, generation upon generation, unto this very day.

God's spies, needless to say, are not listed in this book, because that is the most secret of secrets, known only to the Pope and three special cardinals, each of whom wears over his heart a scapular that contains a minuscule book whose text can be deciphered only with the help of a powerful lens and an inscrutable code. Louis wondered in what form Holst's name was entered there.

What else is recorded in the Book of Rules? Probably the Institute's true set of accounts, to which Aunt Violet, who knows all there is to know about money, has alluded. According to her, the Institute keeps two sets of account books, which is just as well, for if all the figures, all the income and expenditures, were made public for all to see, then the Institute would fall prey to all kinds of malicious elements in the Ministry of Taxes, where the Freemasons pull the strings.

Then there is a geography section with foldout maps showing the boundaries of the Catholic states and of those countries that are still to be converted and are awaiting missionaries. Until two years ago my ardent hope had been that Louis Seynaeve would be sent out to the Orinoco or, if that was impossible, to Iroquois country.

A special section deals with the Jews who, hard to keep track of, swarm out and settle everywhere, in Hollywood and in the diamond vaults in Antwerp. Like nits, Papa said.

"But Jesus was a Jew too," said Vlieghe.

"Not a real one." Louis hoped that Vlieghe hadn't noticed his hesitation.

"The only reason He was one at all was because His Father wanted Him to be humiliated and ill-treated, and that's why His Father chose the Jewish race."

"You don't say," said Byttebier.

Sister Sapristi said that once, years ago, a Jewish boy had been admitted by the Institute and had passed himself off as a normal person from Varsenare. She had found him out when, believing he was unobserved, he had crunched up the Sacred Host with his eyeteeth, his face burning with an indescribable hatred.

"Are we in the Book of Rules as well?" asked Dondeyne.

"No. Everything to do with pupils is put down in separate notebooks by Sister Econome."

"Everything?"

"Everything that they know. It's all kept in the left-hand corner cupboard in her office. File cards, notes, exercise books, cardboard boxes full of information."

Cobweblike threads spanned the Institute, vibrating and carrying signals to the Keep.

"That's why Sister Econome is always busy writing."

"She puts down everything that happens in the village, too."

"Everything?"

"Everything."

"Even that Haarbeke Football Club lost 4–1 to Sporting Waregem?"

"Even that. And road accidents, and that a horse has sprained its fetlock, and the celebration of forty years' service by the newspaper delivery man, and that the Up and About Club has completed its hundred-and-fifty-mile bicycle ride."

"You don't say."

"And that we are the Apostles?"

"Not that," Louis said, but thought, Perhaps that, too. Sister Econome is an electrically charged spongelike brain that sucks up everything, absorbs everything. Even the vibrations of the Mizzlers, who are the Apostles' own devils, and who, though they have no name and leave no trace, are ever present. Sister Econome can sense their vibrations, he decided, but the Mizzlers themselves, no, she doesn't sense those.

"What does the Great Book look like?" asked Eddie, Vlieghe's brother, a little one, who had Vlieghe's hazel, sometimes amber, eyes and his square fingertips.

"Bound in calf. The spine is broken, worms have eaten holes in it, in the parchment. There is a death's-head on the front page. Sometimes the ink is black, sometimes brown."

"Where is it kept?"

"Nobody knows that."

Later that evening Eddie sat down beside Louis, who was sitting under the lantern of the merry-go-round, reading *From Gezelle's Life and Work*, Grandpa's last Christmas present, published by the Davidsfonds.

"If nobody knows where the Book is kept, how can the Sisters read it?"

"There are no flies on you, Eddie. When I said 'nobody,' I meant nobody except the Sisters. I meant none of us. All we know is that the Book was kept in an empty room until 1935, because the Bishop of Bruges ordained that the Book must be allowed to breathe in an empty room. But in 1935, when the Socialist Dockers' Union celebrated its twenty-fifth anniversary here in the village, those heretics came over and yelled outside the gate. Then Mother Superior decided to post one of the Sisters in the room as a guard to raise the alarm as soon as strangers came too close."

And to honk like a goose in ancient Rome, he thought, but didn't say so, in case he had to start reciting the whole history of the Roman Empire for Eddie's benefit.

"Who was the guard?"

"The first time it was Sister St. Gerolphe."

"I don't know her. Is she dead?"

"Nearly."

"Where is she?"

"In a room in the Keep. She used to be a noblewoman. She has four family names."

"What are they?"

"Er . . . she forgot them herself long ago. Her husband, who was a duke, disowned her, and to atone for his sin she turned her back on the world. She can't move."

"Why?"

"Because for a long time she was kept tied to a throne crowned with an oaken eagle."

"The king of the birds," said Eddie eagerly. "What was she tied up with?"

"With three cords around the eagle's talons and around her neck, three around her legs, and twice times three around her arms. Once, after many years, Sister Angel, who felt sorry for her, untied her in secret, but it was too late, Sister St. Gerolphe could no longer move, she stood up and fell flat on the floor, her face was completely disfigured."

"Does she sit on a commode?"

"Of course. She has to."

"Why did they tie her up?"

"Because she had put out her own eyes with a potato peeler. And because she kept licking the walls of her room until her tongue and her lips were raw. So the Sisters tied her up out of compassion."

"What name did she go by outside?"

"Madame the Duchess Catherine, that's all I know."

"Cath-er-ine, where have you been," Eddie chanted.

"For a time two manservants looked after her, two brothers who used to help out in the kitchen now and then, twins, each weighing well over two hundred pounds. But Mother Superior put a stop to it soon afterward because they were found to be unchaste."

"What did they do?"

"Unchaste things, I can't say more than that. They hung around the Institute for several more days, and at night they would stand baying like dogs under Sister St. Gerolphe's window. Apparently they took off all their clothes while they did it."

"And then the Mizzlers chased them away, right?"

"Mizzlers? What Mizzlers? Who's been telling you about them?"

Eddie raised a protective hand to his face.

"Who?" shouted Louis. "Out with it! Was it that fine brother of yours? Come on! Out with it!"

"I'm not allowed to tell."

"What did he say to you? I want to know every word. Right here and now!"

"That . . . that the Mizzlers are everywhere, flying about, but that only you four, the Apostles, can see or hear them."

"Nonsense! There's no such thing as Mizzlers. But don't you dare breathe a word about them. To anybody. Or else you're in for it! Your brother is a birdbrain."

Louis returned to his book. ". . . the West Flemish Consciousness," he read, "fostered the Flemish tongue and asserted its right to be treated as an equal amongst the languages of the Great Dutch-speaking Fatherland."

"Tell me some more about Sister St. Gerolphe."

"Why?"

"Because you like her. I can tell from your voice."

"You wheedler," said Louis, like a grandfather speaking to his grandchild, and shut his book. "She is the most upright, the noblest of the Sisters, and that is why she's been tied up."

"That's sad. What does she do all day?"

"She holds her breviary and pretends to read. She squeezes her pimples because she's covered with sores under her shirt of goat hair."

"She'll soon be dead."

"In an odor of sanctity. What stinks now of rotting plaice will have the fragrance of incense and flowers. Mother Superior will get the scare of her life when that happens, and it will be many a long night before she is able to close her eyes, out of remorse for having had a true martyr under her roof without knowing it."

"She can't move," Eddie said to himself.

"Not an inch. She receives Communion in her chair. The Sisters are very polite to her because she has blue blood. Every morning she is washed and tended before anyone else."

Naturally, Louis had never seen this for himself, since from the foundation of the Institute not one pupil had ever managed to get into the Keep, and no one had ever told him about it either, he just knew. In winter, before dawn, when the Sister in charge of the fires lit the Institute's stoves and walked through the corridors bearing before her a smoking scuttle of softly glowing coal like an offering, with her elongated shadow on the wall, with the rustling of the trembling coals and of her skirts, with the red glow that lit up her features from below, she would go straight to the Keep, and where would she head for first but the room of her Sister held in thrall? Tenderly, devoutly, happily, she would thrust the coals into the opening of the stove, the warmth would reach the encrusted eyesockets of Sister St. Gerolphe, who would quickly whisper, "Thank you, thank you, thank you, for the warmth, Sister of the Fires, the frontiers of the world of darkness have been pushed back once again, thank you, because I, forever blindfolded by Our Lord Jesus, feel your warmth all the more for it."

One day it will happen. Before dawn. Unseen, Vlieghe sprinkles a pinch of myrrh on the glowing coals just as the Sister finds herself on the threshold, on the borderline that divides the Keep from the world. Dazed, the Sister sinks to the floor, the Apostles with Louis at their head step over her in their stocking feet and, following the smell, steal like the swiftest Sioux toward the door and splinter it with a tomahawk. We kneel down before her, I kiss her hand, she fumbles blindly in the air and finds my hair, for one moment she thinks that her two misshapen, naked servants have returned, but I whisper, "Four Apostles reporting, fear not, my kiss is not the kiss of Judas," and then we stand at attention, something she cannot see, although that is not at all certain, for after all we cannot see Christ's loving-kindness with earthly eyes either, and together we call our names out loud, seven nuns rush up in a clatter of dragnets and chains, but we remain at attention and await the verdict. Sister St. Gerolphe says, "Thank you, thank you, thank you, thank you, Seynaeve, Vlieghe, Dondeyne, and Byttebier! I have been living in this darkness for year upon year, and my Sisters scarcely knew that I lived among them, in their world. Thank you! Now they may safely start singing a Requiem Mass for me." Grateful though she may be, we are dragged off to the coal cellars. We offer no resistance as the bass voice of Sister St. Gerolphe is heard intoning, "Now be Thou welcome, Christ our Lord."

Then there would be the Tribunal, with the cross-examination, Mother Superior rapping her table and forty fingers with her jet-black ruler.

Under Vlieghe's supervision and as laid down in the Annals, Goossens wrote his application to join the Apostles in the form of a note folded into a four-pointed star and bearing the following declaration (in a penciled scrawl, overwhelming proof of Goossens's incompetence and also of Vlieghe's culpability—Louis decided there and then to raise the point as his first line of argument): "I, Albert Goossens, son of Theodore, residing in this world at Lovendegem, bear witness to the goodness of Christ. From this day forward, the name day of Petrus Canisius, Confessor and Doctor of the Church, third class, I shall maintain silence concerning all miracles. This I vow by the Forbidden Books. I shall submit to the placing of the sacred star on the spot upon my body assignated by the four Apostles. The reason for my application is that five Apostles are better than four, and that five is the number of the provinces of Flanders."

"Assignated?" said Louis to the ashen-faced Goossens.

"Yes. No?"

"Assigned. Designated. One or the other. Apostles, this application is slovenly and must be rewritten in a fair copy."

When Goossens had gone cringing away, the other three tried to talk Louis around. Things must not be made too hard for Goossens in case he became disgruntled and changed his mind about joining them. What was so terrible about his mistake, anyway? Just a couple of letters out of place. Louis shouldn't be such a nitpicker, they felt, and Byttebier even added, "Just because you reckon yourself an expert in High Flemish and because your godfather got a Gold Medal for Recitation once when he was young."

Louis examined the carelessly folded application form. The letters were all askew, several full stops and commas were missing, and there it was, underlined: "assignated." He tucked the letter away in the file labeled "Apostolic Letters."

The Apostles went and sat down in a row on Vlieghe's bed and raised their bare feet. Vlieghe's toes were long and thin, as if he never wore shoes. Byttebier's were disgustingly filthy. Goossens kissed their feet and was then made to do it all over again by Dondeyne, who felt that it had been done too perfunctorily. Then Goossens swore the oath "Faith and Fidelity," pulled up his nightshirt, and lay on the floor, his buttocks pressed tight together. Louis first, then Vlieghe, then Dondeyne, and then a jubilantly chirping Byttebier pummeled and pinched the pale backside. Goossens behaved manfully and made not a sound. Noting that Vlieghe was proud of his protégé, Louis redoubled his mauling efforts. When the skin was a mass of red weals, Louis said, "Amen." Goossens stood up, made the sign of the Cross three times, and then knelt before Byttebier, who rattled off, "With cross and salt and water sore, I hereby swear to sin no more," tucked up his own nightshirt, and urinated copiously over Goossens's hair. Goossens waited until the water had dripped from his shoulders, and then, carefully and fully briefed beforehand by Vlieghe, crawled on his knees to the head of the bed, found a towel, and silently mopped the floor.

From the town hall the local brass band could be heard repeating an endless series of drum rolls.

Byttebier left to find out if Sister Angel had started on her rounds. When he came back, Vlieghe said, "Now the numbers, quickly," and Goossens counted to a hundred as fast as he could. "The letters of the Testament," said Byttebier, and Goossens began reciting the alphabet, faltered, stuttered, constantly licking his dry lips, and finally gabbled it through in one go.

"Make a sound like a dog," said Louis. Goossens stuffed his handkerchief into his mouth, coughed, and then produced a strangled bark.

"Turn around three times," said Dondeyne.

The village band was now playing "Czar and Carpenter" at full blast.

"Where is your contribution to the treasury?" asked Louis. Goossens fetched a pack of faded, well-thumbed color prints of racing cyclists from under Vlieghe's pillow. On top, held in place by a red rubber band, was Poeske Scherens, six times world champion.

"No," said Louis, "that isn't acceptable. That's for trading on the playground, that's play money. Our treasury can't use that."

"But Vlieghe said that . . ."

"Vlieghe? Who is that?" As St. Peter denied the Savior with careless, assumed indifference, so I now deny my love, my beauty.

Taken aback, Goossens gestured with his chin toward Vlieghe, who was busy picking between his toes.

"The name Vlieghe is not known in this regiment. Apostles are called by Apostles' names during their meetings." Which wasn't entirely true, because the Apostles, and Byttebier in particular, quite often forgot their Apostles' names.

"I know that," Goossens said hastily. "You are Peter and Vlieghe is Paul."

"And what is my name?" asked Dondeyne. Goossens didn't know.

"Matthew," said Dondeyne proudly. "Because I have wings." He stroked a shoulder blade.

"I am Barnabas," said Byttebier. "And don't you forget it or you'll be in trouble."

"And what about me, what am I going to be called? Have you decided yet?" Goossens was sweating, or perhaps it was still the pee.

"That won't be settled until you've been accepted, until you've paid your contribution."

"You should have told me that, shouldn't you, Paul?" Goossens said, close to tears.

"The contribution," Vlieghe said firmly, almost too loudly, "will be here tomorrow." It's just empty talk, he wants me to capitulate, wants me to accept this churl of a Goossens without further ado, he knows that I'll give in because I love him, would offer up my life for him. Louis shrugged his shoulders and slapped Goossens's wet neck with his slipper. "Goossens, Hottentot, henceforth ambassador of God." He took out the Annals and with a lump in his throat read out, "For verily I say unto you, many prophets and men of righteousness have desired to see those things which ye see, and have not seen them, and to hear those things which ye hear, and have not heard them." He added an "Amen," although that wasn't in the Annals.

"*Voilà,*" said Byttebier, "that's it, then."

"So who am I now? What's my name?"

"Olibrius," said Louis.

"That isn't an Apostle," said Vlieghe.

"That's a brand of mustard," said Byttebier.

"Olibrius was the governor who wanted to marry St. Margaret and who worshiped idols."

"But . . ." Goossens looked shaken.

"Until the contribution arrives you may not use an Apostle's name. But I wouldn't worry about it, seeing that your dear comrade, Paul, has said it'll be coming tomorrow. Isn't that right?"

"You're a queer fish," said Vlieghe.

To Louis's annoyance he saw that Byttebier had started to eat an apple. The apple, fruit of Paradise, that, according to the Annals, was to be shared among the four of them. The unity of the Apostles and their ritual had been undermined.

"Paul told me to bring a book," said Goossens. "Shall I get it? Now?"

When he had gone, Vlieghe said, "It's not my fault. He comes from Lovendegem, and down there they are so, so . . ."

The book, which would never, ever do as a Forbidden Book, was an exercise book into which long ago someone had pasted some English and American newspaper clippings. The bulging cover of mottled white-and-black cardboard was labeled "Compositions." Underneath was an illegible name and "53rd Str. Brooklyn NY." Inside, yellowed and crumpled photographs had been stuck onto lined paper. The faces of criminals, soldiers, sheriffs, women with cloche hats and bad teeth.

"It's from America," said Goossens.

"There isn't a single Sister who can read American. That means it can never be a Forbidden Book."

"It's about loose women," cried Goossens desperately.

"I'll study it." Louis tucked the book under his arm. "Let us pray."

They closed their eyes and recited a Hail Mary, keeping time with "Czar and Carpenter."

concerning another child

Sister Kris gave Louis two chocolates from the half-open wall cupboard in which many packets and tin boxes, all marked and numbered, could be seen. The chocolate had already taken on a whitish bloom and tasted stale. Goossens gave him half a bar of his Côte d'Or milk chocolate.

Then Sister Kris sat down at the end of the long table and said that the situation was critical because now that the war in Spain was over, bands of the defeated Red murderers would be fleeing north. And since Christ the King had punished the Communists so heavily, they would come looking for revenge up here. Because they had grown addicted to slaughtering priests, violating Sisters, and killing children with blunt bayonets. Sister Kris liked to talk about Spain, and not only because she knew that her stories kept the boys spellbound. She herself was excited by them, as Louis could tell from the red spots on her otherwise waxen cheeks.

It was the workers in Spain in particular, said Sister Kris, who, blinded by propaganda, had gone completely mad, often sucking the blood from their victims' jugulars. One woman, unworthy of the name of woman, called La Pasionaria, was notorious for having bitten through the throats of several seminarians. The decomposing bodies of canons had been dragged from their consecrated graves and defiled. There are photographs of Flemish men who had been caught at such monstrous acts, and because these hyenas are now marked men they will receive no pardon once back on familiar soil. Hence, boys, it is our bounden duty to report immediately any sign at all of any stranger wandering about our Institute.

Most incautiously, Goossens, who had in the meantime received the name of Bartholomew, was displaying the sign of the star on his upper arm. It was a deformed starfish with pustules and yellowish lumps. Louis hoped it would never heal, that they would have to amputate Goossens's whole arm. After all, the apostle-martyr whose name he now bore had been skinned alive. At the same time, however, Louis deplored the slovenly way Vlieghe had tattooed the sign using a pen nib and purple ink. With the other Apostles the star sign had disappeared after five months.

"Cover up," Louis hissed. "Cover the star up."

Goossens at once pulled the sleeve of his tunic down to his knuckles. Outside, the little ones were singing "Bayard the Steed." The crowned Knight on his White Horse who leads the cavalry of Heaven bears a tattoo on his thigh with the words "King of Kings, Lord of Lords." How often did he not have to pull down his knightly garb lest the heathens spot these words? Many, many times, no doubt. Sister Kris had not noticed Goossens's star. Luckily. For she was one of the dangerous quartet who controlled the Institute.

First comes She who is more than a Sister and bears the title of Mother, Mother Superior, who reigns by Her absence. Even when she is standing right in front of your nose, a white face with a habitual look of faint surprise at the wickedness of her subjects, even then she does not seem to be altogether there. She corresponds with a host of dignitaries and collects the postage stamps that arrive from abroad. She has a passion for gardening, but, constrained by rank, she has to leave it to Sister Imelda. She comes from the poorest dock area of Antwerp, which explains why those who hear her speak find it hard to understand her.

Her three ministers are, first: Sister Econome, whom you glimpse only when you walk past her window which overlooks the playground, provided that the window is open and you dare to stop long enough to look, which is strictly forbidden. Then, if she looks up from her papers and from her writing, you will note an angry pair of spectacles and a narrow little mouth. She does addition with her spectacles, subtraction with her blunt fingers, multiplication with her rolled-up sleeves, and divides the world into pieces with her filed-down teeth.

Second: Sister Adam, that motherly, treacherous, kindly soul. She often picks up the little ones and rocks them on her lap, stroking her treble chin along their cheeks. Her peasant voice lulls you to sleep, cocoons you. Even a Hottentot knows how dangerous that sort of mother is, how quickly that maternal colossus can pivot on her axis and tweak your ears, both ears at once.

Third: Sister Kris, so-called because she is a knife. She never minces her words but goes straight for her target, and that target is you. Yet Louis once heard her singing when she was by herself in the gymnasium.

No matter how these three ministers of Mother Superior may disparage each other, they form a united front. Just look how they approach each other, for instance in the chapel, how they cast piercing glances at each other, how they signal to each other with their eyebrows, their nostrils, how they sail up to each other as if there were magnets under their bodices drawing them together, how slyly their elbows touch when they have to pass each other. Inside the Keep the trio must form a conclave apart, quaffing beakers brimming with mead, that drink of yeast and honey known in the land of Canaan and to the Ancient Belgians, from which they must gain a clear insight into the otherwise impenetrable network of rules, regulations, and decrees they administer. Four Strong Women who, more than all the other Sisters, are the brides of Christ.

"I'd like to have just one look at their rings, those three, to see if they've got any special inscriptions." (Byttebier.)

"They were put in charge out of sheer malice." (Dondeyne.)

"Or else they brought a bigger dowry than the rest." (Goossens.)

"Or passed stiffer exams." (Vlieghe.)

To the tune of the little ones' "Bayard the Steed," the Apostles sang, "The sluggard Steed, he has two mouths, one up north a-and one down south," and then went their separate ways, right arms raised. "Ugh!"

During Geography with Sister Sapristi, Louis felt out of sorts. Annoyed about Goossens's bungled initiation. Goossens had taken everything far too much for granted, he ought to have been made to feel more awe, pain, fear. Vlieghe had presumably made light of it all during the briefings. Louis picked at the encrusted snot stuck to his desk. The borders of the United States. The Arctic Ocean, the Pacific in the West. The climate: frigid, torrid, temperate. How long does a cable dispatched in Chicago on October 5 take to reach Antwerp? What countries are crossed by the Tropic of Capricorn? Chile is rich in saltpeter, the lake region has copper ore.

Sister Imelda and Sister Kris stood in the playground, looking as if something very sad had happened. They fell silent as Louis went past.

Not to be outdone, he said, "Sisters, I'm so unhappy. It's because my mother fell down the stairs."

Both Sisters looked incredulous at first, and then Sister Imelda burst into what was, for her, riotous laughter. "Yes," she said. "Of course."

"How high were the stairs then, Louis?" asked Sister Kris.

He pointed to the window above the refectory entrance.

"And was she badly hurt?" Sister Imelda was unable to keep a straight face. Sister Kris, too, put her hand in front of her mouth. "Where?"

"Where? Yes, where?"

"Her knees and her neck," said Louis.

Sister Imelda wiped her eyes. "Nowhere else?" she said as if with a sob. Once again a wall of mist closed around Louis. He would never learn the meaning of the impenetrable hints, the coded laughter. It was a domain reserved for the Sisters or for grown-ups, and even if you studied it eighteen hours a day you could never enter it. He felt a sheepish grin spreading across his mouth, like a muzzle. He nodded to the Sisters and waited. But the bell rang and the Sisters moved slowly away toward the chapel.

Louis put the blame on his mother, whose fall had given rise to misunderstandings, to inexplicable bursts of laughter. What was she doing right now in Walle? Certainly not housework. She was lying in bed painting her fingernails and listening to Radio Walle, to the comedians Wanten and Dalle.

That evening Sister Angel took him by the arm and led him to the inner courtyard where the conifers were. "I'm going to tell you something, but swear you won't go shouting from the rooftops that I've told you."

"I swear. On my father's head."

"Nothing terrible has happened at home. I can see that you're upset about your mother falling down the stairs, but that is only a figure of speech, grown-ups think they have to put it like that rather than speak the plain truth. Your mother didn't have a fall, she was taken to the hospital because she's expecting a baby, you are going to have a little sister or a little brother, Our Lord still has to make up His mind which one to select, to choose, aren't you pleased?"

"A little sister?" Louis saw a tiny creature in a nun's habit running across the playground, gurgling joyfully, straight into Mama's outstretched arms.

"Or a little brother. Which would you rather have?"

Tears of rage spurted from his eyes, at the humiliation, the dirty trick.

"I'm sure you'd like a little brother, who'd come here to school, too, so you could look after him?"

Louis stammered something. To his mortification a stifled cry escaped from his lips. He ran away. Saw out of the corner of his eye that Sister Angel was trying to catch up with him. Ran harder across the treacherous playground, the cowardly yard, past the pointing fingers of the sneering herd of Hottentots. Oh, how easily, how simply he had been taken in by all of them, most of all by Mama, who as always had conspired with her husband against her only child, shut away in the nuns' fortress.

In the refectory Louis kept his eyes fixed on his buttermilk porridge, of which he ate three platefuls. Sister Adam talked about the Marian Year, about the blessing *Urbi et Orbi* that the Holy Father, sick with anxiety about the clouds of war over Europe, had pronounced in the Maria Maggiore Basilica dedicated to Our Lady. The Virgin has borne a Child of the Holy Ghost, my mother is no better than the lowest beasts of the field.

Not so long ago he had believed (and so had Vlieghe and Dondeyne) that mothers get pains in their bellies, the labor pains, that they totter quickly to the toilet, squat down, and shit, that the turd is immediately fished out of the water by the women of the neighborhood before it has a chance to disintegrate and is put on the oilcloth on the kitchen table, where the parents, chatting away tenderly with one another, model it into a baby, whereupon a wind, summoned by fervent prayer, begins to blow through the window or down the chimney and settles upon the brown clay, the breath of God blowing life into the shit, which takes on color and begins to bend and stretch itself as if made of rubber, and then bawls for its mama to bring its first bottle.

That was what all of them had thought, with slight variations, when they had still been Hottentots and not yet Apostles, as dumb as the black men in the Belgian Congo, who, as the geography book tells you, were not very developed, were still stuck in the rut of their old ways, because they were unable to discover or invent anything new. Their boyish beliefs had been as deeply rooted in superstition as those of the black men, which, taken together with those people's corrupt habits and customs and undisciplined way of life, were the main cause of the decline of the Negro race.

Louis stole into the dormitory, picked up an exercise book with a black moiré cover, and wrote hurriedly, "My Grandpa is the biggest Pharisee of them all. Together with his firstborn, my father, he takes advantage of my ignorance to make a fool of me. I do not want a little sister or a little brother, unless in return I am sent to a school where the teachers are not all abject liars. Except for Sister Angel, who means well."

Then he went outside and sat down beside Vlieghe on the merry-go-round and said, not seeking to meet those almond-shaped eyes, that his mother would soon be better. "That's good," Vlieghe said, and Louis was on the point of revealing the truth that had just burst open like a boil, it was on the tip of his tongue, and whom could he trust more than Vlieghe, who had the beauty of goodness? Not innocence but (like St. Jan Berchmans) the ability to curb malice. Instead, he heard himself say:

"It was my grandfather, who is my godfather, too, because I am the firstborn, who pushed my mother down the stairs, he thinks he will get away with it because he did it where no one could see him, but Madame Piroen from across the road, who was cleaning her windows at the time, just happened to be looking through the bull's-eye of the stairwell. She doesn't dare go to the police, because my grandfather has a great many connections, including police inspectors. Don't you think he should be made to pay for that?"

"Ought to have his legs smashed with a poker," said Vlieghe, goodness personified.

"Or poison put in his soup, just a little every day so that his stomach shrivels up and gets holes burned into it."

Byttebier, whom they hadn't heard approaching, hung like a monkey from one of the poles of the merry-go-round.

"Lupin seeds," he said. "Then he'll be paralyzed." They went to look in Sister Imelda's garden but couldn't find any lupins. It also transpired that Byttebier didn't really know what they looked like. In the playroom the three of them filled in the map of Germany with colored pencils. Vlieghe, who was doing the North in pale green, went over the boundaries, needless to say, so that the edges of the summer sky–blue Baltic became covered in seaweed; Louis used sepia to color in the Swabian Alps and Carinthia. Sister Adam stroked Vlieghe's hair as she walked past. That's all right, she's allowed to. Although he is my Vlieghe, they may admire and touch him.

That baby, that baby about to make its appearance in Walle. If it is a girl, it will be in league with Mama. How does it make its appearance, what is so sinful about the whole thing that they keep going on about storks, cauliflowers, or falling down stairs? Last summer Uncle Omer, who is considered a bit of a card and who looks like Mama, said, pointing to the cauliflowers in Meerke's garden, "Look there, in between those knobbly bits beneath the leaves, that's where children are grown. And the biggest cauliflower in the world is in America in the garden of the Dionnes, there were five there at one go."

But how does the changeover take place? One moment the baby is inside the layers of fat in someone's tummy, and the next moment the tummy gets sore and something tears and there's a pink sausage lying in the arms of the Holy Virgin, something Mongol-like, in swaddling clothes, that reaches for Mary's halo. And what exactly is it that tears? That oozing, many-lipped opening that you see in cows and on Den Dooven's drawings, which, as soon as a Sister appears, he crumples up and swallows? And what if the new member of the family, who is sure to look like Grandpa with a little snub nose, like Papa with thin eyebrows, like me with my ears, and who will be given a name and baptized, what if he turns out to have a hunchback? The Greeks would have bashed his head in without hesitation. Or left him like a foundling out on the rocks for the mountain goats, which are carnivorous in those parts.

And anyway, where is a baby like that made in the first place? In bed, according to Dondeyne, but that's just a Hottentot tall story, in bed they kiss and cuddle, grown-ups, they rub up against each other because they enjoy that, but when a papa takes aim with his jet of piss and sprays at mama's opening, they never do that in bed but in a bathroom or when they don't have a bathroom they do it in the kitchen, so that it's easy for a mama to mop it up.

This brother about to be born was raising a great many doubts, opening up a host of vague, veiled possibilities. Created in the image and likeness of God. But how? Actually, I was not altogether dissatisfied with that stupid explanation about a midget modeled out of shit. It never bothered me, I thought it highly plausible, explicit, clear. Some day the new explanation will no doubt appear just as wrong. A baby plops out of this folded place to a lot of shrieking from these women, right, then the angels turn up for the christening, the angel of the bones, the angel of the muscles, the angel of the nerves, and a whole pile of nameless angels, and they all worm themselves, as invisible as the Mizzlers, straight through the baby's skin and guts, and there they form a stringy sort of clot that stays disembodied and is called the soul. The water that the priest sprinkles over the skull—where there is a hole that does not close up until after the christening, because otherwise the Holy Ghost can't get inside the brainpan—makes this hot, disembodied clot begin to sizzle and to spread like steam through the whole body. That's what happened with the first two people on earth who lay wailing with fear outside the concrete wall that surrounded Paradise. God pretended He wasn't in, wouldn't open up, it was weeks and weeks before He started feeling sorry for those two yelling outside his gate and baptized them in the Jordan and then Adam pissed into Eve's belly, and Abel, who was goodness with the face of a little baby fox, and Cain, who was as hairy as a black poodle, were born. Cain, one of the first devils in human form.

"The devil shall never be my master."

"Nor mine," said Vlieghe.

"We must resist temptation."

"Else we shall burn," said Vlieghe. That night they swore for the umpteenth time that they would go and be missionaries in the Congo, where the Protestants, richer and trickier than the Catholics, might well be gaining the upper hand. But they disagreed about the location of their mission. Louis liked the idea of areas of dense rainforest, Vlieghe leaned more toward those arid places called the bush, with their tough, prickly plants.

_____*the mizzlers*

*I*t was Vandenabeele who pointed to the cow. Vandenabeele does multiplication the whole day long. Ever since he learned how to do it, he's done nothing else, in the margins of books, on grubby little pieces of paper, in the dim light of dawn, under the lamp in the playground where small, white rabbit droppings made of pellets of paper are sometimes found, which, when opened up, reveal Vandenabeele's multiplications; if Vandenabeele is busy and you ask him something, he will cut you short, doggedly immersed in the multiplication of a given number of potatoes by a given number of shoelaces in his gray-penciled, instantly smudged, scribbled numbers and crosses and strokes.

During their school walks he attempts to multiply everything in his head but never succeeds.

"Look," said Vandenabeele, "over there, that cow."

"What about it?"

"Can't you see, that cow over there?"

Louis saw it at once, it was Mary, the dead cow. Not really, of course, but in among those browny-red mammoths in the meadow stood a white

49

cow haphazardly bespattered with black paint by Baekelandt as a sign of mourning, in memory of the dead Mary.

"What a driveling idiot!"

"Why didn't he paint her black all over?"

"He ran out of paint," said Louis.

They screamed with laughter, those Hottentots who passed themselves off as Apostles. Louis joined in. "No," he said after a while, "that was a joke. The real reason is that it's meant to be a double mourning. A Flemish mourning in black, and a Chinese one in white. You wear white for mourning in China." They found this too ridiculous for words. They didn't laugh.

"It's a Dutch cow and that's all there is to it," said Byttebier. The cow moved toward Louis.

Usually their walks took them as far as the boundary of Markegem, up to the hill where Dr. Gevaert's villa stood. Dr. Gevaert was using Socialist propaganda to get elected mayor of Haarbeke. No one who was really sick ever went to him for treatment. According to Byttebier, whose father had been to the Zeppelin Meadow in Nuremberg last year when thousands of party leaders had filed in torchlit procession past their *Führer*, Dr. Gevaerts was sure to get a good beating from the Flemish nationalists one of these days. One night that enemy of our people would have his ugly mug smashed in. "We've warned him," said Byttebier, "but a lot he cares. When we've finished with him, he'll have to treat himself, the doctor will."

But this time the school walk did not get as far as the hill, because the little ones kept dragging their feet and sitting down all the time. Jongbloed and Pauwels had to pull them up and drag them along. The little ones howled, the bigger ones copied them, there was bawling and mewling in the meadows, and the scolding of Sister Adam.

The cow came up to Louis, he who had murdered Mary the cow because he had refused to help Baekelandt. The hairy white of her coat turned gray, though no cloud had passed across the sun. She nodded her head, then shook it: "No, no." Then she turned her back toward Louis, spread her hind legs wide, knelt down on her forelegs, lowed, and stuck her backside with the regular patterns of caked, encrusted cowpats up in the air. The red-and-white cows kept their distance and watched. The gray cow looked around at Louis, her white eyelashes fluttering.

"Mary," said Louis gently.

The cow lifted her tail, the arsehole and the lobes of the mottled slit underneath opened, swelled up, turned purple, as if being blown up with a bicycle pump from the inside, blisters and folds of skin bulged, and a red lump of flesh forced its way outward, a battered and blood-spattered babyface with a triple chin and full-to-bursting cheek pouches and, between two swollen eyelids, two jet-black currants of eyes that lit up for an instant, then went out. The cow sank to her knees and buried the apparition under her flanks.

"Did you see that?"

"What?" asked Dondeyne, picking at his large, diseased red ear.

"What was in that cow."

"What was it then?"

"A baby."

"A calf?"

"A baby."

"Seynaeve," said Sister Adam tartly, "give the little ones a hand. We'll be much too late for Benediction."

By the time Benediction was over and it had begun to get dark, Louis had calmed down. Many explanations of what he had seen had occurred to him.

"I saw the queen of the Mizzlers," he told Vlieghe.

"What did she look like?"

"You know the way the queen of the ants is a hundred times bigger than an ordinary ant . . ."

"You're thinking of bees, you blockhead."

"She had a child's face. I think my Grandpa probably looked like that when he was born, about 1880 or whenever it was."

"And what was she doing?"

"She saw me and immediately ordered the cow to hide her away inside her . . ." He was afraid to say "arsehole." "What that means is that if she allows herself to be seen . . ." His voice cracked.

"Whenever she manifests herself . . ." He faltered before Vlieghe's incredulous expression, then continued anyway. "The Mizzlers ordered her to manifest herself . . ."

"Inside a milk factory's bottom?"

"Inside Mary, the holy cow."

Vlieghe sighed and went into the recreation room, where the other Apostles were busy drawing. Houses. For later on, when they returned to the world. And return they would, deliverance was in sight. They were not allowed to stay on at the Institute after their First Communion except by special dispensation from the Bishop. Mortelmans had been given one, Mortelmans who had already been displaying the beginnings of a mustache. Louis had personally felt the snot-soaked fuzz. Mortelmans was allowed to stay on because his uncle, the canon, had pleaded that his father, who was a widower, could not possibly look after his son. Then one day Mortelmans had disappeared without any explanation. The Sisters refused to say why or how.

The only sign of Mortelmans after his inexplicable disappearance was a picture from an obituary notice sent to Byttebier in an envelope without a return address. The dead man in question was "The Very Reverend Monsignor Kamiel van Ronslé, First Apostolic Vicar to the Belgian Congo and Leopoldville, deceased at Boma, November 14, 1938." Underneath the printed text, the initials M.M., which could only mean Marcel Mortelmans, were written in blue ink that had run.

The Apostles' houses came in all shapes. Vlieghe's were crooked because Vlieghe couldn't draw straight lines, everything undulated, twisted, curved. Even his ground plans. Byttebier produced rooms that were too high, his houses looked like cathedrals, in the corner of every room stood a ladder for cleaning the top windows. Dondeyne drew huts, hovels, their walls entirely covered with ornaments, mostly in the shape of a cross. Louis drew boxes piled one on top of the other because he was providing enough rooms for a family with lots of children, the boxes either cones or cubes. Goossens had a weakness for country houses in the shape of shoes, one of them like the boot of Italy.

Pages full of rows of fir trees, an unending tangle of beams, arches, spyholes everywhere, tall coal stoves, small gardens, toilets, rickety towers for housing prisoners, chapels attached to kitchens. There was almost always a round sun in the right-hand corner of the drawing, with rays that penetrated the walls, and in the top left corner the letters TTGGG: To the Greater Glory of God.

What Louis does not tell anyone is that now and then, secretly, he does a drawing of the Bad House that stands to the left of the wood that the school pass on their walks toward Walle. Every time, without fail, as soon as the column of boys draws level with it, the escorting Sister points to something on the other side: "Oh, just look at those pigeons!"—"Oh, the smoke from the tile works!"—"Oh, what a darling little goat!" And the Sister makes sure that the pupils continue to look in that direction for twenty paces until the white poplars have hidden the Bad House from view. The Bad House is painted beige, has the word "Titanic" written on it in ornate red letters, and has opaque windows behind which, when the sun is at a certain angle, it is said a woman dressed in white can be seen. This woman receives many travelers and makes them pay fifty francs for an ordinary glass of water. Louis draws the façade, the lettering, the flounced curtains on the first floor, a spacious room with six chairs around a low table, but he never manages to get them in proper perspective, and the figure in the white dress never comes out properly either. True, Louis has drawn the woman on a separate page, carrying a dachshund on her arm, something Louis had copied from a print of the Good Shepherd with a Lamb. But when he shaded in the folds of her dress with a soft, Swiss-made Caran d'Ache pencil, he suddenly broke into a sweat, God is watching you, he crumpled up the drawing and for three whole days kept an eye on his right hand to make sure the fingertips had not started to wither. When nothing appeared to be happening, he carved a cross into the soft skin between thumb and index finger with his steel nib and rubbed ink into it.

The Bad House harbors bad men, but they come and go, the only one who stays there all the time is the white-clad Mary Magdalene, who washed Jesus' feet and dried them with her luxuriant red hair. For a time the Apostles thought that Mortelmans had taken refuge in the Bad House during the first days of his escape, living there in sin until the proprietress chased him out of the Evil Temple because his sinfulness had appalled even the most sinful visitors. But then the Apostles changed their minds, Mortelmans was too stupid to sin on a grand scale. Louis thinks that he must have met his death in some distant land, perhaps on the borders of the Tyrol, Mortelmans running through a beet field, a German biplane spots him from the air, dives, skims over Mortelmans, who from sheer panic stumbles over a rock, strikes his temple against a stone, and his brains spill out of his ears.

We could have, ought to have, seen it coming. For there had been something not quite right about Mortelmans. The air in the Institute hadn't agreed with him, the dust given off by the brick walls or by the peeling paint of the windows—hadn't he once had blisters on his face as big as quarter-francs? Or was it the air from the nuns' habits? Or the first (unnoticed) revelation of the Mizzlers?

The Mizzlers had turned up two years ago. Like the origin of children, their provenance had been the subject of determined research. They sprang from sunbeams caught when the sun went down. From the moisture between blades of grass. From the invisible droppings angels scatter when they have diarrhea. From dewdrops. From God's beads of sweat. Thousands are born every second, and eighty percent die at once. All the Mizzlers put together are no more than a grain of sand in the eyelashes of the Holy Ghost.

Mizzlers always laugh, no matter what happens, even at the worst thing you can imagine. Inaudible, invisible, yet you know that they are laughing.

"Tell us some more about the Mizzlers," Vlieghe said.

He used to say "please" once upon a time.

"Come on, Louis," Vlieghe said, and he stroked my knee.

"Female Mizzlers have a skin made of flowers. Their hair changes color from one moment to the next, depending on their mood."

"Only the women?"

"Only the women."

"What colors?"

"When a Mizzler woman gets angry, she laughs, of course, but her hair, her eyebrows, and her eyelashes turn tomato-red. You can tell the age of a Mizzler woman from that, because when they are young and haven't yet mastered the art of changing hair color, their hair stays pink. When they are in mourning, for example when the sun rises and they can see that lots of their sisters have been killed, their hair turns pitch-black with silver specks."

"And when they are pleased?"

"Grass-green."

"When they are jealous, like Sister Kris?"

"Yellow. The color of egg yolk. They eat everything in sight. Except for what moves horizontally, like, say, worms or toads, because they were made vertically out of sunbeams. But for the rest, they gobble up cigars, shoelaces, the little ones' sweets, clothespins."

"But what do they *do?*"

"They don't bother about us, not usually, unless we break their rules, but then it's hard for us to know what their rules are."

"But what do they *do?*"

"Most of the time they stare silently straight in front of them and pray."

"While they're still laughing?"

"Bernadette Soubirous laughed when she prayed, too."

"Why don't they bother about us?"

"Because that's a very dangerous thing for them to do, since if we were to catch one of them at it and look him in the eye, even by accident, he would melt away on the spot."

"Can they speak?"

"They chatter away all the time, but even if we could hear them, we wouldn't understand a word. They talk twaddledy-gobbledygook."

The Apostles laughed. Louis was pleased but didn't show it.

"Mizzlers never brush their teeth, never lace up their shoes, and never button up their celluloid collars. They chew sweet things all day long. They have discovered a chocolate that doesn't melt and never gets any smaller. They sing a lot, with one cheek against the ground. Their national anthem is the *Tantum Ergo.* They are very healthy, mainly because they never wash."

"Like you," said Byttebier.

"They have shops where you can buy feelings. So many francs for an hour of sadness or pride or anger. The mothers of young Mizzlers are allowed to look after their children, of course, but they must always keep at least six feet away from them. And they must do everything their children ask. They have to guess what their children want. Their national monument is a mother dying for her child. Their national dish is cauliflower. I don't know what their national virtues are. But they are easily embarrassed. The smallest thing makes them feel uncomfortable, and then they start stammering and stuttering, though they keep on laughing, of course, like hyenas. Or they hiss like nuns. Lots of them are quite unable to bid their dead relatives farewell and sometimes drag three, maybe four, aunts or cousins behind them, some of the dead are skeletons and then you can hear these corpse-bearers from a long way off, rattling and groaning, though most people think it's a birch tree splitting or a parquet floor creaking. Mothers sometimes carry four or five dead children in their arms, and then they are happy because they don't have to keep their six feet's distance and can cuddle their children as much as they like. Incidentally, when they are little, Mizzlers are allowed to kick and hit their mothers. All they have to do is say one Paternoster right afterward and then they are forgiven."

"Kicking, hitting, and saying Paternosters, what a life!" said Byttebier.

He was grosser and more stupid than ever at that time, the period when the Mizzlers still loomed large in the Apostles' minds.

"Now and then," Louis had told them, "a Mizzler will sit all hunched up with his head between his knees, and with snot and tears dripping onto the ground. That goes on for three weeks, then his hair falls out in handfuls, he sheds his skin, even his mother gives him a wide berth because he begins to stink disgustingly, then his teeth start to fall out, and he can't stop coughing. The week after that, he begins walking on all fours and rubs his shit on his hair to slick it down."

"I did just the same when I was small," said Byttebier.

"I used to eat it," said Dondeyne.

"But why does that Mizzler do all like that?" Vlieghe asked.

Louis paused, then burst out laughing. "Because he is in love."

"You nincompoop!" Byttebier gave an Apache yell, they all whooped and broke into a war dance with tomahawks. That was in the time of the Mizzlers, but now the Mizzlers turn up only very occasionally, and then just for Louis. Like the revelation in Mary the cow's shit this afternoon.

Louis heard one of the little ones being treated in the infirmary, being soothed by Sister Angel. Why had Sister Angel told him the truth about Mama's baby? Was it the whole truth, nothing but the truth, so help me God? In order to thumb her nose at those sneering, underhanded Sisters Imelda and Kris, or because she didn't want him to look so foolish? But telling the truth, isn't that something for beginners in an Institute, for novices, postulants, rather than for a dyed-in-the-(black)-wool nun?

He had run away when he heard about it, about the baby. Feeble, feeble. When would he ever learn to stand firm in the raging sea, to brave evil like Charles of Denmark or Joan of Arc? Take care. Just as you must not give way to all sorts of temptation, so you must not evade the blows that come your way. Even when they come raining down like slaps in the face.

"Be firm," said Louis aloud.

Give as good as you get. As Felicien Vervaecke had done last year in the Alps—Papa sitting beside me on the sofa, the radio had crackled, Papa had said, "This is a great moment for Flanders"—Felicien Vervaecke was two minutes forty-five seconds ahead of Bartali, it was July 23, all the factories had stopped work, so had all the schools and all the offices, and on the radio Bartali and that sly Wardje Vissers were neck and neck and Bartali put on a spurt, Vervaecke was bound to lose, but he gave as good as he got, and that's what I must do, too, all the time. Why do I keep thinking that this is my last spring on earth, when I know perfectly well that isn't true, since the Lord Jesus still has so many plans for me, if only I serve Him well and praise Him?

*T*hen there was a half-holiday, with the Fancy Fair and the annual visit to the village cinema, the Diana, a pagan temple, its lobby full of photographs and posters of toothy American stars of the silver screen, men with lacquered hair, ladies sleek as mica, cowboys socking each other on the jaw. Sister Adam piloted her little troop, dawdling and lingering around the photographs, into the theater. The little ones shouted and chased one another up and down. Louis sat next to Vlieghe, the lights dimmed, that idiot Dondeyne yelled, "Ow, ow, ow, I'm going blind!"

A three-master was rocking in the sea, surrounded by glistening black humps, the backs of gigantic seals. On board the captain was scanning the shore where a nobleman in a tailcoat was waving. "That's William Tell," Sister Kris told the little ones. Rays of sunlight fanned out from behind fir trees. Snow fell across the screen. A waterfall gave off steam. A gate creaked beside a thatched farmhouse. Snow-white slashes flickered across the picture, a muffled rumbling accompanied images of wavering figures plotting something criminal together.

The little ones said that they liked the magic lantern in the recreation room better. Louis remembered how enraptured he and Vlieghe had been by those wooden, sickly little colored pictures, the motionless tales of the gardener who had a flowerpot fall on his head, or the goose that bit the fox's tail, with the late Sister Gabriel providing the voices of the animals, who squabbled continually in West Flemish.

But these jerky grayish-black movements were far more opaque, more mysterious. Vlieghe's profile with its drooping lower lip was turned toward the screen. Heavy clouds. A monk hastened past a lone oak, a churchyard, a seashore. He hid. A dozen trotting horses. Riding them, nuns in flapping, hairy coats. But if this was about William Tell, how could there be a sea? Must look at the map of Switzerland.

"It's a lake," said Goossens. "In Switzerland there are lakes like seas."

"It's about the Czar's courier," said Byttebier, "just watch and see." Narrow mountain peaks, rocks covered in ice and lichens. The nuns, wearing beards, leaped from their steaming horses, stood with legs wide apart in a semicircle, and swore an oath, while the storm raged and letters appeared across their faces: "November 8, 1307, on the Rütli." That was five years after the Battle of the Golden Spurs.

Then there was an argument with a one-eyed man in a fur coat. "Governor Gessler," said Sister Adam, as if he were an acquaintance of hers.

The screen crackled. A tribunal in a vault lit by torches. A thin little man was put on the rack, leg irons were tightened, thumbscrews, the torturer poured a bucket of water over the puny, limp body, the little ones gloated. Governor Gessler approached, he was nervous, the veins on his forehead stood out, he laid his cheek tenderly against the wet hair on the tortured man's chest, listened graciously, then sneered and gave a nod. The torturer, who had Sister Kris's nose and Sister Imelda's full lips, obeyed; he seized the dying man's throat with gnarled hands and squeezed until the sweat ran down his chin, to the piercing cheers of the little ones. Then mercenaries in the flat helmets of Tommies (which always made Papa laugh, "That kind of helmet is only good for eating soup") set fire to some huts. All this was being watched sorrowfully by William Tell, who was lying concealed behind motionless reeds and flickering letters that the Hottentots read out loud in a singsong: "Tell takes refuge in Küssnacht."

"Quiet!" called Sister Adam. "Quiet, or . . . ."

"That was where the queen died," whispered Louis.

"Where?"

"In Küssnacht." (*Küss,* kiss, *Nacht,* night, Vlieghe.)

"I didn't see any queen," said Vlieghe.

"Queen Astrid, dummy." Louis laid the stress on the "strid," just like

Aunt Violet, who kept a musty suitcase full of clippings and magazines about the life and death of the Swedish Swan who had come from the North to marry King Leopold and who had died of it.

When Louis turned back to the screen from Vlieghe's profile, something had changed. The grayish-black picture now had pink speckles, blue-green shimmers. Tartar horsemen clattered across a frozen lake, chasing a scraggy colossus in a bearskin, who, as he fell on the bluish ice and blew steam out of his nostrils, turned out to be Holst. Holst waved his arms about, but the slit-eyed horsemen seized him and bound him in a straitjacket of coarse linen. Holst's undaunted face, powdered with snow, filled the screen and said something to Louis that, even if this had not been a silent film, would have remained unheard because of the noise made by the little ones. With lightning speed a brushwood fire was built, and the Tartar chief heated a broadsword in it, then held the white-hot metal close to Holst's eyes, which watered and seemed to melt.

"No!" shouted Louis. Vlieghe gave him a thump.

As if at Louis's command, the film sputtered and stalled. Lights went up, there was a noise of chairs being shoved about at the back of the hall, and rough, smoke-steeped voices. Sister Adam sprang to her feet. Six farmhands were sauntering down the aisle, apparently drunk. "Convent's taken over t' cinema!" " 'S not poss'ble." "C'mon, little 'uns, out you go!"

"Meneer Servaes," said Sister Adam, "this is a private showing. If you don't mind."

"Whoa, Sister," said the farmhand. "Whoa," as if to his horse.

A younger man took his cap off and said, "Look, Sister, we've got to get this here place ready for the Farmers' Union Ball, got to put up them Chinese lanterns . . ." The gray screen on which the last image to appear had been that of the weeping angel Holst was now wrinkled, empty, dead. The little ones began screaming again. A confused conversation ensued between the sour-smelling farmhands, who explained that the date of their ball had been fixed a year before, and the two Sisters, who finished by clapping their hands angrily.

In the lobby Vlieghe said it was a pity, things had just started to get exciting, what with that one-eyed hunter. Hadn't he realized, then, that they had randomly stuck together odd bits of different films, as they did every year? Louis had never been able to fathom why they did this; presumably they knew that the Sisters and their pupils were only too happy to watch anything that moved in a smudged black-and-white (and this time, amazingly, colored) light, whereas a complete film, of the kind normally shown on Sunday nights in the Diana, with titles and music and a beginning, a middle, and an end, might have had unknown, dangerous effects on young boys destined to grow up bewildered, to remain skewered on riddles, remnants, teasingly incomprehensible, impenetrable, looking-glass fragments.

"That blind man, that was the Czar's courier, didn't I tell you, it's the same film we saw two years ago," said Byttebier.

"A stupid film," said Goossens.

Sister Kris beckoned, and they lined up. Sister Kris asked, "Did you like it?"

"Yes, Sister."

"If the Russians caught you, which eye would you rather lose?"

"Neither of them, Sister," said Louis.

"And you, Dondeyne?"

"The right eye," said the groveler.

She lifted her kris-shaped nose. "All I'd let them have would be a black eye!" she cried triumphantly. There was snickering. Mortification, Louis thought. You were expected to laugh at the Sisters' silly, childish jokes. Many small mortifications make a great love. My name will be entered in the Book of Child Martyrs one day, but I'll have to be quick. Holst, my uncouth giant and guardian angel, begged me in tears to, to do what? To give up my comfortable mission in hot countries. A sheet of ice will be my martyr's death. Freezing to death while wolves gnaw at my toes, I intone the *Tantum Ergo* at the top of my voice. After evening prayers Sister Kris said that this instructive film had shown that the freedom of one's fatherland comes before anything else. "We, too, must swear to defend Belgium at all costs, this little country that has never done anyone any harm, but on the contrary has always ended up invaded, humiliated, and occupied. We shall defend it with the help of St. Joseph, Belgium's patron saint. During the coming term, we plan to go on an outing to Dikkebus Lake, following which we shall visit the trenches and the Yser Tower." (Then she would be able to explain things to them because she came from the area around Ypres, a town that had been laid waste and rebuilt many times.)

"Let us all now pray with a special intention for His Majesty King Leopold, who is having to make difficult decisions in these difficult times, although his heart is not really in it because he has not yet recovered from the death of Queen Astrid." They prayed.

King Leopold was sitting all alone in front of his grate in which the fire had gone out, although he hadn't noticed. His Lord Chamberlain, not daring to disturb the mourner's reverie, kept careful watch over his sovereign.

"Good night, Astrid," murmured King Leopold. *"Adieu, ma belle reine-claude."*

"We must stand four-square behind our king," said Dondeyne in the playground.

"Yes, now is the time," said Goossens.

"Four-square behind the flag," said Den Dooven. Since he had sat down with the Apostles unasked, Louis said, "My dad blows his nose in the Belgian flag," and savored the Apostles' shocked reaction. Byttebier said, "And mine wipes his bottom with it." Terrorized, Den Dooven went away.

"My father is a staunch Fleming," said Vlieghe. "But if he'd heard what you said, he would have gone straight to the gendarmerie and had you locked up, both of you, for insulting the flag."

"My father would, too," said Goossens. "But if I asked him nicely, he wouldn't do it."

"Why?"

"Because he is my friend."

At that the Apostles fell silent. They found it hard to believe. Although Goossens was too much of a Hottentot to invent something like that. Goossens's father must be a Pharisee who could make his son believe anything he wanted. Like my father, who allowed me to believe that his wife had tripped on the stairs, while she . . . while she . . . was actually worse than the landlady of the Bad House.

"My mother will probably die this summer," said Louis. "All her insides were completely messed up when she had her fall. Particularly her kidneys." The kidneys, that's what Aunt Mona and Mama kept going on about, blocked kidneys, swollen kidneys. Mizzlers don't have any kidneys, none at all.

"Listen, a May bug," said Vlieghe and they made for the pear tree and jumped up and hit the lower branches. Louis ambled slowly across to the music room, where Sister Angel, with her porcelain, innocent face, stood at the open window.

"Was it a nice film, Louis?"

"Yes, it was, Sister."

"Are you pleased it's nearly holiday time?"

"Yes, Sister."

"Have you already said your little prayer tonight?"

"Yes."

"For whom?"

"For my mother," he said, because that was what she expected.

"Good," she said and turned to go.

"Sister."

"Yes, Louis."

"I love you." She started, peered to her left and right.

"You're a strange one, you are," she said, leaned forward to take in the whole playground, then blew her whistle. The Apostles and the Hottentots lined up in single file. In the window Sister Angel looked like Charles the Bold. After a battle in the year whatever-it-was, Charles the Bold had found himself caught on a frozen lake near Nancy. He had been devoured by wolves while singing psalms. And yet his name was not in the Book of Martyrs.

Easter was approaching from afar, and the Easter holidays.

The four Apostles—Goossens had already left—went on Sister Econome's orders to give the gardener a hand in the orchard, where he was busy with chicks and piglets, which were overexcited at having just been let out.

"So long, Baekelandt, see you next term."

"Who did you say?"

"Baekelmans, sorry."

"Idiots," said Baekelandt.

"Mind your manners, Baekelandt," said Byttebier cheekily. Baekelandt pushed Louis to one side, picked up a windfall and took a bite. He always gobbled up the bruised fruit.

"You're lucky you little beggars weren't born in Germany, the children there go to school in the morning and work in the fields all afternoon. You'd be planting potatoes, bringing in the rye, spreading manure. That's how it's done in Germany, and that's why they're winning. You don't have to tell me about the Germans, they're a load of bastards, but they mean business, they've got their country shipshape, people have jobs, while the Belgians, all they do is follow the rotten example of the French, they're never happy, they're either on strike or on the dole. Too well off, that's what I say."

After that they had to wash their hands and faces, comb their hair, and get their suitcases ready. The scent of Lux soap and of Ça-va-seul shoe polish wafted through the washroom.

In the kitchen garden they peed for the last time to see who could go the farthest. Dondeyne won as usual. Louis came in last and felt deeply ashamed. It was his punishment for having mocked the Belgian flag.

Sister Kris stood with the little ones, tapping her cheek with a big, heavy key. With the other hand she stroked the shaven head of one who had had lice.

"Attend to your handwriting every day, Seynaeve. A good hand must be practiced daily."

Louis nodded.

"And your arithmetic is the most important thing of all. Without arithmetic you won't get ahead in the world. Arithmetic is the foundation for all that follows." She put the end of the key into her mouth.

"It may be, Seynaeve, because man proposes and God disposes, that we shall never meet again. Things being what they are, indeed, it is quite possible that we may have to close down." She pushed away the little one, who had been clinging to her all the time like the dog against the wounded thigh of St. Roch. "Yes, if the *Führer* keeps acting up we may well have to shut up shop altogether."

"But he has sworn that he will leave Belgium alone."

"And on what does a heathen swear?"

She sucked on the key. Then, with a wet, cool thumb, she made the sign of the Cross on Louis's forehead. What ever was possessing her, this woman who not for nothing had been named after a kris, the Javanese dagger?

"Will you think of us now and then, Seynaeve?"

"Yes, Sister. Of course."

"Of me, too?"

"Of you, too. I swear on my mother's head." You couldn't rely on anyone, that was obvious, you couldn't even tell what people, nuns, were likely to do next, for Sister Kris was truly smiling now, displaying her irregular upper teeth.

The afternoon dragged on unbearably. They watched Sister Imelda planting gladioli, Sister Sapristi rustling past, beating time to an inaudible tune, pupils scrambling for their suitcases and racing away joyfully, one by one.

It was the awful week of the suffering of Our Lord, during which it was forbidden to spin, lest cords be wrought unwittingly with which to bind Our Lord. Den Dooven read out the jokes from *Bravo* and had to keep stopping in the middle because he was hiccupping with laughter. Christ died on the Cross even for Den Dooven.

They watched Sister Econome approach clasping a huge color photograph in a heavy gold frame to her chest, followed her as far as the corridor, and pestered her until she let them have a look. It was a portrait of the new Pope.

"You can tell from his eyes that he's extremely intelligent. Can you see that, boys?" They nodded. It was true. Pacelli had a tight-lipped slit of a mouth and stared out imperiously, sunken-eyed, from behind his spectacles. "Peace is the work of justice" was his motto.

"He wants peace, boys, can you see that? Peace on earth for all men, you can read it on his face."

Then the horn of Vlieghe's father's car sounded. Louis held Vlieghe back.

"What's the matter?"

"You're leaving," said Louis. He walked with Vlieghe toward the corridor.

"You are, too."

"But you're going first."

"Each one in turn."

Louis blessed him as it was laid down in the Acts. *"In nomine Patris."* Although Sister Adam at the entrance could see him, he kissed Vlieghe's cheek.

"Blockhead," said Vlieghe. Papa would have said something like that about the foul habit French and Jewish men had of kissing one another.

"They might close the Institute."

"I won't shed any tears over that."

"No," said Louis. "Me neither."

Vlieghe waved to Sister Adam, to the pear tree, to the white merry-go-round. Not to me. Of course not.

Then he was home in Walle, and she who was never there for him, who had deserted him all these weeks, who had deceived him with Sisterly lies and promises, was there too, and, true enough, she had a big belly. "Mama," he said, and she said, "My sweetie."

Although under that blue dress of hers with the white tassels she was carrying a baby that would look like her and like Papa, an equal mixture of the two of them (and hence would resemble him, Louis, as well), he nevertheless flung himself on her neck, muttering things that remained unintelligible even to himself, smelled her curly hair, and said, "Mama."

"Careful," she said. She had put on a Sunday dress especially for his homecoming, he could see that, blue with white tufts. She was wearing china-blue earrings especially for him. She had painted her lips scarlet for him. Papa had repapered the front room with sunflowers for him, too. There was a newly bound volume of _Ons Volk Ontwaakt!_ ("Our Nation Awakes!") on the mantelpiece, beside the grinning, hunchbacked, plaster figure of Rigoletto, lacquered in black and beige.

Louis went and sat on the sofa in the cozy-corner. In the opposite corner the bust of Guido Gezelle stood on a tripod stained dark brown. The head was a deep green with a broken earlobe and true-to-life bumps, for Gezelle was hydrocephalic, his head overstuffed with brains, which gave the poet headaches all his life. The front room was full of wrought-iron candelabra, copper plates inscribed "The Flemish Tongue Is Wondrous Sweet for Those Who with Respect Her Treat" and "There's No Place Like Home," watercolors by Uncle Leon of windmills and violets, pen drawings of the Belfry in Ghent, the Lake of Love in Bruges. Over the mantelpiece, in fan-shaped patterns, hung a selection of rusty arrows with curious tips and barbs handed over by natives to Father Wiemeersch, Mama's uncle, who was still gallantly, generously, and paternally engaged in the conversion of Negro tribes in the jungles of the Kasai.

Mama brought him a cup of hot chocolate with much more sugar than they allowed in the Institute.

Papa stood in the veranda doorway and took stock of his son, his own, his only, prodigal son, now back at last in his father's house.

"Louis," said Papa, "I must show you our new machine. You'll be bowled over. There isn't another printer in the whole of West Flanders who has anything like it. They'd like to have one, all right, but they don't have the guts to take the plunge. It came from Leipzig."

"Let him finish his chocolate, at least," said Mama.

Wounded, Papa looked away, away from the two of them, from the new alliance being forged under his nose. He leaned back against the door with the glittering leaded panes.

"Right, then," he said, "right. I'll go for a shave at Felix's." Papa had himself shaved by Felix every other day. As soon as she heard the front door shut, Mama rummaged about in her sewing box and brought out a packet of Belga cigarettes. She lit one and inhaled greedily. Then, as if something had suddenly occurred to her, she quickly opened the window and blew the smoke out in the direction of the veranda, toward the wall where mandarins exchanged bows and ladies in flat, wide-brimmed hats sat in boats and played the banjo.

Mama was sticking her stomach out a lot. Or was it the baby that was pushing her so far forward? Of course, the baby now had Mama and her movements at its beck and call.

"That machine," said Mama, "is a disaster. Or rather those machines. His lordship goes to Leipzig, to the trade fair, and comes back home as if nothing out of the way has happened. I ask him, 'Did you do any business over there?' 'Oh, yes,' he says, 'a bit,' but I can tell from his silly grin that he's up to something, well, anyway, Louis, can you imagine it, suddenly the whole street is in an uproar, two cars with German license plates drive up and behind them there's a truck that stretches from here to there, it can't even turn around in the street, they have to get the police. There are two German mechanics there to supervise the whole thing, and what do I see? That machine, Louis, that machine is a monster that could never in your life have fitted into the workshop, a two-year-old child could have seen that, but not your Papa, oh no, so they have to knock down the side wall, the two German mechanics have to stay for two whole weeks at the Hôtel de la Paix at our expense while they install the machine, hanging around the house all day, and they have their meals here, too, in the drawing room, and they aren't satisfied with a cutlet, oh no, it has to be *Wurst,* and *Schinken* in the morning."

"*Schinken?*"

"Ham." Hurriedly Mama lit another cigarette.

"Does the machine print well?" Louis asked, to please Mama and his absent Papa.

Mama sat on the edge of the medieval-style oak table. The Flemish knights had sat at such a table in 1302 planning the destruction of the perfidious French empire. *Wat Wals is vals is, sla dood!* Walloons are false! Put them to death!

"The Germans go back home," said Mama. "The machine is installed. We have to move all the typecases and the paper-cutter. I think, He's happy now with his new toy. But then suddenly there's a lot of noise down below, I can hear the people in the street going Ooh! and Ah! So I look out the window and what do I see? That truck is back, and the police, too, the truck is trying to turn around again in the street, and the same German mechanics are back directing the traffic. I say to myself: Am I seeing double or am I losing my mind? I run downstairs and I say: 'Staf, what's happening? Just tell me. Am I seeing what I think I'm seeing or am I going mad? Is that another machine?' 'Yes, Constance,' he says. I say: 'The same one?' And that clown laughs and says: 'Of course it's not the same one. There's one in the workshop, so this one out in the street can't be the same one.' I say: 'Staf, I'm going to bash the living daylights out of you, you know perfectly well what I mean. Is it a second one of the same kind?' 'Yes,' he says: 'it's a second one.' I say: 'But why, Staf?' 'Constance,' he says: 'This second one is for when the first one breaks down.' "

She waited. Her face floated in the cigarette smoke, the smoke caught in her curls. The most beautiful among women.

"Don't you get it?" She shut her eyes tight, took a deep breath. "A machine that costs an arm and a leg and that he hasn't even got any work for!"

It struck Louis that, as always, she was exaggerating and being very unfair to Papa, who might be unpredictable and unreliable but probably knew what he was doing in a sphere of which Mama—country girl, doll, housewife, juvenile damozel—was totally ignorant.

"I see. You're taking his side. You think he's right." She stubbed out her cigarette in a copper ashtray Louis had not seen before. It was shaped like a flat shell and had a small swastika on the rim.

" 'You know nothing about it,' he tells me. 'This sort of machine is made specially and it costs so much because it's for printing newspapers.' I say, 'But Staf, no one has ordered any newspapers from you.' 'Doesn't matter,' he says, 'we'll print our own.' And that's what he did. One issue. He doesn't have enough money for a second one." Again she blew out her smoke, her distaste, her disappointment at her stolid, uncomprehending, newly reinstated son.

In the workshop, piles of Papa's paper, *The Leie,* had been stacked man-high, four pages full of advertisements of various sizes with, here and there, hoary and unlovely, a joke. The front page bore the legend "Energy from Fresh Food, thanks to SOLO." A goblin leaped over the bold, sloping letters as if over a hedge, and underneath was written: "Her Husband's Overalls Are as Clean as Can Be! Only SOLEIL can wash away grease spots" and "Once he acted like a robot. He had to be helped off with his coat. Now he's more energetic than ever before, thanks to Kruschen Salts."

The machines in the workshop hissed. None of the workers in their long, gray aprons glanced in the direction of the Prince, presumed lost, now returned from his exile in the Institute. Had Papa ordered them not to? Look not in the face of my son, or he will turn you blind! Vandam, the foreman, squeezed Louis's elbow.

"My word, how you've grown! If you go on like this, you'll be a light heavyweight!"

Vandam's tanned face with the broken nose always looked solemn. He used to be champion of southern West Flanders. Now and then he would sniff four or five times in rapid succession. Or make quick-as-lightning feints just in front of Louis's nose. He smelled of cheese and printer's ink. Kid Vandam.

"Well, what do you think of it?" Vandam asked beside the machine. "Nice."

"Nice? *Wunderschön!* Made in Deutschland!"

Louis walked around the silent monster gleaming in all its joints, wheels, suction cups, clamps, cogs, springs, buttons, rods, cylinders.

"She does about twenty thousand revs an hour. *Schnell,* very *schnell.*"

"Let's see it work, then, just for a minute."

"Nothing I'd like better, Louis, but I can't. Only the boss can do that. Not the boss's son." (Recognized after all. As the son, it was true. But recognized, anyway.)

Reams of paper in their sea-green wrapping. Typesetters bent over their typecases. Dusty windows with soot-encrusted iron frames. Concrete floor spattered with oil and ink. The icy sheen of the blade in the paper-cutter. I am returned from a long sorrow.

"Yes, she gleams like a beauty, does our Koenig und Bauer," said Vandam gloomily.

Beside one of the three Heidelbergs, subduing the thundering machine, stood Raspe, who the year before had pulled Louis onto his lap, tickled him on the forbidden spot and cried, "Where's that pretty little shrimp of yours, then?" When Raspe saw Louis, he stuck out a long, coated tongue. Vandam watched Louis turn away and took Louis's arm above the elbow, pressing tightly with his fingers.

"And how's your love life?" he asked.

Louis flushed. The others hadn't heard.

"How old are you now, Louis?"

"Eleven . . . in April."

"You can't start too early. The early bird catches the worm," said Vandam. Louis dawdled as much as he could leaving the workshop. Vandam was a Hottentot with filthy ideas. Forgive him, Lord, he knows not what he says.

In the kitchen he found a clean-shaven and powdered Papa. "This is for you. I brought it along from the trade fair, from the *Messe,* as they call it in Leipzig." Unwrapping a yellowish newspaper with unfamiliar, spiky lettering, he produced a small rubber figure of a boy in short pants and a brown shirt. With a satisfied grunt, Papa put the figure on the dresser and fumbled about with it until the right arm was stretched out stiff, the legs spread wide. Then Papa straightened the loose, feltlike clothes, the armband with the swastika, the brown kepi, the dagger on the belt.

"Well, what do you say?"

"Thank you very much," said Louis.

"Thank you very much, who?"

"Thank you very much, Papa."

Mama picked up the doll, and for a moment Louis thought she was going to eat it, so closely did she hold the pale, grinning little face to her nose. "For the time being we'll keep it in our bedroom, in the wardrobe."

"Why?"

"It's better if people don't see it."

"Why?" said Papa ten times more loudly, more threateningly than Louis.

"Under the present circumstances . . ."

"But I won't show it, him, to anybody," Louis pleaded, "I'll keep him upstairs in my room, and when I go back to the Institute I'll put him in your wardrobe then."

"Better not, Louis. We mustn't go looking for trouble, people talk more than enough about us and the Germans as it is."

"Let them," cried Papa. "They're just a bunch of hypocrites!"

Mama was kneading the doll absentmindedly in her fingers. To his dismay Louis saw that the boy was becoming bowlegged, like a cowboy in the Wild West. Soon she will knead her child like that as it lies helpless in its cradle. What had those carelessly molding hands done with him before he was packed off to the Institute?

At about four o'clock Aunt Mona came to call with buttercakes and the report that she had just bought thirty packets of loaf sugar, thirty kilos of coffee, and thirty kilos of chicory that very morning.

"*He* won't let me do that," said Mama. "He calls it profiteering from the situation."

"But it's forced on us by the situation, Constance! And who'll be the first to come begging when there's no more coffee? You've put on your best dress, are you going to the cinema?"

"Oh yes!" cried Louis.

"No," said Mama indifferently. "I was feeling bored, and I'd been sitting around all morning in my dressing gown. I thought, No, today I'm not going to put my smock on. Belly or no belly, I'm going to put on something bright for a change."

"You look younger every day, Constance."

Louis was allowed to butter the cakes and to pour the coffee. He forgot the Institute. I forget the Institute. This mother, scarcely mine, who did not put on that bright, loose dress for my sake, and this sister of Papa's, who luckily did not exclaim right away how much I have grown and did not inquire about my marks at school, they are two fairies in a wood who can make the whole Institute disappear with a wave of their magic wand. Fairies? That was a girl's idea.

"What are you going to do with him, Constance?" (Him, me, Louis, her child.)

"Yes, what should I do with him?"

"I could go straight back to the Institute," Louis said. "If that's what you want."

"You silly billy," said Aunt Mona, "we're all very happy to have you back with us in Walle. Grandma won't believe her eyes when she sees you. How much you've grown! He's grown like anything, hasn't he, Constance? Grandma said to me this very morning, 'Where is he, our Louis, our best boy? Of all my grandchildren, he's the only one I want to see.'" Aunt Mona's lying face was an unlined, translucent white, as if she had been living in a cellar for a whole school term, surrounded by toadstools, glistening fungi as tall as she was.

"You don't have a lot to say for yourself," she said. "Just look at him sitting there. At your age. You should be jumping for joy that you're not twenty years old yet, my boy, or else you'd be called up! One hundred and twenty million, that's what it's costing us, that mobilization. And who's going to pay for it all?"

"Your man in the street, of course," said Mama. She picked at the buttercake Louis had set out and spread extra thickly with butter for her.

"Anyway," said Aunt Mona, "luckily they've kicked Paul-Henri Spaak out, him and his Bolshevik ideas. What sort of a prime minister was he anyway, with a build like that? And that fat face of his? You could have scraped the villainy off it with a trowel! Where is it all going to lead, where are we going?"

"To the cinema," said Louis.

"All right, then, where are we going?" said Mama.

"Straight to war, Constance. Straight as the crow flies!" exclaimed Aunt Mona. She had bulging eyes because her glands had all gone haywire when her husband, Uncle Ed, had run off.

("It's odd," Grandma had said, "because she and Ed belonged together like a pot and its lid. And it's odd because Ed had popeyes like a frog, and no sooner had he gone than she got them, too." Uncle Ed used to beat his wife. "What? Haven't you ironed my shirt?" "Of course I've ironed your shirt." "What do you mean? Look at that collar, it's creased like an accordion!" And whack! Right on the side of her head. "What? Haven't you cleaned my shoes?" "Of course I've cleaned your shoes." "What do you mean? A bit of spit and a quick rub with your sleeve!" And whack! Right on her chin.

But Aunt Mona stood her ground. "A bump, a bruise, so what? We women can put up with that, we have to, it's the men who faint at the sight of a drop of blood!" She stuck it out, and in sheer despair, after dealing out one last uppercut, Uncle Ed ran off with all his clothes and a deaf and dumb seamstress.

Aunt Mona lived with her daughter Cecile on the Horse Market, behind a façade of gleaming blue-and-white tiles and white-lacquered windowpanes with ED written in dark-blue Gothic letters on each one. Cecile took expensive ballet lessons. She would be leaving for America, for Hollywood, as soon as Shirley Temple grew too old and worn out for children's roles. Already Cecile could sing "Over the Rainbow" and "La Cucaracha" to perfection. A photograph of Cecile, hand-colored by Uncle Leon, hung in the front room: a moon face with beady eyes, a pinched little body in a tutu.)

The afternoon slipped by. The talk rambled on, touching on ministries, the Farmers' Union, the Freemasons, Poland, Spain, Hitler, who may stop at nothing all right, but has he any option? The French, the English, the Russians, the whole world is at his throat! Then Aunt Mona noticed that Louis was still there, and said, "Happy to be at home for a while?"

"Yes."

"Have you been to the workshop yet?"

"Yes."

"And what did they say? That you'd grown?"

"Most of them didn't even say hello."

"That's workers for you," said Mama.

Aunt Mona laughed, the lump in her throat squirming as if it contained a knuckle-sized child. "What did you think? That they'd welcome you home like a princess?"

"No." He blushed, stood up, and began clearing away the cups and saucers.

"You've got to understand," said Aunt Mona, "those boys' thoughts are elsewhere, they could be called up and lose their jobs at any moment. So they couldn't give a damn right now whether the boss's son is there or not. It's not the way it used to be, when the working classes had respect for those who paid their weekly wage. Everybody is equal in the eyes of the Socialists, everybody is boss. And all the working class thinks about now is, How am I going to get the boss by the short hairs?—excuse me.

"And our Staf, Constance, he doesn't want to admit it, but that's how things are right now. He's kind as can be, and that's going to be his downfall. I'm his sister and I get along well with him, but when it comes to this, he's really screwing things up, excuse me. He ought to stick to principles, and the principles are that this one is the master and that one is the servant. Right, Louis? Get that into your head. Principles.

"You must have seen it for yourself, Constance, with that Dr. Martens business at the beginning of the year. He worked with the Germans, Dr. Martens did, in '14–'18, and why? For us, that's why, for Flanders, for Flemish principles. So then he was nominated as a member of the Academy of Medicine. Oh no, said the Liberals, that won't do, he was a traitor, away with him! And the war veterans played the *'Brabançonne'* and couldn't agree, and Paul-Henri Spaak was thick as thieves with the Flemings, to save his prime minister's job he'd sell his own mother, that fat slob, well, there were arguments and fights in the street and what was the result? The Flemings stuck to their principles, they let the Liberals screech, 'Either Dr. Martens leaves the Academy or we leave the government,' and the Flemings said, 'Right, gentlemen, off you go,' and *voilà*, Meneer Spaak fell flat on his fat behind."

"But that Dr. Martens isn't all that he should be, either," said Mama. "They say that his clinic . . . well, you know . . . they come from all over the place, from Germany, France, all those rich women, for . . . you know what I'm getting at . . ."

"I do know what you're getting at, Constance. Best keep quiet about it. There are rats in the rafters."

(That's me, twelve rats and a rat catcher, sniffing about in the rafters, scrabbling about in Mama and Aunt Mona's attic, full of secrets, hints, suddenly broken-off snatches of conversation.)

"Rex will win," said Louis.

"Well, I never!" said Aunt Mona. "Where ever did you get that idea? Rex was all washed up long ago. In '36, all right, he could still pull a string or two, that handsome Leon Degrelle with his hair all slicked down, but how many seats have they got left now of the twenty-one they had in '36? Four! Is that what they teach you in your convent school? Honestly? About Rex? Are the Sisters still crazy about the handsome Leon?"

"No." Louis was afraid that, overcome by the first day back home, he might start to laugh out loud or cry, or slide down along Mama's swollen belly, his chest coming to rest against her thighs. He saw the nuns from the Institute doing a wild, *crazy* dance around Degrelle, who dwindled away until he was no bigger than one of the little ones in the playground, the nuns waltzing with flapping skirts around and around the little one, who kept piping up, "Rex, Rex."

"Rex hasn't got anybody left in Flanders," said Aunt Mona. "Not a single leader, no one with any get-up-and-go. Their only big gun is, what's his name again? Help me, Constance, what's his name? That senator who had both his legs shot off in '14–'18. A decent enough fellow and educated, too, but all the same he's an invalid. It's a cruel thing to say, but Flemings don't trust someone like that, someone without legs."

"What about Roosevelt?" said Louis. "He's in a wheelchair, too."

"That's quite different," said Aunt Mona. "Anyway, the Americans know only one kind of politics, making money."

"We're not all that different," said Mama.

73

"Constance!" exclaimed Aunt Mona. "What do you mean? We have ideals."

Mama smiled and rubbed the football under her dress.

"They ought to make you a senator, Mona."

"I'd show them, all right," said Aunt Mona. "For a start I'd have all those Reds who went to Spain and murdered priests put up against the wall. Then I'd confiscate all the capital that's in the hands of foreigners and Freemasons and divide it up among all the people who have to work for their daily bread."

To lie there against that swelling dome, against the tight-stretched blue-and-white dress, listening to the gurgling and splashing of the floating, swimming baby inside. When he wrestled with Vlieghe, the soft rumbling of Vlieghe's stomach.

"What are you looking at, Louis? My stomach?"

"Your brooch." A silver disc with the purple silhouette of a leaping buck or a dancing gazelle, pinned, right through her dress, to her soft skin with the two bumps.

"A present from an admirer," said Aunt Mona. "But you mustn't tell your father. He'd have apoplexy."

"For goodness' sake, Mona," Mama said weakly.

"A person should be able to have a laugh now and then," said Aunt Mona. "Louis, fetch me two buttercakes from the cupboard, please." She nibbled, chewed. "A person, a woman on her own, likes to have a bit of a laugh."

"But you have Cecile," said Mama.

"Oh, her!"

"She's a good girl, isn't she?"

"A woman on her own, Constance. They always say 'a man on his own,' they never talk about a woman on her own. But when it starts getting dark and you've finished the cleaning and the scrubbing, the dishes are washed and the days are drawing in . . . Ah, well, we musn't complain."

"No," said Mama. And then, bitterly, "Otherwise, we would never stop complaining."

"A person just has to get things off her chest from time to time, Constance."

"Louis," said Mama firmly, "why don't you go for a walk? All right? But not too far. And not through Toontjes Street, either!"

Past the row of low, terraced houses of dark-brown brick. He could have danced. It was weeks since he had last been out alone on the street without boys in school uniform chattering beside him, without giantesses in fluttering, many-layered garments.

He walked very quickly past Felix the barber's, you never could tell if some howler-monkey with shaving soap on his cheeks would come rushing out, pumping your hand and asking all sorts of intimate details about the Institute, about Mama. When he reached the fence belonging to Groothuis the textile manufacturer, he jumped as high as he could and saw a woman in the garden lying on the terrace, on the stones. She was wearing a straw hat, a string of beads around her neck, and nothing else. He was afraid to jump again. In that split second he had seen the woman lying on her stomach. And it was possible that she had lifted her head at the exact moment he had been hanging there, suspended in the air. Who was she? Had Meneer Groothuis married during last term? For one reason or another that was out of the question. Papa had said, "Georges Groothuis may be a Liberal, but he's a real man for all that." And then Mama had given a snide little bleat of a laugh. "Just don't get too close to him, Staf." "Why not?" "I'll say no more, just that Georges Groothuis isn't going to get married in a hurry, mark my words." "Why not?" "Georges Groothuis and women, they don't mix, that's all I'm saying. And I have that on good authority."

Louis missed Vlieghe, friend, refuge, paladin, apostle. Shieldbearer Vlieghe, who was spending the whole holiday away from him in Wakkegem, an obscure little village where Father Vlieghe was lawyer to the local yokels. Louis could have taught, explained, demonstrated to Vlieghe how he, Louis, who had ended up in the Institute by some horrible misadventure, had now been restored to his natural environment, here in Walle, in his own home town. The history of Walle, princess of southern West Flanders, can be traced back to the fifth century, Vlieghe, here alongside the military road of the Nervii. Even then the knights of Walle sported a red shield with a white dragon coiled around a white hemisphere in the middle. White and red, Vlieghe, the colors of the Walle Sporting Club, where my Uncle Florent is reserve goalkeeper.

He walked along Toontjes Street, where bad people lived on Public Assistance and drank all their money away, where the women sat on doorsteps with their children covered in scabies, the little street was an eternal disgrace, that's what it was, so close to the church of St. Anthony, too, and they never saw the inside of that either, except to seek refuge when the police were after them. Louis looked wistfully at the boys playing around and shouting in their hoarse adult voices, coal dust in their ears and eyelashes, kicking a ball made of paper and string, swearing. Although he knew it was a sin, he stopped and stared, was infected by their sin, and copying one of the swearing boys he scratched his crotch and was attacked by the germs of evil. Vlieghe, can you see me? Louis ran behind the church, sought the shadow of the many child martyrs who had resisted similar temptations in the face of torture and death, looked around to see if anyone was watching him, and quickly crossed himself. To make doubly sure, he did it again when he passed the Cattle Market church, the church where his parents had been married and he had been christened.

On the Market Square he gave a wide berth to the Café Rotonde, where Grandpa was probably playing bridge.

Come on, Vlieghe! He took Vlieghe by the hand and pulled him up the soot-blackened cast-iron stairs, the two of them paused and waited on the arched bridge, but then all at once Vlieghe was gone, and there was little point in hanging around waiting for the hot, puffing steam of a passing train if Vlieghe wasn't going to be there. Louis thought, Better the Institute with Vlieghe than Walle without him, but that didn't last very long either, he allowed Vlieghe to fade away, blow away, and went and looked at all the shop windows in the Doornik district.

Through the open door of a café he heard the familiar voices of Wanten and Dalle gabbling some joke about a mother-in-law in strident dialect. He missed the punch line because a young bully in overalls came and stood next to him, shoving him aside with the wheel of his bicycle as he parked it, saying, "Is that Wanten and Dalle?" Louis nodded and turned, strolling, away, away from the crackling applause pouring out in the distance.

Papa was crazy about Wanten and Dalle because they were "the voice of our people," as he often said. The real Wanten and Dalle are medieval statues standing in one of the four turrets of the Belfry. The comedians on the radio program "Walle Lives!" who call themselves Wanten and Dalle are people like you and me.

When "Walle Lives!" was on the air, everyone in the sitting room had to keep quiet as mice, Papa leaning back stock-still in the cozy-corner, the beginnings of a laugh already trembling at the corners of his mouth.

" 'Well, my boy,' says Banker Moneybags, 'I'm told you want to marry my daughter.' 'That I do, sir.' 'And supposing I give her to you without a penny to her name, will you still want to marry her?' 'Of course I will, sir!' 'Well, my lad, my daughter's not for you, then!' 'Oh, really? And why is that, sir?' 'Because I don't want a prize idiot in my family!' "

Papa laughs. Mama says, "Where do they dig it all up?"

"Quiet, Constance," scolds Papa. "They've started again."

Wanten is lumbering and stupid and never catches on to anything. Dalle, his wife, is a shrew and a mischief-maker. But sometimes Wanten is too quick for her.

" 'Funny, Wanten, ain't it, how people can get things wrong? I've just been reading how Columbus, when he got to America, how he thought he'd discovered India.' 'Ah, Dalle, when I married you, I thought I'd discovered paradise.' "

"That's a good one," says Mama.

"Yes," says Papa, "but it's true, too. The fool makes his point with laughter."

Louis came to a smart salute in front of the lackluster bust of King Albert, an indistinct figure with spectacles welded to his helmet. Forty feet deep he had fallen into the ravine, the Knight-King who had so loved to climb mountains. His manservant, Van Dijck, had waited at the foot of the rock, but his Prince never returned. At two in the morning, Baron Jacques de Dixmude had stumbled over the rope, still fastened to the body of the King. According to Grandpa it was the Communists, there are lots of them around Namur and in the Ardennes, where Walloons and foreigners live. And at the inquest the public prosecutor's office had hushed up a great many things. The public prosecutor always covers up for the Franskiljons and everyone else who is against the Church and against Flanders.

Sootje's ice-cream cart rattled past, the pony stopped, frothed at the mouth. Sootje blew his copper horn. Louis had no money with him and cursed the gang of noisy boys from the College who stood around the pastel-colored cart eating pastel-colored ice cream. The College boys had briefcases bulging with textbooks and notes. Soon I'll be carrying a brief-case like that, too, and it can't be too heavy for me. The covers of their exercise books are dark-blue, the Institute ones are brick-red. I have to get back, Mama must be biting her nails. No, Mama would never do that. King Albert conducted himself like a hero in the mud of the trenches during the Great War, which broke out just as His travel-loving Majesty was about to start a long motor tour right across Europe. He had wanted to travel incognito, and his Autoclub of Belgium membership card, made out to Leopold, Count de Rethy, still exists. Of course, it wasn't the Communists who killed the Knight-King. Grandpa is lying. Or else Grandpa is a fool, which can't be true.

Marche-les-Dames, rocky terrain of evil omen. The King is short-sighted, he hangs vertically from the rope and hauls himself up, his spectacles mist over, he gropes with his right hand along the rugged rockface, he snatches at the wet ivy. At that moment a man with a muti-lated face appears at a cleft in the rock, half his face is bashed in, one eye is lower than the other and seems lifeless. "Are you hanging comfortably, Sire?" the man asks. *"Merci, mon vieux,* I am hanging perfectly." "That's good, Sire," says the man, bringing out a breadknife from his threadbare army coat. "Don't you recognize me, Sire?" *"Non, mon brave."* "Yet I was at your side in the trenches at the Yser." "Belgium is grateful to you for that, my good fellow." "On the twelfth of October, 1917, you charged me with a mission behind enemy barbed wire. But in spite of my appeal to be given time to fetch my spectacles from the blockhouse, you ordered me to complete the aforesaid mission immediately. You gave this order in French, Sire." *"Et alors, Flamand?"* *"Alors? Alors,* I leaped out of the trench, and being nearsighted like Your Majesty, I landed on a grenade. Sire, what you did was unjust and must be avenged." "Do what you have to do, bad Belgian," says King Albert the First. "Farewell, bad king," says the mutilated man and cuts through the climbing rope. Without waiting for the dull thud from below, he leaps off across the rocks like a gazelle.

As Louis returned through wicked Toontjes Street, a boy on a scooter rode up close alongside him. "Cross-eyes," said the boy. "Out of my way, cross-eyes!" Louis stared fixedly in front of him. I'm not cross-eyed, that's unfair, stupid, and untrue. The boy rode on, swinging his supple left foot with carefree ease, his other foot pressed steady as a rock to the wooden plank. If I have a little brother, he's going to want my scooter, that's for sure.

Tetje was sitting on the windowsill of 12 Oudenaarde Road, dressed in football shorts.

"Hello," said Tetje, a thirteen-year-old foreigner from the Balkans, a Gypsy, at any rate not a pure-bred Fleming, swinging his dark-brown legs and feet in yellow rubber overshoes with oval holes.

"Hello." Louis could see the front of his own house, the sun on the small lattice window in the front door.

"You're back."

"Yes."

"For long?"

"Until the end of the holidays."

"Coming with me to Walle Stade?"

Impossible. Stade, with its purple-and-white striped shirts, was a club for lame ducks, sissies, and cowards. There is only one decent football club in Walle, and that's Walle Sport, where Uncle Florent is the reserve goalkeeper. Tetje was a Stade supporter because his father sold ice cream at the gate. Bekka, Tetje's sister, with her Gypsy eyes and full lips, came out of the house. She had grown but was still too small for eleven. Since the last holidays there was something quicker, sleeker, about her gestures and about the provocative way she spoke.

"A person would pay to see you," she said. She wore the same rubber overshoes as her brother, a wrinkled flowered dress, and a belt of cracked white leather.

"Coming with us to the cinema on Thursday?"

"If his mother will let him," said Tetje.

"He doesn't have to tell her he's going with us." She hopped up and down on her short brown legs.

"Why not?" Louis asked.

"Because," she said and came so close to him that he could smell the Lutti caramels on her breath. "Because your mother would turn up her nose and say, 'My boy, don't let me see you mixing with those common people again.' "

"My mother would never . . ."

"Common people," said Bekka. "I've heard her say that myself. But maybe she was drunk."

Louis burst out laughing. His mother drunk! How had this little dark-skinned vagabond, who had turned into a woman in just three months, managed to get that idea into her head? He saw the sun move in the front door of his house.

"I've got to go."

"Yes, do hurry along," Bekka drawled. "Or else she'll be cross."

"You're wrong there," he said, starting to run.

"Hurry along and dream of me," she said, laughing shrilly, Rebekka Cosijns, fairground fortune-teller-in-miniature, little desert wife.

"Get inside, brat," said her brother.

"*Allee*, fatheads, *salut!*" said Louis in Byttebier's voice.

*T*he bells came flying back from Rome. Mama hid a chocolate egg behind the toilet bowl, Louis discovered it immediately and ate it up all at once, which he would not have been allowed to do at the Institute because the Sisters held that too much chocolate was bad for the liver. Mama thought that he still believed in eggs dropping out of the belly of church bells, in storks, in Santa Claus, in cauliflowers with babies inside. Or that fairy tale that the Germans had made off with the church bells of her village, Bastegem, in '14–'18 and cast them into cannons.

The bells rang all morning, but when Louis had to go for buttercakes and rolls he failed to detect any sign at all of reverence or awe among the passers-by in their Easter best confronted with all the ding-dong that was making the air tremble and calling for joy because Jesus was risen after all His pain and suffering. The world is becoming more un-Christian by the day, Sister Econome had said, their souls are on the point of perdition and they don't realize it.

Papa put on his light-beige suit and said, "Let's be off, my boy."

Louis was to go along with him to visit Grandma, Papa's invalid mother. Papa walked very fast, only slowing down in the Cattle Market in order to stop in the lobby of the Vooruit Theater, where the members of the Red Youth gathered regularly to sing their seditious songs, and then marched in procession with flags and drums through Zwevegem Street. Papa carefully examined the stills from that week's film: gaudily made-up girls in their underwear, with their arms around one another staring wantonly out at Louis. Sailors singing so lustily that you could see the roofs of their mouths. A fat blonde in evening clothes being murdered by a suntanned hand that protruded from a starched white cuff, the knife pressed into the swelling bulge of her breast, she was terrified, she recognized the killer, her bright blond hair shone like a halo.

"Another bit of French vaudeville," said Papa, his body quitting the lobby with its ungodly photographs but his head turning back involuntarily a few more times.

"You'll never see anything uplifting in these French films," Papa said afterward to Grandma. "It's always something silly or vulgar, *l'amour toujours*. To think that the government allows that sort of thing! But of course these films come from France, and it's the Jew Blum who runs the show there. And all our own prime minister does, that Pierrot of a Pierlot, is dance a jig on the end of a string in time to a French tune."

"Oh, come off it, Staf," said Grandma. "People would much rather see a beautiful naked French woman than the Maid of Flanders!"

"Mother, you may be my mother and I may respect you, but you are wrong here. Of course, your ordinary man, your worker, prefers looking at smut, but that's only because he doesn't know any better. Which is why we have to set an example and make sure our Flemish youth doesn't get poisoned by that foul French pig-swill!"

Grandma shifted her broad, ample figure in the wicker armchair and chuckled at Louis, who at that moment loved her more than anyone else in the whole world. When he had come in, she had clutched at her heart and given him six or seven sloppy kisses on his cheek, his neck. "My little pet, my little pet," she had cried, and despite being tightly clamped in her plump arms, he had put up no resistance.

Four years before, she had broken her hip, and ever since then she had sat in the same wicker armchair next to the Louvain stove. She resembled a bulldog, with watery, alert, twinkling little eyes and drooping cheeks that sagged into the withered, much-wrinkled pillar of her neck. Red ears flat against her head, covered by silky, thin white hair.

"Are you letting them poison you, Louis? What's this I hear?" she chuckled.

"That's right," Louis smiled conspiratorially.

"Mother," said Papa, "don't you have any bread and butter with a little bit of something to put on it?"

"Hélène," Grandma bellowed, and as if she had been sitting waiting on the stairs, Aunt Hélène came clattering into the room. She gave Louis a wallop on his behind.

"Just look at this fine young man! It's time I took him off to the Monte Carlo. We'll make a proper *danseur* of him yet."

"Hélène, the boy is dying of hunger," said Grandma, and Louis didn't know if she meant him or Papa. A large stoneware bowl of pickled herring appeared on the table. Papa tucked in at once, hunched over, bolting the food down, three herrings in a row under the approving gaze of his mother. Mother feeding child.

"I bet your Constance can't make them like that," said Grandma.

"Not in twenty years," said Papa, treacherous spouse.

"Mama doesn't marinate them, she does them in aspic with lemon," Louis said.

"And why not?" said Grandma. "That can be tasty, too, now and then."

Papa drank three glasses of beer. Aunt Hélène examined herself in a small oval mirror with a heart-shaped iron frame, made a face, then turned around with a death's-head grin, pointing to her (for the Seynaeve family, impossibly perfect and white) set of teeth. "So—wha'd'ya think?" she said, holding her mouth wide open.

"Very nice," said Papa and fished in the bowl for the fattest herring.

"She asked her father for new teeth," Grandma said grimly, "first for the New Year, then for her birthday, then for Easter. She asked him very nicely, 'Please, Father,' and what did he say? 'Someone who can put steak away like you did today has nothing wrong with their teeth!' I've had to pay for them out of my own pocket, the child didn't dare show her face in the street. Louis, is that how a father talks to his daughter?"

Grandpa hadn't spoken to his wife for two years. He slept beside Grandma, ate at the table right next to her wicker armchair, sat a couple of yards away when reading his paper, talked to his sons and daughters, but never addressed one word to his lawful spouse. "Florent, tell your mother to get my laundry ready for Thursday." "Hélène, here is six francs, give them to your mother for powders from the White Cross." This while she was sitting right next to him, seething with rage. In the beginning, two years ago, she would come back at him with "Look here, you old fraud, I'm not deaf" or "Blockhead, can't you tell me yourself?" but, confronted with that chilly face of his (the Iron Mask), she felt helpless. For a time she went on calling him "windbag," "stinker," "loudmouth," but then no more. "You've got to try and understand him," said Papa.

"Understand? What is there to understand about a monster who can say things like that to his daughter when her teeth are falling out at the age of twenty!"

"Twenty-two," said Aunt Hélène.

"Look, just starting to talk about him makes me feel breathless, I get palpitations."

"You've got to lose weight," said Papa. "That's all."

"It's all water," said Grandma, "I'm nothing but skin and bones otherwise."

"And you don't take your pills," said Aunt Hélène, speaking as a Sister would to one of the tiniest little ones on the playground in the far-off Institute.

"Why should I take them anyway? What for? Everything is in the hands of Our Lord," said the wobbling, full-to-bursting bag of water. "Or in the hands of Hilter."

"Hit-ler, Mother."

"What's your opinion, Staf, will they be able to stop Hilter? He seems to have gone right around the bend lately."

"They'll have to have what it takes to stop him. There's no stopping an ideal, Mother, get that into your head. If somebody, or a whole nation, is prepared to sacrifice their lives for what they believe in, then there's nothing anyone can do about it."

"Did you see the King's picture in the paper? He looks so sad all the time. That man must be crying his eyes out, that's for sure. And a king, someone like that, he can't just go out to a café or to football, all he can do is sit there in his palace and eat his heart out."

The sorrow of King Leopold was reflected in her doggy face. I must look after her, Louis thought, she'll be dying soon, the water bag will burst.

"Looks as if he's going to attend the National Drama Festival," said Papa, "which is going to disappoint The Sons of the Leie, that's our group, because our president had just decided not to enter the National Festival, seeing that, what with the mobilization, people's minds are not on serious drama. We were going to give either *The Trial of Our Lord* or *Children of Our People* in the Youth Fellowship Hall, but, as our president said, at times of national crisis we shouldn't try to dish up such heavy stuff but go for something light so that lots of people will turn up and we can make a lot of money for our Parcels for Soldiers. So we're going to help out The Sons of Breydel by taking walk-on parts in *The Merry Peasant*.

People will still make the effort to come to an operetta. Lovely costumes, lovely voices, catchy music. It stops you from brooding and helps to pass the time."

"There's something in that," said Grandma without conviction. She is like Sister St. Gerolphe, distant, afflicted, frail, but defiant in the face of the enemy. I will have to look after these two women, that is my mission in life. Papa skimmed through *De Leiegalm, The Leie Echo.*

"Just look at this. All this advertising. The money it must be bringing in! Silvikrin for the hair. Aspirin. Cirio tomatoes. The National Lottery. But if a serious independent printer asks them to put a small advertisement in a paper that's printed a hundred times better and more clearly on the latest German machine, then it's 'Oh, but Mijnheer Seynaeve, we have already placed an advertisement in *De Leiegalm* because when all's said and done we are Catholics first and foremost, isn't that so?' 'And what about me, d'you suppose I'm not a Catholic?' 'Well, of course you are, Mijnheer Seynaeve, but you are more of a Catholic Flamingant.' It's all politics, that's what it is," Papa shouted, "we are infested with politics!"

Grandma winked at Louis.

"Don't let any of that bother you, my pet," she said, "politics and all that grown-up foolishness. Much better to make sure you go out to the privy regularly, every day if you can. If you can't, eat prunes, that'll make you go, and clear you out good and proper. All the rest is just stuff and nonsense."

Aunt Hélène accompanied them up the stairs, to the front door.

"Don't forget, now, Louis, the two of us have a date to go dancing at the Monte Carlo." She tried to slap his behind again, but he dodged. Just before she closed the door, she displayed her new teeth once more.

Outside, Papa took a few determined steps and then turned around. He examined the front of the house (which he had once described to Mother Superior as "my father's ancestral home") from top to bottom, as if appraising it for sale after his parents' death. Or as if he were looking for cracks in the plaster, for pigeons blocking the guttering, or broken windowpanes. Then Papa crouched down and peered through the windows into the basement kitchen. Now Grandma would surely see him, she always kept looking out into the street for a good three minutes after the front door was shut. So she would see her son there before her, she would see the cyclists and half a plane tree behind him, but she would have to guess as to Louis, because her best-beloved grandchild would not take the trouble to bend down and so remained invisible.

"Is she waving at us?"

"No," said Papa. He straightened up and gave a doleful little sigh. He said, "Ah, well, my sweet little mama."

They walked in the direction of the market. Not home, not to Mama. Papa is setting a trap, he is luring me somewhere.

"My mother is a saint," said Papa, making it sound like a threat and as if he would tolerate no contradiction.

So Louis didn't say what he thought. Grandma might be a martyr because of the tortures inflicted upon her by her diabolical spouse, my godfather, but a saint? That was ridiculous and could only be explained by the blind love Papa had for his mother. But could you be a martyr without being a saint? He would ask Sister Angel. Sister Angel would bring her almost transparent fingers, which were usually fumbling with her crucifix, up to her mouth, run her index finger along her lower lip, and say, "That's a good question, Louis."

Sister Angel could also recite beautifully, her clawing, caressing little fingers sketching whole cornfields, seas, ships in the air. "Oh, Belgium, dearest fatherland. How fierce the wild waves' roar. So many cast ashore. Yet steadfast, rocklike, there you stand."

"Louis, how long do you think your Grandma will still be with us? It's a funny question, I know, but I would like to have some idea of what you think."

"A long time yet," Louis said.

"Yes, but how long?"

"Five years?"

"I don't know," said Papa. "She's worn out before her time. And she sometimes says such peculiar things. Every so often she looks at me as if I weren't there. Well, there you are, man proposes and God disposes."

Had God disposed that Grandma was to marry Grandpa and nobody else? Of course. But had God been having a bad day, perhaps? Of course not. He has His reasons, and though most of them are riddles and you must never question them, still . . .

("Your Grandpa," Grandma had said, "the first time I saw him, he was wearing a suit that must have been handed down from his own father for sure, it was shining at the elbows and at the knees. I saw him coming, and I said to my sister, 'Margo, he's coming toward us, he's after you.' 'No,' she said, 'he's after you, Agathe.' He still had a bit of hair in those days, brownish-red curly hair, and it was sticking to his forehead with embarrassment. His celluloid collar with the gray dickey was much too tight, too, and he'd forgotten to take off his bicycle clips. 'Juffrouw,' he said, 'you don't know me, how could you, I'm nobody special but I know you.' 'How is that, meneer?' 'I saw you at the Rhetoric Prize ceremony at St. Amand's College, where your brother . . .' I said, 'Our Honoré?' 'Yes,' he said, 'Honoré, I was giving him private lessons in arithmetic and chemistry. And since then I've often had occasion to walk past your door in Burgemeester van Outryve Avenue.' I said, 'Our Honoré seems very pleased with your lessons!' And Margo, the silly goose, said, 'Yes, he's been doing much better in arithmetic.' Which was a bit of a joke because Honoré had been kept back in arithmetic, he only got forty-five percent. 'If it isn't an imposition,' he said, 'I should like to ask you, juffrouw, I should like to invite you, if it's agreeable to you, that is, one can never tell, to accompany me to the opera, I just happen quite by chance to have a ticket to spare.'

"Louis, my pet, that was the biggest blunder of my life, Donizetti's *Élixir d'Amour* was my downfall. I'm told Donizetti died a madman, well, I must have been even madder.

"Oh, he was so charming, your Grandpa. Chocolates, flowers. But my father said, 'Agathe, a teacher, even one who gives private lessons, can't be right for a Demarchie girl.' But there you are, you're a child, you know nothing, you're bored with your family and your girlfriends, and you have the idea that it's all like Racine at boarding school: *'Il faut que j'aime enfin . . .'* and before you know it, you've got children and there's someone walking around the house who's as cruel and jealous as a tiger, and as nasty. You think, Everyone has his own cross to bear; but after a few years you begin to ask yourself, What for? And it's just like Racine again, only another scene this time: *'Et moi, je lui tendais les mains pour l'embrasser, mais je n'ai trouvé qu'un horrible mélange.'* And new little crosses keep coming along all the time. Like last week, when he, that fine Grandpa of yours, deliberately peed on the floor next to the bowl just so that Hélène and I would have to mop it up. Hélène said, 'Mama, perhaps it's his prostate,' but Louis, my pet, I know him inside out, he does it on purpose."

The smell of ammonia on the veranda in Philip of Alsace Avenue. The door to the toilet is always kept open. The bowl in question is a rusty little urinal painted bright green, with iridescent colors around the milled edges of the plate at the bottom, its holes almost completely blocked up.

"But I've been told by Georges the electrician that it's possible to attach an electric wire to the bowl so that when his stream hits it he'll get a shock he'll never forget."

"But Grandma, you've just said that he pees on the floor."

"Not all of it, of course. A tiny little stream making contact with the wire would be enough . . . But there, you may think about it but you don't do it, you have too much respect, after all, he's the father of your children."

Aunt Hélène's hoarse little laugh. "That's exactly where you should let him have it, Mama, where those children came from."

It offended Louis that Grandma should have discussed such intimate secrets with an electrician, but then he joined in their laughter, the women's laughter.

"He'd get the shock of his life," he said. "It would be like a bolt from the blue."

"Wouldn't it, though," said Grandma, and her face lit up. "Perhaps we ought to try it, just once. Georges says that you have to expose the electric wire and then scrape it clean."

"No," said Louis firmly. "You mustn't return evil for evil. Our Lord didn't do it, not even when the Jews drove nails right through His hands and feet."

"But then I'm not Our Lord," said Grandma, and started to play patience. They were new cards. When she shuffled and dealt them out, it sounded like a far-off pony clattering quickly over frozen cobblestones, no, it was like a boy cycling along with a piece of cardboard rattling against the spokes.

"And what he did when I was expecting Marie-Hélène, God rest her soul!

"It was right in the middle of winter, and I was lying in bed with a belly as big as this. He sent Mona out, pretending he needed a lot of shopping, and he sent the cleaning woman home, too, so that I'd be completely alone, and then he opened the door of the bedroom, the hall door, the door to the upstairs corridor, and then the front door, too, everything wide open, letting the icy wind from the street blow right in, so then I had to get up in my nightgown, all the way down the stairs to close the doors, I had to cling to the banister so as not to topple over with my belly, and then up all the stairs again. And that dares to call itself the father of my children! Would you believe it, Louis! And was he punished by Our Lord? Not on your life! But I was! With the death of our Marie-Hélène, and with my hip ruined for good."

That last bit was sacrilege, of course, but, Jesus forgive her, she means well, she just can't find the right words. Louis said, "God shall repay him even this day or upon the morrow."

"Don't you believe it, my pet. Things have not been dealt out fairly. That may be our fault, but it's Our Lord's too. Sometimes he *deliberately* favors ne'er-do-wells."

"That can't be true. Why would He do that?"

A mischievous, girlish expression appeared on her face. She shifted her bulky body, the wicker armchair squeaked like a baby rabbit.

"If He is all things, that Our Lord of yours, then every so often He can also be a real swine."

Scandalized, Louis exclaimed, "You'll have to confess that right away, do it today!"

"But, my pet," she cried triumphantly, "I've confessed it a dozen times already to the curate, and all he said was 'Madame Seynaeve, don't go on about it, it's long since been forgiven and forgotten in the eyes of Our Lord, but if I can do you a favor, well, then, say twelve Our Fathers and ten Hail Maries.' I said, 'Mijnheer Curate, that's a bargain.' 'Just don't keep going on about it, Madame Seynaeve,' he said.")

When Papa made his way past the Kouter, his ruse became only too obvious. He nudged Louis's arm with his elbow. "Louis, don't drag your feet like that. And stand up straight. We're coming to the Market Square. *Allee,* Come on, a bit *tenue.*" So it had all been arranged in advance, probably three days ago: the two younger Seynaeves, father and son, would come as serfs and vassals to pay their respects in the Café Rotonde on the Market Square to their Great Overlord, Grandpa, who was usually playing his daily game of bridge around this hour. From the Rotonde Grandpa would go on to his other habitual haunt, the Café Groeninghe, which flew the flag of the Flemish Lion.

And, yes, there in the shadow of the Belfry Louis could see Grandpa through the palms in the window of the Café Rotonde. Did Grandpa pee next to the bowl in the Café Rotonde as well?

The Seynaeves, father and son, waded through the thick, acrid cigar smoke toward the grand old man. Grandpa was staring at the cards in his hand, while his other hand, the one with the signet ring, lay on a newspaper, fingers spread wide, as if in search of something to hold on to. There wasn't the slightest doubt that he had spotted his son and his grandson. But it was only right that he should ignore them. They approached the table with the green cloth, with the three ashtrays and the smartly dressed gentlemen, and stopped. Then Grandpa suddenly flung his cards down, and the other three gentlemen immediately started to count furiously. Grandpa threw his hands up in the air as if it were Louis's fault that he had lost. But an instant later he appeared to have shrugged off misfortune, the Overlord of the Rotonde, and said, "Well, well, our Louis."

"Hello, Grandpa."

"So, have you come to read us your New Year's letter?" The other gentlemen smirked.

"No," said Louis calmly.

"No New Year's letter, no tip," said Grandpa.

"I already read it out four months ago."

"Well, I'll be darned, so you did! With all these troubles nowadays you tend to forget what time of year it is." Grandpa thumped the threadbare spot on the green plush bench by his side. Louis sat down, the cards were dealt again. Papa did not agree with the way his father played, his body twitched nervously as if he wanted to snatch the winning card out of Grandpa's liver-spotted hands.

Grandpa lost and paid.

Then the gentlemen talked about Count d'Aspremont Lynden, he would be getting Agriculture again as he had under Paul-Henri Spaak, and what did that piece of Franskiljon nobility know about agriculture? The only tomatoes he'd ever seen were in an hors d'oeuvre! And the Germans are on the move again, what tiresome people they are, hard workers, agreed, and more patriotic than we are here in Belgium, agreed, but you can't feel at ease with them, just look how they swallowed up Czechoslovakia before you could count one-two-three. But then, we mustn't look on the dark side of everything, either Chamberlain did a fine job, they're sure to give him the Nobel Prize. A fine job, yes, but it didn't actually help much, since Hitler still goes on about wanting Danzig back as well as an autobahn to East Prussia. He's crazy about autobahns, Hitler.

But should we rearm, which is what the King wants, or not? We must simply stay neutral, that's the most sensible thing to do. Mijnheer Daels, the director of Public Assistance, claimed that the vibrations in Hitler's voice had been estimated at 228 per second, while a normal man wouldn't even make 200 in a fit of purest rage.

Then Grandpa flapped at the cigar smoke as if shooing away a mosquito. It was a signal. Obediently, the gentlemen resumed their game of cards. Papa and Louis had permission to leave, indicated by the same careless wave of Grandpa's hand. Papa asked if Grandpa would be coming for a meal the following evening. Louis drank what was left of his hot chocolate too quickly and choked. Shamed in front of his bridge partners, Grandpa held his cards close to his waistcoat, coughed as if to drown the barking sounds being produced by his grandson, and said, "Tomorrow? Perhaps. If I can spare the time. What's it to be?"

"Constance was thinking of roast veal."

"With baby carrots," said Grandpa, "not a bad idea."

Out on the street Papa said in an undertone, "Did you have a good look at that red-haired fellow sitting next to Grandpa who kept winning all the time? That's Meneer Tierenteyn. You wouldn't guess it from his looks and that stupid expression of his, but he's in the Secret Service. He spies for the English. Yes. The whole of Belgium is poisoned with the likes of him. They keep going on about the German Fifth Column, but there are a lot more on the French and English side, a lot more spies.

That's why I'm telling you, for your own good, Louis, always be sure who you are dealing with, and think seven times before you speak."

Papa took off his hat and wiped his forehead with a red-and-white checked handkerchief, the classic peasant handkerchief of our people over the centuries. Grandpa used spotless white handkerchiefs that stuck out just a little from his breast pocket like a strip of cardboard. Once used and crumpled, the handkerchief went straight into the right sleeve. Handkerchiefs are used for semaphore, signaling, secret signs. When I'm grown up, I'll be told all there is to know about them. The handkerchief you use to wave goodbye has naturally got to be white, so that it can be seen better. Moses waving from his mount to the tribes below. The red-and-white checks of Papa's handkerchief stand for simplicity, solidarity with the poorest of the poor, rejection of French frills and furbelows. A handkerchief can also be a prop, not to say a weapon, for a businessman like Papa. Louis had observed this twice during Papa's visits to the Institute. Trained no doubt by Grandpa, Papa is, in his own way, a conjuror. First step: say, sweating, "How warm it is in here!" and look for handkerchief. Second: "Ah, here it is!" and fish for handkerchief in trouser pocket. Third: pull out rosary with handkerchief and allow it to fall to floor. *"Tiens, oh, pardon."* Fourth: smile bashfully about your piety, pick up rosary, tuck it away, and assume a contemplative expression as if the contact of your fingers with the ebony beads had renewed your ability to face life. Papa couldn't possibly have thought up these maneuvers all by himself, he was much too happy-go-lucky, too disorganized for that. No, if it is method you are after, then you have to go to Grandpa.

Louis started to drag his feet on purpose, but Papa never noticed.

the moose

T hey were playing, Tetje and Bekka and Louis, in the clay pits created
when some antediluvian giant had kicked the yellow ground with his
mountain boots in a fit of rage and the ground had split open to reveal
ocher clefts in the earth, and then the Nervii had come and taken the earth
away to build their ovens and to plaster the walls of their huts, then later
some ancient Belgian had had the idea of baking wet blocks of clay into
bricks, although the ancient Greeks preferred marble, it's always been
like that, Belgians like to fiddle about with building-blocks, matchboxes,
while the rest of the world builds with granite and porphyry and marble.

They flew a kite that Tetje had taken fifteen minutes to put together
with his oily brown fingers. Louis had tried to make one as well, but it
was no good, his flour paste wasn't thick enough, the newspapers were
wet, the string wouldn't stay in place around the cross of cane sticks as
it did around Tetje's.

Then they explored their surroundings and sang, Bekka the loudest.
No one chased them away. In the cramped hut where the clay-diggers'
foremen played cards when it rained, they came across empty tin cans and

used them as footballs. Tetje tried to make an electric drill work, but it was either rusty or broken, he could nick the walls with the twisting bit but couldn't make any holes. Bekka put on some filthy overalls, rolled up the sleeves and the trouserlegs, and strutted around like Charlie Chaplin with her feet apart, toes turned extravagantly outward. Suddenly a man appeared and said, "Hey, you dirty little tramps!" Immediately Bekka snarled, "Can't you see we're busy?"

"I can see that." The man was wearing gray socks and sandals, a plum-colored sweater, bottle-green trousers stretched tight over his slender legs and bottom. Around his neck hung a St. Anthony medallion. There was something wrong with his wavy, woolly hair, it looked like a cap held on by his ears. The man had just been eating chocolate, his lips were smudged brown.

"Oh, you dirty little tramps." He gave a sigh and sat down on the doorstep of the hut. He kept looking at Louis. "I know you," he said. "You can't fool me, I know you."

"Could be."

"Aren't you one of the gymnasts I saw in the Market Square during the Golden Spurs festival? In white shorts?"

"No," said Louis, avoiding the bright, insistent gaze. Bekka's hoarse, rasping little laugh. Tetje banged nails into the door of the hut.

"No? Then it must have been somebody else. But you come from a good home. I could see that right away. Not like those two Gypsies over there."

"Cut it out, Dirty Dick!" Like a little old woman, Bekka pursed her lips into a disdainful pout. "I am ten times cleaner than you. Right, Tetje?" Tetje went on driving nails furiously into the wood, in the shape of a heart.

The man stroked his chest, the inside of his thighs.

"At it again?" Bekka asked casually. Dirty Dick muttered something. A beaten expression came into his face, reminding Louis instantly of Bernard, one of the little ones, who used to hang around the bigger boys in the playground as if wanting to tell them something sad, but no sound ever emerged, which aroused the fury of Sister Adam and the compassion of Sister Angel, who would make valiant efforts to get him to speak. He grew gradually thinner and thinner, Bernard, he used to take ten or twelve steps and then stand rigid in helpless silence for a quarter of an hour. When Louis had asked him, "Bernard, why are you being so stupid?" Bernard had simply nodded at him. "Bernard, you won't set the world on fire, will you?" Bernard had nodded and his sadness had grown more sorrowful still. If you had given him a push, he would have fallen right over. Louis patted Bernard's shoulder. The boy nodded. Louis put his index finger on Bernard's throat, touched the Adam's apple. "Go on," said Bernard. Whereupon Louis kicked his ankle. For days on end Bernard followed him about, with those sorrowful goat's-eyes of his, getting thinner all the time, as white as a sheet. Then his parents took him away. According to Sister Imelda, he still had to keep to his bed.

"What's your name?"

"Louis."

"I thought it would be be something like that. The sort of name used by the better sort of family. And what school do you go to?"

"Leave him alone," said Tetje, lifting his hammer and letting it descend within an inch of the sculptured waves of Dirty Dick's red and brown hair. The man continued to stroke his tightly stretched trousers as he got to his feet.

"Oh, so he's jealous, he can't bear . . ."

"Ten francs," said Tetje and dropped the hammer right in front of Louis's feet.

"You get more expensive every day." Dirty Dick put on the voice of a sprightly old market trader calling out to her customers. "Seven francs and not a cent more! Take it or leave it!" Bekka grabbed Louis's wrist and pulled him away as Tetje nodded and Dirty Dick walked into the hut. "Come," she said.

For quite a while they tried to skip flat pebbles across the gray-green surface of a pool of stinking, stagnant water, but the pebbles wouldn't bounce.

"What are they doing, those two?"

"What do you think?" They must be fighting, Louis thought, because now and then he could hear a stifled cry and the sound of stumbling about.

"Yes, they're having a fight," said Bekka. They took off their shoes and waded into the yellow mud under clouds of swarming gnats. The earth felt yielding and cool between Louis's toes. Bekka said that her father would soon be going to France for the harvest and that he had asked her to look after her mother and Tetje.

The fighters came out of the hut, and Dirty Dick headed straight for the road without looking up. As he walked past the raspberry-red crane, he gave one of the struts a hard thump. Tetje picked up the hammer, stuck it inside his shirt next to his bare, breadcrust-brown skin, and said they ought to be getting back.

"But we just got here!" So here, too, here in this spacious playground of clay pits, a thousand times larger than the one at the Institute, things are suddenly being brought to a halt for no apparent reason. Why is this afternoon being cut short?

On their way back home Bekka acted as if her brother didn't exist. Until she suddenly gave a little shriek. "What a fine pair you are! Here I am walking around in these filthy overalls and you never said a word!"

She took the overalls off and threw them over a tree stump, like a gunned-down scarecrow.

"Would you believe it! It was touch and go there that I'd walk in on our father like that!" But it didn't sound as if that would have been a disaster, she was saying it only to break Tetje's silence, or to gain time to . . . Bekka is a Sister, Sister Rebekka.

"I thought you wanted to take them home for Dad," said Tetje inanely, unthinkingly.

"Our Dad in that filth? You want our Dad to put on something from out of that hut?" Bekka said acidly. "Not all of us are like you!" When they could see their street in the distance, Tetje started to walk faster. "I'll buy you a Prince Valiant book," he said to his sister. A peace offering.

"And a bag of lemon drops," Bekka said immediately. "Different-colored ones."

"Okay." Tetje walked faster still, head bowed. There were a lot of cardboard boxes, cans, and bottles lying along the road, but he didn't bother to take a kick at any of them.

Mama screamed when she saw Louis's shoes and socks encrusted with ocher-colored lumps. "You've been playing with those guttersnipes again!"

"No, I haven't."

"You were seen, you little liar! Look, you've turned all red. Your head's gone scarlet from all that lying."

She made him kneel on the veranda while holding two bound volumes of the encyclopedia *Ons Volk Ontwaakt!* on the palms of his hands with his arms outstretched. After he had been there for some time, she shuffled laboriously up to him, her big belly sticking out. He wanted to get up, but she put a flowerpot with a hydrangea spotted yellow and pink on his head. *"Voilà.* And don't you budge or I'll take the carpet beater to you."

Out of breath, she subsided onto the sofa. Now and then he could feel her looking at the back of his neck.

Papa and Raspe toiled along, carting reams of paper. Raspe said, "Look at that, Staf, a newfangled flowerpot." They stopped, the paper sagging between them. Papa was panting. "That flower needs a bit of watering," he said. Hooting with laughter, Raspe heaved again at the load. Papa did the same. Louis couldn't stand it any longer. His arms were aching, he had a cramp in his neck, but those were the least of his worries, he could feel the tears trickling down his chin. He tried not to make a sound, but a sharp little sob escaped him, as from one of the little ones alone in his bed. Then he heard the sofa creak, and she came and stood in front of him.

"Now you know what it's like," she said.

I must be someone else. I am not here. This looming shape, this bulging sack in the flowered dress with the lovely head on top, at which I don't dare look or else I will cry even harder, she, she, she is looking at some other boy. Raspe called my father, who is his boss, his employer, by his first name. I would never put up with that. The child in her belly is looking straight at me through those walls of flesh and thinks it is looking at its brother. Nothing of the kind. Its brother, Louis, is somewhere else, cocooned in the safe familiarity of the Institute, miles and miles from here.

Mama was saying a lot of things that sounded apologetic, he found it hard to hear them, as if his ears were awash with tears. She said that they used to give out this kind of punishment in the College of Education, where she was often sentenced although she had done nothing wrong. "Sentenced?" he said.

"All right then," said Mama bitterly, "you think you can make fun of me, all right, we'll see who has the last laugh."

After what seemed half an hour his arms began to twitch, to tremble. He allowed them to drop, went on sitting under the wobbling clay hat, his buttocks against his heels, and called out to her behind him, "Forgiveness. I beg forgiveness, Please forgive me, Mama."

She washed his face with a kitchen towel. He sat at the table and cut out pictures from *Bravo,* which he would later paste into an exercise book, to show to Vlieghe.

"I'm doing it for your own good," she said. "Do you realize that or don't you? You'll grow up like a disobedient savage otherwise."

They ate spiced rusks together at four o'clock.

"The baby is going to be a little beauty. With curly blond hair and blue eyes. I can often picture it in my mind's eye. Three or four times a day I look at a picture of Gary Cooper, it's supposed to have some influence. I really ought to be looking at Jean Harlow as well, I suppose, in case it turns out to be a girl, but I'm sure it's going to be a little boy. What do you think? Nothing, of course, it's always the same with you, it's too much trouble to answer your mother. Is that what they teach you at the Institute? You're not pleased at all that you're getting a little brother. Even though I'm suffering all this just for you. So that you won't have to grow up alone, so that you'll have a little playmate."

You don't have to do it for me. He just managed to swallow the words.

95

She stroked her stomach, automatically, like Dirty Dick this afternoon. So long as she doesn't push the baby out, right here in front of me.

"I just wish it would hurry up. The sooner the better. Because sometimes I can't bear it any longer," said Mama.

Then they heard the rattling of the mussel cart outside, and he was allowed to fetch a bucket of mussels. His arms at full punishing stretch, he heaved the bucket into the kitchen. "You're turning into a strong lad," she said. He was allowed to chop up the onions, she put a match in his mouth against the tears. As if he had any tears left.

Peter Benoit, the greatest Flemish composer of all time, who was born in a miserable little hovel on Harelbeke market, liked eating raw mussels best of all. He had a lion's-head with a beard, and so did his friend the great poet Emmanuel Hiel. Together they would sit at a café and gulp down raw mussels while the one wrote poetry and the other sang his immortal melodies out loud, to the bewilderment of passers-by, who would doff their hats or caps in respect all the same.

On the radio a German voice was making guttural sounds.

"*Jetzt,*" said Mama. "Did you hear that? He said *jetzt*. That's just what that German kept saying, the one who taught me the piano in '14–'18. We used to play duets together. And when it was my turn, he would call out, *'Jetzt! Jetzt!'* and it startled me every time because it sounded like such a strange word. I wish I could go to the maternity home *jetzt*, right now."

They played the Game of Goose. Night fell. Louis cheated, Mama didn't notice.

"I saw the man who was in the car with Papa and Grandpa, that man Holst."

"A nice man," said Mama, "but a bit odd. What did you make of him? Good-looking, isn't he? He used to be after me."

"You mean he came after you in class?"

Her laughter bubbled up, high, in cascades, like one of those songs that came trilling over the radio, Mimi Colbert, Papa's favorite singer, coloratura, in *The Bells of Charleville*.

"No, you silly. He ran after me, to get me to go out with him. It's high time someone taught you what's what. Don't you know what's meant by boys going out with girls?"

"Of course." I turn red again.

"But you can see, can't you, it just wouldn't have done."

"Why not?"

"He was much younger than me. And then, my father would have beaten me black and blue."

"But why?" cried Louis impatiently.

"Don't make me nervous." She swept the pieces off the board into a cardboard box. "Those Holsts are backwoodsmen. They live in the woods. They don't know anything but the woods. And it's much better if people like that stay in the woods."

"But he was in Papa's car."

"Your father is much too kind. Holst only came here to deliver some baby clothes. And he just had to get into Papa's car by hook or by crook and go for a drive, that's a backwoodsman for you. And your father wanted to show off, of course, so he took him along. The baby clothes were hideous, old-fashioned things, I threw them all out. My baby won't be wearing other people's cast-offs."

"Whose were they?"

She was busy putting the Game of Goose away in the drawer at the bottom of the cupboard, along with the cards and the draughtsboard, straightened up too quickly, put her hands to the small of her back, and rubbed.

"Well, now that you mention it . . . Whose? I never bothered to ask. Meerke probably had them from before. No, then I would have seen them at home. I'll have to ask after all."

Suddenly she exclaimed, *"Nondedju,* I do know! No, it can't be. D'you know, Louis, those clothes must have been Jeannette's. No, they wouldn't dare . . . *Nondedju!* That's what she did, those clothes were little Jeannette's!"

Jeannette was the little dead daughter of Aunt Berenice, Mama's sister, who lived in Wallonia and was married to an Arab, or was it an Egyptian? In any case, a convert to Islam, that disgusting religion that once threatened Europe with the sign of the Crescent and had been stopped in its tracks by Charles Martel. Louis, like Mama, thought it disgraceful that Meerke, Mama's mother, had wanted to dress his brother-to-be in girls' clothes still reeking of Islam. And of death.

"I thought Aunt Berenice wasn't allowed to go to Meerke's anymore because she married a heathen and renounced her faith."

"Oh, Louis, that was all over long ago. You've been reading last year's newspaper."

"There aren't any newspapers at the Institute," Louis said crossly.

Just as he was about to go to bed and was putting his wet shoes, from which all traces of clay had been removed, next to Mama's checked slippers beside the dead, lead-colored feet of the stove, Papa came in.

"It's too terrible," he said. Papa's hat fell off his head as he sank back into the cozy-corner, his round, cherry-red face glistening with sweat. "Quick, give me a Pils."

Louis ran into the kitchen, searched feverishly in the bottom of the dresser. "There's no more beer," he called, and cursed his slovenly mother for neglecting Papa just because she was expecting a baby.

"Behind the curtains, you blind bat!" Mama called and went on with her inaudible conversation with Papa. I'm missing the most important part, the beginning!

"Merci." Papa downed the glass of beer in two gulps and continued. "So I had just picked up an ad from the dentist in Kuurne, I was driving up the road, and then I saw that the whole street was on fire. Ablaze. It was black with people and the air was black with smoke, the gendarmes were letting me go through, but the crowds in the street wouldn't budge an inch, I honked like mad, the gendarmes waved me on because they'd seen who I was, and then those gawkers finally made way for me, they moved off to one side of the fire, and, Constance, I could see then that the big barn at the Harelbeke corner was on fire. I could have cried, all that lovely flax burning up, and I accelerated a little bit, I got between the people and the fire, and then the flames leaped out, straight at my car, and just look, look here, feel, half my beard is gone, the whole right side has been singed!"

She, the slave who had been listening open-mouthed, stood up without appearing to be bothered in the least by her swollen belly. Papa took her hand and ran it down his cheek.

"D'you feel it? Louis, come here. Feel it!"

"You're hot," said Mama.

"No, but feel how there's less stubble on this side, Louis!"

"Yes," said Louis, sandpaper against his fingertips. He took his hand away from his father's face. Papa leaned back, his neck supported by the cushions.

"So the flames caught your car?" Mama said.

"My tires, the right side of the body, it's all black."

"Why didn't you close your window?"

"But the heat was suffocating! How could you close the window!"

"You're completely disfigured," said Mama. Papa sat forward, rested his hand on the cushion, and narrowed his eyes.

"It's no joke, Constance. It could easily have been the end of me. I had to swerve to avoid those idiots, and I was within a hairsbreadth of driving straight into that burning barn."

Mama's belly slid along the table, she bent over her husband and, without having been asked, stroked the show-off's unscathed red cheek. "Just think of it, you in that burning barn!" Papa seemed to find this witty and gave the flatterer a wink.

"Was it in Harelbeke?" Louis asked.

"Not far from your Stag."

Louis's Stag was a bronze moose erected in memory of the fallen Canadian soldiers, a beast that looked quite real in the dusk, with its giant soaring antlers. Every time the family went to see Meerke in Bastegem, the car would drive past the moose and Louis would lick his thumb, run it across his palm, and slam his fist into the wet hand with a smack.

That night Louis dug his spurs into the massively heavy moose and rode right through the flames. His mother, in a blue dress with small white gas jets for tufts, spread out her arms as he thundered past her on his moose. At the same moment the wild woolly hair on the moose's forehead caught fire, the flames licked along the antlers Louis clung to, then the antlers were all ablaze, the moose went soft and white like Mary, Baekelandt's cow, and reared up, Louis fell from its flanks and woke up in sheets that the moose had slobbered all over.

_A_fter their Sunday lunch of roast pork, salsify, and fried potatoes, Father Staf and Son Louis Seynaeve repaired to the Café Groeninghe, in plenty of time for the friendly match between Walle Sporting Club and Club Brugge. Many regulars were already seated in the medieval hall with its leaded panes, its oak furniture, its copper pans, its photographs of the Congress of the VNV, the Flemish National League, its signs in Gothic script: "Beef Hotchpotch," "Homemade Blood Sausage," _"Levet Scone"_—"Live a Clean Life," "Never Say Die."

It looked as if Papa wasn't being welcomed as warmly as usual. People greeted him perfunctorily and went on chatting to each other, beers in hand. Papa didn't notice, of course. My father is made of concrete. Papa began telling Noël, the owner behind the bar, at length about his recent brush with death by burning on the road near Harelbeke. Gesturing, and in high-pitched, self-confident tones—since Grandpa wasn't there in the Groeninghe—he related how his brand-new trilby had burst into flames on his head, how his wristwatch had melted, how a front tire had exploded in the hellish heat, but Noël, who had his hands full drawing beer, merely said, "Really? The things that happen these days."

Louis had drunk too much beer at home, and what with the lemonade his father had treated him to, he was dying to pee but he didn't dare to cross the hall toward the beckoning oak door with its burned-in silhouette of a knight through which Groeninghers were following each other in steady procession minute by minute, some with their hands already on their flies.

Mijnheer Leevaert, teacher at the Atheneum, joined Papa at the bar. His ravaged, almost purple face bent down to Louis. "Is this the same Louis I used to dandle on my knee?"

"Yes, sir," said Louis. (If it makes him happy.)

Papa has great respect for Mijnheer Leevaert because he reads a lot of books and is the bosom friend of Marnix de Puydt, poet, pianist, and the most celebrated son of Walle. The two of them are inseparable, Siamese twins.

"Noël, a Pils without too big a head for our Louis!" Papa wanted to object but made do with a half-hearted "Well, since it's Sunday."

Louis knew his manners, and raised his glass to Mijnheer Leevaert. "Santé."

"Gezondheid!" cried Papa.

"Gezondheid, Mijnheer Leevaert." Don't drink too quickly. Don't choke. Another blunder. Toasting him in French, in this café, I'll never, ever forget it, it's all Byttebier's fault, forever raising his glass of water or milk in the Institute and calling out "Santé," at which the Hottentots invariably burst out laughing. When will something ever be my own fault? Later.

"Staf." Mijnheer Leevaert rummaged in his inside pocket and brought out a very thin folded sheet of paper which he opened with delicate, piano-player's fingers. Mama, who used to play duets with an uhlan, *jetzt*, says that real pianists do not have long, narrow fingers, on the contrary, sometimes they have stumpy, short ones, but in any case they have *broad* hands. "Staf, I have a document here from Joris that is going to stand our shaky world on its head."

Louis wondered what would happen if now, with his thighs squeezed tight together, he were to pee in his trousers. Would anyone notice? Weren't all these Groeninghers too wrapped up in their own tales? I'll do it. No. He tried to follow Mijnheer Leevaert's story to fend off the pressure in his abdomen, which was beginning to feel like pain. Joris was Joris van Severen, the leader of the Dinaso party, the League of Dutch-Speaking National Solidarists, men who worked for the creation of the ideal State, the Dietsland or Great Netherlands uniting all Dutch-speaking peoples. From French Flanders as far as Friesland, that was Dietsland—and Holland, Belgium, Luxembourg, and some other bits and pieces, that was the Burgundian State.

But for now—according to the badly typed paper covered with faint penciled scrawls—the party would have to rally under the flag of Belgium, under the kepi of our King and his dynasty. What Joris called for was service to an independent, neutral Belgium, for the formation of a united people, without class struggle, in an aristocratic order.

"*Tiens, tiens,*" said Noël, a tray of brown glasses steady as a rock against his chest.

"A bastion of peace," Mijnheer Leevaert read out, "but also of order and true civilization."

The nearest tables had fallen silent. Louis raced for the door, pushed, but the door that had swung open so easily over and over again for every other Groeningher pisser now refused to budge. The blood rushed to his head, he rattled the door latch, caught sight of a man with spectacles and a beard who was grinning and pointing at the adjoining door, realized that he was struggling in front of the graceful silhouette of a lady burned into the wood, flung himself at the knight, who gave way with a crash.

When he returned, one of the Groeninghers was saying that the Dinasos might not be consistent, perhaps not, but then, political purity wasn't always a virtue. Another said that, no matter what, the Belgian state would collapse, that was the lesson of history. Louis could understand that, his history book told of a whole series of kingdoms that had perished, though most had lasted quite some time. Yet another man said that the Flemish language was the only criterion. A new word, or at least a new meaning, because until then the Criterion had been the bicycle track raced by those two eagles Karel Kaers and Marcel Kint.

Louis saw by the grandfather clock that it was less than an hour till kickoff in the Walle vs. Brugge match and Papa showed no signs of getting ready to go, hanging as he was on the lips of Mijnheer Leevaert, who was now holding forth about the common destiny of the Germanic peoples.

Could you get drunk on one glass of beer? Could you be dying of hunger just one hour after having stuffed yourself with roast pork, salsify, potatoes, and apple tart?

Hazily, Louis saw Leevaert's blotchy face giving way to that of a brewery drayman in a leather apron, who was threatening Papa with a sausage of a finger. What was going on? What was the meaning of those wary, uneasy looks the café regulars had exchanged when the Seynaeves had come in? It was all due to one humiliating, shocking fact, now being put into words by this drayman, this howler-monkey, this aggrieved and vengeful football fan. Yesterday Florent Seynaeve, Papa's youngest brother, had been bought from Walle Sport's reserve team. On the pretext that their regular goalkeeper, Herman Vanende, had been called up,

Stade Walle had offered and handed over a large sum of money to get the turncoat between the posts this very day.

"Big, big money." Louis could see that Papa had been caught off guard, that he was trying to gain time, to concoct a story.

"There's been talk of a motorcycle, an Indian!"

"Not to mention what was passed under the table. *Ni vu, ni connu.*"

"Speak your mother tongue, Hanssens!"

"You couldn't have put it better, Willemijns," Papa said. "Here, as always, it's a matter of language."

Mijnheer Leevaert raised his eyebrows, studying Papa with the suggestion of a mocking smile. He was on his sixth beer.

"I've been talking about it a lot with my brother. I said to him, 'You know, Florent, looking at it properly, Walle Sport is really a bit of a la-di-da club. A good club, a fine club, certainly, in sporting terms you can't say anything against it, but . . .' "

Papa looked all around, not at Louis.

" 'But hostile to our national ideal. No question about it. The directors speak French at home, don't they? And the same goes for the changing rooms, doesn't it? The players all go around with "look at me, how great I am" expressions, don't they? They're all *fils-à-papa,* young playboys turning up their noses at your ordinary man-in-the-street, aren't they?' 'Staf,' my brother said, 'when you come to think of it, you're right. And what you don't know is that we're getting two new forwards next season, one from Charleroi who doesn't speak a word of Flemish and an out-and-out Frenchman from Stade Reims.' "

The Groeninghers fell to discussing the question, all speaking at once. It was true, the Walle Sport players paid more attention to their smart red-and-white shirts than to their public. And they were better at showing off their fancy footwork than at scoring.

Anyway, shouldn't you support a club that might not be doing so well right now but that belongs to us, to our people, like Stade Walle?

Like an orator, Papa can get the masses to change their minds in the twinkling of an eye. Papa, who, sweating and happy, is standing there holding forth, a potential Danton or Hitler. Louis glowed with pride.

"And that is precisely why I'm off right now with our Louis to Stade Walle in order to support my brother."

The ease with which he could utter the lie. The matter-of-fact way in which he could disown his favorite team. The daring of this huge betrayal, conceived on the spur of the moment! Louis took hold of his father's arm and said loudly, "It's time to go, Papa."

"You're right, my boy."

In the street, an empty feeling in his head and a heavy lump in his stomach, he asked, "Are we really going to Stade?"

"That's what I said."

"Who are they playing?"

"We'll find out soon enough," said Papa and belched, the polite thing to do among the Bedouin after a meal in their tents.

"A fine people," said Papa when they were standing behind the goal and behind the narrow shoulders and broad hips of Uncle Florent. "Some may say, a poor people, but I say they are *my* people."

Uncle Florent was wearing a coarse-knit jersey and a beige cap. He did a few kneebends and then, stretching as far as he could, jumped up to touch the crossbar. He was wearing bigger leg pads than his teammates.

"That's because he has delicate ankles," Papa explained. "It runs in the family. That and weak intestines. For the rest we're made of granite, we Seynaeves, aren't we, my boy?"

Surrounded by the tightly packed spectators, he was transformed into a playful, boisterous working man. He waved a casual hand to left and right, at people he didn't know. He seems glad that I've come along, perhaps even a little proud of it. Otherwise why would he be putting his arm around my shoulders every so often in full view of the common people with their caps, beery voices, and hand-rolled cigarettes in the corners of their mouths? Stade was playing S.K. Waregem.

"Break his leg!" "He's putting it on!" "You're borin', Van Doren!"

"*Offside!*" "*Penalty!*" Every time the action flagged, a fat woman would utter a raucous cry, in an inhuman singsong, as if the rag-and-bone man were being tortured on his rounds: "What a load of rubbish!"

Whenever S.K. Waregem were on the attack, all you could hear was the dry, reverberating thud of boot against ball. Whenever Stade Walle went anywhere near the opposing goal, Papa would bellow louder than anyone else.

Uncle Florent parried balls with his fist, his knee, his boot, rather than catch them. "Keep 'em out, Seynaeve!" "Think of your children, Seynaeve!" The football experts let it be known that Stade had made a good buy. "And how!" said Papa but didn't yet dare say, That's my brother.

Only after the match, when Uncle Florent walked into the club bar in his checked knickerbockers, his hair sopping wet, and was being patted on the back by flushed Stade supporters, did Papa come forward. Uncle Florent gave Papa an English cigarette. Papa smoked it to the end, puffing without inhaling the perfectly rounded cylinder between thumb and index finger, like a girl. "Florent, you ought to keep your right foot farther forward when you come off your line, you still tend to stand a little square."

"Staf, you can kiss my arse," said Uncle Florent. "Did we win or didn't we? Did a single ball end up in the back of the net?"

"It's lucky . . ." Papa addressed the noisy tipplers around him, "that you are my youngest brother, or else . . ."

"Or else what?"

"I'd put you across my knee."

"You, Staf? You and who else?"

The fans were nudging each other. Louis felt as if he were Papa's and Uncle Florent's brother. Why wasn't Vlieghe here? Dondeyne, in a pinch, or even Dobbelaere?

A gawky youth with a turned-up nose said that if the S.K. Waregem outside left, who was away manning the defenses on the German border, had been there, Uncle Florent wouldn't have stood a chance, because that outside left had a tremendous low shot, a grass-cutter.

"And you may be able to cope with a high ball, but by the time you get down to a low ball I've said ten Our Fathers."

He was nearly lynched and quickly began buying a round. He gabbled something at Louis, who, blushing scarlet, nodded and had a foaming beer thrust into his hand.

"Oh no, you don't!" Papa shouted and put the beer down with a sickening crack on the glass table. "Are you completely out of your mind?" The spilled beer ran onto the floor. "Hey," said the Waregem supporter, "is that what you do here in Walle when somebody buys you a beer?" Uncle Florent said, "Go on, Staf, let the boy . . ."

"Not on your life!" Papa bawled, as at the football match.

"He'd sooner chop off my hands," Louis said, and the bystanders laughed, Uncle Florent loudest of all.

"You'll turn him into a sissy."

"He's made his First Communion, after all."

"In France they give four-year-old children a glass of wine."

"That's right. To strengthen the blood."

"No, no, and no," said Papa. "They can guzzle themselves to death in France as much as they want to, women and children and tramps in the gutter, the more the better, but not here in Flanders . . ."

"Walle Sport sells you short!"

"War-e-gem lost its phlegm," said a wit.

Uncle Florent said, "You finished, Staf?"

"*He* started it," said Papa, like a Hottentot, and then, "Come on, my boy." My boy. It had never sounded so tender before. It took a long time for the waitress to take their money. Papa turned his back on his youngest brother and his admirers, and, using the little sticks provided for the purpose, he poked holes in a box pasted over with brown paper that hung next to the portrait of Queen Astrid. The first prize was a porcelain figurine of an Oriental dancer with a black and gold fringe around her hips. Papa poked twelve times and missed, his consolation prize twelve small bars of cream-filled chocolate. He ate six of them on the way home, Louis had three.

"Now you've seen for yourself what a vulgar club Stade is. Poor people. We Flemings, what a mess we're in. I'm doing it for our Florent, otherwise I'd never set foot in Stade Walle again. That team is useless."

"What about Uncle Florent?"

"He's not so wonderful, either. Those low balls, he's much too fat for them."

uncle robert

*L*ouis slipped out, but when he looked at the house where Tetje and Bekka Cosijns lived, the shutters were closed. Afraid to ring the bell, he lingered at the front door. Across the road, at the shoemaker's, an old man was helping a young girl to put on a gas mask, smoothing back the fair hair of the round-eyed beast with the trunk. The piercing sound of the knife grinder could be heard in Snellaert Street. Suddenly the thought occurred to Louis—and the thought grew, a savoy cabbage swelling up, filling his innermost being—that Bekka must have died during the night and that the Cosijns family was now at her funeral.

Bekka was sitting in the kitchen that reeked of the engine oil on her overalls, busy shelling peas, when she saw the gigantic angel of death pulling himself through the open window and crouching on the windowsill, his rustling, wide white wings folded behind him. His enormously long, transparent fingers slid toward the pods. The angel began to eat the peas faster than Bekka could shell them.

"Don't do that, Holst," said Bekka. "Please, or my mother will . . ." The angel slipped off the windowsill, gave his shoulders a shake so that his wings stood up gracefully again, and spread his arms wide. Bekka dropped the tin pan with its few remaining peas and sprang toward the angel, to lie against his merciful breast, but at that very moment Holst drew back and vanished so that she ended up on the floor and hit her mouth against the edge of the metal tank that had been standing in the hut at the clay pits, her teeth rolling over the floor like misshapen white peas.

Louis ran over to Mimi at the bakery, who was standing, arms folded, in the doorway of her shop.

"One brown roll and one white?" she said.

"No." A smell of vanilla floated out of the shop.

"What then?"

"Nothing . . . The street's very quiet. Has there been a funeral, by any chance?"

"Not that I know of. There could have been, of course."

"But then you would have heard about it."

"You're in a bit of a state. Is anything wrong?"

"The Cosijnses aren't at home."

"They've gone to the fair."

Trembling with rage, Louis ran out of Zwevegem Street. Never again. I'll never so much as say hello to them again. They are nothing but bohemians, foreigners. Gypsies. They never said one word to me about the fair. But Papa and Mama didn't either, why not? At this very moment Bekka and Tetje are sitting yelling on the *montagnes russes,* the big dipper, with sugar from doughnuts all over their faces.

He walked past the Flandria, the mansion where the French-speakers came to play tennis. He hooked his fingers in the wire netting. Young men with lacquered hair and long white trousers were playing the graceful, incomprehensible game with the white balls, stretching up, swinging their bronzed arms, calling out phrases in French to ladies who were sitting on the terrace eating ices out of crystal goblets. Faced with this carefree, untrammeled, arrogantly self-centered world at play, he felt a great bond with Papa, who called the Flandria "that citadel of the enemies of our people." When I'm grown up I'll play there dressed like that in white, I'll learn to speak that hateful French language better than they do. Soon, one day, I'll pay proper attention at Sister Angel's French lessons.

Although he was not allowed to go there without Papa or Mama, he set off for Grandma's house. Where else can I go? To the fair? Where is the fair? Not easy to ask a passer-by. He'd say, "Look here, young fellow, have you taken leave of your senses?" In any case, I haven't got any money on me.

Aunt Hélène said that Grandma was confined to bed. A confinement? That can't happen to an old woman with one foot in the grave, babies born like that turn out blind. Confined? Aunt Hélène said that it didn't amount to much, there was probably nothing the matter with Grandma at all, she was just pretending to have a cold. Why? Aunt Hélène would rather not say, she raised her eyebrows in the direction of Uncle Robert, who was busy doing the crossword puzzle in *De Standaard*. He had barely greeted Louis, grunting something with his pencil between his teeth.

Uncle Robert had been born one year before Uncle Florent but looked ten years older. He weighed well over two hundred pounds.

"A pig," Papa said. "Not an ounce of discipline, he's let himself go, all he does is stuff himself, he's going to go completely to fat." Mama said that Uncle Robert's "nonchalance" had started one summer night when his fiancée had disappeared and refused to give any explanation the next day, saying merely that her conscience was clear, but Uncle Robert had slammed the front door so hard that it came off its hinges, and he had never returned to her with whom he had sworn to share his life during his earthly existence. The next few weeks he had suffered from a rash, you could still see where the spots had been, rough pink patches on his cheeks and neck.

All the windows were open. Aunt Hélène was about to start on her Big Spring Cleaning. A smell of ammonia hung in the air. Or was it the smell from the little metal urinal again?

"Voilà." Uncle Robert pushed the newspaper to one side. "How's your mother? Getting on with her pregnancy all right, is she? If you ask me, she's going to have twins."

"What do you know about it?" said Aunt Hélène, knotting a scarf into a turban.

"You can tell by her eyes."

"What do you mean, her eyes?"

"They're like this." He became a puffy, half-witted woman with staring, squinting eyes, sucking in his cheeks so that his double chins bulged out. The absence of Grandpa, patriarch and all-seeing lord and master, seemed, as with Papa in the Groeninghe, to have set off a rush of exuberance in this son, too. When the cat's away, the spotty fat mouse will play.

"She must know what she's doing, Constance, she's certainly big enough, I only hope she's not going to copy our mother and end up with seven," said Uncle Robert, still squinting. "Eh, my boy?" The eyes went back into place, fixing upon Louis as if he were a grown-up.

"That's for her to decide," snapped Aunt Hélène. "And our brother has some say in the matter too."

"Some say . . . but that's about all." Uncle Robert stared at a host of

sparrows that had settled in the small garden. Aunt Hélène peeled a banana, gave one half to Louis and the other half to her stupid, fat brother.

"Children! Why don't they go and buy a dog instead, a dachshund. Or a parrot. If they insist on having something living around the place. Eh, my boy?"

One fine morning Uncle Robert will get out of his bed, look in the shaving mirror, and discover that all the spots from his old sorrow have sprouted into little craters, blisters, and boils. A leper whom not even a Father Damian can help. Disfigured for all time, the fat pig in his gray suit will no longer dare go to work in his bank or show himself in the street, he'll have to stay stuck in his chair with his crossword puzzle. But that would make Grandma too unhappy. Very well, then. We will show mercy and spare him.

Grandma had had seven children, like the seven colors of the rainbow, like the seven plagues of Egypt, like the seven brothers of Tom Thumb. We will include the first Hélène, or rather Marie-Hélène, a two-day-old child also counts as a numbered soul in the registers of Our Lord. Still, it had been a bit uncalled for to defy Our Lord by giving a child (Aunt Hélène, who was still fumbling with the hair at the back of her neck, tucking it into the turban) her dead sister's name. As if Grandma had said to God, "You behaved badly when you took one Hélène away from me, so I'm going to do something about it, I've got a spare one here, another Hélène." If I ever have children, I'm going to be careful and choose entirely different names for them so that God can easily tell them apart. Then He'll always be able to do His will with them.

"On the other hand," said Uncle Robert, "the League of Large Families must be kept going. We wouldn't want to see the League go under, because we wouldn't get any more rebates then on the trains. Eh, my boy?"

An airplane skimmed low over the house. Louis ran into the garden, but the plane had gone, the air trembling in its wake. Uncle Robert blocked the way. His stomach looked as big as Mama's.

"We're being thrown out, you and I. Our Hélène has caught the cleaning bug. At times like this, womankind are dangerous. Come on, off we go."

"You don't have to take me home, Uncle."

"I'll go with you part of the way."

Aunt Hélène raised a broom as if about to dub Louis a knight. She let it drop, parted her lips wide, showed her white teeth. "When do you have to go back to Haarbeke?"

"In five days."

"We'll go dancing, the two of us. As soon as I have a bit of time. Don't think I've forgotten."

Uncle Robert made off toward the Bird Market. Louis chose to walk on the inside, next to the houses, which was a mistake because the massive bulk of his uncle, who was afraid of the passing traffic, kept bumping into him. Uncle Florent rode up on a bicycle. He stopped, poised on one leg, did not look at his brother, who said immediately, "We're out for a short stroll."

"He mustn't go to the café, Robert. I don't mind if you do myself, Louis, but if your father hears of it, it'll be my fault again."

"We're only going to the Lost Pastures." Uncle Robert was scared of Stade Walle's new goalkeeper.

"A bit of a walk will do you good." Uncle Florent stood up on both pedals and balanced. That's how the sprinters, those princes of cycle racing, do it during a *sur-place*. And the climbers during the Tour de France, too, frozen on a newspaper photograph, with the towering, snow-covered mountains behind them.

Felicien Vervaecke wearing his little cap. His black-streaked face cleft by a grimace of pain. He'll win the Tour this year. Uncle Florent shot forward, called over his shoulder, "Make sure you're back in time for cards, fatty!"

Silently Uncle Robert trudged on. Louis slackened his pace beside him until they reached the park, where his uncle dropped onto a bench and gasped for breath.

"We've gone quite a long way, eh, my boy?"

A very old policeman came past, looked straight through Uncle Robert, fingered his holster, and disappeared behind the rhododendrons.

"Kaersemaekers from the Second Division. He's only pretending he doesn't know me because you're sitting here with me and he doesn't know who you are. A sound man, but when he's had one too many, hang on to your hat. He always goes to the races with me at Waregem. Out of uniform. After work he does wallpapering for people. Remember that. It may be against regulations, but you won't find anyone better at decorating or papering than a policeman. Or gendarmes for plumbing. And the fire brigade for wiring. Of course, you have to lock your front door, because if an inspector comes around . . ."

Facing them, between the dahlia bed and the roses, stood the spotless white statue of Queen Astrid. Our King was to have been there when it was unveiled last year, all Walle had come pouring in to goggle at their sovereign's grief, but he had had something wrong with his back, and a general, some nobleman, had come in his stead to present the King's compliments.

"You don't have much to say for yourself, do you? Still, I bet you're cock of the walk at your school. Are you afraid of me?"

"No, Uncle."

"Most of people don't feel comfortable with me." He produced a chunk of dry, ocher-colored cheese from a trouser pocket and nibbled at it. "Most people think I'm a lazybones, they imagine that working in a bank is sheer idleness. They're wrong. We work hard in the bank. Though it goes against the grain I'd much rather have been a butcher. I've got a diploma from the hotel catering school, don't forget. But your Grandpa said, 'Robert, first get married, I'll set you up then straightaway.' But darn it all, it takes two to get married! And to be married the way my father, your Grandpa, is married isn't such a great example either. Anyway, why should I get married? I have it easy, I do my stint, and in the evening I listen to the radio or go to the cinema. Or I read my Lord Listers."

"Papa reads those as well."

"They're his." Uncle Robert popped another piece of cheese into his gently undulating cheeks.

"Get married. It's easy for them to talk. We're not in the Congo, where you can buy yourself a woman."

Three nurses walked past, twittering among themselves. Uncle Robert watched them until they had gone by, then began to go restlessly through his trouser pocket, crumbs of cheese had stuck under his fingernails, he cleaned them with a match.

"It's nice sitting here, isn't it?"

"Yes, Uncle."

"I saw two sea gulls here once. Think of it. So far from the sea. And once"—he shifted position, got his breath back—"once, on the exact-same bench we are sitting on now, we played a really good trick on our boss. He always used to come and sit here, you see, every lunchtime, with his meat sandwiches, looking at the roses. So a couple of good-for-nothings from the foreign-exchange section come along pretending they haven't noticed him. They sit down on that bench over there with their backs to him and start gossiping, loud enough for him to hear every word. Thérèse, the boss's wife, was in the Maria Mediatrix clinic at the time, expecting a baby. 'Well,' says the one, 'Tavernier's been to the clinic again.' 'How come?' says the other. 'What's Tavernier doing at the clinic?' 'Come on,' says the first, 'you mean you don't know that Tavernier goes and visits the boss's wife in the clinic every day behind the boss's back?' 'But,' says the other, 'doesn't the boss know about it?' 'Of course not,' says the first, 'Tavernier waits until the boss is safely behind his desk, then off he goes to see Thérèse with some fresh fruit and a bunch of violets.' 'Does that mean that Thérèse's baby . . .' 'Come on,' says the first, 'the whole bank knows that.' And off they go. The boss comes bounding back into the bank like a tiger, drags Tavernier out from behind the counter, and bites him on the ear. Since the boss is raving like a madman, Tavernier thinks he's caught foot-and-mouth disease from him and screams for a doctor. We were in stitches. Nearly died laughing." Uncle Robert lapsed into a long silence.

"And then? What happened then?"

"Then those two owned up. 'Boss, it was only a prank, just pulling your leg.' But the boss can't get it out of his mind. They say he behaves like a brute at home. And he hardly speaks to us in the bank any longer."

Uncle Robert shook his head from side to side, the rolls of fat moving up and down above his collar. He whistled a tune from *The Merry Peasant*, then said, "And they want me to get married!"

Workers came by on their way home, hurrying, not talking. They waited for a tram.

"Well, it is nice sitting here, isn't it?"

"Very nice, Uncle."

"You know, if you were married now, you'd be having to go straight back home. 'Where have you been, Louis? Why are you so late? Have you been seeing some woman again? Take your shoes off, you're ruining my parquet floor! Don't put your umbrella down on the armchair, Louis!' "

Uncle Robert nodded a few times approvingly, as if someone else had spoken, levered himself up from the bench. "*Allee*, up with your bottom!"

Behind the bandstand where the southern West Flanders brass bands competed on Sundays. Past a garden full of shrubs and exotic plants, of which Aunt Berenice, the scholar among Mama's sisters and brothers, knew all the Flemish and Latin names. To a swing.

"Sit down." Uncle Robert pointed to the short, unpainted plank seat.

"We've got to go home, Uncle."

"Don't be a baby." Uncle Robert stooped, got the seat swinging, caught it again in his broad hands. Louis sat on it, lifted his legs. Crowing with pleasure, Uncle Robert pushed Louis's shoulderblades. Louis flew into the air, his shoes high above his head, the world full of trees rocked, turned over five, then six times. Louis felt himself going ice-cold, the savoy cabbage in his bowels turned soft and wet, spreading out like a jellyfish with a hundred eager, grasping fingers gliding greedily into his chest, his mouth. Three times he saw the greenery, the parapets of the post office, the latticework of the bandstand, the marble queen, over and over again he was thrust into the sickening void by the exultant Uncle Robert, he screamed, tried to let himself fall forward, was too afraid, spasms of fear darted through his arms, then, heaving and swaying, he vomited, turned sour and hot and icy cold. Uncle Robert swore and hauled at one of the ropes, precipitating Louis off the seat in a spiraling movement. Clinging tightly to the rope, he fell to the ground, hands burning.

"Leave me alone," he shouted, but his throat, stinging, stifled all sounds. He flopped onto the sand, was hit on the back of the neck by the seat, and let out a sob. The humiliation could no longer be denied, the tears burst out and he lay rubbing his cheek along the sand. He could see the bloated dummy in his gray suit clutching the rope helplessly and saying something to two ladies with a perambulator.

Louis wiped his eyes, nose, and mouth with his sleeve, began to stand up, but his knees gave way, he toppled sideways, crawling on all fours.

Uncle Robert lifted him up and clasped him to his stomach.

"*Allee,* steady now. Eh, my boy? *Allee,* all right?"

"It wasn't my fault, Uncle . . . my body . . ."

"Yes, you've had nothing to eat yet, that's it. That's what it was. And hadn't I just said to our Hélène, 'Give the boy a couple of jellied pork sandwiches'? You won't say anything to your Papa, will you, my boy? Because he's sure to put the blame on me again. And Constance will think I did it on purpose, when I only did it to give you a bit of fun, because you asked me to swing you."

Louis cleared his sour-tasting throat. Took a deep breath.

"Come on, let's go home. Quickly," he said, like an order. Uncle Robert wanted to take his hand, but Louis pretended to be wiping the vomit off his trousers. They walked through the park. Louis whistled the air from *The Merry Peasant* very loudly.

"I got the fright of my life. I'm still a bundle of nerves," said Uncle Robert. "Now I know why people smoke cigarettes. Or take to drink."

the land of smiles
_____

According to Papa, Parcels for Soldiers (a voluntary organization founded to bring a bit of sunshine into the monotonous lives of the men guarding our borders) had been his own invention, and the variations devised by shopkeepers from all over Walle as they sent off parcels with games and sweets and woolen socks and underwear to the frontiers had come about only after thorough consultation with him.

Thus he had advised the Coco (Cooperative Company) stores to fill up their parcels of Lutti caramels, toothpaste, and shoe polish with instructive material printed in his workshop, homework record books, writing paper that had been just a little bit rained on (but then, would our boys over there with their feet rotting in the mud right next to Germany, waiting and straining their eyes for that monster from over the border that, they had to presume, was on its way, bother about a few little wrinkles in the paper before they wrote to their mothers or sweethearts?), magazines dated 1935 and 1936, a tract entitled "The Life of St. Rita," the recently published and sole issue of the advertising paper *The Leie*, and, above all, the not particularly attractive but handy little notebooks (so convenient for addresses or for passing thoughts) that bore in different typefaces at the top of every page the names of various businesses, accompanied by a line drawing of a car, a pack of cigarettes, a can of Mobiloil, women's shoes with straps held up by phantom ankles, spectacles, umbrellas.

Louis helped to get the parcels ready in the workshop, folding wrappers, sticking on tape, making piles. Now and then a shopkeeper or manufacturer would turn up in person to select the right type for his "ad," invariably the largest, boldest letters.

"You'll see, meneer," said Papa, "when our boys come home on leave, they'll have read our little book in the trenches so often, taking note of your company's name in these beautiful letters every day without fail, that they'll simply *fly* around to your business, bringing their wives and children with them."

On the third evening before Louis was due back at the Institute, the Parcels for Soldiers Gala Night was held at the Municipal Theater.

Mama sat in front of her dressing table mirror and clumsily, as if doing it for the first time, applied lipstick to her pursed lips while sipping Cinzano from a small glass shaped like a chalice. She used thick pencil to make the parting in her hair darker and then used it to go over her eyebrows.

"Shall I wear my astrakhan, Louis? I don't have to do it up."

"You won't be able to."

"It's ugly, isn't it?" She pressed against both sides of her stomach and looked in the mirror. Was "it" her stomach or her baby? Although she wanted him to contradict her, Louis said, "Yes, it is."

"Well, am I to put on my astrakhan or not?"

"It's much too hot for an astrakhan."

"I don't care." Her nose was pink and shiny. Louis felt his own nose, which, people said, was like hers. Only men with large, arched, eagle's-noses are capable of great things, of adventure. With an occasional exception, of course. Mama tightened his tie, flattened his ears against his skull, inspected him, then let go of his ears, which immediately flapped like those of an elephant in the jungle sensing faraway danger.

Someone tooted under the window.

"Viens, mon beau cavalier," said Mama.

Uncle Florent drove them to the theater in a Chevrolet. He wasn't going to the Gala himself. That wasn't for him, he said, grown-up people pretending to be Chinamen and singing about dying or being in love. Mama held her elbow out to Louis. He took her arm and pulled her up the marble staircase while she used the banister for support. Once upstairs, where the Walle people in their dark suits and evening gowns were standing about chatting and eyeing each other, she shook off his iron, inflexible, armor-plated arm and snapped, "Leave me alone."

There were moist patches in the powder on her cheeks.

As she glided among the people, a small tight smile on her lips, Louis could see that inside her mouth, inside her head, she was uttering blasphemous curses.

She flopped onto the chair in the box Papa had managed with great difficulty to reserve for her. "You'll get the best seat in the theater, Constance, if I have to pay for it myself." Louis leaned over the red plush edge of the balcony. Smoke was hanging over the three-quarters-full auditorium as if all those present had been puffing at pipes simultaneously or a small fire had been started just before the performance.

Mama looked in her hand mirror and powdered her face, something no other woman there was doing, something out of a French vaudeville show. Slut.

The program, with a Belgian helmet on its cover, was lying against her stomach. He was afraid to pick it up.

Applause. A tall man found his way with difficulty through the folds of the curtain and greeted "all of us gathered together here for this splendid purpose that will bring so much benefit, free of all deductions, to the noblest of our young men in the field, in the presence of Mijnheer the Governor, Mijnheer the President of the Sons of Breydel, Mijnheer the Director of the Groeninghe Museum, Mijnheer the President of the Sons of the Leie, and, last but certainly not least, one who despite his many duties has so indefatigably given of himself, that Great Son of the Leie and guardian of our intellectual heritage, the author of works both spiritual and popular, our very own Marnix de Puydt." In the fifth row a chubby little man with long, light-gray curls and wearing a lavaliere stood up and waved.

"Like a woman," said an acid voice next to Louis.

"Look at that hair, just like a girl's."—"Gerard, mind your manners!" Marnix de Puydt continued to wave a plump little hand. Mama glared at the vulgarians, fanning their offensive air away with the program. The speaker said that Belgium would brave the storm, and then disappeared, hastily and bowing, as if the applause were driving him away. The red curtains glowed, the music swelled, settled in every alcove and niche, washed over the audience.

An elegant salon with furniture radiating a golden light. People in evening dress, slimmer, more graceful than the people just now in the foyer, stood about chatting. A general raised his glass and said something about somebody's daughter who would have made a splendid officer had she not, alas, been a girl.

Dragoons came dashing in with this girl, whose name was Lisa. She had just won a jumping competition on her horse. Three cheers for Lisa! She talked about love. Not flirting, but loving. She and Count Gustav von Pottensterk, "Gustl," were to part, but they would remain good friends.

"Now," said Mama. She laid her hand, in the crocheted white glove, on Louis's bare knee. "Now, pay attention." Her eye, glittering like a wet cobblestone, was fixed on the man who was making his entrance to the applause of the entire auditorium.

He is small like Napoleon, Hitler, Sister Kris. His face is yellow like old piano keys. His lacquered hair, combed back painfully tight, is made of vulcanite, his eyes are the slits of the inscrutable East. He glides into the beam of an unseen light on smooth black pointed shoes, looks with a pained expression into the auditorium, takes a deep breath, and plants his legs wide apart.

Prince Sou-Chong is his name. He enters this room, he declares in song, with a thrill in his heart. His heart beats madly. But his heart should be still. He, Prince Sou-Chong, has taught his heart to be *silent*. And if a Chinaman's heart ever broke, 'tis a secret that none may learn. We Chinamen ne'er reveal.

Louis wants to follow the tormented Chinaman's heavenly song without missing a single one of the lamenting tenor's syllables, and at the same time to hide from Mama. Elbow on knee, he leans forward, his hand shielding his cheek, his eyebrow, his smarting eye, at the very moment that on stage, in the elegant salon, his yellow twin brother, the prince, is bracing himself and warning Louis never, *ever,* to give his feelings away. *"Toujours sourire! Le coeur douloureux!* Fortune may frown, but I keep smiling! I may be sad at heart, but nobody knows!"

And here she comes, that frivolous Western girl. Is His Highness in need of anything? Yes, says His Highness, a cup of tea. It emerges that the salon is in a palace in Vienna. In duet they sing that their talk is *charmant,* that he is *galant,* and they become as one to the swelling of the violins.

Major-General Count Ferdinand Lichtenfels gives as his opinion that Europe and China are like fire and water. What does that matter, Prince Sou-Chong and Lisa cry. Nevertheless . . . they, too, acknowledge that they come from different worlds. Do you not see my stranger's face, do you not see my stranger's eyes? asks the prince. In the moonlit April night he lays apple blossom at her feet. They kiss as the curtain comes down.

"Well?" asks Mama.

Louis wants to say, "Beautiful, the most beautiful thing in the world." Any moment now I shall burst into stupid crybaby tears. Oh, why does she have to talk to me?

"Not good enough for you, as usual? Oh, it is? Then why do you look so glum? What are you sitting there with that long face for? What am I going to do with you?" She greeted a lady with a hat covered with fruit. "Say good evening," she hissed. Louis, who is examining his knee and thighs, surprised that they are not saffron-colored, but who on the other hand can feel his eyes pulling upward into slanted slits, nods like a prince at the befruited lady.

Harps, little bells, cymbals strike up in the twilight. Out of the resonant darkness an Oriental palace rises up: arches, drapery, peacocks. "Ah!" go the people in the auditorium. "My Lotus Blossom," sings the prince; his little sister, Mi, who doesn't look like him although she has the same upward sweep to the corners of her eyes, warbles, "Zig, zig, zig, zig ih!" To Louis's disgust, Mama hums along as the prince and Lisa sing, "Love! What has given you this magic pow'r," and again puts her hand on Louis's knee. Prince Sou-Chong sings, "You are my heart's delight, And where you are I long to be." Thunderous applause, bravo, encore. This is bound to come to a bad end. Anyone who sings so high in such an unworldly, sublime way is doomed, and yes, now Lisa is saying that she must see her homeland again, the land that tugs at her heart like a chain.

Dragons appear, writhing, with snouts like toads and with Aunt Mona's bulging eyes. Mandarins, girls with towering headdresses covered with pearls, priests. And now you can see where the smoke before the performance came from: out of the censer being swung at the audience by a fat, shaven-headed priest swathed in orange. The front rows cough. Slave girls, young brides. Walle has never seen anything like it.

"Ah!" "Ah!" "Beautiful, isn't it?"

"Yes, Mama."

Louis can't quite make out who is getting married to whom in all the hubbub on the stage. Why is Lisa so nervous, pressing her outstretched fingers to her heart? The music has no answer. Why are those children in Chinese makeup throwing poppies onto the road, poppies that leap about like frogs? Prince Sou-Chong appears, he is wearing a cartload of medals on his chest like Hermann Göring. Men in purple and gold surround him, waving peacock feathers in front of his brooding face. Ah, now I understand. He is marrying all three princesses at once, and that's upsetting Lisa. Judiciously the prince puts her in her place. "In China women have no say," whispers Mama.

"This love of mine," Lisa sings, "you have turned to hate! What I felt for you, you made cruelly die!" The prince bangs furiously on a gong. Lisa is dragged away. The prince breaks down. What have I done? What have I done? Because he does not realize how cruel are the customs of the East. We are all of us unaware. That is how we are led into sin. Whether we like it or not. Never before has it been so heartrendingly clear to Louis what takes place in the Institute, in Oudenaarde Road, in the whole wide world.

In the foyer, where the theatergoers are gossiping together instead of giving serious reflection to what they have just seen, Mama sips a Mandarin liqueur presented to her by Mijnheer Messidor the florist, who asks if Louis is going to study medicine later.

"He has strong hands," says Mama vaguely. "He has that."

Mijnheer Messidor says he has heard from a reliable source that in Germany the officers are being made to learn foreign languages more than ever before, including Flemish. Writing on the wall, Madame Seynaeve. And come to think of it, *The Land of Smiles* is set in Germany, since Vienna is German now, and Franz Lehar is a German as well, although he was born in Komarom, Hungary, and was this show really a good choice on the part of the Sons of the Leie for putting on in our neutral zone?

"I think *The Count of Luxembourg* is more sympathetic," says somebody.

"Now that you mention it," says Mama.

"With more feeling," says somebody.

"There's something to that." Louis cannot understand why Mama is going along so spinelessly with all this drivel. Or is it that she wants to show her child, the new one, that other one tucked away in her stomach, how kind she is, how tolerant of all mankind?

Mijnheer Messidor says that Mama must be very careful when buying toys for Louis, for he has heard from a reliable source that the famous Nuremburg toys are being sprayed with infectious germs on Hitler's personal orders and sold at half-price to smugglers who off-load them in our fatherland, in France, and in Holland.

After the intermission Lisa is sad. The dancing-girls try to cheer her up, but to no avail. She laments that everything is over. Mi, Prince Sou-Chong's little sister, who had sung "Zig, zig, zig ih!" so effusively (under his breath Louis had tried to sing it along with her, for he absolutely had to be able to sing it to the Apostles at the Institute, soon, in less than three days), is unhappy as well now as she waves farewell to her white fiancé, or friend, or comrade, the Gustl who appeared at the beginning. Lisa wants to go back to Vienna. Sou-Chong bars her exit. But then Our Lord overwhelms him with His Grace, he realizes that he has to let her go, and he says, yellow saint that he is, "Go then, most precious thing of mine on earth! *Adieu!*" And then he is alone, all alone, and he sings that he is weeping, and once again the treacherous sweet melody is heard that heralds that terrible law: *Toujours sourire, le coeur douloureux!*

More smoke, this time representing morning mist. The front rows cough, splutter. A garden full of noisy children, coolies pushing carts, soldiers, Chinese people cheeping, "Zig, zig, zig ih!" Caterwauling in brocade. Mama is being an insufferable bore. She tugs at Louis's sleeve. "Can you see him?"

"Yes, of course." With a set face, *toujours sourire,* the prince slips into the golden coat bequeathed to him by the Lord of the Ten Thousand Years.

"No, over there." She points. (Don't do that, Mama, people can see you.)

"Where?"

"The one on the right." She gives a chuckle, my mother, rubs her stomach with pleasure in time to the music. "Silly billy." She points again, doesn't she know she shouldn't point when the entire auditorium can see her? ("You can't take her anywhere in public," said Papa.) Mama digs her elbow into his ribs, and now Louis spots, over on the right, a coolie with a wobbly stomach painted an earthy red (like the red you see if you've been sitting in the sun for a bit and look suddenly at something red in the shade). The man with Papa's nose and mouth sings, wiggling and waggling his hips with his belly hanging out over a pair of wide Eastern pants, and his song is taken up loudly by the entire chorus. "Osheen-teen-wuo-men." A coolie. A father. Half-naked and painted. Why doesn't he go around like that at home? She, next to me with her stomach, is proud of him, or anyway she is smiling tenderly at him, at his abandon, his little mincing steps, suddenly light as a feather. He's full of bravado while he's in disguise, Papa-Coolie. Applause. Papa bows, not far from Prince Sou-Chong, who is giving a broad Western grin and whom we can now recognize as Alfred Lagasse, tenor and pharmacist, and looks for his son but cannot find him.

Mama waves, but the coolie is too excited, cannot see his pregnant wife. Mama stays in her seat as the audience throngs toward the exits.

"Come on, Mama." Because people are wondering what is wrong with her, whether she is ill, whether she is about to bring a child into the world right now, to the lingering sound of the little Eastern temple bells.

Then Louis knows what she is up to, this crazy mother of his. She is about to do herself exactly what he had done, years ago, when he had been a little one and had been taken to the theater for the first time, to see the operetta *Gypsy Love.* Then, with the audience shouting bravo, applauding, and joining in the singing of "For as long as I shall live, fate has nothing more to give!" he had cried because he could tell it was nearly the end, and when the footlights, after going dim and then bright again ten times, had finally gone off, off for good, and the audience had left, he had stayed in his seat, would not leave, would not understand, or accept, that those gods and goddesses bathed in that heavenly light, dressed in their tailcoats and diamonds and rustling ball gowns, powdered and warbling, had deserted him. He had stamped his feet, his fingers clinging so convulsively to the seat that he had to be pried loose. Papa had dragged him away by his collar and his hair.

"Come on. We have to go." She powders her nose. She winks at him. Women don't know how to wink. Except for Grandma. Nonchalantly Mama gets to her feet, draws her white gloves on more tightly, moves quickly through the empty aisle on his arm. Louis sees that her dress is all wet at the legs. He smiles at her through thin yellow lips, and she, she fails to recognize the prince who will never, ever, let out what rages in his inscrutable Eastern heart, *toujours sourire.*

On the last day of the holidays Bekka Cosijns said that her grandfather had died the night before. He had been blind for years because he had stroked a loose woman once and had then rubbed his eyes. Bekka had already tied a black scarf over her forehead, like a pirate, and was carrying her mother's shoes, which were too big for her but which she had been told to wear to the funeral.

Uncle Florent came up on his bicycle just as Bekka was bracing herself against Louis's hip in order to pull off her shoes. He braked.

"Necking, are we, Louis?"

"Him? He's still wet behind the ears," said Bekka.

"I've got to join the army. The King is calling me," said Uncle Florent.

"The Belgian army wouldn't be complete without you," said Bekka provocatively.

They all three watched the girl across the road who put her gas mask on every day, she was standing hands on hips talking to herself, her monstrous corrugated trunk swishing to and fro. As Uncle Florent started to stub out his English cigarette on the edge of the windowsill, Bekka snatched it away from him. She inhaled deeply, the little red tip dangerously close to her nose.

"You're starting early," said Uncle Florent.

"Starting what?"

"Smoking. Among other things."

"It's good for the nerves," said the Gypsy girl. She ground the stub under her bare heel.

On the last evening of the holidays, Mama said to Aunt Mona, while Louis was sitting in the cozy-corner reading "The Testament of Dr. Witherspoon," one of Papa's Lord Lister books, "Just look at my Louis sitting there. All he does is sit or walk around, and you never know what he's thinking, there's no expression on his face at all."

"Shirley Temple, now there's a lively child for you," said Aunt Mona. "You can read everything she's feeling in her little face. But maybe that's the new method they're using at the Institute, teaching children from when they're infants not to . . ."

Mama was uneasy. "Louis, did they teach you to make a face like that in Haarbeke?"

"Of course not. That's just the way my face is growing."

"I can't say I'm very pleased about it."

Then the two women talked about the new curtains for the time when the baby would come, about the latest fashion for wearing lots of tartan, and in the evening organza and crepe de chine patterned with quite large flowers, and about a girdle in satin-latex without boning to wear once the baby had come. Mama said that if everything went according to plan, the baby was due right on the anniversary of her father's death, something that was sure to make Meerke very happy. "Although you never can tell with my mother," she said.

_____*a small cudgel*

*L*ining up in the morning once more, obedient once more, surrounded by Hottentots once more. The playground seemed to have become smaller, squarer, more closed in. Sister Sapristi said, "Seynaeve, hold your tongue," although he hadn't said a word. But Louis understood, it was she who had taken delivery of him from Papa late last night, like a mailbag being unloaded from some dusty stagecoach in the Wild West. She had yawned. "I thought you weren't coming, Mijnheer Seynaeve." Papa had laughed heartily, coughing, chuckling. "Sister, we Seynaeves have the courtesy of kings. We may sometimes be a little late, but we're always on time." Sister Sapristi, dog-tired, yawning, had nodded. She had taken Louis to the dormitory, past the kitchen where a lay sister was still up, busy with the pots and pans, Hottentots snoring, someone nearby, Dondeyne? calling out in his sleep, "Hey, hey, it's snowing!"

The playground paving stones were wet from the night's rain. There weren't many little ones in line. Little ones were sometimes allowed to extend their holidays by a few days. Vlieghe isn't there, either. I never gave him a thought the whole holidays. So why am I missing him so badly now? Can he, can I thrive only in the Institute?

"The things that happened to me during the holidays! Really awful, I can tell you," said Byttebier next to him.

"What about you, was it . . . as well?"

"What do you mean, as well?" Get used to the secret language again, to allusions to things surmised.

"Mine weren't so great, either," said Dondeyne. "They kept on laughing at me. As if I'd come from the zoo. They laughed at my clothes."

"Do you wear those things at home, then?" Louis asked. The long black socks, the long shorts, the sailor collar, the straw hat?

"I don't have anything else."

That took Louis by surprise. He was grateful to Mama for sparing him this, for making a distinction between a uniformed Louis in prison and an almost playful, almost boyish child in her home, allowed to romp about in ordinary clothes—although not as dirty and untidy as Tetje's. Mama had been sad yesterday because he was leaving. Or had she?

He would write her a letter tonight, using his rounded nib, paying careful attention to commas and full stops and capital letters. Dear Mother, Why must we always (or: perpetually?) part from each other so quickly (or: so abruptly?)? When I see you next month with my new brother (or: brother or sister?), I will tell you in person how much I appreciate your affection and that I will appreciate it until I die, Your loving son (or: firstborn?), Louis Seynaeve.

That evening Vlieghe was back at his usual place in the refectory. He was suntanned, his shoulders were broader, his hair was combed and parted to one side. When he saw Louis, he gave the Apostolic sign for emergency or danger, a slow horizontal line drawn across his throat with his thumb, but then he suddenly winked. There was no danger.

They ate rye bread with lard and strawberry jam while Sister Kris read out the message of Pope Pius XII, it was always the same message, faith will be victorious in the battle against matter, against materialism, civilization will triumph in the end, those agitators who pretend they are out to change the lot of the poor are, in fact, nothing but atheists. Vlieghe looked as if he were listening to the Holy Father's words, or understanding them, for the first time. As if he were still a little one. Like that time when he and Louis were little ones and had been told one day in class by Sister Kris that there was going to be a competition for drawing the prettiest flowers and painting them with watercolors. You could choose your own flowers. The winner would—imagine, for the first time in history—go on a trip to Rome, the Eternal City, at the Vatican's expense, be received there in His Holiness's apartments by the Pope himself and be presented with a scooter bearing a Vatican license plate, and there aren't many of those around. The choice of flowers is up to you, as I've already said, but everyone knows that the Holy Father likes the humble violet best. Though he always places red roses on his mother's grave. Louis had done the best picture of all, he was sure of that. He had mixed together nearly all the colors in the paintbox but had chiefly used reds and blues. When he half-shut his eyes—and he hoped with thumping heart that the Pope and his cardinals would do the same—he felt he could almost pluck the flower from the paper. So long as the Pope didn't ask him what flower it was. Sister Kris walked about among the desks. Paused somewhat longer by his desk. She wouldn't give anything away. (Just as she never gives anything away while her knifelike eagle's-profile reads out the Pope's message. A savage eagle. The kind Hitler had been given as a birthday present by the whole German nation. Out of respect for the fearless creature, he had at once released it into the German sky.) "That's not bad," said Sister Kris at Vlieghe's desk. It's between the two of us. Vlieghe must not win. With tormentingly slow steps Sister Kris makes her way to the blackboard, turns it around, and, unseen, takes too long to write too many names. Is she giving points to everyone? She appears from behind the blackboard, throws the chalk into the tray, wipes her right hand down her much-washed pale-blue apron. "Who, oh who?" she says. Louis, that's who! With a fierce flip she turns the board around again. A matchstick man drawn in chalk is thumbing his nose with a huge hand, and out of his enormous negroid lips swells a bubble with "April 1st" written inside, and sure enough, it was April Fool's Day, the day when you can pull any fool's leg. Sister Kris laughed, no one else.

Yet Vlieghe seems so meekly, so ludicrously in thrall to this selfsame Sister!

The Apostles' first meeting was held that night in the room where the laundry was kept piled up in wicker baskets.

"*Ave*, Dondeyne," "*Ave*, Byttebier," "*Ave*, Vlieghe," "*Ave*, Seynaeve," "*Ave*, Goossens." Vlieghe was wearing a new tunic, white with cherry-red piping around the neck and the sleeves. He had a picture to show them, cut carelessly out of a magazine.

"*Voilà*. That's why the Germans are the strongest in the world." A forest-green metal grasshopper with a checked muzzle and a turquoise belly.

"The Dornier, 220 miles per hour."

"How many Germans does it hold?"

"Six. They call it the Flying Pencil."

The other Apostles nodded silently. Goossens held the Forbidden Books on his knees, handling them carefully.

"It was really awful at home again," said Byttebier. "The things that happened to me!" "I've got a figurine at home that's banned," said Louis at once. "I'll bring it here after the summer holidays. It's of a German boy swearing an oath to Hitler. It's sacrilegious because Hitler thinks he's God Almighty."

They seemed to find this unremarkable. "I've also got a dagger that belonged to Hitler's personal bodyguard." They started paying a bit more attention. "It's made of stainless steel." He waited, then said desperately, "If you look carefully, you can still see blood on it."

"That'll be from German blood sausage," said Goossens. The Apostles exploded with laughter, and Byttebier slapped Goossens's back three times. "What a wit!"

"Be quiet!" said Louis angrily. "Do you want Sister Kris to hear us?"

"Sister Imelda's doing the rounds tonight." Oh, that Goossens. Didn't he realize that though Sister Kris, the most dangerous of all the Sisters, might be asleep in the Keep right now with a pillow over her head, she can still pick up sound waves through the ramparts, her nostrils can still start to twitch like a rabbit's and she's swooped up to you without a sound before you know it.

"It wasn't so great at home for me either Dondeyne said to Byttebier. Louis, founder and leader, said, "Goossens, take the Acts and write this down." Vlieghe, who was the official Evangelist on account of his beautiful handwriting, did not seem to mind. There really shouldn't be any holidays, they confuse everything, spoil everything, mess everything up. Louis dictated. "A new age dawns. The Apostles here present shall take steps . . ."

"By mutual agreement," said Byttebier.

"Shall by mutual agreement take steps to . . ." He had not the slightest idea what ought to come next. Vlieghe was inspecting his airplane. The splash of the fountain in front of the statue of St. Joseph could be heard far away in the distance.

". . . take steps to pay a visit to a saintly person being kept imprisoned on account of her unshakable faith, namely . . ." Goossens was writing away busily. Louis blurted the rest out. ". . . Sister St. Gerolphe!"

"That's not going to be easy," said Byttebier.

"In her room?" asked Dondeyne anxiously.

"There's no way you can climb in from the outside," said Vlieghe. "At least, *you* couldn't."

"You could, I suppose!" said Louis.

"Yes, I could." Vlieghe said it casually, but his monstrous arrogance engulfed Louis like a wave of salt water. (Last year in Blankenberge the wave that broke and slapped him right in the face.)

"Sister St. Gerolphe is not a saint," said Goossens.

"That was only a manner of speaking. All right, put: a blessed person."

"She isn't that, either." Goossens laid the writing down on the windowsill, pulled a sock out of the nearest laundry basket, smelled it, drew the sock like a glove over his right hand. Mutiny. So he was refusing to go on writing. What had happened during the holidays? A docile hanger-on had been transformed into a rebel although he had only just been elected an Apostle! How had the Governor subdued William Tell? A leader can do anything, but how? I'll flatten you, you'll see. Louis flattened a flapping moth. "The plan I want to propose to you all" (as if addressing a playground full of pupils) "is the following . . ."

Goossens took out a sheet of paper folded double from among the Forbidden Books he had been nursing, opened it out, and showed it to Vlieghe (another transgression). Vlieghe laid the paper on a laundry basket where everyone could see it. A man, his body half-flayed, stood legs apart, gaping or screaming, his fleshless jaws wide open. Dotted lines and numbers radiated from his bare skull like an aureole, there were bundles of yellow, orange, and brick-red muscles and nerves, ribs, veins cut in half crisscrossing each other.

"His willy's been skinned as well," said Byttebier.

"More a William than a willy," said Goossens who had obviously been thinking this up all during the holidays. When he looked at that brazen red member marked with its red nerves, Louis's teeth began to chatter. Cold shivers ran through his body. He jumped up, snatched the paper, and held it behind his back.

"Don't tear it!" cried Goossens.

"No. That's expressly forbidden by the Acts."

"Precisely," said Byttebier. "A Forbidden Book."

"That's the idea," said Dondeyne.

"This isn't a proper Forbidden Book," said Louis uncertainly. "It's dirty, disgusting . . ."

"Oh, Seynaeve, to hell with you and your drivel." In all these years Vlieghe had never called Louis by his surname.

"The names of all the nerves are on it, in Flemish and Latin." Goossens took a step toward Louis. He's going to leap on me like a mountain goat.

"Goossens, you ought to be ashamed of yourself," said Louis. He put the paper on the windowsill. On the other side there was a curved backbone, that of a herring. He sat down on it.

Outside, somebody stumbled over a bucket.

"Give me that paper," said Vlieghe and put out his hand, grabbed

Louis's tunic by the neck, and dragged Louis off the windowsill. At the very moment that the hard, determined knuckles grazed his chest, Louis was aware of something very pleasant, spilling warm as water over his abdomen, spreading, contracting. He was so startled that he did nothing to stop Vlieghe, who grumpily handed the paper over to Goossens. Louis probed under his shirt, and his fingers encountered a small cudgel that had begun to lead a life of its own, it was a soft, blunt sliver of wood, no, a joint that had wormed its way into his willy from the inside, it would never go away again, it would remain glued to his belly, a growth, ultimately a punishment. He could read in the others' eyes that he had been punished by the angels. Panic-stricken, he wanted to shout for help, irresistibly his hand slid again to his crotch, the leprous, hunchbacked, red-hot stigma was still implanted there. The angel of filthiness swept into the room, thrust two fingers into Louis's eyesockets. The angel lifted Louis up and flung him in a frenzied but deathly silence against the door, which opened, Louis crashed against the banisters on the landing, rushed down the stairs, and did not stop until he was at the bottom, still in a turmoil. He pressed his abdomen against the cool, marble-painted wall, crushed the root the angel had planted inside his member against the surface, which turned into warm water but did not open up as the Red Sea had before Moses.

*B*aekelandt came looking for two strapping boys. Needless to say, Sister Imelda picked on Byttebier, whom she regarded as an ox that the Institute could not be rid of soon enough, and on Louis, because she could see that he didn't feel like it in the least. "Might as well take that one, too," said Sister Imelda, pointing to Vlieghe.

"En avant, marche!" Baekelandt barked, and strode off, frowning up at the Institute roof to make certain that no paratroopers were landing on it.

The three of them were to help him put up a barbed-wire fence alongside a ditch. Two-ply, rustproof. Baekelandt sang the praises of his barbed wire, which he had procured from Bekaert's at a sizable discount. By September the whole Institute would be surrounded. The nuns had no idea of the cost of the whole thing. "Sister Econome always starts off moaning and carrying on. But if you don't protect yourself now, it'll only cost a lot more later, right?"

"A tank could go straight through this stuff, straight through your barbed wire," said Vlieghe. "It wouldn't even have to be a German Panzer."

"Hold on, young 'un, the foot soldiers would still have to get across as well!"

"The foot soldiers," said Vlieghe scornfully.

Baekelandt chewed his tobacco, spat. "We've seen some cruel things in our time and we'll be seeing a lot more."

They worked in the sun, drank the heavily diluted buttermilk Trees brought, listened to Baekelandt's tall stories, the ceaseless croaking of the frogs in the ditch. They sweated. Byttebier received lavish compliments from Baekelandt on his skill and physical strength. Then Louis pulled the wire a bit too hard just when Vlieghe wasn't paying attention, Vlieghe gave a stifled scream, the skin of his thumb was torn. "You'll get over it," said Baekelandt when he inspected the wound. Vlieghe brought out a filthy handkerchief and wrapped it around the thumb.

"I didn't do it on purpose."

"It's always the same with you," said Vlieghe.

"What do you mean?"

"Let's not talk about it." Vlieghe picked up his hammer and drove staples into a stake as if he were flattening Mizzlers. No. Vlieghe didn't believe in Mizzlers. Who does? Seeing that his own handkerchief was fairly clean, Louis bit into it, tore off two strips, and tied them around Vlieghe's thumb. He took a long time doing it. When the strips were firmly in place, he picked up the weightless hand, lifted it to his face, examined the pink fingertip and the curved top of the fingernail sticking out from the frayed cloth, and licked it, sucked it.

"Cut it out." Vlieghe did not take his finger away.

"It's against tetanus," said Louis indistinctly, "the rust must come out or else you'll have to have your hand amputated."

"Rust!" called Baekelandt. "Brand-new wire from Bekaert's, straight from the factory!"

"He's a real *infirmière*," said Byttebier. "Baekelandt, if you ever have an accident with a cow, you can always call on our *infirmière*." At which Vlieghe snatched his hand away.

"I only did it for you," Louis whispered.

"Yes, yes. We know all about that," said Vlieghe.

As they walked back toward the convent wall and the hedge, beyond which Sister Sapristi was vainly jumping up at a tree to pick a pear (which couldn't possibly be ripe yet anyway), Louis sang, "You are my heart's delight, and where you are I long to be. You make my darkness bright, when like a star you shine on me."

"The singing *infirmière*," said Byttebier.

"It's from *The Land of Smiles*."

"And where might that be?"

"In China."

"They're really catching it, those Chinese. All they know about is turning tail and running away with the Japanese kicking their backsides," said Byttebier and walked on toward Sister Sapristi. "Yes, but while they're running they destroy everything behind them. Scorched-earth policy," said Louis and took Vlieghe's hand. "You'll have to go to the infirmary with that."

"Seynaeve, you stink," said Vlieghe.

"Me?" Dumbfounded, Louis let go of the hand. Vlieghe sniffed, snuffled, his nose, like a rabbit's, wrinkling up and down like Sister Kris's when she got wind of something sinful. (The rabbit was given a smile by God at the Creation but carelessly lost it. Ever since then it has been sniffing, wrinkling its nose, searching fruitlessly for the lost smile.) "It's your neck that stinks." I'm beginning to rot away. My neck is like the moldy, rotten feet of soldiers with sodden boots down in the trenches.

"That's it." Vlieghe hooked his middle finger into the neck of Louis's shirt. "Your scapular." Louis tore the scapular from his neck, a soaked, greasy, gray rag that had once been blue in honor of the Immaculate Conception. It didn't smell at all. It had all been a trick, a test that Vlieghe had waited to give him and that signified "Thou shalt not wear any token that is not dedicated to me!" Louis flung the scapular on the ground, was too scared to stamp on it, kicked it behind an elderberry bush, burning with fear, I'm not scared of anything, the beetles, the centipedes, and the caterpillars can eat that cast-off token.

"You'll go to hell."

Louis nodded. It was irrevocable now. And yet the garden did not change, the shrubs did not move, no cloud went faster overhead, far off the frogs were still croaking, the little ones still whining.

"And listen, I'd rather you kept your hands off me," said Vlieghe, and started to run with loping strides, more like bounds, like that Negro at the Olympic Games a couple of years ago who had tried to shake Hitler's hand at the end in a show of Negro impudence. Louis ran after Vlieghe but had not the slightest chance of catching up with him, Vlieghe flew across the ditches, Louis lost his breath, he vaulted onto his bronze Canadian Moose and the steaming animal churned up great clods of earth but could not overtake Vlieghe, in despair Louis flung his tomahawk at him but Vlieghe simply ran on, the sharply honed ax planted in his bleeding skull, shouting, not in pain but in triumph, over the meadows where Baekelandt looked up from his fencing.

During break the Apostles played cards. Goossens won, as he usually did these days. Usurper. A word from History. (Next year I'm taking Latin.) Louis looked for traces of his sin behind the elderberry bush, for the revulsion Vlieghe must feel at this sin, but found nothing in Vlieghe's face, fixed foxily on his cards. Why isn't he called Foxy? He's the color of a fox. Though some cats are that color, too.

A fox-colored Puss-in-Boots who rules like the Marquis of Carabas, giving orders with milk in his whiskers. Vlieghe is my mortal sin. He knows not what he does. Isn't that characteristic of all who are loved, Mama, Grandma, St. Francis, Bekka, and the rest? That they don't see who loves them? That only he who loves can take in, cherish, every wrinkle, every breath? Vlieghe was dealt bad cards the whole time.

One day Byttebier had told them about a card game played by adults called "pants down" in which whoever lost had to take off their pants. Louis had found the whole idea so disgusting that he had mentioned it at confession.

"Is that all you have to tell me?" said the curate grumpily. "That you heard the words 'pants down'? Did you take your pants off yourself?"

"Yes," Louis lied.

"And then? Did you do anything dirty?"

"No, no, no."

"What did you do?"

"Just took off my pants. And then put them on again."

"Are you sure, now? Was that all? And what did the others do?"

Feverishly Louis searched for something plausible for the others to have done. "They didn't pay any attention," he said lamely.

"Write two hundred times: I shall not bother my confessor with piffle." Louis had filled up several pages when Sister Adam looked over his shoulder and said, "He is modern, our curate, very modern."

Vlieghe threw down his cards. "Not a single picture card. Nothing's going right today. It's all Seynaeve's fault. He puts a jinx on everything, with those phony faces of his."

"Hey, watch it!" said Louis automatically.

"You'd better keep your mouth shut, because you're in a state of mortal sin. As you know only too well."

"I can hardly go to confession this very evening."

"But you could show a bit of penitence in advance."

"What should I do, then? Put my eyes out with a potato peeler like Sister St. Gerolphe?"

"More lies," said Vlieghe. "That's all you are, lies, lies, nothing but lies. You're made of lies. Sister St. Gerolphe never did that with the potato peeler. You've just . . ."

"Sucked it out of *your* thumb!" cried Louis, pleased. But Vlieghe pretended not to know what he meant.

"She isn't even blind, Sister St. Gerolphe."

"Want to bet?" Louis slapped the back of his hand down on the table. It hurt.

"How much?"

"As much as you like, you doubting Thomas!"

"I never bet," Vlieghe said calmly. His uncle had run up terrible debts on the horses at the Ostend races and would never be able to pay them back, no matter how long he lived.

"We could go and look," said Dondeyne, "then we'd know."

"Look where?"

"In Sister St. Gerolphe's room."

"We'd never be able to get in there," said Goossens.

"Yes, we would," Vlieghe drawled. Bold and cunning strategist. "First we have to go on a reconnaissance to spy out the lie of the land, find out when the best time is, how to beat a retreat, and so on."

Next day in the confessional. "Father, I have sinned, it is my fault, but not entirely, a pupil whom I cannot name has forced me to sin."

"Was it 'pants down' again?"

"No."

"But something like that?"

"No. But I did something forbidden."

"What was it this time?"

"The holy scapular."

"You can take that off as often as you like."

"I threw it away behind a bush."

"Threw it away? But it's a *sacramental!*"

"I can find it again."

"Go look for it."

"It was worn out. May I wash it if I'm careful?"

"Yes. Why did you do it?"

"I was in a state of capital sin. Out of envy."

"You do realize that it is a privilege to wear a scapular? That it used to be reserved for the brotherhoods . . ." And so on, about oblates, tertiaries. He was sweating even more than the confessant. Finally he said, *"Deinde te absolvo."*

That night the burly, grumpy angel sat on the foot of Louis's bed. The white swan's-feathers glistened and rustled in the shadows. "You think you got off lightly, don't you, you puller of phony faces? With your imperfect penance. Because what you were most afraid of was the chastisement, and that can never make for perfect penance. And what about all the other mortal sins you've been accumulating lately, the ones you haven't confessed and that have compounded your guilt? You can't possibly be thinking of going to Holy Communion on Sunday."

"I know you," said Louis. "You pretend to be an angel because you still wear the outfit you had on before your fall. And you also pretend that you're Holst, who delivered those baby clothes to Mama. But your real name is Beelzebub."

The wings rustle as if catching the wind, then slowly they beat the air and swoop right through the wooden partition behind which Dondeyne lies asleep, and vanish, and that wakes Louis up, or so it seems, for he puts his hand over the watery warmth in his abdomen and he rubs, he pulls. Until he can hear the angel bleating again and sits up with fright. He tears the ribbon from his new scapular and ties it around the fleshy twig growing out of him. He pulls the knot tight until a whimpering little squeak escapes him. The twig shrivels up. He reels off a string of Hail Marys in quick succession until he drops off to sleep.

*S*ister Imelda's healthy cheeks can turn scarlet in the twinkling of an eye. The women of certain races, especially those from the North, from the land of fjords and glaciers, have skin that is too thin. The little ones are busy peeling potatoes, mopping the floor. Sister Imelda sits on a milking stool, spread out like a broody hen, issuing orders from time to time in a gruff, warm voice. The Apostles ask if they can do anything to help, and she accepts this at face value. "You can carry those pots through to the refectory in a minute."

"Sister Imelda, how is Sister St. Gerolphe?"

"Oh, boys, what can I say? One person changes more quickly than another."

"You're still young, though, aren't you, Sister Imelda?"

"Boys, sometimes I think that I'll never really grow old, that I'll go on plaguing my Sisters for many years to come. But then, well, I do walk about in the fresh air more than my Sisters, I put all my strength into what I am doing, I am not afraid of working all night now and then."

"Sister St. Gerolphe . . ."

"She comes from a high-born family, she has never known what it means to work, she never learned how, and at a certain age such things come home to roost."

"She never leaves her cell, does she?"

"*Jamais*. We've been through too much with her. But that was well before your time."

"That cell of hers, is that the one there on the left of the chapel?"

"No, that is Sister Econome's. She likes having a view of the walnut trees. She is mad about walnuts. Because walnut oil is good for the brain. Anyway, that's what she thinks."

"Is it the second cell, where the curtains are always drawn?"

"That's the study. No, if you absolutely have to know, you little snoops, it's the cell with the wisteria outside. I pray for Sister St. Gerolphe every day. She was devout and good all her life, and now she is being punished so much. She was rolling in money, oh yes, but she was always devout and good. Ah well, where do these things start? In the brain. And then the rest of the machinery won't work. If you're too busy with your brain, you're bound to come to a sticky end. You can serve Our Lord just as well without brainwork. If you stay healthy and pray a lot, you don't need anything else, Jesus knows that."

"And is she shut up in there, with the door locked?"

"What business is that of yours, Byttebier?"

"I'm only asking, Sister Imelda."

"Sister St. Gerolphe, boys, is something special. She comes from Moeskroen, from a house with three pianos. I used to talk about horses with her. Her father bred them. Not the kind of cart horses we had at the farm ourselves, of course. After a while, though, you could no longer get through to her. It happens quite often in families like that. They say it's hereditary. Mother Superior knew about it, of course, when she admitted her. But, then, of course, you can't refuse someone from her kind of family. And I must say she's been devout and good for years. She always kept to herself, though. And then she started to act funny, she passed out during Consecration. And then she set fire to herself."

"That Keep of yours, Sister Imelda, it must be lovely inside."

"Because we try to wash away our sins there through the mortification of the flesh."

"There must be lots of passages, aren't there, and cellars and attics too, like in a palace of mirrors?"

"Where did you ever get that idea? Just ordinary corridors with cells."

"Because," said Louis, "supposing there was religious persecution and the Sisters were declared outlaws by the enemy and had to hide, then the Keep really ought to have secret cellars and subterranean passages, just in case . . ."

"Who would persecute us?"

"The Bolsheviks."

"They won't be coming that soon. People can say what they like about the Germans, and our Church isn't having an easy time of it in Germany, but they're holding back the Communists all the same."

"Why are there bars in front of all the windows in the Keep, Sister Imelda?"

"That's more to make it difficult for those outside to get in than for those inside to get out. *Allee,* give us a hand carrying the potato pots."

"Right away, Sister Imelda, right away."

_____ *a golden knucklebone*

*B*yttebier, strapping Apostle, bent his knees, laced his fingers together and Vlieghe placed his bare foot on them. Vlieghe crouched against Byttebier's chest, pressed his hip into Byttebier's stomach, then Byttebier, the rustic Christopher, placed his cheek and ear against Vlieghe's thigh and heaved him still higher up the wall. Vlieghe found the window-sill, pulled himself up, climbed the rusty pipe, and swung himself over the small balcony. Success. The Apostles below waited for a scream to pierce the night, a sudden attack by concealed nuns, the boxing of ears, cries for help, but none came. Crickets. From the balcony, as if under a balda-chin at St. Peter's Square in Rome, Vlieghe blessed the admiring faithful at his feet.

"Quick," said Dondeyne. "Quick, all of you." Although it had been ex-pressly agreed that no one was to say a word during the entire operation.

They ran in single file, hugging the wall. Byttebier led the way. Then up the spiral staircase until they stood outside the Forbidden Door of the Accursed Keep. Crickets. The rattling breath of Schamphelaere, who slept closest to the dormitory door.

"Where did that idiot get to?" whispered Dondeyne. In the faint light his eyes were jet-black beads. Sister Adam's steady tread, alternating with the rustling of the curtains as she drew them at every cubicle, came nearer. As anticipated. As anticipated, the Apostles clutched each other when she came around the corner. In a silent embrace the four of them dropped behind the folding screen that partly concealed stacked beds and a mountain of mattresses. Louis's cheek rested against an iron bar, Goossens kneeled awkwardly, Byttebier lay like a sack on top of Dondeyne.

Vlieghe did not appear. Dondeyne opened his eyes wide when Sister Adam, who had presumably been doing the rounds of the little ones, headed for the door of the Keep. Now she will surely hear the thumping of my heart, she must. Don't let her open the door just as Vlieghe reaches the other side, that's all. The nun's billowing habit stirred up dust and cool air under the screen. I'm going to sneeze. Sister Adam cleared her throat, spat, not into her handkerchief, because she immediately ground her shoe against the floorboards. Then, as if on a sudden impulse, she moved over to the spiral staircase, descended, disappeared. Oh, invisible, inaudible Vlieghe, what are you up to! The Apostles disentangled themselves, the floorboards creaked. Was Vlieghe being held against his will, bound, gagged, and blindfolded in the Keep by Sisters hissing out of earshot and lying in wait for his accomplices?

Louis wanted to go. Goossens held him back. Goossens clearly thinks of himself as the new leader. In just one season: Apostle Number One.

Then, without any warning at all, the wall in front of them opened up soundlessly like the veil before the Tabernacle on the Day of Sorrow. Louis leaped backward, colliding with Goossens, who cursed softly. This was entirely unexpected. What had slid apart was a window, painted matte white like the walls and never opened within living memory. It continued to open in an astonishing silence, and Vlieghe chuckled, beckoned. The Keep awaited them.

Walls even whiter than the corridors in the dormitories. Sacrilegiously they advanced, hesitantly they pressed forward, following Vlieghe, who himself was following the instructions of Sister Imelda's gossiping tongue of three days before, as if they had stepped right into the tale of that agricultural nun. Vlieghe stood before the open door and was the first to enter, and it happened in the days of the Wars in Europe and in Asia, during my time on earth, that we saw her sitting there on an oaken throne adorned with ornamental scrollwork, Sister St. Gerolphe, known in the world as Georgine de Brouckère. She sat there, an arm's length away from Louis, asleep on her noble commode, laced up with roughly twisted white and brown ropes. Love in the pit of the stomach, love in the burning head. No one has a right to touch her before me. Louis brushed Vlieghe to one side, like a passer-by in the street. She looks like a pale, bloodless version of Grandma. A head full of dewlaps and wrinkles, tipped to one side as if she were letting water run out of her ear. She sings in her sleep, but that is something only the Mizzlers—if they exist—can hear. The cell is narrow. There is no need for all these Apostles. Although no one speaks, there is an uproar, their panting beats against the tapering walls.

Is she blind, or isn't she? With delicate fingers Vlieghe lifts up her eyelid. The eyes open, dull, milky marbles without pupils. I have won. Or is it the poor light that makes the whites alone gleam?

Sister St. Gerolphe wakes up as if with a small electric shock. She dribbles. She looks right and left, the bloodless fingers fumble, she tugs at her ropes.

"Sister St. Gerolphe," says Louis.

"Yes, Sister," she says, clearly, precisely, in High Flemish. "Yes, Sister. The Lord be with you."

"Sister St. Gerolphe," says Goossens.

Before she can reply with her toothless mouth, Vlieghe has stuck his index finger inside. His thumb—on which you can still see the little pale rings of flesh where Louis had tied the strips of his torn handkerchief—rests against her pockmarked cheek.

She sucks on the index finger, and Vlieghe lets her, with the unassailable gravity of a Hottentot serving at Mass for the first time. The noisy sucking continues placidly. When Vlieghe pulls his finger out with a little plop, Sister St. Gerolphe moans and shakes her head. Vlieghe takes a step back, and Goossens sticks two fingers into the open, deathlike, searching mouth. She slurps, sounding like one of the little ones slurping his soup in the refectory.

"Move. It's my turn." Byttebier's voice is too loud, too strange. Sister St. Gerolphe tries to raise her body, the ropes gleam, stretch, creak, and the stench of sulfurous fumes spewed out by hell spreads quickly through the cell.

Goossens pushes Sister St. Gerolphe down again. "Whoa," he says kindly. "Whoa."

Dondeyne, under orders to keep watch on the whole Keep from his place by the wall, sidles closer. "We must ask for her blessing."

"Hottentot," says Louis. "Sisters aren't allowed to bless. They aren't ordained."

"We aren't allowed to do anything, anything at all," says Sister St. Gerolphe, again in her clear, well-educated voice.

"Just as well," says Byttebier.

"That's true, Sister," says Sister St. Gerolphe. A white crocheted bedspread lies on her narrow iron cot, across which lies an even whiter, shining trapezium of light cast by the small lightbulb in the corridor. On her bedside table is a dusty ashtray inscribed with the words "Roeman Beers," and in it there are two lead knucklebones. Louis steals one of them without anyone's noticing and says casually, as if visiting an aunt, "We mustn't stay too long, Sister."

"The Lord be with you, Sister." She throws her body forward, the throne and the stench sway to and fro. She snaps her gums at nonexistent fingers.

"I swear to you we'll come back," says Louis.

"Time's up," hisses Dondeyne by the door.

"You mustn't swear, Sister. Though He swore. He said, 'Arise, take up thy bed and go unto thine house.' " At this she fell asleep or into a faint, the Apostles nudged each other, jostled the door, ran out into the cool, whitewash-smelling corridor.

Next day, as they were building a crane with the Meccano set after lunch, Louis said, "We'll have to take some action now. You saw for yourselves. But we can think that over quietly for the next few days. In the meantime we'll have to go back there every night. Because you saw for yourselves the kind of hole she'll be stuck in for the rest of her life, and we've got to go to the aid of our neighbor."

"And I'm going to have to climb up that wall every night?" scoffed Vlieghe.

"Visiting prisoners is an act of charity."

"That's true," said Dondeyne, "but not every night."

"Not doing good is the same as doing evil."

They turned back to the crane. Louis winked three times at Vlieghe, the Apostolic sign for: Follow me, if need be through fire.

Behind the kitchens he said, "Here," and stuck out his fist. "Do you want to know what this is?" They sat down side by side on a frayed, threadbare tire.

"What is it?"

He opened his fingers.

"A knucklebone?"

"You're not going to get very far," said Louis. "Not far at all. Because you go through the world like a blind man. You honestly think this is an ordinary knucklebone, no more, no less?"

Vlieghe looked hungrily into the sky, toward the drone of an airplane.

"Shall I tell you what this knucklebone is?"

"Get on with it, then." Vlieghe picked off frayed pieces of tire and chewed on them.

"Sister St. Gerolphe comes from a good family."

"Like you, no doubt."

"You want me to tell you about it or not?"

"Carry on."

"The De Brouckères are Liberals, that is, a family of Freemasons. But she, Georgine . . ."

"Who is Georgine?"

"Just pay attention. Sister St. Gerolphe's name is Georgine. And her family didn't love her because she was the sole believer and she went to Mass in secret. So to be rid of her, her father promised her in marriage to a baron, Stanislas he was called, of Polish descent, who was a pretentious idiot. The two of them had a baby, but instead of forging their love, the baby . . ."

"Forging? Was the baby a blacksmith, then?"

"Shut up. It wasn't anything like that. The baby was nice and quiet and never did anyone any harm, occasionally he might tell a few fibs, and he could be a bit naughty now and then, of course, but in general he was a model of good manners and behavior. Except that he didn't speak all that well, he stuttered, because he needed too much time to think what he was going to say."

"Not like you," said Vlieghe. The drone from the clouds had stopped.

"But what was odd was that the baby's father, Baron Stanislas, was nasty to him all the time, laughing at him and kicking him."

"Why?"

"Why? Because he thought the baby wasn't his but that of a carpet seller, a *shouk-shouk* from Egypt. Because that's where they'd stayed. On the Nile. And the baby . . ."

"What was it called?" asked Vlieghe quick as a flash.

"Gerolphe. Didn't I tell you?"

"No."

"Gerolphe, the poor soul, had a hooked nose and quite a dark skin. That's how the baron got the idea into his head. One fine day, or rather one fine night, when they had just come back home from a ball, Baron Stanislas started going on about it. 'That baby is somebody else's. Somebody from Egypt. Look at his nose, look at his skin! And now you want to go on holiday to the Suez Canal, you slut!' But what they didn't realize was that the little baby, little Gerolphe, could hear everything from his bed. And the little fellow took it all so much to heart that he fell ill. At first he wanted to run away to the land of the pyramids to find his own, his real father, but he no longer had the strength to do it, he just stayed in his bed and wasted away. So then what happens? One afternoon a storm breaks, the bedroom window flew open, the big cactus on the windowsill fell over, right onto little Gerolphe's head, his mother, who was just bringing him some beef tea, nearly died of fright because all the cactus spines were stuck in his face. 'Good God!' she cried and tried to pull the spines out. 'No, Mama,' said little Gerolphe. 'Leave them alone, it isn't worth it anymore,' and with that he died. People flocked to the funeral from all over Europe, whole cortèges of the nobility. But I am running ahead of myself. Before Gerolphe had to be buried, his mother asked the bishop, who was also her father confessor, if she could have her little dead son embalmed so that she could keep him in her bedroom. 'Don't do that, Madame,' said the bishop, 'if you see the child every day your heart will ache more than you can bear.' 'But I don't want him in that pit,' she exclaimed, 'I don't want him in that vault belonging to Stanislas's family, when he has been so nasty to my little boy.' 'Madame,' says the bishop, 'you'd be better off keeping some little trifle belonging to your dead son and leave it at that.' 'Such as what?' she asked. 'Some of his hair in a locket round my neck?' 'No,' says the bishop, 'something you can feel.' 'His right arm which he always put around my neck before he went to sleep?' But that wouldn't have been very convenient to take traveling, so to cut a long story short . . .''

"Yes, make it short,'' said Vlieghe.

"To make a long story short, they didn't know what to choose. They boiled the child, took the skin and the fat off, then his mother was allowed to choose which part of the skeleton she wanted to keep before they put the whole thing back in the coffin. For an entire night she sat by her child's skeleton and wept constantly, and then she said, 'That bit over there, that little joint. Because it looks like a knucklebone and our Gerolphe loved to play knucklebones.' They poured gold over the little joint, and *voilà*, here it is, it's yours.''

"Is that gold?''

"They put a layer of lead around the gold so that the chambermaids wouldn't steal it. But look after it, if you ever need to, you can exchange the gold for money in the bank.''

Louis threw the knucklebone into the air a few times, let it fall on the back of his hand, threw it up again, caught it in a scything motion, and handed it to Vlieghe.

"It was lying on her bedside table. Now it is yours.''

"That poor woman will be looking for it.''

"That's all to the good. Because she was beginning to forget it was there. She hadn't picked it up for a long time, because it was covered with dust. Now that it's gone, her sorrow will be rekindled with a vengeance. And then her thoughts will be turned again to her child, gone for good and all.''

"You're a real stinker."

"I am, aren't I?" said Louis eagerly.

"Not just a stinker but a filthy, dirty liar." Vlieghe dropped the knucklebone into the breast pocket of Louis's tunic, got up from the tire, and walked away.

In Geography, where they were studying Albania, Sister Sapristi told them that Mussolini, one of the worst heretics Christianity had ever known, was plainly feeling divine retribution already, for he had been afflicted with tics and strange stabbing pains, he had begun shouting and hopping around in his palace for no reason at all, it was nerves, no human being could keep that up for long.

Louis wondered what Papa would think about it, he who had shown Louis photographs of that powerful, bald-headed figure helping to bring in the harvest, stripped to the waist amid rough, unshaven peasants, and had said, "Look, now there's a man for you. For the people, of the people. Can you see Paul-Henri Spaak with a pitchfork?" Mussolini had deliberately invaded Albania on Good Friday in order to show that he would crucify the Albanians on the day of Christ's Crucifixion, that coward, throwing in a hundred thousand men, one hundred and seventy ships, and four hundred airplanes against a handful of defenseless mountain folk. Mussolini, said Sister Sapristi, had already been described by Corneille, who had asked, *"si l'on doit le nom d'homme à qui n'a rien d'humain, à ce tigre altéré de tout le sang romain"*—"if we should grant the name of man to one who lacks humanity, to this tiger athirst for all the blood of Rome."

Which was stupid, Louis thought, because the Duce wasn't thirsting for Roman blood but for the blood of the blue-black Ethiopians and of the Albanians. And if he wanted to restore Julius Caesar's empire in the Mediterranean, what was wrong with that? Hadn't they been taught that Julius Caesar was one of the greatest men in history?

Vlieghe's pink tongue came into view as he yawned. (You are lucky, Vlieghe, that I'm not a lieutenant in Mussolini's army. I'd pack you off to the Ethiopian desert in your underpants. "Why, Lieutenant?" Because you are someone who tries to throw sand in his lieutenant's eyes, who claims to follow his lieutenant through thick and thin but who, when called upon to demonstrate his dedication, which is something a lieutenant may demand at any moment no matter where, refuses, no, worse, insults, humiliates his lieutenant. *En avant, marche!* Into the sands. Be sure to find an oasis before sundown, you renegade!)

Mussolini is stupid, says Sister Sapristi, because he imitates Hitler and persecutes and torments Catholics. But at least Hitler does have a new religion, heretical and devilish though that religion may be. Mussolini has put *nothing* in its place. And isn't it stupid beyond belief to try the patience of His Holiness the Pope, who has never put even a straw in that tyrant's way? "He who interferes with the Pope must die!" whispered Sister Sapristi.

On the way to the dormitory Vlieghe did not so much as look in Louis's direction.

Louis could not fall asleep. Lying on his bed, like the Count of Monte Cristo on his pallet in his damp, subterranean cell, he weighed up the different ways of escaping from the Institute, saw himself arriving at the Bad House on the road to Walle, or in Walle itself ringing the bell at the gloomy façade behind which Mama was lying. He looked through the window at the luminous white latticework on the merry-go-round. How often had he sat there, on safe warm days in the past, waiting doggedly through the visiting hours for Mama and Papa to turn up, as they sometimes did. Like that time when, although the Sisters had warned him that Mama would not be coming, he had obstinately continued to wait while the parents of the others chattered and babbled. Until it had grown dark and cold. I have done nothing wrong, Mama. The patrolling Sisters, who had at first felt sorry for him, began to grow cross. "Seynaeve, don't be such a baby!" "Louis, she isn't coming!" "Are you such a little boy still that you can't be without your mama for one day?" "If you don't come along at once, you'll go straight to the coal hole!" "Very well, then, stay where you are." Sister Kris pried his fingers from the metal bar, pulled his hair.

Vlieghe ignores me. His head is reverberating with the Twelve-Cylinder Delahaye without compressor, with the motor-racing circuit at Pau and its seven hundred bends, average speed fifty-five miles per hour, the best oil is Veedol, responds to the slightest touch on the starter, even at twenty degrees below zero . . .

Louis crept back into bed. Vlieghe has no heart. The heart works differently in every person. Vlieghe's is only a little piece of machinery, a cylinder, a crankcase. Mine is like a little night-light, bowing to every draft, what does a heart look like? Cats eat heart, Christ pointed to His heart, a pouch of flames. Richard the Lionhearted. The heart of Prince Sou-Chong, quaking, tempestuous, but held in check. "You are my heart's delight."

He knew that he was half-asleep when he went over to Vlieghe's bed, looked through the slit in the curtain, and saw nothing but an elongated lump under the blankets. He opened the curtain in front of the cubicle of Dobbelaere, Omer. The revolting fat boy was sleeping with tight-clenched fists. Louis pulled his hair, Dobbelaere woke up with a sort of sneeze, propped himself up on an elbow. He was wearing a nightshirt with little tucks and pleats across the chest, as worn by some orders of Sisters in foreign parts.

"Dobbelaere, you've been found out."

"Yes?"

"Yes. We saw you lacing up your shoes crosswise."

"Me?"

"Why, Dobbelaere?"

"You do it, too."

"Only Apostles are allowed to tie their shoelaces like that!"

"Yes."

"As the first of the Apostles, I am Mercy. Beg for mercy."

"Mercy."

"You don't mean it. Not properly."

Dobbelaere crawled on his knees, the blanket fell onto the floor.

"You rat!" Louis grabbed a handful of little tucks, twisted, a springy ball of linen in his fist, tugged, the material gave, Louis pulled harder, Dobbelaere's rounded white chest was laid bare.

"Aren't you ashamed of yourself, Omer?" said Louis. The ritual phrase of Dobbelaere's mother in the corridor when Sister Angel had knelt before her son. The fat boy hesitantly brought his hand up to the torn opening, Louis slapped the hand away.

"Move up." Louis lay down in the narrow bed that smelled of sleep, under the sepia photograph of a gendarme, father Dobbelaere.

"Don't you do anything immodest, Louis."

"I am Mercy, Hottentot!" Louis saw that Dobbelaere's pink nipple was erect, and tweaked it. As he had the teats of Mirza, Aunt Violet's dog, when no one was looking.

"Ouch!"

"Shut up." He pulled harder, pinched tight, let go. "Your punishment will be a light one, not because I like you but because I am Mercy. Lie down. Flat, I say."

Louis sucked the nipple for a long time.

Then Dobbelaere started to stroke his hair. Louis let him, counted to eleven, got up.

"Don't let me ever catch you with your shoelaces crossed again, fatso."

The corridor was drafty. He could see the Great Bear, the Seven Sisters. Mama had always warned him against drafts. He went on looking at the stars until his eyes fell shut and his head banged against the windowsill. Then he stole back to his bed, like the lion in the savanna just before he roars.

The queen of the Institute, Mother Superior, arrived accompanied by her retinue to sit in on Sister Angel's lesson, the retinue consisting of Grandpa (who naturally did not look in my direction) and his bosom friend, the potbellied Canon Vanhoore, world-renowned for his rousing songs for the youth of Flanders. They had failed to forewarn Sister Angel, who looked startled, straightened her always immaculate habit, looked the class over quickly to make sure nothing discreditable was happening as she expanded on Austrian rule, then stepped down from the platform, to be shooed back again with a small royal wave of the hand. Sovereign and retinue made their way, as if in some lackey's sitting room, to the back of the class.

Sister Angel resumed her lesson, ill at ease, pronouncing proper names with more than usual emphasis. Minister Mer-cy d'Ar-gen-teau succeeded Count Met-ter-nich Win-ne-burg.

Louis was afraid to look around, but in the few moments that Grandpa, his friend, and Mother Superior had taken to pass his desk he had nevertheless been able to catch a singular glimpse of a singular grandfather.

Usually when Grandpa came to the Institute and moved among the pupils, invariably accompanied by a Sister, of course, because no stranger, no matter how exalted his rank and station, was allowed to walk around the place without being escorted by a Sister, he would have a jaunty, almost playful appearance. Playful? Well, yes. Do you remember, last year when he and his great mate the canon took lunch in Mother Superior's parlor and he complained of a toothache? "I'm climbing up the wall with it, Mother, it's God's punishment and I must accept it, I know, but it hurts something awful." Mother Superior was in a great state, wanted to send a Sister to the infirmary for aspirin. "Aspirin, Mother? No. Don't bother. I have a more drastic remedy. Short shrift!" And he took his false teeth out of his mouth and placed them beside his soup plate. Mother Superior had given a sour laugh. Sour as a lemon, Grandpa said.

This time, however, a certain irritability could be seen on the battered features.

When the lesson was over, the canon applauded with little slaps of the palm of one hand on the back of the other. "That was good, Sister, very good, I've learned a lot."

"Boys," said Sister Angel, then uttered a splendidly disquieting sound: "Oohoohoo." The boys joined in and sang Canon Vanhoore's best-known composition (which Papa had printed on glossy sea-green paper with a pink cover, *Songs for Our Youth*).

"Oohoohoohoohoo goes the wind, tockatockatock the raindrops fall."

As the company made their way toward the door, smiling approvingly, Grandpa and the canon had a difference of opinion, whispering, the canon putting his hand on Grandpa's arm, urging him, imploring him, and Grandpa shaking his head irately. It has something to do with me. They want something from me.

Grandpa, his hand already on the door handle, took a few steps back again into the classroom and looked nearsightedly—so nearsightedly that the whole class laughed—in Louis's direction. Peering with comical exaggeration, he said, "I think there is someone sitting over there whom I have met before."

Louis flushed, bit the inside of his cheek.

"Yes. I think . . . You there, meneer, you with the curly head. No need to turn red like that. Aren't you a distant relative of mine?"

The class, the canon, Mother Superior, laughed immoderately.

"Come over here."

Louis crept out from behind his desk. "Oh, but now I can see, good grief, if it isn't a Seynaeve . . ."

"That he can't deny," said the canon.

"Tell me, Seynaeve, what is the difference between a fly and a midge?"

"A midge can fly but a fly can't midge."

"Very good. Ten out of ten." A bitter, mean little line appeared beneath the square ancestral mustache. "That was to put you at your ease. Now pay attention. Where was Cyril Verschaeve born?"

"In Ardooie."

"Very good. And the date?"

"It was before 1900."

"Not bad. But not quite good enough. Think about it. Try again."

"1880."

"In 1874, on April 30," Grandpa said portentously. "But you weren't all that far off."

"A mere nothing. Half a dozen years," said the canon.

Grandpa used to be a teacher, you can tell by the way he is walking up and down now with his hands behind his back. He doesn't notice how ill at ease Sister Angel is, now that he has taken over her job.

"Boys, coming here this morning, for we were up and about very early, Mijnheer the Canon and I, I saw a fight, a terrible fight, and one of the contenders was black and the other was white, and then the black one turned gray and the white one turned red. I saw it, and my heart leaped up within my soul, so glorious was that fight, although I see it every day, and know that it takes place every day, come what may."

He wiped the sweat from his forehead with the spotlessly clean handkerchief that he pulled out of his sleeve. "What fight was that, do you think?"

The class was silent. Numb. "Well?" A fight? Louis saw black knights, cowboys in white, white-powdered Roman charioteers. Nobody raised his hand.

"I'll give you a little hint, then. I said very early in the morning. And it happens every day."

"I think that's a very hard one." Sister Angel tried to come to the aid of her class.

"Come, come, Sister," said the canon, but you could see that he didn't know the answer, either. Grandpa shook his head indulgently. "Shall I tell you then? Yes? That daily fight, boys, is the fight between the sun and the black clouds of night!"

"Oh yes," said the class. "Of course. Now that you tell us."

The canon said, "I thought it was two sparrows fighting over a cowpat." The class roared. That canon!

Grandpa caught Louis's eye again, beckoned him, led him into the corridor.

"We laugh, Louis, but that is because of what is going on in our hearts . . . you do understand that, don't you?"

"Yes, Grandpa."

"We must be prepared for every trial . . . you do understand that, don't you?"

Louis nodded. What did he mean? What had he come for, besides selling maps, exercise books, school equipment? Grandpa took Louis's head between two bony hands, mumbled something. Cleared his throat.

"Aunt Nora is in the parlor." He let Louis go, then twisted two knuckles on top of Louis's head, it didn't hurt, it was really a clumsy caress. Louis thought, He is remembering that I am his godchild.

"She will explain it to you." It sounded like a sob. "Off you go now, to the parlor." And indeed, Aunt Nora, Papa's ugliest sister, was standing there, and beside her, like an ally, Sister Econome. Aunt Nora's trumpet nose with the nostrils you can look into, her curled-up upper lip, her white eyelashes, everything was sorrowful, defenseless. "Louis, my little Louis!" Sister Econome took Aunt Nora's hand as if to tuck some secret little present into it. Not so long ago Aunt Nora used to pick me up all the time and whirl me around.

"My little Louis." She sniffled.

"He is a big boy, our Louis," said Sister Econome.

"Louis, it's no good beating about the bush. You haven't got a little brother."

So it's a little sister. A brat.

"Something went wrong, and Our Lord thought that it was probably better that your mama . . ."

"What's happened to Mama?" shouted Louis.

"She's coming back home the day after tomorrow."

Had she been away, then? What exactly was it that Our Lord had thought?

"She's not quite well yet, but the doctors think she'll recover more quickly at home." Aunt Nora sat down, exhausted from a task well done. Sister Adam stood in the doorway with a ledger and said, "Psst!" Sister Econome sidled over to her, the two shapes merging into a single, overflowing black monster. Sister Econome traced the columns of figures in the open ledger with her delicate finger. "But then the cost of the clothes will have to be deducted," she said in an undertone.

"It's terrible," said Aunt Nora, "but that's life."

The Sisters whispered, counted, a litany of figures.

"There'll be another time." Aunt Nora wiped away her tears.

"Is Mama unhappy?"

"What do you expect?"

"Of course she's unhappy, what sort of question is that?" said Sister Adam.

"He was such a little beauty. I saw him myself. Such a beautiful little boy. But Our Lord didn't want him." His aunt is dragging Our Lord in because she is in the parlor of a convent under the searching gaze of nuns and of Pope Pius XII.

There were big drops of sweat in her yellowy-white eyebrows, or tears because she had rubbed her eyes. Yes, of all the foolish virgins, they had had to choose this Aunt Nora to convey these un-glad tidings. Papa, coward of a husband, has sent his unappealing sister and his father. Why couldn't he have come to tell me himself? Aunt Nora had to sign the account book. She had Papa's rounded, slanting, bashful handwriting.

"Through the Bank of Brussels as usual?" asked Sister Econome. Aunt Nora said, "Yes, Sister," like a Hottentot.

In the *pâtisserie* across the road, Louis had a slice of chocolate cake and Aunt Nora three éclairs.

"Did they baptize my baby?"

"What do you mean, your baby?"

"I mean Mama's baby."

"Your little brother. Of course."

"Who baptized him?"

"Er . . . the priest at the hospital."

"Was he there when he was born?"

"Yes. No. They telephoned for him. He came right away."

"Did he know then that the baby was going to die?"

"How could he know that?" She smacked her lips impatiently. "Stop thinking about it. That's what I said to your mother as well. Forget it. As quickly as possible. It was a mishap. It was nature."

The baby, pudgy and all wrinkled like the little Jesus who reclined gurgling with pleasure on Mary's blue-and-gold arm, with the same wide porcelain eyes, sat up, struck at a fly, looked at Papa, and began to kick his legs. Mama said, "Staf, there's something the matter with my baby." "Nonsense, Constance." "Oh, yes, he isn't happy." "Then he'll just have to learn to be happy." The baby heard that and turned away, laid down his little head, and held his breath until his porcelain eyes popped and bled.

"Oh, my beautiful clean pillow," cried Mama, "and the baby clothes Holst brought, there's blood on them!" But the baby could no longer hear. He had breathed his last, my little brother.

Aunt Nora looked at her wristwatch, ordered another two éclairs, and said, "All those boys together at night, what goes on? Do they still play together in the dormitory?"

"We are allowed to play in the refectory until vespers."

"And when the Sisters have gone to bed, do the boys go straight off to sleep or do they get into mischief?" She licked the cream off her fingers and wiped them on the tablecloth. Her cheeks were as red as the strawberry tart on the mantelpiece behind her. She has forgotten all about my mother. According to Mama she'll never be happy with Uncle Leon. Uncle Leon once had his name in the paper, in *Het Laatste Nieuws,* for winning a draughts tournament.

"There must be some with funny ideas. Aren't there? How old are the oldest boys? Thirteen, fourteen? Do any of them have a mustache yet?"

"Yes."

She wanted to say something else but didn't, because the *pâtisserie* lady was passing them on her way to the door. The spluttering of a car could be heard on the street, sounding remotely familiar to Louis.

"How is Uncle Leon, Aunt Nora?"

"You know what he's like. Always happy-go-lucky. Never a harsh word spoken in haste. All he ever asks is to be left in peace. When he isn't solving some draughts problem, he lies on the sofa with his eyes shut and listens to the sparrows."

She looked at her watch again. "Where on earth is he? If there's one thing I can't stand, it's people turning up late. And I have to be back home by six for our Nicole, she's due back from her catechism then."

"Who's meant to be coming?"

She looked at him sharply, somewhat cross-eyed, then a sly little laugh broke through, verily she was Grandpa's daughter.

"Just look around."

Papa took off his hat and came up to them.

"You never expected that, did you now?" crowed Aunt Nora. "I had you fooled, didn't I?"

Papa dropped into the chair next to Louis's. "Have you been here long?"

"An hour!" cried Aunt Nora. Papa ordered a *mille-feuille* and a coffee.

"I couldn't get away. The mayor wanted a ten-by-twelve print for the price of a six-by-eight! Everyone else gives him a discount, he says."

"Well, anyway, you're here now. That's the main thing."

"Is he ready?" Papa asked. As if "he" (I!) were in another room, in another country.

"I still have to get his suitcase, Sister Imelda is packing it."

"You're in luck again," Papa said to Louis. "You can go home before all the rest."

He ate his *mille-feuille* in three bites.

"Home?" That was impossible. They were lying. It was one of their many treacherous little games.

"Yes, for the holidays."

"The summer holidays? But they don't start for two weeks."

"Exactly. Aren't you glad?"

"But why?"

"Because of what has happened . . . to Mama . . ."

"You see, Louis, every cloud has a silver lining. Isn't that right? Another cup of coffee, Staf?"

"No. No more coffee for me. What with my nerves."

"Don't take it so hard," said Aunt Nora, like a wife.

At that Papa signaled her with his eyebrows and with an almost imperceptible nod. She took her handbag and stood up. The bell of the *pâtisserie* door tinkled, continued to quiver.

"I have to explain to you, Louis," Papa said immediately. "In the state I'm in, what with my nerves, I wouldn't dare set foot in the convent, not a single step. Because I would have to tell the nuns every last detail, and you know as well as I do that they understand nothing, absolutely nothing about what goes on in a proper household when there's a tragedy. They would just keep going on about how everything has been ordained by Our Lord and how our trials" (he drew the word out and ordered a jam tart) "are sent to strengthen us, and so on and so forth. And I'm not in the mood for all that right now. I'm afraid I might be rude, and in my business you can't afford that sort of thing."

The jam tart arrived, he cut off an eighth and gave it to Louis.

"Have you been trying your best?" Papa said. "Have you got your report with you? How's the arithmetic?"

"Fine."

"Fine."

Papa chewed, smacked his lips, waited for Aunt Nora. Says nothing about the other child, nothing about the child here, right under his nose.

"I didn't get very good marks in History."

"And you used to be so good at it."

"That's because Sister Kris never tells us anything about the history of Flanders. All we do is learn about French battles and the growth of French industry. And I never used to learn or read about things like that."

Louis's lie had a more electric effect than he could ever have anticipated. Papa immediately sat up straight in his chair, his drowsiness gone in a flash. He drummed on the tablecloth.

"French industry!"

"Yes, Mijnheer Seynaeve?" said the *pâtisserie* lady.

"Yes, what?"

"Oh, I thought you were calling me."

"Well, now that your are here, madame, you might give us another two *boules de Berlin.* I'll come and get them." But Papa stayed where he was, swept the *mille-feuille* crumbs into the palm of his hand, and flung them into his mouth. "I knew it all along. French history, that's how they start. Pumping it into our Flemish youth from infancy. It's all Napoleon's fault. Because he was the first to set up *maisons de la culture française* in the occupied territories to make propaganda for France and to encourage espionage. Yes, Old Boney really got them to bone it up in the convents. That's the way it goes. But, *olala,* that's not the way it's going to be!"

(I ought to show Christian charity toward this gullible fool before me. But I cannot forget that he has forgotten to say a single word about Mama and the ravages wrought upon her. All I get is lies about her falling down the stairs.)

"Sister Angel," said Louis. (If I want to outdo his lies, then I must spare no one. Even the sweetest, the gentlest, must be dragged through the mire with me.) "Sister Angel says it wasn't the Flemings who won the Battle of the Golden Spurs."

Now Papa was truly dumbfounded. His mouth, crumbs adhering to the thin lips, dropped open.

"What? How can that be?"

"Sister Angel says that the Flemish side was mainly made up of Germans and Frisians and Dutchmen and even French-speaking people from Henegouwen."

"That's slander," said Papa.

"That's why I haven't got good marks in History."

I can make him dance like a yo-yo. I just have to stand fast. Louis hummed *"Toujours sourire"* from *The Land of Smiles,* but Papa didn't recognize the tune.

Aunt Nora came into sight on the street. She was struggling with Louis's heavy suitcase, head held high, shoulders stiffly back, but the lower part of her body tottering and staggering. Louis skipped out into the street toward her. Beside him, bent double like a spy, Papa raced panting for the car. "Quick, Nora, in case they see me!" He had trouble with the car keys, fumbling nervously as he tried to keep hidden behind the car.

Three pigeons dropped down and settled on Sister Econome's windowsill. On the first floor of the Keep a window opened and a sleeve with a flapping duster appeared. The street was empty.

The summer holidays are starting for me. Vlieghe is still incarcerated. That'll teach him. Where is he right now? Probably with Baekelandt, in front of the barn door where Baekelandt is nailing up bats to ward off thunder and lightning. Tonight in Walle when I look out of my window at the stars, he will be doing the same, sitting on the windowsill like the pigeons on Sister Econome's, but leaning against the frame, rubbing his back in the white tunic with the cherry-red piping against the wood and falling, falling into the arms of Satan.

The car revved up. The sun shone on the cobblestones. The car slid forward, backfiring past the brick Institute. As Louis looked around at the little towers and the moss-covered roof of the Institute, the sun disappeared behind a cloud. God does not want me to behold His splendor on earth. He withdraws behind the clouds so as not to see my vile face.

*L*ouis let go of the train, plunged through the hot steam, leaped into the arms of his Uncle Florent, crashing into him. The train chugged away, the man covered with coal smuts in charge of the tender waved at the stationmaster, who stood among the rose bushes, gold-braided cap jammed tight on his forehead. The stationmaster took their tickets and said, "She's already here. Look." Aunt Violet stood on the other side of the lowered barrier. The stationmaster stuck his thumbs behind his broad gray suspenders, the voluminous corduroy trousers riding upward.

"She's been talking the hind leg off a donkey. 'Bakels, where is that train?' I tell her, 'Juffrouw, the clock's over there.' 'But that clock is slow,' she cries. I say: 'Calm down, juffrouw!' 'There hasn't been an accident, has there, you'd have heard if there had been, wouldn't you?' I say, 'Juffrouw, this isn't Spain, where the Communists derail trains.' She says, 'But Bakels, why don't you make the clock work?' I tell her, 'Juffrouw, if you want a clock that works, buy one yourself.' 'I've got one,' she says, 'but it's broken.' "

Uncle Florent pushed Louis toward the barrier, toward farm carts, playing children, a seminarian, and Aunt Violet. The smell of steam gave way to a whiff of manure. Aunt Violet was in mourning. For Mama's baby. (Or maybe it was still for Queen Astrid, who years ago had been smashed to smithereens in a car by her husband, the King.)

She weighed well over two hundred pounds, a bit more than Uncle Robert.

"It wouldn't be so bad," said Mama, "if only the proportions were right."

"The flesh is still firm," said Papa, "but as the years go by . . ."

"You look to yourself," said Mama, taking sides with the sister with whom she had once played duets every evening. "If you ask me, there's something wrong with her thyroid." "Better than Mona's, which works overtime."

A bell went ping, and the red-and-white striped barrier rose. Aunt Violet waddled up to them and offered her cheek. "Haven't you grown!" She had a snub nose with blackheads and the bulging, severe eyes of a teacher.

"Fasten my shoe strap for me, there's a dear!" He knelt, first insufferable obeisance in this rustic backwater, air thick with midges, he tightened the leather strap and fastened the button, and the two swollen ankles gleamed, squashed and shackled with perfect symmetry.

"I thought you'd been called up, Florent."

"Yes. To the front," said Louis.

"They'll have their work cut out for them to get me into khaki. It isn't my color."

"You're a Red, we all know that."

"No. I'm all for Violet," said the charmer.

Aunt Violet raised her finger, as she did to the peasant children in class. "Florent, this is the time for every Belgian to do his duty!" Perhaps she said it with so much emphasis because they were just passing her school, a cheerful little building next door to the church tower. There were no railings to be seen, no nuns.

"Not at a franc a day," said Uncle Florent.

And perhaps it was also because they were passing her school that Uncle Florent patted Aunt Violet's wobbling behind and pretended to be about to lift her like some monstrous baby and carry her across the playground in triumph. "How's your love life, Violet?"

"Florent! Behave yourself." He ruffled the hair under her ridiculous little round black hat, dodged aside, expecting a slap.

"Stop it, Florent! My *mise-en-plis.*" Her protest, teasing and half-hearted, was just what Mama's would have been in the same situation. But that's where the resemblance to Mama ended. Or to Aunt Berenice, the youngest of the Bossuyts, who to her everlasting shame had married a Bulgarian heretic. Not so long ago I used to think he was a Mohammedan.

"You must have cried your eyes out when your Mama lost her baby. You probably wanted a little brother, didn't you?"

"Yes, Aunt Violet," he said dutifully.

"I don't even want to think about something like that happening to me."

The fronts of villas clad in ivy. Poplars bent by the wind. Rows of pollarded willows in irregularly shaped meadows. As if there could ever be any question of Aunt Violet's having a baby. Then why does she bring up the possibility, apropos of nothing? One day, Louis was sure of it, he would gain some insight into, some grasp of, all these half-spoken phrases, allusions. If you pay attention, stay watchful, then one day the riddles they let spill out like crumbs with their jokes and lies will begin to come to light, be unraveled down to the finest thread. But not yet. Now they still say, "There are rats in the rafters" every time I come in, a pale wet rat with sharp-pointed elegant little ears plastered to my skull, twitching my scaly tail, scrabbling, furtively among their cursed secrets.

"Would you like me to carry your case?"

"No, Aunt Violet."

"Let him, Violet, he needs to put on muscle."

Uncle Florent winked. Was it a tic? How do you wink if you are one-eyed like Pieter de Coninck, the Sly, doyen of the Bruges guild of weavers in 1300?

They passed Farmer Liekens's house with the sagging thatched roof, the thatch now even more caved in than when Louis had last seen it (on the way to the station, his final glimpse of Bastegem, that gold-and-amber three-foot-thick rye straw), the four Liekens children playing with a piglet, poking its pink-and-white belly with forked twigs. Ivo, the oldest, grinned and called, "Hello," but did not come up to the hedge.

"Keep walking, Louis," said Aunt Violet. "Pretend you don't see them." He looked anyway, to see if he could spot Iwein-the-Cow between the asbestos pigsties, behind the dungheap, next to the stables.

It was forbidden to have anything to do with the Liekens children, and above all to go into their yard. Even though milk and eggs had been fetched from there every day once upon a time. But then father Liekens had done something so unspeakable that not even the socialist newspaper dared to print it.

Sunday afternoon on the village square. The farmers playing whist under the plane trees of the Draughtboard Inn stare at Iwein Liekens, who stumbles, falls, picks himself up, totters about, then sprawls against the concrete edge of the war memorial in a pool of blood that is seeping from the seat of his blue linen trousers. He mumbles that he has been attacked by a bull in rut. Ever since then he has been known as Iwein-the-Cow.

"Hello, hello," called Ivo Liekens after them, only a peacock responding, "Leo, Leo, Leo" (a Pope who was crazy about billiards and who canonized our own Jan Berchmans).

Aunt Violet had a small purplish wart under her chin. Waddling along in her mourning clothes, she looked like one of those tortuous line drawings in *Hebdo* magazine (one of the Apostles' Forbidden Books) of giant women bursting out of their fat, with strawberry noses, warts, and spiky hair, always ready to set upon their dwarfs of husbands with a rolling pin or an umbrella. Louis pointed to his chin. Uncle Florent moved closer to Aunt Violet, looked, snorted with laughter, she saw him doing it, he blew his nose between his fingers.

"It's from shaving," he whispered. Uncle and nephew were overcome with helpless laughter that bubbled up again and again as far as the gate of Villa Heliotrope, the Bossuyt home. The little lane beside the house was overgrown with dahlias of many colors, bumblebees hovered, vibrated, over them. At the barn, which was known as the "garage" and where Louis had once been given twelve hard spanks by Uncle Omer, Hector the turkey recognized his old playmate and immediately began to scrabble in the sandy soil, clawing the ground and shaking his head, wattles flapping audibly.

Meerke sat with both her feet in their checked slippers on the round nickel railing at the foot of the potbellied stove as if warming them, an old habit, Meerke was old. She jumped up, wiped her hands absently down her apron. Only then did Louis realize how much he had grown, he was nearly as tall as Meerke.

"Just look who's here," she said. Toothless, solicitous Meerke, *petite mère*. "Sit down, sit down, sit yourself down," and she pointed to a wicker armchair with a tartan cushion flattened like a pancake by Aunt Violet's mighty behind. Bread with lard and quince jelly. Because Uncle Florent (awkwardly polite and quiet ever since they had come in) doted on quince jelly. Uncle Armand's pigeons skittered about on top of the garage roof, they carry a terrible disease, incurable if a human being catches it. Minute pigeon lice crawl through your pores and wreak havoc inside your flesh. You become melancholy, then feverish, and then you die making cooing noises and twitching your shoulder blades. One of Uncle Armand's pigeons was called Coco, a parrot's name.

"Have you done well at school?"

"Yes, Meerke. I got eighty percent in Geography."

Coffee was drunk from the chased blue-and-white service Uncle Armand had won at archery long ago, before he had turned into a lecher and a drunkard.

"And what about Religious Knowledge?"

"Seventy."

"And Arithmetic?"

"Fifty."

"That's poor," said Aunt Violet. "Very poor."

"And that's the only thing you really need to know well for later, said Meerke. "That and French language and *grammaire.*"

"Yes," exclaimed Uncle Florent, "otherwise you'll get gypped all your life. They don't pay nearly enough attention to arithmetic in our schools, right, Violet?" She did not reply. The moment they had come in she had made straight for the little oval window next to the dresser without taking off her hat or putting down her bag. She was engrossed in what there was to see or what might be coming along in the deserted village street. Meerke reported that Father Mertens had gone into the house next to the dairy at least an hour and a half before. They had noticed that lately he was staying there longer and longer, on visits to a woman with six children.

Aunt Violet had inherited from Meerke an absolute veneration of priests, and, given over as her fat and lonely existence was to piety, education, and gluttony, Father Mertens had become an overriding passion of hers, she followed his comings and goings through the distorted spyglass of love. Father Mertens was her idol and her scourge.

Once upon a time, Mama had been a girl called Constance Bossuyt, and together with her little sisters Violet and Berenice, she had been a day pupil at the boarding school run by the Maricole Sisters. The sparrows fall from the sky, the cows lie steaming in the meadow, and, panting and faltering, Maurits, the oldest son of the ancient Coppenolle farming clan from across the Leie, tells Aunt Violet—who, of course, wasn't yet my aunt—that he cannot live without her, she listens and is flattered, and just because she doesn't run away squealing like a pig, he believes his love to be returned and puts his arms around her and kisses her. Once back home she is overcome with anxiety, the sin of unchastity—for he had stuck his tongue into her mouth—is scorching her soul, and, sobbing, she confesses to Meerke, her mother, who quickly puts on her hand-knitted shawl and speeds to the presbytery. But the priest, whom she reveres and who walks the fields with divining rods before the farmers will buy a single acre and who has electricity in his fingers when he playfully strokes the hair of the little Bossuyt sisters, is not at home, and Meerke is forced to tell her tale of woe to Mertens, the brand-new curate, and he says, "Madame, that will have to be nipped in the bud," or "smothered at birth," or "snuffed out," or "cut off root and branch." Night falls over the farmyard, the oil lamp splutters, and at one side of the table that smells of dough are seated Farmer Coppenolle, his wife, and his parents, on the other side Meerke and the trembling, guilty Violet. Maurits, the culprit, on his knees in the corner of the room next to the brooms and the brushes, keeps his eyes cast down. Curate Mertens sits between the two families, sipping cherry brandy. Lucie the maid pokes furiously at the stove in order to make her displeasure known, in order to smash the priest's voice to pieces. She is sent out.

"Who started it? No, not the kissing, but who took the lead? Where did he put his arm, where exactly? Show us. How long did his arm stay there? But when a boy kisses a girl does he usually put his arm so low down? And what did you feel then, Violet? You can be quite frank, I have heard such things many times before in my confessional. Something warm? You don't know. That's odd, you remember everything else so clearly. How long did the kiss last? Was it a quick peck with the lips like a brother kissing his sister on her name day? It was different. How different? Speak freely. Didn't you defend yourself? Push him away? What else did he want? Remember, you are under oath."

Farmer Coppenolle's smallest children are whimpering. The kneeler is ordered to take them to the room over the cellar and put them to bed.

"Speak freely, he can't hear you. Don't be bashful, he's gone. During the kiss did he put his hand on your neck, around your throat as if to throttle you, to force you to submit to his lewd acts? What did he say to you? You don't remember? Didn't he say, 'Sweetheart, love of my heart, apple of my eye?' Why not? Answer me! We know there was more. We priests are used to our parishioners' telling us no more than half the story to start with."

In a monotone, without apparent menace, Curate Mertens repeats himself and gropes and probes, he is given another brandy and yet another, Meerke nods anxiously, Farmer Coppenolle slaps the table with the flat of his hand, the exasperatingly slow interrogation drags on, Maurits gives stubborn answers, scared to death, and Violet, oh, Violet . . .

Curate Mertens says that many things remain unexplained but that it behooves us first and foremost to forgive, to preserve the dignity of both families, every household has its moment of crisis, we'll just have to draw a veil over the whole thing. As Meerke holds up his coat for him, he says,

"*Te absolvo*, my daughter," and vanishes into a night full of stars and flatulent cows.

"And from that night on," Mama told the breathlessly attentive ladies from Parcels for Soldiers, "my sister was no longer the same. She no longer played the piano, she no longer sang 'Violetta,' she had such a lovely soprano voice, too, and the only thing she still had an appetite for was eating mountains of bread and pan drippings, platefuls of potatoes with cracklings, but that's not what made her get fat, the shame and the panic of that night went to her thyroid so that the thyroid shut down, the very opposite of Mona, my husband's sister, whose thyroid works overtime, with consequences we all know and had best pass over in silence, it seems Mona has taken up with an electrician ten years younger than she is, but there you are. No, our Violet got the horrors about anything to do with men. She still has them. She never beats her girl pupils, only the boys. And from that night on she began to swell up and to be drawn to the curate and to help with the congregation. Sometimes, of course, she hears people laughing at her, calling her 'the balloon' or 'the whale,' and then she eats even more bread and drippings. I feel sorry for her. 'Constance,' she says. 'I'll die without ever . . .' " (Mama's voice in the drawing room grew light, like a butterfly . . .) " 'having known a man.' I say, 'You silly goose, you're still in the prime of life and there are hundreds of men who like their women on the plump side.' " The ladies from Parcels for Soldiers said amen to that.

Aunt Violet, in the prime of life, was peering through the little oval window, her broad back as black and uncommunicative as a nun's. "He's there," she hissed. "He's going to the presbytery. He's in a hurry. It's time for Benediction. No, he isn't in a hurry. He's pulling out a weed and throwing it under the hedge. He doesn't have his keys with him. Oh yes, he has." She came over to the stove, took off her ridiculous hat.

Uncle Florent said that he couldn't wait much longer.

"Oh, but you must stay until Armand gets back," Meerke exclaimed, "he would never forgive you." She made a rattling noise in her throat. She had had seven children, of whom five had survived and the other two, twins, had died at the age of two, they had turned blue with coughing, their throats had closed up, nothing could get through except phlegm and air and then nothing at all, not even their death rattle.

"Armand will be very upset, he sees so few people."

"Oh, he never sees anyone, of course, in any of those five or six cafés he visits every day," said Aunt Violet.

"I mean people to have a serious conversation with."

"In that case . . ." said Uncle Florent, and was given an Élixir d'Anvers.

It was too sweet for him. He was handed a glass of Pils. It was too weak. He was given a geneva. That was just right.

"The Pope would like to mediate between governments, would like to give his opinion of the present situation, but Mussolini won't let him, the Laternan, or is it the Lateran, Treaty forbids the Pope to concern himself with worldly affairs."

"That's just as well, Meerke. Because where would that get us?"

"Then Hitler shouldn't meddle with the Church in Germany!" exclaimed Aunt Violet. "There's always a policeman in plainclothes in German churches putting down the names of the congregation in a notebook."

"In that case they can become martyrs," said Louis. One of the pigeons on the garage roof pecked crossly at the others. Probably Coco.

"It's not nice of you, Louis, to make fun of Catholics," said Meerke.

"But I didn't say it to make fun of them," said Louis, taken by surprise.

Twelve brown cows and a black-and-white one, a Friesian, were wandering along the village street, two boys in bare feet beating them with twigs.

"The King of England had a wonderful trip to America. He and the Queen had tea with the President."

"In the White House?" asked Louis.

"Could have been," said Meerke. "And it wasn't just the tea that came from London, the water did, too. But they weren't allowed to use the water, because the Americans had it tested first and it must have had bugs in it, anyway the Americans got their chemists to copy it using American water so well that the Queen couldn't tell the difference. She was very touched by that, the Queen was."

"That was a nice thing to do," said Aunt Violet. "We Belgians wouldn't have given two hoots. Water is water, we would have said over here."

"Since he came to power, Hitler has made four hundred and thirty speeches. That takes some doing."

"And something different every time. There's got to be something different every time, in that kind of speech."

"The fool makes his point with laughter," said Uncle Florent.

"A fool like that can keep away from me," said Meerke.

"It looks as if he's thinking of paying us a visit anyway."

"You must have heard about the German tourist who had to show his passport to the gendarmes. 'Take a good look at it,' he said, 'it's the last time you'll see it, because any day now *we* will be checking *your* papers.'"

"Would you believe it!"

"They say they're having trouble getting enough to eat in Germany.

They're making margarine out of some sort of chemical muck, there isn't a drop of milk in it. Result: everyone has foot-and-mouth disease."

"And they're so busy with their fortifications and they have to drag so many people in to build them that there are no more waiters left in the cafés in Berlin."

"And the women have to work on the land, so they can't look after their children."

"But then they make new children. In the cornfields. Eh, Violet?"

"For goodness' sake, Florent, don't you ever think of anything else?"

"The Germans are bound to come and make a nuisance of themselves. They can't bear the thought that we Belgians are so comfortable here *entre nous.*"

"We have never bothered any other country. Never in all our history. It's always been the others who have brought their troubles here."

The sky turned slate-gray with glimmers of blue. "*L'heure bleue,*" Mama called it. Louis had often whispered "*l'heure bleue*" at dusk in the playground when the pear tree turned into a dark, tangled mass, a gigantic sponge teeming with noctural creatures and with Mizzlers, unseen.

"No, it's getting too late, I don't want to miss that last train," said Uncle Florent and downed his last geneva. "You can tell that charming Armand of yours that I hung around waiting for him and I'm not too happy about it. Tell him he can go kiss my arse."

"It's not his fault," pleaded Meerke. "He doesn't look at the time. He forgets where he is." Armand, the eldest, is her problem child, her favorite. (If Mama had had that little brother, I'd be the favorite son now, too.)

Meerke made that guttural sound again. Like a jackal choking on too large a chunk of rotting zebra.

Aunt Violet put down her knitting, took off her gold-rimmed glasses. "Remember me to your mother. Don't forget, now."

Uncle Florent said, "So long, keep well." Recollecting that Louis also existed, separately and individually and uniquely, he ruffled Louis's hair, just as he had Aunt Violet's at the station, and growled, "So long, little 'un. *Salut.* And don't let me hear any complaints!" And in that he was just like Grandpa, who as head of the Seynaeves would have growled in precisely the same, almost embarrassed, way here in this outlandish rustic kingdom of Mama's forefathers.

After the buttermilk porridge, Louis sat by the cold stove and looked at the magazine and newspaper clippings Aunt Violet passed him, all about the life, the death, and the funeral of Queen Astrid. The paper felt clammy and smelled of mothballs from the box with the blue-bordered label "ASTRID."

"The Swan from the North, that's what they called her, and that's what she was. It only happened because Our Lord wanted to call her to Him as soon as possible, that's the only explanation. They had such a happy home life, Leopold and she did, such lovely people, look here, there she is in white and he in his uniform."

"The footmen at Laeken Castle said that they never had a cross word, those two," said Meerke.

Uncle Armand still failed to turn up, Meerke grew nervous, and Aunt Violet said, eating buttercakes, "You really ought to read him the riot act once and for all, Mother. But you're too scared to. And he knows only too well that you'll always side with him, so he takes advantage."

"The boy needs to get married, that's all."

"Why should he? He's looked after here like Prince Charles, his meals are ready for him every day, even though he does let them get all dry on the stove like now. His underwear, his shirts, his suits, his neckties, they're all cleaned and ironed on time, and who's it all for? For those women whose shame is common talk in the village and for those girls whose heads he keeps turning and who come bleating to me, 'Violet, couldn't you put in a good word for me with your brother? Why is Armand being so nasty to me now that I've let him have his way with me?'"

"*Violette, je t'en prie, devant le garçon . . .*"

"*Le garçon,*" said Louis with a yawn. His hot cheek lay on his arm resting along the nickel bar of the stove. The air was balmy, pleasantly hazy and tepid and dim, Mizzlers fluttered around soundlessly amid the chattering of Aunt Violet and Meerke and the smell of the newspaper clippings, someone tugged at him and half-raised him up, someone with a rough, mocking voice that half-spoke, half-crooned, "To bed the little fellow goes, off with his cap, off with his clothes."

A merry Uncle Armand emerged for breakfast. He had a long upper lip and a furrowed face full of laugh lines and looked like photographs of Marcel Kint, the Black Eagle of Zwevegem, taken after a sprint to the finish line, beaming, ultrafit, surrounded by panting, exhausted weaklings. Uncle Armand's black hair was combed straight back and slicked down without a parting. He picked at his chalky toenails and said in his rough smoker's voice that he would be taking Louis on the back of his motorcycle one of these days. "We'll really let 'er rip, kid!" Then he scratched long and hard among the gray curls on his chest, ate his bacon and eggs without a word to his doting mother, his envious sister. His eyes were cobalt-blue with black lashes that looked painted, like those of Alfred Lagasse, tenor and Prince Sou-Chong. He rode off on his motorcycle, sounding his horn for a distressingly long time, leaving villagers cursing or crossing themselves in his wake.

In the afternoon Raf de Bock, the son of the ironmonger, came to visit Louis. They walked like tightrope artists along the railway tracks. When he went to the college next year he would be joining the KSA, the Catholic Students' Action movement, Raf announced proudly, the metallic sheen of his parents' shop on his hands and face.

At the Institute Louis would certainly have declared Raf an Apostle, even in Raf's present state of innocence, untouched by guile or circumspection. That was because he had gone to a country school. But his fervent ambition to be part of the Catholic Students' Action movement was food for thought. The KSA, those sentinels of Jesus Christ, were not so different from the Boy Scouts, they had greater ideals, true, but that wasn't particularly difficult, seeing that the Scouts had a fleur-de-lys on their belts and were, anyway, run by the English (because of their founder, Baden-Powell), who imposed their own English ceremonies, drinking tea while starving our kinsmen in South Africa to death behind barbed wire in concentration camps and machine-gunning our coreligionists in Ireland—*fair play,* my arse.

Raf and Louis crept under the rusty barbed wire and set out across a field. Cows began moving toward them, but the two walked steadily on. Louis's heart pounded. They weren't dangerous bulls, of course not, they weren't the same as that monster that had leaped with bestial lust on farmer Iwein-the-Cow and because of which that poor man would be a laughingstock to his dying day, but the horns and the bloodshot eyes were nevertheless drawing too close. "Milk factories!" shouted Louis when he reached the barbed wire.

Along the tree-lined road, past the sanatorium where the idle rich were sunbathing in their silk pajamas, past Bastegem Excelsior's football ground. The grass stood high among the tangle of shrubs. Raf dropped to his knees, Louis followed suit. They crawled through the bushes toward the little pink-brick castle. "Not so fast," said Raf curtly. Louis should never have put on a white shirt, of course, should have worn camouflage like Raf, who had on a dark-gray jersey.

Really it was a pity that their expedition was taking place in daylight, otherwise they could have daubed themselves with mud. The whites of their eyes alone would then have flickered in the light of the campfire. And the glint of silver rifle and tomahawk. They edged forward on their elbows, no sound emerging from the castle or from the outbuildings. "*Godverdomme,* they aren't at home." Raf stood up and ran across the dried-up brook, slashing the bushes out of the way, and, heedless of the fleet Sioux by his side, made straight for an oak tree. No Winchester was trained on them from the leaded windows on the first floor. The gravel on the drive crunched under the soles of Louis's shoes, his moccasins had been left behind in the tepee. He collided with Raf behind the oak, was shoved in the back and found himself exposed out on the open plain. There was a sports car parked nearby with the left-hand door open. No trace of blood could be seen on the stone steps leading to the terrace. Raf came up to join his scout. With extreme nonchalance, hands clenched tight in pockets, fingernails probably drawing blood, he walked past Louis. Louis stepped on Raf's shadow. The little castle seemed deserted. Louis peered into a room.

The lime trees smelled sweet. Raf scrabbled in a dustbin, searched among tin cans, coffee grounds, wet newspapers, a hundred brown cigarette stubs, and picked out a thin, crumpled, torn satin rag. The lid of the dustbin fell shut with a hideous metallic noise that made the birds rise flapping into the air, the clash of sword against breastplate brought forth voices from the basement kitchen, an uncertain cracked bass uttering incomprehensible curses and a woman's shrill voice saying, "Oh, Lord!" For a moment it looked as if Raf, the clumsy oaf, was about to go charging into the house, for he stood poised with one foot on the moss-covered steps and a hand on the weathered railings, but luckily he turned and ran back, without cover, to the bushes.

Noises could now be heard from the first floor of the house, too, noises as if people were moving a wardrobe. As the two wretched assailants fell puffing and panting into the dry ditch, giggling like girls, they could hear the strains of martial music from the invisible castle, strains that quickly made way for the oily trumpet sounds that Grandpa called "bestial," and which were made by American Negroes who, if we didn't look out, would take over our entire culture.

The room that he, quivering with terrified rapture, had glimpsed through the distorting pane of an oriel window, had contained an immense chandelier with dozens of arms and branches hanging from the ceiling, dully gleaming red-brown chairs with green seats, an oval table with a marble top, the bust of a man with a wig from the time of Louis the Umpteenth, and a painting above the mantelpiece of a naked blonde lady on a bright-red bed. Susanna without the two elders. The gleam of porcelain in a display cabinet. An antique crucifix. Somebody had been throwing their money about. In just such a room, minus the painting of Susanna, lived His Eminence Hendrikus Lamiroy, Bishop of Bruges. Why can't I be a prodigal young man? I am ready to renounce everything and to follow Him, but I'd first have to be a rich young man with a room like this one, wouldn't I? Raf lagged behind, now and then flattening a bush with a branch.

"She was at home after all, Madame Laura. But we'll come back tomorrow. You have to see her before you die. With a little luck we might easily have seen her sitting on the terrace. Can you believe it? She comes to the countryside specially for the fresh air and to have a rest without the telephone, without any clients, and no sooner does she arrive than she shuts herself up in her bedroom. She never goes out for walks, just sits around most of the time on her lazy behind smoking cigarettes on the veranda, or sometimes in the shade on the terrace. But we won't be put off, right, Louis? We'll come back tomorrow, and we'll be more careful this time. Maybe we should bring binoculars. Because if she sees us, she'll either have us chased away or get Holst to give us a hiding. Because Madame Laura considers herself very superior, she thinks a very great deal of herself, and you can't help wondering why. Who does she think she is? Her family are ordinary enough people, the Vandenghinstes from Meerhem. Her father had a stroke when she ran off to Brussels with all his savings, *adieu* Father, and *merci*. You just ask your Uncle Armand. He probably won't want to admit it now, but he knows her only too well, Madame Laura, he was crazy about her one whole summer, there was even talk of marriage, what luck that nothing came of it, or that would have been your Uncle's bad luck, what am I saying, the death of him, because your Uncle Armand, although you wouldn't think so from that grinning mug of his, is much too serious. You might think he's nothing but a joker with a lot of charm, but why do you think he wastes himself the way he does on drink and loose women? Because he has problems, Armand has, I'm telling you, and that's why it's just as well that he realized in the nick of time whom he was dealing with—Madame Laura strikes men blind with that muff of hers."

That muff of hers, Louis knew, was what women have under their skirts, at the sight of which some men (men like Uncle Armand?) clap their hands to their eyes, blinded by a flash of lightning.

On the sanatorium terrace a nurse held a bedpan in one hand and waved to them with the other.

"Women don't know the difference between good and evil," said Raf. Where had that self-confident piece of wisdom come from? Raf was an altar boy. And Raf was often beaten by his father, the ironmonger, a little man with a Clark Gable mustache who often had headaches. When he had one, he hit somebody.

They parted on the tree-lined road. Louis stayed behind for a while to watch a mare with pale-yellow hair and little flaxen tufts above her hooves, he called to her, but she wouldn't come. Then in the distance, between the acacias, he saw Raf sniffing and nibbling at the little rag he had stolen from the dustbin. No, he was not after all eligible to be an Apostle.

Aunt Violet said that Mama had telephoned from the Alps where she was staying with her friend Madame Esquenet. She had seen waterfalls and eaten venison though it was out of season.

"Did she say anything else?"

"What did you expect her to say, dear?"

"Didn't she ask how you are?"

"Well, of course. I told her we were very pleased to have you staying with us. That you're being good and minding your manners."

"Didn't she say anything else?"

"Like what, Louis?" asked Aunt Violet testily.

"Didn't she send me her love?"

"Of course, Louis, I've just told you."

"No."

Mama had said nothing about his murdered little brother. Hadn't asked after Holst, who had done the murder, Holst, the archangel who had hypocritically painted his jet-black wings white, who had received orders from the heavenly powers to protect Louis from evil through thick and thin, in fair weather or foul, and who had swept Mama's child to death with a wave of his diabolically flapping wings lest I grow attached to this little brother, come to like him, which I certainly would have done had he stayed alive. So that, instead, I might entirely give myself up to the love of Our Lord, which is my calling, something I tend to forget too often.

He helped Meerke shell peas. She sat with her gray, wrinkled-up feet steeping in a tub of Rodell Saltrates. Louis tried, as he ate peas on the sly, to catch a glimpse of those mysterious things Meerke called her corns, but (ashamed?) she quickly wrapped her feet in the checked towel. Louis flung the milky water at Hector the turkey but missed him.

"At last she's doing the sensible thing, our Constance. She ought to do it more often, leave Staf and all that song and dance of his behind, just do some traveling, because cooking meals day in day out, washing some man's underpants, darning his socks . . . Oh, how lucky I am to have escaped all that." Spiteful Mizzlers huddled in Aunt Violet's throat.

"She hasn't sent us one of her cards this time," said Meerke. "Though she usually does that as soon as she arrives in foreign parts."

"She must have other things to think about," said Aunt Violet.

"We've had some wonderful color postcards from your mother," said Meerke, "from Holland, from Lourdes, from Paris, the Sacré-Coeur, the Panthéon, but that was long ago, how long would you say, Violet? That postcard with Napoleon on his horse?"

"From Paris," said a sulky Aunt Violet, who herself had only been to Fatima, with the Union of Flemish Woman Teachers. She had brought back a ceramic cockerel, colored Prussian blue, which Uncle Armand had carried in his arms to the chicken coop, where he had fallen asleep, cackling drunkenly. "About ten years ago, I think."

"Oh, what a fool I am!" said Meerke. "It isn't all that difficult. How old are you now, Louis?"

"Eleven last April," he said grudgingly.

"All you have to do is count. Nine months extra. Good grief, what a numbskull I am sometimes." Meerke and Aunt Violet both started to count, Aunt Violet ticking off her fingertips with a ring finger that had never worn a ring, would never wear one.

"But, Mother," she exclaimed shrilly, "I remember now, Constance sent the card on the fifteenth of July, because she wrote that the Parisians had danced in the streets on the *Quatorze-Juillet* and that she had danced with them celebrating the fall of the Bastille in 1789. Staf went on at her later for having danced with a Tunisian."

"That was the first time your Mama had been out of Belgium. She was so nervous! She was climbing the wall! 'What shall I wear if we go to the opera? You can never tell. Or to the Folies-Bergère, all the newlyweds go there.' It was the loveliest day of her life."

"Your father was happy as well then," said Aunt Violet. "They held hands all the time, it was all 'my sweetheart' this, 'my angel' that. But they still came back home earlier than expected."

"Too much of a good thing, no doubt," said she who had given birth to Mama.

Mama first saw Papa, Constance Bossuyt first saw Staf Seynaeve, on the train from Walle to Ghent. Bastegem railway station done up with ivy and rose bushes formed the backdrop. Constance boarded the train with Ghislaine, the paint dealer's daughter, who died four years later from cancer of the liver although the poor thing had never drunk a drop of alcohol or even eaten chocolate.

Papa was going to the printing college. And Constance to the teachers' training college because her father, Basiel Bossuyt, keeper of the canal locks, had summoned his wife on his deathbed (following his fall from an apple tree) and said, "Make sure, Amelie, that all five of them go into the Civil Service. Except Berenice, she'll probably end up in the convent anyway. But the other two girls should go into education, lots of holidays, it's a decent job. And on top of that you learn things along with the children every day." (The marrow was leaking out of his spinal column, and you can't fix it.)

Then came the divine, because predestined, moment when Constance's glance crossed that of Staf while she, flippant, tittering, saucy young country girl, was being the most talkative in the compartment (in the middle of the train, for reasons of safety). The spirited young maid took note of the fact that the freckled young man had a pound bag of Lutti caramels on his lap. He munches steadily, cheeks bulging. Week by week this continues, and each time her mouth waters. How could the sweet-toothed boy not notice the greedy eyes being made by the sweet-toothed girl? Week followed week and finally Papa said, "You're giving my Luttis a funny look. Would you like one?" The first words from Cupid's quiver. Ghislaine found the whole thing hardly *comme il faut,* but Constance accepts a Lutti and it melts in the little sweetwater lake of her mouth and he, almost surly with bashfulness, holds the crumpled paper bag out to her again, and this time she takes two. Outside Ghent station their trams separate.

"Au revoir, meneer." "Oh no, *à bientôt,"* says the student of the printing trade, verging on the reckless, and the next day he beckons her from a window wreathed in hissing steam and offers her, in addition to Luttis, cream puffs and sugared almonds, marzipan and peppermints, Ghislaine feeling obliged, so as not to cause offense, to do a little munching and sucking, too. The day after that it is plum tart, which he claims has been specially baked by his mother, but he must be soft in the head, we can read the decorative blue lettering printed at an angle across the corner of the serrated paper: "Pâtisserie Mérécy, Walle." It is ten miles from Bastegem to Ghent, the distance sufficing to win her over, and Constance rises to the bait each day that follows.

Ghislaine spills the beans to Berenice, Berenice to her parents. Basiel Bossuyt, who tries to cultivate the same pointed mustache as Wilhelm II, who, exiled to Holland, chops wood every morning in front of his villa, Basiel Bossuyt, who has fought the Kaiser by spying for the Allies from his ideal position as lockkeeper, says that the fellow from Walle is to present himself at the Lockkeeper's House next Sunday afternoon at half past four.

"He's one of these young gadabouts with too much pocket money, I'd better have a good look at him."

"They think they can do as they please with country girls," says Meerke.

"So he's from Walle," says Basiel Bossuyt reflectively, puffing on his pipe.

"Exactly," cries Meerke. "And too stupid to study in his home town, he must have been thrown out of every school in Walle, which is why he has to go by train to Ghent with bagfuls of caramels to lead young girls astray. She is far too young."

"Don't be so bigoted," says Basiel Bossuyt, but Meerke cannot leave it at that, and Father Mertens, who has only just been inducted, is consulted. "Madame Bossuyt, your husband is right to want to review the situation. It's far safer if the boy comes to your house than if he hangs around with your daughter after school in undesirable places in Ghent. Meanwhile I shall make inquiries from the Dean in Walle about the boy's family, and whether his intentions are serious."

The next day, flushing furiously, Constance muttered with assumed nonchalance that if it suited Staf he might like to come to the Lockkeeper's House for afternoon tea that Sunday.

How Papa must have pranced and capered among the thundering printing presses at his college! How the composing stick must have trembled in his ink-stained hand! That Sunday he brought a bunch of violets for his little dove, a bouquet of pink roses for Meerke—because he is from Walle, don't forget, Walle near the French border, you can sense that, a certain chic, *savoir-vivre,* frivolity, and pretension, in Walle they are men of the world, hence the pink roses—and a box of Dutch cigars for Mama's father, who indicates a chair and says, "Sit down. Do you play whist?" Mama's sisters come, oh, quite by chance, into the sitting room, and each offers a demure little hand to the sweet-toothed stranger. They find him odd and timid, they tell their sister, who thinks the same and wishes the whist-player (who, incidentally, is being trounced by her wily parents) would disappear as soon as possible. The next two Sundays he is back again. Roses and cigars, and for her a bouquet of wildflowers that he certainly never picked himself, as he claims.

She and Ghislaine go and sit in the last compartment of the train, but, armed with liqueur chocolates, fondants, and The Hague coffee caramels, he finds her.

The following Sunday she does not make an appearance in the sitting room of the Lockkeeper's House. From the bedroom she shares with Berenice she has seen him arrive, flowers clasped to chest, briefcase in one hand, striding toward her with those inexorable, inevitable, pointed shoes of his, toward her who dreams of an arrogant Southerner smoking cigarettes from a mother-of-pearl holder and brushing the smoke away from her flushed face with a wave of his hand, singing "Marinella" with the velvety voice of Tino Rossi, leaning a tuxedoed shoulder against the doorjamb, insolently, outrageously sure of himself, then saying huskily, "Come over here, gorgeous."

Clutching the doorlatch, she can hear him ask, "And where is Constance?" and the excuses of her mother, who must be wiping her hands on her apron, and the triumphant yelping of Violet, the subdued sweetness of Berenice, and then the composed tones of her father. "Constance is feeling a little under the weather." "Come on, now, Father," says Violet, "come on, why not tell him straight out? She doesn't want to see him, and that's that." Whereupon the flower-man swallows bravely and says that's a pity for he happens to have brought along a particularly fitting present. "Well, that's a different matter," says Meerke. "A lovely present," says the invisible suitor. Constance presses her shapely pink ear, her unruly brown curls, to the door, but now there is only the scraping of chairs, the rustle of wrapping paper, and then a many-voiced murmuring and clamoring of surprise and admiration. She tingles with curiosity. She is sure it is a ring, even though Staf is not the type to press his suit so insistently.

"Constance!"

"Leave me alone!" she bawls at the beige-painted door.

Her mother comes and puts her ear to the other side of the door panel.

"Leave me alone! Why does it have to be me? What have I got that other girls haven't?"

"You could at least come and say hello. If only for a minute. Have you no manners at all, you rude lump of a girl?"

"I won't!"

"Constance, am I going to have to come and get you?" roars her father.

"Let her be," says the present-bearer. "I'm going. I'm not staying. I understand, I understand only too well."

She is sitting in the front compartment. Ghislaine reports from her lookout post that Staf has made straight for the middle section of the train, looking to neither his right nor his left, making no attempt to find her. He has, however, brought a bag of Luttis with him, about half a pound. And the following Sunday, the last, she sees him again from the room she shares with Berenice, his step purposeful, his soft face sternly furrowed, the bouquet of roses wielded like a club in his hand. He sinks into the wicker armchair and talks. He wants to speak to her one last time. He wants to marry her. She has changed his whole life for the better. She has blinded him for the rest of his stay on earth.

"I don't want to see you!" shouts Mama from the staircase.

He jumps out of his chair, flings his arms around the bony, arthritic knees of her who brought his great love into the world. Basiel snorts with disapproval. He feels like knocking his smoldering pipe out on the kneeler's thin hair. "I can't help it," snivels the young Staf, who has sobbed like this only once before, when he wasn't picked for the match between the Walle Sporting Club Reserves and the Ghent Athletic Association Youth Eleven.

"Constance," orders Basiel Bossuyt.

"Constance, please!" shrieks Meerke.

Staf struggles clumsily to his feet and says with a grimace of despair, "So be it, then." He walks out of the house, climbs over the low thorn hedge, and disappears down the bank of the Leie. Ten minutes later, Mama watches Papa's straw hat with the blue band (the color of Our Lady) drifting by in the waters of the Leie, and doesn't turn a hair. Below her, meanwhile, her family has been following the progress of the silent one, spying on him from between the beanpoles. Sitting ten yards from the swirling, rushing waters of the lock, he whips out a pistol and holds it in front of him as if about to shoot perch in the river.

Berenice and Violet, the two little sisters, clatter up the stairs. "He's going to shoot himself!" they wail.

"His blood will be on our heads," shrieks Berenice.

"He won't do it."

"But supposing he does?"

"Then he would have done it by now. Have you heard any shooting?"

"Constance, am I going to have to come and get you?" bellows Basiel Bossuyt.

The weeping, wailing, and lamenting goes on for an hour, and according to the Bossuyts it is the pressure of their constant clamor alone that brings about the eventual drawing back of the bolt. But I know better. It was actually Holst, who had climbed up a ladder at the back of the house and swung himself in through the window. He chewed on a blade of grass and said to my confused mother, You silly, simple, little minx, aren't you ashamed of yourself? I am ashamed for you. For once there is someone who loves you, you should go down on your knees to that person and beg his forgiveness, yes, you who read books and see films about love and then sniffle with emotion, here you have someone who does love you, right under your dripping nose and you won't see it, you silly goose.— Why don't you marry me, Holst, I'd much rather do that. We could go to the priest and the town hall this very week.—There's nothing I'd like better, Constance, but as you know I have pledged my still yet ardent heart to Madame Laura of the Little Castle.—The one doesn't rule out the other. You can still stay pledged when we are married.—No, Constance, we cannot marry like that. And I do not say it lightly, you know, but that man is your destiny. Go to him, because any moment now there could be the sound of the shot, I have already heard it with my angel's-ears, which cannot tell the difference between yesterday and tomorrow. And I will do you a favor, I will be watching, day and night, unseen and unheard, over your first and probably your only child, he shall be named Louis or Lodewijk, whichever you like, and no harm shall ever befall him, at most a broken rib or two or a touch of flu.—Do you really mean that, Holst?—Word of honor, says Holst and folds his wings tight around his giant torso. Mama hears the sacred rustling, she draws back the bolt of the door and, with her dangerous gray goat's-eyes open wide, goes down to the lock, quite oblivious of the fact that her sisters are dragging her along, whooping like Apaches, then Constance Bossuyt falls into the arms of Staf Seynaeve, just as the pleasure boat *De Schelde* comes sailing down the Leie with catcalling whores and whistling yokels on board who bawl their coarse congratulations across to the loving couple. And as a result, he came to be born, he who would stand up to all the princes of darkness, he, Louis the Fair.

"Traveling, traveling," said Aunt Violet, "I dream of that as well."

"To dream is folly," said Meerke.

"Not to dream is, too," said Aunt Violet.

He walked with Raf past the deserted football field.

A lone man wearing a raincoat and a soft felt hat stood in the goal, legs spread wide. He was catching invisible balls in a nonexistent training session.

"Morning, Meneer Morrens," said Raf politely.

"Bastegem Excelsior!" shouted the man as if a goal had just been scored. "Second Division, here we come!" yelled Raf. The man smiled broadly. His coated tongue hung over his lower lip.

"You can say that again," he said and kicked at the dusty sand in front of the goal, a bare patch in the greenish-gray field. Then he patted one of the goalposts.

"Jantje Vandervelde," whispered Raf.

"It was right here," said the man, "in '35, that I saw Jantje Vandervelde score from a corner. That corner kick was such a beauty that it whistled straight into goal without anyone touching it."

"Will you be buying another Englishman, Meneer Morrens?" Raf's question was excessively obsequious, boding no good.

"This isn't the right moment, sonny," said the man, teetering on tiptoe. "Even though young English footballers are the best in the world."

"And all it means to you is writing out a small check, Meneer Morrens." The man touched his toes with his fingertips, the felt hat staying miraculously in place, the fingertips stirring the sand beside his shoes. Raf waited until the man had done ten vigorous kneebends and was standing up holding on to the goalpost.

"And it would be good for your English pronunciation, too, you have to keep a language up."

"Sonny," said the man. "Haven't I had enough trouble as it is?"

"You must be prepared to take the good with the bad," said Raf.

"We do need a left back badly, and I know a lovely little Chelsea player, he's a dream," said the man, dreamily.

"Well, what's stopping you . . . ?"

The man gave a deep sigh, let go of the post. "Never again," he said. He looked thoughtfully at Louis, who for an instant entertained wild hopes of becoming a left back. Later. Not a forward, I'm not fast enough for that.

"He's at boarding school," said Raf.

"Not for much longer," said Louis immediately.

"With the nuns," said Raf.

"That's a different story," said the man. "Physical fitness is something the nuns don't teach you. Running yourself into the ground and kicking a ball around at random, that they may know, but not physical fitness."

"And the English," said Raf, "they put physical fitness first from the beginning, right?"

"From childhood. And above all," he stuck a finger pointedly in Louis's direction, "the English pick their young boys from the working class, that's the most important thing of all, you get nothing but trouble from rich spoiled brats. No bluebloods. Absolutely not. Leave the bluebloods to their cricket and golf. Or tennis. I know what I'm talking about. I've tried it."

"Nobody can deny that," said Raf. "That last one you bought who gave you so much trouble, wasn't he a baron?"

"An *earl*," said the man in English, and his dreaminess got the upper hand of him again. He shook it off by putting his hands on his hips and performing a wide circular movement with his upper body. "An *earl*, and he was my ruination. They locked me up in Nieuwe Wandeling prison in Ghent for two weeks, on bread and water. If Notary Baelens hadn't mediated with his Liberals, and then with the Minister, I'd still be there along with all the murderers and the arsonists. Just because I stood up for Bastegem Excelsior and for all those young kids who were being exploited."

"But the earl wasn't being exploited," said Raf, pausing obsequiously.

"My only fault was that I was too friendly, too trusting, I had too much love for the rising generation, that's a big mistake nowadays."

He fixed his searching gaze on Raf for a long time, not liking what he saw. Raf grinned at him, then tugged Louis's sleeve.

"So long, Meneer Morrens, *good-bye.*"

"Second Division, here we come!" yelled the man after them and kicked the empty air furiously.

Mijnheer Morrens lived with his mother and had inherited millions from his father, a textile manufacturer. The great tragedy of his life was that after a shady incident on which Raf refused to dwell—"One day I'll tell you the whole story"—and which had landed him in jail, he was no longer welcome at his beloved team's training sessions or matches. All he was allowed to do was pump money into the club and attend board meetings.

Madame Laura wasn't there. The house was deathly quiet, resoundingly empty.

According to Farmer Santens, interrogated with skill by a ferreting Raf, she had driven up in a taxi one night during the week with some VIP and two ladyfriends. There had been the usual shrieking and clinking of glasses and blaring of dance music. From his field, at daybreak, Farmer Santens had spotted Holst half-dragging, half-carrying the elegant white-haired city gentleman to the taxi. And the two ladyfriends? Some three hours later they had driven off, all disheveled, in another taxi along with Madame Laura. How had Madame Laura looked? Nothing special, perhaps a little pale, but straight as a ramrod in her white coat. The one with the gray mink collar? No, the white fur coat, a sort of coney. Are you sure it was another taxi? Because if it was the same one, then they are probably all still together not far away, perhaps with Professor Vandenabeele, who is also something of a partygoer, since it's only natural for even the most learned and pious and upright of Flemings to like a little fling in the evening, having spent the rest of the day cutting up women's insides and then stitching them up and putting them back together again.

"Another taxi," said Raf reflectively when he and Louis were walking back to the village. "So they went back to her apartment in Brussels."

"Where is Holst now?" asked Louis.

"Oh, he'll be back roaming the woods in the fresh air to get rid of the smell of cigar smoke from Madame Laura's distinguished client. There's a lid for every pot, the saying goes, but I haven't seen much evidence of that yet. Take Holst now, a woodsman who has been sweet on Madame Laura ever since he was fourteen, he cleans her shoes, he worships the ground she walks on and if need be her clients as well, but what will come of it all? Especially as Madame Laura is such hot stuff."

Madame Laura, who blazes so feverishly inside that her coney coat bursts into flames, flames shoot from her midriff, gold and red and smoking as they did with Joan of Arc, who cried out in her agony for her confessor.

"She can't stay quietly at home for a single day," said Raf by the railway barrier.

"That's what Pascal says, the cause of all misfortune is that people can't stay in their rooms for twenty-four hours."

"Pascal Geeraardijn?"

"No, the philosopher." Sister Kris had told them about him, about his calculating machine, about how Pascal had renounced his worldly life and how ill he had been, which accounted for his deep understanding of the misery and the greatness of man.

"She's so hot," said Raf, "that she couldn't even leave her own sisters alone," and Louis didn't understand that. It was probably something like the fierce, headstrong restlessness of Sister St. Gerolphe, who had been taken prisoner by the other Sisters because of her hot blood. Not leaving your own sisters alone, plaguing them, torturing them with your piety and the urgings of your soul.

uncle armand

*T*he evenings were getting cooler, and since winter was just around the corner Meerke was knitting a pullover for Uncle Omer, who would be coming back from the Albert Canal one of these days. Aunt Violet was folding and cutting up wrapping paper, which became metamorphosed into tight-fitting dust jackets for the books from the library. Louis was allowed to stick on the purple-edged labels, then she filled in the titles and the numbers with a rounded nib: *The Adventures of Brother Alfus, Father Discipline, How to Combat Our Egoism, The Conscript.* Louis's tongue was coated with a sticky film of glue. Aunt Violet had forbidden him to look inside the books, because they came from the adult section. He recognized *The Bliekaerts* by Edward Vermeulen, a book Papa must have read a dozen times. Vermeulen, also known as Uncle Ed, was one of Papa's favorite writers because he invariably wrote the line "Of our people for our people" under all his titles. His books were full of countryfolk who fell into sudden rages and banged their fists on the table so that the pans danced, uttering curses and imprecations. *The Madman of Poplar Court.*

"Later on, once you have learned proper discrimination, you can read what you like. Right now, unsuitable books can do nothing but harm to your soul," said Aunt Violet.

"If you want to read something instructive, you'll find a pile of books from Uncle Omer's student days upstairs. History and geography," said Meerke.

"I know all the capitals of Europe," said Louis and began rattling them off. He had just reached Lithuania Kaunas, Latvia Riga, when Uncle Armand came stumbling in. Immediately Meerke stood up. "We waited for you. I just have to do the cutlets."

Uncle Armand flopped into the squeaking wicker armchair, glassy-eyed, drooling. *"Olala, olala,"* he gasped and smoothed his shiny flat black hair even flatter. "So I got home after all." A satisfied expression slid across his face. He made a vain attempt to untie his boots. Louis wanted to help but before he had time to move Aunt Violet said, "Pretend you don't see him." Meerke clattered about with her pots and pans. Uncle Armand slept.

"Poland Warsaw, Rumania Bucharest, Hungary Budapest . . ."

"Picardy," said a voice drunk with sleep. The folding and the rustling of Aunt Violet's library paper.

"Pi-car-dy." With an effort Uncle Armand dragged his bloodshot eyes wide open, commanded, "Well, mister know-it-all, what is the capital of Picardy? No, first question: Where is Picardy?"

Scanning the map of Europe with a swift pair of field glasses, the political map, scale one hundred and twenty-eight million. To the right in egg-yellow: Russia, Norway in pink like Belgium and Greece, Finland, France, and Poland in the green of growing oats, nondescript little wine-red dots: Monaco, Andorra, Danzig, then a tiny little lamb's-lettuce leaf: Luxembourg.

Pi-Picardy.

"It's not part of our continent," said Louis. Uncle Armand laughed like the Madman of Poplar Court, the laugh choked off in a guttural rattle.

"Let him be," said Meerke, coming in with the plates.

"Pretend you don't hear him," said Aunt Violet.

Humiliated again, even here, even now. At the pinnacle of his powers the geographer was laid low. If the Germans had divided Austria (colored red-ocher) or Czechoslovakia (violet) in recent months, splitting them up into countries with new capitals, why weren't we told about it at the Institute? Or perhaps I'd have heard about it on the radio a long time ago if I hadn't always been tuned in to the Ramblers and dancing around to their music. Helpless, enraged Mercator.

"Picardy doesn't exist," he said defiantly. "Picardy," he bleated scornfully.

"Oh no?" Uncle Armand was wide awake now, took out a cigarette, held it against the red-hot stovepipe. "Shall I sing you the national anthem of Picardy?" he said, smiling sardonically.

Aunt Violet clutched a pile of dust-jacketed books to her chest. The balcony of Europe. Where on earth could that little piece of confetti, Picardy, be? The old Hottentot was still sneering. He's made a fool out of me.

"In Australia there are koalas, pandas, and kangaroos," said Louis. Uncle Armand, gnawing at his cutlet, held the crooked little bone, a boomerang, delicately in front of his chin. "That's true, but that isn't what I asked you."

"All right then, where is Picardy?" said Louis resignedly.

"Pay attention, now. On the road to Hingene, just past the Mills, the first road to the right, after the poplars, directly opposite the tileworks."

"And that's where they empty his pockets without his noticing, the drunken oaf."

Aunt Violet ate her fourth cutlet ("They are so tiny"), a small diamond of fat twinkling in the dimple of her chin.

The fact that Uncle Armand, who was almost forty years old and had studied agricultural engineering, should have pulled such a fast one on him, should have placed that disgusting café, the Picardy, on a par with those mysterious, beckoning, melodious capitals of a multicolored Europe, made Louis tremble with rage. *Toujours sourire.*

"I've been to the Little Castle," he said.

"What little castle?" asked Aunt Violet, as if she didn't know, as if he had meant Castel Gandolfo.

"The one belonging to Madame Laura, the hot lady."

Meerke's head jerked up, Aunt Violet's lower lip sagged, her crumbling teeth like pieces of turnip.

"Nondedju," exclaimed Uncle Armand. "The hot lady?"

"Everyone knows that," said Louis.

"Nondedju, nondedju."

Aunt Violet wanted to say something, looked desperately at her mother, who asked, "What did you go there for?"

"To say hello to Madame Laura."

Uncle Armand's regular face with its greasy lips and the gray-green irises in the bloodshot whites of his eyes might charm snakes and women and farmers, keep them in his thrall, but not me. Aunt Violet drew a deep breath through flared nostrils.

"And what did she say?" asked Uncle Armand.

"She wasn't at home." (Alas, alas.)

"You have no business there," said Uncle Armand as if to a grown-up, and wiped his lips with the sleeve of his Sunday jacket, something he would never do in the Picardy, where he is known as a dandy, a country squire with charm and good manners, a Willem van Gulik, the martial canon who led the Flemish knights at the Battle of the Golden Spurs in 1302.

"She left in a taxi," said Louis.

"Let's change the subject," exclaimed Meerke.

Later, sobered up a little, Uncle Armand tested him some more. "Who is the president of France?"

"Daladier."

"Wrong! It's Leclerc with his stupid mustache. And who's top dog in Italy?"

"Mussolini."

"Wrong again. You don't know anything. What do those Sisters teach you? The highest authority there is still King Victor Emmanuel, that little runt! And Spain?"

"Franco."

"Right. The Generalissimo. A smart little bugger. You wouldn't think, what with that little rat's-face under his cap, but he's done his homework, Franco has. He got all that gold back, deposited in the Banque de France before the Civil War as security for the Republic. And now the French have been forced to recognize his government as legal, the gold has gone to the only legal financial body, do you follow me? And Japan?"

"Hiranuma."

"Correct. You do know your stuff."

"He's first in his class in Geography," said Meerke.

"A lot of good that'll do him. Geography keeps changing like the weather outside. Not even I can follow it these days. He'd be much better off starting to learn German, because tomorrow or the next day they'll be standing right here in this kitchen. How do you say 'ham' in German, Ludwig?"

Louis hated Uncle Armand, the failed engineer who had been "in the Civil Service" and had been kicked out on account of his disgusting drunkenness. Papa was right, people who drink like fish, like Armand Bossuyt, like most Frenchmen for that matter, ought to be locked up in labor camps, which is what Hitler's doing, and Hitler's never so much as touched a glass of alcohol, as an example to his resurgent people.

" 'Ham' in German was what I asked."

"Schinken!"

"Nein!" roared Uncle Armand. *"Schweine-*poop-*fleisch!"*

And Aunt Violet, bloated virgin, laughed along with him. Even Meerke could not suppress a smile.

Later Meerke took off the shoes of her son, who was snoring in the wicker armchair. "Quick, upstairs with you," she said to Louis, "you with your dirty talk. Where did you learn that dirty talk, from that hot Madame Laura? You're either keeping bad company in this village or else you're bad yourself."

"There aren't any real children left these days," said Aunt Violet. Uncle Armand gave a raucous snore, dreaming of loose women behind wine-red curtains who shrieked with laughter as he told the story of how he had used his knowledge of German to wipe the floor with that little smart-aleck nephew of his.

a carpenter

Mama had telephoned again, and again she had sent Louis incredible amounts of love, she was resting and getting better, but there were still some complications, so Louis was going to have to stay on a bit longer with his Aunt and his Grandmother, but, then, she knew that he liked it there. Yes, those were her exact words from across the Alps, and now off you go to Jules the carpenter and say, "Jules, I've been sent by my Aunt for one of your little bottles, because she is having her heart spasms again."

"But I don't know him."

"He won't bite you."

"What if the little bottle isn't ready?"

"His little bottles are always ready. Louis, you're a big boy now. Go and fetch that little bottle and bring it here. And don't you dare try any, or else you'll end up in the hospital for months with great big holes in your stomach. And if you should run across Raf, just say to him, 'My Aunt doesn't want you to set foot in our house ever again.' No need for explanations. If he must go to Madame Laura's house, let him suffer the consequences all by himself."

185

There was a smell of pigs in front of the carpenter's house, but in the lean-to greenhouse, which was as ramshackle as if it had been built after one of Dobbelaere's drawings (the dream buildings designed on paper in the Institute could be found scattered all over the world if one only looked hard enough for them), there was a strong smell of freshly sawn wood. Louis was standing in the doorway facing the mountains of wood shavings, the carpenter's benches, the shiny pruning saw, the rows of dusty chisels, when he heard a loud squeal behind him, a badly oiled gate or a piglet. A stooping figure in a black cloth coat was running as if battling against a storm, hugging the length of the outside wall of the chimney, and then he was gone, swallowed up by the lumpy limewashed wall, the man, his black, wide-brimmed hat, and the red-and-white checked towel or piece of curtain he had been clutching to his face with both hands.

"Hello." Jules the carpenter came through the orchard toward him, tall, leathery-skinned, with a bushy white mustache. He was chewing tobacco. In the kitchen he kicked off his clogs. "Sit down. How is our Vi?"

The kitchen walls were steamy with the sour stench of pigs. On the stove, on the table, on the windowsills stood little bottles, jars, retorts, most of them apparently filled with urine. Louis sat down next to a birdcage in which a dozen or so white mice were scampering about, making a noise not unlike the one the Zorro-like character had made a little earlier, though thinner and less tormented.

"Let's see, now," growled Jules and handed Louis a dusty, damp, moss-green little bottle with a wet rag for a stopper. "That's for Vi." He grasped Louis's chin between two fingers and said, "Celery. You eat celery by the pound, and you'll be better before the month is out."

"But I'm not sick."

"That's what you think. You can't fool me."

"Did my aunt or uncle say that I was sick?"

"They didn't have to say." The two fingers did not let go, a vise. The crazy pale gaze of the carpenter did not let go, either, he's a sorcerer, he's taking possession of my soul. Help me, Holst! I should never have come here alone. Louis wrenched his chin free, caught sight of himself in an oval mirror wreathed with ivory flowers and twigs, a boy with hair flat and wet with sweat, the bumpy nose of the Seynaeves, an open, shapeless, thin-lipped mouth.

"Celery and leeks," said the carpenter, "as much as you can, together with this here." Louis took a small bulging envelope, the size of a visiting card.

"A teaspoonful in boiling water, on an empty stomach. You can put in a lump of sugar if it's too bitter for you. Every Sunday for three months. And you'll sleep like a baby, all your dark thoughts will vanish."

The mice listened with little heads on one side, little ears flattened.

"It's ten francs for the little bottle. Your powders are a present."

Louis stammered. "She said nothing . . . my aunt . . . didn't give me any money."

Jules's white mustache curled upward. "It's always the same with our Vi. But I'll get my ten francs, all right. Even if I have to come and fetch them with my whip."

Next to the ivory mirror, which had been either stolen from some grand mansion or bought at an auction, hung the sepia-colored photograph of a priest with a little oil lamp burning underneath. "Father van Haecke," said Jules. "I bet they've never even heard of him in Walle. Right? But one day they'll erect a church to that man, perhaps even a basilica, the day the government flings all those doctors and surgeons with their murderous ways into jail. No one has done Belgium so much harm, no one has the deaths of so many children on their conscience as that bunch, not even the Jews." It was a text he was reciting, reading it out from the newspaper in his brain. "And because he denounced them and preached about their doings, they drove Father van Haecke to his grave. But his body will be disinterred and laid under marble in a basilica."

As if to say amen to this, there was the scraping of a shoe against the floorboards overhead. The carpenter shot an anxious look at the smoke-blackened ceiling. His wordless prayer was heard. All remained still above. He put a fresh plug of chewing tobacco into his mouth. "If you can't give it up altogether, my boy," said he, chewing slowly, with emphasis, "it's best to pull it."

Louis began to tremble. To his horror, the pigfood-smelling carpenter bent forward, closer to him. Above them Zorro was kneeling and pressing his ear to the boards.

"Just pull it, your little pigeon's-eggs can stand it. Don't worry, you won't do what the doctors say and turn into an albino, but then they were spawned by Satan and Kaassimolar."

"Who?"

"Kaassimolar, the hound of hell, the chief of the Liberals, commander of thirty-six legions."

Louis wished he could throw the miracle bottle and the herbal powders at the carpenter's head or at the oil lamp with its wooly wisp of smoke, grab the hand of his disreputable friend Raf, and run away. Where had his guardian angel gone? The carpenter spread his knees, placed one hand on the cage of listening mice.

"Yes, you're Constance's child, that's for sure, the same sly look. Sly but blind. Many's the time I've said to her, 'Constance, you delude yourself, whatever you do. You know where to find the truth in life, but you wallow about happily in lies and deceit.' But does she listen? No. She's been heard to say, and in the presence of witnesses, too, 'I refuse to listen to Jules, I have more faith in the Farmer's Almanac!' And those words will never be wiped away, they are recorded for all time. She refused to listen, and you can see the upshot. Not even a second litter!

"I don't like saying it, but she's going to have to forgo a great deal more. Not because of galloping consumption, or piles or cancer, but because of herself. Because the Germans are coming here with their Antichrist, they and the Communists, and Constance won't have the strength of mind to resist. She wasn't even able to resist when the test amounted to nothing more than a fart in a bottle. Because she turned her body and soul over to one of those young doctors no more than three weeks out of university who sang dance tunes from the radio while he scraped about in her insides."

The carpenter was off his head. Louis, who didn't want to hear any more, said quickly, "Are the Germans going to come, then?"

"The Germans have the best doctors in the world, the best mechanics, the best engineers. Sent by Belial in tanks breathing fire and brimstone, Belial, who commands eighty legions and now calls himself Marshal Göring."

It was outrageous that this crazy fanatic should ever have been allowed to follow the calling of Jesus' foster father. In the Middle Ages the carpenters' guild would have jeered and booted him out of the guildhall. Through the dusty window three partridges could be seen hanging from the barn door. They have to be left hanging for three or four days. "And yet there has never been so much diphtheria in Germany, so much measles, diarrhea, infantile paralysis. The men collapse in the fields. But they don't put that in the papers."

The man above Jules's head shifted an elbow or a knee on the floorboards. Jules looked at the spot where the noise had come from. "He can't sleep," he said, concerned.

"But are the Germans going to come to Belgium or not?"

"Yes. Regardless. They can't do anything else. Their Antichrist has ordered them to. It's all laid down in black and white. They may be poisoned with pills and chemical medicines, but they'll turn up, all right. Sure enough. Daladier and Chamberlain don't believe it. They'd do better to read the old books, it's all been foretold. And those three Bossuyt sisters who laugh at me and call me a quack will have to believe in them, too, they'll be gnawing the bark off the trees for food."

"They don't laugh at you!"

"Oh no? Your mother most of all! All I did was my duty, giving aid and assistance whenever they came pleading, 'Jules, you're the only one who can help us!' "

"With what?"

"Later," said the carpenter. "Later I'll tell the world how I helped all three of them."

"Tell me now," ordered Louis. Acknowledging the ice-cold command of Duke Louis the Fair, the quack said almost meekly, "With their women's complaints." Louis looked away from him.

"I cured all three of them," said Jules. "And I asked all three of them, one by one, to marry me after the death of my Bertha, and all three, one by one, laughed at me, your mother most of all."

"Aunt Violet, too?" exclaimed Louis.

"Yes. Vi, too."

It was hilarious and unthinkable at the same time.

"You don't sleep in the same bed as she does, do you? Don't laugh, snotty-nose. Unless you want to laugh along with all those other young boys who have wasted away in the flower of their youth with their blood pressure falling away to nothing because the sweat of women had mingled with their sweat. Why do you think most women live so much longer than men? Because they drain and absorb the fluid from the bodies of young boys!"

Suddenly it came to Louis (like a whisper through the floorboards from the man over Jules's head) that this raving man was right after all, he remembered in a flash that in the twenties a little Rumanian boy had turned up at the Bossuyts' home, sent by a refugees' association, and that this little boy had slept in Aunt Violet's bed, and that Aunt Violet and Meerke had reported incredulously and mockingly that the little boy had clambered out of his new foster mother's, Aunt Violet's, bed the first night and had stolen to a corner of the pitch-dark room and there let go a whistling wind, for that's what he had been taught to do by his genteel, murdered Rumanian parents. And that child, once back in his homeland, had never once replied to any of Aunt Violet's dozen or so letters, which meant he must have been wasting away over there in the East, incurably infected by the poisonous, moist exhalations from Aunt Violet's body. Aunt Violet, who still had a Rumanian dictionary and who could recite the whole of the Hail Mary in Rumanian. Louis resolved not to sit too long beside her on the sofa in the future.

"How is Berenice?"

"Fine."

"Fine? What sort of answer is that?"

"I haven't seen her for quite a long time."

"Of those three she's the one I would most have liked to marry. But no, she had to go get married to a Jewish heretic, just to affront me." He fell into an aggrieved silence. Above them the soft shuffling of stockinged feet. "First Berenice, then Violet, and finally Constance. How is Constance? I often think of her. She was nervous as a girl, but she was good at collecting slugs." Louis took a deep breath. Mama and slugs. He felt like forcing the carpenter to explain, demanding an elucidation of what seemed to be an insult. The man noticed his surprise. "She was the quickest when it came to collecting slugs," he said, "because I used to give her two francs for twenty." He could see that Louis was still put out. "For cough syrup," he said as if to a little child. "Tell her when you see her, 'Jules says that no one else can collect slugs as quickly as you.' She'll be glad to hear that."

The mice went back to scrabbling and squeaking. That evening when he went secretly to the ironmonger's shop to see Raf, and sounded out his one and only Bastegem friend on the subject of the man who had hidden his face in a towel during his rapid flight past the house, Raf said, "That must have been Konrad, he was expelled from Germany."

Louis started. "A spy?"

"Yes. All sorts of odd people came to Jules's house. Supposedly to learn Esperanto."

"Are they fifth columnists?"

"No, you ass. They're against Hitler."

"But they'll be thrown into jail when the Germans get here, or get shot!"

"Put up against the wall," said Raf. "Although by that time . . ."

"Won't be long now."

"Ages yet."

Louis bet his friend that Belgium's neutrality would be violated, as the papers put it, within three months. He staked twelve marbles, polished to a perfect roundness, big marbles obedient to his fingers, alabaster eyeballs in the satin bag with the knotted silver lingerie ribbon Mama herself had sewn for him. If Raf lost, he would hand over to Louis what he had stolen from Madame Laura's dustbin. They slapped the palms of their hands together hard.

"Who's there?" called a man's frightened voice. Raf pushed Louis behind a rack of speckled cooking pans. Rubber boots swished through the storeroom. Raf's father, the son-beater-with-a-headache, shifted a table, then vanished. He had to report for duty next week, said Raf, all reserve noncommissioned gunners were needed to do their bit at the

Liège Water Display, where they would dress up as Roman soldiers and escort the chariots. There would be Algerian horsemen there, too, who would perform a *fantasia,* burnouses flapping as they rode screeching and firing volleys into the air. It was a shrewd move that would actually be bringing crack French troops onto Belgian soil, thus helping to strengthen our border defenses.

On the way home Louis had felt like throwing away the envelope Jules
had given him, but what a stroke of luck he didn't, because through
some misunderstanding—one of how many?—the carpenter had got it
wrong. You wondered how someone like him could ever have produced
a wardrobe that didn't fall to pieces, a table that didn't wobble. The
powdered weeds or herbs had been concocted for Meerke and her dark
thoughts. She sipped the brew, features contorted wryly. Louis did not
let on that she was allowed to add a lump of sugar. From time to time,
muttering, she read out snippets from the *Zondagsvriend,* her weekly magazine.

" 'Delicate health.' My family has never been anything but delicate.
Fortunes we've paid out on Jules's powders and homemade pills. 'Change
of life. A critical period for the man as well as the woman. Keeps melancholy thoughts at bay. When tired organs no longer function regularly.
Blood overloaded by food waste products and poisons produced by the
body itself.' " (She read from the *Zondagsvriend* without her spectacles.)
" 'Physically and mentally down? Kruschen Salts coax liver and kidneys

into eliminating all impurities gently but surely, melancholy is chased away, one hundred and twenty small measures for twenty-two francs.' "

"They print nothing but lies, my dear. Of course, the Germans are going to come for our poor Belgium and our King, just like in '14–'18, uhlans on horseback leading the tanks, and they won't have to ask the way anywhere in our nine provinces, because our King Albert got himself married to a German, and it's a good thing that old bungler isn't alive today to see her bestowing her favors on all sorts of young favorites in his regiments, giving them presents of watches and cigarette cases with her name engraved on them, she buys them by the dozen because of the extra discount she gets on top of the one she gets anyway as a princess. And, of course, she talks to Hitler on the telephone every evening: 'Führer, these Belgians are fond of the good life, their army is weak, the men thumb their noses at their officers, you just come along whenever you feel like it, Führer, and annex this little piece of land to your Reich, then the North Sea will be your frontier.'

"The legs is where it all starts. You want to stand up, but your legs are all cotton wool. You say a little prayer. But that doesn't put any life into your calves. There's fifty pounds hanging on each leg. It was the legs that told me it was going to be twins. Marc and Mariette. Marc arrived a quarter of an hour earlier, it wasn't much, but still, I was glad later on that he'd had that extra quarter-hour of life. In those days pleurisy, especially galloping pleurisy, was merciless. When our Omer was born, my Basiel wanted to call him Marc again. But I wouldn't have it.

"I never wanted what Basiel wanted. It wasn't till the very end, when he had his rosary in his hands, that day with the apple tree, that I realized how much I'd henpecked him all his life. I was jealous of his shadow. 'How long will you be staying out tonight, Basiel?' 'You'll see when I come back,' he'd say. 'How long, I want to know!' I'd say in my jealous rage. 'You want to know to the minute?' he'd shout, and I: 'Yes, yes, yes! To the very minute!' He wasn't even allowed to stay away too long when he went to pick food for the rabbits, I would work out how many minutes it should take, how many steps there and back, and if he wasn't back in time I would pretend not to see him standing there holding his sickle and the clover, and then he would kick his clogs off so violently that I thought each time that they would split in two.

"And when they transferred him here to the lock at Bastegem, that wasn't his choice, because I made the application behind his back and signed "Basiel Bossuyt, Lockkeeper," and then it was too late, he wouldn't dare rub his superiors the wrong way by withdrawing the application, and for just ten francs a month more I made him move here to

Bastegem, where he didn't know anybody and didn't have anyone to play cards with, for the extra ten francs I cut off his air.

"And here in Bastegem I watched him taking longer and longer to polish his boots, he liked to do that, it was a hangover from his army days, his shoes shone so much you could see yourself in them, and it's good for your mind, too, he used to say, when you clean your shoes you can do a lot of thinking, and then, of course, I had to say, 'All you should be thinking about is me and our children, nothing else!'

"He had a sweet tooth, that's why he got along so well with your father, the two of them were always nibbling things together. And he would finish up all the buttermilk porridge with brown sugar if the children left any, quick, quick behind my back, so the children would leave some for him on purpose. It was only after his funeral that they started cleaning their plates. And to think that I had slapped them for that! In those days it was all either crying or slapping, and I couldn't cry in those days, it was as if I'd taken all the sorrow of Belgium upon myself.

"I was strict with myself, I'd been taught no better at home, and that's why I was strict with him, and he, in turn, was strict with the children, the least little thing and they would get the feel of his hand, and I was all for it, except when it came to Armand, he was my eldest and so I always favored him, and that's why he's such a boozer and a wet rag now, who can't stand on his own two feet. I spoiled him by being too good to him, there's no denying that, and that's just what Basiel said would happen, and he's happy now because he was never sent to Purgatory but went straight to Heaven.

"Why couldn't I stand it when he was happy about something that didn't have to do with me? I was even envious of the medals he was given for reporting the presence of German *Landsturm* soldiers, from Lorraine they were, in the cornfields, during the retreat at the end of the war. When he went off to veterans' reunions and checked in the mirror to see that his decorations were on straight, any other woman would have been proud of a man who had received that honor from His Majesty himself, but all I wanted was to tear his mustache off because he was smiling at himself in the mirror the way I imagined he smiled when he was chasing some loose woman. What was it that made me henpeck him his whole life long, and why did he never once box my ears, he easily could have, he weighed nearly seventy pounds more than I did, was it because he enjoyed being treated like dirt? Because instead of being an important person in the village, for that was what being a lockkeeper meant in those days, he'd been turned into a downtrodden stay-at-home with a wife who kept knocking him off his pedestal, or maybe it was, I can hardly believe it, because he forgave me, because he loved me until the day he died."

She lit the dim little lamp on the windowsill, then sat soaking her corns in the Rodell Saltrates. "We've fallen on terrible times," she said. "And my punishment is being saddled with Violet until the day *I* die."

She picked at her toes to release those dratted, blasted roots. "Thank goodness Father Mertens stands by us. Never forget, Louis, governments will come and go for the rest of your life, but the Church will go on forever, and anyone who turns against the Church will perish."

_____*god's great outdoors*

*U*ncle Omer stuck his hand with the glittering wristwatch into the air and clicked his heels. *"Heil Hitler!"* he cried and dropped his suitcase.

"Idiot," said Aunt Violet fondly.

Uncle Omer wore black horn-rimmed spectacles that greatly magnified his moist brown eyes. "You're going to grow as tall as your father," he said. It was meant as a dig, because Papa was not all that tall, something Louis had discovered in recent weeks, for once back in Walle, on the street, the man who had cut so impressive a figure on the the Institute playground had shrunk to no more than average size next to Tetje's father or the woman from the bakery.

"Where is our Armand?" cried Uncle Omer.

"He's a bit late," said Meerke.

"Always the same," said Aunt Violet and helped Uncle Omer out of his jacket, which had modern gussets in the back. Then she fetched his uniform from his suitcase, examined it, and hung it over a chair.

"Hitler is going to take a little breather from his annexations," said Uncle Omer, with his full, girlish lips. "He's shown the world what he's

196

able to do and what he's prepared to do, so that's that for a while. He's too shrewd to bite off more than he can chew." Uncle Omer almost spoke High Flemish, he had been a schoolmaster at Our Lady of the Immaculate Conception, a boarding school in Deinze. "And if any German generals start letting their successes go to their heads, Hitler'll put his foot down. What he cares about first and foremost is full employment, then enough food for his people. It's not like here, where our ministers can only think of lining their own pockets and finding jobs for their pals."

He slapped Louis's thigh. "Are those little nuns still so crazy about you?"

"About me?"

"Come off it, young 'un, didn't I visit you there last year? Those little nuns were dancing attendance on you as if you were the infant in the manger! But good God, what do I see now? He's growing a mustache!"

"Me?" Involuntarily, Louis's hand shot to his upper lip. It was totally untrue.

"It may not amount to much yet, but it certainly doesn't go with short pants. Violet, we'll have to outfit him with a pair of my knickerbockers."

Incredulous, Louis stared at his uncle standing there joking with him as with an equal, when only last year he had spanked him in the garage like a little one.

"How is your mama?"

"Her baby is dead." Obligatory silence.

Uncle Omer ran his hand over his hair, wiped his glistening fingers on the purple-and-green flowered cushion beside him on the sofa.

"Come on," he said. "Let's go out, Louis, out into God's great outdoors!"

"We eat at seven," said Aunt Violet. "Mutton stew, you don't get that on the Albert Canal."

Across the fields. They talked about Bartali, who was sure to win the Tour de France again this year, no one could hold a candle to him. Felicien Vervaecke would win the race against the clock, that was also a foregone conclusion, last year he beat Bartali by two minutes. And how childish the French can be, you remember last year Magne and Leducq reached the Parc des Princes at the same time and rode across the finish line arm in arm.

Uncle Omer spread his arms wide, his chest swelled, his suspenders seemed about to burst asunder, he snuffled like a horse.

"Bastegem air," he said. "*Godverdomme*, you don't get that in Kempen!"

Swearing! The moral degeneration of our Flemish youth, herded together in barracks without supervision, without spiritual instruction, had infected even Uncle Omer, he who only last year had marched at the head of the procession on St. Jan Berchman's Day carrying a gigantic banner with "PX" and "KSA East Flanders" embroidered on it, the photograph was on Meerke's bedside table, Uncle Omer in breeches with shoulder strap and neckerchief, in rigid marching step, knee raised, side by side with choirboys bearing the actual heart of the blessed Jan Berchmans on a velvet cushion, and behind them, freezing in the wind, the virgins in robes and white wings carrying the statue of Our Lady of Diest, before which the saint had knelt every day for hours.

"Your guardian angel heard you swear, Uncle."

"Oh, I don't think he could have been too surprised. If I have a guardian angel, that is."

"But everybody has one. Even heathens. They just don't know it."

"I don't actually see my guardian angel all that often these days. Do you see yours?"

"Sometimes," said Louis, embarrassed.

"What's he look like?" asked Uncle Omer in a matter-of-fact voice, the one he'd used before in the classroom.

They stopped beside a ditch from which steam was rising. There was going to be a thunderstorm. "Oh God," said Uncle Omer in a muffled voice and bent over pretending to tie a shoelace. A red sports car drove past them, a blonde woman at the wheel.

Her hair was streaming in the wind, she had the hollow cheeks of Marlene Dietrich, for one frozen moment her slanting, pale-blue, mascara-rimmed eyes rested on Louis. The gloves on the wheel were of canary-yellow leather, she wore a camelhair coat with a turned-up collar trimmed with long fur. The blood-red lips were turned down, with disapproval or with the effort of concentrating on the road that wound its way between the willows and the white poplars. She was driving toward her little castle. It started to rain, big, cool drops.

"Just look at that," said Uncle Omer. The red car shot along the tree-lined road, disappearing behind the flag-bedecked sanatorium.

"One of these days when she's tipsy she'll drive straight into a tree," said Uncle Omer.

"Then she'll be rid of them all."

"Of whom?"

"Of those men."

Uncle Omer hitched up his trouser legs and jumped over a small ditch. "Which men?"

"All those men who want to marry her."

"There aren't that many."

"Uncle Armand, for instance."

"Your Uncle Armand," said Uncle Omer, "is a ro-man-tic soul."

What did that mean? That he read dirty French novels. Romance is French. We are Germanic. That is how God has divided the earth. Different races, some dearer to His heart, for reasons He alone can tell. So Madame Laura brought out the ro-man-tic, the raw-man-tic soul of men.

"Is romantic good or bad?"

"At his age, very bad," said Uncle Omer. "Did she see me?"

"I don't think so."

"Are you sure?"

"She might have seen you but she didn't recognize you. Otherwise she would have stopped her car."

"Perhaps she was in a hurry to get home." Uncle Omer quickened his pace, took a path leading toward the tree-lined road.

"Are we going to her place?"

"No. Not on your life."

Louis had trouble keeping up with him.

"I think she was probably doing some smuggling again, she must have just come from the Dutch border. Because she was driving in such a hurry. I'd drive like that if I had a carload of diamonds. That's what it is, she's heading for home with a load of Dutch diamonds in her panties."

That must hurt, must scrape your skin inside your panties, or did she wrap them up first in chamois or in cotton wool? Probably. Now Louis understood why Raf had looked so hard for Madame Laura's panties, a precious stone could easily have been stuck in them.

"There wasn't anyone sitting beside her in the car, was there?"

"No, Uncle."

"Not in the back, either?"

"Someone could have been lying down flat."

Again his uncle swore, stepped out even faster than on marches along the Albert Canal with all those Flemish soldiers of his, all of them reduced to degenerates, Godless blasphemers. For a moment Louis thought Uncle Omer was about to take shelter under the lime trees because the rain was coming down harder now, but instead his uncle made straight across the fields, crept panting under barbed wire, ran until he was within sight of the little castle. The sports car was parked in a lean-to shed. Holst came up, leaving sheep and goats baaing and bleating behind him in the stables.

"She's at home," said Uncle Omer.

"She's in bed listening to the radio," said Holst, and his heavyset figure led the way into a low, stuffy room in a small outbuilding. Holst was unshaven, his hair standing up in spikes. He hitched up his corduroy trousers and pointed to the cane chairs by the stove, turned his great back on them, and kicked off his clogs. The room was almost bare, one bicycle wheel hanging on the wall. A withered palm frond. White sand on the red tiles. A jug of milk with a purple-and-gold fly floating inside.

"Blast me," said Uncle Omer, suddenly speaking broad Flemish, "blast me if I didn't just think to myself, I'll go and say hello to Holst."

"You did right," said Holst and poured two small glasses of geneva for himself and for Uncle Omer.

"So she's listening to the radio."

"To the news, in three or four languages."

Rain, rain. The sheep. In his house Holst looked different, younger than he had in the car outside the Institute. He didn't seem to know his way around his own home, he poked the fire, looked for his slippers, kept his distance from the whitewashed walls and the windows, found a red bottle in the cherrywood cupboard, poured from it into a coffee cup, handed it to Louis.

"Here," he said. "You look like a drowned rat, that'll do you good." It was a bittersweet elderberry drink with lemon.

"I've got a hare for you, Omer, if you want it. Twenty francs."

"Fresh?"

"Day before yesterday. She doesn't want it. She's not eating."

"Something wrong with her insides?"

"Her!" exclaimed Holst.

They fell silent. Trees suddenly rustled. Shutters banged against a wall.

"She's following the situation on the radio," said Uncle Omer.

"You took some baby clothes to my mother," said Louis. Holst counted on his fingers. "Three rompers, four undershirts, two caps, one checked woolen cardigan. And not from some cheap shop, either, I saw the label, from a shop in the Avenue Louise in Brussels. Clothes fit for a royal prince."

"Did Madame Laura choose them?"

"She or one of her girls."

"But they didn't look new."

"She sat and played with them for a few days."

"But if she's got her ears glued to the radio," Uncle Omer said impatiently, "that must mean she knows something's up. Or is she listening to the stock exchange reports?"

"That, too."

"It's something to do with her lawyer," Uncle Omer concluded. "With that lawyer Baelens, who'd like to wipe the floor with Hitler all by himself in Brussels, who'd invade Germany right now, him and his Ardennes riflemen, if he could. It's on account of fellows like him that Belgium has had to mobilize, then demobilize again, nothing but misery at the State's expense."

The mention of the lawyer had a peculiar effect on Holst. He seized the poker and brandished it, his eyes lightened, the knuckles around the poker turned white, he picked up the bottle of elderberry syrup, drank from it, and coughed. Then he said calmly, "Lawyer this, lawyer that, I hear about nothing else."

"Does she still want to marry him?"

"Ask her yourself," said Holst. "Asking's free, and so's refusing."

Louis's guardian angel was feeling ill at ease, God was sending him signals and orders he didn't understand. Obviously, the heavenly host had failed to train Holst properly for the job of guardian angel.

In her bedroom Madame Laura was lying on her bed in her negligée, hair wet, playing with the diamonds in her lap. Now that she had no more baby clothes.

"She has enough to choose from," said Uncle Omer, "ministers, bankers, senators, she has only to lift a finger for someone to put a wedding ring on it. It all depends on who makes the first move. The lawyer, perhaps?"

"You," said Holst. "You're pissing me off."

Uncle Omer gave a start, held out his hand with the sparkling wristwatch in a gesture of appeal.

"Move your fat arse," said Holst. Uncle Omer got up.

"Get out of here," said Holst. Uncle Omer downed his glass of geneva, then said, "Laura Vandenghinste is not for the likes of you. Just you remember that."

"Mind your own business," Holst said expressionlessly.

Louis emptied his small cup of treacly sweetness. The rain was letting up. Holst nodded at Louis a few times. "Remember me to your mother."

"I won't forget," said Louis and winked at the giant, who, pockmarked, tanned like the palest gingerbread, continued to nod, then went off and brought back a hare with empty eyesockets. "A promise is a promise," he said.

Uncle Omer looked at the carcass, kept his hand at his side.

"Don't you like it, then?" asked Holst.

"I do, it's my purse that doesn't."

"Just take it, you can settle up with Madame Seynaeve."

Without asking, Uncle Omer picked up *Het Laatste Nieuws* from the table and wrapped the animal in it. Holst, who had killed the hare and also Mama's child, my little brother, Holst, who was responsible for the salvation of my soul, urgently wanted to tell me something crucial, but did not, because of Uncle Omer's presence.

"Mama is in Switzerland," said Louis.

"I can wait," said Holst. "I'm not pressed for twenty francs."

Probably Holst would telephone Mama this evening and tell her, "I met your son, Constance, he loves you, the child misses you, Constance, why are you hiding away in the Alps, why do you prefer the company of that nanny goat of a Madame Esquenet to that of, what's his name again, Louis?"

_____*a fig leaf*

When Louis had said his goodbyes to Meerke—much too early, because he still had to go and wait by his suitcase until Uncle Armand
had finished shaving in the kitchen—the mandolin ensemble Our En-
deavor played the song "Close Ranks!" on the radio. Then came a professor who related the true story of an okapi from the Belgian Congo that
had been refusing all nourishment since the German invasion of Poland,
an expression of unspeakable sorrow in the poor animal's eyes. The
director of the Paris Zoo had stayed up all night, together with eminent
veterinarians, bananas at the ready. But toward dawn the okapi, searching
in vain for a glimpse of the sun in the gray French sky, had given up the
ghost.

"How sad," said Meerke.

"That I'm going away?"

"That, too, Louis, that, too. No, but that poor little beast."

"Okapi steak today in Paris," said Uncle Armand, wiping flecks of foam
from his face.

Despite Meerke's ban, Raf appeared, walking slowly across the farmyard.

He moved like a girl. Louis said, "Just one more minute, please, Uncle Armand," and ran to his friend, who was standing next to Hector the turkey. "Hello, Hector," said Louis, "and *au revoir*, I'll never see you alive again." The turkey screeched, spread his wings, shook himself.

"What's the difference between a woman and the city of Bruges?" asked Raf.

"I don't know. Tell me."

"The city of Bruges only has a Blood Procession once a year." Raf burst out laughing, holding a small limp hand to his mouth, Hector outdoing him with a throat-rending cackle.

"I see," said Louis. But he didn't. Did women go to other blood processions in other countries several times a year? It was as if he were sitting inside a cube of frosted glass, with Raf in fits of laughter pressing his nose against it from outside.

"You can say what you like about me, but I'm a good sport," said Raf. "I heard over the radio this morning that they'll be getting tough in Poland any minute. The King and the Pope want to try and intervene, but Hitler doesn't give a damn about them. So this is for you, *voilà* . . ." He fumbled in his trouser pocket, stuck the scrap of silk with lace trimming into Louis's hand. Louis immediately put it into his coat pocket. No one had seen, not even Hector. "You won. The Germans are coming. You see, I'm a good sport."

"A man of his word," said Louis.

"Always been one. Who knows when we'll meet again? Take good care of Madame Laura's fig leaf."

"Sure you can spare it?"

"I've got two more at home," said Raf. They shook hands, Crusader Louis the Axe leaves his cowardly vassal behind in the rural backwater of Bastegem, surrounded by cows.

Meerke said, "Listen to me, Louis. Always do what your mama says, right away and no arguing."

Aunt Violet waddled along with them as far as the gate and said that Louis would make Meerke very pleased if he wrote her a *lettre de château*. Another puzzle. A letter from the castle. Madame Laura's castle, where she is standing on the steps dressed in white, smiling haughtily at her new bridegroom, the lawyer?

Aunt Violet read the puzzle in his face. "A nice letter, in good hand-writing, to thank Meerke for her hospitality. That's what we call a *lettre de château*," said she who would remain a schoolmistress and a librarian till the day she died.

Uncle Armand squeezed his head into a leather flying helmet, put on gloves, and climbed into the car he had been lent by Mireille from the Picardy. They waved at the house and at the dahlias and at full-to-bursting Aunt Violet who had just eaten half a pound of jellied pork with mustard to drown her sorrow at Louis's leaving.

"Hold tight," said Uncle Armand, "we're doing fifty!" He sounded the horn as they drove through the village. As they passed the Picardy, he slowed down, peered around, but there was no sign of life in that house of ill repute, dripping with rain, shutters drawn. "Next time I'll take you along," said Uncle Armand, "it's about time you learned something about the world. But not on a Saturday or a Sunday, because that riffraff from the racetrack comes then. No, an ordinary weekday. We'll have some fun, the two of us."

Once on the road to Walle, the car gathered speed and Uncle Armand had to shout. "Who do you think is going to become master of the world?"

"Jesus Christ," said Louis.

"Not that, you little prig. The Communists or Hitler?"

It was unthinkable that the Communists, who had tortured priests and nuns in Spain, who wanted to do away with fatherland and religion, should ever rule the nations of the world. God would never allow that. Or perhaps just for a little while, as a kind of test?

"Hitler," he said.

"Agreed. The lesser of two evils." Along the way, while Louis was working out how best to set about asking Mama for a flying helmet, Uncle Armand told him about the various cafés they were passing, places in which he had been at home since childhood, about Marie-José from the Golden Clock who had bitten a client and ended up in jail because a human bite is extremely dangerous, as the gentlemen from the court knew only too well, more dangerous than the bite of a pig, we have so much dirt in our spit, about Adrienne from the Mercator, a girl in a thousand, as good as gold except in her cups, when she got on your nerves something awful, did nothing but complain about her husband, an electrician with one leg, or about Michou, who looked so much like her little sister, Corinne, that she could fool the clients, I'll spare you the details, and about Barbe-à-papa, a billy goat that drank beer and had to be washed every day and rubbed down with eau-de-cologne.

Louis became charged with a mission. Sitting in the roaring, rattling car next to Vlieghe, whose sweet smell came wafting across to him, he could hear a voice humming to the headlong rhythm of the wheels, murmuring hurriedly, Louis Seynaeve, you have been chosen to save your uncle, he whose looks so please loose women, he who is continuing at this

205

very moment with his careless snickering, with his depraved chitchat. With the help of the Holy Virgin you will set him free from that dreadful scourge known as drunkenness, and to this end you will have to root out its cause, as your grandmother roots out her corns, and that cause is Madame Laura, because her soul is rotten to the marrow and she induces forgetfulness in men with the aid of noxious liquors.

Louis's reply to the rapid singsong was without words, he put his hand in his pocket and fingered the slippery thin material with the softly frayed crusts of lace. Uncle Armand rolled down his window to throw out his cigarette stub. The gust of air that blew in reeked of flax and made Louis sneeze, he reached for his handkerchief, the panties dropped between the seats, Louis sneezed three or four times, and Uncle Armand picked up the tawdry piece of underwear. "Hey, what have we here? How did that get in here? I know, Solange must have left it behind, she was the last to go for a ride in Mireille's car. To the Rotary Club. Well, *nondenonde!*" Louis gazed out at the winding Leie, the windmills, the silos, the Walle Sporting Club football ground.

At home in Oudenaarde Road, where the neighbors cast admiring glances at Mireille's car, Mama kissed her brother longer and more fondly than her son. She had lost weight and was burned a light pink.

"I am sorry, Armand," she said. "I'd have loved to please you with a little nephew. And you, Louis, with a little brother."

"Better luck next time, Constance."

"All that pain and all that waiting for nothing."

Papa was wearing a light-gray suit, Mama tightened his tie around his neck, Papa made a noise as if he were being throttled. He had to rush off to attend the jubilee of The Sisters of Charity in Hulle. The Bishop of Bruges would be there as well for the a-ca-demic session.

"Better you than me, Staf, with all those black skirts," said Uncle Armand.

"Did he have a drink on the way?" asked Mama, making cream cheese and shallot sandwiches in the kitchen.

"No, Mama. Not a drop."

"You didn't stop anywhere? Don't lie."

"He may have wanted to, but he did not yield to temptation."

"You sound more like your grandpa every day," she said, "all these high-flown expressions."

Giggles and shouts of laughter could be heard from the front room. Papa's high voice yodeled, "Olala-ettie." Mama ran in, Uncle Armand crowed, *"Paris, c'est une blonde, Paris, reine du monde."* In the middle of the room Papa was dancing, whistling, and yodeling, the tie that Mama had knotted so carefully all askew, on his balding pate the panties of Laura Vandenghinste, chatelaine and lawyer's wife-to-be, his sparse reddish-blond curls protruding from the lace-trimmed legs, his appearance that of some sturdy grandmother from an earlier age who, caught up in a whirlwind, had come to rest to catch her breath in the familiar antique-Flemish front room of the Seynaeves.

What Louis had not expected was Mama's laughter. "Good grief, Armand, what are you doing with my husband? You've hardly set foot in the house, when . . ."

Papa took the flimsy material off his head, looked at it, pulled at it, stretching the elastic.

"Do you carry that sort of thing in your pocket, brother?"

"Yes, sister. It's always with me. For a bit of fun."

"It's from Paris," said Papa.

"It's a present for you, Constance," said Uncle Armand in high spirits.

"Well then, *merci.*"

"It's a fig leaf," no, Louis did not say it out loud.

That evening they had hotchpotch although it wasn't the weather for it. The radio had a report on the nine paltry Polish army units that were standing by at the frontier waiting for the worst without any signaling equipment or antiaircraft weapons.

Sister Angel shook her coif at him indulgently, but that was pure sham, designed to demonstrate to the watching Sisters Adam and Kris how angelic and compassionate she was being in her role as tormentor.

"Louis," said Sister Angel, "I am compelled to punish you. Much though it grieves me. A zero for conduct, an hour in chapel on your knees, then two hundred lines: 'I must learn to be humble, especially in hard times.' "

"That won't fit on one line."

"Three hundred times."

"But Sister, that makes twice times three hundred lines, that's six hundred!"

"_Tiens,_ so now he can count," said Sister Kris.

"Three hundred and fifty," said Sister Angel. "And even then I'm being lenient with you. What ever's happened to you? Since the holidays there's been no knowing what to do with you. You seem determined to distinguish yourself by wantonness."

Louis strolled past the two assenting Sisters. Sister Angel was right, he was being tiresome. Like the Count of Monte Cristo being rebellious in his cell. Like Sister St. Gerolphe being tiresome somewhere in the Keep behind lock and key. (Notwithstanding the rumor that she had been admitted to a hospital for nuns in Limburg, which was nothing but one of their many all-too-well-known diversionary tactics, their transparent fifth column maneuvers. There were good reasons for believing that a cohort of Sisters from all over the country, hastily convened at a secret emergency session, had decided during the holidays to remove her to some poky hole measuring ten feet square, built in a great hurry by nocturnal masons against the Keep wall, without windows, like those punishment cells at the time the convent had been founded by Sisters of the Third Order with the help of Goorik van der Houtstrate, priest, following which Pope Nicholas V had granted the Sisters the right to wear the blessed and accursed habit. The cohort had spoken: "Insurrection against Mother Superior; on your knees, Sister St. Gerolphe, birch in hand; hand the birch to Mother Superior; Sisters, chastise her.")

Louis had seen Vlieghe again. Vlieghe, who should have been called Foxy on account of that dark-red bristly hair of his, much softer than it looked, those restlessly darting predator's-eyes, the pointed, moist mouth. Vlieghe had shaken hands with him, "Oh, there you are!" and in so doing had violated all the Apostles' rules for greetings. The other Apostles, too, had abandoned all the laws and customs of their Association in the fata morgana, the mirage, now vanishing once more, of the holidays, of time spent in an oasis, and now chattered away like ordinary pupils, like Hottentots. The Apostle Peter, their founder and creator, stood alone.

Poland had been overrun. And so? Over there in the swirling sand of the distant desert of the holidays, gallant cuirassiers and lancers had been mown down, stallions and all, in defense of their ludicrously unarmed fatherland, mown down by the indestructible and incredibly mobile tanks of an implacable enemy (in the tank turrets: pitiless Apostles, berets with the death's-head on their death-defying heads), so be it.

"It's the war that makes them so tiresome," said the Sisters, gigantic bats plastered against the chapel wall.

"The holiday assignments . . . a disgrace . . ."

"Even their handwriting has deteriorated."

"The parents . . . no time . . . so slovenly . . ."

"One more reason for teaching their children some sense."

"History has a lesson for them. Especially current affairs."

Mother Superior in the refectory after prayers: ". . . I shall not tolerate this insubordinate behavior one moment longer. From tonight the rules will be applied more strictly. Those who do not obey them will not remain with us until the end of the term but will be removed forthwith. Even if that reflects badly on our Institute. Something I realize only too well. But evil. Must be eradicated."

Sister Econome: "Even if it cuts into the flesh of our finances."

Sister Kris: "We are as poor as church mice, and the existence of our community is under threat. But we are determined . . . Root and branch . . ."

Sister Sapristi: "In times like these we must keep faith with one another, boys, please. Just try and do your best."

Sister Econome: "The rules. Especially now."

Sister Sapristi: "Do not listen to the voice of evil, boys. Do not listen to bad friends who think everything will be permissible in wartime."

The new Sister (a beanpole who either had fled from a stricter convent or had been turned out of a hospital in Bruges or had been sent back from the Belgian Congo with some invisible kind of leprosy, who was called Sister Thérèse but because of her cold face was soon known as Sister Chilly) surfaced in the chapel where Louis, on his knees, was sitting back on his heels, she emerged from the wall as St. Thérèse might out of her niche.

"Don't sit like that." A rustle and a hand tugging at his shoulder. Three days later, again without warning, from out of a soundless, cold doorway: "Seynaeve."

"Yes, Sister."

"What was that I heard you say? Just now in the playground? That word. Say it again if you dare, in my presence!"

"Which word?"

"The word for excrement. Say it out loud, Seynaeve. Or is your unchastity so ashamed of itself that . . ."

He knew it in a flash, the word, innocence itself. Cautiously triumphant, he said, "Sister, I said something about *kaka,* Sister."

"Yes, and . . ."

He interrupted. "The kaka is an Australasian parrot, Sister." He was about to explain that he had shouted the word so loudly because Dondeyne had needed it for the crossword puzzle in the *Zonneland,* when she slapped him without a single fold of her habit moving, knuckle and ring striking his jawbone. She looked as if she were about to kick him, her leg lifting behind her. He put his hands to his face, waited.

"Hands down."

He obeyed and said, "An Australasian bird, the kaka, it's a cockatoo. Like the lory."

"Get out of here, you Pharisee." Her Heavenly Bridegroom had sent Sister Chilly out among the lascivious in order to interrogate, not to learn or to know.

During the next few days Louis kicked the little ones' ankles, took possession of the Hottentots' Meccano boxes and building-blocks in the recreation room, and at night his bed swarmed with lewdly wriggling Mizzlers.

"Vlieghe."

"What is it this time?"

They had been playing tag, were sweating as they squatted in the shadow of the pear tree behind which Sister Chilly could not possibly be lurking. Nor was she up in the branches.

"One day . . ."

"Go on."

"One day I shall not be frightened of anyone anymore." Vlieghe's mouth was open, his tongue pink as a lollipop.

"Nothing shall be able to get the better of me. No sneak shall distract my soul."

"You're driveling again."

"The only thing . . ."

"Well?"

". . . that I still might be frightened of is that there might not be a place in my soul for you anymore."

"You've been reading too many stupid books."

"One day I shall have a house with many rooms, and there will be no parents, or aunts or uncles or Sisters there. Sticks and stones will never drive me from that house. The only person I'll allow in will be you, at night if need be. Because your soul is like mine. I don't love my mother any more than I love you. And when you come to my house, I shall be your servant, you'll be able to order me about, take my stamp collection. You'll be able to walk into and out of my soul as if it were a dovecote. I'll have a tower, and I'll lock myself away there with my Colt and my crossbow, and anyone who tries to take you away from me will die. They'll be able to overcome me in the end, of course, but before they do, blood will be shed, remember that, so said Seynaeve." He knew that he was raving, like a knight in the light of the moon before the battlements and embrasures of a citadel, like Hector the turkey in the light of the same moon. The words stuck to his palate like the cheap chocolate Papa bought in the Groeninghe, before they came blurting out, blurting out.

"We'll go to Heaven together. If they don't let you in, I'll wait in the cold outside the gate until you have done your time in Purgatory. And I shall pray to Our Lady to hurry up and be merciful to you. She'll listen to me."

Sister Chilly came into view from behind the pear tree, but she was reading her breviary and did not see them. Vlieghe's fingernails were black-rimmed even around the cuticles. With a fingernail he traced the line of a scarlet star drawn on his kneecap.

"Are you going to go on gibbering like this much longer?" asked Vlieghe. "Go tell that drivel to someone else." It sounded undecided, unconvincing. "Well, go on then," he said.

"No."

Next day, the priest raised the chalice and the host, and it suddenly came over Louis that His body and His blood were not present in that shaking hand. He looked around him, frightened to death, I am possessed, someone has to drive the devil out of me, those particles of dust swirling across from the leaded windows will become concentrated any moment now into a great, all-consuming flash of lightning that will strike me right here, in the crease between my eyebrows, any moment now the curate will take the chalice from the old man, look, the priest's hands are trembling because my unbelief is flickering through the chapel, if the curate takes careful aim when he flings the chalice at me, it will hit my teeth, the wine will spill, spatter across my face, I will have to taste it then, the blood of Jesus, it tastes salty like brine, I will swallow droplets of it, choke, and drown in eternal perdition.

Jesus did exist. Even Voltaire, who fell out of his deathbed, landing with his ugly heretic mug in his chamberpot and drowning in it, did not deny that. But is He really that small round wafer over there? Isn't that make-believe?

Louis walked, as always, behind Byttebier, hands folded, head bowed toward the altar, at any moment the Anointed, Who is omnipresent, might fling His tomahawk and hit him on his damp neck. Or His dart of scorching, red-hot vengeance, faster than sound, would pierce him from the front between throat and chin so that he would fall against Vlieghe behind him, Vlieghe, the good Samaritan, picking him up and laying him cautiously down on the altar steps, next to the curate's motorcycle boots.

Louis shuffled on, prayed, stuck his tongue out, prayed, and the Lord Jesus took pity on his error and on the doubt that seizes each one of His children (particularly when they have been mortally insulted by a red-haired, foxy miscreant at the very moment they declare their affection) and the God in Haarbeke chapel did not pluck out Louis's stuck-out tongue with the tongs of His cast-iron fingers. Louis's teeth chattered. "Forgive me, I beg you!" "Open your mouth," hissed the curate, standing beside the priest (ready to replace the tottering old man at a second's notice should he slump to the floor, quickly catching the golden ciborium in midair with the strong, hairy hands that rested so firmly on the handlebars of his Indian motorcycle). The Host, His living body, lay on Louis's tongue, a shred of tissue paper. Louis rose, without leaning on the communion rail like that lazy slob of a Dondeyne beside him. He returned to his place without looking at Vlieghe, and it was during the confusion of this retreat that he, pressing the wafer against the gums behind his molars, denied, annihilated the goodness of Jesus, Who had saved him from lightning and death. You did not dare strike me down at Your altar because You were not there, otherwise You surely would have. He bit, chewed, crunched. An immense passionate pride went swelling through his body, I could pee with pride. He swallowed down the cowardly or possibly absent Jesus. Like the Jews, he thought, like the Jews I shall be hunted all over the earth; Jesus, Who has existed and often exists still, will pursue me with His angels. Let them come.

Someone had seen everything. Sister Chilly, a beanpole with a long, leaden face, not unlike that of the Black Eagle, world bicycle racing champion Marcel Kint, was pressed with folded black wings against the wall beside the confessional. She clicked her tongue and beckoned him. He followed her.

They stopped when Sister Chilly held him back at the library door. She peered down the passage. Then she pushed him into the musty room full of blue-bound books. As in a gym class—did the Sisters do exercises behind the quadrupled bolts of the Keep doors?—she jumped onto the table, all at once a carefree creature, and sat on the Persian table mat with legs dangling.

"Confess."

"What?"

"What did you do in the chapel? Confess."

"I took communion."

"As usual? As always?"

"Yes." A vermilion cross began to glow on his forehead.

"Seynaeve, I was no more than six feet away from you. I'm not blind."

"You know everything, so why do I have to confess?" said Louis.

The wrathful Lord has sent one of His brides forthwith.

"I know more than you think."

"I confess," he said and awaited his fate. Denying Christ. Under which excommunication did that place you?

"Who was it?" she asked. And peevishly, when he did not reply: "Which boy touched you?" Touched me. Me.

"Dondeyne," he said. Dondeyne, who always tended to stand too close to you when he was talking to you, had prodded him just before they had knelt.

Sister Chilly was no longer cold, she was breathing hard, digging her hands deep into the short purple and red hairs of the mat.

"And that happened under the eyes of the faithful? In the chapel itself? In the presence of Our Lord?"

Louis nodded. Sister Chilly was being an inquisitor, that was her nature, or rather the nature of her office.

"Did you realize that Our Lord saw you at that moment?"

"God knows and sees all things." His answer came pat as in a catechism class. She searched for a handkerchief among the ample black folds, dabbed her face.

"Come here."

She seized both his ears with bony fingers. "What is my name?"

"Sister Thérèse."

"That's not what you call me when you are with your friends."

"No."

"I know everything. I know what you say about me. That I wasn't admitted to the Order because I had no dowry, and that they just suffer me here." She let go of his ears.

"Suffer?"

"Because the convent in Balen closed down and because they are shorthanded here in Haarbeke. Otherwise they would never have let me come."

"I didn't do anything wrong," said Louis.

She smirked, it was a miracle. I will tell Vlieghe, but he won't believe me. I will never tell him anything again under the pear tree.

"Dondeyne," she said reflectively. "And who else?"

"No one else."

"Liar. Come here. What did Dondeyne do? Where did he touch you? How did he do it? Quickly? Where did he put his hand? Show me. Demonstrate."

Louis's hand, Dondeyne's, prodded her hip.

"And then?"

"Nothing."

"Nothing else? And what does he do with you in the dormitory? Nothing else, either?"

Oh, unchastity, that was what she was looking for! This furtive sniffing around after the sixth commandment, this monstrous suspicion of the sin of lust.

"Sister!"

"Come here," she said for the third time, and her voice broke on the second word, just as the cock crowed for the third time with the Apostle Peter, and again nothing at all changed in the sculptured black waves and folds of her robe when she seized his wrist, pulled him close to her. The material he lay against was no rougher or poorer than that of the other Sisters, though one might have expected it to be with someone who had brought no dowry for Christ.

Sister Chilly clasped Louis's waist between her knees, two giant thumbs encircling his ribs and then squeezing. Her sleeve fanned out, she laid one hand on his neck, he saw two thin trickles of sweat run from under her headband toward her eyebrows where blue swollen veins branched out, the color of the bags under her ice-cold eyes, and then she clasped him to her breast that smelled of cold, nutmeg, and starch. She *clasped* me, Vlieghe. Her knees let go for a moment and then closed again. He was being crushed. A curious punishment. The knees opened and closed more and more quickly, then opened wide as if her entire habit were yawning, and she lay back, a red stripe across her throat where the scarf had slipped to one side, it looked like a newly healed scar. With a smothered smack her legs came together.

When she propped herself up again on one elbow, she was squinting slightly. She let the beads of her rosary slip through her fingers, fumbled at her leather belt, picked up her crucifix, and put it to Louis's mouth. His lips touched the metal breast of Jesus.

"He loves you," she said. "Even though you are such a sinner."

"Yes, Sister."

Colorless lips pursed, she suddenly kissed the crown of thorns and the wavy hair of her God, jumped off the table, slapped dust or fluff from her habit. As, suddenly in a hurry, she held the door of the library open for him like a servant, he said, "A kaka really *is* an Australian parrot, Sister."

"Pharisee," she murmured, almost cheerfully this time, a miracle.

A smooth-faced reddish-blond man with a wavy beard, combed very precisely and parted into two identical points, was berating Louis in Latin. Even though He normally spoke Aramaic? Or was it Galilean? He wore a milky-white robe with, above His heart, a small, rounded, heart-shaped cushion in velvet from which leapt golden flames. In the ardor of His Church Latin peroration, filled with scornful digressions, His gold-speckled thorny crown kept slipping so that the wounds in His scalp broke open and two thin trickles of blood ran down from under His hair toward His eyebrows where little swollen blue veins stood out.

"Is that You?" Louis heard himself ask.

"None of your business. The question is, is that you," said the man in a Bruges accent.

"It's me."

"Then it's me, too."

"Does it hurt?"

"Very much."

Louis fell down before the pierced feet and kissed the elegant, elongated toes set off by four dainty corns. Surely the man had never worn shoes that were too tight for Him. The toes curled up. "You mustn't tickle me so," said the man in a tone too severe for His soft, melodious voice.

A wind blew up, driving sand and snow through the streets of a town that seemed to be built out of matchsticks, so threadbare, fragile, and thin were the buildings of Lucifer's city.

"You call yourself one of the chosen," said the man. "Aren't you ashamed of yourself, you coward, you schismatic? Where are your signs, your miracles, your powers?"

"There." At a nod from Louis, eleven officers wearing five-cornered flat kepis came riding up, their lances pointing at the horizon, where tanks like tortoises and Stuka dive-bombers could be seen.

"The bungling idiots," said the indignant voice by his side.

"They are devoted to You, Rabbi."

"That's not enough."

"Lord, how can I serve You?"

"As a missionary, for example. You seem very suited to that."

"If You say so."

Louis saw Louis. He was wearing a Catholic Students' Action uniform, under his arm a lance, the pole of a flag with the letters "PX" on it. He dismounted from his horse and walked toward the giant ferns and the long hairy gray creepers. The jungle was steaming. Negroes with filed teeth like pointed pieces of coconut squatted among the steaming bushes. Louis called to them, blessed them, knighted them with a tap of his flagpole, they had tears in their eyes, tears for him, the white boy who had come to save them from the eternal fire. Then Louis was suddenly alone in a no-man's-land of savanna, selva, steppes, rainforest, taiga (he recited), there was only the buzzing of giant May bugs and dragonflies and the gnashing of crocodile teeth, and the screeching of cockatoos, and a low sad grumbling of tortoises like tanks.

"They don't want to listen, they've fled," Louis cried in despair. "They are afraid of You and of me, these natives, because they can still recall only too well" (he said in High Flemish) "how Mussolini murdered their ancestors and burned down their huts."

"Mussolini?"

"That's what Sister Angel says."

"I don't know her."

"She's really called Sister Marie-Ange."

"Oh, her. I know her well. A serious girl." The man wrinkled His nose up with a catlike spitting sound. He came from Bruges and had a cold. I must get Him a pocket handkerchief. In Bruges they call that a "pocket nose-kerchief." How can we force those heathens to love Him? I keep wondering about that and at the same time I am probably asleep.

"You chased the Pharisees out of the temple, didn't You?" said a five-year-old Louis.

"Yes. Always had a lot of trouble with those Pharisees." He sneezed, wiped His nose with his milky-white sleeve. "Come here." 'Ere, 'ere, 'ere, came the echo from the valleys between the turquoise-blue mountains capped with snow. Because Louis did not move, the man drew nearer and rent His robe with a tearing sound, a white vaulted chest appeared, with a nipple just as white, without veins, like a marble statue.

"Put your finger on the wound."

"But there is no wound."

"Because you don't want to see. Because you are just like your mother Constance, who only sees what she wants to see."

Louis found it hard to keep his eyes open, but he searched and peered and stared until he could see a thin network in the alabaster flesh—alabaster, that's what it was, not marble but alabaster—like the eight spindly limbs of a daddy longlegs. Against his will his index finger rose into the air and, yes, there was a groove in the chest, a lumpy cleft on which alabaster lips were growing, greasy, shining, bulging. Surely I'm not going to be made to watch his skin burst. His index finger entered the cool, mobile, folded lips, which closed around the first knuckle, the second knuckle, like the trunk of—of—of—. With an electric shock, Louis pulled his finger back, his fingernail caught, tore. Louis propped himself up, I am awake, it happened, where?

A milkman was already busy in the village street with his copper milk cans, but by the time Louis drew back the net curtain, he had disappeared around the corner. There the village street lay, peaceful, untouched. Although not a cloud could be seen, it would probably rain later today. Smoke from the chimney at the bakery. Invisible pails. The elms and the church tower from which the bell would herald the day. The gray Gothic buildings of the brewery catching the first rays of the sun in their dim windows.

Louis felt that he was expected to be grateful for being allowed to stay (not live) here, however temporarily, here in this sheltered corner of Flanders, while the Antichrist and the Communists were giving vent elsewhere to their savagely barbaric, ardently burning passions, dancing over unarmed corpses in a joyous orgy of destruction.

The way I—it's fading while the sun is coming up—was sucked into the

217

body of Christ by my finger. The foolish, timorous smile of Prince Sou-Chong is no help here. Far from it.

"You're up early." Dondeyne stood beside him in his nightshirt, tugging at his sick, red ear.

"You, too."

"I couldn't sleep."

"Because of your sins."

"Probably."

"Because you weren't repentant enough."

"Do you think so, Seynaeve?"

"Because you know you are going to burn in the eternal, inextinguishable fire, a jet of gas burning day and night on your skin."

"Really, Seynaeve?"

Dondeyne's filthy bare feet slid across the floorboards, he stood by the window, shivered. He must have goose pimples, the Hottentot. Gooseflesh. Horribly nimble Mizzlers were swarming around the window, bugs or specks of dust, snorting, splitting up, scattering fear and despair, bursting their way straight through Dondeyne's sick ear into his brain.

"Just go to bed," said Louis. "It won't happen in a hurry. So long as you show repentance." (Show, not feel.) "It's not too late. And hellfire, who knows, it could be just a manner of speaking. No, Dondeyne, you'll be going to Heaven, to the special section reserved for simpletons."

"Do you really think so, Seynaeve?"

"You and all those other idiots will be doubled up there with laughter at all the other creatures writhing in the fire on account of their pride."

"Which creatures?"

"One above all. One will not escape. He will roast like a chicken on a spit."

"Who?"

"Vlieghe," said Louis.

As he uttered the name, a great sadness came over Louis, and the name remained hanging in the brightening dormitory along with the first groans of the Hottentots. Louis tried to chase the name away, to put himself back into the steamy, swampy night that had just been, where there had been no place for Vlieghe. "It would have been better for Vlieghe if he'd never been born," he said, but it didn't sound convincing, it was the sulky voice of his Aunt Violet.

Carts clattered over the cobblestones, the village clock struck, the whole Institute was awake.

_____*a shameful yellow basket*

*D*uring the days that followed, the Sisters could be seen conspiring
together more than ever, whispering in the corridors, a startled ex-
clamation escaping them from time to time (*Athenia!*).

Hitler, theretofore kept at bay by a wall topped with pieces of broken
bottle, now infiltrated the Institute through the breaches, bawling that he
was Germany's number-one soldier, and wasn't that the truth? He could
hardly call himself the last. In Belchatow three bombs had fallen on the
Convent of the Immaculate Conception. One of the little ones insisted
on calling it the Immaculate Confection. Small balloons filled with an
unknown gas and electric detonators were being dropped over Europe.

Ambulances with Red Crosses as clear as day on their roofs were being
machine-gunned. And still those intrepid mounted Polish standard-bear-
ers with their useless lances kept on being mowed down.

Had thirty Polish bombers flattened Berlin, or hadn't they? Everyone
in France was being forced to carry a gas mask everywhere they went,
even to bed, or else they were fined. If the alarm goes off, lie down where
you are, don't move, not even an inch, understand, boys? The weather

is still bad, in the Rhineland hundreds of acres are under water, how can the German army possibly plough through all that mud? The first encyclical of Pope Pius XII proclaims that peace treaties are the hallmark of justice and of equal rights (according to Sister Kris, who has been to Rome), and that martyred Poland shall rise again, and that Italy (where she had been served spaghetti, a sort of thin macaroni, every day for a whole week) is the great garden of Faith, laid out and planted by the Apostles.

The Apostles, who had betrayed their bond, who had forgotten their rules during the holidays, now surrounded Baekelandt. He had redoubled the barbed wire around the Institute and set his dogs and pigs loose every night because in these perilous times they, too, had their duty to do and could sniff out the enemy from miles away.

Vlieghe, know-it-all, beloved and hated touch-me-not, monopolized the conversation as soon as Baekelandt complained about the weather. The floods in the Rhineland had been a godsend, he said, because they had given the Dutch the idea of creating even greater floods if need be.

Baekelandt nodded. "Water maneuvers, like in '14–'18." Which only encouraged Vlieghe, the engineer. "All the Dutch minister has to do is pick up the telephone: Men, stop the pumps! And the whole country is under water. You can't move heavy guns along the roads anymore, you can't get even a bicycle through the big ponds. The only things left above the water line are the big concrete blocks where they stand all the howitzers, the machine guns, and the antiaircraft batteries. And the only way the enemy planes can hope to hit those is by dive-bombing them, which makes them sitting ducks for your automatic weapons."

"Vlieghe, they ought to make you a general," said bootlicker Byttebier.

"It's because Vlieghe means Fly that he knows all about flying," said yes-man Goossens.

"But they fly past you so quickly, how do you tell whose planes they are?" asked Dondeyne, Hottentot.

"The French have red, white, and blue markings on the fuselage, the English have red in the middle of the markings, the Germans have a black cross with a white border on the sides and a swastika in a white circle on a red rectangle on the cockpit. *Voilà.*"

"How do you know all that?" asked Baekelandt suspiciously.

"It's all in the papers."

"If I were you, I wouldn't go on about it too much, people might think you were a spy."

That was it. He would have to be unmasked as a spy, this flying-mad Vlieghe. Handcuffs. Seven years' incarceration in a fortress. After a couple of years, when his spirit has been broken, I'll take him some books and some bananas.

"I wouldn't put it past Göring to paint out his swastikas and put on Belgian colors to trick our ack-ack," said Baekelandt. "I don't trust him an inch."

"The English wouldn't think twice about doing that, either," said Louis. (In his Walle sitting room Papa gives a start and agrees, looking proud of me. And Vlieghe's father, Flemish nationalist but anti-German, has to admit I'm right as well.)

"It took Hitler to teach Göring how to lie and cheat, because in '14–'18 he was well enough thought of as an airman with medals to his name," said Baekelandt. "But then he became a follower of Hitler, and ever since he's done everything his Antichrist's told him, including daily lessons in how to lie and cheat from Goebbels on Hitler's orders. Oh, you can't teach me anything about the Germans."

"They'll be coming here just for the hell of it," said Goossens.

"Mussolini, now, there's a man for you," said Baekelandt, "haymaking and digging dykes and draining marshes, shoulder to shoulder with his people. Mussolini knows you never get something for nothing, you have to sweat and slave if you want to get the best out of the land as well as hang on to it. But that Hitler, he's just an Austrian drifter, he pushes his people around, juggles them. He takes men from the mountains and puts them to work on the land, he takes farmworkers and puts them down in the mines. He couldn't care less for man or beast."

After the French lesson, Sister Adam started to talk about the barbaric behavior of the Communists. About what a disgrace it was that Stalin, because he was supposedly neutral, was now being put on a par with Catholic kings and presidents, on a par with our own King Leopold, who was truly neutral from the bottom of his heart, particularly since that time when he had lost our Queen in Küssnacht in Switzerland.

"Still," said Sister Kris, "there has to be something in it when Hitler says he's Germany personified, because the Germans are all behind him, and an awful lot of them are Catholics."

"Not the Prussians, Sister," said Sister Chilly, "and they're the ones who call the tune."

"The English Bible Society has had tons of pages from the Bible dropped over Germany. The Protestants cross frontiers to help each other. We ought to take a leaf out of their book."

And Vlieghe? He blossomed during that period, drawing airplanes, tanks, and guns in his sketchbook with meticulous, straight, unbroken lines on much-erased paper, and his watercolors no longer seeped across his lines, not by a fraction of a millimeter, unlike Louis's, but then Louis was always in too great a hurry, too Seynaeve-impetuous, spattering colors untidily all over his illustrations of O. Soglow's *Little King*. And as Vlieghe waited patiently for his watercolors to dry, he would bring everyone up to date on what ships had been sunk without warning, the English *Athenia*, for instance, and where it had happened, two hundred miles west of the Hebrides, fourteen thousand tons consigned to the deep. "The whole British Fleet has had it," he lectured the open-mouthed ex-Apostles, "because the Germans are prepared to sacrifice two hundred and fifty planes a week just to destroy one cruiser. And the Germans can build a thousand planes a month now. It takes the English *three years* to build one cruiser. Work it out for yourselves." And the apostate examined his drawing of a submarine, pressed his multicolored blotting paper to it, took up his paintbrush again, the tip of his tongue appeared, he painted. Keeping one eye on Vlieghe, Louis penetrated the wall of the Keep, woke Mother Superior by blowing softly across her face. Seynaeve?—No, Nick Carter, said Louis, I have come to inform you that the person known as Vlieghe is a deadly dangerous secret agent who is plotting the downfall of Belgium.—Is he working for the fifth column, my child?—For the German Secret Service and for the Russians. He may know all there is to know about machines and engines, but he has no sense of honor at all. He is an agent of Satan and wants nothing to do with love.—I know his father is the secretary of the Flemish National League, but isn't he also a Church commissioner?—That's a cover, Mother Superior, a cover for both father and son.

Unperturbed, Vlieghe continued to draw using ruler and compasses in the recreation room, even on the evening when the Russians invaded unsuspecting Finland. Goossens picked scales from the cone of a silver fir, Byttebier slept, Dondeyne read the Davidsfonds book, *From Gezelle's Life and Work*, a present to Louis from Grandpa (in which he had underlined a mysterious sentence in red pencil: "An A at its head has an Angel, I see, yet as saddened as you no Angel can be"), and Vlieghe drew a Messerschmitt, at the same time informing Dobbelaere, the groveler, that all German equipment was inferior, something the Swiss had discovered when they bought Messerschmitts and the engines turned out to be completely useless. And just recently thirteen Stukas—those are monoplanes, Dobbelaere, with thousand-pound bombs under their fuselage— went into a three-hundred-mile-an-hour dive through the fog and crashed all at the same time, making a pretty big hole in the Polish mud. They didn't put that in the papers, of course, and the thirteen pilots were called heroes and given medals as a sop to their mothers. Louis had enough of listening to the smug know-it-all drawl, and went and sat down next to Dondeyne, who, infected by Byttebier, was dozing off. Louis plunged into his Gezelle book in order to consign Vlieghe to oblivion. "No, dearest child of my prayers and tears, none on earth shall ever . . ." "And verily, verily, sit I here thus, without sustenance, without worldly goods, yearning for one thing only, for the eternal bliss which alone can restore my joy, bring about your return, bring back you and no other, to be my only friend."

Who but an angel, not guardian-angel Holst but one of those winged postmen-angels third-class, could have put this right under his nose, this exact formulation of what had been plaguing him? An offering from the great Flemish Mind! Boldly he read on: ". . . If ever I have wronged you in any way, then listen, I, a priest, beg your forgiveness." The signal was unmistakable. If Gezelle, saint, miracle-working artist, genius ordained priest, could humble himself on these ocher-flecked yellowing pages, then surely so could Seynaeve, worm bereft of speech! He half-rose, ready to prostrate himself in admiration of those finicky drawings as a prelude to asking Vlieghe's forgiveness, when he noticed that Vlieghe was looking at him (had been for some time?) (something he hadn't done for days!), while continuing to talk. And then, as they say in books, my heart stood still. "And then," said Vlieghe, "then this young man fell on that easy lay Constance."

That is the last, bitter drop. The messenger-angel is Belial. Vlieghe has signed his death warrant.

"Say that again!" Louis shouted, leaping to his feet.

"What?" (Hypocritical foxy-face!)

"What you just . . . The last thing you . . ."

"Can't you hear properly, Seynaeve? You ought to wash your ears out."

"A deaf Peter," said Goossens.

"Say it again! Right now!"

Vlieghe made as if he were trying to remember. "I said that a Junker had fallen on Lake Constance, in Switzerland: a JU 52 with three engines."

"You're not saying it the same this time!"

"What do you mean?"

"When was it?" Louis asked pointlessly.

"Last Thursday."

Louis picked up his book once more, the letters dancing. A Junker (a young man, young nobleman) has crashed, fallen (like a fallen angel) in (no, on!) the lake (more than water, more a mere, a swamp), into the mere of Constance (wanton daughter of Meerke). The letters ran into each other, redoubled. And still the addle-pated water-on-the-brain Gezelle continued remorselessly with his prayer. ". . . All that has been between you and me was for Jesus' sake and with the purest of intentions, yet now you treat me thus? Oh, I pray . . ." Louis slammed the book shut and flung it at Dondeyne, who caught it between his knees.

"You . . . you . . ." stammered Louis at Vlieghe, who, pencil between his teeth, remained sitting in passive astonishment.

"You . . . Matthew, publican . . . See if you don't grovel at the bare feet of my mother one day, begging her forgiveness . . ."

He left him then, muttering something in astonishment, left him behind, for good.

That evening, in the icy refectory, they prayed for Finland. It was an everlasting disgrace that the Bolsheviks had dared to attack a country with forty-five times less manpower than they had. Sister Kris said that the Germans were now deploying the tanks and troops that had been fighting in Poland along our frontiers under the lying pretext that they couldn't make room for them all in their Siegfried Line fortifications.

Our King and the Queen of Holland have met in The Hague, and together they sent a moving telegram to the nations at war. Because, you see, children, it could easily be our turn next. We must pray. And follow the example of Mayor Adolphe Max of Brussels, who recently passed away to rest in the arms of Our Lord, the very model of the modest but plucky Belgian.

In '14–'18, a German general—during the Occupation!—had offered him his hand. Not on your life, Adolphe Max had said. The German general had then drawn his pistol from its holster and laid it on the table. Whereupon the city father had calmly brought out his fountain pen from his breast pocket and laid it next to the German's weapon. He was flung into prison but escaped with a false passport he had helped himself to from the commandant's desk drawer. On Victory Day in '18, as applause and jubilation rang out all around the Town Hall, he made straight for his office, summoned his aldermen, clapped his hands, and said, "And now, gentlemen, to work!"

Louis said "Psst" to Dobbelaere, like a nun, beckoned Goossens and Dondeyne, raised his eyebrows at Byttebier. They followed him out, Byttebier accompanied by his little brother René, who, at the age of eight and despite his tender years, had been declared "wise" because he had unhesitatingly administered the Last Sacrament when his mother had had a heart attack in their kitchen. He had reenacted the scene several times already, how he had quickly fetched his father's engine oil and applied it, making the sign of the Cross, to her eyelids, ears, nose, and dying lips, and had muttered, "May almighty God forgive you your sins, amen."

They met behind the kitchen in the freezing wind and took refuge in the toilets, squashed together between the stinking stone partitions, bleach stains on the blue-black surface.

"Listen carefully, you, too, René," said Louis. "We have an asp at our breast, a bad Belgian who is passing on military secrets to the enemy. All this time he has been appearing in the guise of an Apostle, but now he has been unmasked."

"That's bad," said Dobbelaere, the drip.

"Worse than bad," said Goossens.

"What are we going to do about it?" asked Byttebier. "Report him to the policeman in the village?"

"No," said Louis. "Apostles take care of things like this themselves."

"Who is it?" asked René. "Do I know him?"

"It's best not to say his name out loud," said Louis.

"He shall pay for it!" cried Dondeyne.

Louis, Peter the Stone, led them toward the kitchen, silent as the grave. In his cruel supremacy he observed little René, as rosy as an apple just before in the toilets, turn white as a sheet, shivering with excitement, Dondeyne stammer wordlessly, the lumbering Byttebier nod his head anxiously. He gave his orders, posted Goossens outside as sentry, concealed René behind the aluminum pots and pans and thrust a bread knife into his hand, stationed Dondeyne behind the door, Byttebier and Dobbelaere in the scullery, took a deep breath like Julius Caesar at a mountain pass about to lure the Ancient Belgians into an ambush, and declared, "Loyal unto death." Only Dondeyne mumbled something in response. Then he walked across the playground, the plane trees jet-black in the garden, a clear trapezium of light falling across the paving stones from the music room, and he found Vlieghe and thought, I must be sure to note down in the Acts as soon as I can exactly what time it was, what the victim said, how he conducted himself before the penance.

"I've got something to show you, Vlieghe," he said and caught himself acting in a slipshod manner unbecoming to Julius Caesar, for he had made no attempt to prepare his approach, whereas a real leader never improvises except in the heat of battle. Caesar planned everything, in particular his first moves, down to the last little detail.

"What is it this time?" (Vlieghe's favorite saying.)

"Something."

"What?"

"Something that'll make you sit up and think." (Said casually.)

"You'd have to be pretty smart to make me sit up."

Louis had run out of ideas.

"Well," he said. "Let this be the last word. The order of the Silent Oath."

No more need for racking brains, Vlieghe was trapped in the spider-web of his own curiosity. He played hopscotch with an imaginary piece of wood, shrugged his shoulders, feigned indifference. "Where?"

"Come along."

It was childishly simple, the fox followed, hands in tunic, close behind Louis. Into the light from the music room: the knee scratched with the cross, a swollen, mottled disc of ivory. Louis could still stop him, send him back with "it was just a stupid Hottentot joke, just something I made up as usual," but Vlieghe's very lack of suspicion cried out for retribution. That he had insulted Louis and Mama paled to insignificance, it was his innocence that called for punishment.

The landing with the short flight of stairs leading down to the evening-still kitchen had grown darker. Your grave, Vlieghe. The banister gleamed. Louis went down first. Dondeyne's breathing was inaudible behind the door. What do I hear? The muffled throb in my temples.

"Well?" Vlieghe pretended not to see Dobbelaere sitting at the scullery table, for some inexplicable reason wearing the faded blue apron of a kitchen Sister and holding his fork in his fist as if about to bring it down on the wood, and who, by Julius Caesar! had left the door open! What had been intended as a tactical ploy now looked like the most idiotic game of hide-and-seek by backward little ones.

"Sit down."

"No."

Louis leaned against the entrance door, feeling with his shoulder that lumbering lump of a Dondeyne right through the wood, and said calmly, "Vlieghe, just who do you think you are?"

"Me? Not a crackpot like you, at any rate."

"It's all your fault," said Louis, and the words were on the tip of his tongue: "that the holy League of Apostles has suddenly withered, that our friendship has shriveled, that . . ." but his voice failed him, the fox facing him had turned suspicious, the fierce almond-shaped eyes glittering in the light of the lamp outside, not at bay but on the alert, desperately on the defensive, and Louis became aware of a sweet, sickly smell rising from his chilly clothes, a soft and melting feeling washed over him, something sinful.

The door at his back creaked, or was it Dondeyne's throat? Louis took a step forward, the door swung free, Dondeyne was holding a poker in his hand.

"What are you playing at, you stupid fools?" said Vlieghe.

"René," ordered Louis, and the small boy, his face bright and flushed once more, emerged from behind the biggest stewpot holding the bread knife out in both hands, like a gift for the child in the manger.

Dobbelaere came into the kitchen, said, "Aye-aye," and began licking his fork.

"Vlieghe, we are going to eat you," said Louis.

"All right, Seynaeve," said Vlieghe, "you've had your fun now."

"Chop you into tiny pieces," said René. Dobbelaere jabbed determinedly at Vlieghe's left thigh, but the fork did not remain embedded in the curve of flesh. "Wait!" exclaimed Louis. "Wait!" shouted Vlieghe with pain or with surprise, a French knight at the Battle of the Golden Spurs feeling the sharp end of a Flemish pike.

But Dondeyne, who did not want to leave the slaughter to the other paladins, who had special rights as an Apostle . . .

But Dobbelaere, who wanted to improve on his first thrust . . .

But René, who believed implicitly in this Last Sacrament and wanted to try the bread knife just once . . .

But Byttebier, who was nowhere to be seen . . .

But Louis slapped René's wrist and the bread knife clattered to the floor, and in the same movement he seized Vlieghe, to whom he had not been so close for months, by the collar of his tunic, drove his other fist into the pit of Vlieghe's stomach, and let the collar go. With surprising grace the boy fell backward onto the shiny kitchen table and stayed there stretched out, legs spread wide like Sister Chilly.

"And then," asked the curate, "after you had threatened your friend with cannibalism?"

"Then," said Louis in the stuffy cubicle. He had not revealed the names of his accomplices, despite the curate's threats and urgings.

"The truth," said the boyish voice of the adult, and Louis did not answer him with "What is truth?" like Pilate, the washer of hands.

"Then we left him in peace, Father."

"Because you had come to your senses?"

"Yes. Yes. That was it, Father."

The curate snorted with distaste or boredom or irritation at this shabby Hottentot transgression. Did he not realize that the sinner facing him was making a false confession, did he not care that the heretic behind the wooden grille was deliberately thumbing his apostate's-nose at the Sacrament of Penance? Did he really believe he could get the whole thing over with the punishment and formulas fit for a child's sin?

Since Louis had been told that very morning that his father was going to remove him from the Institute now that the clouds of war were gathering, were threatening to drive the dove of peace out of our small but beloved country, he suspected—stung—that the officiant on the other side of the greasy, dusty grating had his thoughts more on the map of Europe than on that other war that was raging in his soul, a slimy, inner civil war in which darkness was gaining. Hurriedly he said, "Father, we gave him no peace, I and my accomplices persisted in our sin, the Fat One thrust his fork with tremendous force in the region of his heart, the Clumsy One stuck a soup spoon into the victim's eyesocket, the victim fainted dead away, the Clumsy One scooped about with the spoon as if in a baked potato and threw the organ over his shoulder."

The curate stood up, the wood cracked like a distant woodpecker.

"Meanwhile, the Little One, who has been corrupted to the very marrow of his being by the sight of his dying mother, jubilantly ripped away the shirt, made the sign of the Cross with his bread knife, as his dead mother used to do before she cut bread, and cut a slice of naked, shuddering breast, and appeared to be about to partake of this bodily morsel when an innate feeling of brotherly love stopped him just in time, whereupon he knelt down and cried bitter tears." Louis gasped, he had brought it all out too fast, all in one breath.

"And you? And you, my son, what was your attitude to this wicked act?" The voice sounded firm and attentive but was mocking the tone and style of my confession.

"I wrested the bread knife from the Little One's hand and used it to transfix the victim's heart, a heart that was filled with malice."

"But, child, there was a fork already there, the Fat One's fork."

"Next to it! Next to it! There is enough room in a heart for a knife and a fork." A smell of blood wafted through the confessional, the odor of a vat filled with the steaming pig's-blood that is used to make blood sausage with onions or raisins.

The curate gave three little smacking, sucking noises as if working a sliver of meat out from between his teeth.

"Seynaeve!" The name echoed through the chapel nave. Was that allowed? Did a father confessor have the right to identify a penitent so brazenly? Shall I shout back, "Curate Johannes Maes, what do you want?"

"Seynaeve," the priest repeated more softly. "You're a fine one! Do you really believe you can get away with such arrant nonsense? Do you really think I have nothing better to do than listen to your twaddle? Don't you know where you are, you snotty little boy? I could have you thrown right out of school."

"My father is coming to fetch me anyway, tomorrow or the day after."

"Good luck," said the voice. "You'll go far with that imagination of yours. I wouldn't be at all surprised to find you writing for the papers one day. Or writing books. But you'll have to tone down that extravagant style. Follow the example of Philip de Pillecijn. High-sounding but simple. I'll give you *Pieter Farde, the Story of a Minorite* to take with you, it's one of the Select Series."

"I've read it."

That seemed to annoy the priest. He shifted his position, Louis could hear his stomach rumble, close by, as if it were his own. The priest muttered under his breath, "I am not going to say that joy shall be in heaven over one sinner that repenteth, more than over ninety and nine just persons . . . I shall not say, Arise and be not afraid . . . Seynaeve, for goodness' sake get out of here."

Louis made for Bernadette Soubirous's grotto. He was tired to death. The crown of an oak tree was blood-red. The freezing air was still, birdless.

"Wait," exclaimed Louis, René let his knife drop, Dondeyne laid his poker next to the shuddering Vlieghe, held down by Dobbelaere. Louis wrested the bread knife from the child's clammy hand and held it across Vlieghe's throat.

"Don't do it, Louis, you'll go straight to hell," uttered the snout of the mortally afraid predator.

"Say you're sorry," said Louis in a strangled voice.

"I'm sorry."

"That you deserve your punishment."

"I deserved my punishment."

"Without the d."

"Without the d. I deserve."

René tugged at Vlieghe's tunic. "Yes," said Dobbelaere. Louis pressed the blunt edge of the knife to Vlieghe's throat as Dobbelaere and Dondeyne, gleefully chortling, pulled Vlieghe's trousers down to his shoes. René tore off the soiled underpants. Louis slapped away the hand sliding down the abdomen.

"Take a look at that," he said.

"What a pretty little piglet," cried René happily.

"He ought to get it on his bare bottom," said Byttebier, coming out of the scullery at that moment with a sopping wet mop.

Under the all-seeing eye of Louis, executioner of Flanders, Vlieghe was turned over by eager hands, his pale buttocks with the pink stripe at the top where the elastic had been looked defenseless, more innocent than Vlieghe's face had ever been. Isn't this the humility, the poverty demanded of us by the Blessed Virgin? "Wait," said Louis. Immediately Vlieghe propped himself up on one elbow, the martyr was anything but meek, forever plotting new tricks. Even René, the pitiless little snot-nose, could tell that, he pushed Vlieghe down, cheek to the worn, shiny wood.

Because he was loath to gratify Byttebier, who had been holding aloof in the scullery, who might even have been hoping for the intervention of patron saints or of Sisters, and who was now waving his mop about and grinning, Louis said, "We won't give him a hiding." He dragged a tall basket half-filled with apples toward the table. Head and folded arms first, Vlieghe was tipped in, quietly moaning. "Please."

His backside and despondently floundering thighs stuck out of the basket. René asked if Vlieghe would have to stay like that all night.

"Then we'll have to tie him up," said Dondeyne.

"And gag him."

Fatuous, useless underlings. Something urgent, essential, prescribed, had yet to take place. Goossens peered in from out of the night through the small window, then stood open-mouthed in the doorway.

"But that's . . ."

"That's a snotty rotten Hottentot," said Louis. No one laughed. Louis took the warm knucklebone he had stolen from Sister St. Gerolphe's bedside table out of his trouser pocket and pushed it into the dry opening between Vlieghe's buttocks. Until the base metal had finally disappeared from view. Vlieghe wept, his bisected white body shook, the fruit basket creaked.

"Signed, sealed, and delivered," said Louis. The accomplices looked at him with awe. Vlieghe begged for forgiveness, but the words came tripping out over each other, all jumbled together.

And Louis stammered them out again, in front of the grotto. He was afraid to look at the peeling, weathered, stony face of the Blessed Virgin, and when he did summon up enough courage, he saw that she was sad, so he said the act of contrition twice, three times, but a little tune, like some half-remembered scrap of rhyme in the cold, dark kitchen, kept blotting it out: "A-tisket, a-tasket, a shameful yellow basket."

He was standing talking with Baekelandt by the hedge that the gardener had fitted up with barbed wire hung with rusty saucepans, bottles, and metal rods, so that any Germans creeping up in the dark would be sure to make a hell of a racket with their helmets and rifles and mess kits, when he saw Sister Chilly and Sister Angel waving.

Louis went up to them and up to Mama, who put a suitcase down in the pale sunlight on the edge of the merry-go-round. She was wearing a ridiculous velvet beret with a pheasant feather. Sister Chilly and Sister Angel watched as she held out a hand to her son.

"I've come to fetch you."

"I can see that."

"I came on the bus."

"Did you?"

"Don't you have to say goodbye to your little classmates?"

"I did already."

"Aren't you glad to see me?"

"Yes. Yes, Mama" (blessed among women).

The Sisters babbled on to her about the persecuted Church. An infirm old canon in Munich has been flung into jail for speaking up against the regime. In Germany schools are no longer allowed to teach religion. German women have to sign a letter in the maternity hospital promising not to have their children baptized. No more than one candle can be lit in a church. And the affront to the Pope when he asked them to allow priests to visit their prison camps! "Don't bother with that, Holy Father, that's what the Red Cross is for," they told him, he who had been nuncio in Germany for ten years and had been so well liked there.

Vlieghe shook hands with Mama. "Good afternoon, Madame Seyna-eve." Louis took him by the elbow and drew him aside.

"I came to say good-bye to you, Louis."

"That's . . . nice of you."

"You've hurt me, Louis." Vlieghe put his hand in his pocket, and for one terrible moment Louis thought he was going to bring out the disgusting knucklebone, but what emerged was an ivory penholder. There was a little hole in its flat handle, through which you could see the Sacré-Coeur (basilica or cathedral?) in Paris, in pastel-colored detail.

"This is for you. To show that I forgive you."

"Thanks."

"I can't understand why you did it."

"Me neither."

"But I'm not cross with you. I think you have a kind heart."

Louis was ashamed of the savage, cruel thoughts twirling and tingling in his skin like Mizzlers. Could the knucklebone have come out through Vlieghe's mouth? Was that possible? If you humiliated people, surely they did not beg for more of the same, as Vlieghe seemed to be doing now, more shameful yellow basket?

"I'll always think of you," Louis said, and before the tears could come he ran to his mother and lifted the suitcase off the merry-go-round.

"Keep well!" called Vlieghe after him.

Past the conifers so carefully pruned by Sister Imelda. The copper weathervane. The flower pots on the windowsills of the Keep. Through a gap in the thorn hedge, Vlieghe, waving under the pear tree, waving and waving.

THE END   *November 1947*

OF BELGIUM

*T*imes are bad, the radio says so, and the newspapers. No, things aren't getting any better, far from it.

An airplane with two German officers so paralytically drunk that they mistake the Maas for the Rhine lands right in the middle of the bicycles of our Thirteenth Division. The German officers are slapped in the face until they have sobered up, and then they are interrogated, carbide lamps full in their faces, the third degree, rather you than me.

They answer politely enough, these officers, but suddenly the German major leaps to his feet and flings a small bundle of papers he has been carrying next to his chest into the burning stove. Our Belgian commandant rushes to the stove, burns his hand badly, another third degree, but manages to snatch the German papers out of the flames. What can still be read on these singed pages? That the Second German Air Fleet is about to attack Belgium, Holland, and northern France, that paratroopers are to be dropped, bridges across the Maas occupied, etc., etc.

"When?"

"It didn't say."

The radio crackles with bad news. From parts of the world you never hear mentioned, too. From Canada, for instance; Canadian troops are being landed, without ceremony, at English ports, Canada is taking fifty-five million pounds from its own treasury for a war loan to the English, just see what that comes to in Belgian francs.

"But why should the Germans want to invade us, you may ask? They're not complete idiots. They're massed along a front the length of the French border right now, and they'd have to extend that otherwise by miles and miles. And the Allies would be reinforced otherwise with our Belgian equipment and our Belgian troops. And another thing, *pardon*, Gaston, aren't the Germans doing good business with us right now? Just to mention one instance, those ten thousand railway trucks we're meant to be delivering to them as soon as possible, they're itching to get their hands on those. Business before, Isidore!"

"Strategically speaking," said Grandpa, "it wouldn't be a bad thing for the Germans if they were to attack us. Because the French army, holed up there in their forts and casements playing cards and drinking Pernod, would be forced to *s'é-par-piller*, to disperse, and you know that the Germans are surprise-attack specialists, just look what happened in Poland."

"Incidentally, did you hear about the mobilization of German dogs? Every German who owns one has to take it before a special examination board. Oh yes, they certainly know how to organize things, those fellows."

"Don't be too sure, Arthur. After all, you need supplies before you can organize. And the Germans simply don't have enough fuel. There isn't a taxi to be had anymore in all Berlin."

"They're bound to attack England, definitely. They've been printing English banknotes for a long time now."

Times are bad. Except for the radio shops. And for the Duchess of Windsor. She just spent a fortune at Lucien Lelong's fashion show in Paris. Mostly small turbans. Delft blue is all the rage just now, Constance! And a new shade called Finnish blue, it's like Delft but with a bit more gray.

Finland has been completely flattened, anyway. The Pope celebrated the anniversary of his coronation last week, but he's taken that Finnish business badly, they say.

In any case, this is not the time to be without a car.

Mama was cutting Papa's hair to tidy him up a little for his delicate call on Major Nowé de Waelhens. Papa was in a state. Louis knew the signs, the fiddling with his fingers, the hissing between the teeth, the unsteady voice as he raged against Mama, blaming her for the disaster.

"I never had the slightest trouble with any of my other cars or motorcycles. The Gilette, a dream! The Harley-Davidson, a pearl! Like an airplane! My Model T Ford never broke down once! And then suddenly my DKW wasn't good enough any longer. Her ladyship your mother decided that it shook too much, made too much noise, was too cold inside for her. And idiot that I am, I listened to her! I must have been soft in the head to do what she said!"

"Staf, sit still or I'll nick your ear!"

Papa held himself rigid. Because of all her complaints, Papa had traded the DKW (which Mama had claimed was not only drafty but also unstable, on account of that nasty skid on a country road covered with mud and sludge from beet carts) for a Fiat belonging to Thiery, Major Nowé de Waelhens's son. Plus three thousand francs. "I'll go and get the money from my mother at once," said Thiery. "Meanwhile may I have a trial run in the DKW out on the Doornik road, Meneer Seynaeve?"

"But of course, Thiery."

Thiery shot off, waved jauntily to Papa standing beside the Fiat (the cheapest model), and never returned. After having waited, cursing, for a few hours, Papa went off to the Fiat garage because there was a slight rattle in the engine.

"Just as well," said the garage man. "You can leave the Fiat in that corner over there."

"What for?"

"Mijnheer, I've been waiting three months now for the second, third, and fourth installments on that car."

Now Papa was sitting staring somberly in front of him. Mama clicked away with the scissors. Louis was looking forward to Papa's confrontation with the treacherous Thiery.

"*Voilà,*" said Mama and folded the towel covered with Papa's hair.

"*Voilà,*" said Papa. "That's what you get for trusting people, for being kind."

"Kind?" cried Mama. "Plain stupid, if you ask me. Thiery will have sold the DKW long ago and spent the money on loose women."

The Major's villa was a squat little building of yellow brick, pointed in black. "The Flemish colors," said Papa bitterly as they walked up the drive. He gave a start when a dog set up a deafening bark inside the house.

The Major's wife opened the door to them in person, a tall, morose-looking woman with a long nose and a scrawny neck. They were asked

237

to sit down on a flowered settee. Papa pressed his knees tight together as he outlined the ticklish situation.

"I know, I know, mijnheer," said Mevrouw Nowé, with a French accent. "I haven't had a wink of sleep for three days. Not a wink. Ever since Thiery disappeared. You know how it is, don't you, mijnheer, when you have an only child."

"It's the same with me, Madame," said Papa and gave Louis an accusing look.

"It's as if they can smell that Thiery has gone, mijnheer. They come from all over to knock at this door, they telephone, they buttonhole me in the street, in the Sarma. But he must have done it in a fit of *folie*, our Thiery, yes, in a fit of *folie*. I would repay you the money with the greatest of pleasure, no, more, I'd go down on my knees to you . . ."

"All I want is my car back," said Papa, "and we'll forget all about it."

"Oh, the car!" She raised her eyes to heaven, then placed a bony hand on her pointed collarbone. "He's been besotted with cars from childhood." She looked vaguely out into the garden.

"What are we going to do about it, Madame?"

"I'll be quite honest with you, mijnheer. Right now . . . these are hard times, do you follow me . . .? Especially now that my husband is having to help run the fort at Greben-Smael. And I'm sure you are enough of a patriot to realize that I can't bother him at this particular moment with some trifling sum of money when the Germans could be making their attack any time."

The garden had all her attention again. A long-haired young soldier was working with a garden hose.

"Of course, I wouldn't want to go straight to the police," said Papa brusquely.

She spread her dry, beringed fingers against the wrinkled skin on her neck. "But, mijnheer, what can I be hearing? Have you absolutely no feeling for your fatherland?"

"Indeed I have, indeed I have," said the man who had so often shouted "Bel-gi-um can kiss my bum" in the Café Groeninghe.

"In that case, why threaten a decent family with the police over a mere trifle?"

"A DKW is no trifle, Madame."

She looked Papa up and down from his eyebrows to his shoes.

"*Tiens.* And you looked such a reasonable, refined sort of person, too, mijnheer."

Papa waited. The young soldier emptied the hose by shaking it up and down.

"I wouldn't advise you to go to the police," said the tall woman. "You

238

would come off second best. The Nowé de Waelhens family has a long arm."

"Madame, I, too, have connections," said Papa.

"Any connections you may have aren't going to be able to help you a great deal right now. We know your sort of connections, mijnheer, and connections like that are likely to be put up against the wall any time now. Because you've been noted, Meneer Seynaeve. We know who can be counted on to stand by Belgium these days and who can't."

"You hideous skinny old bag!" Papa leaped to his feet, purple in the face. "We'll teach the likes of you a lesson yet. The Flemish people will hold you to account, Madame, they've been exploited by your kind for far too long! And I will have my DKW back, even if I have to take your Belgian flag and . . ."

What he would do with it never emerged. He choked, swallowed. Mevrouw Nowé de Waelhens ran to the window, waved, and called the young soldier as if in fear for her life, "Arsène! Arsène!"

Arsène came trotting up to the house, clambered through the open window, landed on the carpet with large flat feet, and stood before them, panting and breathing French fire.

"Arsène, throw this riffraff out. And be quick about it!"

Papa bowed. "The riffraff is leaving anyway, *Madame la Majorette. Mes hommages.*"

Because the English are planning to occupy the Swedish iron mines, the Germans have been obliged to march into Norway and Denmark. It's all happened like greased lightning. You simply can't beat German organization.

Mussolini claims to have a few tricks up his sleeve as well. But not until the spring.

In Poland only the Germans are allowed to wear leather footwear. The law of the victor. What would you do in their place?

The French are on our borders, just itching to get into Belgium. Ostensibly to forestall the Germans. They were on their way, the French were, with banners and bugles, when we stopped them.

"Oh, *pardon,*" said the French. "Forgive us, but we thought that your King Leopold had sent for us. *Pardon.*"

A shameless bunch. But what we managed to see of them, the French, was impressive enough. Instead of the mess kits they used to have, they've each got a proper cooking pot now. And they can use their tents as raincoats.

If the Germans come all the same, our government intends to evacuate the *whole* country, everyone without exception. Where to? That's something the government is still discussing.

Theo van Paemel, a plainclothes policeman who joined Papa on the pilgrimage to the Yser battlefields every year, made himself comfortable in the front room.

"The Nowé de Waelhenses do have a long arm," he said, "And what's more, Staf, this is not the right moment. In view of the general situation, you'd better lie low, my old friend."

"Yes, but the injustice of it . . ." said Papa.

"That'll all be taken care of," said Van Paemel. "I'll see to that young Franskiljon ape Thiery myself. If he ever shows his face around here again, he's in for it. But you, Staf, you've got to watch it. There's a dossier on you in our office as thick as my arm."

"What ever for?" cried Mama.

"Constance, you surely haven't forgotten those Germans in your house that time when you got the printing presses from Leipzig? There are some who claim you got those machines as a present from Goebbels to print Nazi propaganda. We've also had a letter to the effect that you had a portrait of Hitler on your mantelpiece. Or was it a bust?"

"A doll," said Louis. "A small Hitler Youth doll."

"People around here wouldn't see the difference, young man. In any case, Staf, you're on the list of people who pose a threat to the security of the state."

"Well, thank you very much!" Papa exclaimed.

"And if you ever get into trouble, Staf, we ordinary civilian policemen won't be able to do a lot for you. You'll come under military jurisdiction, because right now we're in a state of war."

"But Belgium isn't at war!"

"A state of war begins when the army is mobilized. Law of 1899."

"Well, thank you very much!"

"Another letter we received mentioned a sticker on the back of your car. A Rex sticker. And don't forget, either, your DKW is a German car. Details like that all count."

"Everyone is against me," said Papa and poured Theo van Paemel another geneva, his fifth.

The Germans have lost the war. Seven destroyers have been sunk at Narvik, a third of the German fleet. They can never make up for that.

Prime Minister Pierlot has tendered the resignation of his government. On account of the budget. But our King refuses to accept it. "What can you be thinking of, Pierlot! This really isn't the time."

In Finland wounded soldiers are left screaming for hours on the frozen lakes. Elks and wolves prowl close by. In Poland schoolboys Louis's age have been beheaded for tearing up a flag with a swastika on it.

In Paris, City of Lights, loose women walk the darkened streets shining their red pocket torches.

The streets of Walle were suddenly filled with cars being driven by strangers extremely slowly, boxes and mattresses strapped to the roofs, bursting with suitcases, bicycles, and children. Among them, in a Chevrolet packed unobtrusively with all their worldly goods, was Mama's pious sister, Aunt Berenice, and her husband, Uncle Firmin Debelianov, who came from Bulgaria, a land where people grow very old thanks to yogurt and the Orthodox Church. They stopped in Oudenaarde Road. The two sisters sobbed. Uncle Firmin nodded glumly. When Louis put out his hand, Uncle Firmin looked the other way.

Aunt Berenice had a broader, more peasantlike face than Mama. She wore no trace of makeup because her husband had had an extremely jealous streak ever since he had become an Adventist at the age of fifteen. Aunt Berenice laughed frequently, displaying a set of square, milk-white teeth. Her husband was a gloomy man. If he was forced to laugh, against his will, a smothered bleat would escape him. He did not talk much, partly because, in addition to a number of other organs, his vocal chords had been damaged during a near-fatal tonsillectomy. He had woken up the night before he was due to be discharged from the hospital. By his bedside stood an enamel spittoon. A young ninny of a nurse had poured bleach into it the evening before and left it there. Uncle Firmin, only half-awake and dying of thirst, had downed the contents of the vessel— which to his sleep-befuddled brain must have resembled the bowl he had used as a child back in some thatched Bulgarian hovel. The bleach had completely burned up his insides.

They stayed for a few days, sleeping on a mattress in the front room. They were in a hurry to get to France before the border was closed, but Mama begged her sister to stop a while, and Aunt Berenice took pity on her and stayed.

"Why are they in such a hurry to get out of Belgium?" asked Louis.

"Because your Uncle Firmin is a Jew," said Papa. "Jews always make off with their money. Or, rather, with *our* money."

Uncle Firmin was the first Jew Louis had ever seen. In Bastegem, Raf had once pointed out a surly-looking, dark-skinned character standing beside a delivery van full of carpets. "Look, a Jew!" But Louis hadn't really believed him. Uncle Firmin, with his heavy eyelids, his undeniably hooked nose, his full, wet lips, was patently more of a Jew. And because, during supper, the Jew remained sitting at the stove all by himself, vulnerable and brooding, Louis said, "Uncle, it's not fair that your people are being persecuted."

The Jew made a high-pitched sound. A shrill, drawn-out sound that ended like the scraping of a small stone in the chalk against the blackboard. Then he said hoarsely, "My people! My people! What Hitler does with the Jews is his own business!"

"Firmin has a Belgian passport," said Aunt Berenice.

"Why is he running away, then?" asked Mama.

"Because the Belgians are just as narrow-minded as the Germans, Constance," said the hoarse Jew-or-non-Jew. "And that's why it's more sensible, when times are hard, for someone like me, even if he isn't a Jew, to put as much distance as possible between himself and them."

"Thanks a lot, Firmin," said Mama, and later, as Louis went quietly as a mouse through Aunt Berenice's handbag out in the passage, he heard Mama say to Papa in the kitchen, "I don't know what to make of Firmin. Because when all's said and done, he is circumcised."

"How do you know that?" Papa burst out.

"Berenice told me."

"Do you talk about things like that, the two of you? A fine business. And in my own house, too!"

Louis found nothing exciting in the bag, stole twenty francs, tiptoed to the front door, slammed it shut extra hard, and walked noisily down the hall, scraping his feet and singing "It's a Long Way to Tipperary." When he came into the kitchen, his parents were discussing laying in large stocks of coffee, sugar, and coal.

"What in God's name can the Germans possibly want from us?"

"U-boat bases. Airfields. So they can reach England."

"The Danube is still frozen."

"France has to protect her heart, and her heart lies between Paris and Brussels. That's why the French are sure to come storming in on us one of these days with their tanks and their spahis and their filthy magazines."

"Not so long as we stay neutral."

"Our Princess Marie-José has had a little baby in the Royal Palace in Naples. A thirty-one-gun salute, Constance. And Prince Umberto, that idler, arrived too late from Rome. The baby was already in its cradle. A girl. They've already got two children. Maria-Pia, who's five and already knits scarves for Mussolini's soldiers, and the little Duke of Naples, who has the same gentle eyes as his grandfather, our King Albert."

Before starting a meal, Aunt Berenice and Uncle Firmin bowed their heads and closed their eyes for a good minute. During that time, they thought of all the starving children in countries near the Equator, Aunt Berenice explained, because only then did you realize how grateful you must be to God for having chosen you.

Piety had brought those two together. At the time, Aunt Berenice had been keeping company with "Ham" Renard, a corpulent teacher who made a fool of her, turning up impossibly late for every appointment or not turning up at all. After one of these rendezvous she felt quite desperate and was wandering about aimlessly and alone through the streets of the metropolis of Ghent when she heard a voice deep inside her, difficult to make out, as if it were being filtered through a luxuriant white beard. "Cross the road and take the second turning to the left." However, because of the absent Ham (so called because of his opinion, oft-declared in various cafés, that the best things about a woman were her thighs) she was in such a state that she took the second turning to the right. There she found a ramshackle building with an open door, from which issued a rosy glow as from an oil lamp above an altar. Boldly she stepped inside and found herself in a bare little room in which four old women, a postman, and a workman with a black eye who was being propped up by his small eleven-year-old daughter were listening to a preacher with a voice as sharp as a razor. This preacher, Firmin Debelianov, undid Aunt Berenice with his Jewish-Bulgarian glances even as he condemned the use of alcohol and tobacco, even as he proclaimed the Advent, the Coming of God, even as he explained that this Coming had once been wrongly presaged for the year 1843 by the Founder of his Church while he himself put the definitive Coming at about the year 1982.

Shortly afterward they were married and Aunt Berenice sold encyclopedias, atlases, and religious reference works to village worthies throughout West and East Flanders while Uncle Firmin waited in the car and prayed. Uncle Firmin considered Belgians a coarse and dirty people and refused to drink from a glass, eat off a plate, or use cutlery that had not been washed by his wife before his very eyes.

One Saturday Papa brought home some pork cutlets. "Just to see his face." Mama started frying them. When the smell reached Uncle Firmin in the front room where he was reading *Is There Life After Death?*, he rose from his chair, walked into the kitchen, took one horror-stricken look at the pan, and ran out into the street uttering Bulgarian curses.

"You can see that's a Jew," crowed Papa. "That was his gut reaction to an unclean animal!"

Grandpa chewed on one of the cutlets and said, "For a Christian, he certainly has Jewish habits."

"And that stocky figure of his," said Papa. "All Jews get fat in their thirties. Because they don't go in for sports. Who ever heard of a Jewish sportsman?"

"He can't weigh much more than you do, Staf."

"But he's quite a different shape, Father. I'm surprised you don't see that."

"Berenice is not her old self," said Mama. "I've lost a sister."

Our King Leopold, for instance, now there's a sportsman for you. Lean, despite that heavy bone structure he inherited from his ancestors. Although when Meneer Tierenteyn once shook hands with him, he was surprised by how limp his handshake was.

And he is a dreamer, too, our King. Mostly he dreams about the past, about his family's history. That's something commendable in a king because it helps to apply the lessons of history to the present day. Although the world keeps changing all the time, you can never steer a fixed course. But when he isn't dreaming, he keeps his ear to the ground, His Majesty does. And what does he hear? Mainly those Socialists Spaak and De Man whispering in his ear and telling him to keep our noses clean, not to get involved in our neighbors' troubles, to mind our very own, wholly and exclusively Belgian, business. Of course, the Communists and the Walloons are against that. If it were up to them, we'd be asking our so-called Allies to move in with us right now. No, our King keeps asking himself, What is my duty? What would my chivalrous Papa have done in these circumstances? And then Count Capelle, his secretary, says, "First and foremost, Sire, you must maintain the dynasty."

What else could he say, though?

Louis was sitting in the cinema with Tetje and Bekka. The second feature, with Double Patte and Patachon (the small fat one was Harold Madsen and the tall skinny one Carl Schenström), had just started. The two comedians were standing in an immense field of wheat, arguing with jerky gestures about how, where, and when they could do the greatest possible harm to someone or other who had insulted them, when a drunken young soldier started dancing and leaping about right in front of the screen. Waving his beer bottle, he roared in a great, hoarse voice,

244

"You peasant shits, don't try and kid yourselves I'm going to let them shoot my balls off for just one franc a day, the price of one miserable beer!" To the jeers and yells of the spectators, Tarara the doorman chased him outside with a few well-aimed kicks to his backside.

Louis saw that Bekka had turned as white as a sheet. She bit her thumb and rubbed her eyes.

"Aren't you feeling well?" he asked. She shook her head.

"She's certain war is going to break out any minute," said Tetje, in a voice unusually anxious for him.

Next day at dawn, without the slightest noise unless it was the rustle of angels' wings, ten perfidious gliders flew, unforeseen by any member of our General Staff, over Fort Greben-Smael and dropped eighty German paratroopers. The fort was taken. Major Nowé de Waelhens lost his right leg and several soldiers their lives in the sudden smoke, gunfire, thunder, flames.

So that was it, at last. "At last," whispered Louis to the mirror in his bedroom.

Even on the first day, while Guderians's tanks were rolling in, while the Belgian air force was being reduced from one hundred and seventy-one planes to ninety-one in just a few hours, while Louis was sitting by the radio, overwhelmed by an absurd, quivering, jubilant coldness, even on that first day, the French (who had been waiting for the chance since Napoleon) poured into our country.

They hung around Walle, none too eager to make a rush for the fortified line they were meant to establish on the River Dijle near Leuven, while the Belgians were keeping the Hun at bay with their perfunctorily oiled rifles.

The French, their helmets askew, stinking of garlic and Pernod, assaulted Flemish widows and orphans, forced their way into our homes without knocking, demanded drink and women, yes, just as if we were still living in the Middle Ages. Général de Fornel de la Lourencie noticed that our disheveled reservists, dressed half in civvies and half in uniform, were mingling with the refugees, and ordered these deserters to be reformed into companies. *Manu militari!* Under French command!

Hold on. Who in the world does he think he is, where in the world does he think he is?

"Staf, I'm letting the cat out of the bag, and if my bosses ever hear of it I'll be thrown right into jail, but you haven't a moment to lose," said Theo van Paemel, a tot of geneva in his hand. "You've got to leave town right away, Staf."

"Are you serious? But I haven't got a car. Thiery's taken it!"

"Too bad. Just make sure you get away. Or we'll be ordered to come and get you. The new department, State Security, has gone raving mad. Yesterday they arrested a farmer they found burning papers in his field, now he's flat in his cell without a tooth left in his head. And they nabbed a young student, too, for drawing a pair of spectacles on a poster for baby powder."

"Spectacles?"

"They think it's a secret message for paratroopers or fifth columnists. And even if we don't arrest you, that mob from Toontjes Street is likely to come and pester you. Yesterday they ripped the cassock off a priest to make sure he wasn't wearing a German uniform underneath.

"You're on the list, Staf. Along with all the other subscribers to that four-part *History of Flanders.*"

"But where should he go?" shrieked Mama.

"To France, if he can still make it."

"Into the lion's mouth," said Papa, startled.

"Into the cock's beak," said Louis. "The Frenchman is a cock. The lion stands for Flanders and England."

Papa gave his pedantic child a bewildered look. Through the window Negroes in ragged uniforms could be seen dancing the Lambeth Walk, holding their rifles out like lances. Tommies in their comical flat helmets showed them how to do it. Other African riflemen were entrenched behind crates of Roman-Pils beer awaiting the advancing German motorized divisions.

"Louis, my son, I have to go. Constance, my wife, we may never see each other again. Though who knows, perhaps we will."

Mama stroked Papa's wet cheek. Papa was wearing a green raincoat with epaulets, like Gary Cooper playing a war reporter in the Orient.

"If I still had my car, Louis, I would take you along, but Thiery . . ."

Louis broke in. "And who would look after Mama?"

"You're right. You're a good boy." Papa took a few steps toward the gleaming red fire engine Tetje's father had borrowed, bought, or stolen. Tetje's father had said, "Mijnheer Seynaeve, *à la guerre comme à la guerre.* Don't trouble your head about it. The brigade has more than enough vehicles. And this one's tank is full to the brim."

Bekka embraced her father, who then climbed behind the wheel with a sob.

Papa said, "I don't want to leave, Constance, you know that, but Queen Wilhelmina of Holland has left, too." When Papa had gone helplessly to sit down beside Tetje's father, smiling and waving uneasily, Louis saw, lying against the windscreen and within easy reach of his fleeing father, a double bar of Côte d'Or milk chocolate and a large box of Lutti toffees.

Everyone waved. The fire engine had trouble starting, which made the neighbors laugh.

"He's not used to it," said Bekka dully, keeping her eyes fixed on the stocky figure of her Gypsy of a father behind the wheel.

"Let's just hope those two don't fall out during their *voyage,*" said the baker's wife. When the red vehicle, tooting its horn, had disappeared, Louis took his mother by the arm.

"Come," he said, like a man.

The Germans drop dummies dressed as soldiers. That ties up the heroic resistance of our men for hours. Are our troops going to have to withdraw as far as the Yser, as in '14–'18? That's what they'd like to do, but where are the field maps?

All German soldiers have been taught to swim. They swim across our rivers and canals like water rats, keeping their rucksacks and machine guns bone dry.

The Belgians have to withdraw. At least make sure you take your ammunition along with you! But how now, brown cow? There is no transport! Shoot it all off at the sparrows, then! The spring air, black with smoke.

The cars of all those who work in the ministries, in the administration, are crammed with suitcases and children. But our roads, perfectly cobbled, perfectly good for country fair races, cannot cope with so much traffic. Mounted artillery, transport columns, bicycle companies inch their way among the refugees. Engines steam, overheated by the painfully slow pace, drivers fall asleep, horses snort. Everyone thinks no one else will be traveling in the dead of night. In the dark, men shoot everything that moves. Anyone squatting by the roadside to relieve himself is as good as dead.

Bridges are overloaded and collapse. Commandant Serthuysen de Branchard lies squeezed between iron girders and draws his last, tobacco-laden breath, pipe in mouth, trousers full of shit.

Across the Dender. Across the Meulebeke. Across the Maalbosbeek. Back!

Children loiter in the empty villages, crawling into abandoned vehicles still dripping with blood.

In Bastegem, where Meerke, Aunt Violet, and Uncle Omer are entrenched in the cool cellar, our army is putting up a brave show. Pity the soldiers can't take cover in the specially built casemates, but the keys are nowhere to be found. Our army has taken its stand in front of the concrete walls, behind barbed wire. Our field guns are perfectly good, though if you fire them too often they tend to jam.

Leaving the Maginot Line to one side, the Germans advance right through Belgium, making straight for our army's munitions, which are stored in Flanders and guarded by the Ardennes Light Infantry, who, disguised as women, are waiting on the first floor of village houses, machine guns at the ready on the windowsills.

Arab horses clatter along the country roads, pulling dilapidated carts in which Tommies smoking Players sit on each other's knees.

The enemy approaches in rubber dinghies by the light of the moon and occupies the churchyard. Approaches our beloved Walle.

But the river Leie stands in their way. The river is low and choked with planks and plants.

Our troops are having difficulty communicating with each other, who could have anticipated that so much telephone wire would be needed?

The couriers carrying the tactical rescue plans are boys from Limburg who understand not a word of West Flemish, keep losing their way, and end up wandering in the fields, munching salami.

Louis is not allowed to go down into the street but slips out all the same. Along the edge of Harelbeke, where the bearded Peter Benoit gave birth to immortal music, observation balloons float, swaying to the organ music of the guns.

Louis crouches down, points his forefinger, and shouts, "Boom!" A balloon bursts and drops in flames on groaning Germans.

Walle is declared an open city. Policemen visit every district to give out the news. Lie low, everyone! But our infantry, egged on by outrageous radio propaganda, intends to fight on. So what now? The people of Walle cannot flee, because the French border has been sealed off by disgruntled French customs officers who demand documents stamped by phantoms in some strange town at some other time. The inhabitants of Walle curse at the alien Belgian officers. "Scum! If you want to die, go and do it somewhere else! There are hundreds of heavy German batteries out there pointing straight at us, at our Belfry, at our cafés, at our houses!"

The inhabitants of Walle refuse to come out of their houses. They do not want their bridges blown up. Women walk around with men's white shirts tied to broomsticks.

The officers stand about open-mouthed. *Que faire, Robert?* Just imagine, Colonel, if the Germans, those sneaky cowards, worm their way in among our local people, we won't be able to fire at them! Or before you know what's happened, you've hit a businessman from Walle with six children, a school friend of Paul-Henri Spaak. *Mais non, Gaston!*

Machine gun fire erupts in the short, green wheat. It comes from Belgian repeaters, you can hear that, ten rounds a minute. (The German guns fire five hundred and forty rounds a minute.) And then thundering and crackling, splinters and explosions, in the house, in the corridors, in the cellars, right through the walls. "Louis, stay here, Louis, don't leave me alone," cries Mama. But he clambers up the stairs and finds the street bathed in sunshine and flames. He leans against the front of the Bossuyts' house. An airplane dives straight at him. Louis lifts his head to get a better look, the last thing you should do, because up there the gunner can see a bright patch and aim his gun straight at it. This gunner does just that, Louis is asking for it, begging for it. The Bossuyts' windowpane shatters, the brick smashes next to Louis's head, turned away at the very last moment. The plane sweeps back into the sky. A shudder of all-powerful, leaping life shoots through Louis's body. Dazed, he gathers up the warm, twisted shrapnel fragments. With a jagged edge he deliberately gashes himself on the cheek, causing elation and wild pain. He runs into his house and yells, pelts down the stairs to the cellar, where his mother takes her fingers with the rosary away from her face. She looks. She screams. She takes Louis in her arms, pushes him away, examines the bleeding laceration. "It's nothing, nothing at all, my naughty boy," she says in a trembling voice. "It'll heal in no time. Wash it in cold water. Go and do it now."

"I don't dare go upstairs," he says. And again she presses him to her warmth, and then licks his cheek with long strokes, swallows his blood. Tears come to her eyes, little pearls bubbling up suddenly as if she were one of the little ones at the Institute.

The Germans are coming. The good people of Walle are forced to march before them, blankets in their widespread arms. But our infantry won't give in. Why not? So as to give those English rabbits enough time to run back across the Channel to join their buffoon of a Churchill. The English make out that it's perfectly all right for them to run off like thieves in the night because Canadian troops, fresh as daisies, are coming to relieve them. Tell that to the marines, Tommy!

Pamphlets fall like snow over Walle, texts in French and English saying we should give ourselves up, that our position is hopeless, that our leaders have fled the country.

Has our King fled, then? *Mais non, Algernon,* he's a man who sticks to his post, and his post is right here. His proclamation is as follows: "Officers, men, come what may, my lot will be your lot. Our cause is just and pure." Our King has even written a note to his royal colleague, George of England. "Dear George, you know as well as I do that a king mustn't leave his people in the lurch, unlike some whose names I shall not mention but who used to be my ministers."

Churchill, who has waited until all his Tommies have been embarked safe and sound under the flames of tens of thousands of incendiary bombs, declares solemnly, *"Bon, all right, okay,* tell the Belgians we got home all right and they can clean up the mess we left behind now."

King George sends a reply. *"Dear Leopold,* don't be childish, come to London, you'll be well looked after here."

"No, Sir," said His Majesty, our King.

Holland is throwing in the sponge!

Postal money orders can no longer be cashed!

There is no more flour for bread. Those blackguards put in potato flour instead!

Hundreds of wounded are screaming in a hospital train parked in a siding of Walle station. A very young medical student runs up and down trembling amid shouts of "Water, water, Mother!" Any moment now cholera is bound to break out.

For four days Uncle Florent does wonderful business selling tires he has stripped from abandoned cars, and then Belgium surrenders. The first Germans in Walle are reported on the Ghent Road, riding those queer, uncomfortably high Dutch bicycles.

Most of our regimental colors are being burned. The rest are being hidden away in St. Andrew's Benedictine Abbey. The abbot, Dom Nève de Mévergnies, accepts them solemnly and hands them to Dom de Meeüs d'Argenteuil, who will watch over them as if they were holy relics. The colors of the Eighteenth Engineers are cut into pieces; the officers wear them under their shirts, one the Lion, the others the silk, the embroidery, and the fringe.

Tetje, Bekka, and Louis, who are allowed to associate with each other openly now that their fathers are roaming inhospitable French parts together, walk past the department store, where a shouting, joyful crowd from Toontjes Street, bent double, is hurriedly looting radios, fur coats, dresses, bread-slicing machines. The three of them are on the point of climbing through the broken shop windows when a swarm of formidably helmeted Germans in green bomber jackets chases everyone away and the war is over.

Mama no longer cleared the table, no longer put the bedspreads back onto the beds, allowed the cauliflower to burn.

"Shall I make the beds, Mama?"

"How often do I have to tell you? Just leave me alone."

Through the streets of Walle, past the darting glances of people repairing their houses, the German army marched toward England. The cheerful, tanned young soldiers marched in straight lines, in perfect step, swinging their arms and singing in two-part harmony about Erika, not a girl but a flower. In the turrets of the tanks sat knights in oiled black jackets, skulls-and-crossbones glinting on their berets.

Helmeted motorcyclists in sunglasses wore metal plates on their chests.

"No one can stand up to those people," said Uncle Robert. "Because they have the sacred fire in them. And we don't. Never did. Just take the radio. We say, 'Ladies and gentlemen, here is the news.' They say: 'The Supreme Command of the *Wehrmacht'* . . . *Wehrmacht,* the word says it all, *wehrt Euch mit aller Macht*—defend yourself with all your might."

"Will we all have to learn German now?" asked Grandma. "I'm too old for that. And my mouth gets round French better."

"Schweine–poop–*fleisch,"* said Louis. "That's German for ham."

"The declensions are the hardest part," said Aunt Hélène.

"We'll just have to make the best of it," said Grandma.

"We've always had to make the best of it. We've never done anything else in our entire history!"

"Yes, but this is the first time we've been under the Germans. From the same stock, people like us."

"Some consolation! Whenever I hear people say 'people like us,' I know how the land lies."

"Still, Hitler is doing his best to send the Flemish prisoners of war home before the Walloons. That means he understands the Flemish position very well, he knows we've been exploited for centuries."

"Hitler went with Göring to Ardooie, to Langemark, and to Ypres where the little farmhouse he was quartered in during '14–'18 is still standing, and he said to the farmer's wife, who still remembered him from those days, 'Well, madame, is there anything I can do for you?'

" 'Ah, Meneer Hitler, my nephew has been taken prisoner by your people, and we need him so desperately for the harvest. Could you put in a good word for him?' 'Of course, madame, if that's all you want.' And he began issuing orders right away in German, and it was all settled there and then. Surely that's worth a *'Heil Hitler!'* "

Mama had migraine—today of all days—and no matter how much Louis nagged, she refused to go with him, this ghastly first day at the College.

He had been several times during the week to look at the turreted buildings, the property of the Bishop of Bruges. Grandpa had told how King Leopold had been present at the first prize-giving ceremony and how ever since then the College had produced statesmen, scientists, poets, great industrialists. "So, Louis, remember our good name!"

He walked among scores of boys who, like him, carried a briefcase but, unlike him, shamelessly brushed past the priests. In the large corridor leading to his classroom, much better lit, wider, and dirtier than the corridors in the Institute (so that they could keep a closer eye on you), a tall bald priest was waiting for him. His moist dark eyes behind a pair of spectacles with an unusually heavy frame discerned Louis's wish to escape, his wish to run to the Leie and—at his age!—his wish to go back to his Mama. They could also read the sin inside Louis.

"Come with me." Louis walked alongside the well-cut, elegant, perfectly ironed cassock. "A grandson of my friend Seynaeve has greater responsibilities than other pupils. Understood?"

"Yes, Father."

"I will not treat you unfairly, but neither will I give you preferential treatment. Understood?"

Coming to a halt in front of an immense crucifix, the priest fixed Louis with jet-black pupils, enlarged by the lenses of his spectacles.

"His name is De Launay," Louis told Grandma at the end of the afternoon. He had come in skipping and singing because the first day had gone wonderfully well, he had been accepted by the chattering group of pupils in the playground as one of them, and no one had noticed that he had come from a backward nuns' boarding school.

"De Launay, De Launay, that rings a bell. He must be from the Bruges branch, I shall ask Aunt Margo."

"But we call him the Rock." (We!)

Grandma heard his Latin declensions. Then he ate three large portions of jellied skate. As he walked home, firemen were using poles and hooks to fish a bulging sack out of the Leie. It was a dead soldier with a creamy ball full of red holes for a face. The bloated hands paddled fingerless in the water. A rope had been wound around his preposterously swollen belly. According to a postman (whose evening round had been consigned to oblivion), it was the body of a deserter who had been so frightened of both the Germans and his Belgian superiors that he had committed suicide. "Just look at that rope! He must have wound the rope around himself first with a lump of concrete on the other end and then tied his wrists together because he was afraid that if the concrete broke free of the rope he'd have to start swimming for dear life and that was something he didn't want to happen. You've got to be crazy with fear to do something like that. But if you do do it, you might as well do it right."

Then, three weeks later, a stranger opened the front door with a key. Mama stood disconcerted in the passage where the light bulb had gone, hugged him, and drew him inside, and into the kitchen walked a leaner, rejuvenated Papa, burned a deep red, carrying melons and perfume. He shook Louis's hand, wouldn't let go.

Deciding that these two married people, separated for so long by the fortunes of war, would like to be alone during their reunion, Louis went out into the street, where Tetje's father, Papa's faithful companion, was leaning against a lemon-yellow pedal car and crying. Bekka had her arms clasped around his middle and was shouting, "Daddy, Daddy!" above the murmurings of the neighbors.

Louis crept into the car, would have liked to step on the pedals and take a ride around the block, but father and daughter Cosijns remained as if glued in place, the sound of their joy like lamentation. (Just as "This my joy therefore is fulfilled" is also sad, incomplete. Nothing is ever fulfilled, Sister Adam, you can't fool me.)

"What we went through is indescribable, I couldn't begin to tell you in twenty-five years.

"Right through the lines, tanks just two inches away.

"Camps crawling with lice and fleas, not to mention everything else.

"Deep in French shit, I won't say any more.

"The French who threw stones at us because we had capitulated. Who called our King a rotten fish. Who surrendered, with a bottle of wine at the ready.

"They wanted to put us to work! I said, 'Excuse me, we don't happen to be laborers.'

"That we got back home alive just proves there is a God.

253

"It's a miracle we weren't murdered.

"Because the Belgian State doesn't care what it does. Making common cause with the French! No scruples at all. A great man like Joris van Severen put in chains and handed over to those French bastards. It all goes to show, Louis, that when push comes to shove our fine Belgian state doesn't think twice about stamping out us Flemings.

"But Van Severen's blood will be on their heads!"

"Don't keep dwelling on it, Staf," said Aunt Hélène. Mama continued to gaze in a state of confusion and surprise at the stranger filling the kitchen with his complaint, who then added, as an afterthought, "And tell me, how are things at school?"

"Fine, Papa." (If it weren't for the Rock, able to spy out sin in the most secret corners, in the bathroom, in the bedroom, behind a hedge, on the way home.)

The rowdy boys thumping one another with their briefcases by the school gate were calling him, but the Rock detained him. The smooth surface of his scalp reflected the sun, he hitched up the belt of his cassock.

"Sit over there," said the Rock in the chalky salty air of the classroom.

"No, there." The Rock pointed to Maurice de Potter's seat, he knew that Maurice was Louis's best friend.

"You will have noticed that I've been keeping my eye on you now and then during lessons, as well as during break."

"Yes, Father."

"Why do you think I do that?"

The answer seemed so obvious that Louis hesitated but then said anyway, "Because you promised my grandfather that . . ."

"No," said the Rock. His cheeks and chin were as smooth as his scalp. Didn't he have any facial hair, or did he shave every hour? The yelling boys by the gate fell silent, a boat chugged along the Leie among all the bloated corpses still shackled to concrete in the slime. The Rock's cassock—Mama would be able to name the material—is too elegant for a teacher, the collar ivory-white, flawless. Sometimes, during dictation, he uses a small silver implement to push back his cuticles. Why isn't he saying anything?

"Louis, I don't like what I see. Oh, I'm certain you do your best, and you are talented enough, your talent is the least of our problems, no, what I am worried about is your soul." (Worry about your own beardless soul!)

"Do you get along well with your classmates?"

"Fairly well, Father."

"With whom do you get along best?"

"With Maurice."

"I thought I'd noticed that. And who comes next?"

"Martelaere."

"Not Simons?"

"As well. Yes, perhaps Simons first and then Martelaere."

"Yes, that was my impression, too. It doesn't surprise me. You are shrewd enough to ensure the affection of boys more innocent than yourself. Yes, indeed. You'll go far. Thank you, you can go now. Oh, yes, just one other thing. You know that before long you will have to present yourself for examination to the Fund for the Gifted. If I were you, I would do some preparing, I wouldn't count on the fact that my grandfather is on the board. What is it? Don't think of me as your enemy, Louis. Not for a moment. How could I be? Do you believe me?"

"Of course, Father."

"Of course, he says. There is no of course about it. Why should you believe me? After all, I am not infallible like the Holy Father."

"He is only infallible when he speaks from his throne!" exclaimed Louis. What is this priest getting at, this smooth variant of seven dangerous Sisters rolled into one? He wants to trap me, to confuse me.

"Good, Louis. The Council of 1870. Excellent."

"Pope Pius IX!"

"The nuns at Haarbeke have instructed you thoroughly, bravo! An interesting Council, incidentally. Between you and me, Pope Pius had it entirely his own way. Five hundred and thirty-three votes for and two against. *Faut le faire*. It is, of course, possible to question Our Holy Father's soundness of mind, and in certain circles that is just what is happening, do not forget, Louis, he was over eighty at the time and his strength had been somewhat sapped in his youth by a touch of epilepsy, but all the same, Louis, what tenacity, what tactical ability! Don't you agree?"

He twirled the large matte gold signet ring with his family crest on his finger, it possessed the power to smite mosquitoes, pupils, or soldiers with invisible, blistering heat rays.

A servant in a lead-gray apron, carrying two buckets, pushed the door open with his foot and apologized.

"Oh no, it doesn't matter, come in, Coorens, there is nothing here that shouldn't see the light of day, nothing at all! No, we've finished our discussion! Just carry on with your work. We're as good as gone."

The Rock pushed Louis toward the door and, once in the corridor, strode hurriedly off, the unpredictable man of whom the mathematics teacher had said that he was a great scholar but no teacher.

He was in the middle of his chemistry homework and Papa was making a lot of clatter washing up, when Mama, who had gone to bed a few hours earlier, began to sing *"Der Wind hat mir ein Lied erzählt."*—"The wind has told me a song."

"She's at it again," said Papa, folding the dishcloth neatly in four.

"At what?"

"Who'll ever know? And it isn't even the full moon."

Louis found his mother sitting on the edge of the bed in her slip, a prickly, shiny fur coat on her knees.

Her voice was shriller and shakier than Zarah Leander's in *La Habanera*.

"People can hear you in the street," said Louis.

"What of it? What's wrong with that?"

"Nothing." He dropped into a low easy chair positioned like a breakwater among the sea of petticoats, negligées, and towels, gingerly placing his feet among the frills and furbelows of silk, satin, and wool.

"I've finished my homework," he lied.

"Me too," she said with a giggle. The scissors in her hand moved, their points catching the light. "What's he doing?"

"Washing up."

She thought about it. On her shoulders, her neck, you could see deep-red spots as if she had dabbed them on with red ink.

Tufts of black fur, plucked from the pelt of some unknown black beast, lay spread over the bed. Mama returned to snipping here and there at the sleeves of the fur coat.

"Why are you doing that, Mama?"

"I want to tear it to shreds, then I'll put all the little pieces in a bag, take the bag to St. Anne's Bridge, then I'll climb right to the top of the Belfry, and then I'll scatter it all from the top, then for the first time in their lives the people of Walle will see black snow."

A low chortling sound that ended in a snort.

"It's horsehair," said Mama, "from a little foal that was probably beige to start with and was dyed black afterward."

"What'll Grandpa say?"

"If you give someone a present, they can do what they like with it. Anyway, he gave the foal to Aunt Mona as a present. She is his great love."

"Whose? Grandpa's?"

"Least said, soonest mended." She cut triangles out of the collar.

Then she picked up one of the triangular pieces from the floor, looked in the wardrobe mirror, held the small black-haired patch low against her

256

abdomen, and burst into stifled laughter. Louis looked away, at his feet lay the front page of *Volk en Staat*. Clouds of soot and flame were leaping out of London's Cathedral, as Churchill, cigar between pursed lips and a laurel wreath on his bald head, plucked a lyre.

"A modern Nero," read the caption.

Germans marched by right under the window. Boyish voices above the thud of boots. Mama ran to the window, drew back the curtains a few inches, and peered out. Her buttocks strained against the salmon-colored slip.

"Careful. Don't let them see any light!"

"They can stick me in jail for all I care." She let go of the curtains.

"You're crazy!"

"Maybe, but not about you!"

"Don't I know it." She was startled by the bitterness in his voice and came up to him smelling warm, soft. "It's not true, little one, I just said that to say something." Perhaps she had meant to stroke his cheek, but her movement was too abrupt, he felt the ball of her thumb hit his face.

"Oh!" she exclaimed. "Did I hurt you? I didn't, did I? I can't help it. Oh, I do everything wrong!" She examined her neck, her shoulders, close up to the mirror, dabbed at the spots that were now a deeper red. "Just look at these, will you!"

The two of them stood reflected in the wardrobe mirror as if in a photograph in *Cinémonde,* a tousle-haired film star with a cleft between her breasts and a boy in short pants who was lingering illicitly at her side, who had shamefully forced his way into her bedroom, his body filled with an enjoyable guilty, feverish heat.

"Downstairs with you, quickly."

"Why?" asked Louis.

"Go see what your father is up to."

"Can't I stay a little longer?"

"No," she said slowly, almost reluctantly.

Louis threw pebbles at Bekka, who leaped away behind the crumbling wall of a ruined house. He scored one hit, and the street reverberated with her yelp and his fearsome Sioux war whoops. She claimed he had broken one of her little rabbit ribs, he wanted to listen to her chest like one of those perpetually inebriated, top-hatted doctors in Westerns, but she said, "Keep your hands off me." Then they walked to the soup kitchen and got a bowl of soup each from the Germans.

Bekka's father had written. He was doing very well in Essen, the barracks were full of Flemings, the kitchen as well, he could send thirty marks home every week, he asked for hair oil, two bars of Sunlight soap, a rosary, and trouser buttons of the "bachelor" type, the kind you just pressed together.

Papa's business was doing badly, the people of Walle had few printing jobs, there was a shortage of paper, you needed a permit for every hundredweight, but could you get one?

"I'd like to do you a favor, Staf, you know me, but I'll get it in the neck if I let you have paper, unless you can produce a membership card in the VNV or the DEVLag or something like that."

"But I've marched all my life out there at the front, right next to the Flemish Lion, in the front rank, there are photographs to prove it, I can show them to you. And I've never missed a single one of the Yser pilgrimages!"

"A membership card, Staf."

"Am I going to be forced to live from hand to mouth, I, who fought for Flanders against the gendarmes?"

"But why don't you become a member? I simply don't understand it, if you're such a dyed-in-the-wool Fleming."

Swallowing impotent curses, Papa stormed out of the office. But Grandpa was unyielding. The day Papa became a member of any of those organizations, Grandpa would wash his hands of him, "and I'll dig out that whole bundle of IOUs, too."

"But, Father, those were good for before the war, because we could have had trouble then with the Belgian government and the Catholic education authorities, but now that Flanders is about to spread her wings, why can't I be part of it all?"

"Staf, a promise is a promise. You swore it the day I made you that loan of a hundred thousand francs. Just as I had to swear to the bishop that no child of mine would ever become an official member of an anti-Belgian group."

"I could murder him," said Papa at home, and, "I would be within my rights, legitimate self-defense, what he wants is to starve me and my family to death."

"Who? Grandpa?" asked Louis.

"The Bishop of Bruges. And he's a distant relative of ours! He compiles dossiers on everyone who is a member of this group or that. Why are people running down the Gestapo or the GPU when things are just as bad over here?"

"We are bound to love, reverence, and obey our Ecclesiastical Superiors and to assist them in the exercise of their religious duties."

"Louis, learn your lessons and shut up!"

"That *is* the eighth lesson, Papa."

"What do you mean?"

"Of the catechism."

Papa glared and started to read *Gone with the Wind,* but Mama took the book from his hands. "I'm reading that." He started on Stijn Streuvel's *The Flax Field* for the fourth time. So as to exorcize the ghosts of poverty and death by starvation from the house in Oudenaarde Road, it had been decided that Mama would go out to work. On the recommendation of the Dean she had been offered a post in the ERLA, as secretary to the director, Herr Lausengier, and had learned to speak fluent German in less than a month. Declensions included. She was slimmer, used more makeup, but never laughed out loud anymore.

Members of the Black Brigade were playing cards in the Café Groeninghe. Marnix de Puydt and Leevaert, his boon companion, were sitting behind the palms that divided the little side room from the café. Both were red in the face. Marnix de Puydt's bow tie drooped, his thick curly hair lay in strands across his forehead. "*Houzee!*" he mumbled, using the old form of greeting that the National Socialists had revived.

"*Houzee,*" said Papa.

"A Scotch, Staf?"

"No, thanks. Two lemonades, Noël!"

"Dr. Borms," said Marnix de Puydt, "for whom I had the honor to vote in '28 when he was languishing in a Belgian jail, has not forgotten the poet who remained loyal to him, and tonight, Staf, I drink to his health, but not with a lemonade."

"Noël, bring me a Geuze!" called Papa. "If it's for Borms, that's different . . ."

"Dr. Borms has done me the honor of asking me to serve on the Commission for Reparations to the activists of '14–'18, to help establish what is owing to those who have suffered for Flanders. I will not shirk from doing them justice."

"I don't know if that's a good idea," said Leevaert, a personal enemy of Grandpa's. Grandpa disapproved of his beating his wife, Lea. According to Grandma, Grandpa had once planned to take Lea to the Côte d'Azur, where Lea's sister owned a villa that stood empty during the winter.

"Why not, you renegade?" cried De Puydt.

"Why associate the activists publicly with the advancement of the Flemish people as a whole, on which we are now entitled to count?"

"Count? Discount!" yelled De Puydt. One of the Black Brigade men playing cards shouted even louder, "Hey, there, let's have some peace and quiet." His neighbor, who had two silver stripes across his epaulets, said, "Puydt, go home and write your verse, you're nothing but a curse, or worse."

De Puydt looked haughtily at the noisy café crowd, thrust aside a palm frond, a sweating red dwarf in the jungle, and raised a threatening forefinger. "I will not tolerate anyone in this establishment trampling the memory of activism underfoot. The activists laid the foundation stone . . ." The rest was lost in jeering laughter and booing. Marnix de Puydt laid his tangled wet curls across his forearm on the table. "My people, my people," he said in a strangled voice.

"Marnix," said Papa. "There has been some talk about a lecture you are due to give in Wannegem, on Cyriel Verschaeve, I believe, you must need posters and programs and pamphlets. And seeing that I just happen to have a few days to spare and that my machine is awash in red ink, I thought we might perhaps . . . It won't take a moment, I've brought a few models for you." The face of an old woman looked up. "Models? Where? I will judge them in the light of perfection, by the canons of beauty!"

"By your own bloody cannon, no doubt!" bawled the block leader of the Black Brigade.

The Rock pressed a packet of biscuits into Louis's hand. "Here, I find it easier to fast than you do. I'm used to it. Of course, that means that any merit due to me is that much less."

"Thank you, Father." He broke one biscuit, the crisp, crumbly froth melted immediately in his mouth.

"I imagined your first thought would be to share it with your bosom friend, De Potter."

"You are right, Father. I just didn't think."

"It's not particularly important, it's just that I thought he was someone close to your heart."

"Maurice is still a child."

"Perhaps you should spoil him all the more in that case." Through the black horn-rimmed spectacles his eyes looked twice their real size. And yet he doesn't seem to see me. Or does he see me upside down? Grandfather said, "If you take out the eye of a salamander and snap the nerve running from eye to brain and then put the eye back in the other way around, the nerve will grow back but the creature will see everything upside down." Louis wished he could stand on his head quickly and easily, as Vlieghe used to do.

"What are you laughing at?" asked the Rock.

"Nothing. I'm sorry."

"Oh, laugh all you want," said the Rock, with unusual indulgence. "Even someone as serious as St. Jerome used to laugh quite frequently, it is said, without good cause. That's how God Himself laughs now and then, I believe. Because if He is the darkness in us, then He must also be the light in us. Our joy, too, at times." Suddenly, as occasionally happened during Latin or Religious Knowledge lessons, the Rock seemed seized by fatigue, a paralysis of the wings, due to excessive fasting, praying, and penitential exercise.

"The longer and harder I look at you, the less I can see myself. That makes it hard for me to go on loving myself humbly in Jesus Christ."

As usual, the Rock fled abruptly. He strode past the boys who were scuffling dangerously close to the young saplings standing in square carpets of earth between the playground paving stones.

It was said that the Rock's mother had called out over and over on her deathbed, "Rock, Rock, where art thou?" when she would normally have cried out to her son, "Evariste, Evariste, where art thou?"

Grandma complained about the soggy bread and the waxy potatoes. At the same time, Grandpa and his cronies, according to her, were banqueting at Groothuis's, the textile manufacturer's, where not only did they gorge themselves until they couldn't move, but where, after the *crème caramel* and the champagne, women came and wriggled onto the men's laps.

Aunt Hélène was in high spirits because dancing was now allowed again at the Swing-Club Flandria on Saturdays and Sundays. "What ever does she see in those Negro dances? She wasn't brought up like that, after all," said Papa. Uncle Florent made a horn with his hand and imitated a saxophone.

"When are you going to grow up?" Papa barked at his youngest brother.

"Next week." (Because that was when he was going to Bremen to work, together with Uncle Leon, who would, of course, be taking his game of draughts and his watercolors along with him.)

"Do you think you really ought to go, Florent?" said Mama. "I can easily get you work in the ERLA."

"No, Constance. If I have to work for a living, I'd just as soon see something of the world doing it."

"And he'll be learning a trade. Fitter or machine operator or electrician, that sort of thing always comes in handy later on," said Aunt Hélène.

Uncle Leon winked behind Aunt Nora's back. "And we get away from our womenfolk. It'll do us a world of good to taste a different soup for once. It doesn't have to be leek soup day after day. And we've been promised good wages, the same rights as our German coworkers, sports facilities, and entertainment. Entertainment, what do they mean by that? That a young man's needs are catered to."

"So long as you come back home clean," said Aunt Nora.

"Constant medical checks," said Uncle Florent. "It's on the posters."

Aunt Mona sighed. "If I didn't have our Cecile with her dancing lessons, I'd go along like a shot. As a typist. The Germans are so *charmant,* so *galant.* They know how to treat a woman."

Accompanied by his friend Maurice de Potter (top of the class in Latin and mathematics, how could it be otherwise when you are four or five lessons ahead of everybody and remember everything?), whom the Rock had impugned so obliquely and with such insidious nonchalance, Louis rang the doorbell of Marnix—member of the Commission for Reparations—de Puydt. Louis had brought the proof of a leaflet. On top, in eight-point cursive Rondo between quotation marks: "My vastness throttles me, I choke on infinity, Cyriel Verschaeve." In the center, in boldface extended Hidalgo: "Flanders, reality, and prototype." In Egmont underneath: "Lecture by M. de Puydt, poet and playwright." At the bottom in twelve-point cursive Rondo: "Admission free. Groeninghe Hall, Wannegem." Papa had forgotten to add the date.

The poet shuffled ahead of them in red leather slippers, he knotted the braided belt of his dressing gown tight around his waist, straightened his hair.

The dining room was hung with portraits of Flemish writers, elderly men in beards and spectacles, they all looked the same, well fed, with bushy eyebrows, thoughtful. Louis recognized Ernest Claes. And Stijn Streuvels, of course, his picture was in Papa's workshop too. (Papa's secret is that he models himself on Farmer Vermeulen, the capricious, truculent old character from *The Flax Field,* that rock of peasant pride, furrowed like a field by the storms of life, et cetera.)

"Those are all Flemish Minds, aren't they, Meneer de Puydt?"

"Quite so, my boy." With a smack he stuck a clay pipe between his wet lips. "Fortunately for me, I have the gift of admiration. People don't admire nearly enough in this country. Typical of a small country, that. That's why Verschaeve's title is so uplifting: *Hours of Admiration.*"

His calves were hairless and paper-white, the ankles had a violet sheen. He held the proof close to his nose.

"Excellent work, your father is a highly gifted artist, in the line of our great printers who, alas, left for Holland during the ill-starred days of our Spanish occupation."

"Are there any mistakes?"

"With the best will in the world . . . no, there isn't a single mistake."

"But shouldn't the date of your lecture be . . ."

"*Godverdomme,* of course, *dedju,* we nearly . . . *nondedju* . . .!"

He sat down at the table, the cloth was riddled with little burn marks and holes, he panted as if he had just run the five hundred meters. Maurice, who never said anything, said nothing now, but you could see he was impressed.

"Sit down, sit down."

"Won't we disturb you?"

"Young man, I have been working all night, I am certainly entitled to a rest of some sort. However . . . rest . . . if only that were possible . . . is not *irrequietum* man's deepest essence?" Fortunately, he didn't wait for an answer, blowing fierce clouds of smoke into Maurice's face.

"It would give me great pleasure to read you a few passages from the third act of a play that is occupying me at present, a fairly accurate evocation of Zannekin, leader of the Bruges uprising. Dr. Leevaert, who is one of the foremost experts we have on the fourteenth century, assures me that I am doing no violence to the historical truth. But, boys, I am worn to a frazzle. Although I do appreciate that you, the youth of Flanders, would be interested in perusing my glimpse into our past. I take it that you read books, I mean, besides your assigned books at school?"

They both nodded dutifully. Maurice was wriggling uncomfortably in his chair, he probably needed to pee. In reaction, Louis, too, suddenly needed to go very badly.

"Do remind me to give you my *Psalms and Palinodes* when you leave, you are bound to find some of the hexameters amusing. It's a pity that Kogge, the publisher, has let me down so badly, because of the so-called paper shortage, otherwise I could have let you have a first edition of my *Death of Descartes,* five acts in which I, taking the Germanic point of view, definitely settle the hash of that champion of Latin pseudorationality, one who has sapped, not to say stunted, our people so lamentably."

Without pausing for breath, he roared, "Ma-ri-a!"

A stick of a creature, a centenarian orphan in a crackling white apron, appeared and gave Louis a look full of hate.

"Maria, pour these young people a small glass of port. They may not be old enough, but it's never too early to learn how to let go a bit, who knows what tomorrow will bring, isn't that so, gentlemen?" She poured. The port was honey-sweet and tepid.

"Well?"

"A little too warm," said Maurice.

De Puydt took a sip. *"Godverdomme,* you're right, too. Maria, put that bottle in the cellar at once. No, leave it here. How many are left in the cellar?"

"Four."

"There's someone here who, behind my back . . ." With a crash that set the Flemish Minds on the wall trembling, she slammed the door behind her.

"She drinks," whispered Marnix de Puydt. "It doesn't matter to me what she drinks, as long as it isn't this port. Those twelve bottles were specially presented to me after my recital at Mijnheer Groothuis's."

"My grandfather told me about that," said Louis. "He thought it was magnificent."

"Yes, our Seynaeve has a weakness for Debussy."

De Puydt refilled his glass and drank it down in one gulp.

"My friend Joris Diels from the Royal Netherlands Theater in Antwerp was naturally the first to go over my *Death of Descartes* in manuscript form, and he complimented me most sincerely."

"It's in five acts?" asked Louis, because he had to say something, certainly in the company of Maurice the Silent.

De Puydt went on nodding his head for a long time. He drank out of the bottle. "I can see you are wondering, young man, if that isn't a touch too classical. And I am bound to tell you, yes, it is classical, the time for experimentation has passed, we are now facing the age of re-con-struct-ion, not only of our society but also of its forms. I am entitled to speak because I am one of those who dare, one of those who have expanded the frontiers of the language, following in the wake of my deeply la-mented colleague Van Ostaijen. Which among other things has earned me the honor of not being included in Father Evarist Bauwens S.J.'s *South and North,* nor in *The Golden Gate* by Mijnheer the Socialist Julien Kuypers. I can understand the first, our good priest obviously objects to my some-what libertine and frivolous approach, but the only explanation for the second is that I am not one of the congregation of the Great Deaf-Mutes, if you follow my drift."

He took two large gulps from the potbellied bottle.

The Great Deaf-Mutes? I'll have to ask someone . . . yes, but whom? Louis observed that Maurice, who knew everything, did not know, either. "My *Death of Descartes,* really 'Death *to* Descartes,' is not in Alexandrines, no, do not fear, I am not encroaching on Verschaeve's territory, nor is it filled with that soulful nostalgia which is the foundation, the trend, and the mainspring of so much art, no, it is, rather, almost, in a certain sense, and now you will be startled, a classical comedy."

Maurice acted as if he were startled. "About Descartes?"

De Puydt grunted with pleasure and crossed his paper-white legs. "Yes, yes! I do not need to sketch out Descartes's life for you, that is being most ably imparted to you by your teachers in the College, but even so I would draw your attention to the most bizarre last months of his existence, when, after all those miserable peregrinations during which he was persecuted by all sorts of clerical riffraff, he sought asylum with Queen Christina."

Maria pushed the door open a crack and said, "The toilet is blocked."

"Again?" shouted De Puydt. "Maria, what on earth have you been up to this time?"

"Me?" The jaws of the ancient, decrepit angel in orphan's uniform chattered.

"Yes, you, who else?"

Maria's toothless grin split her face. "It was Amadeus!"

"Don't lie to me! Accusing my son, how dare you?"

Her grin did not falter. "Then it must have been Madame."

This possibility gave De Puydt pause for thought. He fumbled with the corners of his dressing gown, pulled them over his knees.

"We've had it all before," Maria persisted with devilish enjoyment. "Last year, as you well remember, Madame blocked it with you know what."

"Maria, leave us in peace with your women's-nonsense, if you don't mind! Just see that it gets fixed, that's all . . ."

"I'll try with a brush," said Maria.

"The Queen of Sweden," said De Puydt, "had not only remarkable intellectual powers but also a singular character, thanks to which her undoubted womanly nonsense, uh, charms, often made way for what we must call preeminently masculine traits, for instance the tendency we men have to explore the limits of human reason no less than those of physical endurance. She would ride horseback, to mention just one example, at four in the morning, in the icy cold.

"Now Descartes was naturally a Latin, you couldn't be more Latin than he was, just take a look at his portrait by Frans Hals, liverish, olive-skinned, raven-haired, thus not at all up to the icy northern climate, a man who was sensitive to the least draft, *vide* his letters, who shivered up there in the far north from morning to night, blue with cold . . ." De Puydt drew the collar of his dressing gown closer as if about to throttle himself, hunched his shoulders and began to shiver, then let go of the gown and swung a bloodless, hairless leg up and down. "But Christina, our feminine Viking of a Queen, was unrelenting. She insisted on seeing him in the saddle at the crack of dawn and having him explain to her as they rode precisely how things stood with two such distinct entities as matter and consciousness, and what else could he do when she, the Queen . . ."

"Nothing," said Maurice, more excited than Louis had ever seen him.

"Nothing!" shouted De Puydt as if he were in the Café Groeninghe. The bottle of port was empty, his forefinger slid down the inside of his glass, he licked his finger.

"And so he dies, which happens in the fifth act where we get a brief glimpse of the last work conceived by the poor man, not a mathematical or philosophical tract but a ballet in verse, the Triumph of Peace, nymphs of every shape and size appear dancing on the stage, something the public, which cannot always follow the subtler nuances of my many historical allusions, will find a welcome diversion, but meanwhile, in a corner, Descartes, spitting blood, has to admit to himself that his twisted Latin intelligence is barren, has the elegance of petrification . . ."

"He thought the air was a liquid," said Maurice de Potter. "And the sun and the stars were liquid as well, otherwise they couldn't exist, that's what he thought."

"He did think that, yes," said De Puydt crustily. "And it was precisely these aberrations of his thought that were destroyed by the vital force, the very bloodstream of Queen Christina. One sometimes wonders whether René, Sieur du Perron Descartes, to judge from his portrait by Hals, mightn't have been Jewish, but I refrained from stressing this point, this is not the moment."

Louis and Bekka had forgotten what games they used to play in the clay pits, or else they had outgrown them. They hung about, threw pebbles but not too far, because German engineers in rubber boots carrying measuring instruments now tramped through their ocher-colored paradise with its crags and quarries. Bekka missed her brother, who had been sent to stay with their grandparents in Roeselare, an inaccessible town inhabited by olive-skinned weavers and brushmakers known as Egyptians.

One day Dirty Dick turned up in the wooden hut, both of his hands in filthy bandages.

"There I was sitting in the Patria minding my own business, reading my paper, when these Black Brigade men came in, drunk as lords, they'd just been to a party, they were all singing, and then suddenly one of them,

Troop Leader they called him, comes up to me and says, 'How come you didn't salute when we came in?' I say, *'Houzee, Kameraad . . .'* and I stick my arm in the air. 'That's not according to regulations,' he says, 'first you have to stand to attention and then hold your arm straight out.' I say, 'Straight? But your *Führer* does it like this!' With the hand tilted back. *'Allee,* to attention!' says he. I say, 'Look, sonny, why don't you just bugger off?' And then they grabbed me, I had to put my hands on the table and they beat them to a pulp with their truncheons."

"They'll get infected," said Bekka.

"My friends say I should go to the police. But they know me there at the police. I don't possess a certificate of good conduct. How is your brother?"

"He's at my grandmother's."

"Does he get enough food there?"

"That's why he's gone."

"I could have looked after him. He wouldn't have gone short of anything."

"You could look after Louis," said Bekka meaningfully, dirty little dangerous witch.

"Please!" exclaimed Louis.

Over the stagnant water of the pool, over the film of green, swarms of dragonflies hovered, light sparkling on their veined wings and metallic bodies.

"You've turned into quite a fellow," said Dirty Dick. Louis shrugged his shoulders. If that dirty old man thinks I'll serve as a substitute for Tetje, he's got another think coming.

"What do you learn at the College?"

"Latin and Greek."

"You're not going to become a priest, are you?"

"Him!" said Bekka scornfully, which made Louis glad.

"I intend to be a writer like Cyriel Verschaeve or Guido Gezelle."

"But they're priests!"

The blunder was monumental. "Don't bother your head about me," snapped Louis.

"We can at least talk about it. After all, your future is important. If anyone had given some thought to my future when I was your age, things might have turned out different for me. What are you going to write about? Country life, stuff like that?"

"No, more like Jack London."

"Writing," said Dirty Dick. "That won't put butter on your bread. Just look at Meneer Vrielynck."

267

Meneer Vrielynck was a doddering old man with a broad-brimmed black hat and tangles of yellowish-white shoulder-length hair, who had studied the Flemish language until he nearly went blind. He often came down Philip of Alsace Avenue with his white stick. Children would run after him jeering, tugging at his grubby black coat, and calling out, *"Het Leeuw, het Leeuw!"* For one day he had spoken on Radio Walle about the emblem of *De Leeuw van Vlaanderen,* the Lion of Flanders, found on banners, shields, and books, saying it should be referred to by the neuter definite article *"het,"* to show that it was a concept rather than a beast, and as such without gender.

"And what did Meneer Vrielynck get for his trouble? A medal from the city, that's all." Dirty Dick wiped his face with the filthy linen rag around his hand.

"What of it?" said Louis. (Will I ever be depicted in sepia, right at the back because I am the youngest, in that standard work *Flemish Minds,* pipe in mouth, head to one side, one finger digging into my left cheek, looking sunk in gloom? Perhaps a mustache? No, a short beard.)

Dirty Dick: "I can understand those louts in the Black Brigade to some extent. From what I heard, they had drunk too much because they were upset that their leader Staf de Clercq isn't long for this world, what with his cancer of the liver."

Mama, who had seen him say goodbye to Bekka outside her house, said, "That girl's keen on our Louis! Something nice'll come of that, eh, Louis?"

"Stop it, Mama."

"Yes, stop it, Constance."

There was a cheery air about Mama these days, she often came home late because it was part of her job to dine with Herr Lausengier and his colleagues in the Golden Crown restaurant on the Market Square, where, typically German, they would spend the time poring over various documents. Now and then Mama would come out with such German expressions as *zweifellos, wunderbar,* or that strange word *ähnlich,* in the middle of a Flemish sentence.

"Make the most of it, Constance," said Aunt Nora. "You are only young once in your life."

"They are so correct," said Mama, "you have no idea, it's always Frau Seynaeve this and Frau Seynaeve that."

"What? Don't they ever call you Constance?" asked Papa.

"Once in a while," admitted Mama.

The Rock was talking about Lucretius, whom the theologians of his day had dismissed as a mad dog. St. Jerome, though, had been somewhat more subtle in his judgment. According to him, Lucretius had been driven mad by a love-potion.

The pupils laughed obsequiously.

"Clinamen." The Rock wrote the word impatiently on the blackboard in angular letters. *"Clinamen,"* Louis did his best to pay attention, but it was hot in the classroom and he also had the impression that the Rock was addressing the entire lesson exclusively to him, as those eyes, sometimes doubled behind the spectacles, swimming in translucent oil, pursued him. *Clinamen,* the ever-present inclination. In the movement of bodies. Thanks to which they escape their destiny. But who cares? *Clinamen* also means declension. Which makes syntax possible. Pay attention, now. Allows words to be declined in their smallest common parts. Common parts, does that refer to me? Declining words. My smallest common parts are declining. Inclining. Altering their function.

It is my opinion that the Rock is preparing some sort of lecture and is testing it out on this servile class of guinea pigs who put up with his incomprehensible gibberish. A lecture for delivery in the near future before learned, pipe-smoking priests.

"So that we may perhaps conclude that most conceptions of life are aesthetic but do not wish to appear as such." The bell rang punctually on the last syllable.

"You were dreaming," said the Rock in the playground.

"You give lessons the boys can't follow."

"The boys?"

"I can't, either. It's not for people our age."

"Once upon a time people your age used to speak fluent Greek and Latin."

"Once upon a time," said Louis. Some boys were looking at them both from a distance—especially at me, the favorite courtier.

"Plus est en vous," said the Rock.

"All you want is for me to become a Jesuit."

"I don't want that. I hope for it."

"And yet you aren't happy." (As if to a Hottentot, in a fortress where unarmed Sisters stand guard.)

"I don't think in those terms. Although I should be a great deal happier if you had a little more respect for the possibilities the Lord has offered you."

"More than to the others?"

"Louis, why don't you want to learn? Why do you prefer what is being proffered so glibly nowadays, allowing nature free rein, giving in to every impulse, why accept force, the lust for power, the love of destruction, everything that glorifies nature and war, so meekly?"

"Who's proffering all that?"

"Our new masters," said the Rock. "They glorify blood. They want to go back to a dark, blood-bespattered past. Haven't you noticed?"

"And what should I choose instead? Mortification?"

"Don't be impertinent. Not with me."

There was a sudden commotion in the playground. A pig's squeal, amplified tenfold, piercing shrieks and yells, pupils and some priests rushing past, jostling around a little tree. While playing tag, Maurice de Potter had tripped, in full flight, over a gap in the flagstones and had landed on one of the spikes of the iron fence protecting the young tree, the heart-shaped point had pierced his left eye, and Maurice, his head impaled and his arms clasped around the fence, was now half-lying, half-hanging, a stranger, white as a sheet. Was the eye seeping out? Was it lying on his cheek? Colliding priests and pupils, bellowing as they had during the bombardments at the beginning of the war, unhitched Maurice and carried him away. Several pupils from the Fifth Latin class then set upon fat Voordekkers, who had been chasing Maurice, like a pack of hounds.

With his class Louis filed past the waxen body laid out, the black eyepatch and the wide-open nostrils stuffed with cotton wool.

"Take his hand, Louis," said Maurice's mother. "You needn't be afraid, after all he was your friend."

He imagined that the hand, cold rubber, was radiating cold from inside, that the cold was contagious, that the fragile, felled pirate was blowing the air of death at him through his almost translucent lips, lips that had once said that even the stars were liquid.

Maurice's mother sat with one elbow on the edge of the coffin. "It looks as if he's asleep, doesn't it, Louis?" Traces of lipstick in the corners of her mouth. Applied anyway, although she knew that her child could no longer see it. Unless the Day of Judgment were proclaimed this very night. I must mourn. Why don't they nail up the coffin? Where is his exercise book, the one he used for pasting in photographs from *Der Adler*? He has the hint of a mocking smile, doesn't anyone else see that? Why doesn't someone shoo that fly away from his neck? Because he wouldn't notice if they did. And what if he looked down at himself from heaven?

"He undoubtedly did that," said the Rock a few days later in the chapel. Behind him a muscular Jesus fell for the second time on a fresco of the Stations of the Cross by Dolf Zeebroeck, one of Walle's celebrities, he exhibits in Brussels, the pictures he does for death and birth announcements are sold as far away as America, he's modern but in great demand.

"Of course, you mustn't take that literally," said the Rock quickly, for he had caught Louis's mulish, peevish, tetchy expression. "You might also think that someone, after his death, becomes part of that great whole made up of the billions of thoughts and feelings that have been absorbed into the Universe, into its very Principle, and that this does not preclude a measure of consciousness. But, of course, that sort of thing just glances off you. Louis, you are much too down-to-earth."

"Maurice is the one who is down-to-earth right now." Louis felt the silly laughter welling up inside him, and for the first time in years he was slapped. His ear roared, tears sprang to his eyes. Mistily he saw the Rock make a half-protective, half-parrying gesture.

"I have been in a state of mortal sin for weeks now," said Louis.

"I don't want to hear about it."

"But you must! As a shepherd of souls."

"Do you want to have your ears boxed again?"

Louis made a beckoning gesture with his forefinger. Come on, then. Just as boys did in the playground, challenging each other to a fight.

"Behave yourself, Louis Seynaeve, in front of the altar."

"I haven't believed in God for weeks." (Because if I did, you would be his agent, the not-so-glad bearer of these tidings!) "Only yesterday I spat the Host out into my hand, rolled it into a ball, and stamped on it."

"You are lying."

"Yes," said Louis wearily. (For there is an evil called God, it has angels of death, like the one who lifted Maurice up and speared him on the iron spike and who now roams about, searching, drooling with the frenzy of the chase, after a fresh new child, and there are jack-booted, bronzed, helmeted angels, too, in tanks and in Stukas who are allowed to kill without having to answer to anyone.)

"Kneel down," ordered the Rock, pointing to a prie-dieu. "And offer up a prayer of thanksgiving to the Lord Jesus for sparing your life." He stood behind Louis's back and placed his hand on his neck. "You," Louis heard him say. "You!" He wanted to stand up, but the cool hand held him down. "You, who have been created good and beautiful in the image of your Maker, you are determined to deliver yourself up to evil, and all because of a rebellious urge that I understand better than anyone else."

(German science has invented a death ray that can penetrate anything, for instance it can go straight through the brick and plaster of my room, the ray has been cleverly mounted on the horn-rimmed spectacles of the man behind my vulnerable back and is about to pin me to the floor.)

"You are impure. Like me," cried Louis in the chapel.

The fingers dug into his neck. Pinned down by Ming the Merciless in his spaceship, who is as bald as the Rock and wears an identical black uniform! Louis, now Flash Gordon, turned around, saw a puzzled, desperate man with spectacles perching askew on a fleshy nose.

"Bugger off, Rock, you bloody bore!" said Louis and ran past the Stations of the Cross toward the light of the open door. B, b, b, that was an alliteration, and alliteration formed a link between lips and language, *dixit* Guido Gezelle, priest and poet.

Uncle Robert, trained by Spinel the butcher in Doornik Street, was getting the knack of the butcher's trade. His pâté was still on the bitter side, too much liver, but his jellied pork . . .

Grandma told Louis to go and bring his homework. "You'd make me more than happy if you just sat here by the stove and said something to me every now and then."

On the day he should have taken the train with Uncle Leon for Essen (or was it Bremen?), Uncle Florent had failed to turn up at the station. Uncle Leon, beside himself, had not wanted to go alone, but witnesses testified that Aunt Nora had literally shoved her lily-livered husband onto the train when the brass band struck up. "Auld Lang Syne."

Other witnesses whispered that Aunt Mona had been seen at least three times in the Michelangelo Tearoom with a stripling of a German corporal who had helped her into and out of her coat like a regular gigolo.

"I'd rather have a gigolo in my bed than a hot brick."

"Oh, you silly goose," laughed Mama, and her laughter died away abruptly.

Grandpa claimed that a reliable source had told him that things were about to start humming in the East. Although he found it hard to believe that Hitler would turn on Stalin, because, as Mijnheer Tierenteyn had said, "a nonaggression pact isn't written on water."

Papa was shown into the parlor. The walls were hung with heavily embossed brown paper that simulated antique leather. Papa shook hands with the Reverend Father the Headmaster and then listened to the verdict. His son was uncontrollable, a moral danger to the other pupils, whom he had attempted to subvert. The College was renowned for its patience and tolerance, and naturally had the deepest respect for the head of the Seynaeve family, but short of a radical change in the immediate future together with an act of public penance, steps would have to be taken, possibly of the most drastic kind. In the end, no matter how progressive the College was said to be, it had to respect a higher order.

The Rock was standing with crossed arms in front of the fireplace, next to the marble bust of Canon Germonprez, who had restored prosperity to the College in 1814 following the infamous dissolution of the Jesuit order in 1773, blessed date.

"Order," said Papa. "But there's nothing I want more than order. I shall personally ensure that Louis obeys on the instant whatever you impose. We have given him a Christian upbringing, he'll understand, and if he doesn't I'll beat him black and blue!"

Behind the histrionics, Louis could hear the pleading. Of a baboon for a banana.

"Ever since he was a little boy, Headmaster, we have aimed for that! A Christian life. Would we have sent him to St. Joseph's Institute in Haarbeke to have him brought up the wrong way?"

"What do you have to say, Louis?" asked the Headmaster, an office clerk with a golden pince-nez.

"Answer when the Headmaster speaks to you," boomed Papa. "Didn't we teach you respect for the priesthood?"

"Yes, so long as they were Flamingants."

Papa ran his hand over his bald head to quench the raging fires within, turned imploringly to the Rock, who uttered not a sound but brought his hands together, the fingertips forming a small pointed arch.

"It's a good thing that the Reverend Fathers know you through and through, Louis, and that they understand you can sometimes be a bit of a wag. He gets that from his mother, Headmaster, I don't understand her either, sometimes, her and her strange little jokes."

"You'd do better to do your Easter duties," said Louis piously.

"My Easter . . . My Easter . . .?"

"You didn't do your Easter duties this year."

"I? I? I didn't do my . . .? May I be struck dead right here in front of you, Reverend Fathers, if . . ."

"Where did you do your Easter duties, Papa?"

"In France," shouted Papa. "I went specially to Lille to do my Easter duties in French."

This was so tall a story that the two priests exchanged incredulous looks.

"Yes, I know, it sounds strange from the lips of a staunch Fleming, but I'd had it drawn to my attention that there was a preacher in Lille, a Dominican, who could preach so magnificently, a second Lacordaire, if that means anything to you . . ."

"We have heard of him," said the Headmaster unctuously.

"You mean the friend of Lamennais who was elected in Marseilles to the Constitutional Assembly after the Revolution?" asked the Rock.

"No," said Papa, "I mean the Dominican."

"They're the same," said Louis, who had divined the nauseating charitableness behind the horn-rimmed spectacles.

"Be that as it may," said Papa, "in any case he preached so magnificently that I was on top of the world, I came out of the church totally refreshed, I couldn't feel the ground beneath my feet."

But the harm had been done, the Seynaevian lie had been pinned like a butterfly to the pseudo-Cordovan leather, and the Headmaster said curtly that the matter would be given further consideration, but that meanwhile Louis must not enter the grounds of the College. For how long? He would be notified.

"The Lord be with you," said the Headmaster, and the Rock handed Louis a book, St. Bernard's *Traité de la Considération,* telling him to make a précis of it.

On the way home Papa trudged along silently, hugging the fronts of the houses as though carrying the weight of the world on his shoulders. At home, still forlorn, he slumped into the cozy-corner.

"Constance, as of today no more bacon and eggs. As of today every franc is going to have to be turned over ten times. That child of yours has made sure of that. I can kiss good-bye any printing orders from the College from now on. As of today we're all on bread and water."

"And jam," said Mama. "I've just been given a pot of greengage jam by a new young man, a dentist's son. They all try to butter me up because they know it's up to me whether they go to Germany or not."

"But they've all got to go to Germany as soon as they've finished their training."

"You can drag it on and draw it out. Provided you are on good terms with Dr. Lausengier. But first they have to go through me."

"Let's have a taste of that jam," said Papa. (But what he was imploring was: Who has to go through you? And why, when I come in, do you never raise your diabolically beautiful powdered face to me?) "Greengage, is it?" He tried some. "Tastes more like cherry plum to me."

Why didn't Uncle Florent turn up that fatal afternoon when Aunt Nora had so resolutely packed her husband off to the Promised Land and then, to assuage her qualms and fortify her nerves, had gone with two sobbing women, who had just waved their husbands good-bye, to the nearest café and there made herself drunk on two miserably small and weak genevas, afterward twisting her ankle? Aunt Nora pointed accusingly at the coward. "It's all your fault, Florent. Look!" Her leg was held aloft. "That's never going to heal again. I know it isn't. I don't have enough calcium in my bones."

"I can't do anything about that."

"And I packed my Florent's bag," said Grandma. "His shaving things, his pajamas, his underwear, his work card, his passport, his harmonica . . ."

"I couldn't do it," said Uncle Florent.

"He didn't want to leave me alone," said Grandma shrilly, wrapped in two or three black knitted shawls, as if it were snowing outside and not steaming with heat.

"I couldn't go. All I could think of the whole time was, it's impossible for me to go there and work."

"But it's good enough for my Leon!"

"Nora, your Leon is used to working for a boss, clocking in his eight hours a day and then playing draughts and painting his watercolors. I can't do that."

"No, but you can live off my back," said Grandma. "He put away two pounds of potatoes tonight."

"And what about Louis?" cried Uncle Florent. No one could make fried potatoes like Aunt Hélène. Brown crusts, not quite burnt. With onion sauce. Louis felt his stomach tighten.

"The boy has to grow!" shouted Grandma.

"And I have to shrink, I suppose!"

"He doesn't want to leave his sweetheart." Grandma made a face as if she had just discovered, stuck between her few teeth, a clove left behind from the cabbage soup whose smell still lingered in the house.

Aunt Nora giggled. "He's going to lose her anyway. Is it still that Jeannot from the hairdresser's?"

"Leave Jeannot out of this."

"I saw her out with Thiery de Waelhens, and they weren't acting like brother and sister."

"Where?"

"In the park. I even thought to myself, Those two, they couldn't have met each other all that long ago, but their hearts are already playing sweet music."

"Jeannot's as dumb as a doorknob," said Uncle Florent. "I think I'd rather go to France. They need truck drivers for the Atlantic Wall, and a driver earns at least . . ."

"Florent!"

"Yes, Mother?"

"What are you hiding up your sleeve?" Grandma cried in a frightened, stern voice.

"Me?"

"Yes, you!"

"From Normandy it's easy to get to England."

The women fell deathly quiet. Grandma poked the corner of one of her shawls into her mouth. Uncle Florent gave Louis a penetrating look, the end of his cigarette dancing up and down between his lips.

"Well, *godverdomme*," Aunt Nora managed to get out, and Grandma immediately crossed herself.

"Louis, swear to me you won't breathe a word, not a word . . ."

"I swear, Uncle Florent."

"But the sea is full of U-boats," said Grandma, "and destroyers." She knew the word because every so often she played battleships with Louis on the squared pages in his arithmetic book.

"I might have guessed," said Aunt Nora. "First he drives my Leon crazy so that he goes off to Germany, and then, like any other coward, he . . ."

"But if the Germans invade England, they'll shoot you!"

"Mother, they'll never get as far as England."

"*Tiens.* Hitler told you that, did he, on the telephone?"

"If he'd gone right after them, then . . ."

"But what do you want there in England?" asked Aunt Nora.

"He just wants to get away from home." Grandma's tears glittered. "Germany or England, he couldn't care less which, so long as he gets away from me. And to think I packed his bag."

"He has no ideals," said Louis.

"How right you are, Louis," said Aunt Nora. "He doesn't even know what an ideal is."

"I won't sleep a wink all year!" cried Grandma.

Louis told the whole story to Mama, who was shocked. "We'll never see him again. A lamb to the slaughter. We'll have to make sure your Papa doesn't hear about it, or I wouldn't put it past him to denounce Florent to the *Kommandantur.*"

Three days later Papa was told that his brother had vanished, together with four other footballers from Stade Walle. "He's always been pro-

276

English, what with his English cigarettes and those English I-I-I-loff-you songs. I won't have his name mentioned in this house ever again. I've always said Stade Walle was a club past praying for."

The Germans did not go to England, as they had sung in two-part harmony while marching up the Oudenaarde Road, but went off in the opposite direction, to Yugoslavia and after that to Russia, on the day Louis wore his first pair of knickerbockers, dark blue with green flecks.

"It'll be a relief to Hitler to be going for Russia's throat," said Papa. "Making common cause with Stalin must have gone against his grain, he was really in a bind, but now it's all out in the open, it's a fight to the finish. That's the way it goes, it's the same way with me, when a man can't follow his ideal he gets ulcers, everything has its price."

"Am I your ideal?" said Mama merrily. "That's the first I've heard of it."

"Silly goose," said Papa, and after a while, bitterly, "The English will be pleased. It's always the same. The whole of history proves it. The English get everyone else to do their dirty work for them. Now it's the Russians' turn. And it won't be long before the Americans join in the dance as well."

"*Le plus beau de tous les tangos du monde,*" sang Mama, "*c'est celui que j'ai dansé dans tes bras.*"

"Churchill will be having a double Scotch tonight," said Papa glumly.

The tall, bald priest in his smart black robe swooped like a black vulture into the Seynaeves' beige kitchen. He wanted nothing to drink, he did not have much time.

"My wife is not at home," said Papa, "she won't be back until later, she has to do a lot of overtime nowadays, that business with Russia has meant full steam ahead for production, of course."

"You don't need me, either," said Louis but stayed in his chair, hoping the Rock would see the St. Bernard book lying on the windowsill. (I read it every day, Father, but I haven't had time to write a précis yet.)

"I came on a bicycle, it's locked, but . . ."

"Oh, they wouldn't dare, they know that I . . ."

"In that case . . ."

"All the same, I'd just better quickly . . ."

"It's only a bicycle, but these days . . ."

"I'd know at once who had taken it, in Toontjes Street . . ."

(His cold eyes, like fishes', no, frogs', jewels of evil.)

"A small cigar, Father?"

277

"No, thank you."

"Go on, don't hold back. I get them by the box from my brother-in-law." (Uncle Armand, Inspector in the Division for the Detection of Concealed Smokers' Requisites, showered with gifts by every peasant in the neighborhood.)

"No, thank you."

"Then please take a few for Mijnheer the Headmaster."

"No, really. Why I am here, Mijnheer Seynaeve, is that it has come to my knowledge that your wife enjoys quite a high reputation in the ERLA Works. Well. Yes, to be sure. To come straight to the point. Something people don't expect from a Jesuit. My question is whether, with her considerable influence, she would be willing . . . to support . . . to help. It's for a friend. If she would recommend him. A distant cousin of mine. I would, if some pecuniary contribution were required . . ."

"Never!" cried Papa. "It goes without saying that we will do what we can, no question of money. We've been put in this world to help one another."

"And would it be possible . . . to . . . within the foreseeable future . . .? My friend, my cousin, has been called up for next week. The destination is Leipzig."

"But, Father, of course!"

"He is a good worker."

"With your recommendation, Father! You can rest easy. It's as good as done."

At long last the Rock looked at Louis, something chastened in the angry eyes. "Oh yes, the other thing I came for was to say that Louis will be expected back at school tomorrow morning."

"Excellent," said Papa.

"One good turn deserves another," said Louis.

"Excellent. We'll wipe the slate clean and begin again at the beginning as if nothing has happened, right, Father?"

"Yes," said the Rock (moneychanger in the temple).

"Tu quoque?" said Louis.

"Jawohl," said the Rock. For the first time, Louis could see, by the weak glow of the lightbulb, how tired and sad the Rock was, how much under the sway of something immense that was gradually crushing him, his shoulders bent, his smoothly shaven cheeks hollow. I will look after him.

"Not a wink," said Grandma. "Not a single minute. Maybe just half an hour toward morning before I have to get up. To have to live through that! And not only live through it but know in fear and dread that things can only get worse and worse. And here I am, with one foot in the grave already, or at least my toes. The only thing that can happen to me now is to fall over out of sheer sorrow and topple into my grave. *La tombe finit toujours par avoir raison,* the grave always has the last word. That is, if they don't burn me instead, all the rage right now, but you'll see to it that they don't do that to me, eh, my boy? Because nowadays a person is cleared away quick as a wink, stuck in the fire and away with him, a tin can full of ashes in the dustbin. Promise me to see that doesn't happen? Because I wasn't brought up like that, and what's more my sister has already ordered the stone, not marble, that's much too la-di-da, dead people shouldn't put on airs and graces, they've had a whole lifetime for that, it's all been paid for by my sister, Aunt Margo from Zegelsem, perpetual mass on Saturdays, the whole works, I'll be giving you indulgences as a present from the grave. But that I still have to live in such dread, that's something I would never have believed, I, who never gave a tinker's damn, or thought I didn't, it's all that Hilter's fault, no, I'm being too hasty and unfair again, I'm too old to put the blame on somebody else. Well, well, we're all in it together, if horrible things are going on, well, well, you might as well put the blame on Our Lord. 'Mother,' says Hélène, 'you must eat, you don't get enough protein, I'm going to drag you to the scales so you can see for yourself. And your hair will fall out, eat a little bit of calf's liver at least!' And Mona, who has a heart of stone, also says, 'Mother, just look in the mirror, under your cheeks, all that skin hanging down like a turkey's.' Hélène is cross with me, of course, because I give my ration coupons to Mona for little Cecile, and Nora is cross because I took my rings and brooches to Foquet the jeweler on the Market, but I couldn't let our Florent go off without a cent, it's cruel enough that he's stuck away in England, must he die of hunger there as well? 'We are entitled to that jewelry,' says Mona, 'it should be divided up fairly!' I say, 'What? What should be divided up, those diamonds the size of flyspecks that I once got from your father?' 'No,' she says, 'the brooch, it's not the money but the sentimental value, it ought to have stayed in the family!' I say, 'What? That brooch? I got that from your father because I was going to run away from him the day I discovered he was having that affair with Alice, the schoolmistress, who only wanted to get a job teaching in the secondary school, and that jackass believed she was in love with him.' 'And the locket?' she says. I say, 'What locket? You're welcome to it!' 'But Foquet on the Market has it already,' says she. 'Well, go and get it back, I'll give you the money.' 'Oh, forget it,' she says, 'it's just that I've looked on that locket all my life as a symbol of the love between Father and you, because there's a snapshot of Father as a baby inside, isn't there?' I say, 'But Mona, poor lamb, that baby isn't your father!' 'I always thought it was,' she says. I say, 'It's time you went to the eye doctor, that was a snapshot of our poor Marie-Hélène as a baby. No, not poor Marie-Hélène my own little girl but Marie-Hélène my little sister, God rest her soul.' People keep telling you that your own children come first and that you always favor the oldest and the youngest, but I think that I loved my sister best of all, at any rate she gave me the most heartache. She couldn't follow her lessons at school very well, our Marie-Hélène, a bit like our Robert, also no shining light at school, so our mother thought to herself, That child is going to have to learn something in life, perhaps we can make a seamstress out of her, and they sent her to the Christiaens family where girls were taught to sew in a farmhouse that had little rooms fitted out on the top floor and where Marie-Hélène was happy. Now there was another girl there, Solange, who couldn't speak Flemish, with a violinist for a father who was always abroad with his orchestra and her parents were divorced, I think, anyway the mother never once bothered about that child and she was so unhappy, and Madame Christiaens says, 'You, Marie-Hélène, you speak good French, please pay some attention to Solange so that the poor child has a little bit of company, I'm afraid she may pine away.' Now, that little girl couldn't sleep at all at night. She kept hearing the shutters slapping against the wall in the wind and because she was so frightened and couldn't sleep she crept into our Marie-Hélène's bed. Our Marie-Hélène comes home after a week and says to our mother, 'Mother,' she says, 'won't you please tell the Christiaenses, because I don't dare to myself, that Solange presses right up to me at night, and she sweats so much, every night she's soaked to the skin and I don't like to say so but I feel sick to my stomach because I get so wet myself.' Well, to make a long story short, one thing led to another, they had Solange examined and yes, my pet, guess what? Tuberculosis. They examined Marie-Hélène, and yes, she had it as well. But Dr. Martens, our doctor, a simple family doctor but an excellent man who has spent a long time in the Congo, says, 'Tuberculosis? Nothing of the kind. What are you thinking of? Nothing of the kind. Just look at her sitting there, that fine figure of our Marie-Hélène, how much would you say she weighs? Perhaps a hundred and forty pounds, look at her rosy cheeks, a true Demarchie, and the Demarchies don't get tuberculosis, you can bet your life on that!' And the curate says to our mother, he spoke with a kind of lisp, 'Madame, it'sh quite shimple, thish girl ish shimply undernourished, tell the Chrishtiaenshesh to give her bacon and eggsh every morning for breakfasht.' And of course our mother told them, the Christiaenses were even a bit insulted, but what happened? Marie-Hélène didn't get any better and our mother brought her back home, she took care of her, bacon and eggs and good red meat and now and then a glass of Burgundy to quicken the blood, but no, she was running a fever the whole time, she wasn't feeling at all well, and one fine day she says, 'Mother, I'm going to benediction, to Confession!' But that was because she'd been sitting cooped up indoors all day, she needed a breath of fresh air, you can understand that, can't you? And she walked as far as the Crossroads Café, and then because she couldn't put one foot in front of the other any longer, she dropped in on Hortense in the café. 'Hortense, give me a glass of lemonade, if you'd be so kind, I'm dying of thirst, but please don't mention it to my father, because I'm supposed to have gone to benediction and I don't have any money on me!' Hortense says, 'Oh, child, when your father comes in to play cards, I'll just add a lemonade to his bill, he'll never notice!' And she comes back home. Our mother says, 'Marie-Hélène, you're sweating terribly!' But she went straight to her room, which she shared with Ariane at the time, and we didn't hear a sound and after a while our mother says to me, 'Agathe, call your sister,' and I call, 'Marie-Hélène, come quickly, your porridge is ready, come and eat your porridge.' No reply. I go upstairs and what do I see? She's lying in her bed and her clothes are lying in a heap on the floor, she who was always so conscientious and so careful with her clothes.

"... wait a minute, it's breaking my heart, wait a minute, pet, where's my handkerchief . . .?

". . . it's so long ago and . . .

". . . just one moment . . .

"I say, 'Mother, you're going to have to come yourself,' and our mother, she knew no better, she was of the old school, she shouts, 'Lazy slut, just because you feel a little bit sick, that doesn't mean that you . . .'

" '. . . that you . . .'

". . . oh, my pet, our mother cried on account of that for the rest of her life . . .

". . . much more than I'm crying now, much more . . .

"Because our mother slapped her then, on each cheek, as hard as she could and she shouted, 'Pick up your clothes,' and so she did just that, Marie-Hélène, that lamb of Our Lord, and hung her clothes neatly over a chair . . .

". . . just a moment . . .

". . . and then she crept back into bed and our mother felt sorry for her after all, she went upstairs again and brought her the porridge, but Marie-Hélène couldn't keep it down, she spewed it out all over the eider-down, and Dr. Martens says, 'I don't like the looks of this.' For the disease was too far advanced, Marie-Hélène was really too well built and because she was so well built the virus settled in her brain instead, she began to see things in the ceiling, 'Over there, Agathe, can't you see, that crooked old man walking along!' and she was cross with me because I couldn't see him. 'Bring me the feather duster quickly!' she called, 'quickly!' and she used the feather duster to point the old man out to me. And on the floor, in the mat that was marbled like linoleum, she could see lions and dragons and crooked old men. 'But Agathe, you just don't want to see them,' and she asked me to go and fetch some tracing paper for cutting patterns to lay over the crooked old men and animals and to draw them, and then she started to rave, clawing at people and at me, too. Dr. Martens says, 'We really ought to call in a specialist from Brussels,' but we didn't call the specialist in and then she was dead and our mother fetched our Gerard, who had just been thrown out of the Brothers of Charity School, and she said, 'Go take a good look at your sister, go and look, and make sure you do your best at school,' and he bent over her to give her a last kiss, but he was pushed aside, kicked out of the way by our Honoré, that clumsy tub of lard who is now a major, no need to ask why the Belgian army collapsed on the tenth of May, and Honoré flung himself full-length on the deathbed, right on top of that little body, ranting and raving, 'Forgive me! Forgive me!' because he had declared his love to her, that big fat stupid oaf, later we found the letters he had written to her in her chest of drawers: *'Adieu, je pars, mais dans mon coeur j'emporterai le souvenir de tes beaux yeux, de tes baisers'*—'Farewell, I am leaving, but I will carry in my heart the memory of your beautiful eyes, of your kisses'—and I say to him, 'What is the meaning of this, you big ape?' 'Oh,' says he, 'that's the words of a song she asked me for.' I say, 'Oh, yes? And what about the other letters? "I shall love you forever even if the sky falls in," and here: "You and you alone are my light on earth!" To your own sister, you fat pig!'

" 'I wrote that when I had to go away,' he says, and I say, 'Go away?' 'Yes,' says he, 'she couldn't bear it if I stayed away too long.' I say, 'And when did that happen?' 'Well,' says he, 'when I had to go to the butcher's or the baker's to do the shopping, she would say, "Write me something, then I'll have something to think about while you're gone . . ." ' "

In the Café Groeninghe many a glass was raised to the crusade, to the *Blitzkrieg* on the Kalmucks.

In the Café Rotonde, Mijnheer Santens, coal merchant, said at the bridge table, "Crusade? I'm not so sure about that. The West is being threatened by the Bolsheviks, that's true, but it's under threat from other heathen powers as well."

"Mijnheer Santens, the walls have ears," said Grandpa out of the corner of his mouth. Mijnheer Tierenteyn arranged his cards on the table, studied them, and then stared out over the steppes, over the tundra. "Napoleon, Napoleon," he said. "Please, Mijnheer Tierenteyn, not so loud," said Grandpa.

There has also been talk about a separate Flemish State. The VNV is against it, they want a Great Netherlands (as if the Dutch would be fools enough to allow themselves to be landed with all those Catholics all in one go). The Dinasos are against it, too, they want a Burgundian Empire. DEVLag is against it because they want to incorporate us into the Great German Reich, soon to become the Great European Reich, and straight after that the Great Thousand-Year World Reich. So who in the world wants a separate Flemish State? One person, at any rate: Papa, holding forth at Felix the barber's.

"Because after all those centuries of slavery and bullying we can finally be ourselves for once. But it means having a firm leadership that knows where we're finally heading. Not like the Belgium of yesterday, with twelve governments in six years and not one of them overturned in the proper way by Parliament. No, every time it was that old rigmarole: 'Ah, you Liberals, you're doing nicely out of all these swindles, all right then, we resign,' or 'Aha, you Socialists, you're taking kickbacks, all right, we're off.' And, bang, another government has kicked the bucket. The only thing they could ever agree on was how many jobs to dole out to their pals. You sit there, then I'll sit here, it was musical chairs!"

"Ah well, what would you have done?" said Felix the barber, soaping Grandpa's face.

"Used a strong hand. But an intelligent hand and a sensitive hand," said Papa.

"That's too many hands for one man," said a mathematician.

"Staf, the leader of Flanders, there's a job for you," said a wit.

"He'd declare war on Brussels immediately," said a strategist.

"Brussels has always been a Flemish city!"

"You'd have to explain that to them in French," said a practical man.

"I'd soon bash some Flemish sense into them!" roared Papa.

"Staf, you're talking a lot of shit," said Felix the barber. Papa looked helplessly at the stony, wrinkled face of his father behind the snow-white foam.

Mama brought a present for Louis from her boss, Dr. Lausengier. A Tintenkuli pen, with a retractable needle for a nib. Papa examined it.

"Pretty clever, that! It doesn't look like much, but it's aerodynamic, it's engineers who developed that, and they weren't stupid, either. A Tinten-kuli, the coolie with the ink. Those Germans, they're engineers and poets rolled into one."

"What do you think of it, Louis? You haven't said anything."

"But Mama, I don't know him, why is he giving me a present?"

"No reason."

"It's because you're the son of his secretary," said Papa. "Is there anything so unusual about that?"

"Shall I tell him you were pleased with it?"

"Yes, Mama. Of course."

"Yes, tell Mijnheer Lousy-gear that Louis got down on his knees, clapped his hands, and barked *danke schön.*"

"Staf, be serious for once."

"You ought to ask that man to come over some evening for a drink," said Papa thoughtfully.

"But there's nothing in the house."

"Then I'll go get a bottle from the Café Pennoen. What's his drink? Schnapps?"

"Courvoisier."

"Well, let's say Friday night."

"Not Friday night, there's a dinner for the *Generalkommissar* for Munitions at The Walle Castle."

"Well, Sunday, then."

"Staf, he doesn't like visiting Belgians in their homes."

"We're not Belgians, Constance, we are Flemings, we belong to a fraternal Germanic people."

"I think it may be because he doesn't like to intrude."

"But he's welcome! Imagine if I were in his place, far from my *Heimat,* I'd appreciate it."

"I think he doesn't want to, because of the way neighbors gossip and things like that."

"It's terrible in wartime," said Papa. "The best of intentions go by the board in wartime."

On the surface it appeared as if the Rock treated Louis as he did all the other pupils, but he was biding his time, preparing the *coup de grâce,* even at this moment as he paced up and down, straight as a ramrod in his cassock, even as he gazed at the bleeding plaster feet on the crucifix, no doubt considering what arguments to use against those who claimed that no nail was used on Golgotha and that people who were crucified simply had their hands and feet bound.

There was a languid, sluggish atmosphere in the classroom because the pupils, who were quick to catch on, realized that this lesson was not one of those during which you had to pay attention or remember things in case the Rock questioned you on them, but just another expedition into a no-man's-land during which the Rock, ramrod-straight, speaking in a monotonous mumble, would talk literally over their heads, expecting neither questions nor interruptions. There is no rhyme or reason to it, they are eructations, allusions to a domain inexpressibly far removed from any conceivable syllabus.

The Rock has already been admonished from on high but is obviously unable to give it up, this delirium that Louis refuses to accept even though he senses that it is intended for him and for him alone.

Then the Rock stopped in front of the casement window. In the lower left corner, through the dirty pane, the branches and sprays and sprigs of the spindly little tree swayed, the trunk invisible like the protective iron fence on which the clumsily suspended Maurice de Potter had been crucified. "That only a god can save us," said the Rock. It sounded like the conclusion of an argument, but that was how all his sentences sounded, as if he ran out of breath with his every digression, gasping for air like someone playing water polo. "We must prepare a place for Him in our thoughts and *in poeticis*. So that we ourselves may be prepared and available for His coming, perhaps very soon now," and then he called God (as he always had during these past weeks) by His Jewish name, not Jehovah, which is a corruption, a misunderstanding, but Jahweh. The Rock casts a direct, coal-black, jet-black, mineral glance at me, *in poeticis* they call that: "carbuncle," because he has, shamelessly, adventurously, ventured out of this dusty cage peopled with pupils in order to entrust his friend, his cousin, his nearest and dearest, his pluto-aristocratic protégé, to Mama's care, this trust in her is a strange thing, what has come over him lately?

"Be available, even should He be absent in our decline."

The frame inside the priestly robe looked brittle. He moved, though still as unbending as an officer, more slowly, more carefully, like a sleep-walker, he doesn't get enough sleep.

"How may we reach Him? Only through the mediation of our fellow men, that's something which cannot be stressed too much in these distressing times, I learned that myself quite recently, with full force, only man can give Him a name and among men only the most humble, something Meister Eckhart forgot when he said, 'He only appears when all mankind calls Him,' forgot, or else he could not have imagined what beasts men would one day become, all of us, because all of us are guilty today, all of us."

(Grandpa said out of the corner of his mouth, "Rock, the College walls have ears.")

"It is in the desert alone that we may expect Him, which means He is near, since the deserts are proliferating all around us, albeit the predominant dimension seems to be one of expansion, of abundance, in which the bestial herd predominates and mediocrity is elevated into dogma." (For God's sake don't go on, shush, s-s-sh, Grandpa hushed, hissed from far away.)

The Rock's sleepwalking words had the shape of his manicured fingers, and they stroked Louis's cheek, touching the down near his ears, and the Rock was asleep on his feet while the lulling, gentle drone continued to flow from him, and the autumn sun grew warmer, flies swarming around Louis's sleeping brow, they were glittering blowflies, because Vlieghe, the fly, was among them.

When the German cohorts goose-stepped down Leie Street and onto the Market Square, Louis had difficulty in recapturing his first excitement, that mixture of dread and delight which had filled him when they, all the same age, all with the same bronzed faces (boys, really, not much older than he was), had marched into the town of Walle "like a knife through butter," Tetje had said. Now they had the appearance of well-drilled men dressed in uniform for good measure. The attack and invasion of Belgium lay behind them. With no enemy facing them now, their fierce, feline, ready-to-pounce ardor had seeped away. He felt vaguely deceived by these ordinary creatures in field-gray, as if, in those shimmering May days full of shots and screams, they had made a false entrance in an operetta, drum majors with death's-heads on their caps. Now the death's-head angels were deployed in the snow and ice to root out those Tartar muzhiks incited by godless people's commissars.

A small door had been cut in the medieval, nail-studded oak portal of the Town Hall, above which hung three flags: a Lion and two swastikas.

Now or never. Now.

Louis pulled the small door open, and in the courtyard beyond he found the board with the rune for "Sol"—victory and sun—and, in Gothic letters, *Nationaal Socialistische Jeugd Vlaanderen*—National Socialist Youth of Flanders. He walked up the blue granite steps, worn down over the centuries by monks, warriors, and magistrates, toward a sound reverberating like the irregular echo of his thumping heart, someone banging his fists against a padded wall.

A freckled boy in a green shirt and a black knotted scarf sat at a small table covered with magazines and pamphlets under a portrait of the *Führer* in his iron suit of armor. The boy said *"Heil Vlaanderen!"* *"Heil Vlaanderen,"* said Louis, and then the sentence he had been rehearsing in front of the mirror for days: "Seynaeve, Louis, reporting for service in the NSJV." The boy folded his hairy arms, inspected the recruit, stood up, tugged down the legs of his short trousers, and disappeared. On the little table lay "The Singing Banners," "The Fight for Popular Values," "Our Great-Netherlandish Future." I have taken the step, the first. Without anyone's help or intercession or advice. That's conviction for you!

"It can't be true! Just look who we've got here!" There came up to Louis a jovial, heavily built young man in black riding breeches, boots, and a khaki jerkin, whose round, light-complexioned face seemed familiar. He was the young man in a light-gray three-piece suit whom, now and then, on his way to school, Louis had seen behind the windows of the Genevoix shoeshop on Our Lady Street.

"Genevoix. Troop Leader. Aren't you Seynaeve the printer's youngest?"

"I'm an only child."

"Did your grandfather send you?"

"No. I have come to enlist, Troop Leader."

"And your grandfather . . ."

"He's got nothing to do with it," Louis said curtly. (Establish my position immediately.) His tone did not please the freckled boy. A Hottentot.

"What's your name?"

"Seynaeve, Louis." (I have already reported in accordance with regulations!)

"Well, I'll be damned." The leader put his hands on his hips, legs wide apart, not unlike Mussolini in the newsreels, then used his outstretched fist to deliver a slow-motion hook to Louis's stomach. It didn't hurt, the young man had pulled his punch.

"Immediately, you must tense those stomach muscles immediately, as soon as you see my hand move."

"I didn't see it."

"Obviously not," said Genevoix.

In a dusty little hall with Roman arches that Louis recognized from picture postcards, five boys in gym clothes were sitting on the floor, legs spread wide, hands behind their heads, pushing their faces down into their crotches. Puffing, they counted out loud, they were up to twenty-three, one of them was having trouble keeping up, his name was Haegedoorn, he was in the Fourth Latin class, he couldn't make it to fifty, stayed sitting there breathless, dazed.

Genevoix introduced Louis. Two of the boys tried to crush his hand, Haegedoorn said, "Seynaeve, who would have believed it?" Then they had to squat down and listen to the Troop Leader, who—presumably adhering to a strict schedule, because he kept looking at his wristwatch—lectured them about runes, signs whose grandiose significance our retrograde educational system had never taught us to appreciate. It was odd that a Troop Leader was expected to lecture on this sort of thing. Every child knew that runes, from the Gothic *runa* (meaning "lost things"), had been used by the Scandinavians to communicate with their God. The Troop Leader called it "the writing with which they reached the Center of their Being." You could put it like that as well. From time to time the Troop Leader consulted a small gray book and explained that Odin, speaking from the mountain where he lived between agony and resurrection, had said, "I have raised up the runes, those branches in which the tokens of Destiny have been engraved. *Verstanden*, Bosmans?"

Bosmans, a weedy, down-at-heel boy, undoubtedly from Toontjes Street, gave a frightened nod.

"Then tell it your way. How will you, once you've been made a *Stormer*, explain it to the *knapen*? Start with Seynaeve here."

Bosmans gave Louis a ratlike, hate-filled look. "This Odin has two ravens that tell him about everything, a horse with eight legs, and two wolves, he only has one eye and most of the time you can't see his face, because he hides it under a big hat."

"Bosmans, we're not here for a laugh. We were talking about runes!" bawled the Troop Leader. *"Verstanden?"*

"Er, yes. Anyway, this Odin knows all about runes."

"Naturally!"

"Because he hung from a tree for nine days with nothing to eat or drink."

"And was wounded by a spear," said Haegedoorn.

"Stick to the runes, Haegedoorn!"

"This Odin," said Bosmans haltingly, "inscribed the runes, er, the tokens, er, of Destiny, er, into our roots."

"Roots," said the Troop Leader. "Bosmans, is man a vegetable?" There was laughter. Louis laughed, too. Genevoix, the leader, was a comrade. He sighed.

"Shall we do some fencing now, Troop Leader?" asked one of the sturdily built boys.

"Mansveld, theory comes first. And it'll be me who gives the orders!"

"Yes, Troop Leader."

Genevoix looked at his wristwatch and then in his little gray book. "What is the Proclamation of Kortrijk? That's a question that's really meant for *Stormers,* but I'll ask you all the same."

No one knew. Louis had never even heard of it. Had the victors of 1302 made some proclamation in Kortrijk after the Battle of the Golden Spurs, creating some sort of independent country, perhaps?

"One nation, one youth!" exclaimed Genevoix. " 'The society we are creating will know no parasites. Only smoothly functioning cogs in the machinery of our national life. Any caste spirit and all party politics must be eradicated mer-ci-less-ly.' So said our Youth Leader, Dr. Edgar Lehembre, and I was standing less than three feet away from him at the time. Any questions?"

Because no one said anything and it seemed discourteous not to give the Troop Leader any answer, and also because he wanted to make an immediate impression as an intrepid, manly, fine fellow, Louis said, "In the College they claim that the NSJV is against Catholicism. What shall I tell them?"

"Who says that? Who are 'they'?" Genevoix's round face had turned pink.

"Teachers."

"Which teachers? Names?"

"Yes, names!" said Mansveld, as if ready to storm the ramparts of the College, Hitler Youth dagger between his rotten teeth.

Haegedoorn said, "You can talk freely, Louis. I know the names."

"Evariste de Launay de Kerchove," mumbled Louis.

Genevoix noted in the back of his little book: "De Launay, De Kerchove, who else?"

"They're the same person," said Haegedoorn. "He has two names."

"Oh, a member of our nobility, is he? We'll soon show him!"

"What are you going to do—" said Louis and then, quickly, "Troop Leader?"

"That college of yours is scheduled for closing down in due course, we intend to turn it into a citadel for the NSJV, political Catholicism has to be destroyed root and branch."

"We'll give the news to the Headmaster, right Seynaeve?" (Crybaby Haegedoorn was a loudmouth *here.*)

"He knows already. He knows already," said Genevoix ominously. He read out, " 'Anyone who fails to appreciate that his life and that of his nation have been directed into certain paths by Providence is no National Socialist. We recognize the Christian character of our people, we strive to maintain and to foster it.' I couldn't have put it better myself. For what are we, comrades, the products of a vulgar, senseless materialism?"

"No," said Haegedoorn fervently.

"Are we nothing but blind instinct?"

"No," said Louis.

"Or instinct giving rise to will?"

No one answered.

"What do the Greeks say?"

Nobody knew. Louis cast about, came up with *agape*, a Rock word, he begged the Rock to give him more light, help, knowledge, but that stupid *agape* was all that stuck in his head, and he wouldn't be taking Greek until next year. Genevoix said, "That there is a struggle, that everything has always been a struggle from the very beginning, a struggle *surtout*. And what does Darwin tell us?"

"He has such a lot to say," said Mansveld.

"That existence is a struggle for existence. Right? So our aim in the world, National Socialist Youth of Flanders, is not to run away from the struggle like cowards! That's as plain as a pikestaff. Right? But the struggle has to be sublimated. Into what?"

"Into superman," said Bosmans with conviction.

"No, Bosmans, into human genius."

"But last week, Troop Leader, you said into superman."

"Bosmans, that was last week. *Verstanden?* In short, comrades, are we beasts?"

"No," cried Bosmans.

"No. And someone has to uphold the image of man in all his greatness and strength."

"That's us," said Bosmans.

"Precisely." Genevoix felt in his pockets. Cigarettes? Surely not. He brought out a copper toothpick and began to pick his teeth with it. "And morality, that's a habit imposed on us by strength. You must realize that. Good and evil, it all comes from the same source. Right? If you were a priest, Seynaeve, and offered up your life for your so-called God, if you absolutely had to be righteous as most people have to be now and then, if you said '*merci*' to life, then strength is what it's all based on. Right?"

"Right," said Louis. It was true. "But in the College . . ." he began.

"Your College," said Genevoix, extracted the toothpick from his mouth and gave a loud belch. "That's my answer."

Everyone laughed. They were laughing at Louis. All at once, however, Genevoix became the comrade again, the all-understanding friend hidden within the hard-as-nails leader.

"You are a thinker," he said. "That won't do you any harm, think, think as much as you can. But don't just think, be a soldier of thought, too, a pillager, a destroyer of thought. Right?"

"Right," said Louis fervently.

That same week, Louis stole some money from the wallet in Papa's jacket on the coatrack in the hall. He used it to pay an advance on his uniform, green shirt, black corduroy trousers, orange scarf, black cap with chin-strap, belt, crossbelt, haversack, and buckle with Delta sign. He polished the buckle, donned his armor, washed himself, and combed his hair in Haegedoorn's room, and the first time he walked through the streets of Walle the whole town knew about it, envious boys from the Atheneum stared open-mouthed, young girls smiled, a German corporal saluted him, *"Heil Hitler,"* dachshunds barked at him, the Lion flag on the Belfry fluttered. Even though the uniform was far from complete, still lacking the Hitler Youth dagger or any proficiency or sports badge. Haegedoorn beside him noticed nothing, the Hottentot.

In the room in the Town Hall, Genevoix was reading *Der Adler,* a cigarette in the corner of his mouth. His face betrayed utter amazement at the sight of his latest *knaap,* and Louis was already tingling with pride when Genevoix began to laugh and to swear. Bosmans, who was practicing fencing on his own with a wooden sword, joined in the laughter. Then Haegedoorn, too, moved away from Louis and pointed at him with a giggle. Then, only then, Louis saw it himself, he had forgotten, how in God's name could he have done that? totally forgotten to put on his boots, he was still wearing those ludicrously pointed, glossy pumps Aunt Hélène had cleared out of Uncle Florent's wardrobe when she had moved into Uncle Florent's room, over Grandma's wails and protests.

"I told you," said Haegedoorn, the rat.

"You never told me anything," shouted Louis.

"A regular *danseur mondain,"* said Genevoix in a foppish falsetto. Louis jerked the wooden sword out of Bosman's hand and pointed it at Haegedoorn, who should have spared him this disgrace. With a catlike leap, worthy of the Hitler Youth proficiency badge on his breast pocket, Genevoix grabbed one of the two sabers hanging on the wall on either side of the portrait of the poet Albrecht Rodenbach and with a single stroke sent Louis's miserable sword flying. Haegedoorn ducked. The sword landed noisily on the floor. Louis started to pick it up but was given a kick in the backside, a clip around the ear, and then Genevoix seized him by his new scarf. "No one interrupts a fencing lesson without my express orders. Right?"

"Right, Troop Leader."

He had to do thirty pushups.

During the slow motion of the cut and thrust no one spared him a glance.

He heaved himself up and down, chin nearly touching the floor, he couldn't make twenty, his trembling arms were crying out with pain, he was gasping for air, the dusty room was spinning, a cramp was shooting through his calves, wouldn't go away, he let himself drop.

"Thirty," said Genevoix. "Right?"

He started again. The Institute with its erratic nuns had not prepared Louis for this. Nor had Grandpa. Nobody had. They should have taught me this iron discipline from early childhood. I will be the toughest of you all, my arms will be like braided steel cables, my head like a steel helmet, my soul will contain its flames in a shell of asbestos—. But his chest would not rise another inch. Kick me, kick me with your regulation boots, I am not worthy.

"Next week you can come for a pair of boots in our shop," said Genevoix when they were alone. "I couldn't say that when the others were around. And that hair of yours won't do." Before Louis was allowed to go home, Genevoix cut his hair as it should be, the length of a match. With gentle fingers, those of a comrade.

Louis was on guard duty in his stiff, new, round-toed boots (he had told the envious Haegedoorn that he could try them on now and then), legs spread wide, hands gripping the pennant. The Flandria, the building where the party was being held in honor of a captain in the Götz von Berlichingen Division who had just been decorated for his valor on the Eastern Front, was the former anglophile, Franskiljon tennis club and lay in a park of hundreds of shades of yellow and green, full of trees all of which Maurice de Potter could have named. The cars, of which Vlieghe could have told you the makes, were crammed with officers and drove right up to the front, braking with a raucous crunch. All the officers leaped up the stone steps, they had been taught to do that for generations. Grandma's brother, Honoré, the Major, should have taken a leaf from their book. Belgians never leap, have not done so for generations. Genevoix is inside, running the buffet. No job is too lowly if it serves the cause. When would there be an opportune moment to let slip to Papa that he had enlisted in the NSJV? The moment Papa noticed the thefts? It would have to be before next month, in any case, because the whole section was due to travel then in the *Organisation Todt* bus to Cologne in order to attend the German-Flemish Culture Festival.

A bridge between thinkers and workers. In Cologne they would be addressed by Wies Moens, a Flemish Mind like no other, who, locked up in a Belgian dungeon, had written his heartrending *Letters from a Cell*, which Louis, moved to tears, had read aloud to himself in front of the mirror. Art in search of beauty. Too long have we believed that the secret of life lies buried in darkness and hatefulness. True beauty springs from the primal source of life, and that source is elementary and dangerous, isn't it?, but that is why it bewitches and intoxicates man, a flame that is brightness itself, isn't it?, a scorching sun, and it is not by chance that a circling sun should be the symbol of the German people and now, in part, of the Flemish people as well. Cyriel Verschaeve says that critical times call for rapid, committed, decisive action! All right, then, priest of genius, I have reported for service, here I stand and do my duty.

Musing thus (said Louis inaudibly), observing the traffic and nature thus (said he under his breath), I, Sentry Seynaeve, dream my dreams, "and observe through the mists of time a great people rising up in the wake of an intense, stupendous struggle."

All those s's.

And over there, Maurice, what are those, oaks? Oaken, olden, golden. Three o's. Common oak? Holm oak? Maurice, I miss you. You would never have come along with me, that brave day, to the office in the Town Hall.

Through the shrubbery Louis saw his mother. She was wearing an elegant beige two-piece suit, one he had never seen before. Did she change her clothes somewhere else, as he did? In the ERLA? She lifted a silvery, glittering little spoon of pistachio ice cream to her mouth, and when she had licked up half the green blob with a waggle of her pointed tongue, she raised the sparkling spoon to the lips of a man in his forties with close-cropped hair and a long nose, in a short-sleeved white shirt. The man gripped the spoon between his teeth, and Mama tried playfully to retrieve the queer little metal object that had made the man look like some sort of spoonbill.

The flagstaff in the sentry's hand did not move, the pennon with the Delta in the claws of the Bluefoot, the fulmar, symbol of Flemish nationalism, did not tremble, although the sentry on guard was stricken with panic. What is my mother doing here? How can I make good my escape? And more to the point, how can I escape if I have to pee? I do have to pee, now, irresistibly. Louis called Haegedoorn, who was passing by bearing a silver platter piled high with meringues, like the nuns in the Institute before sunrise in winter with their scuttles full of glowing coals. "Psst. Psst. Ahem."

Haegedoorn came over and said, "Not now. I've put six of them aside. For later."

"What?"

"These nun's-farts here. Three each, later."

"Haegedoorn, please would you take over for me here?"

"Are you crazy?"

"I'm getting a cramp."

Haegedoorn walked off. Louis sent up a prayer to his mother to go away without seeing him, please, it isn't fair, I can't run away, I can't hide from you, because I'm under orders and have to follow them unconditionally, *nicht räsonieren,* which is why you might come across me, and that must not happen.

Inside the building they were singing, *"Mein Schatz muss ein Matrose sein, und so stürmisch wie die See, und treu sein muss er mir allein, denn ich sag ihm sonst adé!"*—"My sweetheart must a sailor be, and as stormy as the sea, and true must be alone to me, or else I'll bid him gone!"

Stürmisch, stormy. Cold shivers. I am going to have diarrhea. Because the man in the tennis outfit is getting to his feet. And so is Mama. Louis turned his face as far as he could to one side, a sentry in profile, one who happens to have spotted a threat from far across a distant sea. What he saw was Bosmans carrying a landsknecht's-drum that was much too big for him, balanced on his stomach. This the sentry with the gurgling bowels saw.

Footsteps approached, accompanied by the yapping of a small dog and the crunching of gravel. *"Dann schmeckt doch jeder Kuss von ihm, nach mehr, nach mehr, nach mehr"*—"Then with every kiss from him, I wish for more, more, more"—sang Mama in unison with the distant chorus of the soldiers who had come back maimed and wounded from the Eastern Front and therefore had the right to sing songs like that. The man was taller than Papa, who was five foot eight. There was a scar on the tip of his long, thin nose. He had a gold tooth. His narrow eyes were slanting, and two girlish flat ears were stuck to his shaven temples. His otherwise spotless long white trousers had a brownish-red stain on the right knee, the size and shape of a child's hand. He said in a steady, slightly mocking voice, *"Was ist los,* Constance?" *(Konstanz.)*

And Constance, the Constant, the Immutable, the Faithful, spoke to him in rapid, clear German, no, it was to that filthy little white yapping beast on a blue leash who was licking Louis's shoes.

Mama stopped right in front of Louis, as if looking into a cage at the Antwerp Zoo, where she had promised to take him. Her wide gentle eyes. Her mobile, heart-shaped, scarlet-painted lips.

Drops of sweat in Louis's lashes. He did not dare bring his sleeve up to his face, his hand remained resolutely on his hip, a melting, dripping snowman of a sentry.

"Oh," said Mama. And then: "Tell me, young man, what is your name?"

"Louis."

"His name is Louis. Like my son," said Mama in German.

"*Ach so,*" said the man.

"Aren't you too hot in those thick socks?"

"No." (No, Madame. No, Mama, Mama.)

"What smart boots you have. They seem to be new. Aren't they too tight? Just a little? Your feet look fairly large."

"*Heil Vlaanderen!*" Louis snapped out.

"*Heil!* And carry on, young fellow." Mama's scent wafts into his face, she draws his scarf with the leather ring tighter, making the two ends even. "You little rascal," she whispers and does not look at him again. The seams of her stockings are straight. The little dog jumps up against the man's flapping white trousers. "*Tschüss,*" says the man in farewell.

When Louis got home, scowling, with an assortment of explanations on the tip of his tongue, she said not a word. It was only as she was serving him glazed baby turnips that she gave him a wink. Papa was in high spirits because she was.

She entered Louis's room without knocking, something she would not normally have done, and something he had particularly asked her not to do. ("You're right, you are no longer a child," she had said, nodding earnestly.) She sat down on his bed, he was alarmed, her slippered foot with its pink pompom was dangling inches above the towel on which the semen could not yet have dried.

"It was such lovely weather this afternoon, and my boss said, 'What an idiot I am to sit indoors when yesterday's transport has almost been dealt with, I'm going to go and play tennis, would you like to come along?' You little rascal, how long have you been in the Hitler Youth?"

"It isn't the Hitler Youth."

"Oh, no?"

"No. It's the NSJV."

"But that's the same thing."

How stupid can a woman be! "To start with, they have a different flag, they have a swastika on their armband, a buckle that says *Blut und Ehre*, blood and honor, a Victory rune . . ."

"Why did you keep it secret from us?"

"I wanted to get my sports badge first."

"What do you think of him?"

"Who?"

"Henny."

"Henny?"

"Yes. I thought it was pretty funny myself at first. But in Germany, Henny is a boy's name, too."

"He's tall."

"Is that all?"

"Yes."

She stubbed her cigarette out in the saucer under the cactus pot. "I can tell already from your voice. There is no reasoning with you. You're in another one of your moods. What have I done this time?"

She looked over his shoulder at his exercise book, in which he was tracing caricatures of Churchill, Roosevelt, and Stalin.

"You're a difficult fellow," she said. "But we'll make a deal. You won't tell your father that I was at the Flandria, he's been so on edge these last few days as it is, and I won't say anything about your uniform and your new boots. Agreed? Are we sworn allies? Yes? That outfit really suits you. I didn't recognize you at first. I thought, God, how smart that fellow on sentry duty looks!"

"Don't talk rubbish."

"No, no, it's true. I swear it."

"On your child's head, presumably?"

"Oh, you, you do make things difficult for yourself. You're just like your father."

"*Merci*, Mama."

"Don't mention it, my child."

Papa was in the workshop, which smelled of some new kind of acrid printer's-ink, wiping the press with a black oil rag. Papa loved the Heidelberg. Less so the cylinder press, which lay there with all its nerves of metal, dusty gray like a sick monster, waiting for better times.

Vandam, the foreman, was running off an illustrated obituary notice on the platen press. A drawing by Dolf Zeebroeck, the artist who had been associated with the Flemish cause since the twenties and who had adjusted meaningless modern abstracts to accord with the aesthetic sense of our people, rendering them comprehensible to even the least artistic among us. He lived in Canon Vanderpaele Street in a modern house with a profusion of indoor plants and a wife and six children, and he was not nearly as well appreciated as he should have been because he lived among us just like an ordinary man of Walle, an artist should either be dead or living far away, you don't see Rubens or Arno Breker doing the family shopping with a wicker basket in the company of three bawling infants.

Vandam did not look up from his work, he was in a bad mood because the boxing club he had started up in Zwevegem Street, the Kid Vandam Club, was on the verge of bankruptcy after only six months, just when, now of all times, healthy sport and games should be helping to bring people together, making them forget their worries, but it was always the same old story, people, and especially the people of Walle, weren't interested in solidarity, you had to teach it to them, by force if necessary, with an iron fist in a boxing glove. It was quite likely that Vandam, now pulling the obituary notices from between platen and ink roller with a juggler's nimble fingers, considered the suffering Christ shown nailed to the beam's black surface some sort of undertrained welterweight. Dolf Zeebroeck's Savior did not have the bulging, inhumanly taut muscles of, for instance, the discus thrower on the poster printed by Papa last month to announce the athletics competition at which Troop Leader Genevoix had effortlessly won the fencing event. Moreover, this Jesus was standing on a small block of wood, which had been sensible of Dolf Zeebroeck because the palms of a man of that weight—how much did Jesus weigh?—would have torn, he would have collapsed on top of the two bowed women seen grieving in profile (who bore a striking resemblance to the painter himself. Underneath was a legend in the neo-Gothic script also designed by the artist: "He was wounded for our transgressions, and with his stripes we are healed." No stripes were to be seen.

"What's this I hear?" said Papa. "You're in the NSJV? And you never told me anything about it? I had to learn it from perfect strangers!"

"Who?"

"Theo van Paemel."

"He's not a stranger."

"I know you've only done it to spite me. Don't deny it. I've tried to get it into your thick skull that we've given our word of honor not to become official members of anything except the Red Cross. Now I'm going to have to go to Bruges, thanks to you, seven, eight hours on the train, and explain to the Bishop that you put on that uniform either in a huff or out of sheer stupidity. What I won't be telling His Eminence, of course, is that it was only to make me a laughingstock."

"A laughingstock? Who to?"

"To my comrades in the VNV! Naessens, the District Leader, must have asked me twenty times at least, 'Why isn't your Louis in the Great Netherlands Bluefoot Troop?' Every time I've had to tell him that I didn't want to force you."

"But the Bluefoot Troop has been made part of the NSJV!"

"Yes, but it's not for us Seynaeves. We're not allowed to join anything, because otherwise the Bishop will wash his hands of my father!" Papa's despairing lament sounded like the wailings of the Arab women attending a funeral in the B-picture that had been shown before *Hallo Janine,* the Marika Rokk film.

"Staf, just you send him down to the Club on Thursday, I'll soon bring him to heel. After three rounds of shadow-boxing he'll be ready to drop," said Vandam.

Papa continued cleaning the carriage of the printing press.

"As if I hadn't had enough trouble lately."

Bekka Cosijns said that they hadn't heard anything from her father in Bavaria, and that her mother was worried sick because he'd stopped sending money or ration stamps. "Just as long as he hasn't deserted. Because he's so pig-headed he won't take orders from anybody."

Louis pictured what Bekka would be like in ten or twenty years' time, plump, anemic, a Gypsyish laborer's-wife, someone he would no longer care for. She had twisted the corners of the paper wrapper from an orange into four small gray points and slipped it over a billiard ball. The invisible ball trundled along, a headless and legless tortoise in motion under a crinkled skin, and then the billiard ball broke away, sloughing off its membrane like one of the many washed-to-a-shred handkerchiefs that lay around Grandma's armchair, and Bekka bent over to retrieve it from under the sideboard. Her frayed panties and the inside of her thighs showed traces of blood. Louis gave a cry but stifled it at once.

"What's the matter?"

"Have you hurt yourself?"

"Me? No."

"What's that?"

"What?"

"That, there."

"Oh you," said Bekka tenderly. "That's the procession."

And seeing his perplexed face: "The blood procession."

The Procession of the Holy Blood in Bruges, every year, pageants in historical costume, knights, guilds, oriflammes, the Shrine?

"You mustn't look at it," she said. She tossed back her blue-black hair.

In faraway Bastegem, Raf had once said—dusk, mist by the sanatorium, shreds of sentences left hanging in the air, I didn't pay enough attention—that when Madame Laura bled, all the neighboring farm dogs thrashed about in a frenzy at the end of their chains. I thought he meant she had cut her finger with a potato peeler by accident.

Louis couldn't understand why Bekka had not run immediately to her mother or the doctor. He thought about it for days. He certainly didn't love her anymore now, her with her strange Gypsy sickness. At least he had now been shown a glimmer of what Rodenbach had meant, Rodenbach, that pure youth with his sea gull raised to Heaven in his hand, immortalized in the statue on Roeselare market place (where Tetje spread other Gypsy ills among those Gypsies known as Egyptians), when he wrote, "I want nothing to do with the souls of Southern women."

Uncle Omer looked dreadfully emaciated. From time to time his pale face was contorted by a painful grimace as if by a sudden, violent toothache. He had brought two school satchels, real butter, two small bottles from Jules the carpenter, a piece of goat meat, and a blood sausage. And regards from all in Bastegem, except for Uncle Armand. Uncle Armand had turned out to be a barefaced swine.

"You've never managed to get along with Armand," said Mama.

"I know perfectly well he's your favorite, Constance, but what he's done is worse than murder."

It appeared that Uncle Armand had been carrying on with Thérèse, Uncle Omer's fiancée, behind his brother's back. She had gone with him, Uncle Omer counted on his fingers, to the Picardy, the Cocorico, the Swan, otherwise known as the Six Bottoms, and the Mirador. She had even gone with him on one of his farm inspection rounds.

"You can't blame her for trying to wheedle something out of the farmers. Thérèse isn't well off, you know that."

"But she gets everything from me, white bread, horse steaks!"

"And what did Armand have to say for himself?"

"That's just it. Not a word. He knows I'm eating my heart out, and every morning at breakfast he just sits there with that hypocritical smirk on his face. I'm going to join the Flemish Guard. But first I'm going to kick him in the balls."

He was trembling with emotion and drank four cups of malt coffee. He had the same combed-back hair receding at the temples as Uncle Armand but didn't use as much hair oil.

"Why is she doing that?" he cried despairingly.

He calmed down during supper. Mama and he spoke about the old days, about Three Mills oatmeal porridge, about their father, who demanded absolute silence while he listened to "News for Pigeon Fanciers."

The goat meat was a joy, the blood sausage a miracle. "It's all got to be finished," cried Mama.

"Goat meat," said Papa and started to laugh.

"It was a long time ago," he said, chortling. "I'll never forget it, every time I eat goat meat . . ." he guffawed. "It . . . it . . . it may be unkind to say so, but I've never laughed as hard as I did during that time I spent on the road in France with Cosijns from next door."

"Cosijns has deserted his post in Bavaria," said Louis.

But Papa let that pass. Out of sight, out of mind. At this very moment Cosijns was running through the night, ducking along German railway embankments, pursued by the Gestapo, he moistened his forefinger, held it up to the wind, and ran on, consumed with longing for his bleeding daughter, Rebekka.

Papa spread himself, took a deep breath. "Listen. On the 24th at nine in the evening we escape from the camp. Cosijns is scared to, but I say: 'We're not going to let these French get the better of us,' because the French had started talking about making us break stones and dig latrines. I say to myself, I'm not going to let it come to that."

"What's all this got to do with goat meat?" said Uncle Omer absently.

"Listen! When we get to Veurne, I see a beach pedal car standing outside the Church of St. Nicholas. I say: 'Cosijns, that's for us.' Cosijns didn't dare at first. I say: 'Cosijns, after everything they've done to us it's every man for himself now!' So we get as far as Poperinge, and there a farmer lets us sleep in his barn as long as we don't smoke. So we're asleep, Cosijns and I, and I say, 'Cosijns, cut it out!' 'Cut what out?' he says. I say, 'That banging!' 'Me, banging?' he says, and what do we see? I'll give you three guesses!

"A goat is jumping and skipping around and shoving and butting at our pedal car, not a billy but a nanny goat! Well, the sun is up just a little bit by that time, and I say to him, 'We might as well get going,' and we tie the goat to a wall. After five miles or so the sun is so bright, you know that part of the world, beautiful countryside, and the farmer had given us bacon and eggs, and Cosijns says, 'Staf, I didn't sleep a wink last night, no one is chasing us and we're in no hurry to get home, and what with this fine weather and all, why don't we take a little nap right here in the wheat?' So we lie down, we shut our eyes, we snore, and suddenly I say, 'Come on, Cosijns, cut out that banging of yours,' and you know what, I'll give you three guesses, that goat was back again, she had followed us, if you please, and was standing there in love with our pedal car, pushing her two front legs against the front of the wagon, shoving and skipping and butting. 'That's a sign from the Lord,' says Cosijns, who is anything but a Bible thumper, 'it's Abraham's ram,' and he grabs her by the horns and looks into her bulging glassy eyes.

" 'Oh, you horny old goat,' he says, 'do you want to do it with our lovely car?' and in a flash he's cut her throat, and then we roasted the best bits, juicy white meat, there, in the open, as if we were out camping."

"You weren't in any hurry to get home," said Mama.

"Well, in point of fact, Constance, that is, I mean to say . . "

"Best say nothing."

Uncle Omer remained motionless, sitting there with glassy goat's-eyes, withdrawn into himself. Later, when Papa had gone to a meeting of the new dramatic society (actually a revived version of one of the oldest Flemish "Chambers of Rhetoric," called "St. John's Lamb," with the motto "Devout and Gainful"), where he would probably get the lead role of the drunken old clown in *Circus Love,* Louis came into the kitchen, having just finished his homework. Uncle Omer was sitting with his head on Mama's lap, he had been crying, and she was stroking his spiky hair. Uncle Omer wanted to get up, but Mama held him back. "It's all right, Louis," she said, "go back upstairs."

He listened at the stair door. Uncle Omer was sobbing again.

"How could they do that, behind my back?"

"That's life," said Mama, but she didn't believe it.

The Rock took off his alb like an old man, then flung it carelessly on top of the brocade chasuble before Louis, who had been summoned to the sacristy, had a chance to catch it. The gold thread and the scarlet were dimmed by the white lace-bordered linen. Somebody—in the confessional?—had let it slip that Louis had joined the New Order.

"If good and evil are the same thing," said the Rock wearily, "as your chief alleges they are" (chief! we aren't Boy Scouts!), "if evil is to be preferred to weakness because it is a manifestation of life, if, if . . . ."

He snapped his fingers, Louis handed him his breviary. "If inhuman qualities are the raw material, the fertilizer of human achievement, then, then . . . ."

They walked in step to the oak door where, quite recently, someone had made an obscene scratch, jagged and pale, in the form of a cross. In some kind of frenzy? The Rock himself?

"When a guilty conscience is equated with illness, then I can hear the enemy's voice."

"I am not your enemy."

The Rock had blue rings under his eyes. For the first time there was short white stubble to be seen in the cleft of his chin, a poignantly vulnerable, neglected little spot. His shoes, too, were dusty for the first time.

"No?"

"No!" Louis exclaimed, and could not stop his knees from trembling, nor his hands, he knelt, leaned briefly against the knee of the priest in the immaculate cassock, and wiped the tops of the shoes clean with his sleeve.

With a swift, rough gesture, the Rock jerked him up by his collar.

"If you ever do that again . . ."

"Yes?"

The Rock pushed him to one side and fled, robes floating behind him. Alone with the cold breath of incense. Why did I do that? Because no one could see me? I wanted to tell him that he should look after himself, that he should not fast so much, not atone for others, for me, that he should watch his step because there were whispers that he had—covertly, like the first Christians—said Mass in a barn to English airmen who, disguised as peasants, had landed in a field in Moorsele with orders to smash the "Blacks."

Louis put on the alb. The Rock's shaving soap drove out the cold breath of the incense. There was no mirror. He unbuttoned his fly. At every Mass this week you, Evariste de Launay de Kerchove, will carry my trace, my mark on you.

Touching toes, doing kneebends, holding dumbbells at shoulder level, at the thighs, over the head, chopping wood with an imaginary medieval mace, the *goedendag,* doing scissors kicks, bicycling in the air, doing push-ups until the eyes were shrouded in a red mist. Afterward Louis and Haegedoorn walked in uniform to Haegedoorn's house. The town had by then become used to seeing Louis in full array, and anyway there were few people around. In Toontjes Street, where almost all the men and youths had left for Germany, an old man, his cap pulled down over his eyebrows, was sitting on a chair in the middle of the pavement. Louis stopped in front of him. Haegedoorn, who had stepped off the pavement, stepped back up again.

"Well?"

"Well, what?" said the old man.

"Get that chair out of the way. And be quick about it!" snapped Louis.

"The street belongs to us all."

"Exactly. That's why the pavement has to be clear for us all."

The old man dragged his chair to the front of his little house, mumbling and grumbling. Louis pulled his Hitler Youth dagger out of its sheath and held it to the filthy throat crisscrossed by deeply etched lines.

"Come on, Louis, come on," said Haegedoorn behind him.

"Say 'Shield and Friend.' And be quick about it!" barked Louis, hoping the man would have a Spanish, a French, a Gypsy, or a Negro accent, but the "sh" and the "f" came out right, effortlessly. Louis slid the dagger back into its sheath with the masterful, well-oiled gesture he had so often seen Genevoix use.

"And to think that I got your father to print our Gaston's wedding announcement," said the old man. "Just you ask him. Gaston van Remoortere. And visiting cards as well, before the war."

"One of your daddy's clients," said Haegedoorn with a smirk.

"Don't let me ever, ever see that chair in the street again," Louis snarled.

The afternoon, which had started out as triumphantly, as mightily radiant as the Flemish Legion in the snowy battlefields of the muzhiks, had turned sour. At the railway crossing he felt like going back to Toontjes Street and throwing a brick into the old man's miserable hovel, but Haegedoorn held him back, they had to set an example, not add to the misery of the least privileged among the Flemish people. Back in his room, Louis consulted the picture on the wall, the portrait of Reinhard Tristan Eugen, the *Obergruppenführer*. "Least privileged, least privileged," growled the *Obergruppenführer*. "If that's the sort of thing you bother about . . ."

"In my opinion, the Rock is inciting those least privileged against us."

"Well, well," said the man coolly, fingering the Knight's Cross awarded to him for flying ninety-seven missions over England and France in an ME 110.

"In my opinion, the Rock is radioing reports about our formations to Russia, across the border, I mean across the enemy border, to the other side, to the Mongols. And he keeps laughing at me."

"With the sharpened tongue of a serpent?"

"Yes!"

Hitler himself thought the *Obergruppenführer* had spent too many perilous hours up in the air, but the man could not leave well enough alone, danger tantalized him, nor could he bear to stay in the castle from which he reigned over Bohemia and Moravia. His elongated face (the pale, slanting, close-set eyes, the long, elegant nose, the eagle on his sleeve, the skull and crossbones, the oak leaves) proclaimed, "*Schild und Freund,* I play scherzos by Schumann, Schubert, Schmoll, I am a schnauzer, I shave and I shoot, and you, *du, du,* you are nothing but a sheep. Shame! It's your *Schicksal,* your fate, to shine his shoes."

"*Jawohl, Obergruppenführer.*"

"*Scheisse,*" said Mama. She'd been saying it a lot these last few days. She clutched her loins. As if a child were moving inside.

Papa had done it again. He had obtained something mysterious from his brother Robert. "*La crème de la crème,*" Papa had called out as he entered, carrying a strip of entrails torn straight from the pig, with all the bits and bobs hanging off it. He had fried it, stewed it, boiled it, braised it with too little margarine, too many onions, "*Scheisse,*" Mama had cried, running out to the privy every ten minutes in a rage.

She rubbed her loins, her stomach. "And I've got to go to the *Kommandantur* soon," she cried, "I can't just walk in and go straight to the toilet. You and your filthy muck. Ugh! Oh God, I have to go again!"

"It's odd, isn't it," Papa called after her, "that Louis and I, who've eaten much more of that filthy muck than you, haven't noticed anything wrong."

"Just you wait till this evening," yelled Mama. She came back, drained of color. She dabbed scent behind her ears. "I'm going to fast for two days."

"Not a bad idea," said Papa. "It'll do your body a world of good. Get rid of all the filth."

"Aha," cried Mama, "so you admit it was filth."

"What?"

"What you got from Robert to give us diarrhea with."

"That? But my dear girl, that was *la crème de la crème!* Didn't you think so, Louis?"

"Are you trying to make out," shrieked Mama, "that all that filth comes from me, from my own insides, that I'm filthy inside?"

"But Constance, whatever gave you that idea?"

She ran out of the door.

"The fact that we are eating less," said Papa calmly, "isn't a bad thing at all. Dr. de Lille from Bruges has been saying so for years. Raw food, grains, no meat, or anyway very little."

At that moment Sootje's ice-cream cart sounded its horn in the street outside. Papa rushed out. They ate their tasteless ice cream standing next to the cart. The pony never stopped yawning, you could count its ribs.

"Sootje, I know it's neither here nor there, but you put too much water in your ice cream."

"It's the new fashion, Staf," said Sootje. "The Italian way."

Vanilla, pistachio, and chocolate ices made with *water*, and by Sootje, too, who has served us royally all his life, what are we coming to?

We, that is, everyone who still has some feeling for the West, its past and its culture, are going to Russia, cutting through Russia like a knife through butter made in the Russian steppes. The Russian peasants and citizens dance for joy when the Flemish Legion goes by. It's only a matter of months before those subhuman Bolsheviks bite the dust.

The Finns are already shelling Kronstadt, the very name says it all, the "crowned city" that protects the entrance to Leningrad harbor. They've already gone past Karioka and Knokkala. Where, Claire? That's what I said: Karioka and Knokkala.

And Briansk is ours, too, here, down in the south, where Timoshenko is trying to mount a counteroffensive. Further south still, here, follow my finger on the map, in Kiev, the mother of Russian cities, the Ukrainians are getting it in the neck as well.

The Russians haven't got a decent air force, that's what it is. If the weather isn't good enough, they don't fly. Only twenty-five percent of their pilots have learned to fly in all weather, which just goes to show what their flying schools are like! Add to that the fact that the Russian soldier doesn't like to attack, Jack. Marshal Mannerheim himself said so. The Russian soldier is more your defender, a center-half digging himself in just in front of his own goal. The only advantage the Russians have is numbers. Too bad for them quantity isn't what counts.

Frankly, a sore point right now is that the Walloon Legion is already scoring greater successes than the Flemish Legion. Why, Guy? Because it has more regular Belgian officers, cadres who know how to train other cadres. And the Flemings have no one of the caliber of a Leon Degrelle, who joined up as an ordinary private and in my view will make it to general, not in some headquarters office but right at the front, at the head of his men.

Daels, the new teacher of Dutch, who looked like an American and who, although it was strictly forbidden, would now and then smoke a stinking, belching, badly drawing working-man's clay pipe during lessons, came into the classroom in his jaunty way and sat himself down on the corner of Bruyninck's desk in the front row, the desk from which one of the boarders had thrown an inkwell at the blackboard years ago because the night before he had suddenly discovered, without being able to do anything about it, that he no longer believed in the existence of Jesus Christ. That morning, in the middle of the first lesson, he had uttered a piercing, inhuman cry, thrown the inkwell, and then fallen into a coma.

Daels rattled the stem of his clay pipe against his teeth and began giving out marks for the last composition, "Spring in the City." Baetens got eighteen out of a possible twenty, Robert Smetjens, another of Louis's rivals, got sixteen. Louis couldn't understand it. It was Daels's first effort at marking. Hadn't he heard from "Snotty," his predecessor, that Louis Seynaeve was the *primus inter pares* in composition? One by one Daels brought the exercise books up to his nose and his pipe, read out the marks, and placed the exercise book on the tottering pile beside him on the desk.

He picked up the last exercise book and used it to wave the tobacco smoke away, as haughtily and coquettishly as a Chinese lady-in-waiting during the last act in an overheated theater, and it was Louis's book with its dark-blue cover. Daels looked out across the playground where a platform was being erected. "This is a piece of work," he said, as if addressing the carpenters, "to which I have not awarded any mark . . ." (Because it cannot be fitted into any category, because my appreciation cannot be expressed in marks, because I cannot compare it with the wooden, tame scribblings of all the others, Baetens included.) ". . . because zero out of twenty would still be assigning it some value. No, I would like to consign this effort to total oblivion without further comment."

He swiveled around and pointed his pipe in Louis's direction. "Mijnheer Seynaeve junior thought he could make a fool of me, and in the most blatant manner. I don't know which sickens me more, his laziness or his arrogant stupidity."

Louis stood up. As in an empty room, he heard Robert Smetjens snicker.

"Seynaeve, sit down. I have nothing to add. Have you?"

"No. No."

Daels flung the exercise book into the wastepaper basket next to his desk with a well-aimed flourish. Louis clung to his seat.

"Seynaeve, did you really think your new teacher was some country bumpkin who wouldn't be able to tell when a phrase, let alone a whole essay, had been cribbed from some book, you oaf!"

Daels radiated blind, flagrant omnipotence. What had happened? Had Robert Smetjens, imitating his handwriting, secretly insinuated a different text or some different sentences into his composition, a composition Louis had taken two evenings to write, first quickly in a cramped penciled scrawl and then with well-spaced writing in ink, in which he had captured, conjured up, the shrubs, the postman, the servant girls and the rising sun, conscientiously observed during that walk from his home to the Park. The sentences, the paragraphs, the words had simply spurted out of him, oh yes, there had been one short phrase over which he had hesitated, that was true, because it had seemed like something from the book he had just been reading, *The Song of the Scarlet Flower* in the Phoenix Series, something about the day that came into blossom like a flower.

"Seynaeve, I told you to sit down."

"You are quite right, Mijnheer Daels."

The teacher's radiant smile. Fred Astaire dancing with Ginger Rogers, one franc, Thursday afternoon, before the Second World War.

"Absolutely right, Mijnheer Daels, I copied the whole thing letter for letter."

"The whole composition? Are you sure you didn't perhaps omit a few adjectives out of sheer laziness?"

"No, Mijnheer Daels. The whole thing came straight out of a book." Louis dropped back onto his seat, a cheat caught red-handed, a squalid charlatan. The day came into blossom like a rose.

"Just one last word on the subject, Seynaeve. So that there can be no misunderstanding. I take it very hard that you thought you could get past me with that crude deception of yours simply because I happen to have the same political views as your father. Just remember, young man, I am here as a teacher, nothing else."

Robert Smetjens clapped. The others followed suit. Daels, who was too suave, too young, too dashing to deserve a nickname, brushed the noisy applause aside with his pipe. Louis refrained from driving his nib with all his strength into Daels's backside.

The boarder who had thrown the inkwell had been carried out by two monitors and two teachers. They had been on the way to the infirmary when he had come out of his coma, changed into a werewolf, and scratched and bit his escort. It took their combined strength to carry him off to the cellar, which at the time had not yet been blacked out with blue-painted windowpanes or protected by sandbags. Later the boarder was accepted into the Little Seminary in Roeselare. But they had had to kick him out of there as well because he kept throwing hysterical tantrums. So one fine night he had returned to the College, the scene of his calamitous humiliation, and, smiling satanically, had scratched the Cross into the oak door of the sacristy.

Papa boiled some beets to make a custard, mashed the pulp with a fork, tossed in eggs, flour, and milk. "Another hour in the oven and the feast is ready."

Grandpa hated seeing his son do women's work in front of his grandson, the more so as Louis had come home with a bad report. The stove was red and so was Grandpa's face.

"Bad marks," he said. "You're not being a credit to us."

"That's what I told him," said Papa immediately.

"I'm second in the class in Latin."

"And what about this? Mathematics? Do you call that a mark?"

"And I'm top in German. And in the mother tongue as well!"

"Mother tongue, mother tongue," Papa licked the plate, turned it around, swallowed, licked, a strange, bald beast in shirtsleeves and suspenders.

"What in Heaven's name is to become of you?" Grandpa sighed.

Grandpa preferred to visit them when Mama was not at home. "I don't know why, but I get the impression that Constance is not very eager to see me."

"That's all in your mind, Father."

"I know what I'm saying, Staf. Not that I have anything against her, you know I don't, up till now Constance has always been a daughter-in-law I respect, but recently . . ."

"What recently, Father?"

"I don't know," said the Pharisee.

"Just say what's on your mind, Father. Louis, go to your room and do some homework."

"Oh, there's no call for the boy to leave. It's just that recently I keep seeing Constance laughing for no good reason, at least none that I can tell."

"So you'd rather see my Mama cry, would you?"

Grandpa grinned. "That's what I like to see, a boy sticking up for his mother. Very good, Louis. Incidentally, Louis, Louis . . ." Grandpa tasted the name, spat it out. "I have never really liked that name."

"He was named after Constance's godfather, Father."

"And after St. Louis, King of France!"

"France, France," Papa looked at the pudding in the oven.

"You could call yourself Lode."

(Lode! A load! Never!)

"That's more Flemish, of course," said Papa.

"And it also goes better with Seynaeve," said Grandpa, adding in an oh-so-casual and insidiously light tone, "For instance, if you were ever, just supposing, to join the National Socialist Youth of Flanders, Louis, then they would, I feel sure, oblige you to call yourself Lode."

Grandpa tapped the bowl of his pipe against the edge of the table, ash fell on Mama's floor. "But then, that's a silly supposition, you would never join an organization like that, would you now, Louis?"

"In Kiev," exclaimed Papa, "twenty Bolshevik divisions have been surrounded, and if truth be told, Kiev is more the capital of Russia than Moscow!" He turned the pages of the newspaper feverishly. "Fifty thousand prisoners, three hundred and twenty armored cars, six hundred pieces of artillery in our hands."

"In whose hands, Staf?"

"I mean . . ."

"You always mean so many things, Staf." Grandpa gave another sigh, relit his pipe. "I also hear from Mona that Constance has been buying a lot of new clothes."

"She's saved up for them," said the tortured husband, squirming uncomfortably, then going over again to the oven, from which a sweet, mouth-watering smell arose.

"She's probably been working overtime?"

"Yes, Father," said Papa to the sweet smell.

Mama was crying. There was no calming her. Her shoulders were shaking, she was pouting like a small child and had red eyes. And all because that morning when Herr Lausengier had been walking his little dog in the park, a huge brute of a bull mastiff, all of a sudden and without any provocation, had fallen upon Herr Lausengier's little Bibi. Before anyone could intervene, Bibi had been torn to shreds and his entrails strewn all over the gravel. "He was taken straight to the clinic," Mama wept, "but it's ten to one they won't be able to save his life."

"But who did the brute belong to?"

"That's the awful thing. Mijnheer Groothuis. He was terribly upset. Because he had to admit that his dog had been acting strangely for quite some time."

"Were you there, Mama?" Louis knew the answer, of course she had been there. Raf, his disreputable friend from Bastegem, would have said, Of course. Everywhere your mother goes when she's bleeding, the dogs are driven to a frenzy.

"Of course!" Mama sobbed. "And he was such a playful little dog, Bibi, always so happy. And he'd won so many prizes. For looks and for training. He would listen like a child. You could put a hamburger right under his nose, but without a command he wouldn't go anywhere near it, even though he'd be drooling with longing."

"And your Meneer Lausengier?"

Mama did not notice the scornful tone. "He was as white as a sheet. From sorrow and from anger. He would have shot that mastiff on the spot, I think, but he couldn't, because it belonged to Mijnheer Groothuis, who after all is a friend of his and couldn't really help it anyway."

"Did he buy this prize-winning animal here in Walle?"

"Oh no! He brought it with him from home. It was a present from his first wife!"

"What? He's been married once already?"

"No."

"But you said his first wife!"

"I meant the wife Henny is divorced from, Staf!"

"What? Divorced? You never told me that."

"I meant the wife from whom he's divorced for the time being. Because she lives in Bremerhaven and he lives here. That's a kind of divorce. Oh, Staf, one day you're going to drive me stark, raving mad!" She ran upstairs in her new shoes.

"Hamburger," said Papa dreamily. "With capers."

The Rock was standing, as always, by the window, he did his best to keep away from it, he described loops and curves along and between the desks, but again and again he would end up in front of the view of the playground, waiting for something, for someone, for people who were looking for him, who needed him (the lawyer's clerk come to report that the aged nobleman De Launay de Kerchove had died and that his priestly son had inherited millions, whereupon the Rock would joyously take off his cassock and perform dance steps in his short satin pants).

"Some of you will shrug your shoulders and think it old-fashioned, not modern enough, but isn't there some evidence in favor of the devil's existence? Could it not be that mankind has fallen under the sway of satanic powers? That mankind is suffering from a satanic disease? And that we must take pity on all the diseased people, perform the great labor of charity, tend the sick?"

The cassock flapped about his frame, he turned from the window as if shunning it, dropped into his chair with an ashen face. He twisted his signet ring around his thin finger.

"Is it persecution mania to think of the devil as of someone you meet in the street, unexpectedly, around the corner, in uniform? That the unfathomable evil committed by man has been given tangible form?" Unintelligible mumbling. Stammering. He was talking more and more to himself, mainly in the form of questions. Recently, while asking one of these in a monotone, he had drawn a six-pointed star with chalk on the blackboard and then, as if seeing that star for the first time, as if it had been drawn by another, had shyly wiped it off with his sleeve (with his sleeve!).

"All of which makes one dare to think that it must be a singular God who does not put a stop to all that, that, that . . . Isn't that so? In one's despair one yearns for desperate solutions . . . Isn't that so?"

Why didn't he, oh, for the hundredth time, why didn't he say straight out what he meant? What was stopping him?

"And so people look outside the faith . . . no, they replace faith in Jesus Christ with another kind of faith . . ."

That was more familiar ground, priests' language. The last part, that about the desperate solutions, was probably aimed at National Socialism. And that other faith, that is faith in the New Order, the faith I propagate with my uniform. Is he afraid I may give him away? When I want nothing more than to please him? If he were the mathematics teacher I would even apply myself to mathematics just to wring a glimmer of appreciation from him, and why does he keep circling the window so awkwardly, as if he had special arch supports or corns?

After class Louis said, "You were talking about me."

"If you want to take it that way."

"You think that the devil is driving me."

"Whom does he not?"

"You think I have deliberately chosen to do evil! Right, if that's the case then God has made me that way, so there!"

"No. He made you with good as well as with evil."

"Why?"

"If you were nothing but good, there would be no merit in choosing it."

The Rock brought out a snow-white handkerchief, rubbed his spectacles, his black pupils were those of the polyp in the color section of the magazine *Signal*. Jesuits receive instruction in the straight-through-the-sinner look.

"Baudelaire says . . ."

"No," said Louis. (No! Don't go foraging again through that dustbin into which all the long-winded loudmouths of the past have vomited their sayings.)

"Yes," said Louis. "What does he say?"

"That there are only three honorable vocations, those of priest, soldier, and poet."

"I don't want to be a priest."

"Of course not. With me for a model." It was meant to be sarcastic yet sounded like one of Mama's sobs for Bibi. Louis saw the priest pull himself together, don his spectacles like a mask.

"Soldier," said Louis.

The Rock gave a tired nod.

In the chlorinated air of the swimming pool Bosmans was paddling on his back, blowing. Haegedoorn was doing his set number of laps. Genevoix stretched out on the diving board, checked how many of his Troop were left. Three. Seynaeve was sitting on the edge. A head bobbed up and down, that of a German since no Fleming was as blond, as tanned, as muscular as that. Not even the boxing champion, Karel Sijs, who gives the *Houzee* salute in the ring before every fight and who is the doorman at the Ostend casino. Genevoix dived into the water without a splash. A dolphin. *Leistungsabzeichen,* proficiency badge.

Then, brazenly, a loud bass voice started to sing "Go Down, Moses" in one of the cubicles. The swimming pool, which at this privileged hour was frequented by comrades, was startled. Had an English airman, hidden away till now by Communists and snipers, suddenly gone mad with foolhardiness, seized by a death wish? Louis recognized the voice, the half-door swung open, and Dirty Dick came ambling out of the cubicle in orange trunks with a wobbling lump inside. He stood there, legs wide apart, arms akimbo, and Louis immediately dived into the chlorinated water, saw through wet lashes that Dirty Dick was doing a handstand, long wrinkled toes against the ocher roughcast wall.

"Dirty Dick? What was he doing in the swimming pool?" asked Papa.

"Singing."

"Did he have a *Schein,* then, a special permit?"

"Don't know."

Louis tried to imitate Dirty Dick and Louis Armstrong, "Go Down, Moses," but the sound didn't come out raspingly enough, was much too high, made his throat sore, he coughed.

Just as he had expected, his father said, "Aping Negroes, that's what our culture has come to these days."

And to Theo van Paemel: "Singing about Moses! Not only like a Negro but about a Jew, too. It's too much."

Van Paemel added, "That Dirty Dick is riding for a fall. You mark my words."

The first outing of the Walle and Idegem divisions of the NSJV was by bus to Wierebeke, the picturesque village in the Flemish Ardennes praised in song by, among others, Alice Nahon, who wrote poetry even as she lay dying of consumption, and by Karel van de Woestijne, the decadent Flemish Mind with the large, drooping half-caste lips ("The resonance of gardens in hazy autumn days . . ."), who, according to Grandpa, would deliver his university lectures inebriated and still bearing traces of his carousing on his clothes. On the bus, next to the small window just behind the fat driver, who, for a laugh, had wrapped the orange handkerchief of a *kerlinneke* turban-fashion round his head, sat a dark-haired girl who looked vaguely like Bekka, though more refined, middle-class, domesticated. She was the only one on the bus not wearing a uniform, and had on a silky dress with autumn-colored flowers. She was staring fixedly out the window, oblivious of the ever-changing landscape, with fields and woods undulating as far as the eye could see. No doubt she was dreaming of the aristocratic mansion in which her mother lay dying of a wasting disease, the home she had left, unseen, at the crack of dawn, resolved to allow her father—who, gripped by the hand of fate, had been conducting himself bravely and with dignity—time to be alone with his spouse so that he would be able, unencumbered by his daughter's presence, to catch her last words, words not intended for a child's ears, and now she was giving herself over to the often ill-understood, but in her case only too real, sorrow of an only child. Louis would have liked to sit next to her, hold her hand, consol her, perhaps whisper impetuously, "It's terrible, I know, but it's in the nature of things that first they must grow and then they must perish." (Which you could read in the books of Gulbranssen or John Knittel, and to a lesser extent in those of Jack London.) But then he might be intruding upon the musings of her soul. Perhaps, on getting off the bus, he could press a note into her hand: I have been much taken by your demeanor. Your profile is one I have seldom (never?) described (discerned?) before, it is noble? distinguished? true? no, *tender.*

The girl picked her nose, as people do when they become distracted under the burden of a great sorrow.

They were welcomed in the gym of the Wierebeke village school by the headmaster, one of Genevoix's uncles. He was delighted about the unification of Flemish youth in the NSJV which had brought together the General Flemish Youth League, the Great Netherlands Girls' Troop, Young Dinaso, the Rex Youth League of Flanders, the Flemish Youth Movement, the Flemish Folk Art Institute, and many more. They were next addressed in animated and paternal German by a bespectacled man in his forties with a cold, Dr. Bühlen, who told them about the New Order of Europe based on national principles. Bosmans, at Louis's side, had difficulty in following the German, the effort leaving him open-mouthed.

The talk was mainly about *Dietsch* (Dutch) and *Deutsch,* which had sprung from the same *Wurzel,* root, and about the fact that the *neue germanische Ordnung,* new Germanic Order, made it incumbent upon all *Beteiligte im völkischen Schicksalsinteresse,* those concerned with the fate of the nation, to view *Deutsch* and *Dietsch* not as a linguistic-philological antithesis but as a history- and future-determining synthesis. Hence the robust and unreserved resolve to collaborate *mit dem grossen deutschen Brudervolk,* with the great German fraternal nation.

"Nach Ostland wollen wir reiten," "To the land of the East will we ride," was what our forefathers used to sing, and that message remains *der Weg der Natur,* the path of nature.

Next Louis joined in a quadrille and a handkerchief dance, during which a plump girl with round spectacles and straw-colored hair accosted him.

"I've seen you in Roeselare," she said.

"You might have." (Never been to Roeselare, town of Tetje, Egyptians, and Rodenbach.)

"On the New Market. You kept staring at me."

"Oh yes. I remember."

"What color dress was I wearing?"

"Blue."

"Light-blue, yes." Hoppity hop. Sweat. Hop. Hop. Her braids whirled, whacked the air. Sway. Sweep.

"You haven't done much folk dancing, have you?"

"I'm just learning," said Louis.

"You've got a flair for it, I could tell right away."

"Thanks."

She sat down beside him on the flat stones of the open-air theater, a sloping arena dug out of a hill with dense pine forests behind the stage, like the illustrations to Grimm's Fairy Tales, soft watercolors, something Uncle Leon never could have done.

They drank dark Oudenaarder beer and ate the cheese sandwiches Genevoix handed around. Suddenly Louis realized that he had seen the theater before. He is four or five years old, his father lifts him up in the middle of a jostling crowd, sets him down again on a flat stone surrounded by wet grass, Mama takes him on her lap and pulls a yellow-and-black striped knitted cap onto his head. Against a background of phosphorescent pines Smedje Smee, the smith, thrusts a golden sword at the sparkling armor of the French tyrant Chatillon, who screams for mercy in French. Louis screams as well and is consoled. He screams again much later when Chatillon, who you can tell is a Frenchman because he wears a fleur-de-lys on his tabard, lifts his battle-ax and brings it down on top of Smedje Smee's mother, there is a blood-red stripe across her throat, she flaps hands glistening with blood in the air. Screams. Stamping of feet. Mama calms him. Not enough. Never enough. Never again.

"That's local cheese," said the girl, who was called Hilde and who played the oboe with her brothers, could tell your fortune from cards and could pack her knapsack faster than anyone else in her *round*.

"Round?"

"The round, the section, the standard, the district and the region," she recited.

Bosmans went around collecting leftovers and crusts of bread. With bulging cheeks and chomping jaws he lowered himself next to them and handed Hilde a thin slice of cheese.

"Mm, mm," she said. "That's local cheese."

"If you like, I can soon get you some more," said Bosmans, the flirt.

"Really? You're very kind."

"It's a pleasure."

"And another sandwich."

"Two," said all-conquering Bosmans.

"I have an aunt," said Louis, "my Aunt Nora, who's always playing practical jokes. Once, just after my parents married, she put a stinking cheese, a Herve, under their bed."

"I don't much like Herve cheese," said Hilde, "your breath reeks the whole day."

"You get the same with Camembert," said Bosmans, man-about-town.

"Oh, really?" cooed Hilde.

"Yes, you should chew a coffee bean right afterward."

"Would malt coffee do as well?" The two lovers burst out laughing. Louis walked away, over to the stage where Genevoix was pouring out lemonade.

"Bosmans is in love," said Louis scornfully to Haegedoorn.

"She isn't bad," said Haegedoorn. "Nice firm bottom."

"Yes, but what about that big fat face?"

"You put a towel over that."

The girl without a uniform who looked like Bekka was sitting in the shade, the flowery dress pulled tight over her drawn-up legs. Every time she bit into her cheese sandwich she pulled a wry face.

"That one over there," said Louis, "that's more my type."

Haegedoorn immediately went over to the girl. Burning with shame, Louis saw Haegedoorn talk to her while pointing to him.

I will report this. Haegedoorn must be expelled from the ranks for violating the most elementary rules of comradeship.

And what's more, Troop Leader, didn't you notice that Haegedoorn drank *two* bottles of Oudenaarder beer instead of the regulation one, and, Troop Leader, Haegedoorn's father traffics in bacon and butter, and the son, too, is hand in glove with the worst enemies of our people. Haegedoorn put out his hand, pulled the girl to her feet, and with scarcely conceivable acquiescence, she came with him toward Louis.

"Here he is," said Haegedoorn. The girl was almost as tall as Louis.

"I gather you have something urgent to say to me." She was chewing.

"I just wanted to say . . . well, that it's magnificent here, the pure forest air . . . of this region . . . where this cheese comes from . . ." She stared incredulously in the direction of Louis's stomach, at the gleaming buckle with the Bluefoot clasping the Delta sign. Polished like mad this morning with copper cleaner. Hilde left the line in front of Genevoix and handed Louis a bottle of lemonade. (Get away from me, you fat pig!) A whistle blew, they assembled.

"Next time you want to tell me something," said the girl, who had gray-blue eyes, "give it some thought first." She walked to the back of the stage with long, athletic steps that did not seem to go with her slender body.

"She thinks a lot of herself," said Hilde.

"Why isn't she in uniform?"

"Her?" Hilde gave a placid smile. "She isn't one of us. She just came along for the ride with her father, that's all."

Genevoix bellowed, the company reassembled, the Chief Troop Leader appeared, the juniors and seniors formed a circle. Into their midst stepped a man in a brown velvet jacket and flannel trousers. He had unwashed red hair that stuck to his scalp in greasy curls. He looked furiously to left and right, waited until not a breath could be heard, stuck out his chin, sought something in the distance among the fleecy clouds, spread out his arms, then folded them.

"They say . . ." he started venomously, cleared his throat, and shouted shrilly, "They say the Flemish tongue must fail, but never shall that be! They say Walloon speech will prevail, but never shall that be! This we declare, and this we swear, as long as we stand firm and dare . . ."

Birds answered, cows lowed. He shouted them down, barked, bawled, pointed his rigid fingers at the horizon where the nation, hitherto enslaved, was now being aroused by the blazing verses of Guido Gezelle (priest and poet, two of the three honorable professions). Applause. The man mopped his face, smoothed his curls, bowed, exhausted.

"He knows how to put things," said Bosmans.

"Inspired, that's what he is," said Hilde.

"It gave me goose pimples," said a small girl and displayed them on her skinny little arm, right next to the orange rune of fidelity.

"And you ought to hear him talk about the Bluefoot! 'Where no pettiness is descried . . .' "

"I'm always on Troop duty, otherwise I'd go to his evening classes in recitation."

"It's almost unbelievable to think that he's the same man who plays Dalle on the radio!"

"Of Wanten and Dalle? Is that him?"

"Yes. Paelinck the pharmacist."

The girl who looked like a more elegant Bekka went up to the pharmacist and put her arm through his, led him away like an invalid.

Next they were due to pay a call on Geerten Gallens, whose work sometimes appeared in color in *Ons Volk.* One of our most famous landscape painters, Genevoix said, a man who, as is so often the case in small countries, is honored more abroad than at home, his own people don't stand by him, but he bears his lot in seclusion and puts his faith in his art.

Singing, they climbed a hill, toward the Schampavie, the rustic café run by the great Flemish artist in the serene setting of Flemish woods.

The Chief Troop Leader gave them permission to drink one more glass of beer, but not Oudenaarder.

Geerten Gallens was a little man with a clerical air who sidled between the tables, rubbing his hands. Yellow down was scattered here and there over his domelike balding head. Crafty little eyes behind steel rimmed spectacles. His bitten fingernails still bore traces of paint, he chewed on a curly pipe.

They were allowed to inspect his studio in groups of six. Gallens pointed to the hilly landscape outside the large windows, which admitted northern light, so essential for a painter. There were two easels spattered with thousands of little paint spots. Gallens posed, palette in hand, while Hilde took photographs of him and her Section Leader. "You'll have to send me one of those, you little scamp," he said.

"That goes without saying, Master," said the Section Leader.

"Yes, yes, that's what they all say."

The paintings all looked alike, mostly representing a snowy landscape with trees like slender blades of grass in the red glare of a setting sun. There was one hanging in Marnix de Puydt's drawing room.

"Well, what do you think? Tell me the truth now. Come on, no beating about the bush."

"Beautiful," said Haegedoorn.

"I know that myself," grunted the painter. "But what do you feel, what do you experience when you see my work? Is it a sense of peace or is it more of an aesthetic emotion? Just look at them standing there with nothing to say for themselves! Well, well, *merci,* thank you very much, is that the youth of Flanders?"

"It's because our youth isn't used to . . ." the Section Leader began.

"Then our youth will just have to learn to speak their minds!" Gallens exclaimed.

"Well, what's it to be? Spit it out! Perhaps my work isn't modern enough for your tastes? But, friends, modernity, that so-called modernity, has poisoned our lives, my wife's, my children's, and my own! What has modernity brought us? Nothing but modish madness! One picture madder than the next! And is that supposed to be the image of contemporary man?"

He picked up the magnifying glass lying next to his palette and thrust it into Louis's hand.

"Go on! Look through it! Here! Take a good look, *nondedju!*"

Louis trembled, focused the lens, saw the slender blades of grass, the delicate twigs of the tiny trees in the blobs of snow.

"That's what I call craftmanship, meneer! And what does that wretch of a Permeke do, who has been praised, mark you, by Father Stubbe? What does he do? He picks up a broom and a bucket of, I'll put it quite bluntly, a bucket full of shit, and he smears it around and he says, 'Ladies and gentlemen, that is expressionism, that is the way I see the world!' I, Gallens, say, 'If that's the way you see the world, then, Permeke, you'd better go as fast as you can to the nearest eye doctor and from there straight to the nearest psychiatrist!'"

Polite titters.

"And Meneer Frits van den Berghe, the one who daubs monstrosities on canvas worse than Picasso, man-apes, bush Negroes, and monsters with eyes and noses all mixed up, what do you think he did when he made drawings for that Socialist propaganda rag, *Vooruit?* Then he saw fit to draw the Red leaders properly, so that you could recognize them, because the man-in-the-street had to be won over and made to sing the 'Internationale.' But for rich Jews that parasite went back to painting the same con tricks as before, spew and phlegm you can't make head or tail of. Or take Meneer Gust de Smet, who paints faces like bare backsides!"

He pinched Hilde's plump arm. "Come over here. I'll tell you a little secret. Something I don't usually do. A cook doesn't let anyone into his kitchen. Well, Gallens does. Look over here. Can you see that crescent moon, can you see how it's been painted, so delicately? Well, tell me, how was that done?"

With his hand on her hip he rummaged among the jumble of tubes, paintbrushes, rags, newspapers, varnish bottles, turpentine jars, and then held a match before her round face with the round spectacles.

318

"With this. As simple as that. With a match! Making a moon, a celestial body, shine with an ordinary match! That makes you sit up, doesn't it? The simplest means are the best. As long as you know your job, of course!"

He looked at his wristwatch. "Next," he said. And as they made for the door: "When you get home, friends, feel free to tell your fathers and mothers what you saw at Gallens's place today. And if they are interested in an original Geerten Gallens, signed and authenticated, they are welcome to come to the Schampavie any time they like, have a drink with me, and examine my work. As for buying anything, well, that's a different matter. They'll have to look sharp, because a good Gallens is snapped up before it's even dry. Yes, they'll have to be quick, because Gallens won't be around much longer, what with his heart. He's been through too much. *Allee,* friends, *au revoir* and *Houzee!*"

"*Houzee,* Master, that's the VNV salute!"

"By God, you're perfectly right. What group are you again? The NSJV. Yes, of course! Then it's *Heil,* isn't it?"

"*Heil Vlaanderen,*" said Bosmans.

"Precisely. Of course. *Allee, Heil Vlaanderen.*"

They slept in the straw, in a barn the size of a church. The girls were taken to the village school. Summer rain. Louis couldn't fall asleep. The pharmacist and his slender, dark-haired daughter were roaming the fields under a moon outlined with a sharpened match, she fell into a ditch, her thighs spread wide, her snow-white stomach heaved, she rose and fell over backward three or four times more, slowly and obligingly, each time with her legs wide apart. The barn dissolved, became a forest with an open-air stage, Louis's breath gave off a moist heat. After lying for some time on his stomach, he turned to the sleeping Bosman, took the other's hand, and laid it on his belly. He curled the boy's cool fingers around his hard, stiffly erect thing, came almost immediately, flung the hand away. "Get off me, you dirty pig," he said to the snorer and grimly dismissed the image of the pharmacist's daughter sitting in the bus behind the driver on the way to Wierebeke with all the sorrow of Belgium in her wide eyes, which, reflected in the window, seemed to be looking at him. Through a crack in the planks of the ramshackle barn door he looked at the stars, which are not really where we think they are, because light sometimes describes strange curves before it reaches us.

Aunt Mona poured malt coffee for Aunt Nora on the veranda, where they were waiting for Mama to go down into town with them. Because Louis was in the kitchen, they didn't talk about Mama.

Aunt Mona was getting fat. "From *Liebe*," she explained, "from love! Every cloud has a silver lining. I know we're living through awful times, war is grim, but I can't help it, I'm happy with my *Gefreiter*, we go together like bacon and eggs, and when I'm with him I forget the whole hullabaloo, the bombs and the guns. Ulli often says, '*Mein Liebchen*, what more can we ask for?' He's so considerate, Nora! He puts women on a *piédestal*, like all Germans. Because as soon as they've gone off to war, the only thing they want is to be back home with their *Frau*, their *Frau* is the symbol of hearth and home. See if any Belgian's like that! It's quite simple, Nora, I'm in seventh heaven."

"While it lasts."

"I don't care. Only Our Lord knows how long it will last."

"You've always been lucky."

"But Nora, surely you can't be jealous of your own sister!"

"I'm not jealous."

"But sad?"

"Just a little bit."

"I've even mustered enough courage now and then to mention marriage, and that I'd like to go with him to Wachenburg to meet his parents, but he doesn't want that. So I say, 'But Ulli, you can't really know a man properly without knowing his mother.' 'No,' he says, 'later, when the war is over.'"

"And that's not going to be all that soon, what with the Second Front. And the Caucasus."

"Yes." Silence. Cups being moved. Were they whispering? Making signs to each other? Pointing to the kitchen, where the eavesdropper was lurking?

"But, Mona, you can't be thinking seriously about marriage?"

"Why not? He has a bright financial future, he's a civil engineer, bridges and roads, you know."

"Says he. If he were, he'd be an officer."

"*Nein!* He doesn't want to be."

"His wishes don't come into it. They'd make him."

"Do you really think so?"

"Ask him."

"I don't dare."

"So he's got good prospects?"

"Well, his father is mayor of Wachenburg, and that's not some little parish like our own St. Roch."

Louis tried to do his homework. There are somatic cells and reproductive cells, the first are not handed down. That must mean they're mortal.

Lamarck says the opposite, he speaks of the inheritance of acquired characteristics.

"What I'm really afraid of, Nora, is that he might hear that I'm divorced. Because I've let him believe that my husband fell in May '40, machine gun in hand. And that it's really a little bit his fault, because he's a German. Just as well he's a believer."

"You mean he's religious?"

"No, no. I mean he believes what you tell him. The Germans are like that. Their word of honor is sacred."

"So he doesn't go to Mass?"

"No. He's a Protestant."

"Oh, oh, just don't tell our father."

"No, I'm not going to let go of him. Especially now that he's paying for Cecile's dancing lessons and wants her to call him Pappi. No, it's best he goes on thinking I'm a *Witwe.*"

"A what?"

"A *Witwe.* A widow. It may sound silly, *Witwe,* but that's what I am, all right, a woman without a man. Even though it's not down in the registry office. A widow and a merry one at that!"

"Oh, you crazy Mona. You've always landed on your feet. As for me, I'm a born loser. What with my asthma."

Louis stood in the entrance porch to the bank, his back pressed against the ridged granite wall. From time to time across the road a woman would go into the pharmacy.

Paelinck was walking up and down behind the counter in a white coat, handing out bottles and boxes, nodding his solemn red head ponderously, weighing out powders. I could simply walk in like an ordinary customer after some ointment or aspirin, but what if she should happen to step through that inner door with the frosted glass?—Hello, Simone, how are you these days, if I may be so impertinent, immodest, indiscreet as to ask?—*Tiens,* how do you know my name?—I've made inquiries, asked around, sounded out the neighbors.—I can see that.

Roly-poly Hilde had said in a hate-filled voice that Simone Paelinck was too hoity-toity to join the Movement, that her feet were too big, and that she could hardly read or write.

—Aspirins for my mother, please, Mijnheer Paelinck.—Or was it Dr. Paelinck? Pharmacists studied medicine.—*Tiens,* Simone. By the way, Simone, how about coming to the cinema with me tomorrow to see *Music by Request,* with Ilse Werner? If Dr. Paelinck has no objections, that is!

He stepped resolutely into the pharmacy, as if extremely pressed for time, bought some aspirin, the man barely paid any attention. Louis dawdled, pretended to be interested in a dandruff cure, took a long time reading the label, then carefully pulled the jingling door shut behind him, she had gone out somewhere with another boy, one who could hardly read or write but who was wooing her with vehemence and experience.

With his Hitler Youth dagger he scratched white lines into the walls. When he returned home, Papa threw his *Volk en Staat* on the table and half-rose from his chair.

"Did you think I was Mama?"

"No," said Papa. "She's . . ." late. She had to do overtime. ". . . She had to go to a meeting, she couldn't get out of it." *Volk en Staat* had fallen carelessly, the faded, vulgar colors of the cover of a Lord Lister novel could be seen underneath.

"Are you hungry? Although I don't have to ask. You're always hungry."

Papa fried two herrings. The smell made Louis's mouth water. He crunched the bones. He still felt hungry. He pulled out the Lord Lister novel, a masked man in a dinner jacket was leaping out of a moving train into an ashen, turquoise-colored fog.

"Are you going to Mass tomorrow, Louis?"

"Of course."

Louis went every morning at the crack of dawn. The oil lamp, the subdued chanting, God in the tabernacle, the squeaking harmonium, the old women, God in the Host, incense, the other pupils from nearby, numbing cold, God on the tongue.

"When you come out of Mass, have they already started work across the road in the ERLA?"

"That depends on how late Mass is. Sometimes there are quite a lot of people standing around the gate."

"What people?"

"The workers. The staff turns up later. Like Mama. At half-past eight."

"But the bosses?"

"What bosses?"

"The directors!" said Papa impatiently.

"How should I know what time they turn up?"

"Haven't you ever seen them, early in the morning, Meneer Lausengier and the other directors?"

"I've never paid attention."

"You never pay attention to anything, do you!"

Next to his Lord Lister, Papa had a box of lump sugar ready and a glass of water from the pump. The box was three-quarters empty.

"Naturally, they come to work late in the morning, what else would you expect? Merrymaking and carousing all night long, how can they rouse themselves from their beds? And to think that people like that have been given responsible jobs! Now you could argue that they're only repairing spare parts over here. But every spare part of a Messerschmitt counts. If the bosses don't do their duty, then the whole war effort goes up in smoke!"

He drank, held some water in his mouth, pushed in a lump of sugar, sucked.

"You know them, don't you, those directors?"

"Mama's bosses?"

"Yes. That Meneer Lausengier and the other one she talks about now and then, Dr. Knigge. You must have seen them?"

"Me? Never."

"I thought you had. I thought you saw them that time when they were eating pastries, the three of them, on the Market Square!"

"No," said Louis stubbornly.

After another half-hour Papa could not stand it any longer. "Come on!" He put on his hat. In the Vooruit Theater, *Music by Request* had been canceled. They saw *The Valley of Fortune* instead, also with Ilse Werner. When the little girl in the Tyrolean dress fell into the ravine and, abandoned by everyone amid titanic clouds in the forbidding mountains, began to wail for her *Mutti*, Papa chewed on his knuckles furiously. The sailors and their boatswain sitting quiet as mice in the row in front of them in their black jackets were also deeply moved. One day they, too, would go down with all hands in icy water, far from their *Muttis*.

In the Café Groeninghe, Amadeus and Aristotle, the fair, frightened children of Marnix de Puydt, were holding hands. Their inebriated father lay on the green plush bench under the life-size, realistically tinted portrait of *Untersturmführer* Tollenaere, to which a black band had been tied, a mourning echo of the gray satin lavaliere De Puydt wore around his neck. Tollenaere has done his duty unto death, theirs not to reason why, his demise has been a slap in the face to Belgian half-heartedness and a fatal blow to the entire Flemish community. For if Moscow wins, the West is lost. The passionate, bespectacled advocate had been unable to stand by, doing nothing in the face of such a dire threat to our religion, our culture, our economy. For Altar and Hearth. They had had to dynamite the icy soil in order to lower his coffin, over there in the shadow of the little Orthodox church in Podborezhe. Even Radio London, it would seem, has demonstrated *fair play*, declaring his martyr's-death to have been in keeping with his life.

"Europe, Europe, there's no such thing!" said Marnix de Puydt.

"Marnix," said Papa (who, when the poet was sober, invariably addressed him as "Meneer"), "Marnix, you're far gone!"

"Staf Seynaeve, Europe always has been and always will be a pile of little countries thrown together higgeldy-piggeldy which'll always fight tooth and nail for their own national specialities, for their spaghetti, for their Pale-Ale, for their Goethe."

"And yet in the minds of many people a Great Europe is a reality," said a teacher.

"Of course," cried De Puydt, "and it was a reality for Charlemagne and for Napoleon, and it's actually quite an obvious idea, something that's easy to conceive of and easy to govern, but the point is that things now, that things now . . . Noël, a Scotch!"

"You've had more than your ration already," said Leevaert.

"And two lemonades for my offspring!"

"With lots of sugar," shouted Aristotle.

"This piddling obsession with making everything great! Great Ghent, Great Antwerp, Great Netherlands, Great *Dietsland.* The whole idea is anything but new, anyway, gentlemen. Do you remember, the older ones among us certainly will, those jokers Pierre Nothomb, Carton de Wiart, and all the rest? In '14–'18 they set out to create a Great Belgium with Dutch Limburg and the Ever-Great Duchy of Luxembourg. And who else had a finger in that pie? The man with the ill-fated name, *appellation contrôlée,* the man from the Steel Trust, Barbanson, do you remember him, the *'Brabançonne'* had obviously gone to his head. And who else? Oh yes, de Broqueville, who was Minister of War at the time! While our boys, our country's finest, were being massacred in the trenches, these gentlemen sat around with the whores in a Parisian seraglio and dreamed it all up over a bottle of Dom Perignon: Great Belgium! And among these noble gentlemen's pipe dreams in 1917 was a plan for Palestine with its holy places to be brought under the tutelage of this Great Belgium. In the name of our bold crusaders, Godfrey of Bouillon, Baldwin-the-Ax, or was it Baldwin II?"

"Baldwin I and II," said Louis. "Baldwin-the-Ax was Count of Flanders, not a crusader."

"Then who was Baldwin, the Emperor of Constantinople whom the Bulgarians beheaded and whose skull they split in two across the middle?"

The blond twins whooped for joy.

Marnix de Puydt continued recklessly, "Into which they poured wine and then devoured the raw brains?"

"Quiet, children!" shouted Noël, the owner.

"That must have been Baldwin I," said Louis. "In Adrianople."

"I thought it must be Baldwin-the-Ax, on account of the ax in his head . . ."

"Brains braised in wine, that doesn't sound bad," said a surveyor. "But raw, no, that's not for me."

"Still, handing the holy places over to the Belgians wasn't such a bad idea," said Mijnheer Groothuis.

"Bel-gi-um, kiss my bum," said Papa.

"Because you could hardly hand them over to the Jews, the very places where they crucified Our Lord."

"Belgium was within an ace of getting them, too, those holy places," said Marnix de Puydt, "because there were some very prominent people involved."

"Cardinal Mercier," said Leevaert.

"Cardinal *Merci,*" said Papa.

"He went specially to Paris to plead with Clemenceau."

"The Tiger!" said Papa.

"And Clemenceau thought it was quite a good idea, too."

"So why did nothing come of it?" asked a nurseryman. De Puydt shook his head. "That I don't know."

"Because Clemenceau didn't make it to President in the end," said Leevaert. "He went off in a huff to sulk in his country house, he couldn't have cared less anymore."

"So that was the end of Great Belgium," cried Papa triumphantly.

"Still, it wasn't such a bad idea," said Mijnheer Groothuis. "Belgium could have done big business."

"We could all have taken our holidays in Palestine."

"Yes, and for half-price if you belonged to the League of Large Families."

"Noël, the same again all around."

"Basking in the sunshine of the Holy Land with a good Pernod."

"Ah, one can't help dreaming of Paradise."

"Paradise," said Marnix de Puydt weightily, "lasted a very short time. According to the calculations of the Florentine *sommo poeta,* no more than six hours."

Everyone agreed that that was too short.

"What's wrong with you, Staf? You're looking very pale," asked Mijnheer Groothuis.

"He's got a tapeworm from eating too much minced pork."

"That's right. From his brother Robert."

"Don't pay any attention to me," said Papa. "I don't know what I've got."

In Russia, behind the *Winterlinie,* by the Mius and Lake Ilmen, men were freezing to death in their hedgehog positions. Small wonder, then, that the men in the Groeninghe crowded around the roaring potbellied stove kept lavishly fed with coal nuts by Noël.

Figures in field-gray cast envious glances inside. Amadeus and Aristotle seemed to have taken root. The afternoon wore on. The spinning of yarns, the drinking of watery beer, the telling of smutty stories (known as "the black school" in Walle). De Puydt came out with a rambling, confused tale about the British scholar John Ruskin, who had written books as thick as my arm about Greek sculpture and who, still a virgin, saw a naked woman, his wife as it happened, for the first time in his life on his wedding night. "The woman had a pussy, as you might expect, and on that pussy there was hair, what else should there have been? But Ruskin, that art historian, had never in his life come across anything like it in the books with reproductions of Greek art he kept in his library, because the Greeks thought it was much tidier and more beautiful to shave that sort of hair off. Ruskin looks, he looks again, and then he races out of the bedroom lickety-split. He never went in there again, never slept with his wife, who, when all was said and done, was a respectable lady and nicely built and during the whole of his unhappy existence he never dared to tell a soul about it, he suffered terribly from his nerves because of it, for he thought his whole life long that he had married a deformed creature, some sort of hairy woman-ape."

"Would you believe it!"

"And an art historian, too!"

"The poor man."

"I have a *chef-de-bureau,*" said Mijnheer Groothuis, "who shaves his own and his wife's right off."

"It must be hard work keeping that up."

"That's right, because you'd get stubble and it'd make you itch."

"And then when you rubbed against each other . . ."

"Gentlemen," said Leevaert, "there are children present!" Louis felt an icy rage rise up inside him, but Leevaert was referring to the De Puydt twins.

"Oh, but my two know all about life, eh, boys?"

"Yes, Papa," said Amadeus and Aristotle in unison.

"Your Aris is *echt Arisch,* a real Aryan, with those blue eyes."

"Why do you think I called him that? The union of Hellas and Germania, Hölderlin's dream."

Louis nursed the hope that Simone would come walking past and spot him there in the window among the succulents, whereupon he, a regular among regulars, or so it would appear from the outside to anyone who pressed his nose to the window, would clink his glass of lemonade against the glass of Scotch raised by Marnix de Puydt, whose photograph is to be found in Verschueren's Great Dictionary. She would feel a tingle of respect for him right down to her loins, where the hair must be growing, sepia-brown or maybe black as coal. And if an English bomb fell and she were sent flying three feet into the air and then dropped into the gutter and a flaming whirlwind came along and burned up just her dress and her underwear, then he would see it, that triangle of hair, and then the roof of the Café Groeninghe could cave in, the debris could swallow up his ecstatic gaze.

Under Louis's feet, down there in the kitchen, all was quiet. Papa had started sneaking out of his workshop now and then to take him by surprise. Last week he had encountered a motionless Papa standing behind the veranda door, ready to pounce like a panther. At whom? At what?

Louis listened on the landing. In the street outside, three or four women were chattering about ration coupons, their wooden soles tapping, shuffling. From the workshop came the drone and hiss of the printing presses (ten thousand leaflets depicting a smoking, crumbling row of houses, a mother holding her injured child to her breast, the legend in flaming Gothic letters: "Churchill, you monster, why are you doing this to us?").

His parents' bedroom smelled stuffy, acrid. When he fell upon their bed, his warm cheek against the cool, salmon-colored bedspread, dust swirled up into the weak winter sun. He poked his index finger through a hole in the bedspread. He was lying on Mama's side. During the holidays, earlier, released from the Institute, he would hear his parents talking together at night in subdued, calm, unintelligible, tranquil voices, the door sometimes left open just to let him know that they were there, murmuring together, and that he was safe, had nothing to fear from nocturnal Mizzlers. Now and then, in the middle of the night, a soft moan, creaking, Papa sighing from the bottom of his heart. Lately they had stopped talking in bed. Papa would go up long before Mama, leaving her pottering about downstairs, matches scraping, magazines rustling. Sometimes, his face grimacing as he strained to listen, Louis would imagine he

327

could hear her drawing on her cigarette, hear the rumblings of her stomach.

Louis looked in the mirror of the dressing table on which lay the Crème Mimi, a tube of Rose d'Automne, Tokalon powder. He was changing, almost imperceptibly. (Two indispensable things: imperceptibility and changing.) Spy. Panther Seynaeve. On very close examination: pores, *her* nose, *his* small, pinched mouth. Changing? You can forget that, you wishful thinker. Because I can see nothing different, nothing unusual. Even though the most horrible thing has happened to me that can befall a man, well, a boy.

If I were to tell Haegedoorn, he would split his sides laughing just as he did two days ago, when it happened. Is that finally to be my punishment, my penance, am I, as well as being impure because I break the Sixth Commandment, sometimes twice a day, now also to be damned for that as well? Am I now among those they call the damned of the earth?

The women in front of Louis's house began to shriek, the wooden soles clattered, the Walle alarm siren must be out of order, because, unheralded, enemy bombers roared overhead and antiaircraft fire could be heard in the vicinity of Rattenberg. Louis pointed his forefinger at his temple, it would all be over in one fell fatal swoop. His face bore no mark of Cain, nothing of what Jules Verne and Jack London had described as the mark of fate to be read on the face of some submarine captain or gold prospector. And yet I have been punished by fate, every NSJV member knows it and is laughing like a hyena.

Perhaps Mama knows it, too, by now. Unbearable. She must have heard it, of course, but she hasn't said anything, not even to herself, groaning with shame for her only son in the depth of her soul.

Two days ago.

Fencing. Singing in harmony. Theory. About the Judeo-American epidemic that has drifted across to us, degrading our musical taste, we who, ever since the Middle Ages, have sought the harmony of our music in the sounds of nature herself. Next gymnastics, boxing, and then that horrendous moment. Under the shower. For weeks there had been no hot water. Ice-cold drops and suddenly an icy jet. We have to be toughened, and so I pushed myself away from the slightly less cold wall of small square tiles and rough cement and stepped into the middle, right under the lashing icicles, for what were they compared to the arduous conditions of our boys, smeared with lanolin, on the *Winterlinie,* at the gates of Kharkov, Vyazma, Orel, Schlüsselburg? Soaped myself under that Siberian stream. Then Bosmans slipped in and threw his towel on the wall hook and opened his eyes wide and pointed at Louis's crotch, clapped his hand to his mouth like a girl, and hiccuped with laughter. Why? The thin, consumptive Bosmans took Louis's arm and with a curiously violent, cata-pulting movement propelled him through the doorway, whereupon the troop, seven in all, looked up.

"Look, look," screamed Bosmans, "just look at his willy!" He snatched away Louis's hand, which had covered that shriveled little proboscis, frozen in the wind of eternal glaciers.

"A referee's whistle."

"An earthworm."

"A matchstick."

"You can't do the girls proud with that, Seynaeve."

"Troop Leader, just come and have a look!"

Genevoix, legs wide apart, wet mountain boots braced against the cement floor, pronounced it perfectly natural. Roars of laughter. "With me," said Genevoix, "it's exactly the same under the shower, sometimes I can hardly even find the darned thing."

The howl of laughing hyenas. What their Leader was telling them was such a patent fib, so worthy of Baron von Münchausen, that they fell against each other with glee. (I, in my wet clothes, fled through Walle, shivering with fever.)

"All right, that'll do, the boy can't help it," Genevoix had added.

This is the curse of the Rock. Of all priests. That's why they don't marry. Because of that dwarfed excrescence they are allotted at birth. That's why priests offer up their stunted, mutilated bodies to God. And that's why Dirty Dick is accursed, too, he who, before the war, when it was still allowed in Belgium to celebrate Carnival in public, paraded about dressed up as a Spanish *danseuse*. We are a branded race just like the Jews, who are stunted, wounded, down there as well.

Louis detected nothing new when he looked at himself in the mirror. No matter how smartly I may march through the town in my uniform, I am still like Dirty Dick.

He put Mama's onyx earrings on, painted lipstick on his Papa-lips. In the wardrobe, which exhaled a whiff of perfume, next to the pink rubber bulb with the bakelite nipplelike tip, he came across the cut-up fur coat lying in a corner like a shiny, hairy beast. He put it on. Sat before the mirror for ten minutes, neck chafed by harsh fur when he moved his head. He waggled his head, a boy with a gaping, lopsided, scarlet mouth who was not only damned but foolish as well.

In the morning after Mass, on the way to school, he lingered in the bank porch. Black ice had formed, bicyclists rode by very slowly, heads bowed.

Seynaeve, you silly boy, what are you doing here?

Seynaeve, old man, I can't help it.

Why not? Why don't you just forget about it?

I can't. No, I have to see her.

You can't see her, she's still asleep.

I don't care. At least I can see the window she sleeps behind.

But you don't even know which window.

That one there, because once I saw a light there, a little strip above the blackout paper when her father was in the shop in his stupid white coat.

It could still have been her father's bedroom.

No. He would never have left the light on. Everyone knows how tight the Paelincks are.

The sun rose, he was hungry, he walked along Zwevegem Street and gave up talking to that nagging, tiresome, destructive second Seynaeve. By the Cattle Market a crowd of people were bickering and jabbering and pointing. During the night a parachutist had crash-landed against the front of the Akkerman Mills, a dark-red arm and a piece of stomach in khaki were still hanging from it, shredded rags, leather and metal and chunks of flesh, skewered on a length of guttering. White vapor rose from the onlookers' mouths.

"Good job. Serve him right."

"That'll teach 'em."

"How are they going to get those bits and pieces down? You can't even reach them with a ladder."

"The fire brigade, perhaps."

"It'll all fall down by itself."

"Looks like a young fellow."

"Could be a Negro."

"American, anyway, with that light kind of khaki."

"You know a lot, don't you?"

"Me? No, no, I don't know a thing. I'm just guessing."

"He couldn't have known what hit him."

"Oh, yes he could, the moment he realized his parachute wasn't opening."

"That's half a minute at the most."

"Half a minute can seem a long, long time."

"Miriam, imagine, he could have crashed right through your window."

"Shut up, Georgine. I don't even want to think about it!"

"Make sure you close your window tonight, Miriam."

"Shut up, I said. Now I'll be dreaming about someone like that smashing straight into my room."

"Straight into your bed, Miriam."

As Louis was walking through the park, all the trees suddenly gave off a penetratingly pungent smell. As if he were wading through solid fragrance. It's the air, just the air, he thought, and his knees buckled, he subsided with a languid, voluptuous feeling, continued to sag, inconceivably far and deep, he was being covered in a blanket of red cotton wool, was being gently obliterated, his ear was lying against velvet stinging nettles, against a vast boiled cauliflower, his cheek against a ponyskin fur that turned soft and fluid, he heard the marble Queen Astrid shuffling along in her shoes with the wooden soles, she bent over him.

He was taken home by passers-by, he heard them saying something about vitamins. Mama sat at his side, close beside the Seynaeve who lay defenseless, powerless in his own bed. She said, "You did give me a fright, I thought you'd had an accident, but it's nothing, you just fainted, it's nothing, it often happens." He summoned up all his strength and took her hand, kissed the back of the dry, perfumed skin in the black lace glove. He was a knight on the field of battle at Groeninghe who in a fit of panic had thought he'd been hit by an enemy arrow and had fallen into a swoon but who then, cured of his fearful fancies, beheld his companions-in-arms raising the battle cry of *"Houzee!* Walloons are false! Put them to death!" and resolved to return to battle. And so I will! He swung a foot out of bed and stood up. "You see?" Mama said. "You see? It was nothing. Thank God for that. But what are those spots on your neck? Just like blood poisoning. Like what I got from that dyed fur coat."

He missed Mass. He was sent outside by the mathematics teacher. His black mood matched Papa's. "Two bears with sore heads," said Mama, "and I do my best to run a happy home."

"You mean me too?" cried Louis.

"You too."

The electricity was being cut off more often now. They sat without the radio on, eating kidney beans in tomato sauce by candlelight. Mama told them about Bibi Two, Dr. Lausengier's new little dog, a dachshund who had to be walked at least a mile each day for its health.

"Can't he take his dog out himself?" Papa asked.

"I have to do what he says, he's my boss. And he doesn't have the time to walk along the Leie."

"What's he got to do, then, all day long? His work's all done for him."

"He's still the one who has to answer to his bosses in Leipzig."

"He spends all his time reading French newspapers," said Papa.

"How do you know?"

"None of your business. All I'm saying is that he starts reading the newspapers first thing in the morning. I know that. Mostly French papers."

"You're wrong," said Louis. "He starts the day with two slices of toast."

"He does?" Mama's teasing little smile appeared for the first time in weeks.

"How do you know?" exclaimed Papa.

"I know everything."

"Oh yes? Really? Everything?" Mama filled his plate.

"Toast and three cups of tea."

"Tea!" Papa said, startled. "Like the English!"

"Then he smokes a cigarette. And it's not until then that he turns to the most important sections of the world press. Domestic and foreign affairs."

"That's what I'd do," said Papa, "if I had the time."

"At ten o'clock the post arrives. Which has already been sorted by Mama, who has put to one side those items that need his personal attention."

"Don't tell me you're a fly on our office wall?"

"Go on," said Papa.

"He reads the letters. Which include a number of petitions. He takes quite a lot of time deciding who should be helped. Since there's always lots of chaff among the wheat."

My parents hung on my words. Especially Mama.

"There are letters from simple country folk who are worried about their children. 'Bitte, Herr Lausengier, they say that our Willem is on the Punkt of being sent to Germany with the next lot und he is such a good welder und does his Bestes, just ask Frau Seynaeve.'"

Mama uttered a brief mew and lit a fresh cigarette from the end of her old one.

"Or: 'Herr Lausengier, our Gerard has lost ein Finger in the Maschine. Who's going to pay für das?'"

"Stop this silly pretend German of yours. It isn't funny," said Papa. "Only anglophiles do that sort of thing."

"Go on, Louis, go on," said Mama-with-the-glittering-eyes.

"Then he telephones the priest from the village of the people concerned to make sure it isn't all a cock-and-bull story and the family is well thought of in the parish, because people can be really cunning and bad in wartime. Then, at eleven o'clock, he holds an audience for all the foremen. Luncheon is taken in the company of Frau Seynaeve, an egg, fish, meat, beer, and, if there have been no complaints from the *Kommandantur*, half a bottle of claret. Then the car drives up and he repairs to that bastion of the French-speaking citizens of Walle, the Flandria, where he indulges himself in his favorite game, tennis. Although he is a player of quite exceptional ability, he occasionally lands on his knees and dirties his tennis trousers. He is very agile, however, he is able to place one foot behind his neck. After that he steals a lick of ice cream from a lady passing by, but not until he has . . ."

"Not until he has what?"

"Let him tell it in his own way, Staf!"

"I just forgot to say that before he licks the ice cream, he takes a refreshing shower. Not too cold. It musn't be too cold."

The candles flickered. Louis ate a few cold beans. He had lost interest in the story, but Mama was waiting, tensely, immersed in the subdued light-and-shadow play.

"He had finished playing tennis," said Papa.

"Then he drives back to the office, sitting next to the chauffeur, because he is very *gemütlich* with the staff. And he never goes back to work until he has exchanged a little quip or two with Frau Seynaeve. He plays just one hand of patience before supper. Supper always starts with soup. He is crazy about soup. Then the bridge table is prepared in his apartment, and all the leading lights of Belgian finance start turning up. To his regret he is unable to go hunting as much as he would like, in his *Heimat* he never missed the chance of pulling on his hunting boots and setting out with the foresters, enjoying an occasional cup of coffee in a hut along the way."

"You said he drinks tea!" cried Papa triumphantly.

"At the hunt it's always coffee, made by boiling a kettle over an open fire while having a chat with the cottagers. Who keep a proper distance, of course."

Mama began to clear the table. "That's enough now."

"Does he read many books?" asked Papa.

"Never. He used to once upon a time, or so he claims."

"Enough. All right. Enough," said Mama.

"He sounds like an interesting man, from what you say," said Papa.

To Louis's annoyance, Haegedoorn never once came over to him on the playground to ask why he didn't attend NSJV meetings anymore. Nor did anyone from the troop visit his house to ask for an explanation. They probably took him for a rat abandoning the sinking ship just as Europe was engaged in the struggle along the Upper Volga and in North Africa and the plutocrats were stepping up their bombing of Paris, Berlin, and Walle.

He started going to Mass again regularly, almost daily, taking into his mouth the God of Mercy (in Whom you must believe, or you might as well string yourself up), when one fine morning, looking through the half-open door of the sacristy, he caught a glimpse of a short, unshaven young man in shabby clothes gesticulating vehemently with one arm as he harangued the Rock. And there could be absolutely no doubt that it was the tall, heavily bespectacled figure of the Rock standing inexplicably, inconceivably at this hour, in the sacristy of St. Roch's Church, three miles away from his College.

"I saw you in St. Roch's Church this morning," Louis said during playtime.

"Me? No, you couldn't have."

"I recognized you."

"You are confusing me with some other bald priest."

"You are lying, Father."

"No. Yes, I am." Louis's mentor and enemy and leader and spiritual father had turned into a pale figure of a man whose lower lip was drooping like that of a boy with painted lips in a mirror.

"I can explain, Louis. But not now. I beg you, in the name of Our Lord Jesus, forget that you ever saw me there. I implore you, tell nobody."

(What was he doing there, ten steps from the altar? In the sacristy. Celebrating a Black Mass?)

"May I count on you, Louis?"

"I swear, Father."

"I shall repay you."

"No need, Father," and for the first time it was Louis who walked away from the other, from *him*.

"The boy's a shadow of his former self, Constance. Just look at him, white as a turnip. He isn't being fed properly, Constance, I must tell you that straight."

"He eats like a horse."

"Yes, but what? Nun's-farts!"

"No. Meat. And at school he gets milk and vitamins and army biscuits."

"Perhaps he's got a tapeworm from all that meat?"

"Well, the meat from our Robert does often have a bit of a smell. No one can say that Robert puts his family first."

"It's as if he's upset about something. Are you upset, Louis, my pet?"

"I wouldn't know what about, Grandma," said Louis.

"If you ask me, he's in love."

"Good grief, Hélène, you never think of anything else. No, he's coming down with something, Constance."

"It's just growing pains."

"You may be right, you can tell that from his hands and feet. He's going to be a beanpole."

"Yes, he certainly is shooting up."

"Speaking of shooting, they've shot the Mayor of Vernisse."

"Vernisse, where?"

"In the liver. It's beyond repair."

"It's those Walloons, they keep sneaking over here. In Wallonia they've been let loose, they can murder and pillage as much as they want, the whole place is teeming with foreigners and Communists."

"They get money from Moscow so that pressure on the Russian front is relieved."

"And our Mona's Ulli has been packed off to, where is it again? Somalia. She sobs all day long. With Cecile on her lap. That can't be doing the child any good."

"Perhaps it's as well she learns about the pangs of love early in life," said Mama.

Grandma nearly choked laughing. "Really, Constance! The way you came out with that! Like in a cemetery or in court." Sobering, Grandma tugged at her shawls. "The pangs of love, they may hurt you but they're the salt of life."

"I prefer pickled herring," said Aunt Hélène.

The yokel on sentry duty in front of the ERLA front line repair shop was not a Flemish Guardsman but wore a dark-gray uniform like the Luftwaffe. He appeared to look the other way deliberately as Louis walked through the gate. Probably, no, definitely, Mama had told this bumpkin that she was expecting her son, and anyway the rifle in the man's hand wasn't a real one with real bullets. Real rifles aren't being fired here in humble Walle with its scattered turrets, its rows of workers' houses, its villas and little front gardens. Europe's fate is being settled elsewhere.

Young people in gray overalls stood hunched over humming, rumbling machinery.

For once Mama had given proper directions, he found the corridor and the third door on the left with Dr. Lausengier's name on it.

"Herein," said Mama's cheerful voice. She leaped up from behind her

typewriter and in a single whirling movement fixed her hair, stubbed out her cigarette, and put out her hand as if, for the first time in their lives, she wanted to shake Louis's, but ended up merely stroking his cheek. (She was playing mother for the benefit of a thin, white-haired lady sitting at a smaller desk with a paper clip between her lips.)

The office was bright, with large windows through which you could keep an eye on the machinists in the building opposite. There was blond-colored furniture, the *Führer*'s portrait almost entirely hidden behind a potted palm, a calendar with a view of the Alps, metal cabinets with dozens of little cactuses on top. Her paradise, the place she preferred to her home. The thin lady picked up a folder and disappeared.

"Would you like a cup of coffee?"

"No."

"It's not malt coffee, you know."

"No, thank you."

"You won't be a nuisance, will you?"

"No, Mama."

"It's real coffee. I'm allowed to take two spoonfuls, it's locked away in his safe. And, of course, I smuggle just a little bit over to Janine in the kitchen. You have to be on good terms here with the staff."

She sat down on the windowsill. Next to her, framed by the window, out in the garden, Louis could see the tall man who had said hello to him in the Flandria. Hands crossed behind his back, he was talking to himself, or was intoning his Protestant German prayers. He stood still, tapped his waist with the sides of his hands, did a brief kneebend, stood up straight again, and spoke to a brown dachshund with a small black wet spot for a nose who was busy scrabbling under a bush. He waved to Mama.

Seen up close, he had pockmarked skin, a searching, somewhat super-cilious look.

"*Heil Hitler,*" said Louis.

Mama explained that this was her son. Apologetically and proudly at the same time.

"*Ach,*" said the man, and then, in High Flemish, "Good day to you, how are you?"

"Very well."

"*So,*" said the man. Continuing in German, he added that the resem-blance to Mama was striking, yes, yes, you could see it around the mouth in particular. To his great relief Louis realized that this Lausengier had not the slightest suspicion that the boy with the flag on guard duty on the gravel outside the Flandria had been one and the same as this son of Mama's now standing politely before him with an exaggeratedly eager smile. That was why they hadn't sent Lausengier to the real war, he was too blind, too stupid, had too short a memory. And yet he had managed to become a *Doktor*. He must have been an awful grind. Once upon a time. By now he has forgotten all he has learned. All right, tennis, but a sudden fall and brick-red stains appear on the snow-white trousers that have been washed and ironed by Great Netherlands Girl Troopers.

"*So.*" Lausengier emptied the half-full ashtray on Mama's desk into the gray metal wastepaper basket. Then he asked how things were in the *Hajott,* the Hitler Youth. Ah, well. Stammering furiously because once again he had underestimated an adult—my arrogance makes *me* as blind as a bat, watch it, you idiot!—Louis said that he didn't know. Because there was no *Hajott* in Flanders. Although there was talk of starting one sometime in the near future.

"*So.*" He couldn't have cared less. Louis added that in any case he was no longer part of any youth movement whatsoever. Mama quickly interrupted, saying she had seen it coming, had felt right away that Louis wouldn't be able to stand being part of a group, he was far too much of a loner for that.

"*Ach,*" said Lausengier. "In that case, what are we to do about fostering the development of healthy male virtues?" Louis kept his steely expression under control, never let it be seen that I have understood this flippant piece of badinage.

"And what are we to do about those indispensable initiation rites, about trust in leadership?"

"Henny," said Mama. The *Doktor* showed the gold in his mouth. He had exceptionally thick wrists, with little golden curls, which Bibi Two was now licking.

"He'll manage somehow," he said as if Louis weren't present, then turned to greet a slender young man in a worn suit who had entered without knocking. Perhaps because he had only one arm. The young man offered Louis his only hand, he was looking calmer, more self-assured, than when he had been talking so vehemently to the Rock in the sacristy of St. Roch's Church. Bibi Two began to growl softly, his ears pricked up halfway. Lausengier said it was extremely good of Monsieur Donkers to come by.

"It'll take less than a quarter of an hour," said Mama to Louis. She handed Donkers an almost empty file.

"Ten minutes," said Donkers, taking Louis amiably in tow with his one arm. Lausengier winked.

In a small interview room whose walls were covered with regulations and slogans, Donkers said, "Sit down. Make yourself comfortable. I won't bite you."

A poster drawn with thin austere lines, like Dolf Zeebroeck's, showed an SS man leaning forward with *"Vlaanderen Korps"* on his left sleeve, his machine gun pointing at a faceless, hairy, stinking (because wrapped in polecat skins), toothless, dark-eyed Asiatic partisan. Over the soldier's helmet floated a flag with heavy folds carried by a resolute, medieval figure with a clenched jaw, probably Till Eulenspiegel, the spirit of Flanders. Donkers ran his finger down the two poorly typed pages in the folder and nodded approvingly. *"Je vois. Je vois."*

"I haven't done anything wrong," said Louis.

"Of course not. There's no question of wrongdoing."

The little room had bars in front of the windows, and there was just one door, it was a cell for locking up recalcitrant workers or captured snipers.

"The main complaint is dizzy spells, is that right?"

"No," said Louis hesitantly. "Not really."

"But that's what your mother put down."

"I only had one. It was from the smell given off by the trees."

"Oui. Oui."

"A sort of sulfur smell."

"Je vois. Je vois. That doesn't concern me too much. Nor your nocturnal and other pollutions, of course. You are a big boy, nearly a man, in other words. And we are men *entre nous* here."

If Louis had not left his dagger behind on his bedside table, he would have brandished it now, made the one-armed fellow kneel down under the little table, forced a path through the office clerks and the workers, and raced past the bewildered yokel in the gray uniform by the gate, along the railway track, out into the cold fields.

"There's no reason to be ashamed because you dream of girls and your body reacts to that. *Bon. Voyons un peu."* He stood up, and Louis rose as well, trembling as if his legs had rain falling inside them.

"Pull your trousers down, please."

Louis could not believe his ears. He felt his *Untermensch* lower lip drop. "Now?"

"Yes, now."

Incredulously, Louis undid his suspenders.

"It's just to put your mother's mind at rest, all right? So that she doesn't go on fretting over you too much."

Scarlet, he yanked down his trousers and underpants in one furious movement. Oh, wouldn't he just make her pay for this, Constance Seyna-eve-Bossuyt, pay for the slimy toils of her tale-bearing treachery, because now he had proof positive that, going behind his back, she had had contacts with Haegedoorn, or Bosmans, or Genevoix. It must have been

Genevoix, come to think of it. He must have promised to sell Mama shoes, without coupons, without a blush, on the black market, on the sly. *"Voyons, voyons,"* said the one-armed man and pulled, pushed back the foreskin, felt, kneaded Louis's testicles, then patted his shoulder.

"Pas de problème. Everything's fine. And normal, that's for sure, I don't know what sort of problem your mother could have imagined. I suppose you could wash yourself a bit more thoroughly, *jeune homme. Un peu d'hygiène, tout de même."* Louis heard no more, the blood pounded in his temples.

"Well, that was quick," said Mama. Louis didn't dare look at her, the despicable, beautiful woman who had wounded him so callously, continued to wound him now with her honeyed, cajoling little laugh.

"Aucun problème," said Donkers and handed back the limp file.

Delivered over to foreigners, including his mother, who were now speaking French among themselves (Lausengier's consonants being more drawn-out and heavily stressed than those of the other two) while Louis sat on Mama's office chair. In the corridor a German was on the telephone, he said *"Jawohl"* twelve times, *"Jawohl, Ortsgruppenleiter"* twice, it sounded servile and coarse next to all those French innuendos, turns of phrase, secret little pleasantries, rattled off so playfully nearby. As if I couldn't understand them, for God's sake! *"Une insulte au mariage . . ."* (Who had been the insult? He, Louis?) *"Et à la generation et au travail et à l'épargne . . . gâcher l'energie . . ."* With Mama as the chief accomplice— what am I saying, the ringleader—they were going on with impunity about his sin, the sin that he had believed was exclusively his own. Here, part of the flippant chitchat, that sin was being bandied about on Mama's desk, among the folders, ashtrays, pens, telephone, atlas, coffee cups. Louis, clothes drenched with sweat, face itching furiously, heard Till Eulenspiegel declare that this outrage would be avenged with blood, heard the soldier of the *Vlaanderen Korps* swear *Rache,* vengeance, between his teeth. *"Jawohl,"* said Louis, like the man on the telephone. He would destroy her, the adorable one standing there, frivolously French, twirling about inside that transparent, glassy, glittering cocoon together with her fellow conspirators, vipers writhing in her hair.

Louis smiled at her. *Toujours sourire.*

First he drew a one-inch frame around the photograph of the dead *Reichsprotektor* with ruler and pencil, then blacked it in with India ink. Because he was using the blunt, thick brush Papa had used before the war to daub gold onto the scarlet edges of copies of *Ons Volk* before binding them into annuals, the black of mourning was now speckled with golden dots. Which seemed fitting to him.

"No," said Heydrich, "it's got to be silver and black, those are the colors of political warriors." *"Maul zu,"* said Louis, "Shut your trap." "Incidentally, you're a bit late to be in mourning for me. Months too late! But I can understand that, to you Flemings the memory of Reimond Tollenaere comes first. That's why you left me hanging around here unhonored for months." "Tollenaere is one of my father's group, people who fight for a Great Netherlands. Flemings come first." "On the battle-field the god of war makes no distinction of rank. We are all one in death. And yet Tollenaere was only an *Untersturmführer."* "He died on the field of battle, you didn't." "Look out, you're painting over the wallpaper. Be a little more careful, *bitte.* When you're dealing with a hero." *"Ja, Protektor."*

The dead *Protektor* fell silent. Two men with Boy Scout whistles—or were they referee's whistles? no, they couldn't be—who had been flown across from Scotland after a period of training with the British, had hidden grenades and Sten guns under their coats in a suburb of Prague. Heydrich, the brilliant administrator, fencer, violinist, and *Protektor* had pointed his pistol at them, a grenade had burst, amid the smoke and dust he had fired at his attackers, who fled and hid cravenly behind a tram, he collapsed, his spleen had burst, he died a week later, the man with the iron heart.

"Rache, vengeance," said the dead *Protektor.* "If you find my murderers I will pay your father and mother one million crowns. Then you'll be out of the woods." *"Maul zu,"* said Louis to himself.

At dusk, just before the last crucial second after which soldiers were the only ones allowed out in the streets, Louis went to Genevoix's shoe shop with a brick under his coat. But found a metal blind over the windows. He could think of nothing better than to ring the bell and take to his heels, the brick falling and smashing to smithereens.

Bell-ringer! Bah!

The next day he was allowed to keep goal for the College eleven because Hendrik's mother had hanged herself, leaving a note: "No one loves me, or Bolero." Bolero was her Siamese tomcat, whom she had first crushed to a pulp with a sledgehammer.

The College was winning hands down, the Technical School was being surrounded, beaten back, brought to its knees, 3-0, when suddenly, everyone could see he was offside, a lanky lout of a joiner's apprentice broke through and skied the ball high into the air. Louis watched the ball coming down toward him like a melon dropped from an airplane, he opened his arms wide and stood there as if seeing a ball for the first time in his life, dissociated from any kind of recognizable space, a weathered, round leather object (circumference roughly thirty inches, weight nearly a pound), which looked more improbable, alien, out of this world, untouchable, the nearer it came, and he, Louis, was scarcely there and yet was there, eight yards from his goal, he wanted to fling himself at the mysterious object as if to embrace the unknown, it landed three feet in front of him and bounced back into its own space, always out of reach, then sailed in an arc whose perfection turned Louis into stone, over his head and straight into the net.

And then mortification overcame him, and the wild yells of some twenty players and a dozen spectators.

Reverend Father Landegem, teacher of Greek and referee, who ought in principle to have remained neutral, shouted, "What on earth do you think you're doing, Seynaeve?" before running back to the center circle. He looked ready to box Louis's ears. "We were leading three-nil and I thought it was about time to liven things up a bit," said Louis. A little later, when he had a goal kick, his shoe—or, rather, the one belonging to Hendriks, who had great big flat feet—flew off with the ball to the accompaniment of loud jeers. What a day! And more to come. When he changed, he noticed that he had shit his pants. *Rache!*

Theo van Paemel brought a bottle of geneva that had been distilled by an acquaintance of his, and asked Mama to give it to Dr. Lausengier. "He'll know why. And tell him not to worry. It's safe to drink, it's not meths, it won't blind him.—And you, Staf, you ought to watch your mouth a bit. The Germans don't like your trumpeting it about all over the place that you're working for the SD."

"I haven't been trumpeting anything about," cried Papa.

"We have witnesses. You've been talking in Felix the barber's shop."

"Me? At the most I might have said, 'As a member of the VNV, I think this or that'!"

"But you aren't a member of the VNV."

"In a manner of speaking, I am!"

"Staf, just lie low. That's safest for all concerned."

"Well, if a man can't even speak his own mind anymore!"

What Grandpa was prepared to allow and what the Bishopric didn't object to was letting Papa volunteer as a first-aid warden, rushing to his post as soon as the last animal-like moan of the alarm siren had ebbed away. Because he preferred not to be confronted with the blood of innocent Walle citizens blasted by bombs, Papa did traffic control duty, with an armband and a white baton. He roared at the people, and the people bawled, "Filthy VNV-er!" back at him like fishwives. Then, with the theatrical gestures that had earned him such warm applause on the boards as a Chinese courtier, a Tyrolean peasant, or a magistrate, Papa would point to the stars, among which lurked the Flying Fortresses of death, and cry, "Are they VNV-ers?" Whereupon those brainless people would think again and redirect their curses at the sky teeming with murderers.

It was usually toward morning when he would come home and flop into his chair. Each time he would declare, "Now I know what a hard time the police are having."

This morning Mama could sleep in because the evening and the night before they had been celebrating Dr. Knigge's birthday at Mijnheer Groothuis's. Louis poured some brown malt coffee, extra-light. Papa was breathing heavily. He had been clearing rubble.

Keeping an ear open for any sound from Mama's bedroom, Louis said, "Do you do this sort of work to help people, or is it to kill time because otherwise you'd be pacing up and down waiting for Mama to come home? You blame her, don't you, for staying out till morning? But I don't blame her, I admire her staying power, her resistance."

"Resistance," said Papa. "Resistance, don't ever use that word again. Nor 'opposition' nor 'White Brigade,' either, for that matter."

"Why not? There's no one but us here in the house."

"All the same. The walls have ears."

"All right, then, I'll say endurance. It's only natural for her to go looking for a bit of distraction, she has to work really hard, isn't that right? I've been there and I've seen for myself, she's kept busy the whole time, invoices one moment, correspondence the next. She's liked by everybody over there, they even call her 'the Madonna of the ERLA' because she looks after injured machinists and welders in the infirmary. No, the only ones there who don't seem to care are the Germans themselves, which is something I saw with my own eyes, too. And that's because they're the wrong sort of Germans, they're all hale and hearty, yet none of them are at the front like regular soldiers; so there must be some reason why they've been banished behind the lines. What I think, but I could be wrong of course, is it's because they haven't got what it takes, the commanders at the front don't have any trust in these characters. When I was there, I heard them speaking French to each other, I ask you, is it proper to speak our archenemy's language in the middle of a war?"

"French?"

"Yes. Because they were telling each other things that should never see the light of day." (This is the language they use in his Lord Lister novels, the one he understands best!) "Because that way, they think, they can safely spout all that rubbish they're thinking. Well, let me tell you, I understood quite enough of what they said, and it wasn't very nice. No, I think what they are is so many vipers in the bosom of the German Reich. That frivolous un-German talk of theirs undermines all the efforts of the front line. Instead of keeping a lookout for tears and holes in their airplanes and cracks in their propellers, they chatter away in French about *l'amour romantique.* Which could cost the lives of unsuspecting pilots and a lot of money too, because replacing a single Messerschmitt can run to hundreds of thousands of francs."

"*L'amour romantique?*" asked Papa, as expected.

"Among other things."

"What else did they say in French?"

"I'd better tell you another time. You ought to go to bed now."

"No, no."

"Yes, yes. Because you're so tired you could jump to the wrong conclusion about something that may have been nothing more than a childish prank, something we, as outsiders, don't understand."

"What sort of prank?" said Papa, haggard.

"Listen. In the light of what I gathered as an impartial observer I could draw only one conclusion, and that is that some people in responsible positions in those workshops have no business to be there."

"Don't beat about the bush."

"Papa, those Germans in there are not imbued with the Atlantic ideal—that's the first thing. And then they also have contacts with French-speaking doctors, who undermine the morale of the workers with their plutocratic principles, and with priests who are no good, either, because in their teachings, far from stressing the importance of the national spirit, they continue to mouth those empty Judeo-Christian principles that are misguiding our people." (Rock, Rock, forgive me for I know not what I do!) "While our boys are making the supreme sacrifice every day—just think of the two sons of the coal merchant around the corner who were hit by MiGs—while all of us need so desperately to stick together if we are to preserve our Flemish identity, something is going on over there, in what is a crucial area for the war effort, that ought to be stamped on like a rotten apple without thinking twice about it."

"And who is to do that?"

"Not you. That's for sure. Not me, either, but certainly not you. Because you are blind. You deliberately refuse to see that in those ERLA offices your wife is . . ."

"Go on."

"That she is both victim and slave to her passions." (Was he going too far? His father shook his head but kept listening.) "You know her better than I do, you know what she's like. And if you tolerate that, well, that's your business. I just don't want you to turn around and say, 'My boy knew what was going on and never told me straight to my face, man to man!'"

Louis began talking faster because he thought he could hear his mother's bare foot stepping out of bed, the floorboards creaked.

"Why doesn't she do more in the house? There are plenty of women with jobs who try and look after their family after work as well. But she, all she does is stand there giggling while that Lousyguy makes fun of Flemish women in French—he calls them *des pondeuses soumises*'" (an expression Louis had heard Meneer Tierenteyne use to refer to German women during a game of bridge in the Patria). *"Pondeuses,* egg-laying women. With those words he was trying to ridicule the standards, the concepts, the ideals of our race. I couldn't understand how Mama could put up with that! It filled me with horror."

Did Papa realize that this phrase had been lifted straight out of *The Diamond Murders,* a recent Lord Lister? Papa shrugged his shoulders. He shut his eyes. He ran his hand over his skull, black with soot from the gutted houses.

"And it may just have been a game but I did hear that Lousyguy say, *'Je te veux.'*"

"Who to?"

"Je te veux, Constance, à outrance." Louis was proud and surprised that the rhyme had come to him just like that.

"What does that mean, *à outrance?"*

"Till death do us part or something like that."

"I'll kill her," said Papa, but when Mama came down at half-past eleven, he was in no state to kill anybody, asleep in his chair, his back against the wallpaper, open mouth gurgling, and hitting out in his sleep at the whirling Mizzlers now multiplying in those cerebral lobes of his contaminated by my *Propaganda-Abteilung.* Mama had plucked her eyebrows. With a wad of cotton wool smelling of Paelinck's pharmacy, she now dabbed the arched curves above her eyelids, the thin little hairs.

The reason Louis could place the smell was that, at that very moment, the pharmacist, a crotchety, prudish Dalle, was raging against the dull-witted Wanten on the radio.

Uncle Robert's indolent head seemed to swell even more roundly as he listened intently.

"Wanten, d'ye know how to get fifty people from Walle into one rabbit hutch?" "No, I don't know, Dalle." "Throw a potato chip inside!" All the folds on Uncle Robert's stomach shook. "Where do they get it from? Where ever do they get it from?"

Monique, his lanky fiancée (every pot has its lid), wiped her tears away. "A potato chip!" she said, gasping. "Where do they get it from?"

Monique came from a well-to-do farmers' family, but her people were opposed to her seeing Uncle Robert, for the simple reason that, of course, they didn't want to put up a dowry, but that would all be straightened out, and soon, very soon, a few of the twenty cows and fifty pigs from Monique's home would find their way to Uncle Robert's butcher shop, when he had established himself in one, that is, for things couldn't go on as they were forever, in a place the size of a handkerchief. He had asked Grandpa for a loan, but Grandpa had been so snappish of late, all he did was talk about "these perilous times." Nor had Grandpa set foot in the Rotonde these last few months, because too many collaborators went there, so now he played bridge exclusively in the Patria. According to Uncle Robert, Grandpa could sense a shift in the wind.

"He's always been a weathervane," Mama said bitterly. Because Grandpa had also stopped coming to Oudenaarde Road.

"Wanten, I'm going to tell you a really good little Flemish story!" "Yes, but watch it, I'm a Fleming!" "That doesn't matter, Wanten, I'll just tell it to you three times!" Uncle Robert and Monique fell into each other's arms.

"That's a bit off," said Papa. "This is no time to poke fun at Flemings."

"Still, it was a good one," said Monique. " 'I'll just tell it to you three times, then,' he says! Thank goodness we can still have a laugh, eh, Constance?" Uncle Robert peered into the pot on the stove. "I thought so. I thought I smelled braised turnips. When I think that we used to be able to buy a bunch of turnips as easy as a box of matches. And now . . ."

Mama put on her coat. "Are you sure you don't want to come along?"

"No," said Papa.

"I'm going to a concert by Robert Holz," said Mama to her brother and his skinny fiancée. "He's come over to conduct it himself, and since it looks as if he won't be with us much longer after his stomach operation, this may be my last chance to see him in the flesh."

"If I know our Staf," said Uncle Robert, "he would just doze off. I'm the same. Ten bars of violins and cellos and I'm done for. What's more, Staf, with all the turnips you've eaten, you'd be joining in the music. Because turnip and beet make you fart a fair treat!"

Monique spluttered violently, Uncle Robert laughed along with her, their wedding was in sight, full of peals of laughter, heart-warming chuckles.

The reason Papa wouldn't accompany Mama to the concert became clear when the bell rang an hour later and Raspe walked into the kitchen. Louis hardly recognized him. The man with the coarse face who had fumbled with Louis's fly and whom Papa had thrown out of his workshop sat down in the drawing room where Papa had lit the open fire as soon as Uncle Robert had left with his Monique, a gray man with hard, sharp features honed by the snowstorms of the steppes. He was wearing a much too large pinstripe Sunday suit, his army boots sticking out at the bottom. His uniform was being washed and ironed, he said, because tomorrow he had to go to Vindernisse, where they were paying tribute to a brother-in-arms who had been killed last month, face turned toward the East. He had been out all afternoon visiting comrades to try and track down a recording of "Siegfried's Death" because in that backward hole of a Vindernisse they didn't have anything like that, of course, and it was the least he could do for his comrade-in-arms. The hymn to the dead hero.

"I have seen hell, Staf," said Raspe.

Papa poured him an Élixir d'Anvers, from the last of the hoarded bottles.

"I keep telling myself all the time, 'Pieter Raspe, you're home,' but it's no good. I'm still over there."

Clumsily Raspe rolled himself a cigarette from a dented tin, one of his hands in a woolen mitten from which three dark-blue fingers protruded.

"And when I think of those damn democrats sitting here on their backsides watching which way the wind is blowing so that they can go on doing business as usual . . ."

"I have often been on the point of joining up," said Papa, "but my left kidney . . ."

"I didn't mean you, Staf, needless to say."

Raspe sucked the white air deep into his chest. Not like Mama, who took short little puffs into the front of her mouth. Raspe ate the dense white smoke.

"Nothing will ever come of that Flanders of ours as long as none of us have the guts to look death in the eye. As long as we allow that cowardly, take-no-risks, yellow-bellied system of self-interest to get the upper hand. It's only on the battlefield that you realize that. There and there alone. That's where you realize that as a Fleming you can't leave your German brothers to fight on their own. And I say brothers without a qualm. In the beginning, well . . . During the first few months as a recruit, I often cried my eyes out, Staf, I'll be honest with you. Have you ever had roll call with a German NCO during training? One speck of dust on your rifle and it's straight to the stockade. They break you, Staf. You think you are somebody, somebody important, and they break you, and after a while you become somebody else, somebody who toes the line without question."

With his blunt left claw Raspe grasped the golden-yellow bottle. "Over there you'd better not try any tricks with us. You're either a comrade through hell and high water or else you're just full of hot air, a shit trying to save his own skin, and that's not going to keep you alive very long."

"What's the food like over there?" Papa asked.

"There's nothing to eat over there. Except for lice. If the forage truck doesn't get through for a few days . . ."

"What happens?" Louis asked.

He had put his question too eagerly, Raspe grinned sardonically at him. "Louis, my boy, without an ideal, an ideal you can feel down to the marrow in your bones, you wouldn't be able to close your eyes at night over there, from sheer terror. We freeze over there, we're blown up over there, we're forced to cut men down like firewood, but we have our ideal. The chances are we'll be done for, it's not that we can't see what's under our noses, but the *Führer* needs us and we need him."

Louis could feel his eyes burn. "I wish I could go with you."

"First do your homework," said Papa.

"Yes," said Raspe in a tired voice. "And that's something done best over here in Belgium, your homework. By people who still believe that you can run the world on tactics and slyness and trickery. And it's true that you can get everything you want with a bit of trickery. It's true for all of you over here. Not for us any longer. We're going after our goal with our eyes wide open."

Much later, when the bottle of Élixir, long since emptied, contained two buzzing flies, when Papa had looked ostentatiously at the clock several times, when the steely names of Kerch, Voronezh, Dnepropetrovsk, had resounded over and over again and Louis was glancing at his algebra, Papa said, "The ones who ought to be taught a good lesson are the profiteers, the ones who are getting away with trampling their own race into the mud over here while you're working your balls off for a united Europe and for history over there."

"Who do you have in mind, Staf?"

"Quite a few."

"Now I'm a lot wiser." The sarcasm of the knight from the Eastern Front was lost on his former employer.

"Quite a few, that's all I can say."

"Then you'd best say nothing, Staf."

"Quite a few whose job it is to look after the home front, even strengthen it . . ."

"So what are they doing instead? Smuggling a little bacon? Felling a few saplings?"

Raspe looked at the fire Papa had allowed to go out an hour before. If Raspe had turned up in uniform, with all his medals pinned on, Papa would certainly have fetched a few more logs from the small pile in the cellar.

"We'd better go and sit in the kitchen," said Papa. "I can give you a slice of bread and lard. Or aren't you hungry?"

"I'm always hungry. I'm used to it by now."

"It's better to fight on an empty stomach," said Louis to his father, "in case you get shot in the belly."

With his boots on a chair, Raspe said, "I haven't even seen my mother yet. I arrived in Wachteren yesterday, people barely gave me the time of day. Not that I expected a red carpet, being the prodigal son, an idealist, but even so. My mother is at her sister Emilie's place in Vichte. I stood there in front of a closed door. I could have climbed over the courtyard wall, broken a window, if necessary, I wanted to, I was silly enough to want to put on my Sunday suit with a colored tie after all this time, but then I thought to myself, Who for? What for?

"Because if I walk into a café in Wachteren there is every chance that I'd take those malingerers who can't think of anything but how to smuggle and make a profit and smash their brains out against a wall. So I went to a comrade's house in Waregem, but his parents began to cry and I've never been able to cope with that, and then I thought, I'll just go and call on Staf, who's made a monkey of me all my life behind a Heidelberg press, perhaps he'll offer me a piece of bread and lard. I like the taste, Staf," he lay the piece of bread like a jewel on the kitchen tablecloth, "but I don't like it enough." The hobnails on his boots scraped against the floor. His head nearly touched the lamp. Papa stood up as well.

"If I can do anything for you, Staf . . ."

"There are some German officials . . ." Papa said.

"In the ERLA. The directors of the ERLA!" cried Louis.

"What are they up to?" Raspe asked.

"They are paid large sums by the parents of boys who have been called up. They are showered with presents, several whole hams at once sometimes, by people who want their sons kept off the transport, Louis will bear me out."

"Are you saying that these gentlemen sabotage the war effort?"

"Sabotage is a strong word," said Papa.

"They sabotage it, all right," said Louis, "egged on by a priest and a Franskiljon doctor. Under pressure from the White Brigade."

"But we can't prove anything, of course," Papa said quickly. "And anyway, they're the top brass."

"Top brass," Raspe repeated. "Only last month we cut a *Hauptsturm-führer* down to size. And how! You'll never read his name on another report."

He nudged Louis's collarbone with his frozen, crippled hand. "Do your homework," he said.

"Where are you off to? Where are you going to sleep?"

"Staf, Staf! The Flemish Legion can look after its own. I'll be surprised if I'm not eating lobster or turkey within the next half-hour, even if I have to go and shoot up the Swan Hotel's whole kitchen."

When Papa came back in, he opened the window a crack, despite the cold weather, to drive out the stuffiness from Raspe's cigarettes and the smell of death and honor and loyalty. "You've just seen a hero," he said. "Remember that all your life." He nibbled at the half-slice of bread and lard the hero had left uneaten. "If it weren't for you, I would seriously be thinking of going there myself, to the Crimea, Orel, Dyep-nostrok . . . But as a driver with the NSKK. That way you see more of the country, the lakes, the mountains, the different tribes . . ."

Louis was awakened by softly quarreling voices and by Papa's fist pounding a pillow. Not as in the old days, when he had cried in bed and Papa, dreadful ogre, would come tearing into the room, roaring, "Are you going to go to sleep this minute, or aren't you?" and thump the pillow right next to his petrified son's head six times with the rhythmic swing of a woodcutter. Tonight the voices were subdued, Papa's rather plaintive, Mama's defiant. Louis knew the expression on her face that went with it, a detached, pigheaded glee. He felt it flit across his own face sometimes, like a small cloud.

A little while later he woke up again. Raspe pushed one of his blue, almost black, stone-hard fingers into his ear and whispered into the other that the milk doled out at school would give him foot-and-mouth disease, and that he, Raspe, would smuggle in some butter from the Ukraine, just for him. That gave Louis such a fright that he leaped out of bed. He pushed the stiff blackout paper to one side, saw a yellowish, brightening vapor rising beyond the dark-gray roofs, there was rustling, Papa's drawn-out snores, two dogs a long way apart signaling to each other. Simone was asleep, dreaming of a young, talented violinist.

In the kitchen Louis licked at the rim of the Élixir bottle, with its lingering suggestion of something syrupy. The bottom of the bottle is called the "soul" of a bottle.

He crept back into bed and almost at once found himself sitting on the squeaking white Institute merry-go-round, which, screeching, began to spin, Louis waved at Hottentots, at smugglers, at Mongolians in huge bearskins, and, sliding off the merry-go-round because a Sister had put the brakes on, he lay against the uneven paving of the playground between lazily rolling marbles. Come on, said a hairy voice, open your mouth. A hard, unripe, sour little pear from the pear tree was pushed into his mouth, he swallowed pieces, cores, stalks. But it was not the Institute merry-go-round that he had been twirling around on, it was a toy magnified a hundred times and made of vividly lacquered little tin airplanes that hung whirring at an angle from thin metal cables, rusty holes appeared suddenly in the wings, the propellers melted, Louis began to laugh weakly with nerves. "Jump!"—he let go of the swelling, creaking crate, his parachute opened and turned into a bellying bright bed that he sank into without ever having touched ground, and, sinking, he heard: *Komm,* right in front of his nose one fold of the parachute began to billow, turning into a breast with amber-colored makeup, the breast bulged inside a tunic of the same color whose buttons burst off but continued to cleave to a body with neither head nor legs, the tunic was studded with decorations, Louis recognized the Iron Cross, the Palms, the Oak Leaf, the Pour le Mérite, the nipple is the softest of pacifiers, sweet and redolent of almond milk, Louis recognized—but how could there ever have been an "earlier" occasion to remember?—the breast of *Reichsmarschall* Hermann Wilhelm Göring, a fat peasant woman (but immaculately conceived) squeezed into a uniform that grew ever paler and paler until it was as white as snow. *Komm, Sündensklave Mensch,* Come, slave of sin, says the *Reichsmarschall,* and he bends his many chins down until the braided chinstrap of his cap touches the top of Louis's head.

Machine guns rattled in the meadows behind the College. Exercises. Bawled commands, cheering.

The pupils made a few notes. No more than were strictly necessary. Just enough to give the Rock the impression that they were listening. Because the Rock, it was whispered, was going to be removed to a rest home for priests. You couldn't really call his mumblings a lesson any longer. Today's lesson, about original sin, was again aimed exclusively at Louis: one may have no doubt about the reality of original sin, although it is sometimes difficult to accept that all of us are beset with a hereditary moral flaw. Adam and Eve happened to have eaten of the forbidden fruit and in so doing infected every newborn person from that day onward.

Now, that, however, poses a problem. Because the story of the forbidden fruit and the serpent and so on first saw the light of day nine hundred years before Christ. When Israel was being threatened from the north by the Syrians. When the very heart of Israel was being threatened from within by a worm, namely the persistent practice of the Baal fertility rite. Understood? So it was to keep the people of Israel in check with a telling bit of propaganda that this tale was first told. Since the story with the serpent was something the people could readily understand, the serpent was the symbol of the Canaanite peasant religion—"Understood?"

A few students in the first rows nodded absently.

"Yes, but in that case what are we to make," the Rock murmured and avoided looking at Louis, "of St. Paul's claim in his Epistle to the Romans that sin entered into the world through one man, by which he meant Adam? What do we make of St. Augustine, who says that all the world's misery has its roots in this single deed?"

Yes, what do we make of that? The bell sounded. While the others rushed outside, the Rock rummaged in the folds of his cassock and quickly pressed a note, no, a number of ration stamps, into Louis's hand.

"These are for you. For nobody else, understand?"

"Dearest darling Louis, you probly often have wondered Where has my Bekka got to recently but Darling I couldnt write earlier since I've been with my aunt Alicia in Baudroux-sur-Mere because something gastly has happened that is my Daddy the fool has been STUPID in Deutschland and made trouble there with his Deutsche Chefs and was thrown into a Deutsche JAIL without apeal or mercy and nobody knows where and maybe for years because he had a KNIFE on him but he always carries a knife because its handy to have one you know Louis, I must stop myself from crying, wait, dearest little Louis of my heart, I know that you carry me in your heart but you dont talk about it me neither thats why I am writing for maybe we'll never see each other again in this life because my aunt Alicia she says I must stay here all the war time but I want to get away maybe to Deutschland to seek my Father for no one know where exactly he is kept in chains. Acording to aunt Alicia its all because he said something against the government or against the Furer not on purpose but I think its because my Daddy look like a Gipsy or an Egiptian and thats like a Jew and the Deutschers dont want such people to work in the factories with the other workers. I am so sad every day especially at night but one fine day well be happy together, you can look at other WOMEN so long as you continue to carry me in Your HEART. Dearest Louis, I must go now to look after the children of Maitre Laveyron, they are little brats the children but I get paid and Aunt Alicia say every franc helps for my keep. To the end of my life I'll be true to you. Rebekka, YOUR DARLING Cosijns, 3 Rue Arsène Houssaye, in the town Baudroux-sur-Mere. From my dear brother I never hear anything. He has to stay in the monastery of the Redemptorrists. Mainly cleaning the coridors. That is in Kempen. And how is your dear Mother, Madame Senave? Is she still cross with us?

"Kisses and kisses. And EVER TRUE."

Genevoix, the Troop Leader, now also sporting the marksman's badge, the ungainly Haegedoorn, Bosmans the Anemic—all behaved as if they had not seen Louis. They stood in the regulation manner, it was a solemn moment, but even so one of them might have glanced sideways at their former comrade, standing beside his father among such leading figures as Marnix de Puydt, Dr. Leevaert, and Mijnheer Groothuis *cum suis.*

Bosmans cried when a fat, toadlike boy with heavy spectacles and a sonorous voice recited: "Here are they scattered, like seeds in the sand, promise of harvest, oh, Fatherland." Bosmans must have wondered what would be the most propitious moment to wipe his wet face.

Sacrilegiously, during the memorial ceremony for Staf de Clercq, leader of his people, dead of cancer of the liver, Louis heard the strains of Django Reinhardt's guitar with the Stan Brenders orchestra, Swing 41, that had come over the radio this morning while Mama was explaining why she wouldn't be coming along.

"What would I do there?"

"Nondedju," said Papa, "you could pay homage to Our Leader who fought his whole life long for us."

"For you, perhaps, but not for me."

"How can you, Constance?"

"You didn't even know him. You never even once met him."

"Me? What do you mean? In '37, when we were battling against the Belgian Gendarmes during the Yser Pilgrimage, I personally dragged him out from under the horses' hooves, as I live and breathe!"

Mama wrinkled up her nose and with safety pins fastened to Louis's arm the strip of black material she had cut from a petticoat.

At the entrance to the Municipal Theater, past the many banners and pennants, marched Louis's former comrades-in-arms, chins out, knees raised in unison. Pharmacist Paelinck arrived with his daughter, both in mourning, stood next to Papa, and said that for the most ridiculous reasons he had been prevented from giving an address. "Instead they had to choose a boy with no voice. Could you understand what he said, Mijnheer Seynaeve? He swallowed all his consonants."

"I can't tell," said Papa, "because I know the words by heart."

"There wasn't the slightest bit of life in that voice."

They walked side by side down the middle of the street toward the Market Square. The Lion over the Belfry hung at half-mast. Paelinck said that the demise of Staf de Clercq was a catastrophe, "because whom can we get as a leader instead? Surely not Dr. Elias? We don't need a scholar, we need someone at the tiller." (Killer, thriller.)

Simone kept her mourning eyes fixed on the cobblestones.

"Mark my words, Mijnheer Seynaeve, we must be vigilant when it comes to choosing the executor of his will!"

"It didn't amount to all that much," said Papa, "and that in itself shows you the sort of life the man led. Un-self-ish. Ten thousand francs to his godchild. The burial plot bought for his wife for when she's ready to lie beside him in the Kester churchyard. And a hundred Masses for the salvation of his soul."

"I meant his political testament, Mijnheer Seynaeve."

"Oh, excuse me."

Louis slackened his pace, Simone remained by his side.

"I haven't seen you for quite some time."

"Me neither," he said. "Did you want to see me, then?"

"Why not?"

"The music was impressive. Beethoven is always impressive."

"I thought it was a bit heavy."

"Still, it was fitting."

"I'm not crazy about classical music."

"Me neither. Normally."

"You're not in uniform."

"We had some differences of opinion." (That sounded important, mysterious.)

"I prefer you like this. In knickerbockers."

"Me too. What I mean is, I like you better like this than in that stupid Great Netherlands Girls' Troop costume."

"It doesn't suit me."

The backs in front of them, those of her father and of his. Their own two backs were being admired by a mourning Walle. He heard himself sing, "I'd love to have your photograph."

"Do try and be serious!"

Braving her gray, almost anxious look, he continued to sing, "No matter how small, so long as it says, 'I'm yours alone.' "

"That's by the Ramblers."

"Yes. And it says exactly what I . . ."

"What?"

"Feel for you."

"This isn't the time," she said and quickened her pace, catching up with her father, who was busy describing the outskirts of Stalingrad. In the distance Amadeus and Aristotle could be seen sitting on a terrace like good boys, waiting for their father in the autumn sun. Then they rushed up to him. De Puydt said, "Staf, would you be kind enough to pay for my two little ragamuffins just this once? In the hurry of putting on my black suit I completely forgot to bring some money. And we're all off to the Groeninghe, where we can feel more at home."

On the way he said, "Staf, you are well *reçu* by the Gestapo, aren't you, so could you do an old comrade a favor?"

"But, Marnix, you know that you can ask anything of me."

"It has come to my notice that someone has been passing slanderous allegations about me in these circles. That there's even been a complaint. And all because I drink whisky."

"Come, come, Marnix," said Paelinck.

"Can I help it that I have a confirmed taste for Scotch?"

"But what can there be wrong about a glass of Scotch?" Paelinck exclaimed as if standing on a platform. The De Puydt twins were skipping along holding on to Simone's hands.

"I think they feel that Scotch . . ." Papa began.

". . . is the drink of the enemy!" Paelinck exclaimed scornfully. "How petty people can be! Would you believe it, they wouldn't let me appear in the theater because the District Inspector for Culture and Style thought that people would recognize my voice as Dalle's and start laughing. As if I had only one voice. As if, goddammit, I hadn't played Richard the Third at the National Drama Festival!"

"I could understand it if I were actually helping the British economy," said De Puydt. "But the Scotch I get is mostly distilled over here. Tell that to your German pals, Staf."

As they drew level with the statue of Guido Gezelle, he added, "A little while back I tried some Canadian whisky, appropriated from some Canadian plane that had been forced down. I have to tell you quite honestly that I didn't like it, the corn and the malt, no, just give me an honest drop of Scotch that doesn't make your head spin, doesn't make your tongue babble or your teeth chatter, doesn't blow up your guts, and keeps your arteries nice and open."

They had all collected outside the Groeninghe, the sound of a funeral march echoing from inside.

"Staf, try and get a peek at my dossier, so that at least I know what the Gestapo have against me. And if you can, put in a good word for me. Because right now what I need is peace and quiet, I'm working on something that's going to make the world sit up."

"How is *The Death of Descartes* coming along, Mijnheer de Puydt?" Louis asked to dazzle Simone.

De Puydt's puffy, womanish face showed signs of confusion. He didn't recognize Louis. "Descartes? What put that into your head, boy? That's not my line. No, I'm totally absorbed in a comedy."

"Surely not French vaudeville?" Papa asked.

"I couldn't write vaudeville if I wanted to. No, it's something a great deal more spiritual, light but consistent. The surface, all grace, but beneath lurks a skeleton, the framework of death, something in the genre of Purcell's cantata 'Soft notes and gently raised,' flutes and continuo, if you follow me."

"You're right," said Papa. "It must be elevating but not too heavy. For the man in the street, I mean." He seemed suddenly to have fallen into a somber mood, decided against joining them in the Groeninghe. "No, seriously, Marnix, on a day like this and after such a ceremony, I wouldn't be able to get a drink down my throat."

"I have to go home," said Louis.

"I don't," said Simone.

"I'll come and see you at your place one day. If that's all right with you."

"Why not?" she said. He put out his hand, but she had already turned around to walk into the café, pushing Amadeus and Aristotle ahead of her. Through the leaded window they watched the plump figure of De Puydt flop down on a seat, framed behind glass as in a secular temple for Flemish Minds.

Papa shuffled home like an old man.

"Are they going to put up a statue to Staf de Clercq?"

"The VNV hasn't got enough money for that."

"A commemorative plaque then, on the front of his house?"

"That would be a disgrace. Just a commemorative plaque. For someone who offered up his life. The Flemish are an ungrateful people."

His thoughts were elsewhere. They walked past the Flandria, the tennis court was deserted.

"Do you understand your mother? Refusing to pay her last respects to so great a man? She has no heart. My whole life long she's left me out in the cold. Her whole life long it's been too much for her to show even the slightest bit of affection. She doesn't understand what a man needs. If you think of all the sacrifices I've made, money, presents, nothing was too much for me, I lay at her feet, and what did I get in return? Cold comfort. That's because she never got any affection in her own home. She was brought up all wrong! Meerke never taught her how to treat a man. D'you know that when we'd just been married and went to visit friends, she wouldn't use the toilet there? As sure as I live. She held it all back."

He stopped. "As sure as I stand here. You don't believe me, do you? Then ask her yourself! I'll tell you something else, you're big enough, we went to the vicar's jubilee, more like a reception really, and she held it back there too a whole afternoon and we got back home and she couldn't go to the toilet anymore, her bladder was blocked, the doctor had to come with a probe. What's the matter? You've gone all pale . . ."

"*Louis,* couldn't you come here and fetch me? Its so horrid here. Aunt Alicia says its better if her brother my FATHER never gets out of jail in Deutschland because before when they were small he was no good, she said that tonight on account of she was cross with me on account of I slapped the face of Gaston Laveyron, one of the children of Maitre Laveyron who droped his plate on purpose so I would get the blame. If you dont come and get me I'll run away from here even if its under a train. Dearest, Dearest, Dearest, do you still think of your Rebekka Cosijns? Take the tram to Doornik after that you take the slow train to Charleroi, the forth stop in Baudroux-sur-Mere then ask in the Café La Fleur et Papier Doré, oposite the station."

It was snowing. Louis was coming back from school when he saw two German soldiers outside the Cosijnses' door, the smaller standing with his boot on the doorstep, having apparently just rung the bell. The other, who had a very small head and a long neck on top of an abnormally broad chest, was leaning against the front of the house like a street urchin, whistling *"Nur nicht aus Liebe weinen."* When the smaller German saw Louis coming up, he turned around and said, "Who do we have here, then?"

It was Dirty Dick. Louis felt like turning tail and running away, because a person could be shot for disguising himself in German uniform as if it were Carnival time. And anybody caught in the company of such an unscrupulous saboteur would most likely be considered an accomplice under the Geneva Convention. Or some convention or other.

"It's Louis," said Dirty Dick to the other one, who was likewise illegally disguised. Still, Louis was proud that Dirty Dick had remembered his name.

"Aren't they at home?"

"Bekka is with her aunt in Wallonia and Tetje is in a monastery."

"In a monastery?" Dirty Dick guffawed. It was snowing. In the bakery window, which years ago had bulged with towers of pastries and brown-crusted milk rolls and chocolate cake and éclairs and nun's-farts and buttercakes and *speculaas,* spiced ginger biscuits, there now stood a lone dwarf palm. Dirty Dick's *Wehrmacht* uniform looked as if it were made to measure, but it was still a Carnival costume.

"I wanted Odiel to meet Tetje, I told him so much about him and now he's in a monastery. Oh, well, *merci.* Another time, Odiel. Come on, we're going to the Graaf van Heule." Louis was included in the command.

Louis had never been in the Graaf van Heule, because Papa maintained that there was still a whiff of Jenny's grandfather about the place, and all Walle knew that he had died of yellow fever and that the late Dr. Devilder had failed to notify the Public Health Inspector. And actually the place did smell of some feverish, very old man.

Odiel took off his cap, his head now even smaller. If you had to choose, then the hydrocephalic head of Guido Gezelle was better anytime. They drank *hengstenbier,* the light-brown brew of which Dirty Dick had so often dreamed in El Agella, on the Gulf of Sidra, where they'd had to escape from because of the heat. "How hot was it? Odiel, Odiel, how hot did Montgomery make it?"

"Hotter than we could put up with, anyway," said Odiel in a boy's voice.

Dirty Dick ordered a second round. Louis knew for certain that he wouldn't be paying. Jenny knew it as well but naturally didn't dare open her hereditarily tainted, feverish mouth. Odiel only wanted a mineral water.

"That boy doesn't know how to have a good time," said Dirty Dick. "Believe it or not, ever since we've been back in the *Heimat,* he's talked of nothing but going back down south. The desert, the desert, that's the only thing he's interested in."

"Did you see the Foreign Legion, in North Africa?"

"Odiel, did we see the Foreign Legion?"

Odiel nodded.

"Mostly just their heads," said Dirty Dick. "The Tunisians were playing football with those."

Jenny asked if she could join them in a little drink. She could.

357

"What didn't we see!" said Dirty Dick. "In Tripoli. Two bombers, that's all it took, and everything went up in smoke, the whole harbor, torpedo boats, freighters, our own boat was dancing around like a Negress."

"A Negress at Carnival," said Louis, who was getting drunk, having a good time, feeling clear-headed and befuddled by turns.

"Carnival, that was a long time ago!" The shy man who had hung around the clay pits had given way to a completely new person. As with Raspe, the training, the baptism of fire, had fashioned him into a different man, dressed as a soldier. Would I change into something so bronzed and self-assured, too?

"Dick, you've always been one for a good time," said Jenny.

"Madame," said Odiel, "there's no one like Richard, they don't make them like that anymore."

"If I'd taken everything to heart, well, my friends, I'd have been buried in the sand long ago," said Dirty Dick.

"But what he makes you put up with, madame," said Odiel like an anxious housewife. He was wearing two gold watches with the faces on the inside of his wrist (that way when you're lying beside a machine gun you don't have to turn your hand over) and a broad silver chain on his right wrist.

"You love people for their faults," said Jenny.

"What faults?"

"Come, now, Dick, you've got to admit that you're a bit of a gadabout."

"You're absolutely right there, madame."

"Shut up, Odiel, *Schnauze!* Or we'll have a few things to say about your failings! But we don't want to start on that, do we, Jenny, come on, how about another little one, then. It isn't really hot in here, but I'm dry as a cactus all the same. We've seen quite a few of those, eh, Odiel, cactuses?"

"More than enough."

"Many's the time we've said, that cactus over there would look great in our living room in Ostende, but just try and take one along with you! Although some fellows from the *Afrikakorps* did send them home, in special crates. Whether they got there is another question. I'd be surprised."

"And annoyed," said Odiel.

"But aren't you in the *Afrikakorps?*"

"Come off it, Louis," said Odiel.

"They aren't wearing tropical helmets these two, are they now?" said Jenny. It was snowing.

"The best time we had was in Greece," said Odiel, his unusually broad shoulders held squarely back, he strode in a white tunic between Ionian columns, Aristotle was sitting in a trireme in the wine-red wine-dark sea.

"Where he bounced a lot of checks," said Dirty Dick.

"That's something we'd rather not hear about," said Jenny.

"For a hundred and eighty thousand francs," said Dirty Dick tenderly.

"I did it for you just as much as for myself."

"My little butterfly," said Dirty Dick.

They had cleared out of Greece in a great hurry, taken off their *Organisation Todt* uniforms and gone on to Egypt and from there to Tunisia, and one could still see the effects of this vagabondage, since both could think up a fresh masquerade at the drop of a hat, turning into zookeepers, tram conductors, at the switch of a cap or tunic or belt. But at the drop of a hat, too, the military police might raid the Graaf van Heule. Were these two carrying loaded pistols? The blackout started at twenty to five. The first batch of workers from the ERLA, released from the cages Mama watched over, arrived in the café and were listening in.

Louis toyed with the idea of taking these two unreliable paladins and quick-change-artists home and surprising his parents with them. But he forgot it, accepted a drink from one of the young men from the ERLA who said that his mother was blossoming like a flower, the remark intended to be offensive, teasing, provocative, but maybe also to be conciliatory, comradely, flattering, the beer sloshed around in Louis's entrails, a voluptuously sleepy feeling crept sluggishly over him from every corner of the café, the mock-velvet curtains closed in, wrapped themselves softly around him, the voice of Dirty Dick, more and more belligerent and shrill over the past hour, reached him with difficulty, as through a fleece of snow.

". . . and so, off I go in perfectly good faith with an *Oberleutnant* after the RAF has peppered us with high explosives just as I was cooking dinner for the *Oberst*, because my *Oberst* wasn't one for canned food, and I rush outside still wearing my apron, and the *Oberleutnant* says, 'Come on, quick, get on the back of my motorcycle.' I hold on tight, we're doing more than forty through the sand, and suddenly, not a palm tree in sight, he stops and he says, 'Hand over your money.' I hand it over to him and he races off, never to be seen again, I say to myself, 'Dick, you've had it,' and I was gone for three weeks, what I went through then I cannot describe. Odiel says, 'Come on, you can tell me, what did those outlandish tribes get up to with you?' I say, 'Dear boy, I can't, but I cried many a tear into my apron . . .' "

". . . They have no mercy, any SS man who touches another, even fully dressed, or tries to give him a kiss, gets a bullet through the brain right away . . ."

". . . We're going to settle down, my Odiel and I, not far from the Market . . ."

"You aren't thinking of opening a café?" said Jenny, and asked if she could have another little one with them. "You go right ahead," said Louis.

"No, a shop selling dress materials and curtains."

"Here, in Walle?"

"No, no, dear girl. In Ostende. By the sea. Where the sailors are."

"The l-l-last time I s-saw you," said Louis, "was in the shwim' pool, you s-s-sang 'Go Down, Moses.'"

Dirty Dick sang it again, the ERLA workers clapped.

"Encore, encore!"

Jenny shouted, "You idiot, the Germans will come in any moment, and I've already had to report to the *Kommandantur* once this week!"

Odiel said, "Woman, Richard may sing as loud as he likes."

"Swing low, sweet chario-ot."

"Woman, we don't keep quiet for anyone!"

"Bravo!" called the ERLA boys.

"Ol' man river" followed Louis far down the street, as far as the front of his house, white with snow.

Mama was coughing in the downstairs hall. Too much smoking. She said in a thick voice that she had only been out for a walk. "Can't I do even that anymore? I'm still allowed to breathe, I suppose?"

"Why didn't you want any herring tonight?" cried Papa. "Tell me that."

"It's always herring."

"Oh, so it isn't good enough! It has to be entrecôte steak at the Swan!"

"I wasn't hungry."

"Because you didn't want your breath to smell of herring!" roared Papa.

The light flickered on in Louis's room, she flopped down onto his bed. She looked hot in her dress with the deep décolletage and the black sequins, her scarlet mouth opened and closed as if she were accompanying a distant song.

She had landed on Louis's feet, but it didn't hurt.

"He is mad, mad," she said, and then the madman came storming into the room in his shirtsleeves, crying out, "Tell him, tell him, tell your son how you're deceiving me with the Occupier!"

"He's no occupier, he's a decent man."

"You hear! She admits it!"

"All I admit is that he's charming and attentive to me."

"And I am not?"

"No, you're not."

Papa pointed at her, the wide black sleeves of his robe swung, his advocate's bands stood on end, the courtroom held its breath, the boy's bed was the dock. The made-up, overexcited accused had the hiccups.

"She persists in her denials, she'd rather bite off her tongue than tell the truth and nothing but the truth, but, Constance, you simply reek of the truth!"

Mama leaned back against the creaking bedposts. Then she allowed herself to fall forward against Louis, flung her arm around his neck. The truth reeked of wine and face powder. Her warmth reached him through her silk dress.

The man, neither father nor husband, shook the bedposts as if trying to tip the woman and the boy out. Then he stood up, red in the face, under the lamp that lent his sparse, fair hair a platinum halo.

"Constance, look me straight in the eye . . ."

"No." (Mama, the recalcitrant teenager.)

"Look me in the eye, I said!"

She wound her hair around Louis's neck, snorted briefly as horses do in the meadows when the evening mists come up.

"I can't, Staf."

"Get out of that bed. The boy needs his sleep."

Her one wide-open eye, with the little veins, with the spiky, black-daubed lashes like those of the little foal on its back in the meadow.

"I'm going to teach you a lesson, Constance, I'll show you what's what once and for all!"

"If only you could do that for once, teach me a lesson!" She burst out laughing, hooves thudded in the matted grass. What did she want, then? For him to kill her? Why and how did she, laughing so vilely, want to be taught a lesson? Why did Papa now utter this snarling cry, grab her hair and pull her up, and then shout "Ouch!" because he had struck his knee against the iron edge of the bed?

With a grimace of pain that failed to extinguish the last remnant of her mocking laughter, Mama was torn from Louis, given a kick and a shove, the door of their bedroom was slammed shut, Papa stumbled down the stairs, and a crooning, inarticulate singsong rose from her bed.

Papa sat on the sofa in the front room and bit into a fist-sized lump of bread pudding, which he must have fetched quickly from his secret storage cupboard in the workshop.

"I can't get to sleep with all your goings-on," said Louis. "Shall we have a game of draughts?"

"I'm not in the mood."

"Try thinking about something else."

"All my life," said Papa, chewing, swallowing, biting. "All my life from the day we got married . . ."

"It's all because of my little brother's death," said Louis.

"That's right, take her side, why don't you." When he had finished the pudding and was licking his fingertips, he added, "She doesn't want to confess, but she doesn't have to confess, it's known all over the ERLA, all over Walle! She's been seen! She's been heard! Do you know what he calls her?"

"No." (Not "Who?")

"Flämmchen, mein Flämmchen, if you please!"

"My little Fleming?"

"Wrong! Madame is his little flame! If you please!"

He went to the kitchen, I followed him like a little dog, he took the narrow red carton with the lump sugar, filled a glass of water from the tap, and was about to start sucking. Louis said, "How about making some sugar candy?"

"Not a bad idea."

The sugar spluttered in the little pan, caked together, dark-brown. Papa tested it. "Another little drop of vinegar." Then he poured the steaming, sticky mass onto the blue stone slab. When it had become pale and harder, Papa rolled it between his chapped, black printer's-hands into a long sausage, then cut it into equal, twisting little pieces. They both greedily ate the candy, which was too hot and too acid. Papa read from a Karl May book.

The ticking of the alarm clock, the crunching and the cracking of the sour-sweet pebbles, boots past the front door, and now and then from the bedroom above a snatch of song, followed by silence. Old Shatterhand and his blood brother Winnetou stalked the prairie, the silver rifle kept the Sioux and the Kiowa at bay, a tomahawk whistled through the air, herds of buffalo trampled and stifled the adultery in their clouds of dust.

Now and then the Rock would stay away from the College for a few days, the mathematics teacher said he was taking a rest with his noble family. (In this new age, incidentally, are we not all of us noble? Work is ennobling, too, and hadn't Aunt Nora, following the new fashion of digging up one's ancestors, proved that we were rooted in the people and, retracing our family tree, full of branches and branchlets, that the Seynaeves had appeared as early as the seventeenth century in Wevelgem, as witness the local municipal archives, and with a bit of luck and, above all, time, she might even look into the records of the guilds and corporations.)

When he came back that Monday, the Rock was without two front teeth. During the study period, soft scratching and coughing, rustling of pages, he sat on his throne in the large, cool study hall and read from a book called *Ergophobia*, which he afterward handed to Louis for his parents. Louis leafed through it as it lay on the school bag across his knees while he sat, despite the cold, in the little park by the Church of Our Lady.

A study of two thousand public children's-homes in New York had shown that most children were not so much lazy or work-shy as suffering from a hereditary defect, a pathological tendency. I, child of skyscrapers and of Mama, can therefore do nothing about being work-shy. Two factors are to blame, temperament and environment. Aha, so the family tree has spoken! And the experience of Dr. Hanselmann, director of the pedagogical seminary in Zurich, has taught him that the blame lies mainly with the debilitating effects of certain environments. The environment of that noble-and-ever-shabbier-mumbling-signet-ring-wearing Rock does not, of course, suffer from such effects!

The book was not meant for Louis's parents, the Rock knew perfectly well that Papa and Mama would never read it. It was for me, the lazy child, to browse through, to study my own tendencies, like some unhousebroken kitten I must have my nose thrust into my work-shy, sinful pee by my own ego, which has to make the diagnosis on the orders of the Rock.

"Once the lazy child is allowed for some time to enjoy advantages (including creative play) of which he was previously deprived, he will feel confidence in, respect and certainly fondness for those who have facilitated this course of events." Point taken, Dr. Rock! Advantages of which he was previously deprived, I know no others.

And according to you these advantages can be enjoyed again. *Voyons, voyons,* as your colleage Dr. Pants-Down, with whom you are in cahoots, would say.

Aber, aber, and yet, and yet.

He was afraid to throw the book away. Do you know what, Seynaeve?—What, Seynaeve?—Well, Seynaeve, I've got a strange feeling.

In some ways I am partly responsible for the Rock's heart-searching (or decline). He has chosen me, the lazy child. He sends me signals I cannot decipher. Why does he speak more and more often about the dignity of man under threat, man being trampled upon? What is he up

363

to with those three or four individuals, always the same ones, from the Rhetoric class? Sometimes they retire to the gym, and when I just happen to come by and *catch them at it,* they shoo me away disdainfully, as if I smelled bad. I miss Bekka. I will teach her to read and to write. I have a terrible longing for chocolate. They shouldn't put chocolate flavor into vitamin pills, it only makes the longing worse. Longing for Simone, but I can't go there in that stupid checked shirt of Uncle Florent's (now in England, a country inexplicably left in peace by the *Führer*). And I don't want to go to Uncle Robert, either, even though I would get minced meat there, because I would have to listen to all that sloppy drivel about his Monique, whom he is going to marry just as soon as the loan from Canon Voordekkers comes through. And I don't want to go to Aunt Nora, either, who keeps nudging me and asking about my love life. *Dies irae, dies illa.* Death is always a way out. Another, a mother. Not long ago she had a bundle of twenty-franc notes in her handbag. She'll never notice anything.

Resolutely he stepped into the Groeninghe and said, "Noël, a glass of your light beer. And not too much foam, please."

Stalingrad.

How Ethiopia has declared war on Germany. And Brazil as well.

How there must be a change in the supreme command of the Gendarmerie, because some of those majors and commandants there aren't any good, they're more anglophile than Churchill, they're doing their damnedest to see to it that any saboteurs slip through the net.

Stalingrad.

How the VNV football team isn't up to much. Politics and sports don't mix.

Stalingrad.

How sometimes you can hear Radio London in broad daylight in the middle of Walle, I won't say where, everyone has to decide what risks to take, but it makes your blood boil when you hear them inciting that rabble in Toontjes Street to lay waste our fields of rapeseed, just because the oil is supposedly needed by the *Wehrmacht.*

How—and this from Dr. Leevaert, who the more he drank the more he became the doctor with the special flair for Germanic languages—how, "having investigated the matter and with my analysis, having demolished all the traditional proofs of the existence of God . . ."

"Yes, but which God?"

"That of Aristotle."

"Aristotle!" groaned Marnix de Puydt. "He was crying, that poor little mite, I took him in my arms, I told him, 'Aris, my little lamb, Papa has to earn some pennies, and that's why you must leave him in peace, otherwise he won't be able to write his comedy!' 'Everything you say is a comedy,' said he, my little seraph, 'I don't want to be sent to those nuns.' I said, 'Aris, Papa and Mama can't look after you as well as they ought to. And over there in the Institute in Haarbeke you'll get new-laid eggs and freshly made butter straight from the Institute's cows."

"Yes, but which God?"

"The abstract God, *godverdomme*, why don't you listen when I talk to you, the prime, unmoved Mover."

"Noël, get a move on for once and give us the same again."

"You can't have the same again, because you've got that inside you already," said Noël, something he said ten times every day.

"Immanuel," shouted Leevaert, who got drunk on two Pale-Ales but was able to stay at the same level for two days and two nights.

"*Gott mit uns!*"

"Immanuel Kant . . ."

"Couldn't . . . ?"

". . . was talking to a peasant . . ."

"The peasants squeeze us dry, granted, but we'd find it hard to survive without them."

"He said, 'Peasant, let us assume that there is a God, a Great Conscience.' "

"A great *concièrge.*"

" 'But that, Peasant, does not imply that the soul is immortal.' Now, the Peasant had a prune he was munching on, and he said . . ."

"It was *her* prune he was munching on, Leevaert."

" 'Why does He exist then?' "

"Leevaert, you're drunk."

"And yet it's very simple. Our essence is nothing more than the effort we make to survive as human beings, the effort to ward off death."

"You've hit the nail on the head, friend," said Marnix de Puydt. "The not wanting to die. King Albert said that to me. De Puydt, *mon ami*, he said, under your princely *nonchalance* I can sense the resilience—the *ressort*, he called it—of someone who laughs at death. In your conversation, *mon cher*, I can hear the tune I used to sing in the trenches in '14–'18: '*Viens, poupoule, viens, poupoule, viens!*' I said, '*Je vous remercie, Sire,*' and I meant it."

"Kant refashions this god, who corresponds to the '*zoon polipkon*' . . ."

"He had a son with polyps?"

". . . but this time into the God of conscience. . . ."

"A bad conscience if you ask me!"

". . . into the creator of the moral order."

"Ah, so he was in favor of the New Order as well!"

"Precisely. An immortal *salto mortale.* He rebuilds with his heart what his head rejects."

"King Albert," said Marnix de Puydt, who was often received at Court because he was the Prince of West Flemish Letters, "King Albert," he said, "was so nearsighted as well as clumsy that he never ate at official banquets, for fear of being shown up when he used his spoon or fork. The reason his appearance was described as chivalrous and as one of natural *noblesse* and why he held his royal head erect with so much dignity was that he couldn't see farther than eight inches in front of him. It was only when he returned home with his Queen and a few trusted attendants after such banquets that he would fall upon his special Meissen porcelain tureen and, happy and napkinless, slurp up a quart of onion soup. His greatest delight, however, was traveling by train. At the most improbable moments, if his crowned head was so inclined, he would repair by royal train to, let's say, Geneva. Immediately all international railway connections and regulations would have to be revised, turned around, adjusted. His Majesty would set off with his Swiss watch and a train timetable written specially for him by a calligrapher in large capital letters, and would hold it up close to his pince-nez, being able to remain seated like this for a very long time since the royal scarlet velvet underneath him had been fitted out with a *lunette,* and then it might happen that at, say, the forty-two kilometer marker, Albert I would with his own hand pull the emergency cord. The Viscount–*cum*–Chief Engine Driver would then come running up to pay his respects, and the monarch would say, 'You bungler, according to my specially designed chronograph you are one minute, so many seconds late!' Trembling, the Viscount would stammer out something about the wheels overheating, about viaducts, about imponderabilia, about the concept of time, in short, that when all was said and done it wasn't his fault. 'What? Even I, the King, have to shoulder responsibility for any possible mistakes I may make . . .' "

"Puydt, my boy, that's not the way a King would talk. Only ministers talk like that."

"Go on, Puydt."

"The railway incunabula would be consulted, breathless engineers and secretaries would prepare new timetables. *En avant,* the Royal Mountaineer would say, and the train would again deliver itself of its triumphant smoke signals. Until the next stopping-place. Until the next session with the vellum book of rules that covered time anticipated, time hoped for, time despaired of, time dislocated, and time regulated, just like European railway traffic. In Geneva the King would take a shower while the train did an about-turn. In fits and starts, laboriously, it would go thundering back to Brussels, that miserable bone of contention in the very heart of our country. Worn out but satisfied, the *Roi Chevalier,* more erect and more slow-moving than ever, would reenter his palace, where his wife would be playing the violin in a democratically, pluralistically composed quartet, each of the three male musicians having in his pocket a flat gold cigarette case bearing her monogram."

"Noël, a whisky for our Marnix!"

"Because positivism reduces facts to mere fragments, to the dust of facts."

"It's been a long time now since there's been any bombing."

"Yes, there has been. In Etterbeek."

"Maurice Chevalier, who when all is said and done is looked on as the soul and *esprit* of France, claims he owes it all to his mother. Well, his mother is Flemish, to her fingertips!"

"And if man is an end and not just a means, then . . ."

"Easy, Leevaert, easy does it," said a glassy-eyed Marnix de Puydt and fell asleep, his head with its Flemish Mind wobbled, sought and found the shoulder of Leevaert, who was having trouble bringing his glass of beer to his mouth. The snores leaving De Puydt's mouth became a drone that swelled and rumbled ominously, that would blanket the town of Walle several hours later, dense as smoke, the bombers' assignment was the destruction of Walle railway station, to which end a square had previously been drawn in Covent Garden, England, inside which everything was to be flattened, and in the southwest corner of that square lay the Haarbeke Institute, where the tower burst asunder, where the white merry-go-round was flung into the air as high as the guttering, a true *salto mortale,* and where three Sisters and seven children died, among them Aristotle de Puydt, seraph.

One half of the Institute had disappeared, the other was unrecognizable. The playground lay pockmarked, cratered, an awful, stinking meteorite having blown up like a chocolate puff, a disemboweled piano lay filled with little unripe pears, villagers using pickaxes pried and scraped among dented milk cans that looked like bombshells.

"Sister Eve-Marie and Sister Marie-Ange were praying in chapel for a special intention. I was furious with them: 'Sisters, your special intention must be to stay alive for Our Lord!' But they wouldn't listen." Sister Econome sank onto a lump of concrete, one side of which was painted in imitation marble. "The statue of Our Lady of Sorrows is untouched. If I weren't so sad, I would call that a miracle."

Grandpa crossed himself, Papa followed suit at once.

"The boys who were in the wine cellar are all safe, I counted them."

Sister Econome looked like Our Lady of Sorrows, glistening pearls dipped in oil rolling from the blood-red rims of her eyes.

"Our Lord is cruel."

"And Sister St. Gerolphe?" asked Louis.

"Not a scratch."

"And Sister Imelda?"

"With her brother in Avelgem."

Baekelandt came past, brandishing his pickax, and said gruffly that the masons would be around next week. "But this time the walls will have to be twice as thick and made of reinforced concrete."

"Baekelmans, can't you see we're busy?"

"Yes, Sister Econome, but I wanted you to know that there are quite a few people here in Haarbeke who are only too pleased to see the convent flattened. So what we've got to do is show them this isn't going to get us down! Reinforced concrete is what I say!"

Grandpa tugged at the two points of his vest, rubbed his head, asked for details of the funeral, he wanted to leave, and Sister Econome, who notices everything, walked toward the parlor that was no longer there. "It's not fair, Mijnheer Seynaeve."

"We must pray, Sister," said Grandpa, his head bowed as if he had been occupied with the appropriate prayer for some time.

"Can we do anything for you, Sister, anything at all?" asked Papa.

"I can't think of anything."

"You have only to ask, Sister."

"If we'd only crept into the loft, up there, under the beams . . . that roof is still there . . . Or into the cowshed with Baekelmans. But who can know these things beforehand? And all my papers, all my administration, years of my life, up in smoke."

"Churchill," said Papa. "Churchill!"

"Louis, dear, offer up your heart to Jesus, morning and night."

"Yes, Sister Econome."

Papa and Grandpa repaired to the parish hall, where Sister Adam and Sister Angel were lying in state. Louis wasn't allowed to join them, because he wouldn't be able to recognize them now anyway. He tried to find the exact spot where the pear tree had been, and stood on it. I am a filthy swine because I want to jump up and down and dance and yell in this ravaged citadel, this blown-up Keep.

Like a lump of lard. Like some giant nun-doll won by someone at a fairground shooting gallery, inflated with a bicycle pump and then dumped in the living room—outlandishly, there Sister St. Gerolphe sat, next to the stove, less than six feet away from Grandma. She was wearing blue-tinted spectacles pushed lopsidedly into her wimple. A white stripe of dried porridge ran from each corner of her mouth down to her collar. Aunt Hélène said, as if talking to a baby, that Louis was here, Mijnheer Seynaeve's grandson, but she didn't react.

"She's a good sort," said Grandma, whose own ponderousness seemed greatly diminished by that of Sister St. Gerolphe. As if wanting to look less bulky and inactive than the nun, she was wriggling, almost jumping about, in her wicker armchair.

"She's very easy to deal with and listens to everything we say."

"She does nothing but listen," said Aunt Hélène.

" 'It's an act of charity,' is what he said," Grandma grumbled. "I say to him, 'Act of charity, what kind of charity?' But off he went. To his lady-love. Or one of his lady-loves. Or to Mona. I've wracked my brains about that act of charity, believe me. First I thought it was 'sheltering the homeless,' but now I think it must be 'tending the sick.' Because she's more sick than homeless, don't you think? Because as soon as the Institute is rebuilt she'll have a roof over her head again, even better than the last."

"Easy enough with government money."

"Hélène, most of the money is coming from the Roeselare Bank, and that is tied up with the Bishopric."

The nun had the appearance of a younger, more vigorous sister of that monstrous nun so greatly, so fervently revered in the Institute's past.

"Yes, we've been saddled with her. But, then, we like her. We wash her from head to toe every two days."

"We?" said Aunt Hélène sharply.

"In a manner of speaking. She also gets the choicest bits from Robert."

"Liver," said Sister St. Gerolphe.

"And cutlets," said Grandma, looking proudly at her sister in adversity who had spoken. "But she knows nothing. In the convent they treat the Sisters like babies. I can understand that, what with their having to concentrate on religion, but they go too far. She didn't even know about our King getting married again last year, for just one example."

"To a princess," said Sister St. Gerolphe.

"And what is her name? See, she's forgotten already."

The nun's eyes searched the four corners of the room.

"Princess Liliane," Grandma bellowed.

Sister St. Gerolphe brought out her rosary from among her folds, the precious black stones of the joyful, sorrowful, and glorious mysteries rising and falling.

"He just dumps her here in our house. An act of charity, he says. Without so much as a by-your-leave. Just so he can play the Good Samaritan in the Institute."

"But, Mother, you're only too pleased to have somebody around, admit it."

"That's right, take your father's side, just like Mona. But she is a good sort. I've been trying to teach her patience, but it doesn't sink in. Or maybe it's because she thinks it's a sin to fritter away time she ought to be spending on reading her breviary or saying the Lord's Prayer."

"But, Grandma, she can't read."

"Why not, Louis?"

"She's blind."

"Oh, the good-for-nothing! And all the time she's been pretending she could read!"

"I've had an operation," said Sister St. Gerolphe. "I was given the eyes of a dead person."

"What? You didn't say anything to us about that!"

Much urgent and prodding questioning accompanied by exclamations of surprise elicited from Sister St. Gerolphe the explanation that when her father had died, she had cried so much that she had gone blind, but that after years of devotion and mortification the Lord Jesus had given her back the eyes of her dead father, she couldn't see much, but more than enough. "God has operated on me."

Louis walked through the smell of drains in the scullery to the privy. There he brought out Simone's photograph.

("Here, this is for you. It's what you asked me for when you sang."

"It's a lovely one of you."

"I cut it off, at the legs. I was wearing my ugly shoes."

"You look much more beautiful in real life."

"That's what they all say."

"I mean it."

"You mustn't show it to anyone. My hair doesn't look nice, it needed washing.")

He lifted the photograph to his lips. If you love a person you love them faults and all.

The worn, wan, decaying head in the wimple spat at Louis like a cat, her way of laughing.

"She wasn't pleased to see you go out," said Grandma. "You're going to have to stay here and live with us."

The cat subsided and recited a lesson memorized in her cat's-head: "They say we must be sick to withdraw from the world, that we are too ugly, too stupid, or too foolish to get ourselves a man, they are mistaken." Then she tilted her head, hooked a finger inside her wimple next to her spectacles, and shook it furiously.

"She's bothered by a ringing in her ears. I say, 'Sister, it's from the bombing.' 'No,' she says, 'it's Our Lord hissing at me.' "

"Whistling," said Louis, and Grandma recognized her husband's pedantry as he insisted, "Hissing is what snakes do."

"Her blood pressure is too high," said Aunt Hélène. "She's not allowed to have any salt."

"They are mistaken," said Sister St. Gerolphe. "Our calling is not of this world."

"Oh, come on now, what's wrong with this world, Gerolphe?" Grandma exclaimed.

"Everything," said the nun.

"What do you know about the world, Gerolphe?"

"I wanted to see something of the world before I entered the convent. The Vatican, Assisi, but it was too late, Jesus already had his hooks into me. It has to be all or nothing. Jesus isn't interested in leftovers."

"She's never said so much before all at once," whispered Aunt Hélène. "It's because you're here."

Did the Sister, desecrated, resurrected, reawakened, and rendered human by the bombardments, recognize Louis? As the boy who had stolen the trinket from her bedside table? Vlieghe lying on the table, pale buttocks, a martyr.

"It's you women who don't have it easy. Especially mothers. Because although they're not children themselves, they have to be children to their children."

"That's easy for you to say," said Grandma. "All you had to do was think about your Jesus, while you had your bread buttered for you and as often as not with Ardennes ham on top."

"It is hard to love you," said the pale voice. "But also hard not to love you."

Grandma stuck out her wobbling chin like Karel Sijs facing Gustave Roth in the ring last week on the newsreel. "Now, look, you're not in your convent anymore!"

"In the convent I wouldn't love you more than anyone else, because no one is allowed to have a special friendship."

"And that, Louis, is what I have to put up with." Grandma leaned back, well satisfied. *"Allee,* go and do a bit more praying for us, so that we don't have to hang around in Purgatory too long."

"If," said Sister St. Gerolphe, and with a practiced gesture she threw her rosary up in the air and caught the falling jet-black raindrops, "if you tell me about the princess."

"Which princess?"

"Liliane."

"How many Hail Marys will that get me?"

"A chaplet."

"That's five times ten. How many is that?"

Louis didn't hear, the answer lost because Aunt Hélène said, "That's how they go on all day long, the two of them."

The two battered war goddesses with the identical fleshy, hunched shoulders were observing a truce because Grandma was telling a story. Aunt Hélène was laboriously filling in a crossword puzzle, wrongly; "ancient Belgians" should have been "Nervii," not "Gallii," as she had scrawled in.

Liliane, the daughter of the governor of West Flanders, had been presented to the English King at Buckingham-of-the-Three-Musketeers-Palace, she had danced at the court ball in Vienna, where the *Führer* comes from, and then a little later she had broken her leg while skiing. Sister St. Gerolphe didn't know what skiing was, Aunt Hélène had to explain it to her, but the Sister refused to believe such a thing was possible. "Your Jesus walked on water," said Grandma and went on with her story. Liliane first saw our King in Nieuwpoort, and it was like being struck by lightning, her heart leaped into her throat and never stopped leaping, so that three years later, when Prime Minister Pierlot attacked our King so foully after the capitulation, her heart almost failed her because it was leaping about so much with rage. She had so set her heart on the royal widower—and when Liliane gets something into her head, she doesn't footle around—that she wrote a letter to his mother.

"Elisabeth, Majesty, isn't there some little job you can give me at Court?" And one thing led to another, a *déjeuner* at Laeken, a *tea party*—"A what?" Aunt Hélène didn't feel up to defining this exotic word—a drive in the open Mercedes to Knokke, and *voilà,* Cardinal van Roey had it announced from all the pulpits in all the churches in Belgium the day after St. Nicholas's Day that three months before he had had the honor and the privilege of blessing the royal marriage in the chapel at Laeken and that Liliane would henceforth be known as the Princess de Rethy. But if they ever had a child, it would never be able to wear the crown. And the priests had only just read it all out when a few hours later the Japanese attacked the Americans, at, where was it again? At Peer Arbor, in the inscrutable Orient.

"You see how one thing leads to another. *Allee*, you can start your Paternoster now."

In the workshop a pale-yellow sun lent the Prussian-blue windowpanes a green sheen following some obscure laws of chromatics. Louis was doing something that was absolutely forbidden, running blank quarto sheets of extremely expensive white paper between the ink rollers of the treadle machine. Because he had first crumpled the paper and then smoothed it out, the paper absorbed the ink unevenly to produce veined leaves, stormy skies, salamanders, dwarfish figures, fleeing mothers. When the bell rang at the front door and he could hear Papa shuffling out from the veranda, Louis sprang up, lithe as Mowgli, silent as Winnetou, catlike as Sabu, to hide behind the jute-wrapped bales of paper.

"*Tiens*, it's worth paying money to see you," said Papa. "I thought you'd already fled to Spain."

"Times are grim, Staf," said the bad-tempered voice of Theo van Paemel.

They were standing by the platen press. From the veranda a commentator could be heard shouting that Standard Liège was now leading 2-0.

"Staf, we are sworn comrades. But for heaven's sake, man, what have you been up to this time? You've stirred up a whole hornet's nest, Staf, I'm telling you. It's dynamite, Staf!"

"I don't know what you're talking about," said Papa.

"Oh, yes, you do! Pieter-Raphael Raspe, 61 Nightingale Lane, Wachteren, your employee, is the one who lodged the complaint."

"I still don't know what you're talking about."

"Your Raspe, and I hope he's left hanging by his balls from the end of some Russian bayonet, has handed in a whole dossier."

"You amaze me. I'll have to talk to him about it."

"But he left for the Eastern Front ages ago! The whole ERLA management has been implicated! Staf, how in God's name could you do that?"

"I swear I don't know anything about it, this is the first I've heard."

"You didn't know anything about that Jantje Piroen affair, either."

The intoxicating smell that rose from the bales of paper, the smell of printer's-ink and of machine oil. Almost as nice as the smell of the stuff Mama used to remove the polish from her fingernails. That business with Jantje Piroen had been Mama's fault. A *crime par négligence*. Jantje Piroen had been a boy from Toontjes Street, a little wild but a good sort, his father had fought with the Reds in Spain, but Jantje himself wasn't interested in politics. "Oh no, not at all, Madame Seynaeve, what do you think? I'll do my best, Madame Seynaeve, you won't hear any complaints about me." And as a fitter in the ERLA he did do his very best, always courteous, opening the door for Mama, until, eight weeks later, he was transferred to the ERLA main works in Leipzig, one of the fated hundred a month. He came into the office to have a bruised thumb bandaged by the Madonna of the ERLA and asked, "Madame Seynaeve, what's going on? My name's down on the transport list."

Mama looked at the list. "Yes, Jantje, so it is, what's wrong with that?" "But Madame Seynaeve, surely you know?" Mama examined the swollen, purple thumb. "All I know, Jantje, is that you did this to your thumb on purpose." "But, madame, didn't you talk to Madame Kerskens?" "Madame Kerskens from across the road? Yes, now that you mention it, she asks about you now and then. I tell her you're doing your best." "And is that all?" cried Jantje in despair. It turned out that Madame Kerskens, who lived across the road, had been asked by the lawyer Meester Vrielynck (a notorious Freemason, the heartless son of the great linguist Vrielynck of *Het Leeuw* fame, who had allowed his father to pine away in misery) to find out from Mama, her neighbor, whether Jantje Piroen might not be granted a deferment. In his extreme distress, it appeared that Jantje Piroen had turned to the anglophile advocate Vrielynck, reputed to be a Red, and Meester Vrielynck had claimed that he knew Mama well and would put in a good word for Jantje since Mama quite often intervened in this sort of affair, for a consideration, of course. So, if Jantje would just let him have two thousand francs, he would duly hand the sum over to Madame Seynaeve minus his commission of ten percent. Mama was so taken aback on hearing this that she reported it to Lausengier, who, in a Wotan-like rage, bellowed that the ERLA and the *Wehrmacht* were being compromised. At the trial the chic set, elegant perfumed knights in uniform, marched in: *"Heil, Heil, Heil."* Mama, too: *"Heil."* Madame Kerskens from across the road also said *"Heil"* but was so overcome with laughter that she was nearly thrown out. Mama listened to the whole rigmarole of accusations and turned round and saw Meester Vrielynck, face contorted, making signs to her, his red beard streaked with white, like some dirty old man who had been dribbling red cabbage. She had to give evidence and swear to tell the truth and nothing but the truth, so dear to Papa's heart, but when she turned and saw Meester Vrielynck sitting there looking so huddled up and miserable, tears sprang to her eyes and she said, "I'm so sorry, meneer, forgive me, but I'm afraid I have to tell the truth." And Lausengier, too, was consumed with pity when he saw his *Flämmchen* sob. Anyway, Jantje Piroen and Meester Vrielynck were given three and six months respectively. The lawyer said he would appeal. What with the sky-high piles of dossiers and all those Masonic accomplices in the administration, it would be quite some time before the appeal was heard. Jantje Piroen opted for prison and was thrown in with saboteurs, shirkers, and murderers. Mama talked every week about going to see him one of these days.

"It isn't the way it was in the golden days anymore," said Theo van Paemel, standing by the platen press. "Staf, you couldn't have chosen a worse moment to try your monkey tricks. At least old von Falkenhausen was someone you could reason with, you knew where you stood with him, we had freedom of action within limits, depending on his instructions, of course."

Papa gave the wheel of the paper-cutter a few turns, acting as if he didn't have a minute to lose. Louis was breathing hard with his mouth wide open.

"He's a kind of Chinaman, Von Falkenhausen, spent years in China with Chiang Kai-shek.. Not a joking man, a real Christian, always takes an interest in his subordinates. But he's being shunted out because they've caught on to the fact that he's been throwing any ordinance aimed at the Freemasons straight into his wastepaper basket."

"Oh, so he's one of those, is he?"

"Of course."

"They're everywhere," said Papa grimly.

"What's more, the nobility isn't respected nearly as much as it used to be. Monocles, and coronets on your writing paper, are rather *passé.* Perhaps that's all to the good, all those *Von* Thises and Thats getting together and conniving with their Franskiljon relatives. The war practically doesn't exist for those people, or borders either, they stick together, big money and blue blood do. Although I have to say the Old Man was fair. He would close his eyes to the black market when it involved the little man, what we call the gray market, but he really went after the big boys trafficking in metal."

A handsbreadth from Louis, who was getting a cramp in his calves, a file of small red ants hurried by, crossing another column just as unswerving, heavy congestion around a dozen or so crumpled toffee wrappers on which no dust had settled. Papa, secret, selfish nibbler.

"Raspe must have been busy with his dossier day and night. Or did he have any help? Who from, Staf?"

"Not from me."

"What about Groothuis?"

"Never. He wouldn't have soiled his hands."

"It's all about corruption, Staf, you dimwit! The acquisition office of the Four-Year Plan is implicated. That dossier is going to go straight to Jungclaus."

"Jungclaus!" exclaimed Papa, and then: "Who's that?"

Van Paemel's voice sounded fractionally slower, deeper, more loaded with menace. "If you don't know who Jungclaus is, my friend, then perhaps it'd be better if you didn't concern yourself with our affairs."

And without the slightest warning a bale of paper was thrust to one side. Dangerously alert, a lady's pistol in his hand, with the unblinking, glazed-over stare of a codfish, Van Paemel stood over Louis, legs planted apart. He raised one foot as if about to stamp on him.

"What in the world are you doing there?" shouted Papa.

"Spying on us for the British Intelligence Service," grinned Van Paemel. "Or for the Sûreté Générale."

"I was asleep."

"Does he always sleep in the workshop?"

"Never."

"And I never heard anything you were talking about, either," said Louis. Van Paemel turned away. Louis scrambled to his feet.

"I don't know what to do with the boy. He doesn't study, he doesn't take up any sport. All he does is lie around all day long with his nose buried in a book."

"If he were mine, I'd soon give him something to remember."

"The principal of the College told me they hadn't come across anything like him for years. One year up with the very best and the next year right at the bottom of the class."

"Perhaps he ought to have his mind changed for him during the holidays. Why don't you send him out to the countryside with the *Kinderlandverschickung?*"

"That's often crossed my mind," said Papa, who had never heard that blighted, fateful word.

Eleven o'clock Mass on Sunday in the Church of Our Lady, an occasion for the citizens of Walle to meet and for the ladies to parade their latest creations in hats and dresses and shoes, had lost much of its former attraction since Marnix de Puydt, who used to play the organ, sometimes facetiously interposing a jaunty little waltz motif in the middle of the more solemn passages, had been replaced by a music teacher who kept strictly to Bach, and while there was nothing wrong with that kind of chorale or prelude, people missed the unexpected.

The night disaster struck Haarbeke Institute, Amadeus wet his bed for the first time in years; during the days that followed he refused to eat or drink, and then he ran away, they didn't discover him until a week later, miles from his parents' home. He was lying with his mouth in a shallow puddle of muddy water, fieldmice crawling out of his stomach.

Aunt Nora, who had been so looking forward to Uncle Leon's return, was in a terrible state. Her husband had found himself another sweetheart in Germany for sure, because when he had come home he had hardly looked at his wife or at his daughter with her thyroid trouble, he had played a bit with Valentine the rabbit, and then he had left for his draughts club.

Aunt Nora produced a slice, the size of a packet of cigarettes, of the cake she had baked specially for him. The cake was as hard as rock, but Papa said it was nourishing.

"It's because you don't look after yourself, Nora, I mean look after yourself in the way a man appreciates," said Aunt Mona, and the whole afternoon, under the guidance of Cecile, who was learning about makeup at her ballet school, Aunt Nora was taken in hand by Mama and Aunt Mona. Her eyebrows were plucked, creams were applied, her hair was titivated and tinted, fluffed and frizzed, her elbows were pumiced, she was decked with chains and earrings, her bosom was pressed in and pushed up until the Sorrowful One was ready to be sent back to her Leon with a glimmer of hope in her suddenly almond-shaped eyes. "We'll get to hear the details soon enough, and if it doesn't work, well, that's when she can start thinking of a divorce."

"But where will she find someone else with such a good income and double ration cards?"

Sister St. Gerolphe, who in a first wave of gluttony had wolfed down everything that was set before her and then licked her plate clean but had now suddenly gone on a fast, no longer asked Grandma to tell her tales. Her armchair had been moved to a corner of the veranda, according to Grandma because of the view of the garden and also because it was easier to get to the big linen chest, according to Hélène because her mother could no longer bear the sight of the obdurate faster. With her back to the kitchen the nun sat praying out loud. With a view of her back, Grandma sat telling stories out loud.

"Oh, loving Heart, how much You suffer at this time, suffering the cruelest pains of all, a suffering commensurate with the millions and millions of sins committed by the whole human race."

377

". . . so he throws his jacket into a corner, after first taking out his money of course, because meneer does not deign to carry a *portemonnaie* like other people, oh no, meneer thinks that's a vulgar and petty-bourgeois thing to do, and he says that his jacket has to be sent to the cleaners because Hélène doesn't clean things nearly well enough for him, only Mona, the apple of his eye, can do it properly, but he can't bother his darling Mona with things like that, her plump little hands might get dirty, well, I pick the jacket up from the corner because leaving it lying there doesn't look very good, suppose someone comes to visit, you never can tell, and I can smell something, I say to myself, That isn't perfume, that isn't face powder, that isn't eau-de-toilette or after-shave lotion—have a guess, it was the smell not of a peony, not of a garden rose, no, one of those with the tiny buds, is that an eglantine? and I take another sniff and it comes from the buttonhole for sure, which means that he walked right up to our front door with a rose in his buttonhole given to him by some Rose of Jericho or other which he'd then quickly thrown into the gutter . . ."

". . . oh, love beyond praise, oh, adorable one, You who love Your heavenly Father with an unending love that floods Your Heart with infinite happiness yet rends it, too, when You behold the countless sins committed against the inexpressible goodness of Your Father . . ."

". . . so he turns up at the reception since he's due to give a lecture about native customs in the Congo, what does he know about that, I ask you? at most whether his shares in the Kasai are going up or down, and he certainly got burned with those despite the advice of his cousin the missionary, so he comes in and the headmaster says, 'Mijnheer Seynaeve, we are fortunate this evening in being able to welcome a good friend of yours.' 'Of mine?' he says. And who should be standing there out of the blue? His lady-love. That's right, the one from Koekelare, the one who works in the rubber factory there as, what is it again? a secretary? we all know the sort of thing, personal assistant, need I say more, and do you know what he did, that coward, he pretended not to see her, not to recognize her, not to know her, he said, 'I'm sorry, I'm afraid you've made some mistake, I don't know that person,' like Peter in the courtyard in Palestine, because he had seen that the canon was present, the one from the Bank of Roeselare, and for no amount of money would he have the canon suspect that he might have been getting some on the side, and she, she was so taken aback that she turned red as the setting sun, because what a letdown *en public,* because the poor girl most probably had declared beforehand, 'The distinguished speaker on the Congo this evening, well, I know him, I'll go further, he is my lover and our relationship is hole-and-corner because his wife is still alive,' and she picked up her *sacoche,* her handbag, and was about to whack his bald head with it, so they told me, but Madame Kerskens held her back, and then the ninny ran off, poor silly slut, I really feel sorry for her, even though she is his ladylove . . ."

". . . And Your Heart rejoiced at the prospect of so many other souls being saved for eternity by Your suffering, and the salvation of but one single soul is ample recompense for Your love, because Your Heart brims over with tenderness for mankind . . ."

The operations on the Tunisian front may be said to indicate a systematic improvement in our position. You don't say, Desirée.
In the eastern Caucasus our troops were able to disengage themselves systematically in the context of our mobile-warfare strategy. Pipe down, we've heard more than enough!
Despite stiff resistance, the defenders of Stalingrad could not stem the enemy advance from the West, with the result that our forces have had to be redeployed several kilometers to the rear. Tell me another, brother.

"Dear Heart, make me love You more and more."

According to Uncle Robert, the quality of the two pounds of minced pork he had given Papa for Grandma (at risk to his life, because the stronger the smell of burning that rose over crumbling Sicily and thawing Russia, the more officious the Germans and the inspectors grew, and in order to carry on your butcher's trade in peace many little packages were having to change hands here and there) had been first-class. Because the neighbors, the hard-to-please officers at the Flandria, and above all he himself and his wife Monique had eaten some and been none the worse for it.
According to Aunt Nora, a great deal of minced meat nowadays had poor-quality fat mixed in with it. "I'm not saying that you do that, Robert, all I'm saying is that some minced meat on the market has been tampered with." She also said that what Mama and Mona had rubbed on her face hadn't been *crème de Payot* because it had raised blisters. At which that little horror of a Cecile says, "I thought the intention was to raise something of Uncle Leon's." Smack! She got a slap, but not a real one because those two go together like bacon and eggs, they're thick as thieves,

speaking of which it seems that the Americans in North Africa are being fed *powdered* eggs. "Where's it all going to end? Any day now people won't be eating anything but little powders and pills, no, give me minced pork any day," said Grandma.

According to Papa, he hadn't wanted to hand over all the minced meat at once, because, knowing what gluttons his family were, he had decided to give us a pleasant surprise by producing another pound three days later. This he had hidden away for our own good in his workshop. "We have to think about tomorrow, don't we?"

"But why in your workshop? Why not in our cellar?" asked Mama.

"Because there are rats in the cellar. And because otherwise that one" (his pink unshaven double chin gesturing in Louis's direction) "would have gobbled it all up!"

"So where is the pound of meat now?"

"I had to throw it away. There was a maggot in it."

"One little maggot, what harm would that do, Staf?"

"You hang a hare for three days, after all."

"Negroes even bury their elephant meat."

"And Roquefort with maggots, there's nothing like it."

"It's all good protein, we can't get enough of that."

"In Stalingrad they would have danced the tango around a bit of minced meat like that!"

"I tasted it," said Papa, "and it was definitely off."

"You were wrong, Staf," said Grandpa. "We have to reconsider our attitude to food. What we used to think unfit for human consumption may well turn out to be the most nourishing food of all."

Grandma stuck her tongue out at him behind his back.

"Just think of the late Firmin the Bulgarian, who turned his nose up at us when we ate a dozen snails each with parsley butter."

"The late?" asked Mama. "What makes you say that?"

"Oh, but, Constance, no one's ever set eyes on him again."

In the empty corner, where lately Sister St. Gerolphe had sat with her face to the wall praying to the Sacred Heart, there now stood a hat rack.

Aunt Hélène had been the first to get up that morning. She had turned on the radio for the program "Slept well?"—mostly mandolin music—she had read in *Woman's Realm* about how to make soap at home, and she was talking more to herself than to the immobile figure of the nun when she said, "And now we'll warm up a bit of last night's soup," before she noticed that Sister St. Gerolphe had had diarrhea on the tiles and then that she had turned blue and vomited minced meat into her lap.

"How on earth did she manage to lay her hands on that, I'd put it on the top shelf behind the little statue of Father Damian!"

"If people are hungry, they'll stop at nothing."

"They'll even let their only son starve to death while they keep caramels hidden in their workshop," said Louis.

"You're going to feel the back of my hand," said Papa half-heartedly.

"What really is a shame, more than a shame if you ask me, is that only two days ago she said she'd decided to stop fasting because it was not Our Lord's intention that we should neglect ourselves."

Aunt Mona, Aunt Nora, Uncle Robert, and Louis walked behind the coffin. Women went on cleaning their front windows, bicyclists whistled, railway workers quarreled, the town of Walle did not stop and stare. No duke exclaimed, as at Louis XIV's funeral, "Croak, frogs, the sun has set!" Papa had wanted to print a fitting obituary notice, but he had nothing to go by, she hadn't carried an identity card.

"Straight into the pit, without kith or kin," said Grandma and rummaged in her handbag with the silver clasp representing two entwined snakes. She pressed a twenty-franc note into Louis's hand. "Go to the bakery and buy us some nun's-farts with that. It's the only thing we can do in her memory."

In silence each one ate the brittle, foamy meringue that melted on the tongue. Louis licked the last crumb out of the paper bag, the milky white ash flew into his nostrils. "You can tell all right that they've been made with egg white from chickens fed on fish meal," said Papa.

"Makes no difference," said Grandma.

"You can tell me, Constance, I won't be cross, I promise to keep calm, I'm not going to lose my temper, but for the love of God, out with it! Where was it, the first time, you don't have to give me any details, but where was it?—I know you don't want to tell me, it's a delicate matter, but when was it, at least tell me that!"

Papa bawled, "What did he *do?*"

Their bedsprings squeaked, Mama turning over.

"Please, Constance, we're still friends, after all!"

"It was during the Yser Pilgrimage," said Mama hoarsely.

That rat in his maze, that low-down sneak of a Theo van Paemel, kept his word. The *Kinderlandverschickung* sent the apostate Seynaeve junior to the Strelenau lake district in Mecklenburg. There games and folk dancing awaited him, handicrafts and amateur dramatics, nature study and drill. Papa had to sign a letter declaring that Louis had no strange diseases. Louis was annoyed by the efficiency and dispatch with which his mother had his suitcase packed a week in advance.

"I'm going to the Far East."

"Germany isn't the Far East," said Simone. "The Far East is where the Chinese live."

"Even so, have a look at the map, it's way far to the east of here."

"You'll have to give me back my photograph."

"What's given is given."

"If you say so. I must go in. To make syrup."

"Cough syrup?"

"No, a tonic. One of my father's recipes."

"Will you think of me?"

"When?"

"Tonight."

"Yes."

"Really?"

"Before I fall asleep I always think about what I've done during the day."

"I won't be seeing you for a long time."

"Four weeks, that'll soon pass. Your hair is too long."

"I'm having it cut."

"At Felix's?"

"No, my mother will do it," said Louis and felt ashamed. Simone was wearing an almost transparent blouse, you could see her brassiere. He kissed her on the cheek.

"All right, that'll do," she said, her melancholy expression entirely appropriate, it seemed to him, although most things made her sad. He took her hand and tickled her palm because Haegedoorn had said that women found that irresistible. She didn't notice. The bell of the pharmacy tinkled like the sort of bell with which well-to-do families in Mecklenburg villas summon their butler, who then turns out to be Lord Lister in disguise, irresistible to women because of his steely gaze.

Mecklenburg.

Sixth day. How quiet it is here. At night I sometimes hear the clatter of horse's hooves. The beet fields stretch farther than the eye can see. It's foggy a lot of the time. The dialect here is a bit like Flemish. They say *"vertellen,"* not *"erzählen,"* for "tell." Most of the men walk with a stoop.

As if they're looking for something in the soil. The man I'm lodging with is called Gustav Vierbücher—"Fourbooks." But he can't read properly. He's too short to be called up. He goes around sticking an iron rod into the soil and then examining the end. Is he prospecting for oil? His wife is called Emma, like Göring's wife, and she's as fat as her, too. She's always nudging me and telling me to hurry up. But she doesn't say what for. It rains a lot. If I behave myself, Emma says, I can take back the figurine of a dancer, made by the SS porcelain works in Munich, as a present for my mother. They have funny stoves over here, tiled and built into a corner of the room. They sleep under a bolster (?), too, which is much too hot. There are also lots of insects in strange shapes and colors that keep buzzing through the house. Maurice would have had the time of his life studying them. I often cry at night, but I'm learning to control myself.

Seventh day. I'm woken up five or six times every night by Gustav peeing laboriously into a tin can. He sighs and groans while he's doing it. Yesterday Emma said I was ungrateful. Because I didn't like the pink soup, which, according to the packet, was made of strawberries.

Eighth day. Gustav and Emma made me go to the town hall where the youngest members of the Hitler Youth are taught choral recitation, how to cut out figures with a jigsaw, and to make little wooden airplanes. This afternoon I recited the poem of Guido Gezelle's that goes "Oh, crinkly, wrinkly, wat'ry thing, with your black cap on," etc. But when I had to repeat it, I said, "Oh, stinking, winking, paltry thing, with your knapsack on." No one noticed any difference. Later, a kind of Solstice celebration with a campfire. Which is allowed here. Because Allied aircraft don't fly over this area.

Twelfth day. I help Emma with her household chores and Gustav with feeding the livestock, but even when there is nothing to do and Emma knits and Gustav sleeps by the stove she can't bear it if I just sit and read *Simplicissimus* (ten issues). She says I'm lucky not to be a German boy, or else I'd be taught what's what.

Fifteenth day. Emma says I'm as dirty as a Jew. That just like the Jews I don't change my underwear often enough. I have the definite impression that Gustav is shrinking day by day, that soon he won't be able to look over the table.

Sixteenth day. I taught the Hitler Youth to sing "Ti-yi-yippy-yippy-yay." They think it's a Flemish folk song.

Eighteenth day. I have discovered a forest in this flat countryside. I'll go and have a look at it tomorrow.

Nineteenth day. What a story. I am writing it down now so that I can laugh at it later. I set off to walk toward the forest in the distance. For hours. It was like a mirage. I tried getting there as the crow flies, climbing through thorn hedges and wading through brooks. For hours and hours. Then I got tired and fell asleep in a cornfield. After about an hour I resumed the expedition but finally found I couldn't go on anymore because I was in the middle of a bog. So there I stayed, stranded on a kind of small island. Midges, dragonflies, and horseflies attacked me. Then a school (?) of water rats swam close by. I retraced my steps, but when I reached the spot in the cornfield where I had rested before, three peasants jumped out at me. I couldn't understand what they were shouting, it didn't sound anything like German. But I did make out the word "parachutist." Me, at my age! One of them was carrying a scythe, like the Grim Reaper. I was taken to a farmyard. The youngest peasant, who was called Ernst and was lame, seemed to be some sort of village policeman. He took me home (home, sic!) and ordered me never again to stray beyond the center of the village.

Twenty-second day. The days are very long. I found the Evening Star, the Seven Sisters, and the two Bears. The Milky Way, too, of course. Gustav the dwarf never takes his eyes off my fingers when I draw ink caricatures of Churchill, Roosevelt, and Stalin. He doesn't know how I do it.

Twenty-third day. What next! I heard *"Der Wind hat mich (mir?) ein Lied erzählt"* on the radio and told Emma that Zarah Leander had a wooden leg. She was so shocked that she ran screaming out into the street and brought several villagers back to the house with her. Including two with wooden legs, one with only one lung, and the local party secretary, who must have weighed well over three hundred pounds. They all started yelling and cursing and looked as if they were ready to lynch me. The secretary, who was acting as camp squad leader, seized me by the collar of my shirt and tore it. He began interrogating me. Among other things, he wanted to know what sort of father I had to bring me up so badly. I said that my father was with the Gestapo back home. That made a great impression. If Papa only knew, he'd be crowing with pride. They went on at me a bit longer but finally slunk off. And the best part? Emma has never been so friendly. She even made doughnuts, but they were too heavy and Gustav had them all.

Twenty-sixth day. Gustav and Emma say that they're upset I'm leaving, that they've grown used to me. *"Wie ein Sohn,"* they say. I said that I can never be a good son, not even to my own parents. Emma started to cry. That's when I called her *"Mutti."* Gustav said, *"Und ich?"* So I called him *"Vati."* Tomorrow I'll be given the porcelain dancer and Gustav will take me to the station on the back of his bicycle. *Good-bye,* Strelenau.

Drunk with sleep, Louis stood at the window that must never be opened, not even to wave at your happy parents in the distance, because at the last moment a cinder from the engine could get into your eye. And then, waving the little swastika flag as instructed, he rode into Antwerp on the footboard, wreathed in steam, overwhelmed by all the shouts and calls in familiar, homely Antwerp Flemish, and spotted Mama standing on the platform as promised. How small she is, I will put it down in my notebook tonight; she doesn't even come up to the shoulder of the Flemish Guardsman beside her, and she has dyed her hair dark-red.

Mama tried to lift him up, kissed him frantically on the cheeks, the neck, pressed him to her bosom. He let his little flag fall to the ground but nobody noticed. Although it was against the laws of nature, she looked a bit like Papa's sister, Nora, she had no makeup on, and there were pink spots on her cheeks as if she'd been rubbing them with that torn-up fur of hers. She was up to something, because she was skipping, humming, whinnying, linking arms with the young Flemish Guardsman, who picked up Louis's suitcase with a oafish grin.

On the train to Walle, through the black landscape for hours and hours, the thick smoke of the overcrowded compartment, the chitchat and the swearing of the cardplayers, which died down only when inspectors came by.

"Oskar has been kind enough to come along with me, to make sure nothing happens to me, that I don't lose the tickets or hang around waiting for the wrong train. He's been looking after me very well."

The oaf mumbled bashfully that he had done no more than his duty.

The train stopped in the middle of rapeseed fields. The only light came from lit matches and from the reflected glowworms in the hollow-eyed countenances of the cardplayers. In the distance, searchlight beams. An old man sitting pressed close up to Louis was belching the whole time, it never stopped, eructomania. Cursing men waving lanterns examined the hissing, steaming undercarriage of their compartment. Chained dogs in distant farmyards. The sudden, violent rustling of invisible tree crowns. This was Belgium, and immeasurably far away, almost nonexistent, lay Mecklenburg, a flat, virgin planet with here and there a cripple straying across the beet fields. Belgium was here and now, crammed with bleating, smelly, frightened people. Louis drew Churchill in the steamed-up window, three semicircles for the chins, a small circle for the pug nose, the drooping lip with cigar, a high round forehead with six hairs on the side, then the bow tie underneath.

For the third time Mama asked what the food had been like, the beds. If he had brought back all his washing, both his pairs of shoes, his pajamas. What the people had been like. Downhearted about Germany's losses?

"Once they came after me with a scythe."

"Well, I never!" But she did not ask why, when, how.

Some men and women were taken off the train, they were ordered to put their bags and cases down beside the track. One of the smugglers grumbled, a gendarme went up to him, caught hold of his nose, tweaked it, went on tweaking. Louis saw the tears spring from the man's eyes.

The train rumbled jerkily on, the old man beside Louis told a series of jokes in a hurried, hoarse voice.

"It's only because I have you, Louis . . ." said Mama to the window-pane.

"If I didn't have you, my boy, I know what I'd do then . . .

"I'd put aside some chocolate for you, Swiss milk chocolate with nuts, to give you at the station, but it hadn't been on the table ten minutes when he made off with it.

"Meerke has had all her teeth pulled. Uncle Omer has gone mad, he's with the Brothers of St. Vincent.

"It's as if you've been away for years."

These were the opening skirmishes. Something has happened to her, to this cigarette-puffing, unmade-up woman facing me. She's like this chaotic train, which is traveling ever farther from that foggy realm, flat as a pancake, where choral recitations resounded, where order and regularity reigned, among the maimed, where I struck the only disorderly note. We must be approaching Waregem, one of Grandpa's lady-loves lives there, a teacher who was once given a good hiding by Aunt Mona. Why do I suddenly remember that? Because, just like Mama sitting opposite me now, it involves adult-er-y, that adult game, the game that erring adults play.

"He's done it now, your father. He's finally managed to get the better of me."

"Shush!" said Louis as if to a little one.

"The better of *us*. Oh, he can rub his hands now, pat himself on the back, congratulations!"

"Sh, sh!"

"It doesn't matter. Oskar might as well hear it all." Oskar pretended to be asleep, as if he had no wish to listen to her frantic outpourings, those words that tumbled out, as urgently as from the old man just now with his tired jokes, before they could arrive at that cursed little town of her sorrow, in the night air of her downfall.

"He had it all fixed up with his pal Theo, the one with his dirty fingers in every pie. And they had to fix it, because what evidence did they really have against Henny? Not a blessed thing, and yet he had to justify himself, a man of his caliber, appointed by Von Falkenhausen himself and turned down for military service by the strictest of army doctors on account of his chronic *Magenschleimhautentzündung,* his gastritis. How could they say that a man of his moral stature took money to get rich men's sons off the transports? That he supposedly spoke out against the regime? What exactly was it he reportedly said in the restaurant at the Swan Hotel? He never denied it, on the contrary, even when I begged him to deny it, '*Liebchen,* swear you didn't do it, tell them you never said anything of the kind.' '*Flämmchen,*' he said, 'if I can't tell the truth to my own people!' "

"What didn't he deny, Mama?" asked Louis.

"That he had said, 'Total victory is its own undoing.' And it wasn't even his own saying but some big German thinker's, you must know which, you've always got your nose in a book."

"All right. What else?"

"That he drew attention to himself by drinking too much *Sekt,* champagne, in public." (*Sekt, Sekt,* Mama, like the *Jetzt, Jetzt,* you used to say in '14–'18, a girl sitting at the piano.) "But it so happens that he's not allowed to drink *Sekt* on account of his stomach, and even if he had drunk *Sekt* by the bucketful, surely he can do what he likes with his own money that he inherited from his family."

"Has he left Walle?"

She wiped her face, the train slowed down.

"*Kriegsverwendungsfähig,*" she said bleakly, "fit for active service."

"Where is he?"

"An antiaircraft battery. But I'm not saying where. He's going to write to me. But I won't say where he's going to send the letter. I wouldn't put it past you to tell your father."

"Me, Mama?"

Papa came down the stairs blinking, a Belgian army sweater over his pajamas. "Well, well, well."

"Did we wake you up, Papa?"

"No. Of course not. I was waiting up for you. What else! I just lay down for a while to read my copy of Cyriel Verschaeve's *Judas,* because there's talk of my playing one of the members of the Sanhedrin, which means that I've got to go through the whole thing at least once, of course. And believe me, it's heavy going!"

Mama yawned. "Not too early tomorrow, Louis."

"Doesn't he have to go to school?" asked Papa in a reed-thin little voice. Mama took off her coat and fell onto the sofa, which had blankets on it, and a lipstick-smeared pillow. She kicked off her shoes and pulled a blanket over her head. "Turn off the light," she said in a muffled voice. Papa said, "Come on." In the kitchen he asked, "Did you get along all right? We'll talk all about it in the morning. But not too early."

Mijnheer Tierenteyn, together with leading anglophile citizens, had been arrested and held hostage because some prize idiot had stuck a butcher knife into a German corporal's back in the dark. And that's the sort of person who calls himself a member of the White Brigade!

It would not have surprised us to hear that Eric, the son of an insurance agent and Aunt Hélène's suitor, was involved in such affairs, directly or indirectly. He listened to Radio London every day, reported that the coal output in the Ruhr was dropping off, which meant, of course, that arms production was declining as well. And that the German national debt was running close to two hundred and fifty billion, which meant that within a few months their debts would be as great as all their national resources put together. He might be good at counting, that young man, but he was too scared to ask Grandpa, the patriarch, for Aunt Hélène's hand. He was afraid of Grandpa because the old man had turned on him one day when he'd come to our place and, with the front door still wide open and thus in full view of all Walle, had made the V-sign with two fingers. "It was just for a laugh, Mijnheer Seynaeve!" "For a laugh? What's there to laugh about, you blithering idiot?" said Grandpa, so furious that he forgot his High Flemish.

Eric also declared he felt sure that Uncle Florent had sent them a message over Radio London. "Listen to what I picked up. Pom-pom-pom-*pom*. The Flower sends greetings and a sign from the Grottos of Han. What else can that mean but 'sign' plus 'greetings,' which is *'ave'* in Latin, making Sign-ave or Seynaeve. And Flower in Latin is *'flor,'* the Grottos of Han, Han is pronounced *'ent'* in French, making Florent."

"Bless my soul!" cried Grandma. "My poor heart!"

"He can solve crossword puzzles in three minutes," said Aunt Hélène. "Cryptograms as well."

"But what is Florent trying to tell us?" asked Grandma. "And over the radio, too! That must have cost him a fortune."

"That he's alive, Mother. Isn't that enough?"

"It's enough," she said. "Although all that Latin, that doesn't sound like our Florent."

"An officer in the BBC probably did it for him, Mother."

Grandma cried softly. "Even if it isn't our Florent, it still makes me happy."

"I, who'd do literally anything I could for her," said Papa. "And what do I get in return? A slap in the face. And that hurts, my boy, believe me it does. I was eating my heart out trying to think of something that would get her back to normal, healthy, the way a woman should be in her home, and then suddenly I hit upon the very thing. You may or may not know that we're no longer putting on *Judas* in the Municipal Theater because *Monsieur le directeur* Alfred Lagasse is of the opinion that people like us can't speak verse and that *Judas* is over the head of your average Wallenaar, when we all know that Monsieur is actually shitting in his perfumed evening trousers for fear that the wind may be turning against the Germanic people so to speak, so he doesn't want to pay tribute to that great Black Priest and famous Fleming in his theater any longer. Right, I said to our dramatic society, 'Why don't we put on Heijermans's *The Good Hope* instead? That always goes over well, and I've just been reading the play, it's magnificent, it may be Dutch, but it has Flemish seamen in it as well, and all I want is a fisherman's role,' and then I suddenly thought, Why shouldn't Mama join us and take the role of a fisherman's wife, she can be both melancholy and charming, I mentioned it to the society and everyone agreed, except who? Your mother. I said, 'It'll do you a world of good, when you're acting you're being somebody else and you can forget all about who you really are.' "

" 'You go to hell,' she said. And do you know what happened next? Somebody from the *Kommandantur* came to see me and said, 'It's just as well we know you, Mijnheer Seynaeve, or we'd have thrown you in the clink right away.' And why? Because it turns out that Heijermans was a Jew! Who'd ever have thought it! With a good Flemish name like Heijermans, almost like Heymans, who got the Nobel Prize in Stockholm."

"What for?" asked Louis.

"Something in chemistry, or was it metabolism? And then it turned out that this Jew, like all Jews, was actually called Samuel, yes, really, Samuel Falkland, if you please! And wait, this tops it all. I mentioned my little mishap to your mother and all she did was fall down laughing. There she was, helpless with laughter for a good quarter of an hour, like some sort of crazy woman, and all because I'd nearly ended up behind bars.

"If you ask me, though I've been of two minds about it for some time, your mother must be going through the change of life. It's a bit early, I have to admit, but it's the only possible explanation."

The Rock asked, "And how were things over there?" and meant, Over there in enemy territory. He looked less and less like a teacher, emaciated as Father de Foucauld in his flowing cassock, wasting away in a desert, inconsolable.

"Are they having a hard time, the ordinary people? Where did the Flemish boys stay? I thought they were being put into camps, and that only the little ones under ten were being boarded out with foster parents. What were the people like in that village?"

"Just like here," said Louis.

"Can't you be more precise?"

"No."

"Are they resigned, for instance? More so than the Belgians? Yes? Understood. Are they more irrational, more intolerant, more megalomaniacal? Yes? Understood. Did the farmer who put you up admire Hitler?"

"He worshiped him."

"Exactly."

"There will always be leaders, Father."

"Yes. Always this mimetic longing. The passionate embrace of leaders. People want to admire, to be swept off their feet by fairy tales, by that one sanctifying myth. Understood? Because in that sort of trance, reality slips away, fear becomes anesthetized. Understood. You may go now."

That afternoon the Rock told the class about the Romans, whose sense of duty made them take up arms against the State. About how desperate and how obstinate they were. How, so as to be capable of doing the tyrant to death, they first disparaged him, made him look less than human. I am the only one who knows that he is talking about Hitler. At least in this class. The close-knit group of young men in the Rhetoric class would have caught on right away. They are the Rock's bodyguards, in their company he can let himself go, with them his mumblings about the old Spirit of Europe, about the Promethean longing, strike straight home. If you come from one of the better families or are an aristocrat like the Rock, you find it easier to believe in a God embodying unworldly ambitions, hovering over, under, outside economic and social conditions, a God who is will and energy and what else? Oh yes, beauty. Something has been happening in the College since my German holiday, that is quite apparent, and at the center of it all is the Rock, stricken and reckless all at once.

The Rock said, without losing any of his fragile, tired grace, "My kindest regards to your dear mother."

His dear mother cast a look of mutual understanding at . . .

Mama looked in a peculiar manner at . . .

Louis's mother caught the meaningful glances of the pharmacist Paelinck, who had come to have labels and folders printed for his blood-strengthening, vitality-enhancing, fortifying St. Martin's Syrup, his own formula. Canon de Londerzeele had solved the problem of the name. St. Martin could be shown on the label as a young soldier rending his cloak in twain and holding it out to a poor shivering old man. Couldn't Papa see, bending over his screens and plates, that the pharmacist was giving Mama looks like caresses and that she seemed to be asking, no, begging, for more?

"What was it like in Germany, Louis? It must have been grand, eh?"

"Yes, Mijnheer Paelinck. And strange . . ."

"That's what I thought. To us it seems strange that they should follow their leaders so singlemindedly. It's a big country, and that's why they think big, too. We, Belgians or Flemings, being a small nation, cannot help thinking in small terms, because we don't count for very much and could be swept away at any time like pieces of dirt. That's why we take international problems with a pinch of salt. But the salt corrodes our vision, of course."

Mama knitted her eyebrows, with their bristly new growth. "Staf, won't you show Mijnheer Paelinck the little dancing figurine Louis brought back with him?"

"I thought you didn't like it, that you didn't want it in the living room . . ."

"I would like to hear what Mijnheer Paelinck thinks of it."

"Oh, all right then, you'd better come along with me to the workshop, Mijnheer Paelinck."

"No, Staf, you bring it here. You can see the man's just having his coffee."

As soon as Papa had left, Mama put her finger to her lips, stroked Louis's hair, and moved close to the pharmacist, who gave her a small brown bottle of pink pills. *"Motus,* Louis, movement," said the pillmaker, who then declared that the porcelain dancer was too Jugendstil-like for him. "That sort of thing is a bit out of date, but even so it's good for its genre. In art, too, we can't stick to what was modern yesterday. Although, of course, we have to learn from the past. So long as we preserve our own identity. And that is what I have against the German-Flemish Labor League, it wants to crush our own Flemish soul with its pan-Germanic paganism."

It was Sister Imelda who was sitting in Louis's room, because although her face had been replaced by a featureless, pumicelike tumor, he recognized her peasant bosom, her smell of manure. She spread her knees, and from between the black billows she carefully pulled a skinned rabbit, or was it a cat? Unfortunately he couldn't see the skull properly, she stroked the naked, blood-spattered carcass to which tufts of fur still clung, the pupils were not slit-shaped but round, like little pink pills.

He was woken up by the siren, the antiaircraft guns and Papa calling him. Papa always called him, vigilant watchman of the night, even though he knew that Louis would still not follow him and Mama down to the air raid shelter with its crowds of quaking, praying neighbors.

Through the attic window he caught a brief glimpse of Mama's flowered peignoir. Had she waited for me even an instant before fleeing to the shelter? A fraction of a second? Had she looked back at the house?

The town went up in flames and clouds of soot, thuds and reverberations. Louis shouted the pom-pom-pom-*pom* of the English radio at the top of his voice. Beams, exploding meteors, lava gushing over Walle, St. Roch's tower tilting, falling. From his lookout in the attic of his shabby parental home the budding tyrant watched a piece of Europe vanish, his whole body overwhelmed by the utmost exultation. *Rache*, vengeance.

When things died down, both in the pit of his stomach and in the air, while the voracious sound of the flames mingled with moans rising to the sky, he walked on tiptoe, though there was no need for that, to Mama's bedside table. In the glow of the fiery town he fumbled in her crocodile-skin bag and found a diary in which every day of the last two weeks had been marked, a comb with a wisp of red hair, a mother-of-pearl powder compact, some tubes, an almost empty little bottle of Vendôme eau-de-toilette, an eyebrow pencil, lipstick, matches, six broken cigarettes, a small handkerchief that rustled when he unfolded it, hairpins, safety pins, a bill from the Golden Lamb Hotel in Waregem, double room with breakfast, a picture postcard of Munich without any writing on it, a picture postcard from Stettin of a Greek hero, elbow on knee, contemplating a woman with the lower body of a dragon, Mama's name written in round, almost typographically perfect letters on the address side, without street or town or postage stamp, and next to it, almost illegible—smudged by tears—such words as *"zunächst beschlossen,"* "provisionally decided," and *"stümperhaft,"* bungling," and the signature *"Dein Henny,"* and the ground plan of a small house, poorly sketched. The little bottle with the pink pills wasn't there, his nails scraped up grit.

"The pills are for calming me down," said Mama. "I'm not very well, if I don't take them I start climbing the wall. I hope you never get like that, walking around completely out of your mind because someone isn't there. But I know you, nothing like that will ever happen to you. You, you're an eel, you wriggle your way through anything, and that's the best way to be. If only I'd been born like that, but the blood of the Bossuyts won't be denied, it was our Omer's ruin as well.

"I wonder how long it takes to get certified as a nurse. A couple of years? Or aren't they all that fussy these days? According to Mona, the clinical training alone takes about four months and you have to sign up for the duration. But that doesn't get you certified, of course. And the worst thing is that you aren't allowed to smoke. Even so, I'm going to join the Red Cross, but only on certain conditions, or else I can see them sticking me in some maternity home in the middle of nowhere. No, I want to go to Russia, it must be lovely there now in the summer. Yes, if you must know it's to be back with him. He's on the Don, but I'm not going to tell you where. Because he's right on the front lines, that's the sort of man he is, not the kind to sit on his backside behind some desk in Norway. No, Louis, I'm not saying where he is. You're not *forced* to help me. I'm big enough to buy a good map and to ask passers-by for directions. Will you spare a thought now and then for your mother stumbling around in the cold, from one icy train to the next?"

"It's summer there now."

"But it's so short. The summer there is so short."

But she never left, she was too indolent, too frightened, too disorganized to pursue her ideal through fair weather and foul. And because she did not go and was unhappy, she turned on her only son. "What in God's name is to become of you? You have no prospects, you don't do your homework, you're not interested in how the war is going in Russia, you never bring any friends home, I never hear you speak about girls like other boys your age . . ."

"Our Louis is a late bloomer," said Aunt Nora. "And God help us when a late bloomer blooms, there's no holding him then."

"Look at Victor Hugo," said Eric, Hélène's official fiancé, "he was a virgin until he married at the age of twenty-five, and from then until the day he died in his eighties he could never keep his hands off a woman."

"Our Louis? He isn't going to let any woman lead him by the nose, eh, my boy?" said Aunt Mona, who, miracle of miracles, had heard from her Ulli, in a hospital in Cairo and thinking of only one thing, of her. So there was still such a thing as true fidelity.

"Louis will never become a skirt-chaser," said Aunt Hélène.

"I'm not so sure," said Mama.

"Victor Hugo ate two oranges every morning, peel and all. And when he died, they found a notebook in a secret drawer in his desk with the names of all the servant girls he had had, together with how much he'd given them in tips."

"That'll do, Eric."

"To me, Louis is more of a Thijs Glorieus type."

"You mean the Glorieus family in Little Pope Street, the corset shop?"

"No, Mona, from the book by Walschap that I lent you."

"Oh yes, *merci*. You said that it was spicy. I'm used to stronger fare. A few passages perhaps, but there wasn't really enough meat in it for me. Not that it wasn't well written, it's true to life all right, but it's more about human feelings in general."

(If you've kissed someone properly six times and have taken her bra off twice, can you consider her your sweetheart? Last time, I lifted Simone's skirt, but she slapped my hand away. It was a full moon, though.)

"You're not interested in anything. You can't spend your whole life just reading books. What do you really want? Your report cards couldn't be worse, yet you aren't stupid. You need to have some aim in life, something to work for, something you can cling to, that's what you have to go out and find. Otherwise it's all a waste of time, day in day out, gray and drab. Is there really nothing at all you want to do? You draw so well, why don't you develop that?"

"Like Uncle Leon, Mama? Is that my model?"

"Leon has done some magnificent watercolors, they'll still be around hanging in people's homes long after he's gone. That's art."

"And suppose all those houses got burned down, razed to the ground?"

"All of them?"

"Yes. Where would Uncle Leon be then with all his art?"

"That'll never happen. It can't. People aren't that stupid. They throw bombs, yes, but there are limits."

One house that was still left standing was Dolf Zeebroeck's, the most modern in Walle, designed by the master himself, a copy of the Castle of the Counts in Ghent, with its battlements and turrets in egg-yellow glazed brick, but naturally with all modern conveniences, such as a bathroom and two toilets, you need that with six children, though the house isn't easy to heat.

One of the six, a cross-eyed, fair little fellow, blocked the way when the neo-Gothic door swung open. He looked suspiciously at Louis's briefcase, crammed with colored pencils and paper in various sizes and shades from Papa's workshop. "Do they know you're coming? Yes? What time? For how long? No longer than half an hour. Because Dada is going to the country with us, to collect potatoes."

Around the walls of a winding staircase, wide enough to allow swordfighting knights in armor to pass, hung hundreds of black-and-white prints in that nebulous, streaky style so renowned far beyond our borders. Dolf Zeebroeck, the creator of all this, wrapped in a brown monk's-habit, was at work behind an immense drawing board. His spiky white hair, his large-pored, turned-up, red nose, his pockmarked skin, were those of a Flemish Mind, there could be no doubt about that. He wore a broad copper bracelet with Arabic motifs around his wrist, which must have made it awkward to draw. The room was exceptionally clean and smelled like a hospital. An antique crucifix looked down on Louis with compassion, almost like Dolf Zeebroeck himself, who inspected Louis as if wanting to memorize his lamentable features forever, sketch his miserable proportions after just one glance.

The still wet drawing on which he was working showed one Norman setting violently upon another with a raised ax, their coats of mail flapping, the clouds rushing by.

"D'you see that cactus? Well, sit down there and draw it. You can interpret it any way you like. So long as it doesn't turn into a Picasso, of course, haha." Louis laughed, too. "No, no," he managed.

The cactus was made up of three lumpy parts, there was gray wool around its spines, the pot was red earthenware. What else is there? I must concentrate, banish everything that is not cactus from my mind, give it the full attention with which all great masters focus on the world. Louis tried to look at the cactus just as Dolf Zeebroeck had done a moment ago at him, absorbing it, his look being transformed into sheer brainpower. He kept his eyes fixed on the cactus as he spread out his drawing implements.

When he had done the outlines of plant and pot, the master said: "Your cactus is too big for that sheet of paper, the proportions aren't right, can't you see that?" Quickly Louis erased his sketch. The master continued to fill in the gleaming black robes of his Normans. Louis applied shadows with his Conté-8.

"I said draw, not fiddle about. The line, young man, the line."

The eraser. At last the thing began to look like a cactus, even like the one in front of him, especially when Louis squinted at it as you often see visitors doing in galleries. But the color of the pot was quite unlike that of the real pot, because Louis had no pencil in that shade of red.

"No, no," said Dolf Zeebroeck, a small brush between his teeth. "No coloring during the first lessons." He snatched the paper away, crumpled it up, and threw it with a sure aim into the wastepaper basket at the foot of the Crucified.

After a quarter of an hour a new, black-and-white cactus appeared. The little spines with their slanting shadows, the wooly tufts, the way the light fell across the table in the shape of a Zeppelin, the little halos around the spines. Louis leaned backward.

"And he saw that it was good," said Zeebroeck.

"It's a bit too black, but I can always erase it."

"What do you want to erase?"

"Where it's too dark."

Zeebroeck lit a pipe. "It isn't up to much," he said, not unkindly. "You've just been sitting there fussing with the details, these little bubbles over here, those little dots over there. But what about the line, man, the line?"

"Shouldn't I draw the details, then?"

"Only to serve the line!" (Of course! The stiff, elongated black line of the master's own drawings, woodcuts, stained-glass windows!)

"I could have drawn it in your style, too, Mijnheer Zeebroeck."

"Young man, for forty years I've been slaving away at that line, day in, day out, Sundays included, and you think you . . ."

Louis took a new sheet of paper, just as the cross-eyed little boy came into the room. "Dada, it's getting dark. And you promised . . ."

"Just a minute, Godfried!"

"No, not just a minute! Now! A promise is a promise!" The boy slapped his own cheek with the flat of his hand. As if to quell an uncontrollable fit of temper.

"Right . . ." sighed Zeebroeck. "That'll be forty-five francs." Louis paid, Mama had thought it would be thirty francs. And for a full hour.

Godfried came and looked at the cactus from Louis's standpoint. The smudged shape with the little spikes remained in place, did not go up in smoke.

"It's another Picasso, Dada."

The master pinched his red, turned-up nose. "He has a lot to learn." He noticed Louis's confusion, rubbed the paper cactus with the bowl of his pipe.

"That's what you get when you do your work in bits and pieces, you don't see the wood for the trees. The essence escapes you."

"What essence?" exclaimed Louis. "If all the bits and pieces are right, doesn't the essence emerge by itself?"

"My poor boy," said the pockmarked monk.

"It is another Picasso, isn't it, Dada?"

"My poor boy, what should you have noticed right away, drawn before anything else? Come now, think, look at the plant, at the spines, at how the spines are planted in the cactus, in every cactus, as it happens." Something began vaguely to dawn on Louis. The demonic master sucked on his pipe.

"He doesn't know, Dada."

"Can't you see that the spines are distributed *evenly,* that the distance between this little spine here and that little spine there is the same, that there is a pattern?"

"A pattern," said Godfried. Zeebroeck pulled his habit over his head. Underneath he wore workmen's overalls, which he started to unbutton.

Oh, my ignorant, impotent, backward, nearsighted stupidity! It was true, the little puzzle yielded its ridiculously obvious secret to everyone except a brainless idiot like myself! The perfect harmony of those diamond shapes! God creates regular patterns! And all I did was copy bits of wooly thread.

"Thank you very much, Mijnheer Zeebroeck." Seething, Louis ran down the winding staircase, left the front door wide open. He failed to see connections between things, that was true. For one reason or another he found this proof of his inability to recognize the basis, no, the very structure of things, incredibly depressing. He swore all the way back home. Others were able to gain an immediate, coherent, rational picture of complex, fragmented objects, facts, incidents all around them, but not he, no matter how hard he tried, but then he didn't try very hard, because he didn't know how to. Patently obvious superficiality, that was his way, how humiliating! His cactus would never have become a real cactus, just some strange, scruffy, improbable growth, one of those cactuses from North Africa that Dirty Dick and his friend Odiel (actually *Odile,* something else he had not grasped until later) kept dreaming about, a little fantasy of a homemade castle in the air, a sandcastle of mirages. And for forty-five francs! Less than half an hour! By the ruins of St. Roch's Church he noticed that he had left his briefcase with the colored pencils behind.

But never, never would he go back to that modern version of the Castle of the Counts, where the truth was dealt out like a slap in the face.

As he reached home, Vandam, on whose shoulders the once flourishing Seynaeve printing works now rested, was slipping through the door. The passage still smelled of the turpentine Vandam had cleaned his hands with. There was no one at home. Vandam was playing truant.

Because he had seen his father only yesterday with a suspicious bulge in his cheek, Louis went in search of toffees in the workshop. In Papa's small office he came across crumbs of fresh cake among all the accounts and bank statements. He looked behind the bags filled with waste paper, the cardboard boxes full of oil rags, tried to imagine what his father would do before he took a postprandial nap in his office, as he walked from the paper-cutter past the dusty remains of the rotary press to his desk. Where and when did he scrabble somewhere for his always replenished supply of honey-sweet toffees with nuts and pieces of nougat? In a rickety cupboard that had been put up around the washbasin there was a carefully arranged pile of books by Zane Grey and John Knittel that certainly didn't belong there, absolutely not, Louis rummaged about and triumphantly turned up two already opened packets of shortbread, half a bar of fondant chocolate, a fist-sized bag of toffees. Something started to crow deep inside him, Erwin Rommel, the Desert Fox, gave Louis a field marshal's salute. Louis broke off a finger-sized piece of chocolate, stole four toffees and a piece of shortbread, and was about to make off with his booty from Tobruk to northeast Cyrenaica when he spotted some rolled-up magazines behind the neat little pile of books. *Ciné-Revue, Le Rire* of March 1924, *Lustige Blätter,* and a well-thumbed, thin little volume, *Les Aventures d'une cocodette,* Papa's stock of smutty books. The cocodette was nearly naked, wearing an orange straw hat, gray stockings, and extremely high heels. On every page, even when just sitting there on a swing without panties, she was pictured terrorizing some poor, fat, bald fellow in a three-piece suit. In one illustration she was riding horseback on the man, who seemed to have had no idea what had hit him, because his cigar had shot out of his mouth. Elsewhere she strutted about with bare buttocks, usually being fondled by the avidly clutching, shirt-cuffed hands of some bald lawyer or businessman. At some point the dream-woman looked Louis straight in the face, playfully and provocatively raising her finely drawn eyebrows, urging him on, whispering that he must continue with his senseless, itching, release-seeking, clamoring, sour-sweet friction against the jute sack full of curly wastepaper, and then she uttered a hoarse little smoker's-laugh, just as he came and flopped onto the voluptuous, rough sacking.

Papa held the watch, a miracle, up to the lightbulb above the sink, where Louis was scrubbing saucepans. "You can tell the date on it, you can use it as a stopwatch to time a race, you can even go swimming with it, though to be on the safe side I wouldn't do that for the time being. Well, what do you say?"

"Thank you, Papa."

"Is that all?"

"Thank you from the bottom of my heart, Papa."

"That's better."

It was the watch that the jailed Mijnheer Tierenteyn had given to his ancient mother, who was over eighty-five and fit as a fiddle because she took a spoonful of yeast every morning, with instructions that it be handed on to Papa. In case of sabotage, Mijnheer Tierenteyn would, thanks to Papa's intervention, be the very last in line of hostages to be tied to the fatal stake. This request had put Papa in a pickle. Up till now, in the neighborhood and at Felix's barbershop, he had done nothing to deny the myth of his membership in the Gestapo, on the contrary, whenever the subject was raised he would nod in a rather abstracted fashion and say, "Yes, well, there is quite a lot we could say about that, but we won't," thus drawing attention more than ever to the dangerous association and to the oath of silence he must observe or risk hideous physical retribution.

"In fact, I really shouldn't be giving you the watch until you're eighteen. Because you don't deserve it. Not yet. Your report card. Your conduct. Your slovenly ways. And now you've lost your briefcase! You're just like your mother with her keys. But I'm not going to buy you a new case. You can carry your books in a cardboard box. We never had leather briefcases in my day."

"This watch belongs to someone who is about to be executed," said Louis to Simone. "I can't tell you who. But his last words in prison were 'Give this watch, which is ticking my last seconds away, to Louis, my bridge partner at the Rotonde.' "

"My grandfather has one just like it."

"Don't you find it touching that the old man's thoughts should have turned to me at the very end? It's like Socrates—before he drank from the poisoned chalice, he said that he still owed a cock to, to . . ." Louis stuck his broad, manly, albeit hairless wrist out from under the porch on which they had taken shelter. The rain poured onto his new treasure.

"What are you doing that for?"

"It's waterproof."

She removed his hand from her hip.

"At the very moment that the volley rings out, this watch by rights should stop. Like time itself. His time will be up. But things are unfaithful."

"Why did you say that?" she asked abruptly.

"What?"

"About things being unfaithful. Did you mean me?"

"Of course not, Simone."

"Has somebody said something to you?"

"About what?"

"About me. Me and Jacques van de Sompel."

"No."

"Oh yes, they have. You just don't dare tell me straight to my face!"

Van de Sompel was the only son of a timber merchant, a man who was a regular at those parties of Mijnheer Groothuis where women bathed in champagne. Louis suddenly remembered that he had last seen Van de Sompel in the pharmacy.

In the twilight, with the rain in her tangled hair, her eyebrows, and her lashes, Simone looked vulnerable and touching. He would look after her, protect her from Van de Sompel's attacks. For ever and ever, through all eternity.

"I can't help it. I'm fond of both of you," said Simone. He wanted to tear out her wet hair, roots and all.

"I've talked to my mother about it. She thinks it's a bit odd but quite normal."

"Which is it? Odd or normal?" he managed to bring out.

"I'm fond of you as if you were someone in my own family. I've always wanted to have a brother, just ask my mother. And anyway, you're too young."

"And what about him?" (Papa in the marital bed, plaintive, *Untermensch.*)

"He is more . . ."

"More what?"

"More of a man. You can't help it, Louis, but you don't know what a girl really likes."

"But you won't ever tell me what you like."

"A girl shouldn't have to say it. A man should sense it."

"How long has this been going on?"

"Not very long. A month or two. But I like you, too."

"Merci."

The rain-pearled face slipping away from him, a face that belonged to another, worse, to that boor of a Van de Sompel, he drank it in, absorbed it, it was the worst and the most beautiful thing that could have befallen him. *Rache,* vengeance, he mewed.

"When Jacques touches me and puts his fingers here . . ." the slut was stroking her left breast, "it's as if I'm spinning away, as if I'm about to swoon. And with you . . . Look . . ." The incredible happened, she took his hand in her wet fingers and pressed it against the soft, full spot, he couldn't feel any bra and his teeth began to chatter. "You see, it doesn't stand up, my little bud, it doesn't get hard. With him it only takes a second." (I can time it with my hostage's-watch.) He snatched his hand away so violently that she fell against the wall and the nail of his forefinger tore.

"You're cross. I knew all the time that you wouldn't be a good sport about it."

"Oh, I am, I am." (He was standing in goal, the ball was dropping like a slow, perfect meteor, he reached for it, it bounced and swept over his beseeching hands.)

"We went for a walk along the Leie and Jacques said, 'Why don't we lie down on the grass?' It was very hot, so we lay down on the grass. He said, 'You're wearing such a lovely brooch,' and he took hold of the brooch and then he stroked my neck, and then I knew that he was the one for the rest of my life, for evermore."

"Silly cow." Either she hadn't heard him or else she must have thought he'd said, "Surely, now."

The rain was stopping.

"He makes me laugh all the time. You never do."

But that was her fault. He had simply sucked in the melancholy she gave off like bad breath. To be like her, from love, he, too, had wallowed in a mire of quiescent, groundless gloom. I should never have allowed myself to become absorbed into her.

"What exactly does he do to make you laugh?"

"He clowns around."

"And that makes you laugh?"

"Or he tells jokes."

"What jokes? I know hundreds of jokes."

"You've never told me any. You're always going on about Socrates or Guido Gezelle. It's all very educational but not terribly funny." She burst out laughing. "Only yesterday he . . ."

"Clowned around, did he?" (Fumbling under her skirts, clawing at her, making her laugh.)

"No. He told a good joke."

"Which one?"

"I said, 'Jacques, isn't it terrible about those two railway men who were killed by that German patrol in Varsenare?' And he said, 'Do you know the one about the priest of Varsenare?' 'No, Jacques,' I said. 'There was a farmer in Varsenare,' he said, 'who'd been married for twelve years, but there was no sign of any child. One day he comes home unexpectedly from the fields and what did he see in the bedroom? His wife with her legs up in the air, and between her legs the head of the priest of Varsenare. The farmer ran straight out into the road, shouting, "Gather 'round, folks, come quick and have a look. No wonder I haven't got any children, no sooner do I make them than along comes the priest and gobbles them all up!" ' " Her peals of laughter ebbed away and ended in a sigh. From the lips Louis had kissed, from that face he had thought undefiled, veiled in some indefinable sorrow, there now streamed this nauseating language, the filth of a whore of Babylon.

"That doesn't make you laugh, that's obvious."

"Does your father know?"

"About Jacques? Yes. He's allowed to come to our house."

"No. About that dirty talk."

"Heavens, no. He'd kill me. He thinks I'm still ten years old."

Louis looked at his watch, the second hand had stopped, he realized that all the time she had been talking he had been winding the little stem, not feeling any resistance, so strong had been his desire, in his shameful excitement, to turn away her treachery, her monstrously lewd pleasure taken without him. And as a result he had put an end to the hostage's time! Mijnheer Tierenteyn cried, *"Vive la Belgique!,"* reared up, and toppled forward as the soldiers reloaded, the steely susurration of time.

In the Groeninghe, Papa and Louis finally managed, using elbows and knees, to reach the counter, where Noël was too busy even to say hello. By the door to the w.c., De Puydt could be seen skulking behind, or perhaps sniffing at, a succulent plant. When the rush had abated a bit, Noël said, "You'd think if you were in the state he's in, you wouldn't want to come out and mix with other people, you'd rather hole up somewhere and mourn for as long as it takes, but on the other hand . . ."

Papa kept his back to the drink-sodden, grief-stricken De Puydt.

"I can't get a word out of him," said Noël. "I'm always having to explain to customers that he isn't trying to be rude, he just doesn't want to answer if someone speaks to him."

"He doesn't say anything at all?"

"No, he just looks at you, straight through you."

"How does he order his whisky, then?"

"He lifts up his glass."

De Puydt was wizened, his hair, once as wavy as a woman's, was plastered flat to his skull. He kept stirring a finger in an ashtray that bore a picture of Peter Benoit.

"So long as I can keep an eye on him, I don't worry," said Noël. "So long as he's under my roof, I'll see he's all right. But what if he goes and jumps under a tram outside . . ."

"Yes, what then . . ." said Papa. "And what about his best friend, Mijnheer Leevaert?"

"He's got something wrong with his insides."

"Who pays Marnix's bill, then?" Papa asked.

"I'm not bothered about that," said Noël.

"You make enough out of us as it is," said a Waffen-SS man.

"I just send his bill on to Groothuis."

"The first evening of my leave, the first day," said the SS man, "I go across to him over there in his little corner and I say, 'Well, Puydt, how are things with you?' because I was pretending I didn't know anything, understand? Because sometimes it's better to act stupid, and *godverdomme* if he doesn't throw a glass of mineral water in my face. If it had been Pale-Ale, I'd have put him straight into the hospital. Because our *Scharführer* only has to see one tiny spot on our uniform and he starts bellowing like a walrus. And what with my wife being away . . . I can just see myself washing my own uniform!"

"Sometimes he falls asleep," said Noël, "I just let him lie there."

"To see such a fine Fleming reduced to this," said Papa. "The English have a lot to answer for as it is, but this . . . And he never says a single word?"

Noël thought. "The last I heard was to Leevaert, who had been going on about Stalingrad, you know what he's like, and suddenly De Puydt said, 'Words are the garments of thoughts.' I'll always remember that."

"In which case he would have no thoughts left. I can't accept that," said Papa.

"Not words but actions, there's something in that," said the SS man.

A special bulletin came over the radio, the Sixth Army was in trouble, but that was nothing new.

"Here I am lounging about with a glass in my hand, while my comrades over there . . ." said the SS man.

"What's keeping you? The station's only ten minutes' walk away," said Noël, more peevishly than anyone had heard him sound before.

In Bastegem a row of children in blue tunics, mostly too short for them, walked along in single file holding on to a cord behind a flushed, kindly-looking nun. The gray-faced, frowning children weaved about, reeling, shoving one another. One of them stuck his tongue out at Louis, another had a black smudge on his forehead, an Ash Wednesday cross that had never been washed off.

A heron stalked beside brownish-red cows. Louis thought he could see Farmer Iwein Liekens ducking behind a faded curtain. An unguarded antitank gun stood in his farmyard. And there, as always, was the Villa Heliotrope among the dahlias.

Meerke said that Louis's hair, brushed forward now in a big quiff thick with hair oil, looked ridiculous. "It's exactly what women used to look like twenty years ago, exactly like you know who, I won't mention her name . . ."

"Better not," said Aunt Violet.

"Mention her all you want. Go around rattling skeletons in the cupboard, why don't you," said Uncle Armand.

"That's because you used to go around with old skeletons," said Aunt Violet.

"And still does," said Meerke.

"Angelique is three years older than me," said Uncle Armand in his gray flannel suit, the all-powerful inspector who had made all the farmers in the neighborhood jumpy because he so seldom accepted any of their bread or butter or black-market meat. Meerke had provided him with a widow, Angelique, but she could have bitten off her tongue now for mentioning her in the first place, because during the course of all her careful wheeling and dealing, her scheming and her matchmaking, no one had dared to tell her that Angelique had to swig nearly a quart of geneva in secret every day or else she got headaches. On top of that, Angelique and her family had lied about her age. Now Meerke's favorite son was saddled with a boozer and went off to the Picardy even more than before, while his spouse went about burbling to herself, *"Oh, je suis swing, zazou, zazou."*

"To nail those peasants down you have to be a bigger bastard than they are. That's the only way you'll catch them at it, with all their wangling, their double-dealing, their back-door slaughtering. In order to be fair, you have to be a swine. And if I call on a local hostelry now and then, it's because that's the only place I can get wind of what those swindlers are up to. Because once they've had one too many, their tongues start wagging."

"You can twist anything to suit your book," said Aunt Violet.

"You're being unfair," said Uncle Armand. "And you're a fine one to talk. Didn't I bring you copper sulfate for your garden, and sardines, and honey?"

"That's because it was your honeymoon." She gave her brother a sweet smile.

Aunt Violet was much more animated than she used to be, and she also looked much smarter in her mouse-gray two-piece.

"Honey?" said Louis, and was given two slices of bread and honey. He told himself to chew them very slowly but gulped them instead, wolfed them down as fast as he could.

"I'm off." Uncle Armand put on his bicycle clips.

"Give my love to Angelique."

"I won't forget, Mother."

"Or aren't you going home?"

"Mind your own business, Mother." He patted her gingerly on her fragile, brittle little back. As he rode off, she went over to the window to follow him with her eyes, and started coughing, which lasted a very long time. "I never rest easy about that boy. They're quite capable of knocking him off his bike with their flails."

"He's not going home," said Aunt Violet.

"No. And to think I was so happy that he was finally married and wouldn't be clinging to my skirts anymore. All I thought to myself was, She comes from a good family, she's been brought up properly. She can sing like a dream, Gounod's 'Ave Maria,' a voice like a bell, and the other classics, too. But when she's drunk, it's all *swing* here and *zazou* there, and Charles Trenet. Still, it isn't her fault that she drinks, she learned that at home, her mother comes from around Roubaix, that means red wine with lunch and supper, and then between meals, too, of course. It didn't take Angelique long, mind, to discover what sort of a fellow she'd married. They hadn't been two days in their house, newlyweds, when he dragged a commode indoors, a huge leather armchair with a pot built into it, something he'd bought at an auction for sixty francs. 'But, Armand,' says Angelique, 'we'd agreed we wouldn't have children right away in these terrible times!' 'Who's talking about children?' says he. 'It's for me!' 'What do you mean, for you?' 'Well, for when I get old!' " Meerke coughed with laughter, cleared her throat, slapped her thin knees under their black bombazine. Louis didn't dare slap her on the back. He went out into the garden, and to his surprise, close by, on the little tiled first-floor terrace, he saw a blond-haired young man in khaki swimming trunks rubbing something greasy into his bony, white shoulders. Louis immediately slipped behind the barn. The young man fell forward, landed on his hands, then lowered himself slowly. Louis stole along the back of the barn, past the coalshed to the kitchen.

"That's Gerhardt," said Meerke. "The nicest officer you could imagine. Both his parents are teachers in Werdau in Saxony, and they wrote to me in French to thank me for looking after their son so well. Needless to say, those bellyachers in the village are jealous because they think we're taking advantage of the situation, that we're getting paid for it, or get extra food. That's slander. Just like with our poor Omer in the beginning. The things they dreamed up about him, but that's all died down a bit since."

"How is Uncle Omer?"

"Louis, I only have one heart and that's already been broken into a million pieces."

"Isn't he allowed to come home sometimes?"

"Omer is just fine where he is," she said curtly.

Gerhardt had put on a grass-green dressing gown, he said that Louis was *ein netter Bursche,* a fine fellow. Seen from up close, he had a thin, cruel mouth. He had no earlobes, either, the mark of the Devil, according to Sister Sapristi.

Meerke said that Fräulein Violet would be back at seven. Gerhardt didn't seem to care, he hoisted himself up the kitchen wall, clambered back onto the terrace. "Violet is mad about Gerhardt," said Meerke eagerly, her eyes shining like coffee beans. "And he, well, he's polite, of course, in his German way, but he doesn't care for her, naturally. What with her figure. How would you yourself feel, Louis, as a man?"

Because Meerke was such a shrew, Louis made a point of telling Aunt Violet, as soon as she had flopped down breathlessly at the table and asked about Gerhardt, that she had lost a lot of weight, he had noticed it at once.

"Oh yes, she's melted away. Nothing but skin and bones," said Meerke sarcastically.

"Do you mean it? Really? I thought I must have." said Aunt Violet. "I thought, Do I dare go and stand on the scales in our school gym? It's all due to nerves. On account of that Father Mertens, who keeps treating us like shit."

Aunt Violet's defiantly audacious gaiety had, of course, everything to do with the blond officer's presence in the house. In the past she would never have used a word like "shit."

"Father Mertens has publicly turned against us, Louis. Against Meerke, but most of all against me."

"It's your own fault, Violet. Kissing a German, when Madame Vervaeke of the Union of Liberal Women is standing right next to you!"

"Mother, I'm of age. And as for that kiss, it was done with the best and most honorable of intentions. Like brother and sister. Anyway, if Father Mertens is egging his parishioners on against us, it's because of our Flemish principles. I made that absolutely clear to His Reverence the Vicar, but, of course, he had to stick up for his subordinate.

"When he teaches my class in Religious Knowledge, Louis, and I have to cough, he says that I only do it as a signal to the children that he's been talking nonsense. And when he preaches in church, he claims that I make faces to make him lose concentration. If he doesn't stop annoying me, I'm going to go straight with Gerhardt to the *Kommandantur* in Ghent."

"But the *Kommandantur* isn't interested in that sort of thing, Aunt Violet!"

"That's what you think! Not even if I tell them that he listens to Radio London? And that he wants to turn our youngsters into Boy Scouts? He's always been against our Flemish ideals. From long before the war! He got Felix Baert, a farmer with five children, kicked off his farm in '36, a farm that belonged to the Bishopric, just because Felix had been flying the Lion! And he also tried to get Mijnheer Godderis, the secretary of the Flemish Ex-Servicemen, fired by making out to the Ministry that he was a Dinaso. And Mijnheer Beulens, because he accompanied the singers on the piano at the Golden Spur Celebrations . . ."

"Don't work yourself up, Aunt Violet."

"And he took my congregation membership card away from me!" she cried.

"But Violet, you didn't go there anymore."

Aunt Violet ate four bowls of buttermilk porridge with apple slices.

"He's banished me from the choir, from the congregation, and from the Third Order. And when he exposes the Blessed Sacrament, he looks at me with great fiery eyes like carbuncles. And the worst thing of all, Louis, is that he accuses me of having walked arm in arm with Uncle Firmin at the fair!"

"Who did he say that to?"

"He just let it slip out casually at the Red Cross conference, where there are always lots of Flemish nationalists."

"But surely there's nothing wrong with walking arm in arm with your sister's husband?"

"Not when he's a Jew! But the worst part is, believe it or not, it isn't even true! On the contrary. Meerke can bear me out. She and I did all we could to stop our Berenice from getting married to a Jew. And when they did get married all the same, Meerke refused to give her signature. All of us, the whole family, tried everything, nice and nasty, threats and sweet reason, to keep Berenice away from that Jew. Her parents' home was closed to her for years."

"She wasn't allowed to set foot in here," said Meerke.

"So how did she manage to get taken back? Because Mijnheer Alex Morrens, who had pestered our poor Omer in the showers at the Bastegem Excelsior and was punched in the jaw for it, went around everywhere saying . . ."

"Why did Mijnheer Morrens pester Uncle Omer?"

"Violet," said Meerke and gave a quick cough.

"Because he . . . er . . . a question of money, I believe." (She believes? She lies!) "Anyway, he spread it about everywhere that Berenice and Firmin were legally separated and that he personally had seen Berenice at three o'clock one morning coming out of the Cocorico with some fellow, blind drunk. And it was only to give the lie to these slanders . . ." Aunt Violet raised a plump finger, her voice rose as if to reach pupils in the last row, "and to expunge the shame of it all, that we thought it expedient to allow her back into our house, and it was for that reason, and that reason alone, that I decided to show myself at the fair, *en plein public,* in the company of my sister and her lawful husband. But arm in arm? I ask you! With that Firmin, of all people, who's been the bane of our lives all these years?"

"And still is," said Meerke. "Sometimes I get the cold shivers when I think that he might turn up right under our noses any day now."

"Or that he might get arrested by the Germans and we all get interrogated at the *Kommandantur* on account of the anti-German things he says."

"You could hide him. In the loft or in the cellar," said Louis.

"Like a dog!" Meerke cried.

"And what about Gerhardt?" cried Aunt Violet even more loudly. "He can smell a Jew a mile away. He'd go straight for the kill!"

Meerke was knitting. The evening, the evening with the joyful shouts of the village children in the distance, the train rumbling by, filling the garden with steam and smoke, the uprooted, floating pear trees and cherry trees, the flashing, dark-cherry-red sparks of the coals from the train, Meerke coughing, Aunt Violet nibbling and sucking at a pig's trotter.

Because there were no curtains in the little room over the cellar, Louis woke with the first rays of the sun. Barefoot, he ran out into the wet grass, like the ancient god who drew his strength from the earth.

But after a dozen or so dancing steps it became too cold, besides, tiny creepy-crawlies can get stuck between your toes and multiply there, hatch little eggs there and then forge a passage through your flesh before settling in your spinal cord. Pelting through a field of millions of teeming Mizzlers, he raced inside, dried his feet feverishly with the kitchen towel.

There was no honey left from Uncle Armand's honeymoon, the greedy women had left not a single drop. He took a lump of sticky black bread, rolled it into a sausage between his palms, the sausage completely filled his mouth, the tepid mush slid slowly down his throat. In the kitchen shaving mirror he saw a pasty face with large red earlobes. The cock crowed. Today he would go and see Raf. If they'd been a little older and it weren't wartime, they might have gone out shooting together. Supposedly after game, but once out in the fields, flash, bang, straight into the swollen, reddish-brown bellies of cows. A farmer comes running toward them, cursing. The heaviest shot there is explodes right in his black-marketeering peasant's-face, his head bursts open. Next year I'll look eighteen and I'll enlist in the Flemish Legion.

Louis stole six five-franc pieces from Aunt Violet's handbag (her *sacoche*), ran doubled over like Rigoletto back to the little room over the cellar, and immediately fell asleep again.

A bill from the Brothers of St. Vincent lay in Meerke's lap. "Omer is costing us the earth," she said mournfully. "Where am I supposed to get all that cash? Especially since I doubt that any of it does any good at all. Not that I begrudge it to our Omer, but he's never going to get well again. He's been smitten by Our Lord. All he gets to eat is kidney beans, and they bleed us dry for that. His hair is falling out. At his age. He says one prayer after another. And he sits there all day with his head between his knees. The Brother says that Omer thinks it's good for the circulation. I brought him a lovely book, *The Knight of Laarne Castle,* but he doesn't want to read it, because if there was anything in it about a young noble-woman riding a horse in the Middle Ages, he says, he would start getting strange ideas. He asked the Brothers to tie his hands together in the evenings, but they wouldn't hear of it, they said, because if the others saw it, they'd all want to be tied up, too."

Aunt Violet was late leaving for Mass but all the same was first frying herself a duck egg while she examined the bill.

"Armand must help pay," she said. "At least the laundry bill."

"He doesn't want to."

"He must, Mother. If only out of Christian remorse for what he did to his brother."

"He didn't do anything to him. It just happened. It was in him from

409

early youth, in Omer. He got it from his grandfather, that one wasn't all there either."

"Oh dear, oh dear," exclaimed Aunt Violet, shaking the frying pan. "Mass must have started already!"

They could hear chanting, it sounded as if Ceulemans the sacristan, nicknamed The Goat because he sounded like some tortured, starved, unmilked nanny, was intoning the *Tantum ergo,* but when they looked out, they saw that he was in fact chasing a stray cow, trying to pacify her with psalms. It was a black-and-white cow, a Friesian. The sacred cows of India. If you were allowed to slaughter them, not a single Indian would starve. The nomads in Africa are more cunning, they open one of their cow's veins, tap the blood, make blood-sausage pancakes with it, then close up the vein with mud. If you want to study the rumination and digestion of the cow, you can cut a small rectangular window in her stomach, fit a pane of mica into it like in a slow-combustion stove, and then make scientific observations of the way the grass is transformed.

Louis sneezed, brought out his handkerchief, the stolen pieces of silver rolled over the floor, chinking. Guilt, like a towel soaked in blood, flooded across his face. One of the coins continued to roll in a graceful arc.

"It's my savings," Louis said quickly.

"It's out of my *sacoche,*" said Aunt Violet icily. "I noticed at once this morning. Do you think I'm an idiot? On your knees!"

"Is that our thanks after all we've done for you?" cried Meerke.

"On your knees in the corner," said the fat schoolmistress. He laid his forehead against the wallpaper.

"And that's how I get one sorrow after another," coughed Meerke.

"You can count yourself lucky that you aren't my child!" The very idea of Aunt Violet having a child, let alone that it might be him, made Louis shriek, scream with silent laughter for the umpteenth time. Her trained pedagogic eye noticed it, she slapped his cheek as hard as she could. *"Schweinhund!"* she cried and gathered up the coins, looked for one under the table, then straightened up with a groan.

"The sorrow of Belgium, that's what you are," said Meerke and gasped for breath with a raucous snort. Then with his own sticking-out ears he heard Aunt Violet curse under her breath: *"Godverdomme,* you nasty little sneak, poking about in my *sacoche,* prying about in my photos and my letters!"

(Her *sacoche!* Again he snickered and chortled inwardly, because not far away Vlieghe was saying, in that far-off, monotonous, funereal, musty-smelling time in that other Women's House, in Haarbeke, "You've been poking about in her *sacoche,*" meaning that purse of skin and flesh and hair that women have between their legs.)

His cheek glowed. So long as Raf didn't arrive unannounced.

After an hour he was let out of his corner and told to fetch beer for the four men in bathing trunks, Gerhardt among them, who were sitting in the garden playing cards. *"Danke, Bursche. Herzlichen Dank."*

When Aunt Violet came back from school, she asked the officers if they would like a *schnapps.* Only if she would serve it wearing a bathing suit, said a fat man with a fleece of gray curls down his back. *"Aber, Ulrich, doch,"* she said with a blush. When she returned with the geneva, she had changed into a little blouse with short sleeves. Her flabby underarms shook when she made as if to drop a curtsy. Gerhard placed a casual hand on her buttocks. Aunt Violet turned suddenly to stone, did not move, peering steadily at the hedge as if the terrible Father Mertens were hidden in the dense foliage. Then the four sun-worshipers sang, *"Sie hat die Treu gebro-o-chen, mein Ringlein sprang entzwei,"* "She has been unfaithful, my ring has snapped in two." Fat Ulrich looked through his field glasses in the direction of England.

Had some cloud of Mizzler-like bacteria alighted on the village of Bastegem and its inhabitants from out of the smoke of gunpowder and war?

Much as Aunt Violet had been improbably transformed into a cursing, ear-boxing maiden, as Uncle Armand had turned from ladykiller into the righteous scourge of farmers, as Uncle Omer had become a hairless imbecile who, at one time, had kept running through the streets of Bastegem with a cowbell, bawling at the villagers, "Off to Mass with you, please," whereupon Father Mertens himself had called in the village policeman with the result that the poor ninny, crushed like a rotten tomato by unhappy love, was now a resident at the extravagantly expensive Brothers of St. Vincent, where he occasionally mounted his fellow patients, "like one bull on top of another," said Uncle Armand, so Raf de Bock had also changed, and into what?—into a *dancer.* He attended ballet classes in Ghent.

They walked together along the tree-lined road, Raf with a spring in his step that Louis thought exaggerated, to say the least.

"When I stand at the *barre,* I am a different person, I weigh less than fifty pounds." He held his arms halfway out in front of him, his fingertips touched, he raised one leg, swept it back, spread his arms wide. *"Arabesque!"* he cried, *"Assemblé!"* and flopped down on the grass. He paid for the classes in Ghent with what he got from the farmers to whom he demonstrated his dance steps. Twenty francs for ten minutes. *"Bourrée!"* The farmers couldn't get enough of it, it usually took place out in the middle of the fields, where their wives couldn't see them. Sacristan Goat also paid.

"If it were up to The Goat, I'd have to dance all afternoon. His eyes pop out of his head."

Jules Verdonck stood at his bench, sanding a small oval windowframe. He seemed not to recognize Louis.

"Don't you have anything better to do, you two, than bother someone who's got his bread to earn?"

"Oh, Jules, you are a wit!" Raf threw a handful of wood shavings up in the air, pretended to file his fingernails with a large rasp, fiddled with the wheel of a machine that looked like the proof press in Papa's work-shop. Ink and rags. But no letters.

"Keep your hands off!" snarled Jules.

"Did you get out on the wrong side of bed, Jules? What's become of your usual amiable self? Is it because I've brought our Louis along? Is that it?"

Jules grinned, baring scarlet gums. "These days they can't get enough of us, these fine young city gents! Because their tummies are rumbling with hunger, that's why. Right? These days the farms are overrun with them. And they don't come for our beautiful eyes, either. Right?"

"Is he in?" asked Raf.

Jules stared at Louis with fierce, pale eyes under eyebrows like two yellowed mustaches. "You . . . you'll be getting it in the neck one day."

"Why?"

"Don't you know?"

"No."

"You surely don't think, young man, that they'll make an exception for you? You'll be getting it in the neck, like all the other heretics who go astray."

Raf picked up a pair of pincers from the pile of dusty tools and pinched Louis's sleeve with them.

"Is he in?" he asked again.

"Look outside!" said Jules violently. "Is it dark?"

"No."

"Well, then, he's in!"

"Is he asleep?"

"That man can never sleep, what with all the sorrow that he feels for the world."

"Like Jesus of Nazareth." Raf crossed himself solemnly with the pinc-ers.

"He's studying." Jules went on sanding the clean young wood. "He asks about you, almost every day."

"Goodness gracious!" Raf fluttered his thick, curly lashes.

"Don't be too long," said Jules.

In the side barn they climbed a rickety staircase up to a landing. Raf drummed on the door, three short, two long taps. A smell of vinegar drifted out to meet them as the door opened and a man spread his arms wide. Louis's immediate thought was to run away, but Raf had anticipated that and pinched his arm hard as if with Jules's pincers. The man was wearing a black woolen cloak like Zorro. Around his head he had wound a red satin cloth, half turban, half woman's scarf, his right ear peeping out, notched and covered with scabs. His face, an ivory-white mask tied on with elastic, gleamed. A perfect, small, pink mouth, molded into a shop-window smile, revealed a dark slit that gave out a hissing sound. On the unlined, smoothly domed forehead, two elegantly painted stripes formed the eyebrows, in the eye-slits two black eyes with bright-red rims glittered. The man stood ramrod-straight. His bare feet were long and white like the hand resting on Raf's shoulder. "Darling," said the seared voice. "Darling."

"My love," said Raf. And enjoyed Louis's consternation. He would have pushed Louis toward the man in black, Louis had already taken a step back, but then the man said Louis's surname and first name, it was an invitation. (I am at the rehearsal of a historical play, and this Knight in disguise from Laarne Castle will be unmasked in the last act as the prince of Raf's dreams. Darling. Darling.)

"I am Konrad."

In his room the man sat down on a milking stool, suddenly stood up again, offered Louis the stool, and leaned against the whitewashed wall next to a potbellied stove and a row of shelves filled with stones, sand roses, goblets of bright-colored powders, and, wonder of wonders, a row of large wooden block letters, the old-fashioned Hidalgo type. Smells of vinegar, medicine, a whiff of straw.

"How is your aunt?"

"Fine," said Louis.

"But you have two aunts. How did you know which one I meant?"

"I thought you were asking about Aunt Violet."

"Violet doesn't interest me, or rather, she does, but I know too much about her, if not all there is to know. No, what I wanted to hear from you, my dear, was if there's any news of Berenice."

He's pulling my leg. My dear. Does he come from some part of the country where they talk like that to all and sundry, including perfect strangers? The unearthly face, with the smooth cheeks sharply set off against the red pimply throat and neck, moved, went over to the barred window, looked outside, and bent over Raf, who was drumming on the table covered with pebbles, stones, books, papers full of tables and calculations, a map of the sky and its constellations, a pair of black crocheted gloves, four small pencils with faded, chewed ends.

"We think Berenice is in France, in the free zone. We haven't heard anything from her."

"Or from him?"

"Or from him."

"A remarkable woman, Berenice Bossuyt. When I knew her, long before your time, there was no one who surpassed her in piety and mortification."

Raf picked up a sharp-edged, shapeless, brown lump of rock and turned it between his fingers. "If you can guess what this is, Louis *mon ami,* then you're a clever fellow. You'll be eligible for membership in the Club of the Chosen."

"A stone, some rock from the desert."

It was a piece of shit, Raf shouted. Konrad's asexual, unassailed, unassailable mask nodded, which caused the headscarf to slip back and a pink skull with rust-colored spots to be revealed. Konrad had at some time sustained severe burns. He adjusted the scarf with a brief affected gesture.

"But Louis is right as well. It was excrement and now it is stone."

"Konrad is mad about shit. He smears himself with goatshit."

Louis couldn't stop himself laughing. "With turds?"

"Mixed with oats, honey vinegar, butter, and nut oil."

"He'd drink it, too!"

"Mixed with white wine. Very good for jaundice."

The little room was filled with the gloomy humming and buzzing of Mizzlers.

"Konrad owns a real diamond. When he dies, I'm going to get it, it's in his will, and that's deposited with Baerens the notary."

"What animates our dear friend most . . ." (All these dears and darlings. Was Konrad a Jew? Jews are nauseatingly intimate like that with one another all the time, too.) ". . . is avarice. But after I have passed on, Raphael will be transformed by the diamond. He will become completely immune to the devil."

"And to poisonous toadstools," said Raf. "And to rotten mussels."

"His failings will be metamorphosed into their very opposite. His pathological lechery will vanish by itself."

"*You* can talk about pathological lechery!"

"Mine is for you alone, *amore.*"

"Once at night we saw Father Mertens on his way to administer the Last Sacrament to the signalman. Konrad got the fright of his life, he choked and careered off like a mad cow across the fields and clung tight to the barbed-wire fence."

The village could be seen through the window, small houses crammed together like the dominoes in the Institute's recreation room. I must make out a will as well, and as soon as possible. Would there be thirteen large candles around my coffin? It's an unlucky number.

"What is it, angel?"

"Nothing," said Louis.

"You mustn't think about death. Mustn't be frightened. I'm not infectious."

"Not your body, in any case," said Raf merrily.

"How are those Teutons in your house?"

"Fine, I think."

"They disport themselves before the populace from your terrace. It's unwise of Violet and her mother to let them."

"There's nothing they can do about it."

"You mean Violet didn't encourage them to take their clothes off and worship the sun?"

"Of course not. The terrace floor was broken, it was letting in rain, the Germans offered to mend it. They fixed the leak with their own blowtorches, and since it was boiling hot the day they did it, they took off their clothes to make it easier to work. And the next day as well."

"Because they are sun worshipers," Konrad snapped through the horizontal slit. "That's why they'll be exterminated by a black sun."

The Mizzlers buzzed, came near.

"Why?"

"They bear the sun in their sign, and they're wholly malign." It rhymed.

Raf and Louis walked past the front of the Lockkeeper's House, on which a wanted-poster picturing Gypsies had been stuck. Bekka's father was not among them. Gerard, the lockkeeper, said, "Well, well, the good-time boys!"

(A week before, Louis had been pulling turnips in the little field behind the Lockkeeper's House. It had been agreed that he could take twenty, he pulled five extra. When he went into the house to wash the turnips in the scullery, he heard a rasping male voice in the normally deserted front

415

room saying, "The whole of Europe has become a slaughterhouse, Gerard, a migration of nations straight to the abbatoirs, there can't be any God, we'd best keep a weather eye open or else we'll get nothing but tears, Gerard."

The door had swung open, and Gerard had been visibly startled to see Louis.

"Well," he had said. "Well, well." Behind him had sat a hollow-eyed bargeman. "Well," Gerard had said again, "quick, back home with you. My cousin has come for a visit." Cousin, my foot.)

Raf walked close by the river, alongside the turquoise duckweed out of which escaped little bubbles of gas, under which lay the corpses of May '40, of '14–'18, of the Spanish Mutiny, of serfs and villeins. Raf whirled his arms like a windmill, standing on one leg, graceful as a monkey. *Bourrée!* If he falls into the Leie, will I have to go in after him? Dive into that green sludge?

They walked side by side along the bank. In the distance a barge brought the news from Europe.

"Your friend with the mask and Jules are doing undercover printing."

"It's possible."

"Where do they get the paper?" (Papa's daily laments about the paper shortage.)

"I don't know."

But Raf couldn't resist letting on that he was at the nerve-center of a highly perilous conspiracy. "They get the paper from the sacristan, from The Goat."

"And where does The Goat get the paper?"

"From Father Mertens."

"And what about him? From the Bishop?"

Raf shrugged his shoulders.

"Why are you telling me all this? And your friend . . ." (I'd rather drop dead than mention his name.) "Why does he tell me, a complete stranger who could easily go straight to the Gestapo, that the Germans will be exterminated?"

Raf pulled his lower eyelids down with thumb and middle finger and pushed the tip of his nose up with the forefinger of his other hand. That's what his friend looked like underneath his smoothly varnished artificial skin.

"You're no stranger, darling."

Holst was standing, legs planted wide apart, by the gate, behind him the conifers, the ancient oaks, the flat, gray lawn strewn with weeds. He was wearing a brown corduroy suit and clogs.

"You're not in uniform," said Raf.

"I'm on leave," said Holst.

"You should look after your lawn properly."

"I'm doing it," said Holst apologetically as to an officer.

"You should keep rabbits on it."

"Then I'd have to sit out on the grass all day and night. What with that riffraff in the village these days. They'd steal the shirt off your back."

"How much leave have you got?"

"None of your business."

"You're getting a lot of leave lately."

"Nobody's business. Why do you ask?"

"It's a bit obvious, that's all."

Holst closed the gate behind them, peered out at the meadows, the fields where men of the White Brigade and their Communist People's Commissars lay in wait behind haystacks, machine guns at the ready.

When I was an Apostle, Holst looked like a giant; he is at most five feet ten, barely four inches above minimum SS regulation height, but outside the Institute he had looked at least six and a half feet; this Holst no longer has the slightest connection with the angel I used to summon up, to worship from my narrow, evil-smelling little bed in the Institute, to whom I addressed my soundless babblings: Come and fetch me, you angel disguised as my tyrannical grandfather's manservant, come and fetch me, and in turn I'll be your paladin, deliver me, and I will carry your pack through the taiga, the erg, the llano, all the crossword puzzle deserts and plains.

In the kitchen—walls of square white tiles, dark-green cupboards, copper taps, a sink full of dishes—hung two hams.

Raf couldn't take his eyes off them. He would be breaking in here tonight. They drank a bitter chicory brew. Holst said awkwardly, "Listen, Louis. Listen carefully. Tell your Grandpa that I wrote to him twice, but perhaps the letters didn't arrive. Tell him that I know he won't like it, but I joined the Flemish Guard anyway for the reasons I put in my letter, in the letters. But that I also realize perfectly well that it wasn't a sensible thing to do."

"You're right, they've started shooting at people like you lately."

"Who says so?"

"I heard it."

"Who from?"

"From a Flemish Guardsman on the train."

"His name? Which unit?"

"They called him Oskar."

"And he says that sort of thing in public? We've had orders about that."

Beside the big kitchen dresser full of china, two sagging, black, dusty boots stood next to a mop. Someone had put them down there a long time ago and forgotten them. Doleful relics.

"Are you still at the Coucke and Goethals barracks?" asked Raf.

"None of your business," said Holst mechanically and fetched a forest-green bottle from the dresser and shook it, churning up little black twigs and sprigs and flecks. When the swirling mass had settled back to the bottom, he poured each of them a drink. It was both bitter and sweet, and very strong.

"Tell your Grandpa . . ."

"Tell him that Holst is a traitor, full stop," said Raf.

". . . that I couldn't do anything else."

"A man is responsible for what he is, Holst, full stop."

"You have no right to talk, you of all people!" said Holst.

"*Allee, allee,* Holst, you enlisted because Madame Laura asked you to, full stop."

"Not on your life!"

"If she didn't actually ask you, you kidded yourself that she would have wanted to ask you. Or maybe just wanted you to. You got it into your head that she'd rather see you in a blue uniform, with a thirty-five millimeter bayonet and that stupid Dutch helmet on your head, than as some clumsy country bumpkin turned gamekeeper."

Holst stared at the blue floor tiles. "You have no right to talk, you don't." He pushed the bottle across to Raf, who drank.

"Have you sprayed your lawn?" asked Raf. "No? It looks as if you have. No, are you sure? Not with that stuff against the Colorado beetle?"

"An English airplane flew over a month or so ago," said Holst. "It might have sprayed something. It looks as if they're trying to poison the whole harvest with their filth."

Into the labyrinth of *la belle dame sans merci*. Behind Holst's massive back, across the badly fitting, broad, varnished boards of the first-floor corridor. Raf flapped his hands, imitating a bat. The newly painted dove-egg-white door. A smell wafted down from the shut-off attic as if from a winter garden growing there, a jungle up against the roof tiles.

Her bedroom? The expanse made Louis think of the gymnasium in the Atheneum, where he had once watched a flag-waving display, the same honey-yellow floorboards, the tall French windows with their casement catches, the beige, feminine color of the bare walls and varnished doors.

Looking oddly lost, an iron camp bed stood against the chimney breast, a lady's satin shoe lying on its gray pillow. Yes, she usually slept here, said Holst. Near the legs of the bed, in a heap, flung off by some furious giant, lay a blue uniform, a haversack, puttees, two crumpled handkerchiefs. Also a color photograph in a small aluminum frame of two young ladies arm in arm wearing large white hats.

"Is that her sister?" asked Raf. "Beatrix?"

"Don't touch."

"Well. So that is Beatrix," said Raf and returned the frame to exactly the same place. "Beatrix, I'd have you know, Louis, is the mistress of *Standartenführer* Hebbel, and at this very moment she is at her apartment in Paris, *vingt-quatre,* rue Saint-André-des-Arts, right, Holst? And without her dear sister Beatrix, Madame Laura would long ago have been kicked out of her house in the Avenue Louise lock, stock, and barrel, for all her wonderful connections. Because she goes a bit too far sometimes, right, Holst?"

"The time will come," said Holst heavily, "when you'll discover that you know a bit too much for your own good."

"But I do know, right, Holst?" Raf gave a childishly proud little laugh. He sat on the squeaking camp bed, put his hand into the small green satin shoe, waggled the mangled, dog-chewed toe.

"She doesn't mean to go too far. It's just that she's unhappy. People do strange things when they're unhappy."

"You've hit the nail on the head there, Holst."

"She is too trusting."

"So are we all, Holst, so are we all."

"She used to be happy, business was booming, her girls worked hard, no problems, the clients paid on the dot, the champagne flowed, Moritz came every day in his Mercedes, and then all of a sudden . . . oh, boys, the war, the war."

"Where is Moritz now?"

"In the troopers' heaven."

"I never knew that."

"He's buried in his own garden. In a small town in the Black Forest. Special dispensation by the *Führer.* He was made *Hauptsturmführer* after his death. You see, even a tram in Liège can be regarded as a field of battle. His orderly was promoted posthumously. Madame Laura sensed it coming, that last week we were in Liège she didn't want Moritz to leave the house in the evenings. I can still see her standing there, buttonholing him, but he didn't listen to her, of course not, he'd only just come back from Belgorod with two holes in his calf. And that day she kept pacing up and down, drinking one glass of champagne after another. 'I don't know what's wrong with me, I'm itchy and tingling all over. Could it be nerves? There's no reason for it at all. Could Moritz have someone else? How long does it take from Liège to Brussels, in this weather?' The bell rang, and she turned white as death. 'Don't open the door,' she said, 'please. No, tell them I'm out. No, I'll go myself,' and there stood the *Standortarzt*, the doctor, and told her that Moritz and his orderly had been on their way to a festival, the *Obstfest*, and that the White Brigade must have known the Mercedes had been left in the garage and that he intended to take the tram from the Council of Ministers. 'I know,' she said, white as death, 'he often takes the tram, because he likes being with Belgians, he thinks Belgian people are so colorful, but where is he now, why didn't he come along with you?' 'You haven't understood me, Frau Laura, the tram got blown up, four Liégeois and the conductor lost their lives, as well as Moritz and Ruwein, his orderly.' Then she began to wail, her false teeth fell out and she couldn't shut her mouth anymore, all she did was wail until the *Standortarzt* gave her an injection. Two days later the girl from the cleaners stood outside the door with Moritz's parade uniform. Luckily I was able to hide it without her seeing it. And because his wife in the Black Forest had told them to, they came to collect everything he had left with Madame Laura, his jewels, clothes, bags, cigar boxes, books, and in her stupor she let everything be carted off, down to his underwear and socks, and all she's got left of his things is that over there."

"Where?"

Raf opened the bow-fronted wardrobe. A field-gray uniform was hanging up, spotless and carefully ironed, like some distinguished, elegant scarecrow. Because the kepi with the three stripes under the silver oak leaves had been hung up above it and two immaculately polished black lace-up shoes were standing at the bottom of the trouser legs, it looked as if the man in the suit had been incinerated, dissolved, by some secret ray fired inside the room by the English that had pulverized everything except for cloth. A white shirt with a very pointed collar, a firmly knotted black tie, the oak leaf with the three stripes on the jacket lapel, the Knight's Cross, the Sports Medal, a swastika on a small china button, all seemed to confirm the presence of the absent Moritz. Raf gave the clothes a quick shove, they wobbled, the belt with the eagle buckle fell resoundingly onto the bottom of the wardrobe.

Holst grabbed Raf by the throat. "You have no respect, you!" Raf freed himself with a dancing movement.

"Take it easy, Holst."

Holst's eyes grew moist, his eyes were sweating. "Yes. All right. But still . . . I can never do right by you, or by Konrad. You always manage to make a fool of me, the two of you."

"Because you are a fool," Raf exclaimed, "a complete fool, when it comes to that bitch Madame Laura!" and walked out of the room. Louis followed, then Holst, too.

In the kitchen, after another gulp from the forest-green bottle, Raf said that Holst ought to get out more and see people, that it was undignified for a man to brood over Madame Laura here all on his own.

"I go to the Picardy now and then."

"Those aren't people," said Raf. "And anyway, screwing, what good does that do you?" Louis looked up. Wasn't screwing what most people were preoccupied with day and night, or were assumed to be preoccupied with, didn't great sorrow come of it, and now and then a little happiness?

"No good to you perhaps," said Holst.

"Not to me, no," said Raf.

"Not everyone gets his kicks from dancing," said Holst.

Raf was quiet as they walked back. When Meerke's house came into sight, he said, "Now you've seen for yourself what women can do to you. He may say that Madame Laura stood there wailing, but I don't believe a word of it. Madame Laura never cries. Never. Not even if you were to horsewhip her."

They could hear Hector the turkey. Raf said, his voice reminding Louis of the drawling pedantry in Konrad's voice, "When you're screwing, Louis, and you're too exhausted to go on, just take a look at Hector, hang on till he's made his neck swell up three times, and then you'll be able to get going again."

The strange being leaping about in front of him was quite mad, but Louis was still proud to have been counted among the screwers of the world.

"I'll keep it in mind for when I need it," he said.

Raf took out a small book with a blue leather cover and golden letters from his inside pocket. "Here, this is for you." The title was *The Ugly Duchess*, the author, who'd ever heard of him?, Lion Feuchtwanger. "A small present from your comrade Raf, whom you won't love but who doesn't hold that against you."

He had stolen it from the kitchen. "Holst doesn't read that sort of thing, not books like this," he said.

"*Merci.*"

Raf's light-brown hand held on to his. "I must be off to Farmer Liekens. *Le grand écart* for a quarter of an hour. Write me a postcard sometime." And off went Louis's guide to masked, seared magicians, to women in wide-brimmed white hats. He wanted to run after Raf, "Don't leave yet," but the devil of chill pride (as he called it that night in his notebook) stopped him; Louis Seynaeve asks nothing of anybody.

That evening, remembering Raf's nonchalant, whimsical and feminine, interrogation technique, he tried to learn more about Madame Laura from Meerke, Aunt Violet, and Jeanne Renesse, a cheerful neighbor who suffered from arteriosclerosis and chewed garlic for it throughout their game of whist. The three of them were too immersed in their game of cards to gossip at length, but even so he gathered that Madame Laura ran a house of ill repute in the Avenue Louise in Brussels, where the chic, the sham, and the chichi from all over the country left their cash, German officers as well as black-marketeers and anglophile industrialists, that she was a millionairess, that she had made Holst, her manservant or gamekeeper, a slave to her foul habits.

"One thing's for sure," said jolly Jeanne Renesse, "she's older than we think."

"She looks after herself, of course," said Meerke.

Aunt Violet, greenish and bloated in the light of the oil lamp, said, "She rubs her face with hemorrhoid ointment every day, that tightens the skin." Probably they talked like that about Mama, too, when Louis wasn't around. Mama, who, just like Madame Laura, had been left by a German warrior, and who also had cried out in despair, jaws frozen, when no one could see her.

"I heard someone say she has false teeth," he said.

"I wouldn't be at all surprised," said Meerke.

"She's false from top to toe," said Aunt Violet.

Although it was as much as your life was worth, because there were no curtains in his little room, Louis lit a Christmas-tree candle and read about the ugly duchess. Feuchtwanger used several adjectives with each noun, then the letters began melting away, and after an extremely short, violent sin he dropped off into sleep with Madame Laura's blurred face looking at him from under her white straw hat, she opened her lips in a loving pout, Louis murmured, "Wait a moment, you woman of ill repute, wait a moment." "Come, then," she said and went red like the wattles of Hector the turkey. Without her noticing it, field-gray snowflakes settled on her shoulders, tattered, tiny shreds of uniform, while a tram bell rang, the altar bell from when I used to go to communion with Vlieghe.

"We could go to the cinema, but nothing's on," said Papa. "*Reitet für Deutschland* with Willy Birgel might be interesting, it's about a man who rides for the glory of his country, it teaches you that you can make yourself useful no matter where you serve, but I'm not in the mood for horses right now."

"At the Cameo they're showing . . ." Louis began.

"Louis, please!"

"*Étoile d'Amour.*"

"Precisely, French vaudeville. The French don't know how to make a film unless it's about *toujours l'amour* and women in their underwear. That the Flemish people of Walle allow that sort of thing in their own town is a shame and a disgrace. Before the war if they showed decadent films we would all go there together and throw inkpots at the screen, people took things more seriously in those days."

Louis made up his mind to go to a matinee at the Cameo someday soon. If only it really were decadent! Like the decadence of the Jews and the plutocrats in America who gave parties to raise money for their war effort, parties where, hook-nosed, fat, cigar-smoking, they threw fistfuls of dollars at dancing girls wearing American flags the size of postage stamps on their quivering, galvanized bellies, at those shamelessly squirming, heaving, clawing women who wrestle in the mud or in a tank full of silvery fish, every wrinkle, fold, groove, luxuriantly amplified, magnified, or at a row of dancers in black stockings and garters that cut into their large, milky thighs, and all these brazen creatures multiplied, spread their knees wide to the sound of saxophones that beat, beat like the blood in his temples, and in the gimlet that was sliding insufferably up his underpants.

"Or *The Rider on the White Horse,*" said Papa. "Although that doesn't interest me much either, that classical period around the year eighteen hundred or whatever. It's more for your Grandpa, he likes the classics, but I don't take him to the cinema anymore, all he does is sit there carrying on and asking questions the whole time because he can't follow what's going on. He can't understand the simplest things at the cinema. If a woman comes on, he can never remember if she's the wife, the daughter, or the mother. 'Why is she crying like that?' he asks. 'Two minutes ago she was laughing!' But many fine minds are like that. Once they step outside their own speciality, they're like big children. They're always searching for deeper reasons. Hundreds of difficulties about something that doesn't give us the slightest trouble. No, I think I'll go to that meeting at the Groeninghe instead, and as for you, you'd better go and do your Latin or your mathematics homework."

In the Cameo that night, Ginette Leclerc, a child-woman with hair cut square over her eyebrows, stood for several minutes in her underwear and black stockings, a workman with the face of a rat consoled her as he stroked her hip in a slip trimmed with little black feathers, Louis stroked along with him, over his trousers. During an endless police chase through the Paris Metro, with shrill French voices re-echoing from the unending walls of gleaming white tiles, he looked down from the first row in the balcony and clearly, although more dimly than the garish black-and-white images on the screen, made out the balding pink pate of his father sitting motionless, with his hat on his knees, only his hand moving, mechanically bringing toffee from a little bag up to his invisible mouth.

Just before the end, which was bound to go on and on about the reunion of the two French buffoons, Louis ran back home.

"How was it?" he asked his father.

"How was what?"

"Your meeting."

"Oh, the same old squabbles between the VNV and DEVLag. How can they ever hope to form a united movement? Everyone for himself and against the rest. That's the trouble with Flanders, we've been left with the legacy of all those years of democratic monkey business."

There was an unwonted stir in the playground, the Rock gesticulating in the midst of other teachers, and Louis thought, That's it, the Rock's overstepped the bounds now, he's gone right around the bend, which was only to be expected—but it all had to do with the arrest of two boys from the Rhetoric class. The boys were walking along, heads bowed, both chewing gum. Four men in hats (one a familiar felt hat) held them by the arm. They were marched to the gate, past the tongue-wagging pupils.

"They say Ceusters has Jewish blood."

"They had a radio transmitter in their desk."

"Maybe they've got to go and work in Germany. I always thought that De Coene looked older."

"They're in for it now. The Gestapo don't pull any punches."

"Going in for heroics is all very well, but you can't complain when the chickens come home to roost."

"They found chalk in their pockets, they'll check to see if it's the same chalk used to draw those hammers and sickles on the walls."

"Let's hope they catch a few more, then they'll have to close the College, hurrah!"

"And what about our diplomas, you dimwit?"

Theo van Paemel held the door of the car open, the boys were hustled in. Van Paemel slid in next to the driver.

The Rock looked ashen. Guilt weighed heavy on the narrow, sagging shoulders, hollowed out his face.

"Father."

"Don't talk to me," snapped the priest. "Go away."

Vitamins flavored with lemon were handed out. Louis sucked one after another, hunger gnawing.

Because he was tired, the sounds and expressions of his native dialect, never heard before, slipped into the Rock's Religious Knowledge lesson. It sounded vaguely like Ostend, and he, the shepherd of souls, had turned into a fisher, not of souls like me acting the Apostle Peter, but of whiting, fried herring, sprats, pickled skate. Louis's mouth watered.

"If you love the Church, you must renounce the world, thus is it written. Renounce, not only for her, for her sake, but also *through* her."

"Then go defrock yourself," murmured Bernardeau, next to Louis.

Sister Rock in flapping monk's-habit, cowl, owl glasses, cassock and all, ran like an elongated bat, tore off his frock, cassock and cowl and, familiar bald head bared, flung the black garments away as far as he could.

"I am a priest first and foremost. How I was chosen is the mystery of grace. Just like some secular callings, it has no logical explanation. Now, boys, some secular callings have been made manifest among you, by boys who have turned into men overnight, in a single day, a day like today, and who have had to pay the price. Reflect, reflect on the fact that God, in His mysterious ways, sometimes delivers up those He loves best, those He loves for their fearless longing for justice and truth, to . . ."

(Say it, risk it, shout it out loud!)

". . . the forces of darkness."

(Coward! Names! Examples!)

On the playground, when the two boys had been led away, the Rock had made the sign of the Cross in their direction. Louis had been unable to see how the boys had responded, whether they had caught that signal in Allied code, because at that very moment he had ducked behind the back of the chemistry teacher, afraid that the all-seeing Theo van Paemel with his soft felt hat would spot him.

"So that we, boys, today more than ever before, must hold our noses, not only to ward off the smell of our own accidie and inertia, but also to bury our dead, the dead in the heart of Europe." (The hollow-eyed seaman in the front room of the Lockkeeper's House had said much the same thing.)

What did he look like, this angel Holst who had now descended upon Walle! It was outrageous, embarrassing, pathetic. Just as the Crusaders used to receive from the Lady of their dreams and songs a small, generally green, scarf that they never once washed during all the years of their attempts to drive the Turks from the Holy Land, so Holst had donned a pink ski sweater of Madame Laura's, which she had probably given him to take to the dry cleaner's. From the blue trousers of his Flemish Guard uniform protruded a pair of bicycle-racing shoes that looked much too small for him.

He sat down by the dead stove, with a little parcel on his lap. Louis said that his parents were not in.

"I've got lots of time. You just go on with your homework." He picked up *Volk en Staat,* read something in it, flung the paper onto the stove, and stared into space.

They played *manille.* Louis lost six francs.

"You're getting bad cards," Holst said magnanimously. "Oh yes, last time you came to my place, did you by any chance go off with a historical novel about a duchess?"

Louis immediately began to flush furiously. Holst noticed. "Oh, you can keep it, I don't need it. I only wanted to say that if anybody asks you, you have to swear not to let on that you got it from me."

"Of course not."

"Because I'd really get it in the neck then."

"I won't say a thing."

"Have you finished it?"

"Not yet. Almost."

"You know what you should do? Write your name in it, at the front. And if they ask, just say you found the book in a dustbin in the street."

He pointed to the front page of *Volk en Staat.* "Just look at that, look." An impossibly slim Aryan in a black uniform was in the middle of beating up panic-stricken, fat-nosed dwarves, Jewish stars fluttered about like butterflies.

"That's bad," said Holst.

"Yes. And silly. Stupid."

"Very badly drawn," said Holst. "The epaulettes are all wrong, and you can't even tell what that comrade's rank is."

He handed the little parcel to Louis. "This is for your mother. Don't forget to say it comes from Madame Laura with her compliments."

"Thank you."

"Did you find it exciting, that historical novel?"

"Very. It's very well written."

"Do you want a couple more?"

"Oh yes, yes. By Feuchtwanger?"

"And some others. I'll probably be able to find them. At a good price. But you mustn't tell anybody, not a soul. It could cost me my head."

426

He put on a loden coat. Another hand-me-down from blown-up Moritz?

The small parcel contained a long, thin pork sausage. Louis read in *Volk en Staat* about the Walloon Legion, which had broken out from encircled Cherkassy, it had very nearly turned into a second Stalingrad. As he read, he nibbled at the sausage. Neither Papa nor Mama turned up, he drank one glass of water after another. Then he had eaten half the sausage, and Madame Laura's present suddenly looked so meager that he wolfed down the second half of the sickly stuff as well. He threw the wrapping paper behind Papa's paper-cutter.

Mama asked nothing about Papa, about school, or about his homework. She sat down on the wicker armchair, on the hollow left by Holst's solid weight, but she didn't notice, she stared fixedly at the seat next to Louis where his little brother was sitting, the little brother who had grown alongside him all these years, a never-crying, never-complaining (not even silently), never-eating (whether sausage or sticky black bread), pure and cuddly child.

Neither Ceusters nor De Coene reappeared at school, those two boys-turned-men-overnight. If Ceusters was really part Jewish, why had no one noticed before?

How could you tell, anyway? Louis was able to guess fairly accurately from what part of the country somebody came, and not from dialect alone. People from Aalst, for example, are sarcastic, suspicious, confirmed pessimists, people from Ostend are men of the world quick to call you their friend even as they pick your pocket, because they've been taught from childhood to fleece tourists, but you can't really get cross with them, because they're always so cheerful, people from Deinze are lumbering and warm-hearted and laugh loudest at their own jokes, and people from around here, from Walle, are flirtatious and energetic and edgy because we live so close to France, and people from . . . The bell in the Church of Our Lady began to toll monotonously, a wind sprang up, the sound of the bell fading from time to time. Aunt Mona was frying potatoes. Not cooked potatoes, making floury, almost charred little crusts, but raw, for the vitamins.

"That bell is getting on my nerves, Louis, I'll go stark raving mad. They're burying him deep, that fellow, what with all that ringing."

Cecile set the table. "It can't possibly be some ordinary worker, the way they're going on ringing."

"Don't touch the potatoes, Louis!" cried Aunt Mona. "Surely you can wait until they've been put on your plate."

The surviving members of the free citizens' army climbed up into the tower of the Church of Our Lady to avenge the arrest of Ceusters and De Coene, one of them handed the sacristan an indelible pencil soaked in an American poison, having spied previously on the sacristan and discovered that he was in the habit of sticking his pencil into his mouth.

The bell played a lament for their friends, heroes now languishing in jail for aiding and abetting the enemy. Louis shoved a wad of cloth soaked in benzine under a slowly passing Mark III tank and set it on fire. Dying German cries for *Mutti* re-echoed through the street where Grandpa (in the porch of the bank across the road from the pharmacy) stood gaping at the flames in stupefaction.

But later that evening Mama said that the bell had been ringing at the commemoration service for Odiel, Dirty Dick's friend with the small head, killed during the Allied landing at Salerno while defending those perfidious Macaronis who had meanwhile, to their eternal damnation, declared war on Germany. "There are no friends, no allies in this be-witching yet so corrupt world," wrote Louis in his notebook. Then crossed out "bewitching" and replaced it with "wondrous."

Papa and Louis sat in a train full of shouting men in uniform. At the last moment Papa had told Louis to take off his white socks because that sort of thing could spell trouble, Brussels would be completely under Flemish control that day, and wearing white socks as the anglophiles did would be considered a provocation. "But they're tennis socks!" "Makes no difference," Papa had snapped as if he knew they had been handed down from the exiled Lausengier. "Don't ruin them, those socks," Mama had whispered.

"Ah, wouldn't I just love it if one of those Brussels frog-eaters hangs out a tricolor, then you'll see some fun, nothing'll hold our men back then. One medal with a Belgian ribbon and they'll burn Brussels to the ground, Palais de Justice and all. We'll show them what our troops can do!"

"Our troops? You don't belong to any troop."

"You don't have to be a member of any particular unit to feel like a Fleming. Can't you widen your horizons a little? If you're going to contra-dict me every time I open my mouth, you'd better get off at the next station. You can find your own way back home. Have you got your passport on you?"

"My identity card. A passport is for going abroad."

Papa said nothing more. The young people in shorts walking past the compartment with furled banners and pennons had reawakened Papa's sorrow that I, his only son, introvert and loner, was excluded from their ranks, fated to languish without sharing in that all-pervasive, burning ardor which can only be found where there is a common purpose.

Louis and his father were allowed to take their place far to the rear of the procession, which started from the Petit Sablon in Brussels, far removed from the drums and the flutes and the men in uniform, behind closed ranks of solid citizens in their Sunday best. The men around them irritated Papa, they looked like a gaggle of parliamentarians, he grumbled as his metal-tipped heels rang out on the cobblestones. He did not know the words to the songs, and his loud "lalala" was drowned in the general uproar.

An hour later Papa, tired and sunburned, knotted the four corners of his handkerchief and pulled it over his head. Like the tissue paper wrapping an orange, when if you roll the orange across the floor it becomes a legless, pale crab running through the room.

"Everyone is staring at you, Papa."

"Do you want me to be burned alive?"

"Any minute now someone from the Black Brigade will get it into his head that you're doing it to poke fun at them, and he'll snatch it off."

Papa immediately removed the handkerchief. He mounted the pavement to stand among the citizens of Brussels and gave the Olympic salute. The last rows were thinning out and trudged along as if following a coffin.

Then it emerged that Papa had left his coupons behind. All they could manage to get with Louis's was two large jam sandwiches. "See how anglicized we've become, *sand-wiet-jes.*" But his anger was forced, he was too tired.

"I'm dying of hunger," said Louis.

"People eat much too much. Belgians have never been as healthy as they are now that they've had to tighten their belts. There are countries where they have nothing to eat but mud, and find it tasty to boot. Still . . . we could go to the Cattle Market, they sell horse-blood sausages there without stamps. But where is the Cattle Market?"

"We could ask."

"One of those Brussels frog-eaters, no doubt!"

They sat down on a bench in a small park with hundreds of different flowers and plants, where the dead, one-eyed Maurice de Potter was bending over in search of corn mint or ivy-leaved toadflax or pasque flower. Louis was waiting to catch his father in the act of stealthily extracting some of the nut chocolate in his pocket. The few locals who passed them all spoke in French.

"It's high time Brussels got a good clearing out. Ever since the Middle

Ages, Brussels has been ours, Flemish. Ever since the time of the Dukes, Jan I and Jan II and the rest."

"The Dukes spoke French, Papa."

"Who told you that? Is that what they teach you at College? And I was reading about it only this week! About the battle of Woeringen and Jan I, who fell off his horse during a tournament. You don't know your history, you! They didn't speak French, that's for sure. And Jan II, who built the Drapers' Hall in Leuven. Are you trying to tell me he gave orders to the workmen in French?"

"Jan II spoke English."

"That takes the cake. Now you're really making my blood boil."

"He grew up in England. His father-in-law was the King of England."

"I'm not going to talk to you anymore," said Papa, and added, "We could wring the neck of one of those pigeons and use those dry twigs over there to make a fire. Like in the good old days when Cosijns and I were tramping through France."

The birds of the Holy Ghost sat on the roof and in the gutters of the Hôtel d'Angleterre bearing olive branches in their beaks.

"What's there to stop us? Come on. We'll pretend we're staying in the hotel, we'll go up to the top floor, we'll climb onto the roof . . ."

"I don't even dare think of it. Not since your mother made me climb the rocks near the Grottos of Han in '36 . . . And anyway, the locals stuff the pigeons full of poison so they can catch them for their pots. Those pigeons are brimful of arsenic, and the locals have become immune. But if you and I simmered them in a pot all night long, just one bite and we'd have had it, boils and ulcers . . ."

Black Brigade men bicycled past, singing. Dusk began to fall, a pink glow in the sky transformed the silhouette of the Basilica into a deep-blue mosque. Papa suddenly woke up, waved his hat to dry his sweating face.

"Come along. Comb your hair. Time we went. And remember, keep your mouth shut about what we're going to see, not a word to a soul or there'll be hell to pay."

The closer Papa came to the Avenue Louise, the more diffidently he held back, the more nervously he threaded his way between the bicyclists and the overcrowded trams.

"Look ahead of you, straight ahead," Papa hissed as they passed a patrician mansion with German army trucks and an armored half-track parked outside. Papa kept a wary eye on the building as they walked on to the next corner, where Papa suddenly broke into a run and turned into a side street, holding on to his hat. Panting, he stopped in front of a narrow door, straightened Louis's tie, inspected him. "From now on you're under the Oath of Silence."

A Black Brigade man opened the door and looked at his watch.

"You're too early."

"Holst said eight o'clock," Papa lied.

"Holst can say what he wants, I'm on duty here."

"We're expected at eight o'clock, meneer."

"Meneer?"

"Comrade, I mean."

They were ushered into the apartment by a slight, freckled Brussels youth who said Madame would see them directly and smoking was not allowed. Despite that, there were two duck-shaped frosted-glass ashtrays full of butts and filter tips. The head of a blind Egyptian goddess in bronze. A small cabinet in the shape of a skyscraper, the doors forming the storys with the windows picked out in pastel colors. A screen on which gazelles and flamingos drank together at the golden waves of a lake. A mirror with cut-glass feathers. A fox-fur thrown over an apricot-colored divan. Papa examined a small box with enamel flowers.

"That's at least a hundred years old. Or more. Napoleonic."

Then Madame Laura was in the room. She took the box from Papa's hands.

"Seventeen hundred and forty-four, Louis XV," she said with the smile of a bronzed Egyptian goddess.

"I thought Louis XIV," said Papa.

"No, Louis XIV didn't like tobacco. No one was allowed to take snuff in his presence. He ate pastilles himself the whole time because of his bad breath."

"I'd heard about that," said Papa.

She was wearing a peignoir with black-and-gold motifs that went with the furniture, stylized swallows and chrysanthemums. From the wide, obliquely cut sleeves, full white arms emerged, unadorned. I must describe her hairstyle to Mama, all combed to one side, with one wave half-covering an eye. The skin was stretched taut over her wide cheekbones. Hemorrhoid ointment. She isn't looking at Papa.

"I've heard a lot about you."

"From Holst?" asked Louis.

"He says that you not only read books but remember everything that's in them." Because he was being laughed at again, because he had turned scarlet again, because he wanted to blot out this veiled, mocking, skirmishing small talk, he allowed his lower lip to droop, squinted a little, and lisped, "What I really like reading are stories about Ukky and Wappy, Or maybe Fik and Fok. But Ukky and Wappy are my favorites."

Papa was dumbfounded. He had introduced a gibbering village idiot into this elegant Brussels residence. He coughed furiously.

431

Madame Laura narrowed her cloud-gray eyes into tiny slits as if bothered by tobacco smoke. "I see, Ukky and Wappy. And what do Ukky and Wappy do?"

"They get up to all sorts of tricks. Like all the other Red Indian boys. And every time Wappy gets frightened, he yells, 'Holy cow!' "

"You're very nicely settled in here, Madame Laura," said Papa forcefully.

"Holy cow," repeated the woman who drove Raf and Holst and Uncle Armand and Moritz-of-the-blown-to-bits-tram wild. She laughed, surprisingly, infectiously. "Holy cow!" she cried and Aunt Violet hated her and Louis wanted the wide, full lips to brush his hot cheek.

The slightly built Brussels youth, who might have been a Walloon Legionnaire in civvies, poured port into sparkling little square glasses. Papa fumbled with his cufflinks. "Perhaps we should start getting down to business, Madame Laura. And to get straight to the point: how much are these books going to cost each? I'll have to look them over first, of course, to see what they're worth . . ."

"I'm not doing business, mijnheer."

"Oh, I thought, am I wrong then? I supposed . . ."

Louis cast off his mongoloid mask. She was aware of it. He was aware of the tip of her tongue.

"I'm doing it solely, and I know the risks I'm taking, as a favor to your son. Holst drew my attention to his . . . er . . . to Louis's voracious reading habits. I consider it my duty to make sure he reads something other than what is being inflicted on young people, the rustic tales that are being inflicted on young people these days. "Another small port, Mijnheer Seynaeve?" Suddenly the raucous tones of a barmaid broke through her veiled voice (shall I put that in my notebook, perhaps being read at this very moment by Mama, who is snooping around my room, no, Mama doesn't give two hoots for my inaccessible private life.) I have never seen a barmaid up close. So that's what they're like. I'll have to write down later that she has cat's-eyes, feline eyes. Or is that too banal? And yet it's true. They light up.

"No, *merci*, no more port, *merci*, Madame Laura. That one's gone straight to my head."

"Come, come, a big, strong fellow like you."

They sipped their ports.

"Recently I myself greatly enjoyed a couple of books by Aldous Huxley, Louis. I can recommend them. You'll see, there must be at least twenty copies of *Point contrepoint*."

The legionnaire, who had witnessed the charge of serried ranks of

Asiatics on his position in Cherkassy, came in to announce that the hair-dresser was in the drawing room.

"You must promise to come back soon, Louis."

"I promise," he said.

"Or perhaps I shall see you in Bastegem. Because I shall shortly be getting married to André Holst. I hope you'll find the time to come to the reception. The wedding itself will be strictly private, but the reception is for all my friends." Louis left her, she whom God had created on the seventh day for him, Louis, for his trembling fingers that would be hacked off like the claws of the crab under the orange-paper. Her shadowed gray eyes followed him with a mocking sorrow, if there is such a thing, so that he turned his head away, and because she thought he was peering at the Louis XV snuffbox like a pawnbroker or a dealer, she said, "It's only a copy, of course." Her infectious laugh. "If it were genuine, I'd be a millionaire."

The Black Brigade man from the front door (a mere concièrge, since he was unarmed) led them along empty corridors and stairs to a coal cellar with mountains of anthracite.

"That'll see them through a few winters," whispered Papa. They clambered across the coal. "If you want to heat this entire building, with all those high ceilings . . ." said the concièrge. "And a pound of coal here or there is nothing to them."

He put his shoulder to a door that was stuck. "*Voilà*. You know the agreement. For God's sake keep your traps shut. Not a word." The two slavishly silent dogs, traps shut, nodded, *down*!

"Not even a cough!"

"No, no," said Papa. He tumbled headlong onto a pile of books and dragged Louis down with him. They heard the key.

The door was locked. A dirty gray light fell into the room from a small cellar window.

For days on end some demented and overworked librarian had been flinging hundreds and thousands of books into the room. The floor held a hill of them piled up higgledy-piggledy, hurled inside or perhaps tipped in like coal through the cellar window with a giant shovel. No, that couldn't have happened, because against one wall they had been stacked right up to the ceiling, the prisoner who had been detailed to do the work must then have escaped and the towers of books had collapsed. Papa scrambled to his feet and went and sat down on a pile of dictionarylike red leather volumes—the *Werke* of Heinrich Heine—and switched on a pocket torch.

Louis's job was to pick out all leather-bound or illustrated books and put them in a pile. Collected works had to be put in numerical order. "If they're not complete, they're not worth a cent. And French books are the first choice, I've got more clients for those, it's degrading, but most moneybags read French."

It appeared that the French did not publish expensive books bound in leather. And unfortunately Volumes IV and VII of Cuvier's *Le Règne animal* were missing. All the animals had been drawn by hand in scrupulous detail. "Complete, I told you!" Papa tore out a few plates, of an anteater, a penguin, and a boa constrictor. "For your mother, she's so crazy about wildlife."

"Henri Barbusse," Louis read out. "On *japon impérial.*"

"No soft covers, I told you."

After a couple of hours Papa decided they had enough for the time being, two tall piles, he made himself a nest between the books and lay down, knees pulled up. When he was snoring, Louis fished the pocket torch out of his jacket pocket and skimmed through *Point contrepoint,* it was all about witty and boring Englishmen. Through *Der Querschnitt,* a review with passages that looked like the poems of Paul van Ostaijen. Through Remarque's *Drei Kameraden.* The three comrades threw rings over a wooden pin at the fair and won all the prizes, because for years they had been doing nothing else in the '14–'18 trenches. The owner of the booth was furious, but they kept on playing and the poor sap had to hand over doll after doll. When one of the three comrades woke up before his sweetheart did, he would quickly clean his teeth to freshen his breath for her. Louis read a bit of Barbusse's *L'Enfer,* about a hotel room with a hole drilled in the wall so that you could see everything in the room next door, even that black, hairy triangle. He read more quickly, picked out a few random paragraphs from Robert Neumann's *Struensee,* from Israël Querido's *De oude Waereld,* his head began to ache from reading too quickly, too greedily, and then he looked at pictures, of naked fat women with reddish tufts of pubic hair and weals across their buttocks. Grosz. "Fat women, of course, take their pleasure in curious habits, crazy habits . . ."

In a copy of *Sélection* he discovered stylized, blown-up women painted by Fritz van den Berghe, a man about whom, once upon a time, on the day that Simone and her sadness had first come into his life, some red-haired ape had made such sneering remarks. Tits with nipples like haddock's-eyes, an ungainly naked woman lay stretched at full length while a man with a bow tie smoked a cigarette on the edge of a ravine. A peasant woman breast-fed three little boys at the same time. His eyes fell shut. His eyes shot open. A prolonged scream. Dull thuds. The screaming man was defending himself. Three or four gruff, strident voices barked out hacked-off commands, imitated German orders, mechanical, practiced, brooking no argument. "Hurry up, get going—bastard—we know all about it—keeping your mouth shut, are you?—out with it—want some more?—two o'clock on the night of January twelfth."

"Christ Almighty," said Papa softly. "They're letting him have it!"

"It's in the room next door."

"No, no, on the other side of the courtyard."

It could be Holst being tortured for having smuggled them into this forbidden domain, into this exciting paradise of decadent Jewish propaganda.

"It's Holst."

"You blockhead," said Papa. "Flemish Guardsmen don't do that sort of thing. It's not their line. Anyway, can't you hear they're Limburgers?"

There were gurglings and murmurings in the water pipes, iron doors slammed shut. Then the man screamed like a woman, it ended in a long wail: "God, God, God." The Rock said, "God only comes when His creatures call Him." Boots ran up and down iron stairs, a truck revved up.

"They've killed him."

"Shut up."

"By accident. They didn't realize. But he had weak blood vessels. And a single blow to his temple . . ."

"Of course not. They're leaving him alone now. He's confessed, names and addresses."

"Some heroes! Four against one!"

"It isn't a boxing match. And there is no alternative. That bunch can't be allowed to go on shooting down innocent Flemings, putting bombs under trains. We have to find things out."

"But suppose they got the wrong man, that he didn't know anything?"

"They wouldn't have picked him up in that case. And if there was a mistake, and they realize when they interrogate him that he hasn't done anything, then they let him go and apologize."

"How do they realize?"

"They're experts. They've been to special universities. And shut up with your stupid questions."

For the next quarter of an hour Papa kept breaking wind. "It's nerves. And anyway, if you must, you must. A man has to let off at least seven farts a day. Otherwise he's going to need the doctor."

One of the books Louis had put to one side, *Die Puppe,* contained a photograph he had at home in his folder of clippings of articles, cartoons,

435

and illustrations. It was at the bottom right of the two complete pages illustrating the difference between classical and Jewish art. Victorious naked warriors with thick, evenly curled pubic hair like flames of marble, flourishing torches in the air, maternal women with a child at their breast, splendidly weatherbeaten sailors, were set opposite watches as limp as omelettes, fragmented robotlike dwarves, panels with nothing on them but little squares like dishcloths. The photograph in *Die Puppe* was very sharp and in color. In a forest full of autumn leaves stood a naked figure that, though fleshy and voluptuous like a woman, was actually a doll, you could see the joints at knee, groin, thigh, midriff. The doll had neither face nor shoulders, because above her navel, but upside down, there rose another belly and full thighs and legs that looked just like the ones underneath. At top and bottom the doll ended in feet with rolled-up white socks and little black patent-leather shoes. Next to the bottom feet, which were splayed out like Charlie Chaplin's, lay a crumpled striped dress on a bed of golden leaves. The lightish umber area that swelled up between the thighs and that could also split apart for an *entrechat* looked fuzzy in the first light of day breaking through the cellar window, Louis couldn't make it out properly. Somewhat farther back in the forest a man was standing behind two birch trees, likewise without a head, hands in pockets. In his dark coat, he was leaning forward against a tree trunk. Although he could not see the doll, since even if he had had a head his view would have been blocked by the birch in front of him, he was nevertheless a voyeur, an accomplice in the crime that had been committed. His figure resembles Holst's, but it is *I* who am spying on these torsos and abdomens hastily reassembled into a monstrous whole after an autopsy, I with my superfluous head, with my convulsively stretched thing that pokes against this birch bark, against all manner of hindrances.

Papa took the book out of his hand. "They're perfectly right to pulp this filth, burn it."

"Give it to me!" yelped Louis, and Papa, taken by surprise, handed it back to him.

The concièrge came to release them and brought them two new cardboard suitcases. "It stinks in here," he said reproachfully.

"I thought you'd never come," cried Papa like a happy lover.

"Usually we don't work here on Sundays, but there was something urgent going on, possibly you heard it."

"Vaguely," said Papa.

"Did they shoot him?" asked Louis. The concièrge bristled. "You've heard nothing, absolutely nothing, get it?"

"You don't have to tell us twice," said Papa.

The suitcases were as heavy as lead, their train was hours late.

They unloaded the books in the front room. "We'll put them in alphabetical order tomorrow," said Papa. "Right now I'm off to bed."

Louis dreamed of two pastel-colored armadillos rooting among paradisiacal bushes and then awkwardly mounting the wooden scaffold that had been erected beneath the Belfry in Walle, a wobbling platform with flags and wreaths on which stood Ceusters and De Coene, chewing gum, wearing their Boy Scout belts with the fleur-de-lys buckles. Drums rolled softly. An overture. He wanted to go to them, since they were throwing him imploring looks, Mama said, "Right, off you go, you may go to their aid, but first you must comb your hair, come, let me do it."

Louis could not resist this, he laid his head on her lap as on a chopping block. From beneath her peacock-eye dress she brought out a pair of red-hot curling tongs. "Mama, I'll be too late. Listen, the drums are getting louder! Please! Let me go!" But she went on curling his hair, the hair oil sizzled.

They never caught another glimpse of Madame Laura, who had been married in the meantime. A very private affair, according to Berwouts the concierge. Every Saturday evening for five weeks they went to fetch books, but they no longer spent the night there. The cardboard cases were wearing out.

Louis stroked the many-colored spines of the books he had put in his bedroom. He skimmed through most of them, he had given up *Point contrepoint* halfway, but he read every line of George Hermann's *Jetje Gebert en Henriette Jacoby.* "What's wrong this time?" asked Papa, when he caught him with a tear-stained face on the veranda.

"The Jews, they're always in someone's way, they're always being chased from pillar to post, it's not fair."

"Is that in this book?"

"No. But you can tell."

"Jews are fine ones to talk."

"But what they say is true."

"You must always take the truth of a Jew with a pinch of salt."

"And not yours, of course!"

"It's nothing to cry about."

Louis was positive that this man was not his father. And I am not Mama's child, either. They don't even know it themselves, but when I lay in swaddling clothes in the maternity home, I was exchanged for another child. Grandpa is the only one who knows, and he keeps his mouth shut, or perhaps he did mention it just to his favorite, Aunt Mona, she's always acted so strangely toward me.

"And what about the Boers in South Africa being starved and martyred in concentration camps by the English? Or the Irish, the Indians, all of them slaughtered by the English? And our boys in the trenches in '14–'18? I don't hear you mention them. You have no tears to spare for them. There always have to be scapegoats, and this time it's the Jews."

"Always, Papa?"

"Yes, always, don't you pay any attention? That's life. It's tough if it happens to you, but that's just the luck of the draw."

"Most laws are based on chance, the whole state system is, anyway," said Grandpa.

"And the scapegoat was a Lamb," said the Rock.

"No! No!" cried Louis obstinately.

The Rock was talking more slowly than ever, that day. "You need only look around you to see how unjust our society can be, and yet it may still turn out to be our salvation. I shall not be there to see it, but society can be saved. Equality and justice, those concepts so glibly mouthed by the very people who trample them underfoot every day, can only be achieved by society, by the state, but which state? God's? Which God? He who has the face of the other. What revelations have we to look forward to before we realize that there is something divine in man's works? No revelation? No? Yes? No. The bestiality that assails us, boys, the horrors without equal to which people prefer to turn a blind eye, I must admit there is not one spark in that of the light that I call God, and that I believe burns in every man. And yet the God who, as St. Paul says, remains unknown, where can He be found if we seek him out? In the most humiliated among us."

"In Ceusters and De Coene," Louis said out loud. His somnolent classmates pricked up their ears. The Rock said, "Yes," and fell silent for a long time. Then, as if he had been transplanted to another lesson, to another class, he embarked upon a long story about Moses, and how amusing it was—which he said with a forced smile, his thoughts patently elsewhere—that Michelangelo should have depicted the prophet with horns, misled as he had been by an error in the translation of the Bible: *facies cornuta* instead of *coronata*.

In the teachers' common room the Rock gave Louis two dozen cigars for Papa. It was so unlikely a gift that Louis thought, He must really be in hot water now. Does the headmaster know? This stuff must have set him back thousands of francs.

"Did you follow what I said in class about the face of the other? No. I could see you didn't."

The Rock sank deeper into the leather armchair in which generations of priests had sat before him. He looked helpless.

"There is no other pupil who has given me as much sorrow as you have. Perhaps that is why I pray for you most of all. Don't put on such a blasé expression. I have been a friend to you. Because you have been wounded, although you yourself are not aware of the nature and extent of your wounds. You put fresh dressings on them every day."

"Speak for yourself," said Louis.

"Pay attention, you young pup. I haven't much time left. I can't tell you why." His pebble glasses misted up. When he took them off to wipe them with a bedraggled handkerchief, he looked more defenseless than ever.

"Louis."

"Yes, Father."

"Study Greek. Every day."

"Is that all?"

"This coldness of yours frightens me. And fills me with pity. Go now."

At the door Louis said, "I did understand. The others, that's the key."

The Rock blessed him rapidly, as if chasing something away. "I will pray for you. Go now. Quickly."

Two days later the Rock was taken off to Germany, no one knew where. Now Louis spoke freely to him.

"Reverend . . ."

"Don't call me Reverend."

"Father . . ."

"I wasn't present at your conception."

"Sir . . ."

"I may be of noble descent, but I do not wish to be addressed as such."

"Evariste de Launay de Kerchove . . ."

"Say 'Rock.' "

"Rock."

"What is it, you whippersnapper?"

"I am studying Greek. Every day. The word for togetherness, for the others, is *koinonia.*"

"The stress is on the third syllable."

"*Koinonía.*"

"That's it. *Go now. Quickly.*"

The Rock went away and Bekka came back. From the way she acted she might never have written a single letter. Impatiently she ate four slices of bread and mulberry jam, followed Louis to the attic, and rummaged with him in the two boxes marked "The Sons of the Leie," Papa's prewar drama group, and came up with rags, ribbons, gloves, velvet cloaks, domino masks, hats with white plumes. Louis put the postman's-cap from the operetta *Spring in Herentals* on her head. She pulled on musketeer boots, which came halfway up her thighs. She lifted her skirt to see the effect, the postman's-coat came down to her ankles. Louis wriggled into a flounced orange dress and donned a broad-brimmed white straw hat. In the dusty mirror he was a rawboned version of Mama-of-yesteryear, a poorer specimen of Madame Laura. He hid behind a screen to which hundreds of cigar bands had been stuck in concentric circles. Bekka raised her right arm. *"Sieg Heil!"* she said to an immense hall filled with invited guests in gala dress. "I am the *Obergruppenführer,* and I have come here to Bohemia for a rest. It's not very sunny, but we're not worried about that, we've seen worse. I don't know what is going to happen to me, ladies and gentlemen, we'll just have to wait and see."

She sat down, pulled the uniform coat over her lean, strong thighs. She drank from the copper goblet used in Verschaeve's *Judas,* in which Papa had been so acclaimed as the mute rabbi, and belched. "I'm very comfortable here, the Bohemians do as I tell them, and so do the Egyptians. If they start acting up, they'll get what's coming to them in a camp." She leaped up, seized a centurion's wooden sword, and waved it around. "Are you listening to me, brothers from Bohemia? But what is that I hear? The telephone? Hello, oh, it's you, *Führer!* Well, *Führer,* I've arrived safely, the weather could be better but everything else is just dandy. *Heil!* We're going to crush those Gypsies, all right, don't you worry. *Heil, Führer,* you'll be well satisfied."

She threw the telephone far over the roof of the reconstructed gendarmerie building, stopped in front of the screen, and knocked. "Is anybody there?" She stepped back, particles of dust floated up. "I am just going to go back to my castle, Harkany" (Hradčany, he had coached her so carefully to say!) "with two telephones and two bathrooms, to eat some cauliflower, where little babies come from. Who are you? Speak, *Donnerwetter,* speak, madame! Who are you?" Louis gave a deep bow, holding on to his hat with lace gloves. "A poor peasant woman from hereabouts, most noble Herr *Obergruppenführer.*"

"Oh, you *verdammte* lying swine!" screeched Bekka and brought the flat of her sword down on the white hat. "Ouch! Ouch! I haven't done anything," cried the partisan disguised as a peasant woman disguised as Louis.

"Shut up! On your knees!" The sword touched his neck.

"Oh, please, mijnheer, I am too old, and once I've knelt down I'll never be able to get up again! *Bitte, bitte!*"

Bekka kicked at his ribs until he lay down on the floorboards, gray bits of grain in the wide scuffed cracks. The postman swung her sword in a circle. "Raise your Bohemian head one inch and off it flies."

"But . . ."

"No buts. You have no right to talk, you're no more than human refuse, you with your black eyes and stunted bodies . . ."

She stopped, either because she was thinking of her father, who was in a labor camp, or else because she had heard something downstairs. Then she goose-stepped around to the rhythm of a fanfare. "Halt!" He pulled out a Sten gun from under his dress. She put up her hands and mumbled, "Comrade!"

"Me your comrade? Not on your life, *never.*" He drew himself up to his full manly height. "Your time is up, Reinhard Tristan Eugen. I flew straight here from my Scottish training camp to savor this moment of vengeance!"

She looked around her, wild-eyed, but then, realizing that there was no way out, prepared herself for death and started to pray. From a wicker basket he pulled out a globe of the world the size of a melon, one of those Grandpa had sold before the war. "Say your last prayer. This grenade has been steeped in the blood of the innocent."

"Mercy." Bekka trembled. Suddenly there was a draft in the attic. He threw the grenade and flopped down on a pile of damp, musty costumes. She stayed on her feet, globe in hand, and pointed at the colors. "Alaska, Greenland," she said.

"You're dead!" cried Louis.

"No."

"Mortally wounded. Pieces of iron and glass in your liver. They are telephoning the *Führer* at the Eastern Front to say you're having an operation."

"No," she said obstinately, annoyingly, just like a woman. He knocked the globe from her hand, the dented planet rolled toward the stairs at the edge of the abyss.

"The grenade failed to go off," Louis said. "American rubbish. The pin didn't engage, that changes all our plans."

He, the peasant woman, throttled the *Reichsprotektor,* the skinny girl. She let him go on throttling her until she finally, motionlessly, ardently, died, rattling, and he lifted up her dress and said in a muffled voice that he would bury her in hallowed ground, and, humming *"Dies irae,"* tugged at the elastic of her panties, worn to the point of transparency.

"Don't touch," said the corpse weakly.

"Shut up." He pulled the panties down. All the violas, cellos, harps, trombones of the monster orchestra from *The Golden City* struck up. At long last, after all that baffling, secret hunger, his first glimpse now of the golden slash between booted thighs, but there was not enough light, so he dragged the corpse with the clenched thighs toward the window. Then a fat rat came running up the stairs.

"Carry on, carry on," said Cecile, chest-high in the stairwell. "Don't mind me." Bekka pulled her skirt down with a practiced gesture and an air of relief that the playacting in which she had taken part for a few slices of bread with mulberry jam had been broken off prematurely.

The three of them squatted by the ancient camera that had belonged to Mama's sainted uncle, Father Wiemeersch, and with which he, at risk to his life, had snapped wild beasts and Negro tribes in their natural surroundings to add to the Bishop's collection.

Cecile said that Louis looked silly with his knickerbockers under the skirt.

Louis wanted to explain that this was precisely the intention, because: (a) that is how women went about in the countryside beyond our eastern frontiers, and (b) it indicated that he was disguised as a woman, but he thought better of it, Cecile was a stupid cow. He had seen them himself in Mecklenburg, those women who came from Poland and Russia, drab and shapeless in jackets, headscarves and army trousers under their skirts, trudging past houses with low thatched roofs in which their lords and masters lived, women in workmen's-smocks and puff sleeves, and maimed, debilitated men wearing leather aprons, the old round Storm Trooper caps on their heads, weaving swastikas for the Eastern Front from twigs and sprigs and bits of foliage.

Cecile, who was so stupid that long after it was obvious that her game of patience would come out she nevertheless dutifully, slowly, obtusely, continued to lay every last card down in the right sequence, said that she'd been thrown out at home. No, not for good.

"Mama was sitting on Pépé's lap," she said. Louis grinned at Bekka.

Pépé, Spanish for Peter, which was the Flemish for godfather. I'll call Grandpa that next time I see him. Pépé!

"Pépé gave me money to go to the cinema. He doesn't realize they're closed on a Wednesday. He lives on a different plane with all his book-learning. He says he's much too good for this world. And that's true. Last week he spent a whole evening in mourning, Pépé."

"What for?" asked Louis, astonished.

She ignored him and said, addressing herself exclusively to Bekka, like an Aunt Mona in miniature, "On account of her extra-uterine. It took three hours. But it all went all right."

"Nowadays that sort of thing is no problem," said wise old witch Bekka Cosijns.

"If it's done properly."

"A curettage."

Then they talked about cancer. Like women. Like all women except Mama. Who did not have any of this uterine business.

Louis smelled Cecile's breath. *"Godverdomme,"* he shouted. "You've been eating our mulberry jam downstairs."

"Just a little spoonful," she said, found a tutu among the colorful musty clothes and held it up.

"That must have been for a really fat female." She threw it over Louis's head and began to dance, a farrago of inane little leaps.

"Shirley Temple herself," said Louis.

"Dimwit. All Shirley Temple can do is tap-dance."

He saw that Bekka was completely captivated by Cecile's prancing about, following her swoops and hops with twitches of her shoulders and knees. The others, the others, said Rock. All the others dance, except me. Even my dreams, when I remember them in the morning, sink, sag, seep. Downward. Ponderously. Like the pictures in *Sélection.* Those blundering, clumsy clubfeet in the mud. Is that what the *Entartete,* the degenerate, do, drag you down, into their own image, remodel you in their own image? Before you know it, you've become one of them. The holy, the sacred, the glorification of courage and energy in those works of Kolbe, Thorak, Breker he had pasted in his scrapbook, was that only for those who believed in it? Yes. Was he (still) one of them? No.

With lead in his calves, screwed to the floorboards, Louis was forced to acknowledge that, while Cecile had been tripping and swaying, he himself had been infected by international Jewry, it had crept into his brain, cunningly, unstoppably. If there are any "others" to whom I belong, want to belong, they are the ones, those fragmented Cubists, Expressionists, all the other ists. Your heroes with their swords and torches made of lard, they melt away.

Bekka clapped as Cecile remained standing on one leg, the upper part of her body leaning forward, on the point of flight, she might take off any moment, as in all the photographs Grandpa had taken of her which were displayed in a fan shape in the front room or stuck into his wallet, over his heart.

Mama was furious. "But you get enough to eat! More than all the other children on our street!"

Louis was just about to explain how he had seen a little old woman in the street who had been on the point of collapsing with hunger and that he had given her a few pieces of bread and butter with mulberry jam, when it appeared that Mama was going on about a sausage. The minced pork sausage Holst had brought!

"Not only are you greedy, thinking of no one except yourself, but you've put me in an extremely awkward position. The very least you could have done was confess it, but no, like a thief in the night . . ."

"That's death," said Seynaeve the lightning conductor.

"What's death?"

"Death comes like a thief in the night."

"That's all I need!" she cried. She sucked fiercely at her cigarette. "And that's not the end of the story. Far from it! Lucien van Capellen, his name doesn't mean anything to you, I suppose? No, of course not, the work I do at the ERLA just so that you don't go without, you don't give two hoots for that, do you?"

"Lucien van Capellen," said Louis thoughtfully, without thinking.

"The gentleman-farmer's son. His parents sent me four pounds of sausages as a mark of their gratitude."

"Two pounds at most!"

"Four pounds," yelled Mama. "Lucien van Capellen doesn't lie. Not like you, lying all day long. He says, 'Madame Seynaeve, did you like those sausages?' I say, 'What sausages?' I didn't have the faintest idea. And he says, 'Oh, I see. So that's how you're treating it.' and he turned his back on me, I just stood there open-mouthed! And ever since that Jantje Piroen affair, all the boys assume I go in for funny business and that I'm too big for my boots."

"It wasn't even a pound and a half."

"So who ate the other two pounds, then?"

"Holst."

She quieted down at once. Like boiling milk when you turn off the gas. That's how the Expressionists would have put it.

"Holst, that's possible."

"On his way here," said Louis. "Holst is always hungry, with that great carcass of his."

"The trouble is that Lucien van Capellen is in the White Brigade."

"Have him thrown into jail then, and that'll be that!"

She was startled. By the ruthless beast in him. He was excited by the disgust he could read in her as in a book.

Papa was helping load the serious casualties onto a truck. Walls blazed, clouds of soot showered over screaming people, mostly soldiers. Something had gone wrong with the siren. Although the bombers had been gone for over an hour, it kept giving breathless, plaintive yelps every now and then. All the soldiers, even those left untouched, shouted as they scattered, searched among the lumps of flesh. Two churches had been hit, they said, there wasn't much left of the railway station. The soldiers were in khaki shorts, most had been on their way home after two years.

Papa sweated and puffed but showed no signs of the Seynaeve haste, supporting the soldiers with almost tender gestures and calming a Red Cross nursing assistant who was flailing around convulsively. Some soldiers had crept under a broken railway carriage, a lieutenant yelled at them and then came looking for them with a pocket torch.

Suddenly, in the stationary truck where Louis was supporting a dying soldier who clung to his knees, he heard Papa swear. He had hurt his foot on a twisted tram rail. But then he went on carrying, stroking, soothing the injured.

The dying man was young. He rattled something about *Blumen*, he stank, his intestines, held back by his belt, were spilling out of his coat in several places. Facing Louis sat a stupefied German captain in a Luftwaffe uniform, holding a severed arm in both of his hands like a baby. The soldier beside Louis had lost his chin, as if cut off with a razor. Between his fingers hung something frayed, a bloody white goatee. The dying man said clearly, "Benjamino," and listened intently to something close by. He made as if to get up, Louis held him back, intoning, "*Ruhe, Ruhe, bitte, be still.*"

Louis rode six times from the station to the military hospital and back again in the truck, until he fell asleep among the mangled soldiers, after which the driver would not take him along anymore.

Papa was sitting under a thick layer of black-and-gray dust in the rubble as the sun came up and drove the smoke away.

"My big toe is broken," said Papa. "I can't walk. But when I see these boys, pining so for their *Heimat,* I know I shouldn't complain. But it does hurt."

He held his hand out to his son, and his son, who saw that he was gray and old, pulled him to his feet, a friend in need, through thick and thin.

"But, Staf, you look as if you're limping!" exclaimed Uncle Robert.

"I've done my ankle in," said Papa and let himself drop into the chair, his right leg sticking straight out.

"Just now it was your big toe," said Louis.

"I can't feel a thing, it's all broken inside my foot. But perhaps it will grow together again all by itself."

When they had come in and he had seen Uncle Robert and Aunt Monique in their bloodstained white butcher aprons, Louis had thought for a moment that all on their own these two unsung and unassuming heroes had turned their home into a private hospital, that in this monstrous night, cleft asunder, they were helping to relieve human suffering. But nothing of the kind. Uncle Robert poured Balegem geneva, Louis was given a quarter of a glassful with a lump of sugar by Aunt Monique. In the garage two flustered apprentices were chopping at yard-high chunks of meat that snapped like young birches, Uncle Robert rubbed his bloody hands. With his wife and his helpers he had carted away three horses from the bombed train, and not once had his fairly decrepit van acted up. "And you saw what the ground was like there around the station!"

"I'm worn out from all that rattling around," said Aunt Monique.

"I had my eye on a few foals as well, but the military police were watching us. If they hadn't been so busy with the people pilfering coal, they would have nabbed me for sure. I'd estimate that twenty thousand pounds of coal must have been taken. Let's say there were a hundred people and each one had a fifty-pound bag, and they came and went three times each . . ." He counted, couldn't work it out.

"But then those people weren't properly organized."

Papa nodded, exhausted.

"One ought to organize things properly, with about five boys and two small trucks and be ready the moment the siren goes . . . But then you can never tell if they're going to hit another coal warehouse . . ." Uncle Robert fetched two large steaks of horsemeat.

"How much do I owe you?" asked Papa.

"But, my dear brother, what are you talking about! We've been put in this world to help one another. *Allee,* another drop, we only live once."

"No, not you, Louis," said Papa. Louis was given a glass of goat's milk instead. He wondered if the goat was still alive, in this house of slaughter.

"Any minute now our father will be coming for his meat as well."

"Does he eat horsemeat now?" said Papa, suddenly wide awake. "Who would have believed it!"

"No, no, for him it still has to be *entrecôte.*"

"That's what I thought," said Papa. Grandpa had an unholy fear of horses, claiming that they became hysterical because they saw everything nine or twelve times life-size, so that a butterfly on the road was as big as a duck, and also because a mare belonging to Mijnheer Tierenteyn, God rest his shot-down soul, had once bolted with Mijnheer Tierenteyn in the saddle, out of sheer jealousy.

"He does love his *entrecôte,*" said Uncle Robert with a faraway look. "Especially the cut close to the bone, he gnaws away at it with such relish it's a pleasure to watch him. When I see him dig in like that, I say to myself, George Bernard Shaw can say what he likes and stick to his nuts and vegetables, but when all is said and done, man is a carnivore."

(The captain lifted the Luftwaffe sleeve, the stump of the arm had been chopped off like a birch tree, the captain brought the gnarl up to his contorted open mouth.)

Louis vomited into the toilet. The apprentices hacking and scraping away at the fatty tissue laughed at him. "It's strong stuff, that Balegem geneva, hey?" Horse's-teeth lay scattered over the floor.

On the way home they had to produce their special *Schein*, the elderly German patrol obviously didn't trust their armbands. A gendarme on a bicycle joined them.

"I thought you were such pals with the Germans, Staf."

"Oh well," said Papa, dead-tired. "They have their duty to do. And the regulations are the same for everybody."

"There's something to that," said the gendarme and cycled on.

"The suicide rate is highest among gendarmes," said Papa. "I'm beginning to see why."

"Why?"

"Because nobody likes them."

The house in Oudenaarde Road seemed miles away. The siren had not finished its drawn-out caterwauling.

"That Robert is getting really ugly-looking," said Papa, "what with putting on all that fat. He always was on the fat side, but now he's gone over the top. And he always eats his meat and his potatoes, and his sandwiches, with mayonnaise. 'So long as it's tasty,' he says and laps the sauce up like soup. If you ask me, it's his wife's fault that he's put on so much weight. A man changes because of his wife, we've seen that sort of thing before. I'd be surprised if those two ever have children."

Mama fried the horsemeat steaks. Papa bared his foot, and it really did look bruised, blue all over. When Paelinck the pharmacist was called in and had taken Papa's foot in his hand, he said, "At least it's nothing like as bad as what happened to Jantje Piroen."

What had happened to Jantje Piroen? Just one bomb had fallen on the jail and that nincompoop from Toontjes Street, who hadn't had enough money for an appeal and so had opted for imprisonment, had been under it. "He's lost both his legs, he'll pull through, but it'll take time and money," said the pharmacist, adding, "Staf, my diagnosis is that you should wash your feet more thoroughly in the future." Because the blue was from the dye in Papa's socks.

When Paelinck had left, Mama said, sweet as honey, "Would you like me to heat some water to wash your feet?"

"It's only because you buy such cheap socks!" shouted Papa.

"A decent person washes his feet twice a week," said Mama.

"Wash your backside!" yelled Papa, voice breaking, and slammed the door shut violently. Mama listened to his steps fleeing down the street. "Hypocrite," she said under her breath.

Although the Allies came overhead now even in daytime and the pupils often had to rush off to the College cellar, the priests doggedly refused to close the school. We all have to die like Xenophon's ten thousand Greeks in Asia Minor.

Louis walked through the park on the way to school. His step slowed, he stopped.

He had seen Marnix de Puydt lying curled up next to a metal litter basket, his small, bare, golden-haired feet sticking out defenselessly from gray flannel trousers on the gravel.

("Don't touch," said the gym teacher, "you never know if there might be internal injuries.")

Louis stood and stared. De Puydt's ear was resting on his hat, his stomach swelled and subsided, the man was laboring in his sleep.

"Mijnheer de Puydt."

Raise him to his feet as a Samaritan would? Run away? And if he then breathed his last, laborious breath, would I be a murderer to the end of my days?

De Puydt's pudgy little hands fumbled in the air, found the scrolled cast-iron foot of the bench beside him. He pulled himself along the bench, found a foothold, his little sausages of toes curled on the gravel.

"Mijnheer de Puydt."

"It is most strange," said the Flemish Mind.

"You fell asleep."

"Yes. But I managed to get up all by myself. It is most strange. I thought, Marnix, how about a short nap? And then there I was lying on the grass and, it is most strange, I heard myself speaking in the very words of Guido Gezelle, our divine Pastor, our Phoenix on his deathbed—proof that on the brink of this self-sought coma I was comparing myself with the incomparable—I heard myself say, you won't believe me, in a voice that was certainly not my own, 'With gladness I hark'd to the flutings of birds.' Now to be sure I have never been a stranger to bifurcation, who are you, come to think of it?"

"Louis. Seynaeve. The printer's son."

"Good at essays. Right or wrong?"

"Fairly," said Louis, taken aback. He sat down beside De Puydt.

"A talent for essays. I know that from . . ."

"My Grandpa!" Louis exclaimed. He tingled. De Puydt nodded with a thoughtful expression. Incredible, my Grandpa blatantly singing my praises behind my back. My praises. Or rather, the praises of his grandson, the boy who had inherited his grandfather's qualities, talent skipping a generation. At that point he became aware that De Puydt had been speaking in, that is, delivering himself of, a series of familiar rhetorical flourishes. Did he never shut up, then, except in the Café Groeninghe? Was he holding forth now because this College boy by his side, still wet behind the ears, was not a real conversational partner, out here in the wide, empty spaces of the park?

"Where are we?"

"In the park, Mijnheer de Puydt."

"Of course, Queen Astrid Park."

"No. The Golden Spurs Park."

"*Tiens,*" said De Puydt.

"Have you hurt yourself?"

"Very much," said De Puydt and fell silent. Behind the oaks, from near the town hall, came the familiar, steady sound of marching soldiers. Suddenly they burst into ". . . *einen neuen Marsch probier'n.*" They hadn't enlarged their repertoire in all this time.

"What is your name?"

"Louis Seynaeve."

"Louis, Louis, like the great and sainted king who had Sainte Chapelle built for the Crown of Thorns. Listen, Louis."

"Yes, Mijnheer de Puydt."

"I've done everything wrong. Everything. And it's my fault and nobody else's. There are no mitigating circumstances."

He got up and stood on the gravel. Louis did, too. De Puydt took Louis's arm and began to walk. Louis felt deeply embarrassed. He walked through Leie Street with De Puydt on his arm like a fiancée as far as the Market Square, and his dead friend Maurice de Potter was up there in the Belfry, training his binoculars on him and the chubby, sweating poet on his arm, and what sort of plants were those swaying about over there? Cow parsnip and angelica? Or two purple marsh thistles with strange heads like balls of wool? I still have Maurice's notebook with all the names, and the one thing I could do for my dead friend is to learn to identify plants and flowers, not just to rattle off their names.

De Puydt dropped into a cane chair on the pavement outside the Ghent Arms and bawled, "Two Pale-Ales" in the direction of the war memorial.

The owner brought the drinks quickly but grumpily.

"Louis, I used to have talent . . ."

"You *still* have talent, Mijnheer de Puydt."

"Ah, child."

"You do, you do, Mijnheer de Puydt."

"I had more than that, a kind of verve, a drive. And pride and impatience and a destructive urge. Louis, I had the motive power of the headstrong, of the quarrelsome, which is what, incidentally, they called the successor to St. Louis, Louis le Hutin, the quarreler, they called him, and then, well, then . . . I could have made my works sing, not with the phenomenal precision and Chopinesque lyricism of Van Ostaijen, of course, but something not far off. But then I sold myself."

"Across the moon glides the long river . . ." said Louis.

"Across the long river glides our Mother the Moon. Ah, child." He fell silent. Louis, *le hutin?*

"My grandfather says that what Van Ostaijen writes may be infantile, but it's art all the same."

"Your grandfather can kiss my arse," said De Puydt. "All my life I've had to listen to all your grandfathers. To grandfather Herman Teirlinck, among others. 'Marnix,' he said, 'you and I have had the bad luck to be born in a misbegotten little botch of a country, there's no place here for poets, the Belgian steamroller is bound to crush us right into the macadam, make sure, Marnix, that you're sitting pretty first, I'll be making sure on your behalf anyway, what do you say to a library inspector's job?' I told him, 'Herman, so long as I don't have to join the lodge.' 'What an odd bird you are, Marnix, who said anything about that?' I asked for two Pale-Ales!" He shouted it out into the Market Square.

"You've already drunk them," said the owner reprovingly, addressing Louis. Then, apparently still nursing a grudge, he brought more beer, rubbed thumb and forefinger together, and gave Louis a questioning look. Louis shrugged his shoulders. Inside the café the owner grumbled loudly to his wife, cursing and swearing that it was always the same and that De Puydt had debts from here to Waregem and that this was the last time. De Puydt did not hear him. ". . . and then I was saddled with Maria, and that is how I came to lay my own inner castle in ruins, to pluck the feathers from the nightingale in my innermost soul, to silence its rippling song. Yes, young fellow, I took the job in the ministry. Yes indeed, he who now sits beside you sweated away in Brussels to better the lot of his fellow artists, and in so doing he drew a covering of cork, a corset of cotton wool, over his own soul. And where are the two Pale-Ales?"

"Who's going to pay for them?" asked the owner's wife, bringing the beer. De Puydt thumped the marble tabletop with all his might. Louis felt like running away across the large, wide, empty Market Square.

"Who? I! I, a member of the German-Flemish Labor Alliance!"

"I quite understand, Mijnheer de Puydt!" said the owner's wife. "That's fine."

"By the way," said Louis, "I've been reading a few interesting books lately on Expressionism. By Hermann Bahr, among others."

De Puydt attempted to focus drowsily on Louis.

"And that has prompted me to delve into what goes familiarly by the name of 'degenerate' art." The pedantic words rolled elegantly off Louis's tongue, it was much easier than he had thought, all you needed was a little nerve. And a few Pale-Ales.

"*Erfolg* by Feuchtwanger, *Joseph und seine Brüder* by Mann, the father, of course."

"What d'you mean, the father?"

"The father of the other one."

"Which one? Heinrich?"

"No, that's his brother. The son is called Klaus. And *Christian Wahnschaffe* by Wassermann." All these Manns! He quickly came up with a non-Mann. "And *Point contrepoint* by Huxley."

"I used to read a lot myself," said De Puydt, a namby-pamby boozer who couldn't even acknowledge the amazing erudition of a schoolboy. I'll just get up and leave him to his stupor. "Read a lot," said De Puydt dully. And did not pursue the whys and wherefores of Louis's being the only person in all Walle to be acquainted with this *Mann* trio, those exotic and above all forbidden names.

"I've been stealing books from the eyrie of the German eagle in the Avenue Louise in Brussels," said Louis. "While they were under guard by armed sentries. I saved those books from being pulped or burned."

"Burned," said De Puydt. "If only I could burn the collected works of Herman Teirlinck. As Diego de Landa did with the Codex of the Aztecs."

Louis called out brazenly, "*Patron*, two Pale-Ales, please." When no one came, he went inside. The owner and his wife, equally grim-faced, were sitting over a game of draughts. Louis said, "I happen to have no money on me at the moment, but I'll bring it tomorrow without fail. Perhaps even this evening. I'm the grandson of Mijnheer Seynaeve, who plays bridge in the Patria every day."

"Then why don't you go and drink in the Patria?" asked the owner's wife. "Mijnheer de Puydt's bill stretches from here to Waregem," said the owner but got up from the table all the same. "These are the very last ones. If I haven't seen the color of your money by this evening, there'll be trouble. Big trouble."

Louis carried the very last ones out to the terrace himself. De Puydt aning far back, once more in a coma. A noisy *Organisation Todt* group came by, but Dr. Louis Seynaeve, with his resolute and distinguished bearing, stood up to their bluster, which, although profoundly human, justifiable, and understandable (since if you managed to escape the icy hell of Smolensk, where the temperatures were thirty below zero, you would not be likely to remain unmarked by the experience), could not be allowed to disturb his patient. The aroma of the Pale-Ale wafted across to De Puydt, who sneezed. "Aha." He tossed the drink back greedily. Then said, "I did everything . . ."

". . . wrong," said Louis.

He nodded. "My engine is worn out, the battery is flat. The immense power of mediocrity, the mastodon of stupidity has rolled over me. I often used to . . . used to . . . think, Alone, without ties, I'll salvage something, who knows, perhaps one can also do the tango alone."

Passers-by on the Market Square froze to the spot like blocks of ice (dead Russian partisans in the snowy wastes) when De Puydt's song rang out. From absolute silence to this incomprehensible bellowing was progress indeed, the path to the light had begun.

"It was more a paso doble," said De Puydt then, and emptied Louis's glass. "Off with you, now," said De Puydt, "you have done your duty, and for that you have earned the gratitude of my worn-out heart. I shall linger here."

"Isn't there anything else I can do for you, Mijnheer de Puydt?"

De Puydt's attention was now totally absorbed by a tall, red-haired nurse striding past in her white-and-blue striped uniform, her eyes fixed on the Atlantic Wall where she was expected.

"*Voilà,*" said De Puydt. "What are you waiting for? Look how she walks. Like one of those big birds they call *demoiselles de Numidie.* What are you waiting for?"

To please De Puydt, Louis walked off and followed her, but once out of the poet's sight, he turned down a side street.

Louis packed his briefcase full of the forbidden books. In the street he swung it as if it only weighed five pounds, to put passing Germans off the scent. Like an enemy of the people, he sauntered along recklessly with the works of the Bolshevik Ehrenburg and the Jewish brothers Zweig, books that could really get you in trouble. More so than smuggled butter, for instance. Would they shoot you for it, or did they only do that to soldiers?

Aunt Nora was waiting in front of the door and let him in. ("She's heartsick," Papa had said. "So just let her read till she goes cross-eyed.

It does her morale a world of good, even if it is Jewish and a lot of democratic propaganda.")

"I've nearly finished that book about the Medicis. A fine family, that," said Aunt Nora. "Not that it isn't interesting, on the contrary, you learn a lot about life at Court in those days. And all sorts of details about the aristocracy, what they ate and what sort of clothes they wore. Even if they did have nothing better to do in the palace than go have a tickle as soon as it got dark, with the cardinals setting the pace. It's instructive, I will say that, but it's no great shakes on the subject of love, and when all is said and done, look at it any way you like, a book's got to have something about love, no, give me something by Vicki Baum or Gerard Walschap anyday."

She went into the kitchen. Louis pictured to himself how, now, while she was busy in there, or later, when she had to go to the w.c. (which was inevitable, since women had to go six times as often as men), he would sneak up to the sideboard, hold back the little gold-colored leaded-glass door so that it didn't squeak, and grope in the tin with the late Queen Astrid's portrait for some of the tight-packed little *speculaas.* He stole the whole tin, shoved it under his jacket, for the toilet had already flushed. Or had it? Was Aunt Nora as stingy as Groothuis the millionaire, of whom Mama said that every morning, before he left for his factory, he gave orders to his family and domestic servants not to flush more than once? Be that as it may, the stealthy secret agent Louis Seynaeve sidled side-long, sideways, along the outside of the house, giving a wave and humming *"Auf Wiedersehen"* to himself as he craftily held the tin full of the fragile, mouth-watering *speculaas* clamped under his left arm to conceal it from his father's still eagle-eyed sister.

Lingering in the room, he suddenly took in the fact that Aunt Nora, standing by the kitchen door, had just—not absentmindedly, since she didn't stop looking him in the face, and not calculatingly, either, since it seemed quite matter-of-fact—lifted her skirt up slowly and adjusted her stocking and garter. Matter-of-fact, as if she were all by herself in the house, with at the most a dim wraith or memory left in the room, and that was him, Louis, the shade of a nephew. She was gone a long time. Came back with coffee. Not real coffee, of course, that was only brought out when there was a different kind of visitor, a more highly valued, more cherished member of the family.

To filter the coffee, she had probably used the foot of an amber-colored silk stocking like the one now stretched tight up her leg. The coffee tasted of her leg. She inspected the new load of books. Feucht-wanger, Zangwill. "Aren't there any spicy ones?"

Books about spices? Peppery books?

"Spicy!" she said, and her ill-proportioned face with the swollen, wet lips was baffling to him.

"You must know what I mean! A boy your age has surely started to feel something or other when he reads a spicy book, hasn't he? You don't have to be ashamed, your aunt knows all about life, don't you worry."

He really had to save some of those *speculaas* for Mama. For a mama who right at this moment was pacing up and down nervously at home, terrified that something might have happened to him. For a Mama, the real one, who was sitting at home right at this moment smoking cigarettes, playing patience, and never even giving him a thought.

"Isn't there a single Walschap in that lot?" Aunt Nora asked. "At least he writes about living as it really is."

What was Aunt Nora getting at with this "life" and "living" business of hers? Or had she perhaps all the time been using the words as they did in East Flanders, to refer to what men did with women? ("They've been *living* together this afternoon, the pastor and his maid, the master and his jade.")

"He says things straight out, Walschap! He doesn't beat around the bush. And he's quite right. We should always speak our minds. Although some times, it's true, that just can't be done."

She planted her legs apart, rubbed the glimmering amber knees, went on looking hard at him, discovered something in him that hadn't been there before.

"You'll have to start shaving soon."

"I already have shaved," said Louis. "Three times."

A black rabbit with a slate-gray tail hopped into the room. It was thin and trembled. Aunt Nora said, "*Allee,* little Valentine, off you go. Go back and play in the yard." The rabbit obeyed gravely, ears flattened.

"She'll never know love. Next week she goes in the pot."

"Shouldn't she get a bit fatter first, Aunt Nora?"

"That's something we can't wait for, my boy." Her eyes followed the rabbit, still dawdling on the terrace. "Unless you want to take her home with you, that is."

"I can take her home with me?" Louis didn't believe it.

"Provided you ask me over when you've got her in your pot."

"Does it still have to be next week?"

"You'll have to decide that for yourself. You're big enough." She kept on talking, her voice taking on a hoarse, urgent sound that muddied the words. She fumbled at the edge of her skirt, stroked her knees. (The skulls of two very small Oriental children.) She said something that ended with "Right?"

"What?"

She laughed, showing narrow teeth, deep-pink gums. "Do you want me to ask you again? Oh, you little tease, you little touch-me-not! Then I'll say it again. If you get the rabbit, then I get a kiss from you. Right?"

"Of course, Aunt Nora!" (I'll boil potato peelings for the rabbit at home. But how can I get them away from Mama, since she always cooks potatoes with the skins on so that I get all the vitamins I need in these terrible times? Uncle Robert says that any day now the animals will have nothing to eat but newspaper. He's a butcher and ought to know.)

He was about to get up to give her the agreed-upon kiss when she pointed an accusing finger at him. "Sit down!" It sounded unaccountably brusque. He drank up the dregs of his coffee too quickly, making a loud slurp. The rabbit on the terrace pricked up one of its ears. It was doomed to death, perhaps not in the next couple of weeks but sometime this year for sure.

Aunt Nora, who did not resemble Papa—she was more sparely built, more alert, and usually much more cheerful, at least before that business with Uncle Leon—continued to stare at him, without blinking. A red spot had appeared at the base of her throat, in the shape of a map of France. Her right hand with two wedding rings was kneading her right knee.

Any minute the siren could go off. Then he would have to go down into the cellar with her. Or perhaps at the first wail she would turn her eyes away from him and run moaning out into the hall and down the stairs? In that case, with explosions all around and above him, he would be able to open the tin of biscuits at his leisure, stuff his mouth full of the sweet, soft *speculaas,* getting them stuck between his teeth. Perhaps the sideboard also contained the Union Minière shares that Papa was always going on about and which, if the British and the Americans ever won the war, would be worth a fortune. No, they were over at Aunt Mona's, and the shares belonged to Grandpa.

"I told you to sit down, didn't you hear me?" Although he hadn't made a single move. Louis lowered his eyes, read in *De Dag* about the heroic struggle of the Sixth Army on the Volga, while Aunt Nora swallowed a pill she had taken from a bottle, washed it down with coffee, jerked at the window catches, let down the dark-blue roller blind in front. He could no longer make out the letters. Aunt Nora's swaying skirt took on a blue sheen, she lifted her elbows and pulled pins out of her hair, it fell loose over her shoulders in waves and curls.

Aunt Nora went to the mantelpiece and gave Uncle Leon's photograph in its narrow aluminium frame a quarter-turn toward Hanover, where Uncle Leon, although *vom Arbeitseinsatz ordnungsmässig entlassen*—officially discharged from labor service—had become involved with some lady who, despite the fact that she came from a good family, was of loose morals.

Aunt Nora turned the radio on, a children's choir was singing in Latin, she switched it off again. She took two egg-yellow candles out of the sideboard, inserted them into wooden candlesticks that had been painted with garish flowers in Hanover, and lit them.

"Voilà," she said gaily. She dropped into the armchair by the stove. Louis felt his heart, it leaped up, he could hear the blood in his ears, he swallowed.

"You needn't think," said the woman gleaming in the candlelight, "that I don't know what you get up to in your room over there in Oudenaarde Road when you read those spicy books. God can see you, and so can I. Well, have you lost your tongue? You could at least admit it: Yes, Aunt Nora, it's true, I confess my sins."

The clock on the mantelpiece ticked audibly. A motorcycle outside. And an old woman screeching at somebody to come and get his food, it sounded like the cry of the man with the mussel cart.

"Come here," said Aunt Nora, "there's another little rabbit here."

Where? Not in her lap where her hands were lying. Under the sideboard? Scrabbling between the nickel lion's-claws on the legs of the stove?

"And it's hungry, that little rabbit," said the hoarse voice, "quickly, it must have a little sandwich."

Ever since she had lit the candles for this Black Mass, Aunt Nora had been going out of her mind. She had created an artificial dark-blue night, and she was raving. Papa would say that it must be the full moon, when all women, including female professors, mothers superior, Great Netherlands Girl Troop Leaders, go completely mad, shouldn't be touched with a ten-foot pole.

"Can't you hear me?" The voice clawed at Louis, drawing him out of his creaking chair.

"Yes," said the gratified voice. "Yes, here."

He was seized with uncontrollable hunger. He went and stood in front of this contentedly purring woman who had been his aunt just a moment ago. She tapped her ankle against his calf, a sign that he was expected to play something out of Vicki Baum's *Grand Hotel* or Gerard Walschap's *Marriage,* but which scene?

She tugged at his jacket so hard that he fell forward, his hand breaking his fall on the warm velvet back of the armchair.

When he immediately tried to break free (as he had done not so long ago on the ice-coated playground at the Institute, when he had slipped and ended up against the billowing black skirts of just such a sorceress, just such a nun, just such a Black Mass celebrant), she seized his tie and hung on until he fell back into her odor and her clutches. She clasped his head between her hands, pressed his cheeks together so that his lips stuck out. Now the kiss. A promise is a promise. Seen so close up, her eyes were bloodshot. She smiled. As if at a child. It infuriated him. He pushed his mouth toward hers. She turned her head away, his mouth touched her cheekbone. She took his left ear between thumb and forefinger and shook it. "Mind your manners, d'you hear? I'm in charge here. You don't think you can kiss me anytime you feel like it, surely?"

"I thought . . ." (that I must pay my debt and then be allowed to go home). She smelled of Mama's shiny underwear, symmetrically folded and stacked in the second drawer of the mirrored wardrobe in her bedroom, smelled of face powder. (I ought to be able to escape now, because there is something slack, lax, something abandoned, about her body, something inattentive. But why would I want to? If things go on like this, I might have the kind of experience described in Papa's secret "spicy" books. Full of sentences ending in three dots . . .)

"I thought, I thought, *nicht räsonieren*, don't reason why!" said Aunt Nora. "Didn't you learn that at school? It's by Albert Rodenbach."

"*Albrecht,*" said Louis.

"You always know better," she sniffed. "And how does the poem go on, do you know that as well, little mister know-it-all?"

" 'Put up a good fight and end up a soldier.' "

"Quite right. Exactly," she said. "*Allee,* then, put up a good fight." She twisted herself around, pulling him with her as she turned. His shoulder was pushed down. She was lying on top of him. Beyond her wavy hair he saw her low-heeled shoe rising in the air, then teetering up and down. She kissed his nose twice, softly and damply, then rubbed it with her finger. "With your red nose you look just like Little Gaston, the clown from the Circus Minard."

"Little Gaston is the one with white powder on his face, in a silver costume. The one with the red nose is Titi."

She let herself slide down alongside him. He hoped she would find a comfortable position soon and not change it again.

"Enough of this nonsense," she said. A bitter line appeared around her mouth, which had become thinner and wider. She had ruined the look of her mouth by smearing its lipstick on Louis's nose.

With a determined but not unfriendly gesture she placed his hand between her thighs. Then she squeezed her thighs together tight. She was wearing nothing under her skirt. While taking her time making coffee in the kitchen, she had taken off her panties and stuffed them in the drawer beside the knives and forks. "My goodness, what next?" said Louis inaudibly in Papa's voice, both derisive and apprehensive.

When his fingers, independently of his will, moved, he felt dry folds, dry grass. It surprised him, since the boys at school always went on about women being wet down there, the reason being that when women laughed too hard they had to pee, they couldn't just turn off the tap like men, or had those boys meant something else? Was the wetness the blood that trickles out from down there day and night, even when they aren't indisposed down there? I really must find out all about it as soon as possible.

Aunt Nora tried to raise the lower part of her body, but when he moved to give her room, she fumbled at his clothes and pulled him back to her.

Her hand with the two wedding rings searched inside his clothes and found his crotch. "Well, well, well, what have we here?" she said. Louis did not feel like replying to such a childish question, but he could see again the text in his mind's eye—in Perpetua bold, ten point, lower left, in Klaus Mann's *Flight to the North*—that had made him gasp when he had read it the first time, and which he must have reread at least ten times during the past week, and he said, "Aunt Nora, that is *mein ragendes Geschlecht,* my rampant sex."

As he had expected, she was startled and withdrew her hand as if from a hot stove.

"My little man, are you trying to make a fool of me?"

He protested. But his mouth only uttered an indistinct moan, because she was covering his face with the hand that wore the two wedding rings.

Uncle Leon had solemnly slipped his own ring over her middle finger at the station when he had left for Germany the last time. She had sobbed with emotion, she who had borne up so bravely until that moment. Only later, when it became clear that Uncle Leon had chosen to remain attached to that distant Hanoverian trollop from a good family, had she come to see that gesture of his as a crime committed with malice aforethought.

"No," she said. "No. Not another word. From now on, little man, I don't want to hear another word out of you, or you'll get it with Victor's leash."

Victor, the dachshund, had pined away with grief when Uncle Leon failed to return. That was Aunt Nora's story. According to Papa, she, knowing that Victor's affections belonged exclusively to her husband the traitor, had throttled the beast with one of her husband's shoelaces and had then eaten the whole dog herself. Papa claimed that he had discovered both a shoelace and a gnawed dog's-bone at the back of Aunt Nora's little garden.

"Take off your trousers," said Aunt Nora. But since that had an affectionate sound to it, she snapped immediately, "And be quick about it!"

"My jacket as well?"

"Your jacket as well. And your shoes and your socks."

The British and American bombers kept away. No neighbor rang the doorbell, no *Sicherheitspolizei*. Valentine the rabbit did not tap on the glass of the garden door with a plump paw. One of the little yellow candles was burning faster than the other.

"That's better," she said. "But just look at that, he's still got his little cap on."

Now what was she talking about? Little cap? I don't want to talk to her anymore. I'm only just back from the Urals, I watched my comrades in the Flemish SS being cut down at my side in the snow. When a Flemish SS officer finds himself in a ticklish situation, he voices his arrogant rage, his confusion, in the clipped language of the front. *"Wie meinen Sie, gnädige Frau?"* Louis asked, "I beg your pardon, dear lady?"

"Aha. In German again! All right then, what is the German word for your foreskin? A *Hitler Youth* cap?" She roared with laughter. "Well, mister know-it-all, what about it, you who are so learned and read all those Jewish books that are not meant for boys your age?" With deft fingers she took hold of his foreskin, waggled it. Her sudden high spirits bode no good. *Hitler Youth* cap. What on earth did she mean? There are such an awful lot of things that I'll never learn.

Aunt Nora pulled the foreskin down, then up again, shook it sideways. "Oh, crinkly, wrinkly, wat'ry thing," she recited, "with your pink cap on."

Guido Gezelle walked past, he had water on the brain and was reciting popular rhymes to himself in a whisper. Separated from us by just a brick wall, he stopped in front of this house of shame, of, we might say, debauchery. The word "debauchery," the negation of the discipline that reigned, had to reign, in the ranks of the Great Netherlands Bluefoot Troop, excited Louis. Aunt Nora was staring so closely at the now indeed *ragendes Geschlecht* that she began to squint. "Ah, we're there at last," she said triumphantly, let go of the foreskin, and lifted her skirt.

It looked like the drawings little Herman Polet produced with a lot of small lines in black and red pencil, which he would sometimes let you see quick as a flash in class, between two pages of his atlas. Herman Polet sold these drawings or swapped them for chocolate-flavored vitamins, to which he was addicted. I'll have to compliment Herman Polet tomorrow before lessons start. It's a good likeness. Although there isn't quite so much hair in this case. Nor those grubby little curling penciled worms that start right up under the navel. Aunt Nora's navel, for that matter, was invisible, it remained hidden in a creamy fold. Louis would have liked to examine at leisure the little color print, the illustration right under his nose, particularly because that little image, that groove, moved of its own volition, was an inhaling and exhaling deep-sea plant and gave off the smell of the sea. (Mama absorbed in peeling shrimps on the terrace of the café on Blankenberge dyke. She snapped at me because I, impatient as always, was eating the shrimps, shells, claws, and all. Blankenberge is sealed off now with field guns and barbed wire to protect us from invasion.)

Aunt Nora opened the fold with her wedding ring fingers. She said faintly, almost lost in the darkening room, "*Allee,* put up a good fight."

Louis lay warm, stuck fast. She barely moved, a calmly heaving springy eiderdown that murmured against his neck.

"Yes, my little man—I've watched you ever since you were a toddler with those fat little bent legs of yours in Oudenaarde Road—and here you are now, in my house—where I am so alone and think of you so often— and here you are now—no, not so fast, please—we have all the time in the world, my angel—I can't believe it—I thought I would never, never again—because they're all against me, those people—I don't exist for them—you can't imagine what that's like, little man—please don't come—hold yourself in because otherwise it happens so fast—I want nothing, nothing except to keep you warm in my little cubbyhole—can you feel it, my little soldier?"

Little soldier. Louis went rigid. Even if the allusion to Albrecht Rodenbach's idiotic verse had escaped her thoughtlessly, involuntarily, without ill intent, perhaps even flatteringly, it had struck home. Little tin soldier, little lead soldiers, chocolate soldiers. He watched her whisper, puckered eyelids shut tight, he rammed his torso against hers and said, "Silly, silly cow."

The bloodshot eyes. The sluglike little tentacles in her entrails enveloping his, *jawohl, ragendes Geschlecht, du Ungeheuer,* you monster, squeezing and squeezing it ever more tightly.

"You are my aunt," he said.

"Be quiet," she cried.

"Who do you think I am?" he said. Never before, not in his parents' house nor in his grandfather's, not at school nor on the way to school, and certainly not during all those years at boarding school had he ever had this triumphant knowledge that he could unashamedly, fearlessly, call out whatever he felt like. He raised himself up, his elbows in her clothed flesh. "You think you're dealing with your rabbit, with someone who knows nothing, but I screw more than you'd ever believe, just ask Bekka Cosijns, and don't think I won't tell everything tomorrow to . . ." He was being swept along by the train (the roller coaster full of screaming children at the World's Fair in Liège, with me outshouting them all) of his simmering, burgeoning, seething rage, he wanted to say, . . . to my mother. But that he would never dare to do, nor did he want to drag Mama into this room that smelled of face powder, the sea, and candle grease, he said, ". . . to the people in your street, just so they know what sort of person you are."

She looked at the sneak, the executioner, the soldier lying half on top of her as on a hastily put-together camp bed in the field of battle, the field of slaughter.

"Oh, you naughty little rascal," she said. She flung her arm around his neck, and, as on the roller coaster at the World's Fair, their little two-seater of skin and flesh and hair and clothes dipped forward and forced Louis to topple over, they uncoupled, she supported herself on her knees, scrambled, nipped, pushed, until in one wonderfully supple, flowing movement their carriage and pair fused again, only now in reverse, she on top, panting at her show of unaccustomed force, a rattle in her throat.

When does this sort of thing stop? There has to be some agreed-upon signal after which the two wrestlers are uncorked, a final whistle, a siren, but precisely when that happens is something I still have to find out. I must pay attention.

"Do you like me just a little bit?" Her wavy hair covered his face, she was not all that heavy, weighed as much as a small foal, no, a St. Bernard.

"Of course, Aunt Nora."

"Merci," she said and licked inside his ear, which must taste bitter.

A new phrase had been obsessing Louis for a whole month. He felt like shouting it out loud whenever he heard the sound of rustling branches, of the radio, of threshing machines. That phrase was "peristaltic movement," and it was happening right now—in the churning, bobbing, sucking, hissing drone reminiscent of Papa's Heidelberg press.

She whispered.

"You don't know how to—you pretend that you do, but you're a cheat—anyway you'll never know what it is to be a woman—not just me but other women as well—don't move—you're no rabbit—although I sometimes wish you were just in and out and *après nous le déluge*—but I love you and that's something you can't bear—it's natural for any male to feel like that—but meanwhile that's the way it is and since I love you I must find a way—'let's go on to the end of the line'—don't tell me I'm being stupid or silly—because I love you—I want to ride on you to the end of time—let me or you'll get another kiss—I am stupid I know to love you—let me just let me go babbling on—it doesn't do you any harm—you're right all I'm good for is pissing and babbling—but I'm no bother to you after all—oh little man why did you run off—with all your lies—and there I was thinking that you'd be thinking of me now and then in Germany and *godverdomme* all you were doing was making a fool of me with that other one—you're even more of a rascal than my mother said—but that doesn't matter, my sweet—because you're with me now and I'm with you and you and I are stuck with each other, hooked to each other—you can't get away anymore can you feel that?—you can't break free—*godverdomme* I'll teach you you rat—you dirty bastard can you feel it?—it's coming it's coming but wait oh no not so fast."

Louis waited, as asked. He had already been waiting for quite some time, since it was she who had brought on this swirling, moaning, pounding. Valentine the rabbit was sitting on its hind legs, patiently trying to reach a dahlia. Always nibbling. Once upon a time God had presented the rabbit with the gift of laughter. But because he turned up his nose at it, God took the smile away. Ever since, the rabbit has been trying all day long to find the smile again, nibbling on air.

No sirens. The RAF isn't being punctual. The candle flame licks at *De Dag,* the newspaper catches fire, the carpet begins to smoke.

"Yes back onto our little trolley—*allee* little coachman giddyap—you do love me I can feel it you can't hide it—ah this can't go on it's more than flesh and blood can stand."

Her crumpled face. Her lips, swollen again and chewing on air, nibbling. Part of my body is now inside somebody else's body, it's amazing, how does anyone have the trust, the barefaced abandon, to dare to do such a thing? My belly is gurgling and growling. A tin drum full of neatly stacked *speculaas.* It was on this planet in the third year of the Second World War that the ice-cool *Hitler Youth* cadet Louis Seynaeve had intercourse for the first time in his life with a person of the opposite sex. He is the first in the Germanic *Reich* to be decorated—you can read all about it on the front page of *Volk en Staat,* next to the photograph of the submarine, the *Heidelberg,* whose rough, unshaven crew had been blown up, torn up, swallowed up—with the Iron Cross. Leon Degrelle, general, has invited him to inspect the guard of honor at his side.

A signal had been heard, but not by Louis. Aunt Nora was the only one to recognize it. She reared up. She moaned. "To love—that's the easiest thing in the world—I'm coming—can't you feel it?—Love is what I want, I don't want to know you—oh don't speak please don't—I am all *verrückt* inside, all crazy—oh."

If she goes on like that, I'll slip out of her, that won't do, that would be dishonorable.

The body of the Knight of the Iron Cross fitted so closely that he became the groove into which she, the manly stranger, thrust, flattening him under the weirdest shudderings of a mazurka danced on the spot.

"No, no," cried Aunt Nora. The three-deep row of neighbors who were listening outside on the pavement, their long pink ears pinned back. "No more, oh yes, more, please, more, oh, oh."

She propped her chin in his eyesocket. He saw whirling spots of light. She bit his lower lip, he tasted blood. She rubbed her cheek against his, and for a moment he thought she had not shaved properly. Then with a bound she freed herself and landed with her elbow across his throat. "Aunt Nora!" he cried. She slid down the armchair and flopped full length onto the carpet, which, amazingly, was not smoking after all. She was crying. The neighbors outside crowded up against the brick wall at the front of the house, which trembled, the wall itself sobbing and moaning with the voice of her who would not be pacified, the wailing wall in Jerusalem.

Aunt Nora knelt and buttoned up his trousers. She wrapped up what was still standing on end in his shirt like a little doll. She wiped her tears away with her sleeve. He blinked his left eye and could see with it again.

"I am wicked," she said. He was about to agree, but she added, "Because I didn't look after you properly. I thought only of myself."

Louis sensed that this was the moment to come straight out with it and to ask for the tin of *speculaas.* But he stopped himself, it would have looked too much like tit for tat. Tomorrow he would compliment Herman Polet on the likeness. He would say, "Polet, she went on her knees and swallowed up my tool."

"Your bodkin, no doubt," Herman Polet would retort, atlas under his elbow.

Calmly the woman now crossed the room, switched on the light, looked for her hairpins, put her hair up, and became something like his father's sister again, saying softly, "This will remain between the two of us, won't it, my little man? Promise?"

Little man. Uncle Leon in Lilliputian form. She handed him his school bag. And six cigarettes for Mama.

"In '14–'18," Aunt Mona declared, "Hitler was hit by a stray English bullet. So they had to amputate one of his balls."

"What I think is that the ball never descended when Adolf was little and that it's still up in his belly."

"That's why he's always so bad-tempered, the *Führer.*"

"That sort of thing is bound to prey on your mind."

"That's why he never married."

"Like priests. A priest can give himself up entirely to his calling and to his ideals."

"That's why he's so against the English."

"But, Mona, he's never been against the English. It's the English who are against him. Von Ribbentrop offered them his hand, but Churchill just spat into it."

"What's the matter with you, Louis, you seem so restless?"

"His voice is breaking," simpered Cecile.

"Fathead, nitwit!" shouted Louis.

"It's growing pains. He's going to be a beanpole like his grandfather."

"That's normal. A man is five inches taller than a woman on average."

"I can get nothing but grunts and groans out of him these days," said Mama. "It's not my fault he's always hungry."

"He's got a tapeworm," said Cecile, and ducked Louis's clawing hand.

Aunt Berenice was sitting in the kitchen. Sternly, without the smug smile of her faith in the Resurrection. "Staf Seynaeve, you can go to bed happy tonight. The devil has given you what you've always wanted. I'd like nothing better than to see you drop dead before my eyes, but my religion forbids thoughts like that. All the same, I'm not going to offer you my other cheek."

Mama poured a strange infusion of lime blossom tea that Aunt Berenice had brought along. It seems that the Dutch drink it regularly.

"But it's not my fault your Firmin got himself arrested. He shouldn't have been carrying a false passport."

"You expect him to tell them his real name, Debelianov?"

"Forging a passport, there's a law for that. Against that."

"It's not God's law."

"I won't argue with that," said Papa. "It's a Belgian law."

"Is your heart so stony that you're just going to let Firmin rot in prison in Liège?"

"What do you expect me to do?"

"Put in a good word for him with the Gestapo. You're in with them, after all."

"That's putting it a bit strongly, Berenice."

"If the German judges are the decent, upright people you seem to think they are, then they'll listen to you, even if you are speaking up for a Jew who isn't even a Jew but a Bulgarian. The Germans will respect you for standing up for your own kin."

"By marriage."

"There's nothing he can do. He doesn't know anybody in the Gestapo," said Mama matter-of-factly.

"Oh no? I suppose I don't know Rathaus?"

"You shook his hand once at a DEVLag party. And when you said, *'Angenehm,'* the man didn't even understand what you meant."

"What about you, Constance, can't you do anything?"

"Perhaps," said Mama. "I can't promise, Berenice, but I'll do my best. Perhaps I'll try Mijnheer Groothuis."

"Oh no, leave Mijnheer Groothuis out of it," cried Papa.

"Doktor Knigge, then. He's a fairly understanding person."

"God will repay you, Constance."

When Aunt Berenice had gone, Papa poured the lime blossom tea down the sink. "Her God this, her God that. Why doesn't she telephone her God, then, and get Him to plead with the Gestapo?"

"It's a fact that the Jews did have a stranglehold on the newspapers, the cinemas, and the banks, they and the Freemasons," said Grandpa. "And now they're having to foot the bill."

"It only goes to show that they were smarter than the Belgians, Father," said Mama.

"And that it's going to be quite some time before they're accepted back in the commonwealth of nations."

"But that's just what they don't want," Papa exclaimed. "What they like is getting in a huddle together, ganging up, with all that swank about being the chosen people, and their funny manners and ways."

"And what about you with your Flemish solidarity?" said Mama.

"Constance, you can't compare the two."

"Why not?"

"They're termites," said Papa. "Fine words, and all the while they're grabbing a Flemish little finger first, then a hand, then an arm, and finally the whole body. And it's written in their special Ten Commandments that they're entitled to seize all another race's womenfolk, that's what their rabbis teach them. But what are we going on about them for? There are ten Jews at most in the whole of Walle!"

"How did it come about that Firmin was picked up here in Walle?" asked Grandpa.

"He was on his way here with Berenice," Mama said sadly.

"What we'll have to do," said Papa, "in these difficult times when it's everyone for himself and forget your fellow man, is to rekindle solidarity in the neighborhood. We're all in the same boat, no food or only a little, bombers overhead, we should all stick together and do our best to make what time we've got left on this earth as pleasant as possible. And that's why I've brought along this proof I've run off, it's an invitation to a Grand Variety Evening for the district. Our people are too materialistic, something has to be done about it. Here, printed on top in Garamond, it says, 'God Helps Those Who Help Themselves.' I've left a bit of space above that for advertising, I was thinking of Mijnheer Groothuis, his carpets are far too expensive, but he's keen on advertising, he can put it down to general expenses." Papa read out loud in High Flemish. "Grand Winter Fête in the Groeninghe Hall presented by the local inhabitants under the leadership of Staf Seynaeve. Program. One. Prayer for Flanders. They probably won't know that, but I'll have it printed out for them, and for three francs a copy they can join in. Two. A word from the President. I will say that I'm happy to see all of us pulling together, no matter what we may think about the war and its possible consequences. Three. A hilarious farce in one act, I still have to look one up in the book. For instance, *Andy the Foolish Village Policeman.* Four. And here, Father, I've printed it already without asking your permission: 'Outstanding lecture by the renowned orator, well known to one and all in these parts, Hubert Seynaeve, on Seltic culture.' "

"Celtic, Staf."

"Celtic culture. In eight-point underneath: 'For the first time in Walle. Extremely instructive and entertaining.' "

"Go on, Staf."

"Five. Comic song. 'To our Mayor.' Pharmacist Paelinck will take care of that. A series of little digs about that piece of ground the mayor has bought in Hoogeland. But not too pointed, because lately the mayor has been rather quick to take umbrage. Next, an intermission of fifteen minutes with some nice gramophone music."

"Jazz," said Louis.

"Louis, please. Try and be helpful for once!"

"Du und ich im Mondschein auf einer kleinen Bank allein," sang Louis, and Mama joined in, They swayed in unison, heads close together. Papa waited for his degenerate family to finish. "After the intermission, a song by Mona Vercauteren hyphen Seynaeve: 'There's Just One Mother For Me.' "

"Cecile could dance while Mona is singing."

"That would be splendid. Most appropriate. Yes. Then comes the local duo The Lazybones performing a comic number. And finally the closing address by the Reverend Dean from the Marine Artillery. Well-Heated Hall. An Exceptional Evening. Doors Open at Four Colon Thirty. Retain Ticket for Readmission, et cetera, et cetera. Published by Staf Seynaeve."

"Your name's mentioned three times," said Mimi the baker's wife.

"It's a little bit old-fashioned perhaps," said Madame Kerskens-from-across-the-road.

"I first thought of a flag-throwing display, but that's too Flamingant for this neighborhood," said Papa.

Drawling, Grandpa said, "And you, Constance, what are you going to do at this feast of fun for the whole family?"

Mama sent him a devastating signal with her gray, gold-speckled eyes. "Me?" she said. "I could do a dance with a bare bottom."

"Constance," said Papa. "Can we never have a serious discussion?"

Aunt Nora said, "Well, Louis, don't you say hello to me anymore?"

"Hello, Aunt Nora."

"Constance, how thin you've grown! I go without for the sake of our Nicole, and yet I keep putting on weight, I can't get into any of my summer dresses. Louis, you let me in for something with your last load of books. All about the peasant revolts in 1700. And that other one, about the man who changes into a beetle. He wakes up, Constance, and he has feelers like a beetle. You have to expect anything these days, I know, but all the same that sort of stuff must be for feeble-minded children.

"Don't look at me like that, Louis. Have I turned black, by any chance? Does he always act so oddly, Constance? If I'm not welcome here, Louis, just say so."

"Marnix has been barred from the Groeninghe," said Leevaert.

"Is he speaking again?"

"He never stops. He can't actually be gagged, of course, though sometimes I feel that would be the best thing. Last week he was chatting with Noël at the bar, incidentally a model discussion on stochastic processes, I even passed it on to my pupils the very next day, but what Noël didn't realize was that, all that time, Marnix was pissing against the bar. Without so much as moving a muscle in his face.

"And he's been barred from the Church of Our Lady too. He's quarreled with the new priest, who scolded him last Sunday for playing 'Mon légionnaire' by Édith Piaf during Mass. All the women sniveled, and the priest thought at first it was because of his sermon. I said to him, 'Father, each of us must be allowed to mourn, to rue, in his own way.' 'He's not going to set foot in my church ever again,' he said."

" 'Rue,' " said Mama. "Louis, 'rue' is one word your father will never understand. 'Raw,' yes, that he does know—raw mussels, raw mince."

In civvies Dirty Dick seemed to have shrunk.

"I really wanted to see the world. Well, I've seen it. And now I'm going to stay put."

"Won't they come looking for you, from your regiment?"

"I'm not going to sit around waiting for them. I've seen enough. I've had enough hollow laughs. Don't talk to me about Italy. We shot out of there like a cannonball. Just one consolation, we'd left those macaroni shits behind us. But laugh! We captured six New Zealanders. The thirst those boys had! They just couldn't do without their Coca-Cola.

" 'What's your name?' says one of them, who was a gynecologist. I say, 'Dick. Dirty Dick,' and every time they saw me they would sing, *'Dirty Dickie from Bizerte, fucks the captain, makes me flirty, oh, he's very very purty, is our Dirty, Dirty, Dick.'* And as for me, you know how romantic I am, I did a dance for them in my pumps and my two-piece on the night they all bit the dust, all six of them. All six of them had to be finished off, we couldn't drag them along with us. Our lieutenant crept into the Honey . . ."

"The Honey?"

"A Stuart M-3 tank we had captured, and he just ran them over and into the ground. Thirteen tons over those six boys. I've seen too much, I'm going to stay put at home."

"Doktor Knigge has asked me to go to Paris with him," said Mama. "I'd like to, but I can't do that to your father. He calls me 'you whore' all the time now as it is. In anger, admittedly. But all the same. No, if it had been to Lille, now, or Reims with the cathedral. But Paris? No, your father'd never forgive me. Because we spent our honeymoon there."

"Surely you can understand that, Constance, my brother wanting to hang on to his beautiful memories of the place?" said Aunt Mona.

"And what about my memories? Rushing around all day, the Sacré Coeur, up all those steps, Napoleon's Tomb, and the rest. But there came a point when I just had to get back home. Staf had paid for a week in advance, but after two days I simply had to go home because they had a French toilet in the hotel, just a hole in the ground, and I couldn't use that, I tried three or four cafés, but it was the same everywhere, a porcelain hole in the ground, and I just couldn't, with the best will in the world, I got cramps. 'But Constance, darling,' he said, 'that's the way it is in France.' I said, 'I don't care, I can't, I haven't been brought up that way.' "

"But he must have managed all right."

"I never asked him."

"No, in those days newlyweds didn't ask each other that sort of question."

"And when we got back to Walle, I couldn't go, either. Rhubarb, prunes, nothing helped."

"On my wedding night," said Aunt Mona, "I crawled into the wardrobe and locked the door. And Ed kept thumping and swearing outside. In the morning he cut out the lock with a chisel."

"And made me," said Cecile, sucking her thumb, as she had been doing for years, no matter how much tincture of iodine her mother painted on it.

"Churchill," said the English teacher, "is coming into his own at last, the old bulldog. His ancestor Marlborough had already been compared by the poet Addison to, note this down, yes, you too, Seynaeve, note this down: 'an angel guiding the whirlwind.' That was at the battle of Blenheim."

"Seynaeve," he said, and it was Papa's name rather than Louis's that he pronounced with such loathing. "I am to give you regards from the Reverend Father de Launay. He asked me to clear out his room and to divide up his possessions among his acquaintances."

"Where is he?"

"In a camp. I can't tell you any more than that."

"But you know where?"

"The less someone like you knows, Seynaeve, the better. This is for you." He handed over a yellowed, well-thumbed soft-cover book. Louis sniffed at it in the corridor. Mold. Glue. The Rock's cassock with a touch of shaving soap? No. Moldy, smoky. *Anthologie grecque*, Éditions Garnier Frères, Paris.

Next to the title page was a folded sheet with notes in the Rock's careful, slanting, well-rounded hand. "Let us flee, unhappy loved ones (lovers?) while the arrow is not yet (placed) on the string (bow). Soon, as I have come to bear witness (prophecy), there will be a great fire (conflagration). Philodemus. (Marcus Argentarius? Bassus?). The library of Philodemus: half-charred under the lava in the villa of Pisos, Herculaneum."

On the fly-leaf, in red pencil: *Koinonía.*

Together. Togetherness. "Study Greek. Every day. Go now. Quickly."

"Here, Louis, that's my boy, have another little spoonful of mayonnaise, you won't find much anywhere as good as that, homemade. You'd have to go a long way to find it.

"Ah, I, too, was slim when I was young. And books, I used to read books like you. Oh well, that's life for you.

"So what do you think of my mayonnaise? Made it myself, because our Monique isn't allowed to go near it when it's the wrong time of the month because mayonnaise curdles then, just you remember that. But, well, you're still young, what do you know about mayonnaise?"

"That the word comes from Mahon."

"Mahon?"

"The capital of Minorca."

"*Tiens,* who would have thought it?"

No more reserves, the Germans? Come on, take another look at those boys. They've got gunpowder in their blood! And how about that for a new uniform? Never seen that before, all leather.

We're coming, that's what the English radio says. But just wait till they land and see the skull-and-crossbones on those boys' caps, they'll make off like kangaroos, those Tommies will. They'll be so scared they'll shit in their little flat helmets!

"I'm getting old," said Grandma, "and it's happening fast and it hurts. You can see your family calculating: 'So many years, or so many months to go.' But I've got to be with you for a little while longer, I don't want to go before he does. Louis, he's going to have to go before me. I pray for it every day, early in the morning, before I put my teeth in. And he'll burn in hell for what he's done to my children, otherwise everything would be so topsy-turvy that you'd have to start doubting in the good Lord. Because he's living quite openly now, for all Walle to see, with his own daughter, and the whole town is scandalized, even Mijnheer the Canon de Londerzeele, who's always stuck up for him, has said *en plein public,* 'Perhaps it's not the most sensible thing to do.' And Mona, she's never been so sweet to me, 'Mums,' she says, 'wouldn't you like some stewed gooseberries? Mumsie, do you have anything to sew or to wash?' I say, 'Mona, how are things with your husband?' 'But, Mumsie darling, Gaston van den Driessche isn't my husband, even if he does hand over every last franc of his weekly wages to me, he's my *amant.*' I say, 'Mona, you know exactly who I mean. Your husband, the one who was my husband all his life.'

" 'Mother,' she says—because when she's cross she calls me 'Mother'—'Mother, you're stirring things up again and trying to make trouble. My father lives with me because he wasn't being looked after properly here, he only had a couple of socks left, and they had holes that big in them. And I can look after him properly now, I have time now.' I say, 'That's because your *Feldmarschall* has gone.' *'Feldwebel,'* she says, and 'Mother, it's no use putting on airs, because you weren't too proud to accept bread and bacon and margarine and chocolate from the *Feldwebel.'* I say, 'Yes, sour bread!' 'It was nourishing all the same!' she cries. I say, 'Yes, but it happened to be sour, and if you're a Belgian and not used to it, you don't like the taste.' "

Raspe's hand had been amputated. "At first they thought I'd done it deliberately because those were my trigger fingers, that I'd let them get frozen on purpose. I've just come from Wachteren. They're all turncoats there. I tried to explain things to them, but they don't want to listen, they're waiting for the government to come back from London, they say. I say, 'Come on, fellows, what has the Belgian State ever done for you? Humiliation. Look, what can we lose? If the English, that is to say the Russians, ever win this war, what chance has Flanders got?' They laugh. If I say, 'Fatherland' or 'Labor,' they laugh. I say, 'Look, what is Belgium? At the most a pile of gold reserves, and the political scum who control it divide it up among themselves. What is that compared with our nationhood . . .' "

"Our what-hood?"

"Oh, you can laugh. Our nationhood, yes, if necessary under the symbol of the sun as part of the greater whole. One nation from Lille to Poland."

But later, after he had had several glasses of Aunt Hélène's pea concoction (boil for three hours, cool, filter, add a large packet of sage and allow to ferment), Raspe said, "The Germans have taken us for a ride. They don't give a damn for our idealism. Flemish Legion, that's easily said, but we were actually commanded by Prussians and Bavarians. And we can't get out. We've sworn an oath of loyalty. Me with the hand that I no longer have."

"Louis, do you get the impression that your father is seeing a lot of Madame Kerskens-from-across-the-road? He prunes her roses, he cuts her grass, I think he must even polish her shoes, I can't find the tin. Of course, you don't know anything as usual, you Jesuit, you. Not that I care one way or the other. Let him look for his amusement elsewhere, he won't be getting it from me. But you ought to tell him one day, just between you, me, and the lamppost, that his little Madame Kerskens-from-across-the-road regularly turns up in a bath full of champagne at Mijnheer Groothuis's little parties. He may be a pansy himself, Mijnheer Groothuis, but he still gets women in for those other businessmen. He always bets on two horses. Because after the war people are sure to need textiles and carpets again.

"Right, you'll tell him then, Louis, about Madame Kerskens-from-across-the-road? Because you're good at that, aren't you, telling tales and snooping on people? You're a real whiz at that."

"Dear Mijnheer Seynaeve, I have read the three poems you sent me with the greatest interest, and in my humble opinion you have a pronounced talent. Your work has not, however, come fully into its own, because it is in free verse, a form which, in my view, has had its day in Flanders. A meticulous study of classical morphology such as may be found in W. Kramer's *Literary Works* and A. Verwey's *Rhythm and Meter* can only be of benefit to you. I assume, in view of the oversensitive and melancholy tone you adopt in your work, which is certainly not devoid of merit, that you are a fairly young person. If I am right, I wish you much good fortune and strength of will because you embody the future of our nation. With Great Netherlands salutations, Yours, J. Willemijns, *lic.*, Literary and Arts Editor, *Volk en Staat*. P.S. Am I in error in assuming that 'A Cloud' was inspired by Hölderlin's *'Es hängt ein ehern Gewölbe'*?"

"In error, error, error," Louis yelled at the walls of his room. The echo of his voice awakened the trumpet of the ice-cream cart outside. Young idlers with nothing better to do were already licking their ice cream by the cart with the scraggy pony. Hölderlin's plagiarist ran downstairs.

"The Atlantic Wall," said Pharmacist Paelinck, "has a number of serious holes in it. And the reason for that is—and you know that I am weighing my words carefully—that the Germans were stupid enough to use Dutchmen for the work. I am all for Great Netherlands, everybody knows that, but getting those Dutch in was a grave mistake. Just consider for a minute. A Dutchman is a businessman first and foremost, which means that from the foreman down to the humblest bricklayer every last one of them is out to make a profit. Take an example. A bunker's designed to be six feet thick, but the Dutchman builds it a couple of inches less, and doing that for the entire length of the Atlantic Wall means that he'll pocket a small fortune in guilders. He takes a profit from the concrete, the steel, the screws, the timber. The Germans out there are blind as bats, most of them are either on convalescent leave or they're such complete amateurs that if they lay a land mine they'll probably fall over their own feet, trip the wire, and end up in the air.''

"They caught a young fellow, a man from Walle, he still had the white pigeon in his hand. An English pigeon with secret messages on rice paper round its leg. They put him up against the wall right away.''

"Right away? They'll have slapped him around a bit first.''

"Your ears? What's the matter with them?'' said Aunt Hélène, who had cut Louis's hair much too short.

"They stick out too much.''

"But that's the fashion. Just like Clark Gable. Women like that. And anyway, all Seynaeves have ears like that. Just look at your Grandpa. But he has a bit of a hangdog look these days. Mona doesn't give him a minute's peace, she's more jealous than any wife could be.''

"Aunt Hélène, is Cecile Grandpa's daughter?''

"Are you crazy? Who's been saying that? Louis, don't you dare listen to tales like that! All the same . . .''

"All the same what?''

"Cecile certainly takes after the Seynaeves more than she takes after Ed. She hasn't got Ed's thick lips or his little piggy eyes. Though that doesn't necessarily mean anything.''

"No. I don't look like my father, either.''

"More than you think.''

"Me? Me? That isn't true. You're making fun of me!''

"You can't hide the fact that you're a Seynaeve.''

"It's not true! It's not true!''

A careworn little old woman rang the doorbell.

"Madame Seynaeve, I waited until I saw your husband go out. I know you have more than enough on your plate, because you have the boys in the ERLA to look after, and you may well say, 'Madame, don't even start, that's my husband's department.' But you don't have a telephone, and I've sent three postcards already to this address, which your husband no doubt threw straight into the wastepaper basket. It's not an easy thing to say, but your husband, Madame Seynaeve, is a scoundrel. The last time I saw him was at the printers' meeting, where he pretended he didn't know me, I felt mortified for weeks, being snubbed like that in front of all the other printers. I'm only telling you because you're probably aware of what's happened to my own husband, a good man but born unlucky, he's had a cerebral hemorrhage, but up till now he's behaved quite normally most of the time, though now and then he does get a bit worked up as he sits there brooding about this and that, he's an emotional man, Madame Seynaeve, suddenly it's all fire and fury and worrying about the others and then I have to lock him up in the cellar where no one can hear him, his sister Ottilie suffered from the same thing, she could hear glass tinkling inside her head all the time and used to run around with a brush and a pan looking for the splinters. *Enfin,* Madame Seynaeve, I've become reconciled to it now, my husband isn't going to get any better and we'll never be able to bring him out of the cellar, because I'm afraid that if we do I'll have to cart him off to the lunatic asylum, and they do terrible things on purpose to the people in there with their new medicines, because they think it isn't the brain that's gone wrong but the liver or the gallbladder, *enfin,* to cut a long story short, Madame Seynaeve, I've gone through my husband's papers with the lawyer, and we've found your IOU for one hundred thousand francs, and what are we going to do about that, madame? What with my four children, I need every little bit I can scrape together."

"A hundred thousand francs," said Mama.

"Please don't say you know nothing about it."

"All I know is . . ."

"Please don't say you'll give it back to me after the war!"

"Calm down, madame."

"If I don't get it, I'll come and set fire to your house!"

"Madame . . ."

"Your husband earns plenty of money. He gets double the amount of paper the other printers do, because he's the only one who works for DEVLag, he said so himself at the meeting!"

"Madame, my husband . . ."

"Hasn't heard the last of me," snorted the old woman.

"A cup of coffee, madame?"

"Is it real? Yes, please. Thank you. You're a good woman, Madame Seynaeve."

"You're right, Staf, I signed the IOU with your name, and I ought to have told you about it," Grandpa said. "But you might also ask yourself just why I borrowed that money from the printer."

"I am asking myself that, Father."

"Because I preferred not to take out an official loan. And why did I need the money? To give it to you so that you could buy this house, that's why."

"Give? But the rent we pay you, Father, is much higher than the interest you're paying the printer," purred Mama.

"Constance, let Father finish."

"It's quite simple," said Grandpa. "If we have to repay the hundred thousand, then we'll do it. We'll sell the house, there are enough likely buyers around with black-market money."

"And what do we do with the profit?"

"What profit, Constance?" asked Grandpa.

"What's left over after the hundred thousand francs . . ."

"You mean you'd want a share of that? A properly worked-out percentage? That's something we can discuss."

They discussed it. When Grandpa had gone, Papa suggested that they might use the profit to buy a charcoal-burning DKW.

"You're even more stupid than I thought, Staf."

"Or a nice fur coat for you."

"I don't need anything from you. Far better to look after the house and Louis."

"We're on top of things again, for a little while at least," said Papa.

"Your father wasn't wearing his wedding ring."

"Perhaps it doesn't fit his finger anymore, you can see how thin he's getting."

"Because of his bad conscience."

"Constance, when are you ever going to stop carping?"

"When I'm dead and gone," said Mama. "The sooner the better."

"They've landed in Normandy, exactly where Field Marshal Rommel expected them to, and what with this fine weather and no wind, those paratroopers are going to be sitting ducks."

"When that Germanic lust for victory really gets going, it'll scare Roosevelt right out of his wheelchair."

"It's mostly Negroes who've been landed, they're always being put in the front lines to do other people's dirty work, poor suckers, all that black flesh getting caught on the barbed wire of Europe."

"It's a matter of Europe's very survival."

"Pierlot admitted it himself from London. 'The time for the greatest struggle has not yet arrived.' That means they're just having a trial run,

like they did in Dieppe. 'Suffering and privation will increase,' says Pierlot. And he says that what we need is courage, discipline, and confidence.
How dare he, with all those murderers in the sky bombing Walle every
night? Cardinal van Roey himself—and if there's anyone waiting to see
which way the wind blows, it's him—has written a pastoral letter protest-
ing that what they are doing to us is inhuman."

"It's a disaster," says Aunt Monique, "the price of meat has dropped
thirty percent in two days."

"Butter, too."

"It's a terrible thing when your business has to depend on some
landing in Normandy. But Robert refuses to take it to heart. Even if the
price goes down by half, he says, he won't lose a moment's sleep over it.
You only live once!"

"Now that the Russians have done their worst in their part of the world
with millions dead, those Anglo-Saxons, those Americans, have to turn
up here. Make no mistake, they're coming!"

The Ku Klux Klan in their white pointed hoods with black holes for
eyes, who hang Negroes and then roast them,

the drum majorettes with their silver-plumed shakos and shameless
soft thighs, waving the Stars and Stripes,

the belly dancers with diamonds on their nipples and their pubic hair
shaved in a V (for Victory),

Al Capone and Legs Diamond, sprung from Sing Sing,

the Comanche and the Sioux and the Apache and John Wayne,

they are all coming, raining down their forged dollars and their phos-
phorous bombs,

they are coming to destroy our St. Martin's Towers, our Roman and
our Gothic pride, our Castles of the Counts and our Lakes of Love, they
are coming to stifle our Gregorian chants.

Just as they laid waste to Rome, no, *nearly* laid waste to it, because,
needless to say, the Pope made a little deal with them, birds of a feather,
he made sure Rome was captured by a British general whose family name
was Alexander, like Alexander the Great, the Conqueror.

As soon as she knew that the house in Oudenaarde Road no longer
belonged to them (although it had not yet been definitely sold to Canon
de Londerzeele's nephew), Mama did even less housework than before.
If Papa did not wash the dishes, encrusted crockery piled up. Mama said
she had her hands full as it was, now that overtime at the ERLA counted
as normal business hours.

Even so, at times she would sit there in the kitchen for long periods just gazing into space, saying that she intended to sign up an assistant nurse in the army, which meant peeling potatoes and tending broken legs in Schwerin for a month and then working in a field hospital in the East, which crept closer on the map day by day. Or she talked about hanging herself from a lamppost.

"Wait until the Americans get here and put up a Christmas tree on the Market Square," said Louis, "then everyone in Walle will be able to see you hang."

"You can laugh," she said. "You'll see."

Herman Polet, who intended to study law at the University of Ghent and then, once he had taken his degree, to become a sword-swallower and a fire-eater, said, "Those are dime-a-dozen poems, Seynaeve, there's no depth to them, they're all about sorrow, who gives a damn that you feel like hanging yourself because you don't have a girlfriend?"

"I do have a girlfriend."

"Who?"

"I'm not telling you."

"Stop pulling my leg."

"I promised her not to tell her name."

"How old is she?"

"A month younger than me."

"Blonde or brunette?"

"Brunette, with Prussian-blue highlights."

"That's presumably when you have a blue light on?"

"In the evening, she undoes her plait."

"Oh, I see, she's in the Great Netherlands Girls' Troop!"

"No. They all wear their hair up in a plait, in her family. Her mother, too, she's a pianist. But when I see her in the evening, she undoes her hair and lets it fall over her bare shoulders."

"Does it reach as far as her bottom?"

"No. No."

"There's no need to blush, Seynaeve. What's her bottom like, is it big, is it high and firm, or does it sag?"

"Polet, that's none of your business."

"Go on, then. After the hair it's usually the eyes."

"Almond-shaped with lashes that cast shadows like little fronds across her cheeks."

"Does she squint at all?"

"Of course not."

"Pity."

"Why?"

"Because squinting women look straight at you when they come. What color are her eyes?"

"Black."

"How common."

"With golden speckles."

"Fronds, speckles, cut it out, Seynaeve. Does she use perfume? What brand?"

"I don't know."

"All right, but does she stink or doesn't she?"

"Wait. I remember. *Imprudence.*"

"That doesn't exist."

"I'll show you the bottle tomorrow."

"What does she do in the evening under that blue light?"

"She doesn't say much. She reads. She's a very good chess-player. She's mad about nature and animals. That's why she always has her dog with her."

"A bushlicker, no doubt."

"No. A borzoi."

"Oh, you dirty liar. A borzoi, he says. And he's never even set eyes on a real live borzoi. You've been unmasked, Seynaeve, 'borzoi' comes from the anthology of Dutch poetry. Ah, you thought you were the only one in Walle to know that, but it so happens that not all of us are boneheads. Borzoi, my foot!"

"It's a Russian dog, Polet. It's used for hunting wolves. She got it as a present from an older man who was in love with her, but she wouldn't have him, so he left for the Eastern Front."

"Where his little pecker's been frozen, presumably. Why didn't she want him?"

"Because she's in love with me, Polet."

"Does she say that?"

"She looks for me in town all day long, she says, although she knows that I'm at school. When the Americans fly over, she dies a thousand deaths, she says, because she can picture me lying under the ruins."

"Is her family rich?"

"I think so. Because she wants to buy me a very expensive watch."

"But you won't hear of it, because you don't want to make us green with envy here at the College?"

"No. Because I don't want to be dependent on her money."

"Is she knock-kneed?"

"A little bit, I think. Yes."

"Aha! And her crack. Is it wet?"

"Please, Polet, mind your manners."

"You have been there, though?"

"What do you think?"

"Aha! And tell me, what did she do to you?"

"Last time she went down on her knees and she took hold of my prick, wrapped my shirt around it, and put it back inside my fly."

"There's something about women these days," said Herman Polet.

Louis was playing draughts with Uncle Leon. They were both squatting on the carpet, Uncle Leon still wasn't used to his house. On that other carpet full of scorchmarks into which Germany had been turned, he had always sat cross-legged on the barrack floor. The heavier the load of bombs that rain down on Germany, the louder the Germans sing the Horst Wessel Song down there in their cellars full of water and soot: *"Die Fahne hoch, die Reihen fest geschlossen."*

Aunt Nora was pretending to be in high spirits, she who deserved to be horsewhipped for having fornicated with a very much underage minor. "Uncle Leon, I have mounted your wife." Wasn't that how it was put?

"And she gave you a good time, eh?" said Uncle Leon bitterly.

"Why not?" said Aunt Nora flirtatiously.

"You just took what was available, eh?"

"What would you have done in my place?"

"And there I was in Germany, breaking my balls."

"Don't exaggerate, Leon." She stroked his hair.

Our Great Dead, Staf de Clercq, Van Severen, Tollenaere, were shown shadowless on black-and-white panels, like woodcuts. Smaller, but still twice life-size, in a black velvet frame, the photograph of Victor Degelijn, treasurer of the Hulp Organization, wearing a Dutch helmet, the lion shield just visible on his left sleeve, the silver number 44 on one epaulette. A faint, incredulous smile on his lips: "Do I really look so gigantically, two-dimensionally dead to my surviving comrades?" The breast pocket of his jacket bulged, his paybook was inside. Clarions and drums, familiar mourning sounds. Vic Degelijn's widow was supported by a *Wehrmacht* captain. The assembled Flemish Guards, mostly in field gray, sang, "The Great Dutch Nation wakes at last, the time of slavery is past." Papa wiped his tears away.

German officers stood less stiffly to attention than their Flemish brothers as a message from Freiherr von Brentano was read out, promising that the dependents would not be forgotten. They had loaded the bits and pieces that had once been Vic Degelijn—who had been on guard duty outside the coal store in Haarsten just before the anglophile bomb went off—onto a wheelbarrow. Papa sobbed. (What has happened to me this last year? A year ago I, too, would have been deeply moved; now Vic Degelijn has become just one of a host of people I don't know from Adam. It's a reasonable death, perhaps sometime I will come to find it absurd. Like that arm in Luftwaffe uniform that lay, independent of time and space, on the knees of an unknown person. The bloody stump turned around, rose, kept rising, toward my mouth. Manna.)

"Regions of Great Netherlands, link hands, the Guard keeps marching on." "Forward march, *houzee!*"

An NSJV youth with a flame-decorated drum dangling from his waist detached himself from the group waiting to follow the soldiers with the coffin, saluted Papa and Louis, clicked his heels, and said, "*Houzee,* Seyna-eve!"

"*Houzee,*" said Papa to the sunburned, sandy-haired boy with protruding teeth and hazel-colored (almond-shaped) eyes, shining (egg-white-blue-milk-white, my love) gaze, it was Vlieghe. On his chest the Hitler Youth proficiency badge.

"Well," said Louis. "Hello." He drove his fingernails deep into his palm until it hurt.

Trumpets blared, the ranks lined up. "I'll see you in a moment," said Vlieghe in the muffled, hurried, and commanding tone of the red-haired schoolboy of old. He tightened the strap of his drum. A hundred iron feet pounded off together. Stupid, brutish, surly sound.

Papa walked slowly beside Leevaert and Paelinck (whose daughter—what was her name again? Simone—was wearing spectacles, I've seen that girl somewhere before but I'm damned if I know where, she looks really miserable, lacking love, lacking a prize stud to ram her against the floor-boards, Simone, yes, that's her name, Simone of Bethany, the Leper, and I am the nine-banded armadillo, armored against anything she may send my way, with my scales and my digger-claws I shuffle away from her toward the cemetery.)

At the cemetery the sergeant-major, the mother of the company, the *Spiess,* as they called him, said that decadence would have to be rooted out, that our spiritual life, which had cost Vic, our Vic Degelijn, his life, would need a new beginning, now more than ever, that was certain, since some ever-burning questions demanded an answer, namely: What is our place in history? What is man's true identity and nature? Must we not create self and truth with our own unshakable resolve?

The piece of paper in the *Spiess*'s rough hands trembled. "The desert," the man read from his paper, "is spreading all around us, but it is from the desert that the gods will return. *Sieg Heil* . . ."

He looked up with relief and added, "Amen."

When the troops had dispersed, there was Vlieghe (formerly Foxy), who said: "*Godverdomme*, Seynaeve, it's a small world."

"Yes."

"And yet . . ."

"Well, that's how it goes."

"Who would have thought it?"

"Not me."

"No."

Papa gave an estimate, based on format and print, for the obituary notice.

Eye to eye with a Vlieghe who swore and said, "Yes, where has the time gone, Louis?"

How untouched, unsullied, unspoiled, we were when we were small and depended on each other, or rather, I upon you.

"Do you still remember Sister Sapristi, hey, Seynaeve, *dedju!*"

"I do."

Ensign Vlieghe had a cold sore. His short white socks, rolled down according to regulations over his long gray ones as far as his mountain boots, were covered with brown splashes.

"We went through one hell of a lot in the Institute, us two, *dedju, dedju.*"

"But we had fun, too."

"That's for sure, *verdomme.* Even if the chocolate was moldy."

"Too true."

"And we were blue with cold in winter."

"And boiling hot in summer."

"Do you still draw so well?"

"Me?" (He must be mixing me up with somebody else! With Dondeyne! With Goossens who was the Apostle Bartholomew!)

"Sure, you used to draw those houses all the time, castles mostly, with trees and flowers, very detailed, women sitting on sofas, that sort of thing. Don't you remember? The women always wore big white hats."

"Possibly."

"You're at the College, aren't you?"

"I had to repeat a year."

Papa gave a short cough. Like Sister Chilly in the gray corridors.

"Do you have to go?" (Vlieghe responded to the signal, as he used to.)

"I think so."

"Me too," Vlieghe said at once. "Look, see that one over there? That little beauty there, see her? She's mine."

A pudgy girl in pigtails. Her large blouse with mother-of-pearl buttons was stretched tight across large flat breasts.

"Day before yesterday I bought her some earrings, cost nearly a hundred francs. I won the money from our Troop Leader. At whist. We play for big stakes. He's the doctor's son."

"She isn't wearing them, your earrings." (Peevish. Jealous. Hoity-toity. Stop it!)

"That'd be out-of-uniform," said Vlieghe. "You don't know about those things, of course. I bet you're a bit of an anglophile, a bit of a White. I can tell that sort of thing straightaway from the way people behave."

"Me? What ever gave you that idea?"

"Seynaeve, you can't pull the wool over my eyes. You never could. I could always see right through you."

The girl came up.

"That's her, my little *kerlinne*. In two months' time, if the Americans don't get here first, she'll be a *Stormster*."

"*Houzee,*" said the *kerlinne*.

"I thought it was '*Heil Vlaanderen,*'" said Louis.

"We are Great Netherlanders," said Vlieghe's girl, giving off from under her skirt a translucent vapor that curdled mayonnaise and made dogs tear at their chains.

"It is imperative that we make up our minds whether we are able to preserve our identity as Flemings and Great Netherlanders or whether we should be incorporated in the German Reich," recited Vlieghe under her benevolent gaze. And then, putting his arm around her waist as she began running a little clothesbrush over her unpleated skirt: "*Allee,* I know where to find you. All the best. *Houzee!*"

"*Houzee,*" said Papa.

"Keep your nose to the wind, Vlieghe," said Louis, as a Boer might, taking his leave on the vast South African veldt.

Now that Rommel has died from the effects of his accident on Route Nationale 179 near Caen, clasping his marshal's-baton on his deathbed to the last, face to face with his Creator, the Americans are advancing rapidly.

The Whites are getting bold as brass, just look at the walls of the Gendarmerie, there's not a brick that isn't covered with inflammatory slogans against the New Order, the Whites smoke special bittersweet cigarettes that were parachuted onto Stade Walle football ground along with their weapons.

General Frissner has ordered the Sixth Army to withdraw across the River Prut. The Prut? The Prut.

Madame Kerskens-from-across-the-road is washing and ironing her Belgian flag.

All over Europe the *Wehrmacht* is being forced to confine itself to defensive actions.

"We have to start being afraid of our own people," said Papa. "We, who have done nothing but aid the people from the day war broke out. We, who put our very last franc into Parcels for Soldiers. Not to mention my wife, who, today as always, is continuing to do her utmost to keep the young folk off the transports to Germany."

"People don't like her," said Theo van Paemel. "With her nose in the air. And that air of don't-touch-me-or-I'll-bite."

"It's only because they don't really know Constance."

"Staf, I'm going to be blunt. You've burned your fingers badly."

"Burned!" cried Papa.

"If you like, I'll give you my Luger. With a *Schein*. For your own protection."

"Not on your life," said Papa. "Against my own people?" He produced Louis's *Hitler Youth* dagger from the trouser pocket of his overalls. "With this . . ." Louis wrenched his property from his father's hand. The blade smelled of green apples.

"You might as well put your trust in a St. Christopher's medal," said Theo van Paemel.

"Don't mock it, Theo. We've all heard about bullets being deflected by medals like that."

"Staf, my boy, I'll tell it to you straight. Your time is up. The hatchets are out for you and your family."

When Mama came home, Papa said, "Constance, it seems our neighbors don't like you. It's not nice of them, it's ungrateful, it isn't your fault, but we're still going to have to face the consequences."

With Grandpa present, the Seynaeve clan held a council. The air raid siren wailed more shrilly than ever, sounding a new kind of sorrow.

"My mother has told me to burn all my scrapbooks and my copies of *Der Adler* and *Simplicissimus*," Louis said, and Bekka said that that seemed like a good idea. They were dawdling along, chewing straws, not a farmer in sight. Three silver airplanes circled watchfully, not diving. Two thin cows walked with them along the barbed wire. Cows were eating rats. Pigs were eating each other. And children would soon be eating the bark off trees.

"I won't be seeing you for quite a long time," he said.

"Who knows?"

"I'm not allowed to tell anyone where we're going. But I can tell you."

"I'd rather not know."

"Aren't you interested in where I'm going?"

"The less anyone knows, the better."

"You're the only person I'll miss."

"For a day or two."

"No, for my whole life.—Does it feel hot to you, too?"

"Me? No. I must get back home."

(Now that I'm leaving, I'm seeing a lot of her. When she was there all the time, I never saw her. Is that a law of nature? She is wide-eyed [like a doe? in *Breviary of Flemish Lyric Poetry*?], angular, with thin, bronzed legs and grazed knees, and soon I'll see her no more among the ruins, the Russians are advancing to the North Sea, the Americans will be presented with France and Italy because the climate there is like California, Russians in Walle, we'll all have to give the clenched-fist salute, there'll be elk steaks, bear steaks, vodka, Tartars.)

"I'll write you a letter now and then. Don't look at the mistakes," she said.

"To what address?"

"I'll find out in good time."

"Villa Kernamout, 8 Dorps Street, Glijkenisse," said Louis.

The airplanes had left a magnificent curved white thread behind in the sky. The antiaircraft guns by the Leie were firing at the thread.

"There'll be a huge conflagration over Europe," said Louis.

"And what about our King? They dragged him off to Germany. The only thing he was allowed to take along was his crown. It weighs twenty-five pounds."

"In Hirschstein Castle."

A farmer bicycled past and chased them away with angry shouts: "Get off my land! Everything is mine from here to the Leie polder!"

They sat down beside the gray water with its shards of light, the air bubbles welling up and bursting. "Now or never," thought the crusader, who was leaving for Turkey and Jerusalem, where ten to one they would split his skull and spoon up his brains steeped in wine, and quickly opened his fly.

"Look."

"Put it away, hurry up," she said placidly.

"Fare thee well, my love," he read from a page full of ornate Gothic letters.

She wrapped her skirt around her knees and flicked her thumbnail against his pink stalk, like a little one from the Institute who was not very good at marbles.

"That's what the nurses do when they have to wash a wounded soldier and that thing gets in the way," she said and flicked harder, it didn't hurt, didn't change anything about the way things were.

"*Allee,* hurry up and put it away."

"Let me see yours, then."

"Are you out of your mind?"

"Come on."

"What's there to see?"

(A lot. Everything!) A devilish, impatient exasperation spread through his body.

He buttoned up his fly.

"Are you sulking again?"

"Just for once I asked you to do something for me!"

"But it was such a stupid thing."

"Don't, then. But I'll give you my binoculars."

"What good are your binoculars to me?"

"You can give them to Tetje."

"When do I get them?"

"Tonight if you like." And the languid heat from the water beat against his face. She pulled up her skirt, sat on one buttock, pulled her panties down.

"I can't see anything like that."

"Oh, what a nuisance you are." She pulled her panties farther down over her ankles, her muddy shoes. "*Voilà,* are you satisfied now?"

"Open your legs." She did it so abruptly that he was startled. There was not a lot to see, a fold that was darker than her thighs with little hairs curling up, but his heart thumped, his mouth went powder-dry.

"No, don't touch."

She wanted to get up. "Just a minute!"

"What is it now, stupid?"

"I'll give you my Scottish scarf as well." (Aunt Hélène had said, "Louis, that scarf is out of fashion. It makes you look like a prewar schoolboy.") He continued to stare. It was for this that men knocked one another's heads off, that they raged with despair, for this peaceful, docile little fold, which had nothing to do with that thing of his as it unbearably, impatiently, chafed against the rough material of his trousers because in his exasperation he had only half-pulled up his underpants, he released the miscreant from his clothes once more.

"Oh, you little swine," said Bekka tenderly. She put two fingers on her slit, spread her fingers, pulled the dark lips apart, little pink and red grooves appeared, a glistening, fleshy little crater.

"Say hello. No, don't put it in, just touch with its little head." She raised her buttocks. The two parts greeted each other, touched each other. With surprising ease the one part slid into the other.

"But only for a moment," said the damsel of his dreams and he, Knight Roland, obeyed, always prepared, my word is my honor, and pulled back, but she pushed her body forward with all her might, the rubbery, oiled sheath did not let go. The sun scorched the field. A screech of gulls, so far from the coast, from the dunes, and the sea continued to surge until he fell back onto her trembling body, the sea-salt hair at the nape of her neck.

She whispered, "Who am I?"

"Bekka," he said, ten, twelve times over.

Kernamout was an English country cottage with bay windows, two verandas, and a patch of grass that the neighboring farmer who looked after it called a "lawn." It belonged to the Goethals family, who were away in the South of France and were grateful to Mama for having looked after their son Henri and given him protection right up to the last days of the ERLA. A strange peace prevailed in Kernamout now that Papa had left to go into hiding on a farm in the Veurne district, where the butter still tasted of the corpses from '14–'18 and where you could still find truly humble Flemish Christians, Good Samaritans.

The Germans withdrew on creaking carriages, spoke in Russian and carted away agricultural machinery, cooking pots, filing cabinets, typewriters, the old horses yawned ceaselessly.

Louis was not allowed to go out, because he was too tall, he looked seventeen or eighteen, Mama thought. Sometimes he lay in wait between the cauliflowers and the rhubarb, like a White Brigade sharpshooter, for the creaking carts, the angry, pale Germans sitting on the gun carriages. He listened to Mama gossiping brightly with Angelique, Uncle Armand's wife, who bicycled over from Deinze in the evenings with news and food. Aunt Angelique was worried because Uncle Armand was insisting on carrying out his job as inspector to the bitter end, only last week he had had a farmer arrested for neglecting his pigs, the poor beasts had been found lying with their legs sticking up in the air from swine fever because the farmer had been celebrating the coming of the Allies to our Fatherland, in a nonstop drinking session. Giggling and reeling, the farmer had been taken away by the gendarmes, on the village square he had yelled, "You can all come kiss my arse, starting with Armand Bossuyt. Long live the Independence Front!"

During their last get-together in Walle, Grandpa had decreed that Louis enroll with the Hieronymian Brothers in Waffelgem to learn typography. "Let's not fool ourselves, Louis won't get anywhere studying academic subjects, he's already been kept back twice, his heart isn't in it, he doesn't have the slightest practical sense, he's no *commerçant*" (the worst thing you could say about a person in West Flanders), "let him at least learn the rudiments he'll need to run his father's business one day."

"Business!" exclaimed Mama. "Those moldy printing presses!"

"Constance, you keep out of this" had been Papa's last words.

Mama made a mistake though, she who did have that so-called practical sense. She and Louis turned up at the Institute of the Printing Brothers of Waffelgem five days before the beginning of the school year.

The Brother Superior, a rotund man with curly white hair, stroked his cassock hesitantly. His allegiance to the Seynaeve family was beyond dispute, he said. Certainly to our patriarch, he smirked, with whom I have shared many a bottle of Burgundy. For any other apprentice, no matter who, he wouldn't do it, but with Louis he was prepared to make an exception. Louis could certainly stay at the Institute for the next few days. Mama kissed the Brother's hand as if he were an archbishop with a ring.

Brother Alfons, a timeworn little man, took Louis under his wing, cooked pancakes for him, and lent him *L'Histoire de la typographie belge*.

Invariably, when Louis went wandering through the empty classrooms, he would chance upon the Brother. Louis wrote: "Tedium fills these halls of learning / but for all my inmost yearning / I scorn the chance to stay alive / Why am I supposed to strive? / Why keep struggling so to thrive? / When my closest friends are earning / Eastern death, should I survive?"

It wasn't modern enough.

"Tedium and gray walls merge / Wretched life unreal / The East aglow, the stench of steel! / Oh, deathly dirge!"

In caps, twelve point, sans serif?

"These are terrible times," said Brother Alfons.

"Yes, Brother."

"Especially for a boy like you."

What did the old man mean by that? That it's hot and that a boy like me would rather be off swimming with his pals? Or that it's high season for young men who like to have fun with girls? Or that I, deserted by my parents, am pining away here all on my own? Or that I have been cast out by the community in these terrible times because my father has to hide like a criminal for his Flemish ideals?

Just then an open car with young people in white overalls waving submachine guns drove into the playground.

"Well, if it isn't Bernard!" called Brother Alfons gaily, running up to the car and helping the driver out. "Bernard, my boy!"

The broad-shouldered youth wearing a French Resistance armband came across the playground with an inquisitorial look. Brother Alfons exclaimed that some double-strength *trappiste* beer had been saved up for this very day. Bernard came to a halt in front of Louis and inspected him, Louis held two widespread fingers in the air.

"Who would have guessed it?" cackled Brother Alfons. "I thought you were in the Ardennes."

"The Flemish Ardennes!"

"On the Kluisberg! We smoked four of them out of their bolt-hole there!"

"Bless my soul, you young rogues!" said Brother Alfons happily.

The oldest White Brigade youth, who was wearing a white-painted Belgian helmet, cradled his submachine gun like a baby in his arms and asked, "Aren't you related to the mayor of Dentergem?"

"No," said Louis and blushed.

"I've just come to make sure, Brother Alfons, that you haven't been sheltering any Blacks," said Bernard, "you with your gingerbread heart."

"Me, Bernard? I am a patriot. Always have been."

"The one does not exclude the other. Anyway, we've heard them singing 'The Flemish Lion' in the classes here. I think we'll just take a look around." They crossed the playground looking to the left and right and veering from side to side as if taking the square of a besieged town.

One hour later Louis stole a bicycle from the Institute shed and rode without stopping, sometimes pedaling steadily like Marcel Kint, sometimes putting on a quick spurt like Poeske Scherens, calves aching with fatigue, past olive-green tanks full of Tommies, past deserted antiaircraft batteries. Near Aalter he rode through an area of scorched trees, rows of smoking houses, the monotonous thud of gunfire over the horizon. It was dark when he reached Aunt Mona's house in Walle. Grandpa, wearing his cotton nightcap, hissed that Louis had gone completely mad. Cecile was wearing a white dress and a scarf with the Belgian tricolor. Aunt Mona gave him sandwiches of jellied calf in tomato sauce.

"But did you really ride right through the lines on that ridiculous bike?" Cecile asked.

"What did you see on the way?" Grandpa asked.

"I didn't look."

"That boy has sawdust in his head!" exclaimed Grandpa, putting in his false teeth.

"Tommies," said Louis. "Lots of Tommies in tanks."

"Those aren't Tommies," said Cecile. "They're Poles dressed like Tommies."

"Poles and Negroes," said Aunt Mona.

"Where is my father?"

"We don't know."

"He's somewhere near Veurne!" cried Louis in despair. "Mama got the address from Theo van Paemel, but she lost it."

"But what do you want with your father?"

"To tell him they're looking for him. That he mustn't come back to Clijkenisse under any circumstance."

"He knows that already. A child knows that. They're looking for everybody."

"Where is my father?"

"Calm down, Louis. Sit down. Over there."

"Louis," said Grandpa, steadily dribbling, "it's better for you if you don't know where your father is. The Whites are running around foaming at the mouth right now, and they would only torture you until you told them where he is."

"With burning English cigarettes against your nipples," said Cecile.

"You don't want them to put your father up against the wall, do you? It's admirable of you to be so concerned about your father, to tell you the truth I'd never have expected it of you, but then, you do have sawdust for brains."

"You've always been against me, Grandpa," Louis shouted.

"Mona, give the boy some of that leftover rice pudding."

"Here," said Aunt Mona. "It's *riz condé* with stewed fruit. See, your Grandpa's going without, just for you."

Eating, he calmed down. Grandpa asked how his mother was. Louis lied, saying that she cried a lot because she was missing Papa. Grandpa nodded, satisfied.

Because people these days often confused compulsory labor service with sympathy for the Third Reich, Uncle Leon had gone to stay with his brother in Wallonia, accompanied by Nora, his dissolute wife. Uncle Robert, notwithstanding the fact that he had fed so many starving people in Walle, had moved to his country house near Doornik, where they only knew him as someone of independent means.

Louis was sent to bed early. In the attic, on the little camp bed, he glanced through the new newspaper, the *Volksgazet,* full of stupid caricatures of the *Führer,* crudely drawn and not at all true to life, in the shape of a snake being flattened by Allied boots. In Waffelgem, Brother Superior and Brother Alfons, clinging to each other, were out looking for him in the misty meadows. Yoohoo, yoohoo, Louis! More and more worried because they had lost a pupil before school had even started, they blundered about in the white mist, and when Major-General Gerhard Count von Kleist suddenly appeared on the scene, they shit in their cassocks from sheer fright, moaning that they were Hieronymian Brothers, that is, *Brüder.* Of course, said the officer, who looked like Dirty Dick, and shot them down without making a sound.

Mama barely glanced at him when he rode up the drive and flung his bicycle down on the patch of grass. With a cigarette dangling from her lips, she was poking around in the mouth of a cat that, according to her, had eaten something bad for it. Louis announced that he did not want to return to Waffelgem under any circumstances and that he could learn printing much better in Ghent, at the technical college.

"Ghent," she said. "Your father learned printing in Ghent, and see what came of that."

Then she shook off the cat with a smile. "Pack your suitcase."

"Why?"

"We're going to Bastegem, to Meerke. Come what may. This villa is getting on my nerves."

They bicycled side by side, bags dangling from the handlebars, she putting her hand on his shoulder from time to time. When she had difficulty in negotiating Drongen Bridge, he gave her saddle a push. "Hands off my bottom!" she cried and burst out laughing. With streaming hair and bright-red cheeks she freewheeled past whistling Canadians. She gave an Indian war whoop, and they returned it.

In Bastegem, Father Mertens had taken charge of the official Resistance Movement. Aunt Violet had heard from reliable sources that he would be coming around tomorrow or the day after with handcuffs to take her into custody. All the roller blinds in Villa Heliotrope had been lowered, Uncle Armand had fitted a crossbar over the front door just before he had the incredible stupidity to toast the Liberation "in quotation marks," as he had put it, in the Café Picardy. His truest friend and mistress, the owner, Antoinette, even as she filled him up with beer, had secretly sent her little

Alfred around to Father Mertens. Now Uncle Armand and all the other traitors from Bastegem had been locked up in the dairy.

"They ought to have given Armand a medal," Aunt Violet cried out. "It was he who saved the people's food by fending off those vile peasant black-marketeers!"

"You and your Germans," said Meerke.

"Is it my fault that they were billeted here?"

"You were much too familiar with them."

"If you weren't my mother, I'd slap your face!"

"You seem to find that amusing, Constance," said Meerke, as if to a fourteen-year-old Mama, long before the war.

Mama went on smiling.

"And if they get orders from Walle to take you away?"

"They can do what they like with me," said Mama, whose thoughts were with Lausengier as he ran along ravines in crystal fields, crying, "Constanz, Constanz."

You could see Uncle Omer through the small garage window, lying on a mountain of straw. He had had a fight with another lunatic in the Institution run by the Brothers of Charity because of an offside decision during a football match, and the other lunatic had kicked him in the head and given him a bad concussion. In the sick bay the doctors, in the euphoria of the Liberation, had declared him cured. Cured was perhaps a little exaggerated. At least he no longer ate his own turds. He had been released on two conditions: (a) that he was not to be let loose on the village, and (b) that he saw as little as possible of his brother Armand, preferably nothing at all, because such contact would probably give him the same kind of shock that had sent him to the loony bin in the first place.

Uncle Omer was not at all bothered about being locked up in the garage.

"Uncle, it's me, Louis."

"Uncle, it's me, Omer," he replied serenely.

"Louis, Staf's son."

"With his staff in his hand, St. Joseph walks the land."

"But Uncle . . ."

"Carbuncle."

"Dear Maurice, my old friend," Louis wrote in the notebook with the label "To M. de Potter." "Writing to a dead person is far from being the easiest thing for an apprentice writer who is to become an apprentice printer just as soon as the effects of the nightmare of the Occupation have abated. Because all this time we have been living in a nightmare, did you know that, you old rascal? That's what it says in the new newspapers.

"It appears, according to these new papers, that the nightmare will dissolve once the Nazi beast has finally been slain. We are heading for a dream of equality, fraternity, and liberty. Yes, with the same people.

"Have you, from up there, also noticed that Belgium, the concept of Belgium, I mean, is gaining ascendancy? Do you still remember how we always used to compare the map of Belgium in our school atlas to a stooping, doddering old man, with the province of Luxembourg as the stump of his leg, our own West Flanders province as his head in profile, and our North Sea coast as the outline of the cap on his head?

"The problem is getting used to this new fatherland of ours again. It's hard to see Belgium written up everywhere now instead of Flanders. Other than that, all I have to report today is that I have my eye on a girl who does the cleaning here in the house and who, I believe, just may become well disposed toward me. Before you turn your paradisiacal nose up at the smell of dish-water and ammonia, please remember that Goethe, who now inhabits your Titans' division, was also married to a woman from the so-called socially disadvantaged classes. Let me have the benefit of your wisdom on this matter. Is devotion not a better guarantee of harmony during our earthly existence than passion? Although I am waiting to be consumed by the second, because I am quietly getting to be old enough, I mean, young enough. Keep your eye on me from up there. And give me your blessing. I'll keep you informed. Your friend and brother in Jesus Christ, I am adding that last bit just in case He sticks His nose in your correspondence. Your comrade, the widely sought sex maniac, Louis."

Uncle Omer was on his knees playing with a beetle. His fingers walked, formed railings, the beetle ran around in a circle. A passing goods train made him look up.

"Hello, Uncle Omer."

"Hello, Uncle Omer. Any *Chicklets?*"

"No, Uncle Omer, not today." Nor yesterday, nor tomorrow for that matter. Uncle swallowed chewing gum. Uncle Omer got up, stood by the little window, scurfy with dried rain.

"You couldn't get in last night, eh, you and your comrades, to catch me."

"Last night I was asleep in my bed, Uncle."

"Uncle, Carbuncle, I heard you calling and knocking."

"That wasn't for you."

"Not by a long shot!"

"It was for Aunt Violet, your sister."

He tilted his head, listened once again for the nocturnal brayings of the villagers who gathered outside Meerke's house as soon as night fell, sometimes to be chased off by the village policeman and a few Canadian military policemen. The yellow-brick front of Villa Heliotrope had been daubed with dripping swastikas, a few the wrong way around, the hammer of Thor the God of Thunder twisted in this fashion no longer preserved the house from fire and lightning.

"Do they think I am Violet, then?" asked Uncle Omer and winked. He flattened his nose against the glass, his bright, girlish eyes, Mama's eyes, not leaving Louis. He licked at the glass, which made it glossy and easier to look through.

"The Japanese are being kicked in their Japanese balls." He knew that from the radio.

"The Germans, too."

Uncle Omer pointed to the orchard where a kitchen chair painted cobalt-blue stood under a pear tree. "That's where they're going to sit me down and tie me up and then ploppety-plop, upsy-daisy, hoppy-de-hop, shoot me down like a pigeon."

"Why would they do that, Uncle?"

"A thousand whys," he said.

"Tell me one, just one."

"Because I am Violet," he cried triumphantly.

The charges against Aunt Violet were twofold, she had not only been in league with the Huns but also committed an offense against morality. A score of Bastegemmers had declared on oath that she had danced stark naked on the terrace in front of young Boche soldiers, a few of whom had turned away in disgust. The acting magistrate dismissed both charges. Father Mertens raged from the pulpit against the, alas, Belgian evil of corruption, now also rampant in legal circles. For wasn't the acting magistrate dancing to the tune of Commandant Konrad, now an extremely important personage in Brussels? And Konrad had saved Aunt Violet for the sake of Aunt Berenice, that sainted woman. "It's as simple as that," Raf explained.

"But," asked Louis, "does that mean that Konrad is gallivanting around the ministries in Brussels wearing that mask of his?"

Like a condor, an airplane had alighted. Its name, too, was Condor. This time no minister stepped out of it, no one who, like most members of the Belgian administration, was in the habit of using the plane to fly to Brittany with industrialists for the purpose of smuggling in more than a few cases of Scotch and cigars and nylon stockings, no, it was a bronzed young man, a fair-haired ephebe in a white suit, who stepped out across the runway, his arms too long, at least by Greek standards, a young man carrying an initialed conjurer's-box of turquoise leather containing miraculous electrical instruments that could give off rays and concentrate them with superhuman accuracy, rays with which the young doctor, following directly in the footsteps of his father, a specialist in burns, and of his grandfather, who had treated *gueules cassées* in the ill-lit Hôtel des Invalides in Paris, had cured Konrad. Konrad still wore, but only because he was vain, a pair of dark-blue-tinted spectacles, although otherwise you could scarcely see a scar. Unless it was in the sunlight or under strong studio lights.

Raf had celebrated the astounding result with the young miracle-working surgeon and with Konrad at Maxim's in Ghent. The doctor, by that time drunk, had promised one belly dancer that he would transmogrify her breasts by magic into those of a sixteen-year-old, and another that he would make her appendectomy scar disappear. He had also claimed that one of his ancestors had bonded a golden nose to the face of Tycho Brahe, the Danish astronomer, to replace the nose he had lost in a duel with one Passberg.

Raf now lived in the house of the headmaster, who had fled to Argentina. The day before the Poles took Bastegem, the liberated populace had smashed to smithereens the beclawed lion and the Delta sign hewn in stone that had graced the front of the house, and had also cut off the electricity supply and the hot-water system. Now the Independence Front held its meetings there, and Raf lived there with none of the comforts to which heroes were legitimately entitled.

"You did know that I was in the White Brigade, didn't you, Louis?"

"Of course."

Holst was standing by the gate. War or peace, he always stood by the gate in his forester outfit. Louis shook his immense, dry hand. Raf said, "Morning, my friend."

A painting of Madame Laura in a white fur coat made her look ready to throttle a panting bulldog that was staring at a chandelier in the background. She wore a flat white Chinese hat to which a dead hummingbird had been pinned, and looked at Louis in mocking expectation. The bulldog wore a pink ribbon with an Iron Cross.

"To us," said Raf.

"To us," said Holst.

Tears came to Louis's eyes because he had downed the bitter-cold champagne too quickly. He tried to quell a swirling, sour wave in his stomach, lest the other two realize that he was drinking champagne for the first time in his life. "Champagne in beer mugs is really rather chic," said Raf. "And Veuve Cliquot—an excellent choice, Holst, most appropriate."

Louis's questioning face seemed to amuse Raf. "Holst himself being a widower, my young friend. Isn't that so, Holst?"

"Drink up," said Holst. "There are cellarfuls of the stuff."

"And how is the minister?"

"Fine. He's coming next week with his press attaché, his principal private secretary, and the rest. To hunt."

"What's happening to the apartment in the Avenue Louise?"

"What do you expect to happen to it?"

"Well, Madame Laura doesn't live there anymore."

"Who's to say she won't live there again?" cried Holst.

"Yes, why shouldn't she?" said Louis almost as fiercely. I'm getting drunk. My stomach is rumbling. Drunk as a lord. I'm going to vomit any minute all over the flowered carpet. No, no.

"If Madame Laura isn't found, and there is a good chance she won't be, then it's highly possible that Notary Baerens, I beg your pardon, His Excellency Minister Baerens, will demand politely but firmly that his lawful property in the Avenue Louise be restored to him."

"She'll get out of it somehow," said Holst.

"You bet she will," said Raf. "No two ways about it."

Raf split into two, separated, like the proof of a prospectus in Papa's ink-smelling workshop. Louis seized Raf's proof and crumpled him up, flung him in the basket under the paper-cutter, then rediscovered Raf safe and sound back on the sofa. Holst filled their glasses. "There are whole cases of it. I could even put in a shot of Cointreau if you like."

Louis's neck fitted exactly, as if made to measure, into the curve of the sofa, how was that possible? Louis XV had given orders to his cabinet-makers to use the pattern made by a head spinning in a cold sweat when designing the velvety lines of a sofa.

"Where is Madame Laura?" Louis asked.

"He doesn't know anything," Raf said at once. "He isn't just asking to make you uncomfortable, Holst."

"He might as well know," said Holst. "She stayed in Brussels, that's all."

"In good health and fit as a fiddle?" Raf asked.

"Of course."

"Which means she could turn up here any day?"

"And why not?"

"But then what do you make of those people who told the police that they'd seen her in Bastegem, in her usual white, riding a bicycle near the sanatorium?"

"Who said that? A couple of drunks."

"Vermaercke, the furniture manufacturer, D'Haenens, Roger, and the postman."

"On a bicycle!" crowed Louis. "Madame Laura on a bicycle! Why not a tandem?"

"The investigating magistrate himself said it was all idle gossip."

"People are wicked," said Raf and drank discreetly, fastidiously, not in greedy gulps like Louis. "They're wicked and nosy. They make a big deal out of nothing. In my opinion they're put out because you two got married on the quiet. Like King Leopold and his Liliane."

"They should . . ." Holst belched. "They should show some compassion for someone who wed and lost his wife within the year."

"Compassion is hard to come by nowadays," said Raf pensively. "Incidentally, the last time you saw your wife she was on roller skates, right?"

"Yes. She was skating, I testified to that."

"Was that for exercise?"

"She's skated ever since she was ten."

"That explains why she had such muscular legs and thighs," said Raf. (Marble her thighs / dulcet her sighs.) Louis felt certain that Madame Laura was dead.

(A woman lovely as the dawn / yet one for whom he did not mourn / he who was bound to her for life / what villain put her to the knife? / da-dum da-dum in dead-man's row / another world she'll henceforth know / her aftermath / a starry path.)

In the tents the Americans had pitched in the fields beside the Lockkeeper's House, Louis was known as "Lew." They invited him to come along with them to Germany in three weeks' time. Robertson, an electrician from Iowa, promised to present Louis with the right ear of every German he shot. That was because Louis had told them that his *"Daddy"* had been caught by the Gestapo and was still languishing in a prison in the Black Forest. He was showered with chewing gum and Mars Bars and Lucky Strikes. *"No kiddin', Lew!"* Sometimes he would go for a ride with them in a jeep, staring fixedly past the villagers, an unflinching guide speaking fluent American. He knew all the lyrics of "Don't Fence Me In," "I Walk Alone," "I'm Gonna Buy a Paper Doll That I Can Call My Own," slow, ponderous songs that sounded as if they were being played at the wrong speed.

It also became obvious that these agreeable, mellow sounds, the smells of Lucky Strike and machine oil, the nonchalant gleam of the Sten guns, and the dancing, springy, casual, childlike, catlike, film-actor soldiers would crush the Third Reich, the German leather and steel were too taut, too hard, they would snap under the indolent multitude, the incessant supply of engaging, easygoing material.

In the faraway rural village near Veurne, it happened that Papa, out of recklessness or boredom, ventured into the local café. Nobody recognized him, he just sat in a corner, drank his beer, and curbed his loquacious soul. A local White Brigadist, who wished the most gruesome tortures on all members of the Black Guard, raised his glass to the execution of all Dinasos. "But, my dear sir," Papa said, "excuse me, but Dinaso ceased to exist just before the war."

"What? What are you talking about?" Papa explained that those Dinasos who had favored the resurrection of Flanders had joined the VNV, but that many of the others had held aloof, confused and disheartened by the death of their leader, who, my dear sir, had spoken up in 1940 for Belgium and her king. The Resistance man pulled Papa up by his ear and emptied his glass of beer over Papa's thinning hair. Papa broke free. "Step outside if you dare!"

"Right," said the hero. "You go outside, but it'll be in a box."

Black and White fought, the bystanders pulled them apart, then pushed them back at each other again. Plainclothes policemen. Identity cards. Amid jeers, Papa was dragged off to the police station and from there to the Flandria in Walle, a former Gestapo hangout.

"It was his own fault," said Louis.

"How dare you?" cried Aunt Violet.

"He who does not honor his father will be reviled by his own son," said Aunt Angelique.

"How can you be so cruel?" said Anna, the girl who helped in the house and who was a blonde version of Bekka Cosijns.

"Perhaps Staf's father will intervene, he has a fairly long arm," said Aunt Berenice.

"He's sick," said Mama.

"They say he's going downhill fast," said Meerke eagerly. "He doesn't shave anymore, or wash."

"Mona has taken it very much to heart."

"Mijnheer the Canon de Londerzeele got the fright of his life when he saw him."

"It all started during a game of bridge, he couldn't add up the score anymore."

"Yes, he put down his cards and said, 'Gentlemen, I've got holes in my head like a gruyère.' "

"They say he does nothing but talk about his father for days on end."

Louis's great-grandfather had been a dignified lawyer with a flowing white beard who sprayed spittle around whenever he argued a case. Meerke still remembered him. Mama, too, of course, but she was wreathed in American cigarette smoke, hardly listening. Lausengier, leave her here.

". . . and his two daughters, Rosalie and Myriam, your great-aunts, that is, Louis, didn't want to live in Roeselare. And so they began buttering him up. Papa darling here, Papa darling there, why don't we get out of this little peasant town? Now that you're retired, we'd be so much better off living in Bruges, where you can still have a little fun in your old age, in a little apartment on the Lake of Love, because a big, cold house like this one costs the earth to keep up. And he said, 'All right, but my pigeons come, too.' And so his pigeons went along, but it's an odd thing, the pigeons fell sick, one after the other, convulsions and cancer and lung trouble. He had a lot of sorrow from that, your great-grandfather, Louis, so much so that he, who was so proud of his long, white beard and always washed it so carefully and put it in curls and kept it looking nice, allowed his daughters to fiddle around with their scissors until he was left with just a small square beard that needed hardly any attention, all they had to do was comb it, and a month later even that had been thinned out to a silly little goatee, and when he laid his head down for good, that poor man, he was clean-shaven, I saw him myself on his deathbed, he was a different person, I didn't recognize him anymore."

"Dear Maurice, Here I am again, pen in hand. My father has been incarcerated. In the Flandria prison camp, where the White Brigade has its tennis lessons now. Because he did not want to be a permanent burden to his host, he betook himself to some local hostelry out in the polders. To the awe of the patrons, he stepped tall as a tree into a taproom that smelled lavishly of army Chester cheese. An innkeeper draped in spider webs approached and croaked, 'What can I do for you, stranger?' A piteous parrot, its feathers singed with a candle by a ten-year-old girl, repeated the publican's entreaty in its filthy cage, and it was to this bedraggled cockatoo that my father replied, 'A beer without much of a head and a hard-boiled egg.' This last raised a laugh among the villagers, who, illuminated only by the flames of the hearth, were fondling each other, and now turned their countenances flushed with drink and debauchery toward my father. With a severe look he reprimanded the shadowy, tangled knot of rustics. It annoyed him that a hard-boiled egg, an item you could find freely available on the counter of every Parisian café, that an egg, the entity from which all of them had emerged in the fullness of time, should have become the object of their derision. My father, in more salubrious times a strong man, a jovial husband, a cheerful neighbor, a generous *commerçant,* felt threatened by his own people. He also thought, and this greatly broadened the field of his melancholy, of his son, who, he sensed, was at this very moment, in another place . . ."

Was Mama coming upstairs? Louis hid his notebook under the *Lustige Blätter, Mémoires d'une cocodette, De Gazet van Antwerpen.* Downstairs someone was busy with pots and pans. Anna? He looked in the mirror, combed his hair, made a face like Mussolini, put his hands on his hips, stuck his chin out, raised his eyebrows, curled his lower lip: *"Lavoratori!"* He saw Anna lying on his bed, she drew her knees up and said tenderly, "Oh, you little swine!" he brought out his less-than-virile member, tied a string around it tight, and attached the string nervously to the doorhandle. If Mama should come in unexpectedly, which she would never do, what did she care what he was doing? that he existed? then she would, something she never would do, because Mama never moved abruptly, then she would with a single jerk pull the door open with so much force that his thing would be torn right out of him, aghast, she would see the thing dangling between door and doorjamb, mouth agape, she would see the bloodspots on her white Madame-Laura-dress. He waited, tied to the door like a calf. Softly he sang, *"A doll that other fellows cannot steal, and then the flirty-flirty guys with their flirty-flirty eyes . . ."* But nobody came. Nobody ever came.

"Hi, Lew!"

That was him. The Americans were playing poker in a stench of steaming clothes that floated in the tent like mist. Today was Lucille Ball's birthday. It was drizzling. They toasted Lucille Ball and quickly became drunk, rowdy. The day after tomorrow they would be leaving to join up with the Russians, or at any rate to take up positions opposite the Russians.

Then they swarmed out toward the village, which was off limits, climbed easily over the barbed wire, through the marshes along the Old

Leie. Only Gene, the cook, who was doing some ironing, and Jay-Dee stayed behind. Jay-Dee listened to the war news while slowly running his hand over his long, sad Jewish face. Gene tidied up. He was about to throw away a newspaper in which tomatoes and onions had been wrapped, when Louis saw that it contained the "Arts and Letters" page. He read a poem by Johan Daisne, printed in italics. It rhymed.

"Look, that's mine," he said to Gene. "I wrote that."

"No kiddin'!" Gene pointed to the words Johan Daisne and asked if that was his name. "Jo-Ann Daynee?"

"My pen name."

"Oh, a different name. For the tax man! You writers are rich, huh?"

"This sort of thing doesn't pay well," said Louis. "I did it for nothing. Because they asked me to. I wrote it in a single evening. It just came to me."

"If I could write," said the cook, "I'd use my own name. Gene Murphy. So that everyone, all my friends, could tell it was me."

"At the paper they think I'm an older man. If they knew I still go to school, they wouldn't print it. But actually that pen name is my name as well. D apostrophe Aisne. I come from the Aisne region in France. My early ancestors used to have, still have, a castle over there."

"No kiddin'. And what does the poem say?"

Louis translated it into English, but not the rhymes, so a great deal was lost. *"In one town I was a child / in two towns lives she that loves me / in three I walked to work / what death, eh, eh, eh, rings at church?"*

"Tolls," said Jay-Dee. *"For whom the bell tolls."*

"Exactly," cried Louis. "Thanks very much."

"What period is your family castle?" asked Jay-Dee. "Does it have seventeenth-century towers by any chance?"

"Right!"

"Did Louis XVIII stay there during the Hundred Days?"

"He might well have."

"And a lot of dukes got murdered there, right?"

"That used to be the custom."

"And the terrace overlooks the cathedral and the valley, doesn't it?"

"You've been there," said Louis.

Jay-Dee smelled his hands, flattened the creases in his long, melancholy face. He had blueish cheeks like a Jewish gangster after an afternoon's interrogation by the FBI. Jay-Dee never did drill or turned up for roll call, something the others took for granted. He was a special security agent in the Counter Intelligence Corps.

Jay-Dee pulled the tent flap open, the marshes lay under a blanket of silver with rainclouds in the distance. He shook Louis's hand five or six times. "In the name of the Twelfth Infantry Regiment I consider it an honor to have met a young poet of this *fuckin' land.*"

"*Thank you, sir.*"

"*Take care.*" He pulled up his wide, shapeless trousers and walked off, his bony shoulders and his broad, lean back bearing resignedly and patiently all the falsehood in the world. Louis wanted to run after him, ask his pardon: If I am *Louis the Impostor,* it isn't altogether my fault. From my early beginnings, *in the town where I was a child,* I have seen nothing but deceit. *Please.*

"I never heard him talk so much," said Gene. "That's because you're a writer, of course. He's always scribbling away in his diary, too. And also because your family owns a castle, of course."

Uncle Omer was beginning to get some color and to talk a bit more sense. Sometimes, when he had washed in the scullery sink, he was allowed to sit down in the kitchen, but he couldn't bear it for long, disappeared quickly into his garage, blowing kisses at Mama.

"You shouldn't encourage him, Constance," said Aunt Violet. Despite the fact that Meerke ate two pounds of carrots a day for her eyes and had never in all her born days drunk alcohol, not so much as a drop of wine or beer, she was seeing more and more flickering black spots. High blood pressure, probably.

Het Laatste Nieuws announced a competition for a short story with a personal flavor, connected directly or indirectly with the war. Contributions had to include a certificate of good conduct and morals as well as a maxim, because the author had to remain anonymous until the accompanying sealed envelope was opened. Louis spent hours thinking about the maxim but couldn't come up with anything cryptic, distinctive, or intriguing enough to get his entry selected even before it was read. Because *Het Laatste Nieuws* often carried serials by Abraham Hans, Meerke's favorite writer, Louis took a pile of historical works by this fairly liberal Flemish Mind out of the Bastegem library, to the rage of Aunt Violet, who considered this to be high treason since she had been dethroned there as queen-of-the-books by that *éminence grise,* Father Mertens.

His grandson's education as a printer was to be paid for by Grandpa, but he was keeping them all waiting. Mama was annoyed about Louis's getting underfoot at home. "Reading and eating and lying around and being rude, I've had enough now, I've telephoned the Provincial Commercial College in Ghent, you like speaking English with your Americans so much, you can get a diploma there in shorthand-typing and foreign languages, that'll always come in handy, even for a printer, no, I won't be coming along to Ghent, no, I won't be taking you to the station, it's high time you stood on your own two feet."

All sorts of smart-looking people, teachers and students, were walking in and out of the grim, gray, august edifice that housed the Commercial College. The boy from Haarbeke, Walle, Bastegem, in the too-warm coat Mama had made from an American army blanket with the help of Uncle Omer, whose pestilent smell of wet straw and dung impregnated the garment no matter how much Mama protested to the contrary, the boy was afraid to go in. He would stutter, choke with shame. They would spot his father's treason in his peasant face in less than a minute. Louis waited until the street was clear, approached the front of the building, and looked through a wide gap in the frosted glass. Boys and girls were sitting in a classroom, heads bent, filling in figures.

Louis trudged along the Grass Quay, the Corn Quay, the most historic places in Europe, with Roman, Gothic, Austrian, Renaissance, you-name-it façades, with ships, anchors, and garlands carved in stone, with baroque arches and Ghent people walking about in long velvet gowns, leading greyhounds and bearing falcons on their mailed fists. Louis bought half a pound of cheese, was about to consume it like a page waiting for his bonneted lady on the terrace at the Court of Egmont, when he noticed the bright-colored poster for *Song of the North*.

The usherette shone her torch in his face and pointed out acidly that her tip was not included in the price, in his accursed sweaty haste he handed her a five-franc piece instead of a one, and then his first American film in color filled him with horror and bewilderment. It was outlandishly garish, the heroes and heroines tinted ocher, the red-and-blue checked lumberman's-shirt worn by George Brent was louder than the screaming of the lady he was then blowing to smithereens, while fir trees shot like fireworks (a paler yellow than his teeth) across the screen. Just as George Brent, heralded by violins, appeared to be on the point of conquest of the rancher's reluctant daughter, Louis unwrapped the cheese from its paper and began cramming small pieces of the sticky, pungent lump into his mouth. Wiping his greasy fingers along the velvet seat, he was absorbed in the puerile, because American, story, when the two students beside him started swearing in Ghent dialect. And at him, there could be no doubt of that. When he continued to stare fixedly at the screen, they got up and found seats three rows behind him, still muttering to themselves. Oh, inhospitable city of Ghent. A pretentious place ever since the Middle Ages. And they'd turned up too late at the Battle of the Golden Spurs.

Then a bald man in the row in front of Louis suddenly rose and, also uttering Ghent curses, moved to the back. With the vague suspicion that he must have done something awful yet to be revealed, Louis fell asleep, pleasantly warm, the cheese had formed a lump of peat fueling a rosy, snug, glowing little stove inside the seat, the Rock was reading a book and ostentatiously (not to show off, but to deceive, to take in, *ostentatio*) allowed the title page to be seen: "Is indolence sin or disease?" in the cheese shop Louis had pointed to a creamy object, "Herve?" the saleswoman cried, and he, in a hurry again, nodded, there are German cheeses as well that look like Herve, the name was on the tip of his acrid tongue, Limburger? and Swiss cheeses, too, to which goat droppings are added that decompose into small blue stars and spider webs, and now I can smell it, did I have a cold before? the stink is growing stronger, rank and rampant like stinkweed, the people in their comfortable seats hit out furiously at it, shit and ammonia float through the auditorium, the people edge in silent lines toward the exit. George Brent's gigantic face with pimply cheeks and cracked lips also notices something just as he is about to kiss the crumbling chalky mask covering his dying mother, oh hell, his mother is mumbling curses with her very last breath and the son, George Brent, widens his nostrils, the hairs inside trembling as in a breeze, he pushes himself away from her bony shoulders, and he, too, flees into some stable, mounts a gray horse, and gallops off over the prairie, his mother's corpse rises up and sneezes, which makes the lights come on, the two usherettes are baring their teeth like vicious dogs.

Louis was out in the street, it was dark, trams were ringing their bells, and he stank as he walked all the way back to the station, afraid to get onto a tram, and there he was dying of thirst, *sitio,* and all because of the Herve cheese, made in Belgium, and the envy of the French.

Aunt Violet came back from Brussels downcast. All her frantic attempts to speak to Commandant Konrad at the Ministry had come to nothing. Minister Baerens had intervened and given orders to fend her off. And Baerens in his turn had been taking his orders from Father Mertens, as one good Catholic from another. Sadly she went upstairs to take off her Sunday dress.

Immediately Meerke whispered, "Now that he's cured, of course he doesn't take the slightest notice of her anymore."

"Did he take much notice of her before, then?"

"From the first moment he arrived in Bastegem. She and Berenice were after him like chickens after corn. Just think of it, a man who, for love, had had vitriol thrown into his face by a woman and who discovered Our Lord as a result! The more his skin peeled and blistered, the more he loved God and all His blessed Saints. And then, of course, when he founded his own church, which he named after the Huguenots because he was distantly related to them, he had Berenice, for whom the Catholics are not good enough, eating out of his hand. And then, because he had picked up with Berenice, Violet, who's been jealous of her sister all her life, just couldn't let well enough alone, she had to try and gain spotty-face's attention."

She shook her head as if she had had an electric shock, had seen another black moth fluttering by.

"It's a good thing," said Louis, "that they didn't breed, Aunt Violet and Konrad, they would have spawned a real baboon."

As expected, Meerke uttered a cry. "Louis, how could you! You get nastier by the day. Isn't there a spark of decency in you?"

Then a second traveler—Flanders had missions for her daughters—returned home. Mama had been to visit her husband in the Flandria, where once she had tormented her sentry-keeping, Flanders-serving son.

"Your father has lost heart. They don't know when his trial will be. There are mountains of dossiers. On the other hand, it's a blessing in disguise, because there's a conveyor belt of people waiting to be shot. Anyone unlucky enough to come up now is going to get the death penalty for sure. And all those witnesses against him! Complaints going back to before the war. Three or four depositions saying there was a Hitler doll on our mantelpiece. Felix the barber has stated on oath that he saw handcuffs and a pair of pincers for torturing White Brigade members in your father's coat pocket. Mijnheer Groothuis has promised Grandma to do his best for your father. But what is Mijnheer Groothuis's best worth? Who would have believed that Groothuis was on the telephone to London all through the war?"

"On the telephone to England?"

"Or sending them telegrams. By some special cable under the sea. I didn't listen all that carefully. But all through the war he was taking orders from the government in London. Telling him what to do."

"How is Staf's father getting along?" asked Meerke.

"He's very weak, he goes cross-eyed every so often, Mona says."

With a calm and blissful gesture, Meerke took up her knitting. "His chickens have come home to roost. Always high and mighty, Staf's father. Do you remember, Constance, at your wedding dinner, that speech he made about the marriage feast in Cana, as if we were in a Bible class? And then he sat there picking at his meat. I said, 'Is there anything wrong, Mijnheer Seynaeve?' 'I have the distinct impression that what we have been served here is horsemeat,' he said, cool as a cucumber. In the Pomme d'Or! Staf must have told him that we were too poor and stingy to eat anything but horsemeat."

"And we used to eat very well indeed," said Aunt Violet in her dressing gown. She smelled of Sunlight soap.

"Lots of bacon."

"Vegetables from the garden."

"Pickled herring for supper now and then."

"And boiled beef on Sundays. With carrots."

"With the bouillon from it on the Saturday before."

"Or chopped tripe."

"And rice pudding."

"And we used to go to school in clogs."

The three women, the three widows, sighed almost in unison. Louis hummed, *"Floody, floody, floy, floy."* Cab Calloway.

"Do you remember, Constance, when you needed a satchel for school and I got that cowhide from Liekens? I took it to Edgar the shoemaker, God rest his soul. And that ninny got it all wrong, he used the wrong side of the hide, so that the hair was on the outside."

"I cried about it for days. The other children all shouted, 'Silly cow! Silly cow!' after me."

"With a love that's true, always," silly cow.

"Every Saturday, into the tub in the kitchen," said Aunt Violet. "And one day the schoolmaster walked in all of a sudden. He saw me, I must have been about seven. 'A real Rubens,' he said."

"And then, quick, quick, soaking wet, into bed in our nighties because it used to be cold enough to freeze the stones those days," said Mama through the smoke of her Lucky Strike.

"I'll be loving you, always. With a love that's true, always."

"One day I came out of school and it was raining. But, of course, I didn't want to go out in my school tunic, in case the boys from the technical school saw me. And so my summer dress, I only had one at the time, got soaked through. I hung it up by the stove at home to dry and I didn't watch and it got completely scorched. Our Dad beat me black and blue. Got a lot of smackings from our Dad."

"He meant well, Constance. But he was quick to lose his temper," said Meerke.

"That's the truth."

"And money ran through his fingers like water. If I hadn't kept him under control, the bailiffs would have thrown us out in the street. I always put something aside, every week. Every week when I went to cash my check, I deposited a little in the savings bank. I'd bring food back for the whole week, and then your father would come home with a pal, they'd sing *The Pearl Fishers,* drink all the beer, and eat up all the week's food. Then it would be herring for the rest of the week. Most of his pals were fishermen. He laughed himself silly when they told him how some stinker of an engine had blown up right in the middle of the sea, by the Green Bank, and how the Russians had to tug the ship away and made fun of the stupid Belgian crew who had to be towed all the way to Russia. 'Give my friends another beer, a little Pearl,' he would call out then, my Basiel. *'Allee,* another little Pearl.' And I would pour them Pearls as if they were in a café. And they'd sing *The Pearl Fishers* in two voices, what am I saying?, in six voices. Filibert was there, too, a blind fellow, who always went on about Floris, his dog, he'd starved him to death. I said, 'But, Filibert, why didn't you ask me for some scraps for Floris?' 'Ah, Amelie!' he says to me, 'I keep asking you for so much food for myself.' I say, 'So what?' 'No,' he says, 'you can't canoodle with two at the same time.' I say, and it slips out before I have time to think, 'And why not? So long as you share and share alike!' They all of them laughed, but I got such a slap from my Basiel that I could still see stars the next day. Now I'm seeing stars as well, but different ones, these ones are black stars.

"Actually, they aren't stars at all, they're black moths."

Louis described his walk along the Grass Quay and the Corn Quay, the guild halls, the Renaissance façades, the baroque elegance, the flights of steps and the porches and the golden ship on the ridge of a roof. "It was like a dream! Like the Middle Ages!"

"Clodhopper," said Raf. "Everything was all thrown together there at the beginning of the century, all sorts of styles all jumbled up, for the World's Fair, specially for tourists who can't tell chalk from cheese, just like you, clodhopper!"

The sky ought to be painted sea-green, slapped on over the roofs of the Institute with slapdash abandon by a painter belonging to some forbidden academy of the arts, a Black School. The walls of the Institute are far too high, and I am too small to see the sky. "Look at that little sheep over there, Lou darling!"

Two figures that must be my grandfather and my grandfather's son. A black-and-white photograph that moves but which has been colored in here and there by Grandpa (the outline of the pear tree, the hedge where Baekelandt might turn up any moment with his scythe) in mignonette and old rose applied with those delicate little brushes made of real sable, which, after use, Grandpa stored next to foul-smelling, iridescent phials in a purple velvet box, a present from Canon de Londerzeele.

Grandpa is the smaller of the two figures, and that is odd, I always thought he was a head taller than Papa. "He has shrunk," says an eager Meerke. How many inches does the average Belgian shrink per year? Does the process speed up with age?

Grandpa, who walks with an inquiring, reproachful air around the gently revolving merry-go-round, with never an Apostle, a Hottentot, or a little one in sight. Grandpa's spotless Prince of Wales suit with the trouser creases as sharp as if there were an iron wire running down them. The dove-gray tie with the broad knot and the pearl has been tied too tight, his Adam's apple is being squeezed, oh, how furiously Grandpa swallows, tries to gulp in more air. And still he continues with his auto-cratic eye to track down hidden children behind Bernadette's grotto, and Papa by his side does likewise, how can that be when he lies fettered on straw far removed from his father and lord and master? Golden wrinkles has my Grandpa, he who is also my godfather. The veins in his temples are golden worms. He carries himself ramrod-straight, he learned to do that well before '14–'18. A wintry light.

Grandpa stops. He listens. His son speaks, saying, "I have lost heart." "You must think of your son," says Grandpa and says my three forenames and forgets the most important, the fourth, that of Peter, the renegade Apostle. Papa looks down at his father's shoelaces, stands meekly in the smooth, gray light of Grandpa's shadow. Grandpa slips two fingers into his waistcoat pocket and brings out a passport photograph. "Is that him?" Papa looks at the photograph of a boy with large ears and nods. Grandpa dabs his own ears with a snow-white handkerchief, a Seynaeve gesture.

"You're going to flee the country?" he says. "Go to Ireland."

"Argentina," says Papa.

"Ireland," says Grandpa with emphasis. His tailor-made suit comes from Ireland, land of missionaries and martyrs. Mama has ironed that suit, sprinkling water over it first, holy water for the peace of Christ in the kingdom of Christ, nuns singing to the accompaniment of a small organ or a harmonium.

"Why do you want to flee, Staf?"

507

"Because they'll sentence me to death."

"Who says so, my child?"

"Barber Felix."

"Who will pass sentence?"

"The Jews."

"They are quite right," says Grandpa.

"Yes, Father."

"The Jews are back. Is that a good thing?"

"Yes, Father. And it's a good thing that Minister Gutt is calling in all the Belgian money, he's a just man."

"I have to go, Staf."

"No! I'll be sentenced to death!"

Two figures in the wintry light, chatting amid the ruins, the craters in a street in Haarbeke. Among the broken lumps of concrete lie pastries, buttercakes, boxes of Meccano.

"It is written, Staf, that a man can only be sentenced to death if the seventy sages of the Sanhedrin vote unanimously for his death."

"Seventy!" The echo reaches the music room, where Sister Angel is dusting the piano, she buries her face now in the veil of her wimple.

"But, Father, there are bound to be seventy against me!"

Grandpa grins. "In that case, Staf, you'll have nothing to fear, the sentence will not be valid, because, Staf, the Jewish book says, 'All unanimity is suspect.'"

"They are right," says Papa. Grandpa reaches into his waistcoat pocket for the golden toothpick presented to him by the Papal Nuncio to mark many years of loyal service to the Vatican, and pokes about with it between the bricks of the Keep wall, he comes up with the silver bullet that I once fired from my silver rifle at Papa's car in days gone by, at Holst behind the wheel. Or is it a knucklebone?

The hissing and rattling of the slow train and a monotonous, subdued roll of thunder, the same noises that had lulled him, now woke Louis up, that and a pain in his stomach. Opposite him sat two traveling salesmen, each with a pipe in his mouth and an attaché case across his knees. Flat and green, the landscape hurtled by. He was sitting in a train, and for the first time in his life it occurred to him that a train, more so than the idea of a train, was a box so many feet high, so many feet long, so many feet wide, a fragile, futile, and above all simple thing on wheels. Stay where you are without moving. I could touch the ceiling of this carriage, who would have thought it? Only a moment ago I was in the playground, in the shadow of my grandfather, who is now lying on his deathbed.

With difficulty Louis got to his feet, clutched the broad, dusty strap for opening the window. He looked in the luggage rack but could not remember what he had brought with him. He tugged at the strap, but the window was jammed, rusted in, cemented in. He remembered that he wanted to open the door. He pulled the handle toward him with all his might. ("No, clodhopper, push the door, don't pull.") He pushed.

("No, clodhopper, first turn the handle down.")

The younger salesman put his attaché case down next to him. Louis thought he was about to lend a hand, but the man tugged at Louis's sleeve. "Don't do that, young fellow," but Raf commanded, *"Clodhopper,* turn it down," the wind swept through the compartment. The salesman shouted and pulled at Louis's sleeve and collar. Telegraph poles sped past, the backs of houses, small gardens, and the entreaties of the two pipe smokers died away.

The sweet air of the hamlet/bamlet, kamlet, stamlet/ no rhyme would come to him, do rhymes spring naturally from nature, who invented them? The Teutons use nothing but alliteration, Romance languages use rhymes. We are all Franskiljons, we poets.

The letters BASTEGEM in white pebbles set among flowers and shrubs whose names poets ought to know. Bakels, the stationmaster in suspenders, had told a farmer that the Germans were coming back. Advancing on Antwerp from the Ardennes, which they had just reoccupied. I have kept the photograph of Reinhard Tristan Eugen. Should I pin it up again beside my wardrobe? Is the age of iron returning? The age of iron lasted for half a minute. The nature of things dictated that blinded horsemen of steel and leather should be destroyed. Morality, too. Louis Seynaeve, Lodewijk, de Lode, Lew, would look upon this and intone elegies, epithalamia, but for whom or to what? I must buy a rhyming dictionary next time I'm in Ghent.

An elegy for Grandpa, for example.

"Right up to the very last moment, right up to the sacristy, his comrades . . ."

"That's a word the Blacks use, Mona."

". . . his friends, then, let me finish, went on arguing. Because his friends wanted to have 'The Flemish Lion' played beside his coffin."

"What ever were they thinking of? This really isn't the time, what with von Rundstedt in the Ardennes!"

"But the Dean wouldn't hear of it. He said there are many, many Flamingants not yet in jail. Or already released. They are quite capable of coming to the church and joining in the singing of 'The Flemish Lion.'

And before you know it, they'll be singing *'Wir fahren gegen Engeland.'*"

"The bishop is right. This really isn't the time."

"But they didn't want to sing it in church. Just at the graveside."

"So what did they play at the graveside? Surely not the *'Brabançonne'*? "

"They finally came to an agreement. 'Far and Wide.' That wasn't played so much during the war, but it's still fairly Flemish."

"Wasn't that what the Rexists used to sing?"

"I thought the coffin looked really small. Or was I just imagining that?"

"He'd shrunk, it's true, but no more than the next man."

"He turned all blue, like a plum."

"While he was still alive?"

"Of course, silly. Afterward he was white, like everybody else."

"At the very end he went sort of purple. The Sisters saw it and made faces at each other, they didn't dare say much, because he could hear everything, you could see his eyelashes move when they said, 'Mijnheer Seynaeve.' "

"His head was completely shriveled up, it really gave me a turn, you don't expect something like that."

"And he didn't have a thing to eat those last five days, Mona. Nothing to eat and nothing to drink."

"But injections round the clock."

"The last thing he ate was that little sponge. He bit into it, Sister Gudule tried to fish it out from between his teeth, but it was too late, he'd swallowed it."

"How did that happen? Did he still have his dentures in, Mona?"

"Yes. I wanted him to look decent to the last, in case of visitors."

"And that rattle in his throat. I know it's natural, but I was so embarrassed."

"The Ward Sister took hold of my hand. 'Madame,' she said, 'he's with Our Lord.' "

"It was for the best."

"Yes. Because his mind had begun to wander so badly. And what a temper! He'd bark like a dog at the slightest little thing going wrong."

"If he ever comes back, the way those Hindus believe, you can bet it'll be as a Belgian sheepdog."

"Yes. For sure he won't be a pug, like Nora's."

"You carried on something dreadful, Mona."

"I couldn't help it."

"Ranting and raving at the doctors the way you did! I was so embarrassed."

"It was all their fault."

"What do you mean? They didn't give him the wrong treatment, did they?"

"They ought to have given him those monkey gland injections. I'd been asking for them since last year!"

"But isn't that against the law?"

"Not the law, just the bishops."

"But he was more Catholic than the Pope. I can still see him going up to Communion. It gives me the willies to think of it. With his eyes shut. I used to think, Oh, Lord, he's going to bump into somebody! You could see that he wasn't holding a wafer of baked wheatmeal on his tongue just then but Our Lord Himself!"

"Unleavened wheatmeal, Mona."

"Yes, yes."

"Well, that's life."

"Everything that lives must die. Even the stars."

"I didn't put on my veil. I thought of wearing sunglasses at first, but you know the Walle people, they'd have said: Look at her, what a show-off!"

"And they wouldn't even give Staf leave from prison to go to his own father's funeral."

"Excuse me. Staf himself didn't want to. 'I'm not going to show up in Walle flanked by two gendarmes, not even plainclothes gendarmes,' he said. 'And,' he said, 'my father didn't want a big, showy funeral like that with an eleven o'clock Mass in the Church of Our Lady, he wanted to be buried in Noordende, in the little parish church there, without all those people!' "

"How could we do that, his own family? To our mother? Go to Noordende, miles from anywhere, just because Antoinette Passchiers lived there."

"We might as well have buried him in Schorisse, where that Mylene lives, he had an affair her, too. And it's closer."

"Yes. If you take the Waregem road."

"Anyway, he didn't want the Church of Our Lady, he said so often enough. It's too great an honor, he said."

"And yet that's just what happened. Thanks to Canon de Londerzeele."

"We could hardly do everything he wanted! Supposing he'd asked us to throw him in a dustbin?"

"I'm only saying what Staf says, Mona."

"He's never spoken the truth yet, that one."

"It seems that Antoinette Passchiers was determined to go to the funeral by hook or by crook. But her husband knocked some sense into her."

"She would have thrown herself onto the coffin, you know her."

"Did he put her in his will?"

"Need you ask? But we'll soon scotch that. There are four or five wills, all of them legal."

"Incidentally, I heard that the proprietess of the Titanic was at the church, too. But I don't know her, and what with all that crowd I didn't spot her. A fat blonde, rather showy, they say."

"Some people have no sense of shame."

"In those last few months she must have wheedled close to fifty thousand francs out of him. Not to mention the gold."

"What gold?"

"The gold he kept lugging to the Titanic at the end, when he was losing his marbles. He used to walk bent double with his two suitcases."

"Suitcases full of gold?"

"Of course not. He'd get the blonde from the Titanic and two others, a Frenchwoman and one from Martinique, to undress, and then he'd scatter the earth he'd brought in his two suitcases all over the floor and they had to scrabble about in it to pick up the Napoleons and other gold pieces with their bare backsides."

"What's the price of gold these days, Mona?"

"What's the difference now? Look in the paper."

"It was only a question."

"He caused me a lot of grief."

"And his wife, too. He didn't show any respect for her until the very end. When it was too late."

"I felt so sorry for her, sitting in that wheelchair in the church with her chrysanthemums in her arms."

"And no one had taken the brown paper off those chrysanthemums, I was so embarrassed."

"Yes, well, at the very end he did repent. 'I have done wrong,' he said, 'and now that I am about to be called before the throne, I realize that I must give an account of myself. I never listened to Monseigneur de Beaulieu, who said when he came back from Katanga, "We should be like the old Negroes who, sensing the approach of death, summon their children and grandchildren and tell them everything, but everything, they feel ought to be handed down to future generations." And now that it's my turn to tell, I don't know what there is that I can hand on. I haven't been a good example.' I said, 'Don't worry, Dad, something will probably occur to you.' 'I don't think so,' he said. And the next day he called the telephone company and asked them to install a telephone in his grave, in case something should occur to him. The assistant manager came by, and he said, 'It's all right, Mijnheer Seynaeve, we'll see to it, we'll put in a line, you won't even have to pay for the calls, just the rental.' "

"Stop it, I'm wetting myself."

"You won't have to pay for the calls!"

"Give me your handkerchief, Mona."

"Oh dear, oh dear, just the rental!"

"Yes, we can laugh now, but by the end he'd caused me more than enough grief."

"And what about me?"

"And as for our mother, it was as if she'd gone around the bend, too, at the end. She went with me to the hospital. I could tell right away in the corridor that something was wrong. Sister Andrea, who was normally so polite —'Do sit down, madame, lovely weather we're having, madame'—was turning her nose up at me, she barely gave me the time of day, and the same with the other Sisters, I said to myself, Uh-oh, what's going on here? there isn't any shit on *my* shoes, you know how you imagine all sorts of things, and what do you think it was? He'd been turning the whole hospital upside down with his shouting. Now, they're used to that sort of thing, the Sisters are, that's what they get paid for. But what he'd been shouting was all in French, the man who'd always sworn 'All for Flanders, Flanders for Christ!' But the worst of it was, it was nothing but foul language and smut, *minette* here and *soixante-neuf* there, a real sewer!

"And the Ward Sister says, 'Mijnheer Seynaeve, at least lower your voice!' *'Je vais t'enculer,'* he shouts, 'I'm going to bugger you.' They had to give him a pill to stop his tongue. Now comes the best part. Our mother, instead of keeping quiet and acting deaf and dumb, began to laugh out loud, there in the hospital, but laugh isn't the word, there was no stopping her, she was shouting with laughter like a backward child. I had to take her straight out to the car, her and Cecile, but she went on screaming with laughter, all the way to the car, *'Il va m'enculer!'* "

"Well, I never."

"Our Staf looked healthy enough in the camp," said Leevaert, doctor of Germanic languages, now engaged in canvassing advertisements for the paper *Het Volk,* without, of course, being officially registered. "I would really have liked to take my leave of him properly, but you know how it is, Madame Seynaeve, the authorities wait until the last moment before informing you that your release has come through, and the prisoner is then in such haste to return to his beloved home. They are turning us into egoists, Madame Seynaeve."

Mama gave a nod, and Aunt Violet said, "It's quite understandable, Mijnheer Leevaert, no need to apologize."

"The main thing is that we now know that he isn't grieving too much," said Meerke.

"He's grieving all right, like the rest of us, but within reason. No, the only one to whom I was able to say good-bye properly was my old friend De Puydt. I had to wait for the first tram, so I had time to play a duet with him in the parlor of the Flandria, a simple little piece by César Franck. I must tell you honestly, I did shed a few tears then. Not so my friend, he has no tears left. And now I am treading God's byways, begging a few advertisements. Luckily, those of our comrades who have pulled through are sticking together. But I've put all my hopes in my book. And in the comrades who are going to help me."

Louis was startled. "Your book, Mijnheer Leevaert?"

"The novel that I wrote in the Flandria. The price will be thirty francs, but anyone subscribing in advance will be able to have it for twenty-five. And if you should order ten, Madame Seynaeve, I'll go down another two francs apiece. What are ten copies should you be thinking of giving your friends a nice New Year's present? And each book will be signed by me and personally inscribed to the recipient."

"What is it about?" asked Mama.

"About a woman whose only wish is to put an end to her life."

"People like to read that sort of thing," said Mama. "It's a good subject."

Louis could have throttled her. How could she seriously go along with something like that? And how could that waffling, drink-sodden pedant possibly write a book? And about suicide, of all things. Just because he was getting bored in the Flandria prison camp.

"My main character is a woman, whom I present at various important phases of her life. A woman predestined, despite the most arduous trials, to see the light in the last chapter."

"Does she die in the end?" asked Aunt Violet.

"No. She learns, despite everything, to accept life, of which she has experienced only the most wretched aspects, with all its pros and cons. As all of us must do."

"Let's hope it isn't put on the Index," Meerke said anxiously.

"Madame Bossuyt, excuse me, but you're not keeping up with the times. Index or no Index, I wipe my backside with it, to use plain Flemish."

"Yes, but then the libraries wouldn't be able to buy it," said Aunt Violet, dismissed librarian.

"Catholic libraries, no."

"The public libraries wouldn't be too keen on it, either, if everything wasn't completely aboveboard."

"As a writer, one cannot lose sleep over that, Madame Violet . . ."

"Juffrouw."

"Juffrouw Violet. All I know is that it is a plea for a purer inner life, and, that being the case, I do not mince my words. My characters are flesh and blood, they can be cast down and they can rise again."

"What's your book called, Mijnheer Leevaert?"

"*Jenny.* With the subtitle: *A Tale of Destiny.*"

"I'm in the middle of writing a story myself," said Louis. "I'm thinking of sending it in for the *Laatste Nieuws* competition."

"That's good," said Leevaert. Aunt Violet missed not a single bite of her minced-meat sandwich, Meerke's knitting needles did not slow down for a single moment, Mama continued to suck at her coffee-soaked lump of sugar, she would get holes as big as peas in her teeth.

"My story, or short story, actually, is going to be called 'The Sorrow.' "

"Ah, my boy, and what do you know about sorrow?" said Aunt Violet. "You haven't lived yet."

"Why such a sad title, Louis?" said Meerke. "People want to be entertained."

Mama went to the stove, and while pouring coffee (because she didn't want to say it to her son's face) she said, "The only subjects Louis got good marks in were Composition and Language."

"Language is important," said Leevaert and lit his pipe, and in truth he was beginning to resemble a Flemish Mind, what with his triple chin. "But the principal point is essentially what you have to say about man, society, our relationship to the Divine. And for that, don't take this the wrong way, Louis, you simply have to have all the experience it takes. Before you are forty, you can't . . ."

"What about Rimbaud?" said Louis angrily.

"Hands off Rimbaud!" exclaimed Leevaert so fiercely that Meerke nearly dropped her knitting.

"A little glass of Élixir d'Anvers, Mijnheer Leevaert?" asked Aunt Violet.

"If you'll join me, juffrouw." Leevaert coaxed hissing, wet noises from his pipe. "Rimbaud was a miracle. A man like him appears only once a century. Something so spontaneous, arising out of nothingness in such a way, so . . ."

"When he was my age he began by copying Victor Hugo and Alfred de Musset."

The pipe was jerked out of the mouth. "Who says that?"

"I read it."

"Where?"

"In the *Nouvelles littéraires,* my friend," said Louis rudely. "I read it every week."

Leevaert took a deep breath. Accepted the small glass. Tasted it. Put the glass down. "They cannot leave well enough alone," he said despondently. "They simply have to drag down every great man, every genius they can't understand, can't even begin to understand, they have to try and belittle him, to reduce him to their own miserable level."

In the garage Uncle Omer sang, as he usually did when evening fell, "Should auld acquaintance be forgot, and never brought to mind?" and as always the eight-year-old turkey Hector joined in.

Leevaert had downed three plates of hotchpotch, his pipe was belching smoke again. "It's quite simple," he said, "and it's something I have often explained to my pupils when they have thought that, just because they'd written a few good compositions, they automatically had some idea of what language was . . ."

"I only took the little ones in the fourth and fifth forms," said Aunt Violet.

". . . that is to say, language can be all things to all men, isn't that so, Juffrouw Violet . . ."

"Certainly," she said uncertainly.

"Pay attention, Louis," said Meerke.

"For example, you can express an emotion. Right? You can also imagine that you are addressing me or, perhaps, your dear Mama . . ."

Mama, *don't fence me in.* Mama coughed.

". . . and that you want to reach, are able to reach, the other. Right? Then you can also say something, anything, without any, or with hardly any, meaning. For instance, 'Hello' when you are on the telephone. Finally, and for us this is the most interesting possibility, Louis, you can evoke a poetic feeling."

"Oh, you can do so many things if only you pay attention," said Meerke.

"It's quite simple," said Leevaert.

"You can also use words so as *not* to be understood," Louis said.

Mama smiled at him. "Yes," she said. "Oh yes."

"And Esperanto," said Meerke. "That's something the Pope is very keen on. So that the Gospel can be spread quickly and easily."

Coming in to land, the airplane chugs. (Like the goods trains beyond the garden.) The passenger cabin is a shuddering, olive-green wooden crate.

There is nothing to be seen through the round windows but fog. The harnassed paratroopers, with their healthy teeth chewing Wrigley's peppermint chewing gum, are not afraid. One of them looks like little Dr. Donkers, Franskiljon and spy in the ERLA, which is why he, in contrast to the others, who are staring at her with burning looks, gives Mama an encouraging nod. For it is she, this woman in the corn-yellow cotton summer dress with a beige scarf, with the dyed, dark-red hair, the cigarette dangling from the left corner of her mouth, patting her *shingle*. A shrill whistle sounds. Under the mocking glances of the men, she looks, muttering, cursing, for her parachute.

Through the round peephole beside her you can now see clouds and, if you bend forward, a German town, a gray mass of stalagmites, of thawing snowdrifts, the airplane skims over them, not a car, not a bicycle, not a human being is about, melted gray candle grease lies over toppled houses, the airplane hovers like a mosquito. Yelling, the paratroopers plunge out of the open doors, then my mother's skirt blows up as well, she presses her skirt against her belly, her thighs and her legs in beige silk stockings quiver, she howls for joy, the pilot sticks two fingers in the air and disappears into the rising sun, his name is Harry, from *Harry Goes Flying* (Select Series, wood-free paper). "The old crate's done it!" cries Harry, and the crate was his coffin. *Remember,* Maurice?

My mother lands in a meadow of ashes and chalkdust just as the little Donkers slams against a soot-blackened factory wall. From the holes in the walls, the cellars, the craters, wailing voices can be heard, a steady pounding like the beating of a heart, the crack of horsewhips. Mama apparently knows where she is going, she makes her way unhesitatingly, summoned by the iron god of love. Quadrupeds of all kinds rustling about her stiletto heels do not trouble her. Do we hear a voice calling, "Constanz, Constanz!" a voice that has become thinner, more boyish, leaner after the years of yearning? With her shoes in her hand, on her last legs, she arrives in a little square by the harbor, Gothic façades shot full of holes. "Is this the Leibnizstrasse in Brunswick?" she asks.

"*Nein,*" someone answers in the blue mist.

"Who are you?" "I do not wish to identify myself, these are dangerous and loveless times."

"I am looking . . ." "I know who you have been looking for all this time, for whom you have at last left your husband, still languishing in jail, and your son, who practices self-abuse." "Take me to him, then." "Give me your hand." "Don't tickle." "I have only your interests at heart." "I've heard that often enough." "Don't be afraid." "I will pay you handsomely, take me to him. Is he well? Is he maimed? Even if he has no arms and legs, even if his chin has been shot off, I will still . . . I hope it is like that, then I can love him even more."

"He is as he is," says the furtive, skulking voice in the mist and leads Mama into a cavern with a counter, a cash register, and empty shelves. She waits. In the suburbs the American paratroopers have taken a bridge. Tanks nearby. Antiaircraft guns.

A man in snow-covered oilskins stands in the hole that used to be a shop door with a bell. He drags his feet as if hauling a cannonball behind him. "My darling," cries Mama. Lausengier reaches for her with a groping hand, puts on his goggles and recognizes her, does not believe his moist, immensely magnified eyes in the Rock's bulging spectacles, he shakes his head with the snowy hair. "Such a long time, such a long time," he murmurs.

"A whole lifetime," she says, and wants to embrace him, but he turns away with an incredulous smile and stamps the tiled floor with his boots because he does not want to see, nor to be seen by, his dream, his only possession. Then he plucks up courage and looks into the hell of her eyes.

"*Wie geht's Ihrem Sohn?*" he asks. "*Dem Louis?*"

"*Meinem Sohn? Never mind,*" says Mama, and says, flustered, that she has come to take him back to her mother, brothers, and sisters in a little village by the Leie, and cries. He dries her tears with a dingy, olive-green handkerchief.

"*Never mind,*" she says.

The day begins like every other. Mama asks Aunt Violet whether Louis has brushed his teeth. "Did you actually see it, Violet?" "Louis, pass me the milk, please." "I didn't sleep a wink with that train in the garden. For God's sake, turn that stupid radio down."

Two White Brigade men with their Sten guns were lounging around the gate to the Mills building, where the Blacks were interned, without the self-important, challenging air of the first days of the liberation. Even so, Louis crossed over to the Picardy, just missing oncoming cars that made no effort to slow down on this, the most dangerous road in all Belgium. You could never tell. The sentries might get it into their heads to grab him by the collar out of the blue, from sheer boredom, and to drag him inside. The dog kennel beside the gate, in which they had kept the curate of Ravenhout for a whole week, had been dismantled on Father Mertens's orders.

As he drew level with the fortresslike villa that a tax collector had erected after winning five million francs in the lottery, a bicycle braked behind him.

"Well, don't you recognize me?"

She rode beside him, blonde under a straw hat, bright-red lips, crow's-feet in the corners of her eyes. Never seen her before.

"You don't recognize me."

"Vaguely," he conceded.

"Michèle! I'm a friend of the Thérèse who almost married your Uncle Omer."

"Oh yes. Now that you mention it."

"Where are you going?"

"To get some papers. *Les Nouvelles Littéraires.*"

"*Tu veux qu'on parle français?*"

"No, no. I can speak it, of course, but . . ."

"Are you in a hurry?"

"No."

She pedaled slowly and placed her hand on his shoulder.

"This is the most dangerous road in Belgium," he said.

"Listen. Have you got a moment?"

"What for?"

"I'm looking for someone to help me clear out my cellar. If you'd like to earn some pocket money."

"I can come just as soon as I've bought my papers . . ." (No, Raf, the way she rode off then, with her firm flesh protruding over the saddle, no, Raf, it isn't a baggy rear end, it's, it's, there isn't a word for it in the whole of the great dictionary of Van Dale, it's Rubens and Memling all rolled into one, that undercarriage, I said it to her in French: *voilà un édifice bien royal.*)

The windowless cellar was filled with kindling, broken furniture, a rusty motor scooter, rabbit droppings. He toiled away, wheeled the barrow, threw everything in a pile behind a hedge. She called him inside, into the opulent villa. He was to call her Michèle. Her husband, a doctor, had died the year before. She poured him a glass of beer, drank one, two martinis herself.

"Wouldn't you like to wash your hands?"

She perched on the edge of the bath set with small Delft tiles as he took a bar of Lux toilet soap out of its checked wrapper (nine out of ten movie stars withstand the harsh glare of studio lights on their complexion by using Lux, Claudette Colbert among others), and scrubbed his hands harder and longer than ever before, dried them quickly so as not to make the bath towel too wet.

"Don't you have to . . .?" She nodded in the direction of the toilet. The blood rushed to his head.

"You've been working for over three hours and you haven't pissed once. You can see I was keeping my eye on you."

The dirty, coarse, working-class word that had spilled from her nonchalant lips took him by surprise, it was repellent and exciting at the same time.

He laughed like a working man in a crowded café. He was no longer surprised when she ran her oxblood-colored fingernails over his fly, fumbled with the buttons, impatiently knit her brows when he gently pushed her away. "You'd rather be a big boy and do it yourself, all right, that's fine with me."

But perhaps he wouldn't be able to, she must be nearsighted, which would explain the crow's-feet, because during those three hours he had, in fact, had a quick pee behind the barn, even two, and what was she going on about anyway, what was there to see (said Bekka in the clay pits) and we aren't beasts after all, there are gods, immortal, and men, who die like beasts, but in between there is surely a category of men who carry divinity within them, for instance those who are gifted with the fire-tongued language of the gods? He resolutely buttoned up his fly, cleared his throat like a nun.

"Are you ashamed? I've seen it more than once, you know."

"I realize that," said Louis, "after all, you are a doctor's wife."

"Was," she said curtly.

"I'm sorry."

"Don't mention it."

She flicked her forefinger against his left nipple. ("Against my indestructible heart, Madame Michèle!")

"You don't dare," she said. "But I do."

In full view of all the thunderstruck Olympian gods, she hitched up her skirt, she was wearing nothing underneath, she sat down, a stream gushed from her.

"Voilà," she said. "A good example."

She stayed there, sitting. ("Surely she doesn't expect me to get onto her lap!")

She raised her forearm and covered her eyes. Then her lower body slid forward on the lavatory seat, her knees parted, the lips there were bulging and bedewed and blubbery and oily, they opened and a riddled palate appeared, a second little mouth. Her calves were taut, only now did he see that she was supporting herself on tiptoe, her buttocks free of the vanilla-lacquered seat. An acrobat with a cramp, awaiting plaudits.

"Enough? Have you seen enough?"

"Yes," said Louis. "Yes. Thanks a lot," he added stupidly, like a peasant.

"Come with me."

The bedroom was that of an extremely tidy maid, or a spare room. Michèle gave a quick look in the wardrobe mirror, shook her blonde mane.

"Lie down, then." She drew the baize-green curtains and undressed him in the dark room without walls and furniture. In all those spicy books, rakes consumed with lust leaped upon at first unwilling, then billing and cooing, women. Yet these women, first Aunt Nora and now this doctor's wife, had both assaulted him! Did he exude so much servility, then? This one kissed his erect member with little catlike licks and pushed and slid and gripped his loins until he was driven inside her under her dress, and whispered that he was dear and that he was sweet and that he was all sorts of unintelligible things, and it was wetter, smoother, hazier than with his hand. Was he making children now? Twins, Aristotle and Amadeus? Douglas, Gene's pal, stood shaving in the tent, while Jay-Dee sat reading on the same kind of camp bed as this in khaki underpants, and Douglas turned around and said, "Lew, the one thing you've got to learn to do is hold it back, no matter how much they thrash around and beg for it, hold it back, that's why the women are all so crazy for me, I can always go on longer than they do, *that's fuckin' all.*"

Tanned legs (from bicycling?) swayed in the air. She swore when he slipped out of her, grabbed him and the rocking and thrusting started again, she seized his buttocks, squeezed. He pushed his hand under her brassière, felt the wide, flat breast, flat, Raf, like a pancake. She bit into his arm, pinched his hand with all her might.

Then she fell silent, in lukewarm suspended animation. He withdrew. His testicles hurt. Hold back, easy to say, Douglas, keep going, the pain kept going, for sure.

She buttoned up her dress, stayed lying on her back and, with the violence of yesterday's sudden summer rain, gave a series of long, high-pitched sobs, burying her head under the pillow.

The little book that Jay-Dee was reading on his camp bed was called *Harmonium*, I had a look inside. "*A man and a woman / Are one. / A man and a woman and a blackbird / Are one.*"

"What did I do wrong, Michèle?"

She sat up, nose and cheeks wet, her hands crossed over her chest. "Now you know, now you know. You're such a nice boy, and you don't want to say anything about it . . ." she said.

"I wanted so much to give you pleasure . . ." she said.

"But it's all because of little René. He couldn't help it, either. And yet . . ." she said.

"They used to be really big, beautiful and full. I was so proud of them . . ." she said.

"Little René ruined them. They never recovered. If only I had bottle-fed him. But my husband wouldn't let me, and being a doctor he ought to have known. I'm so ashamed. You're not saying anything. You're probably thinking, She tried to put one over me with her padded bra. But I can't help it."

"No," he said.

"You don't mean it."

"Yes, I do."

"You are nice."

"Stop it now." He put his clothes on.

"You see, you're cross with me!"

("Apollo, oh, is this the female way?/ Unchecked and unperturbed she wheedles/ Makes my balls ache with her needles/ Pricks my bag of tricks for play!")

She warmed up some chocolate, fetched waffles and syrup, put on a record by the Andrews Sisters, "Chattanooga Choo Choo." On the dresser, on the mantelpiece between mica roses, on little low tables, stood photographs of an anxious young man, a few showed him in swimming trunks waggishly imitating a *bodybuilder*.

"Is that him?"

"Yes. Next month they're going to put up a stone plaque on the front of the house where he was born. The Governor will make a speech. They're even talking of naming a street after him. They want little René to come to the ceremony, but I'm against that, he's not big enough yet. A stupid cousin of mine took him to one side and said, 'René, your papa was a hero and that's why they executed him.' Luckily he didn't understand. He asked me, 'Mama, what's that mean, executed?' I said it's the same as having an operation. He's not big enough yet."

When Villa Heliotrope came into sight in the distance, beyond the railway track, he discovered that he had left his *Nouvelles littéraires* behind and that Michèle had not given him any pocket money. But he would be seeing her again, the pain down there was easing. *Chattanooga Choo Choo, won't you choochoo me home.* I have a *sweetheart.* No, that sounds too rustic. A *lover,* too important, too much like Ivanov's True Romances, a *beloved,* too much like the *Breviary of Flemish Lyric Poetry.* I have a *maîtresse,* that's what it is.

"Clodhopper, what you mean is *mattress.*"

Meerke, Aunt Violet, and Mama were making jam in the kitchen. Thrifty Meerke wanted to boil the apple cores along with the rest. Violet thought only poor people did that. "No, it improves the taste, Violet!" Mama said that, once the sugar had dissolved, the pulp had to be left to boil for a very long time. Louis's task was to pull the cellophane discs over the pots, first moistening them, but not too much. Thus was his time on earth being whiled away. Mama kept on nagging him to go back to school. Did Jack London know anything about trigonometry, what did Van Ostaijen understand of chemistry?

"You must get a diploma," said Meerke. "Then you can always be something in the Civil Service, have holidays, a pension, everything settled."

"You're dreaming," said Mama. "What are you thinking about?"

"About getting up to no good," said Aunt Violet.

"No," said Mama, "he's wondering what to do with the money from the *Laatste Nieuws* competition and about how much of it to give to his poor mother."

"And to his aunt, who used to sit up with him at night when he had the whooping cough."

"Five thousand francs. Is that tax deductible?" asked Meerke.

"I'll never win. There must be at least a hundred entries."

"As long as the story's a moving one," said Meerke. "Moving or historical. Is it historical, your story?"

"No."

"Is it about the school in Haarbeke?" asked Mama lightly, lightly, on stockinged feet, and Louis saw her crossing his room in her pompom slippers, coming upon *Les Mémoires d'une cocodette,* finding the notebook under the wardrobe and the little bundle of stapled newspaper clippings that made up "The Secret of Merivale Castle," published as a serial in *Het Laatste Nieuws,* his inspiration, his style.

"About a boarding school?" exclaimed Meerke. "That's only going to be interesting to children who've been to boarding school themselves."

"So a detective story's only interesting to detectives?"

"Take it easy, I can give an opinion, can't I?"

"Or else," said Mama, "or else he's spying on us here with his mean little eyes and listening to us with his rabbit ears and writing down everything we say and do."

"Making a laughingstock of our family?" said Aunt Violet.

"Our Louis would never do that, would you, Louis?" said Meerke.

"What in God's name is there to write about you?" said our Louis.

"What we went through during the war," said Mama.

"What was that?"

"Our sorrow. Your story is called 'The Sorrow,' isn't it?"

"The only thing you went through was making sure you got enough food and clothes and coal."

"Thanks for nothing," said Mama.

"You ought to be ashamed of yourself," said ex-teacher Violet Bossuyt. "What with your father languishing in jail for his idealism."

"I'd like to read that book of Mijnheer Leevaert's," said Mama. "As soon as possible."

"It can't be all that marvelous if he can't even find a publisher and is having to print it himself. Anybody can have his book printed."

"He's been stripped of his civic rights. No publisher wants that sort of thing associated with his company," said Aunt Violet.

"And what percentage would he have been entitled to, in any case? Now all the profits'll be his own," said Meerke.

Rancorous, jealous Louis had been driven into a corner. He shrugged his shoulders. "If you're so interested in some woman called Jenny who commits suicide, you might as well read *Woman's Realm.*"

"Does Jenny commit suicide?"

"Mijnheer Leevaert never mentioned that."

"At the end of the book!"

"But she's supposed to see the light at the end," cried Meerke.

"No, no, no. He said quite clearly that it's about a woman whose only wish is to put an end to her life."

Silence. The three woman looked at one another, Aunt Violet had hiccups, gave a squeak, it was a signal, the three witches around the cauldron of glorious-smelling, steaming apple pulp grinned, giggled. Mama was the first to stop. "Louis, my boy, life, that's something else again. Mijnheer Leevaert meant to say that what Jenny wanted to get out of was her bad *way* of life."

"Like those women in the Picardy," said Aunt Violet.

"Leave Armand out of it," snapped Meerke at her bloated daughter. Louis stretched the rubber bands around the pots of hot jam. The battle of the Ardennes had gone wrong, the Germans were nowhere near Antwerp. Oh, V-bombs, why do you give Bastegem such a wide berth? What about a direct hit on this household of foolish virgins? This kitchen blown to smithereens!

"Look! Look!" giggled Aunt Violet. "He could eat us up with rage!"

"If I took a bite out of you, I'd drop dead from poison."

"Hey, watch your manners," she said. "You forget I used to change you and wipe your bottom when you were a baby."

Harmonium. The river is moving. / The blackbird must be flying.

"They say that Goebbels poisoned himself, and his Magda, and their twelve children. To start with, they thought he'd gone on fighting the enemy until he had no more bullets left, just his bayonet, but then they did an autopsy."

"Twelve? I thought six."

"His adopted children must have been there as well. Or maybe some bastards who were never mentioned."

"What did he give them?"

"They didn't say on the radio."

"Some powder in their milk, no doubt."

"And Magda just stood there watching."

"Or she did it herself."

"They were all found half-burned."

"Not enough kerosene, probably."

Adieu, warriors, deluge of pride, desperate clutching at heroism, *adieu,* leather-and-steel corsets, death's-head berets, the beautiful cadences of Goebbel's address on Christmas Eve, '41: *"Unser schönes Reich, so weiss, so weiss, so weiss und wunderschön,"* *adieu* cruel Reich, benumbed by the murmuring of these three tame housewives, among them she who is also declining, slackening, decaying, becoming absorbed in her sister and her mother, all her sorrow having been in vain, all the sorrow that made her thin, beautiful, pitiless, once upon a time in another town and another time.

Much as Mickey and Minnie in the animated cartoons shown at the Youth Fellowship Hall in Haarbeke would move jerkily about in star-shaped explosions, so three little manikins, one fat, one thin, and one short, were dancing inside the thick black lines outlining their silhouettes. They were skipping through a storm-tossed wood, Snow White's twisting, lashing kingdom of branches. The fat *field marshal* with all his medals, the rake-thin *traitor* Rudolf Hess with a smear of shoe polish for eyebrows, and the *Head of the Ministry,* the skeletal little dwarf with arms reaching down to his ankles, were running, running, running, beating back snakelike twigs and octopuslike branches, playing tag, Goebbels was the nimblest, color flowed into the drawing (by David Low, the collection of cartoons that had startled Louis in the Avenue Louise book cellar).

Khaki slipped into the uniform jackets of Hess and the dwarf, field-gray into the marshal's bulk and silver-blue into his baton, the color made them stop their little game, there was something happening on the tennis court of the Flandria, something was surging out of the changing rooms, swirling toward the outside world, and before it could turn into a dragon or a witch it was Franklin Delano Roosevelt in his wheelchair, jawbone, white-toothed smile, cigarette holder, and all. On his broad back sat a rabbi. The three fled in panic, Goebbels overtook the lumbering, laboring Hess, Göring hid in a windowless cellar full of kindling. At long last Goebbels, on his ultrashort legs and in his parade uniform with the satin stripe, reached the Chancellery and was aghast to find his *Führer* lying there dead. He gave the Olympic salute and said, "Our retaliatory weapon is nothing but a big fart in a bottle, *Führer,* we brought it out much too late, we should have woken up earlier." Phosphorescent smoke, light-green like young oats, rose from the *Führer*'s clothes. Goebbels whispered, "Who art thou now, *mein Führer,* Christ or John?" Answer came there none, Goebbels lay down, reached his long arms behind his shoulders as in a gymnastics exercise, pulled his legs up, and in this doubled-up position looked at his orthopedic shoe, which had caught fire. "Get up," said Magda.

"I think I'm over it now," said Uncle Omer, a civil, docile man sitting at the table in spotless pajamas. "From now on I intend to shave every day and to try and read the paper."

Meerke was overjoyed. "It's because the war is over. That's what got you down."

"The best tunes are the short ones," said Aunt Violet.

"If my luck holds a while," said Uncle Omer, "I just might see if I can't find some work."

"As what?" said Aunt Violet.

"He's done his studies, after all," said Meerke.

"When the beasts still had the gift of tongues."

"You have all the time in the world, Omer," said Mama. "No need to hurry."

"I love you, Constance."

"I love you too, Omer."

Meerke spooned out buttermilk porridge with apple slices, gazed at the table, her eyes filled with tears, she had to sit down.

"It's only our Armand who's missing now."

Uncle Omer nodded.

"Wouldn't you like to see our Armand back again one day, Omer?"

"Yes, Mother."

"Truly? From the bottom of your heart?"

Uncle Omer was lost in thought.

"You have a heart of gold," said Meerke.

"My Papa is missing as well," said Louis.

"Of course he is, little one, but for the moment I was just thinking of our family, the Bossuyts."

No one said a word about Aunt Berenice.

Holst stood waiting in the middle of the blue salon next to the dining room on an Oriental carpet, as on a little island. He put a pistol in his pocket.

"Are you alone?"

"You can see I am," said Louis.

"Is there anybody else waiting outside? Did you see anybody?"

"No, look for yourself."

"I wouldn't be able to see them. They're usually behind the rhododendrons."

A Browning lay on the marble mantelpiece, next to the porcelain figure of a Scottish piper.

In the spacious kitchen, where Holst poured dark beer into crystal goblets, a double-barreled shotgun leaned against the wall by the door. Holst said that Alex Morrens and the juniors from Bastegem Excelsior had formed a White Brigade unit and had surrounded the house. He didn't know what Morrens's motives were. It might well be that Morrens thought that Holst, as a former Flemish Guardsman, had been let off too easily thanks to the good offices of Commandant Konrad. Or that Morrens held Holst responsible for the disappearance of his legal spouse. The young footballers took aim whenever they spotted Holst's shadow, but so far not a shot had been fired.

"They're waiting," said Holst. What for, he did not know either. For him to step out of the door perhaps. That was why he had not turned up for Grandpa's funeral. The grocer's wife brought him bread and canned food. For the rest, the cellar was crammed with Burgundy, champagne, Cointreau.

"I wash the dishes and do the laundry myself. As usual."

"But what do they want?"

"Ah," said Holst. "The big purge." The Rock stood beside Holst, just as disheveled and unshaven, and said, ". . . the theocratic dictatorship of Savonarola . . . the Dominicans, in an ecstasy of purgation . . . the children following in his wake dragged ornaments, jewels, lace collars, into the street . . . the citizens burned their possessions just as Seynaeve burned

his books of clippings . . . and they burned Greek and Hebrew manuscripts . . . the germs of heresy."

"Her clothes, her jewels," said Louis. "Didn't Madame Laura take
those away with her?"

"No," said Holst suspiciously. "I am taking care of those."

"But you must have some idea where she might have been heading for
when she vanished into thin air. To America, with an American?"

"Into thin air," Holst spluttered, and said it again: "Into thin air."

Louis turned the knob of the radio. A children's choir with pinched
little voices was singing *Miserere,* ten or twelve times, one after the other,
then all together, the lament swelled, splintered, miraculously the fragments engaged again, an Institute full of angels.

Aunt Violet was back from Brussels for the umpteenth time.

"The fifth time," said Meerke.

In her too-tight gray two-piece, with a slightly paler gray Tyrolean hat,
a frivolous, flowery silk scarf covering her chins, in nurse's-shoes with
round toes and sensible heels, she came shuffling in, threw her snakeskin
bag thuddingly into Meerke's wicker armchair, and stamped off upstairs.

"Without so much as a how-de-do," said Meerke. "Since she stopped
teaching, she's forgotten all her manners."

"She eats too much because she can't find a man, and she can't find
a man because she eats too much," said Meerke. "Just as well that impostor's taken himself off to France now or wherever it is. No one in the
Ministry is allowed to give out his address. It seems Violet made a terrible
scene in their office."

"On account of her Huguenot?"

"You mean: her Protestant."

"Huguenots are Protestants, Meerke."

"In that case why do they call themselves Huguenots? At the Ministry
they don't know where he is, but where to forward the presents from
Violet Bossuyt, the cufflinks, the silk shirt, the subscription to the *Winkler
Prins* encyclopedia, that they do know. Now we have to say about Konrad
right away, he's done a fine job, he's been a real St. Francis, nothing's
been too much for him, day in, day out in his jeep all over the country
calling on all the politicians and the judge advocates to plead for pardons,
he's saved a lot of the Blacks, you have to give him that."

She put her wool to one side, looked through the window to the garage
where her favorite, Uncle Omer, sat, lay, or paced up and down. She
picked up her knitting needles again.

"Huguenot," she said contemptuously. "Lucky he took to his heels. Or he'd have been thrown into jail, too, and she'd be visiting him every day with bananas and nuts and clean underwear."

"Took to his heels, Meerke?"

"Ah, my dear, least said soonest mended. That's life." But she came back to the subject, of course, the high priestess of gossip, and after a great deal of malicious beating about the bush she said that Konrad, even during the war when he was in hiding with Jules the carpenter, had never stopped his open-air preaching, mostly at night in the barns. All through the war he would bless farmers and their wives and command them to eat buckwheat. But now his heretic teaching had caught up with him, because a jeep full of Polish soldiers had found farmer Vissenaken's daughter in a small country lane, bleeding and with a baby still attached to her by its umbilical cord. She hadn't wanted to go along in the jeep, but she was too weak to resist. Because that was one of those diabolical Huguenot rules. When they were sick, they weren't allowed to call a doctor. When they felt a baby coming, they had to rush out into the open until they could go no farther and then lie down with their stomach pointing up toward the sun or the stars.

"And did Vissenaken's daughter's baby . . ."

"It survived. But that makes no difference as far as the law is concerned. Our Lord must have his complement of souls, and everyone can practice his own religion, that's the law, but something like that is going too far."

"But was it his baby, Konrad's?"

"How can anyone ever tell, my dear? He blessed a lot of farmers' women in those barns, and not just with Huguenot holy water, either. And your aunt, one fine day she started to get cold sores on her lips, one after the other. If you ask me, she got them from him. She put cream on them and they went away again, true, but even so I went to Father Mertens and told him behind her back. I keep saying that he's escaped to France, but he often spoke about Switzerland, about Zwingli in Switzerland. Father Mertens is bound to know where that is."

He roamed in ever-narrowing circles around Michèle's house but without daring to ring the doorbell. Even if he did ring, she would never open the door to him. And if she did open it, she would greet him with "And what can I do for you, young man?" In any case, it was she who was ashamed of her bosom, so it was she who ought to come and hang yearningly about Villa Heliotrope on her bicycle. It annoyed him that he had had to buy another copy of *Les Nouvelles littéraires*. Raf was not at home. He did not feel like visiting Holst, disturbing him as he knelt before a photograph of Madame Laura illuminated by a little Christmas-tree candle.

From the driveway, between the dahlias, he heard Mama reading out a letter from Papa, a familiar, soothing sound. In the scullery he stumbled into a row of clogs, the reading stopped abruptly. Incredulously he took in the sight of Aunt Violet, Meerke, and Anna sitting around the table. On the oilcloth in front of them stood cups of coffee and a yellow sponge cake, the women were looking at Mama, who was standing with his notebook in her hand, that oblong cashbook bound in faded brown linen. She shut the book with a ghastly little smack.

"Sit down, Louis," Meerke said. "A little slice of sponge cake? Anna's mother baked it."

He leaped at his mother, she evaded him, held the notebook out of his reach, she would throw it to Aunt Violet like a basketball player, and she to Anna, it was a women's team. The harm had been done. But the women, over whom he reigned and whom he had called his "harem" to Raf, seemed to be quite unaware of the monstrous extent of their transgression. So be it, then.

He slashed into the cake, stuffed his mouth full.

"It's terribly good, your writing," said Meerke.

Aunt Violet nodded. "We've been enjoying ourselves here for a good quarter of an hour, especially Anna. But she doesn't understand some of the expressions you used."

"It's all about us, I knew it," said Mama and tucked the notebook under her arm. The hot notebook.

"It isn't about you at all," said Louis. Half the cake had gone, Aunt Violet quickly cut a crumbly slice.

Mama leaned her broadened bottom against the sink unit, lifted the notebook to her nose, and read from it in a solemn, detached tone: " 'An element of marked selfishness prevailed among all the inhabitants of the grandiose villa.' "

"Grandiose," said Anna. "Is that a Dutch word? I've never heard it before."

"It means pretentious," said Aunt Violet. "Be quiet now."

" 'Each one was wrapped in satisfaction as in a banana skin, cared not a fig for what was being enacted in the outside world, their main concern being to provide themselves with everything that fashion and luxury could offer. This was particularly so with the woman who neglected her most basic maternal obligations and was in danger of falling prey to the worst sort of obscenity.' "

"Absurdity!" Louis cried.

"It's because your handwriting's so bad," Mama said, raising her voice.

She continued. " 'To wit, she passed her entire life in the sun of her own egoism, giving never a thought to the shadows that her selfishness cast over her nearest and dearest, who were forced to endure her self-glorifi-cation, that gilding of her being, every day of the Lord's Creation . . .' "

"Where ever does he get those sentences and those words?" said Meerke.

"He has such a fine turn of phrase," said Anna.

"That may be, but it's my name he's blackening," said Mama.

"Fashion and luxury, that's a bit exaggerated," said Aunt Violet. "We don't do without, but fashion and luxury, Louis . . . what's the matter?"

He couldn't hold it back. He had thought that he would be able to drink the dregs of this cup with the same detachment she had put into her reading voice. He burned with shame that Anna should be a witness, but he was seeing the kitchen and the traitress through a mist, tasting the salt of his tears.

"You mustn't take it to heart."

"We all think it's lovely."

"Louis," said Mama as if talking to the dachshund Bibi Two.

Now he knew why his tear glands had reacted. Because Mama's unfeel-ing, monotonous rendering had made it abundantly clear that what she was reading was so much untalented, worthless rubbish.

"I don't know if people really like reading that sort of thing," said Meerke. "Because we know who wrote it, we know you."

"Read a little bit more, Madame Constance," said Anna.

"No, that's enough!"

"Don't be a baby, Louis. The people at Het Laatste Nieuws are going to read it, so why not us, too?"

"Read the end, Constance, so we can get an idea of the rest of it."

Mama turned the pages. " '. . . almost effortlessly Mevrouw Horforêt let the melody swell and pour from her throat, as from an organ, until the last note died away, clean and pure as the ringing of crystal, then sank spent but elated onto the sofa. Meneer Horforêt, whose mood had been so sunny, now wondered what orders would come flowing from her lips and if he should follow them with blind obedience.' "

"Is that the end?" asked Meerke.

"That's all there is."

"It's a funny ending," said Anna.

"Just one comment," said Aunt Violet. "The note died away, then it sank onto the sofa, is that right?"

"Oh no, Mademoiselle Violet. It was the woman, of course," said Anna.

"I was the one who sank onto the sofa," said Mama. "It was me." She moved away from the sink unit, pressed her heaving bosom in the cotton-muslin apron against the table, and lay her face, matte with Tokalon powder, on the oilcloth, and opened wide her mocking gray eyes in which little golden speckles had once sparkled. "That's how I was lying, spent but elated."

She drew herself up. "You'll win the *Laatste Nieuws* prize. Want to bet?"

"If the rest of it is as well written as that, of course he will," said Meerke.

"That woman, that Mevrouw Horforêt, reminds me of the Duchess of Windsor," said Aunt Violet. "The same sort of egotistical person."

The cake was finished. Louis squashed crumbs with a wet forefinger, ate them. The cake was dry, stuck in his throat. He had to sneeze. He tried to hold it back. Tears, sneezes, sperm—all to be held back. *Toujours sourire.* Two large drops of blood fell onto the knees of his corduroy trousers, the blood ran into his mouth. Meerke was the first to spot it and cried, "Louis, dear!"

He caught Anna's look full of revulsion and fear. Meerke pressed a wet towel to his nose. "Leave it to me," said Mama. She pinched his nostrils shut with two warm fingers, held his head back against her breast. "Wait," she said. "Keep still, it's nothing."

She took one of her ridiculously fine little gossamer handkerchiefs out of her apron pocket. It turned red. Then she washed his cheeks, his lips, with the wet handkerchief. He bit into it. Squinting along the top of his Seynaeve nose, he saw the almost impassive, cruel look pinning him down, even while she murmured and pressed him to her. For years he had not been so close to her.

"Frau Seynaeve," he said like one of those malingerers in the ERLA infirmary who maimed themselves in order to be near her. As if no part of him, his hand rose and crept like a freed, cool, calm, plump little animal along her shoulder, her throat, the line of her jaw.

"Keep still," she said.

His fingers stroked her cheek. He saw the watchful females around them and shut his eyes, rubbed the nape of his neck against his mother's breast, I must never forget this, bliss exists. Mama.

"Hush," she said, but she meant the other women, who had begun to tidy the kitchen. He kept his eyes shut. She turned her upper body so that his hand dropped off, and then he was again a child like any other, or like Ivo Liekens, of whom they said that he had hung to his mother's breast into his fourth year, or like the children on the Orinoco whose mothers place a woven grass mat full of termites across their shoulders to harden them to every kind of sorrow in later life, she pushed him gently, very slowly, away from her velvety, perfumed warmth. "Go and lie down on your bed for a while," she said.

He took his notebook with him. Tilting his head far back, he tore the book to shreds, like the Strongest Man in Flanders tearing telephone directories apart at the fair in Walle. He burned the notebook in his little potbellied stove, poked about among the carefully written lines, in the blue flames, the white smoke.

He woke up with a crust inside his nostrils. He picked at it. Started a new notebook. Mama hadn't been all that stupid when she had asked if his story was about the Haarbeke Institute. As hasty as Papa, as cold as Grandpa while he was still alive (and certainly now, Louis smiled sardonically), he wrote: "Dondeyne had hidden one of the seven Forbidden Books under his tunic and then coaxed me into coming along." He scratched out the word "me" and substituted "Louis."

Theo van Paemel grimaced as he gripped his calf with both hands and moved it two inches forward. "It's no joke, a leg like this, particularly with my having to be up and about all the time, here, there, and everywhere, I don't know whether I'm coming or going anymore, but I simply had to see you, you know how much I've always respected you, Constance."

He said that he had only just returned from Holland. The SD had done unspeakable things there, and he had had his work cut out for him explaining his position. "You see, those Dutchmen don't know a damn thing, Constance. They're not the slightest bit interested in Belgium. You were with the Rexists, they said and what they meant was the West Flemish *Einsatzkommando*. A lot of nonsense about Flemish collaboration, but they don't even know the names of the different formations. Anyway. I said, 'Yes, I was with the SD, officially, you can look it up in the files.' They wanted to put me in handcuffs there and then. I said, 'Hold on, first phone such and such a number.' They wouldn't do it. I said, 'Hold on, my young friends,' and dropped two or three names. And when they had telephoned those, it was all 'Excuse us!' and *'Sorry,* okay?' Anyway. Now, what I've come about. The day before yesterday I happened to attend a meeting of our League, which was founded in August '40, which shows that we were the first to start working against the Nazis, Constance, we didn't wait for Radio London. And what do I hear? That our party comrade, Police Superintendent van Dieken, whom we naturally call 'The Deacon' among ourselves, has been seen the day before in the company of John Wallaert van Outryve, that's perfectly normal, Van Dieken and Wallaert are as thick as thieves, two dirty swine who've found each other.

And, now and then, once or twice a week, they do the rounds of all the wives of Blacks who've been locked up. I don't have to tell you what sort of reception they get, the tippling and the greasing of palms, not to mention the rest of it, you get my drift, all these women seem to think that if they only keep on the right side of the Judge Advocate . . . Well, all right, just another drop, then. Although the doctor says I absolutely mustn't, on account of my leg . . . Now, here comes the best part, Constance. This damned baron, Wallaert van Outryve, comes back to his house from his rounds one morning, and what does he find? Only his whole family, his mother, his sisters, his wife's mother, the whole kit and caboodle, because that very night his wife has had a little one, and tipsy as he is, he flops right down on the floor and cries for joy.

"Anyway, the problem is this, Constance, and that's why I've come, because I respect you, this Wallaert, especially now that his wife is out of circulation, is a horny old goat, or to put it in High Flemish, he is highly susceptible to feminine charms. So it might not be such a bad idea if you were to call on him personally, with the most honorable of intentions, naturally, that goes without saying."

Mama nodded. Louis nodded. Van Paemel drank.

"But Meneer van Paemel, if you were against the Germans so much, why did you come with the SD into the College to arrest Ceusters and De Coene?"

Theo van Paemel twiddled the empty little glass between his fingers. Louis poured him some more.

"I'm against everybody," he said. "Because everybody needs me." And Mama nodded as if she understood, as if she agreed with him.

"You must learn to see past your own nose," said Van Paemel. "That's why I'm waiting a little while before returning to Walle. Most people only *think* they saw me working for the Germans."

"But, Meneer van Paemel, they actually *did* see you."

"But doing what? Sometimes I don't know myself which hat I'm wearing anymore, what with the SD and the *Sûreté Générale,* so how can other people possibly tell?"

A dark-blonde woman, hair dyed chestnut now with a hint of the earlier red rinse still showing through, well preserved despite her thirty-seven years, although marked by that secret malaise called melancholia, stepped resolutely into the office of the representative of Belgian justice.

(If your are looking at my new notebook, Mama, please desist.)

A woman of a certain age, my mother, walked smartly into the Judge Advocate's chambers.

(Off you go, Mama, I told you!)

In the shadow of the Belfry, close by one of the two emblems of Ghent-strong-as-cement (the first being the fire-spewing dragon), viz., the *Mammelokker,* the Suckling, which shows an emaciated old man at the ample breast of his daughter in his prison cell, the judge advocacy had its offices on the second floor of an imposing nineteenth-century building. Mevrouw S., chain-smoker, out of breath after climbing the rather short flight of stairs, pushed open a padded door and stepped into the room streaming with sunshine where the Judge Advocate awaited her.

The man was not only of the lower nobility but also of undistinguished mien. As is usual with little people in important posts, he continued to pore over his papers with a portentous air for some considerable time. Mevrouw S. refused to draw attention to her presence. All the same, she did flush with annoyance. She was unable to get up and leave on the spot, because she had slipped in when the gendarme on the first floor had his back turned. What if, having dealt a resounding slap to the Judge Advocate, who then went in full pursuit, she should fall into the said gendarme's arms, he might take her for a Black Charlotte Corday, with the Baron de Pushmuck as the humble Marat? Mevrouw S. was faint-hearted and gave a cough.

The Judge Advocate said, "Mevrouw, things don't look very good in your case."

"My husband's case."

The Judge Advocate gave a superior smile, adjusted his glasses firmly on his nose. "Naturally, I have not yet been able to spare the dossier more than a cursory glance, but what I have discovered is enough for me to advise you in all seriousness to moderate your insistent demands. There have been intercessions, leading political figures, doubtless under pressure from the Bishop of West Flanders, have given favorable testimony, but all that notwithstanding . . ."

"Even a cursory perusal must have allowed your lawyer's-eye to register that the allegations . . ."

He raised his hand with its golden wristwatch in a supplicatory but awkward gesture, like a traffic policeman on his first day's duty in some quiet backwater. "The charges are legion. And must be gone into dispassionately one by one."

From behind a tight-stretched Oriental silk screen on which cranes and hibiscus were transfixed in an eternally frozen plane (the Oriental does not know, or does not want to know, anything about perspective), Mevrouw S. could hear someone clearing his throat, which she took for a sign of agreement, and then the scraping of a chair.

"You are impatient, mevrouw. In your place, so would I be. But elementary fair play dictates that everyone should be treated alike. See for yourself." He used the sweeping gesture that would presently serve him with his wide black sleeves in the Palais de Justice as he demanded the head of a traitor. "And we're only up to the letter D."

Involuntarily Mevrouw S. stretched out a hesitant hand in the direction of the large pile of files.

"You can't possibly be insinuating that I should ignore the alphabetical order."

Without asking permission, the woman lit up a Lucky Strike.

"And speeding the case up would simply mean throwing caution to the wind. Luckily we employ competent people, but our time on earth is limited, Mevrouw S." (The "S" hissed as by a witch, menacing, sardonic.)

"So you have no time?"

"Mevrouw, I work here day and night without the overtime payments customary in the private sector in which your husband was engaged."

"At what time did you arrive here this morning, mijnheer?"

From behind the oriental panel came a warning but amused little cough.

"Mevrouw, it really ill behooves you to interrogate me. I am afraid you are attempting to reverse our roles."

"What time did you roll out of your nest?" said Madame S. with a thumping heart. "And what time did you roll in *here?*"

"Mevrouw . . ."

"Of course you don't have the time to examine the files when you're out on the town all night, pestering the wives of good Flemings and getting plastered with your pals at the prisoners' expense."

The nonplussed, alarmed face of the Judge Advocate exhibited those human lines puckered by pain that one finds marked on the soles of feet whose toes have corns like startled human eyes with little radiating streaks and stripes, advertising Rodell Saltrates, healing salts to soften the corns deep down to the roots so that soon afterward you can wear shoes a whole size smaller, as the mother of Mevrouw S. was hoping to do in the very near future.

"He got the fright of his life!" Mama, jubilant, swept an ashtray off the kitchen table with her sleeve. "It doesn't matter," she cried. "I'll pay for five new ones."

"You'd do better to give up smoking altogether, then we wouldn't need any ashtrays," said Aunt Violet.

"Go on with the story," said Meerke.

"I was wound up tight as a watch. I couldn't stop myself. I really gave him a tongue-lashing. I said, *'Godverdomme,* you bastard, you leave your missus alone to have your kid while you go out and get plastered!' 'But, madame,' he squeaked, 'for God's sake, think of my position.' I said, 'You, you ought to have been thinking of your wife when she was in her position!' 'But I promised her a holiday in Nice, you can ask her yourself!' "

It was known to Mevrouw S.'s immediate circle that once she had boarded the thunderous train of her rage, it was no easy matter to apply the brakes. This had to do with the fact that in such cases she felt a migraine coming on (something that occurs frequently in the animal kingdom, *vide* the papers presented to the Pennsylvania Veterinary College on the relationship between discontentment and headaches in cattle).

Mevrouw S. swept her choleric left hand over the pile of files, the files let loose their dossiers and the dossiers let loose their contents, among which were issues of *Paris-Hollywood,* and these sailed up in the air and landed all over the office. Mevrouw S. flung herself at the screen and pulled it to one side.

Later she declared that in this moment of blind rage she had guessed from the panic-stricken expression of the Judge Advocate, battered both by lack of sleep and by liquid spirits, that behind the screen (with its self-evident connotations of frivolity and libido that thrust themselves upon her, not least because she had seen a photograph of the interior of the house formerly owned by Holst's wife in Brussels and furnished by a decorator on the instructions of the man who had since become Minister Baerens) she would find one of those unhappy women with whom he had been painting the town the night before, the wife or the sister or the daughter of a leading collaborator, and hence a sister of *hers.* Not that she wanted to save that sister from dishonor. It was more a case of feminine curiosity and above all blind instinct, defiant rage (just as there is a region in New Zealand where the earth's crust is so thin that a jet of steam will spurt up when a person pushes his walking stick in to a certain depth, so Mevrouw S. had a thin skin and Judge Advocate Wallaert van Outryve was the walking stick).

The screen tottered, tilted, and toppled onto the source of the coughing, who leaped up, holding the silk cranes at bay. It was a clerk with an inordinately large head. He put the screen back again and bowed, uttering a polite formula that must remain unrecorded since he was holding a Tintenkuli fountain pen between his teeth at the time.

"May I present my friend Daniel Villiers de Rodebeke, who is at present my articled clerk but is to become my associate in the very near future."

The fountain pen found its way behind the articled clerk's ear. "I didn't hear anything, anything at all," said the near-hydrocephalic clerk.

"Nor did I," said the Judge Advocate, looking just like someone who normally wears a hearing aid.

"I said 'What?' " said Mama. " 'What? Do I have to wash out your ears?' 'Oh, please, madame!' he said. 'I only wanted to say that what has been uttered in this office must not leave these four walls.' I said: 'What? Why shouldn't it? I'm going to go straight out and telephone *De Gazet van Antwerpen* right now.' 'Madame,' said that charlatan Villiers de Rodebeke, 'may of course submit a statement to us that she is ill, certified by a reputable doctor.' 'That could make a big difference," said the other one, 'all the difference in the world.' "

"Villiers de Rodebeke, don't I know him?" said Aunt Violet. "Isn't he from the branch of the family that lives in Lootenhulle, in the White Castle?"

"Now I have to go for a certificate to Dr. Vandenabeele, the sooner the better."

"Say it's your kidneys. That they're blocked up. They can't check up on that," said Aunt Violet.

"Or that I have a serious calcium deficiency," said Mama. That was directed at Louis. She turned her gaze on him, on the teeth, the fingernails that had used up all her calcium while still in her belly.

One afternoon like any other, Aunt Berenice rang the bell at the front door of Villa Heliotrope, where no one ever rang.

"I didn't dare go around to the back," she said.

"I got the fright of my life," said Meerke. "I thought it must be a telegram."

"May I come in, Mother?"

"For goodness' sake, Berenice!"

"I would have written a card first, but I thought to myself, What if they don't reply?"

"You're more than welcome here."

"Louis, you look different. Like somebody else entirely."

"What do you mean, Aunt Berenice?"

"I'll tell you tomorrow. I'll have to think about it. You know me, everything has to be just so. Or did I say something wrong?"

In the kitchen she put down her suitcase, propped her umbrella in the corner against the wall, lifted her skirt an inch or two, and knelt down. Head bowed, she said, "Mother, I have come to beg your forgiveness."

Meerke made the sign of the Cross on Aunt Berenice's forehead with her thumb. Aunt Berenice jumped to her feet and took off her coat. "Good," she said. "Are there any dirty dishes?" and walked into the scullery.

"She hasn't changed one little bit," said Meerke. "I'm glad. Because she can look after our Omer. The two of them used to be inseparable when they were children."

But Omer refused to come to the garage door or to the window. Aunt Berenice called in a little child's voice, "O-mer-kins, O-mer-kins," and pressed her face to the glass. But he probably thought that this stranger was mistaking him for Meerke. He was having one of his bad days.

"Is this a good day or a bad day, Uncle Omer?"

"A good day, Louis. Yesterday was a bad day."

"Your sister Berenice has arrived."

"I used to know her well. Very well."

"She called you."

"That's a shame, because yesterday was a bad day."

"It was three days ago."

"That just means she can't call right. Hector can call right. Why can't she?"

"She'll be coming back tonight."

"We shall see. We shall see."

"Are you coming into the house to play cards, Uncle Omer?"

"No, I don't think I'll go outside today."

"But you haven't been out for a whole week."

"Those bad days don't count toward the week. Brother Benjamin couldn't understand that, either. 'All days are the same,' he would say and crack! he hit you over the head with the rubber truncheon. 'It's not a truncheon,' Brother Benjamin said, 'it's a *goedendag*, a mace, and a good day to you, too.' And crack ! on your head again. 'I don't like to see sad faces, you have a roof over your head and food in your belly, and if necessary we even wipe your bottom, the least you can do is not to make such a miserable face when I come by,' and crack with the *goedendag*, 'you have to say good day to life,' he said, '*allee*, come on, then, all together, good day, Life! good day, Life! and good morning without mourning!' and Brother Benjamin would sing loudest of all. Sometimes we were happy. What do you think, Louis, were we happy? You're right, I shouldn't ask, I ought to know my place. I'll never be as happy as I used to be, now and then my mouth gets all twisted up and I hear something like a rattle or a mussel in my throat wanting to get out, but it's never laughter, not even if it's one of the best days, and that sort only comes when it isn't day anymore but night.

"Konrad said, 'Look in my eyes, you won't be able to help laughing,' and they say that I did laugh, but if you don't know yourself, Louis, how can you tell if you really did laugh? And even if I did laugh, does that mean I was happy? 'Look into my eyes,' Konrad said, that's easy to say, but you yourself know you are going to drown in his eyes and that they'll suck you down into the dark, and before you know it you've keeled over. And I don't mean Kiel in Silesia, either."

"In Schleswig-Holstein, Uncle."

"Thank you. Well, well, well. But why is it well? You tell me that."

"It's getting dark, Uncle."

"That's because of the women. Have you ever heard me say one bad word about women, Louis? You're right, I shouldn't be asking. They've led me astray, women have, because otherwise I would have taken my studies seriously, I had a head for ideas."

"It'll all come back to you, Uncle."

"We'll see. We'll see."

"It's dark, I have to go and eat."

" 'You shouldn't be so on edge,' says Thérèse, 'just because I went out dancing with your brother, with the most honorable of intentions.' I say, 'Come on, Thérèse, I've got eyes in my head.' Even in those days, and I'm speaking now of before the war, my mouth was all ready to laugh, I could feel it stretching like a rubber band but I couldn't laugh. 'And,' she says, 'what if I did do it just once with your brother?' I say, 'For pity's sake, Thérèse!' 'Just suppose,' she says, *'supposons.'* I say, 'For pity's sake, girl.' 'Because you never can tell,' she says, 'you can't always control these things, Cupid aims his bow and you just happen to be standing in the way.' Sister Claudine said the same thing in the infirmary when she was holding my head tight in her tongs. 'It's Cupid, Cupid, Cupid,' she said, 'that's brought you to us.' And Brother Benjamin held me tight as well. 'Are you still struggling?' he shouts, and he has strong arms all right from all that bowling he does, and Sister Claudine who is holding me tight says, 'Lie still, just think of Chinese *minette* and it will pass,' but it didn't pass, when I thought of Chinese *minette* I began to squirm and to shake, and the more I thought of it, the more . . ."

"What is that, Uncle, Chinese *minette?*"

"I thought it was dark and you'd gone to eat."

"No. What is Chinese *minette?*"

"He who corrupts the innocent is to be drowned with a millstone around his neck. And if he has seven lives, then let him have seven millstones."

"You don't know yourself what Chinese *minette* is."

"Oh, that I know. That I know. That I used to know."

"I'll go and get you ten cigarettes."

"And matches?"

"No, I'll come and light them for you one at a time."

"In Violet's room, in that cake tin with Queen Astrid on it, that's where you must go. You get that photograph, it's in there in the middle of all the others, the one with Thérèse waving to me with that lady wearing a white hat next to her. She's waving to me, you can see that, very clearly, I'm just getting on the train to go to my exams."

"Uncle Omer, that's the hundredth time you've asked me for that. You know you can't have that photograph. You know it's bad for you."

"Promise me you'll think about getting it for me some day. Some day like today."

"I promise."

"Swear it on the head of your unhappy mother."

"I swear."

"Why are you swearing?"

"Because I want you to tell me about Chinese *minette.*"

"Thérèse never did Chinese *minette.* Never, never, *jamais.*"

"Uncle, I will go and get you ten cigarettes."

"*Bon. Explication.* Chinese *minette,* as everyone knows, is when you put a little balloon inside a woman."

"Is that all? A French letter?"

"Louis, did I say that? Don't you understand plain Flemish? Must I tell you in that fancy, pretentious Flemish you speak? A little balloon, any old color you like. That's all. No, excuse me, it isn't all, once you've put it in you have to blow it up. I must have bought a good hundred francs' worth of little balloons for Sister Claudine, I got them in the Grand Bazaar's children's department. 'It's for a party,' I said. And so you just blow. *Et voilà.*"

"And how long does that go on for?"

"After a while you stop blowing so hard. After a week or two. When the novelty's worn off. Your heart isn't in it anymore. But you have to go on. Because she asks you to so nicely. You're not made of stone, after all. And so you just blow. My eyes used to pop out of my head, I could feel my veins bursting and my head got like a balloon itself, like a football, and my brother who came on a visit that week because they thought I was going to die, yes, that selfsame brother, I won't mention his name out loud, he said in the parlor, 'What's the matter with you? Your head is getting so puffy you ought to go to Switzerland for a while, you're not getting enough oxygen here.' Because he liked me, my brother did.

"Thérèse said, 'Even if I did do it just once with your brother . . .'

"The psychiatrist, Brother Ildefons, said it was because of Thérèse and my brother that I, that I, that I . . . but that isn't true, he still has a lot to learn, and so do you, it was by the tram stop in Hooregem, in the Halfway House Café. That's where it happened and nowhere else. She said, 'Even if I did . . . Just suppose,' she said, *'supposons,'* and I wasn't feeling comfortable, that's true, I even went outside, to the tram stop. Not angry, just sad. She came out a quarter of an hour later. I said, 'Did you pay in the Halfway House Café?' 'Yes,' she says, 'I paid.' We were waiting for the tram and then Blanche came, she came, and then Blanche came from that Halfway House Café out to the tram stop and yelled at Thérèse, 'You dirty hussy, you filthy slut, who do you think you are?' And I thought that Thérèse hadn't paid after all, and Blanche screamed, 'Do that in your own house, put that in your own toilet!' and Blanche flung a little packet at Thérèse but it landed on my white shirt, here, here, and I caught it, the little packet, and it was a rag full of blood, and all the blood on my hands and on my white shirt and I can still hear Thérèse saying, *'Mais c'est naturel,'* and in my, my, my nervous state I gave a scream and because I could hear myself scream I thought, Why is that fellow screaming like that? and I stuck the rag in my mouth. Thérèse pulled it out and everyone waiting at the tram stop said that I must have said ten, twenty times that it was *naturel, natural, lel lel,* as if that were all I had on my mind but my mind was empty and then I laid my head down right smack in the middle of the dandelions."

"Come and e-e-eat!" called Aunt Violet.

Uncle Omer helped to push the washtub out of the garage. "Heave-ho," he cried.

"Take care you don't strain yourself," said Aunt Berenice.

"I always take care, madame," he said. "Take care of yourself."

In the pale sunlight Mama was washing her and Louis's clothes. Sometimes she slapped the wet clothes, making the sound of the crack of a horsewhip that re-echoed three or four times from the woods around the sanatorium. Then a man in a raincoat that was much too big for him, and with a hat pulled down over his forehead, was standing there motionless, looking at the busy, sweating woman. He was carrying a rectangular wicker basket from which a pair of checked slippers dangled.

Mama took her red arms out of the suds, rubbed them dry on her apron. Hesitantly Papa came forward. There was a crease between his thin eyebrows that had not been there before. Mama continued to dry her hands.

"Well, Constance," he said, and moved as if to embrace her. She came closer. "So," she said.

"Yes, Constance."

"I am, I was, doing the washing."

"Hello, Papa."

"Ah, there you are." They shook hands, Louis took the wicker basket from his father's hand, searched for traces left by imprisonment, and found a somewhat grudging, dazed-looking man with baggy trousers and sluggish gestures designed for other dimensions, another environment, another ambience. And how small his teeth were.

"They said I could go," said Papa.

"That's what they say. Yes, but we'll see. We'll see," said Omer, turning away and calling to the pigeons. They flew down and skimmed past Papa, who shooed them away anxiously with a wave of his arm. Then Aunt Berenice came running out of the kitchen. Jubilantly she cried, "Staf! Staf!" kissed him on both cheeks, and put her arm through his. Mama took the other arm. Like a patient, more hoisted than pulled, Papa allowed himself to be ushered into the kitchen. Meerke said that he looked well, no doubt he'd been put to work in the fresh air there?

"I will write the Baron a card to say thank you," said Mama. "With a bottle of Burgundy."

Papa sat down in Meerke's chair, refused to take off his raincoat, in its frayed pockets he was carrying treasures that he would conjure up at the right moment, a belated Santa Claus.

"We had such awful potatoes to eat over there," he said. "You know, flabby, thick chips. And they were never hot."

"*Allee*, Constance, go and fry your man some chips," Meerke exclaimed. "With jellied pork!"

"In a minute," said she who had been the cause and the effect and the blame and the retribution. "In a minute, first we've got to get a bit used to him. Don't you agree, Staf?"

"But the man is dying of hunger!"

Bacon and eggs were fried. Everyone watched. As he ate, Papa filled out, became stronger, more self-assured. Not just because of the food but also because of their presence. The Seynaeves and the Bossuyts were feeding him, very soon he would be lording it over Louis's harem again, filling the house with his entire presence. Because he was under house arrest. And he had gone much balder.

"Is there anything sweet?"

"How about some bread and jam, Staf. Or . . ." Meerke climbed onto a chair and from the top shelf of the kitchen cupboard she fetched a large piece of frangipane she had hidden away from Aunt Violet.

"Don't eat too much, Staf, we're having supper at seven o'clock," said Mama.

"You can tell it's been made with real butter," he said, bolting it down greedily.

"With *l'essence d'amande*, of course," said Aunt Berenice.

"Frangipane," said Papa. "It's been a long time."

"Don't eat so much, Staf. And not so fast."

"You should give thought to the victims, Staf, all those Jews who are turning up in Antwerp," said Aunt Berenice. His mouth fell open, full of frangipane.

"Don't start that now, Berenice!" yelped Meerke.

"All I meant, Mother, was that it's for his own good not to eat so much all at once. Like the Jews in Antwerp back from the camps. They were warned, all of them, but their families stuffed them full of food, and lots of them died from having too much all at once."

"I'd rather not think of the Jews," said Papa. "But I'm going to have to. We were fools during the war, there's none so blind as will not see."

"Talk about something else," said Meerke, on the way back to the kitchen cupboard with the last small triangle of cake.

Papa was expanding visibly. The shabby man in the raincoat disappeared, the man in the wicker armchair took on a familiar air. Even when he felt pains in a stomach that used to be made of concrete, even when he said he had suffered so much in the camp that every night, well, almost every night, he had prayed to Our Lord, and now he knew from his own experience that there was such a thing as human solidarity, that some of the prisoners had been real saints, he named their names and good works, and noticing that after the third or fourth name in his calendar of saints the women's attention wandered, he said, "Perhaps that last little piece of frangipane will help settle my stomach."

He was given it, smacked his lips. "It's been a long time. You can taste it hasn't come from a shop."

"It's St. Francis's cake," said Aunt Berenice.

"It comes from bread, *pane*, of Francis, *frangi*," Louis said immediately. (Because you see, Aunt, I, I am the King of all such scraps of obtuse and trifling inanities, country almanac truisms and pettifogging platitudes that my late grandfather, despite everything, has bequeathed to me like some African chieftain.)

"He used to adore it," said Aunt Berenice, as if St. Francis were breathing his last in the front room. "He asked for it even on his death-bed, and because he was too weak to keep anything down, the other Fathers and all his friends stuffed themselves with frangipane, whether they liked it or not, so that he could see them doing it."

"*Tiens,*" said Papa. "Something else I didn't know."

Jay-Dee arrived with cardboard boxes full of canned army food, which he wanted to swap for vegetables from the garden. The smell of the chips seemed to trouble him.

"*My daddy.*"

"*Hi.*"

"That's a Jew," said Papa. "Am I right? I can tell them straight off. Mijnheer, I wish in all sincerity to offer you my personal apologies. Louis, translate that."

Jay-Dee's oblong blue jaws were moving up and down. "Personally and in the name of Flanders. I did you and all your kinsmen a grave injustice. Translate."

Kinsmen. What was the English for that? *All your race fellows?*

Jay-Dee could see that Louis was searching desperately, that Louis would be buying a Dutch-English dictionary the next day, and said "*congeners.*" Never heard the word. Louis repeated it a few times, it still sounded strange.

"*Verstanden?*" said Papa. "Uh, excuse me, I mean *compris?*"

"Yeah, yeah," said Jay-Dee.

That night Louis married Michèle. They sat at a table covered with snow-white linen in the shade of an apple tree, surrounded by excited wedding guests. In front of Papa stood a golden dish with a gold-roasted duck. He eyed it gloatingly. Jay-Dee's dark figure rode slowly by on a gray charger, and when he had disappeared to the left of the screen Michèle said, stammering with emotion like Uncle Omer, "*Le con, le con, le con-génère.*" Louis was shocked, he thought his bride looked common in her white hat, he turned away from her, and on the sparkling dish there now lay the gnawed carcass of a duck, Papa was regarding it gloatingly, with goggling eyes and a lipless, open mouth. "Have mercy on us," said Aunt Berenice, and Papa sat there dead for a little while, with a napkin under his chins glistening with duck fat, then from his dead face there arose a childish wail, it filled Louis's room, Michèle ran with bridal veil stream-ing—what had become of the white hat?—to the folk-dancing wedding guests, Papa wailed, Mama soothed him, Papa groaned, Mama said very clearly, "I did tell you, Staf," whereupon he said almost as testily as in the old days, "It's all because of those chips, I tell you!" Then everything went quiet in Mama's room. Except for her heavy panting, and then she went on gasping for breath for a long time.

"There were all sorts there," said Papa, sitting beside the overnight stove in the front room.

"There was one very thin, bent, meek little woman in a khaki coat she had been given by a Canadian. She had to put the slop buckets out every day. The male prisoners, who never laid eyes on any other woman, would bray mating calls at her, interrupted by the jailers and the guard dogs. In June '43 she had denounced the six White Brigade men who had set fire to her house, her husband, and her sixteen-year-old son. She didn't have a tooth in her head. A collection had been started to buy her some false teeth, but there wasn't anywhere near enough money.

"Then there was an oculist who had studied criminology in Germany and who spent his days in the Flandria in the governor's office drawing up a more efficient administration scheme for the prison camp, using charts and graphs. He'd been sentenced to death, but you couldn't have wished for a more cheerful prisoner. He had a small notebook in which he'd entered hundreds of jokes, all numbered, using abbreviations that no one else could understand, and he often brought it out. He was three-quarters of the way through his collection when he was taken out in front of the Belgian firing squad. We all roared out together, *"Levet Scone!"* live a clean life, because that's what he said jokingly every morning washing under the pump.

"Then there was Wanten, from the 'Wanten and Dalle' radio program, and everyone remembering that slow, stupid oaf with the grumbling voice who was always being interrupted by that giddy, horny old witch of a Dalle, was amazed to discover that he was a well-spoken engineer, graying at the temples, who couldn't remember a single one of his hundreds of radio quips. 'All I did was read them from a sheet of paper.' He spent most of his time hunting through an atlas, working out how many miles Walle was from New Guinea or Valparaiso.

"Then there was Milou van Dentergem, the NSKK man, who cracked his knuckles even in his sleep.

"Then there was Ambrosius, whose glasses had been stepped on and who refused to wear new ones right up to the day they put a bullet in him. 'I've seen more than enough of all of you as it is.'

"Then there was Van Rossum, who was given Dolf Zeebroeck's monk's-habit when Zeebroeck was released, and never took it off. 'You have no idea how pleasant it is walking about without underpants. At last I can understand those Fathers.'

"Then there was Roel the Ram, who was called that because he'd bang his head against the doors and walls every time an airplane went over,

"Musical Joe, who sang, 'Flanders, day and night I think of you' the whole time and didn't know the rest of the words unless you count the occasional lalala,

"Sootje, who talked to his pony as if he still had his ice-cream cart.

"Then there was Poeske, called that after the fellow who was world sprint champion all those times, Poeske Scherens, because he had once won a stage of the Tour de Flandres. He claimed that he had often eaten parts of Russkies. 'Which parts?' 'I'll give you three guesses! With shallots and a squeeze of lemon they taste like sweetbreads.'

"Then there was Piet the Camel, who slept on the floor because of his lumbago, and who would get kicked accidentally-on-purpose whenever someone went out for a piss at night,

"and then there was Maurice the Ass, who wrote poems, all of them about Jacqueline of Bavaria, who according to him was hot stuff in her day."

And they all of them peopled Meerke's house, turning toward the sun in Villa Heliotrope, these acquaintances of Papa's about whom he had considerably more to tell than he did about his wife or his son and who almost made him smile, every night in front of the stove that was now filled to overflowing with coal and the last of the coke nuts: "Ah, there were times when we could crack each other over the head with a bucket, but an hour later we'd be throwing our arms around each other again."

"And Dalle, Papa?"

"Who do you mean, Dalle?"

"Paelinck the pharmacist."

"How that man has suffered. Because what nobody knew was that he was on some kind of pills from his shop, and, looking back on it, that explains a lot, the way he was always firing on all cylinders, remember, Constance? Those lectures and his radio work and running his pharmacy, how else could he fit all that into one life? Eventually they caught on that Simone was smuggling the pills in and they put him into solitary, you could hear him shrieking as far as the Upper Town."

"And Simone?" Mama asked.

"I don't know. Something about a Canadian, I think."

One evening, when the family had long since become reconciled to the idea that it might go on like this for many more weeks, this cat's-cradle of chattering, twittering, and chortling about his companions and their peculiar complaints, Papa had just started to tell the story of Jack the Calf, an electrician who had a second stomach with which he chewed the cud, when he suddenly stopped, stared, took the cigarette from Mama's lips, and started to puff at it. He went on staring. No one, not even Aunt Berenice, asked what had happened to Jack the Calf. And then Papa went to bed early, together with his whole retinue of friends-in-need, his only kin, and never mentioned them again.

"Agreed," said Papa. "Hitler did do some nasty things, he butchered his own ideal by butchering the Jews, it was inhuman, if you look at those photographs your stomach turns right over, but you can't really expect me to believe that there were so many of them, a hundred thousand perhaps, even two hundred thousand, I'll give you that, and out of those how many were criminals and the sort of people who plotted to overthrow the State? Surely the State had to do something to defend itself, it was a question of life and death, just look at other States under threat, look at us, if . . ."

If. No ifs. The Jews continued to come back, the air of the pestilence inflicted upon them descended upon Bastegem, and a procession of some thirty men, with the Belgian flag and all eleven of the Bastegem Excelsior juniors, led by Mijnheer Morrens and Father Mertens, protested against the premature release of the Blacks, marking time to the strains of "Toreador" from *Carmen* and hurling imprecations in the direction of the house, its façade liberally daubed with swastikas. Goossens, the village policeman, ordered them to move on and came to Villa Heliotrope that night in plainclothes, the selfsame man who had known Constance as a small girl with a calfskin satchel, and now advised Papa to lie very, very low, and not even to venture out into, say, the kitchen garden, let alone leave Bastegem.

"It's mainly Mijnheer Morrens, you know what he's like, he hates all Blacks."

"So-called Blacks," said Papa, the renegade.

"He wants to clean up our village. Because he wants to become mayor in the spring."

"But I've never put so much as a straw in his way!"

"It's nothing personal, Staf. He's against Nazis. Everybody has something against someone."

"Morrens has something against me," said Aunt Violet calmly.

"When will people stop attacking each other?" said the policeman.

"It's all aimed at me," said Aunt Violet still more calmly. "Morrens not only gave evidence against me to the Commission but together with Father Mertens he has also spread lies and slanders about my personal life. If we lived in less troubled times, I'd sue him."

"Think of the cost," said Meerke.

"Some people can't stand other people, and they can't even say why," said the policeman. "If you ask me, it was something like that with Hitler and the Jews. To tell you the truth, if I look deep in my heart, I'm like that myself. I'll go further than that: I'll admit that when I meet Dr. Vandenabeele in the street, a man who has never so much as examined me, let alone cut me open, well, I look the other way. I don't let him see that, of course, I do have some manners, but I can't stand the sight or smell of that fellow, and if I ask myself why . . ."

". . . you're damned if you know," said Louis.

"Right. Now try to explain that. My blood starts boiling the moment I lay eyes on him. D'you think that's because he comes from the part of Oudenaarde where my wife was born? It could be."

He had not yet reached the gate before Papa was discussing emigrating to Argentina, Mijnheer Byttebier had started a timber business over there with Mijnheer Groothuis's money. This branch of the Seynaeves would build itself a new future, in Spanish. Or was it Portuguese? Louis looked it up right away in Aunt Violet's Larousse, it was Spanish, which is easy if you know your French vocabulary, all you have to do is to add an "o" here and there at the end and everybody understands you. Argentinian meat is very cheap and very good, and a lot of comrades were over there already. Even Mama allowed herself to be carried away that night. "Because all we have to look forward to here is sorrow," she said.

"The sorrow of Belgium," said Papa.

"I was nearly engaged to Morrens," said Aunt Violet. "I was eighteen years old, and he wrote me letters."

"The same old story," said Meerke.

"Lovely letters. Taken from a book, but with something of his own soul in them."

"I don't remember that, Violet," said Mama.

"Me neither," said Aunt Berenice.

"Well, it was very short-lived. Couldn't have been shorter. Because the first day, I repeat, the very first day, he escorted me back home and as we were walking beside the Leie, he told me that before he joined his father's textile business he wanted to travel around the world, Macao, *l'enfer de jeu,*' Zanzibar, the Cape of Good Hope, and carried away by his geographical excursion he put his hand around my waist and I, being in love, did likewise and *that one over there* "—her bulbous white chins indicated the righteous, judgmental mother who had chased men away from her all her life—"saw us and she said, 'Violet, I won't have that, a boy you're with for the first time and who does a thing like that, he won't do, he can't be much good.' And in those days you were obedient and Christian and you listened to your mother. I wrote him a letter saying that it would be better for the two of us if he didn't come visiting anymore. He never got over that, ever, because afterward he took off in the wrong direction."

"The question is," said Papa, "how do we get to Argentina?"

"By ship."

"No, I mean how do we get that ship, what channels do we go through? I can't set a foot outside the house right now. I need to find things out from my comrades, but they're all being watched."

"I'll do it for you, Staf," said Aunt Berenice softly. "Give me the addresses and I'll go and see your comrades."

Louis could see Papa thinking, Oh yes, all the addresses and then straight to the Judge Advocate with them. Because her Bulgarian has disappeared.

"All in good time," said Papa slowly. "The first thing we should do is buy an Assimil course so that we can speak a little Spanish when we get there."

"I understand." Aunt Berenice wraps herself up again in her little cloud of mortification and clears the table.

Either Grandma was sitting much deeper in her chair or else she had shrunk dramatically. A smell of wet leaves rose from her black shawls and her dressing gown. Tears rolled down her flabby cheeks. "Oh, Staf, oh, Louis—oh, Louis, what a fine young fellow you've turned out to be! All the women must be running after you already. Don't look at me, I haven't washed yet, Hélène would be here but there's a sale on at the Sarma, she'll be dilly-dallying there, oh, Louis, dear heart, how I love you!" She groped for Louis's hand and pressed four or five slobbery kisses on his wrist, then lifted her rosy dog's-head, and all her wrinkles sagged. "Good-for-nothing," she said.

Wounded, Papa turned to *De Standaard.* She said immediately, "You're looking better, too, Staf. The fresh air must have done you good. You look very fit." Papa resembled his mother more than ever, not so much in the structure of his face as in the movements his face made when it reacted to something, for instance the thin, jealous lips right now. So I must look like Mama, too, because right from the beginning all I did was mimic her, I would lie at her breast, bite into her, she'd be cross because I was hurting her and wrinkle up her nose. I'd see that and copy her. And so . . .

"I'll never see him again," cried Grandma. "I knew it the day he left." Papa picked up the crumpled, dirty, typewritten scrap of paper. Was it yet another of the many wills Grandpa had scattered in bank vaults all over West Flanders?

"In French," Papa said acidly. In French the English authorities reported that Sergeant Florent-Marie-Pierre Seynaeve had died in 1942.

"He couldn't have had a single friend over there in Glowsesterschire, because no one ever came to tell us one word about him."

A pietà without a corpse in her arms.

"Maybe he got married over there."

"It would say so in the letter," said Papa.

"And the mortal remains?" she said delicately.

"We'll have to make arrangements. Robert could take care of that. I can't myself, what with my house arrest. I'm not even supposed to be here."

"Wouldn't he have a pension? He was working for the English government, after all."

"The English, Mother, the English!"

"They wouldn't wash their hands of Florent!"

"An Englishman just takes care of his own. That's how it is with islanders."

"The only silver lining is that his father never knew about it. He loved all his children the same, but Florent was his special problem child. Couldn't Robert see to it that Florent is brought over here from England and laid next to his father? What else have we got a family plot for?"

One single bouquet of chrysanthemums for both, both together under a single gravestone, both alike prey to the damp animal kingdom beneath.

"I almost don't dare say this, but it's a load off my mind. You keep hoping and longing and listening to the English radio. *L'espérance,* Louis, *l'espérance,* it's a terribly cruel thing, it hurts, it won't leave you alone."

Papa said that he and Louis had to catch the four o'clock train. At a quarter past four he was sitting beside his son on a barstool in the Café Groeninghe, now called the Chez Max. The wallpaper was brighter where the photographs of Staf de Clercq and Raymond Tollenaere had once hung. Noël's wife said that her husband was in good health in Lokeren camp, but that it would be better if they left it at just the one beer, "because you know what people are like nowadays. My blood pressure is much too high, Mijnheer Seynaeve, I'll tell you straight, I'd rather you didn't come back, I can't help it. At least not for the time being."

"We mustn't cave in to the mob," said Papa fiercely, "we must . . ."

"We must each of us sweep our own doorstep," she said.

The Town Hall was draped with the Belgian and French tricolors. The shops were full of chocolate, wine, pineapples, entrecôte, skinned rabbits.

"High blood pressure," grumbled Papa. "As if I didn't have high blood pressure myself. My ears buzz all the time."

Louis looked for Bekka down every street. She was nowhere to be seen.

L'Espérance, if you ever go on a world cruise, is an island off Madagascar.

Next to the Belgian and French flags the Canadian was also run up, the one with the green maple leaf, and when it was hanging there the people of Walle rejoiced, for once again the façade of the ancient *stedehuus, scepenhuus,* that is the town hall, built of Brabant freestone with the ornate niches in Valency stone like tabernacles in which painted and gilded saints had once stood, was decked out as it should be. On the southeast corner of the building, as in most municipal buildings and halls built since 1600, stood the Virgin Mary, crown on head, scepter in hand, the Child on her arm, her feet supported by the Lion of Flanders.

It was Sunday. The Truce of God, which commanded that all hostilities and plunder cease from Saturday night to Monday morning, and once a year, out of respect for the days in which Christ had suffered His Passion, from Wednesday night to Monday morning, was not observed in Walle.

The populace roared with pleasure when the third truck drove into the Market Square. "It was a quarter past eleven, I looked at the Belfry clock," said Mimi the baker's wife, "and because the other trucks had been fairly full and *he* was the only one in that truck with two Whites on either side of him, the people thought he must be an important Black, famous, what with that truck all to himself, anyway, before it had stopped they'd all rushed forward, there were lots of people from Toontjes Street, of course, but respectable citizens, too, from the Doornik district, I can't tell you who they were, but I've got a picture of them in my mind's eye, and he, he just stood there with his hands up in the air until they pulled him off the truck like a sack of potatoes, even the two Whites were nervous, they said, '*Allee, allee,*' but the crowd didn't budge. And that was when Georgette, Jantje Piroen's sister, recognized him, she called out, 'My God, it's Dirty Dick!' and all the people cried, 'Dirty Dick! Will you look at that, it's Dirty Dick! Gestapo! Gestapo!' and Jenny from the Café Graaf van Heule leaped at him and gave him a big thump on the back of his neck and screamed, 'Why don't you come over to my place and sing some more American hit tunes so that the Gestapo can come and get me?' 'Gestapo!' they all yelled, you could hear them for miles. Then some joker said, 'He always wanted to be a woman, didn't he, let's cut his hair off like we do with the women.' 'Good idea,' they shouted, and they laughed as if they were at the circus. The fellow with the scissors began snipping away, but, of course, it didn't have the same effect as with a woman, because his hair was already German regulation length, and I still thought to myself, He's going to get off light, all he'll have to do is sing the *'Brabançonne'* and take a good beating, but he was shaking so much from nerves, Mijnheer Seynaeve, and the man with the scissors was trembling so much as well that the scissors slipped right into Dirty Dick's eye, the fellow with the scissors cried out, 'It wasn't my fault, he wouldn't keep still!' and that crowd from Toontjes Street called, 'All right, Dirty Dick, are you satisfied now?' and Mijnheer Seynaeve, he was looking straight ahead of him with his bad eye, and the blood and the eye were running out, and the other eye was like some blue stone, because he had lovely eyes, do you remember, Louis? he used to look after them, put droplets in and paint his eyelashes. 'Satisfied?' they asked. And he tosses his head back and nods yes. He nodded and kept nodding with that blood all over his face as if he wanted to say, I'm finished anyway and all of you in Walle can kiss my arse. So, of course, they went beserk. They pulled him down, and ten or twenty of them, including Jenny, kicked him until they grew tired of it. Then the White Brigade men came out of the gate, dragged him inside, and took him to the hospital, with a ruptured lung and his spleen split, of course, because it got pierced by a rib.

"And what I think, Mijnheer Seynaeve, and you must give me your opinion, is when they'd asked him, 'Are you satisfied now?' he had meant to say no, which is what they'd expected him to answer, but he was all flustered and, having lived in Greece, both before and after Africa, he answered in the Greek way, that is, just the opposite of us, nodding for no. Because he was mad about Greece, he brought me photographs of the scenery and the mountains there. So what do you make of that, Mijnheer Seynaeve?"

Because Louis's and Papa's excursion to Walle had been reported by the juniors of Bastegem Excelsior who kept watch on the railway station, the village policeman, who had faithfully come to pass on the news, said that

Papa would have to leave the village at once. "You mustn't give them any excuse to come here and smash the place up. And you ought to spare a thought for my responsibilities as a policeman as well."

Papa did not want to go. "I can't just leave these four women alone here."

"But we've got Louis," said Mama.

"I know that, but . . . Do I really have to make myself scarce?"

It was decided that he would go and stay with Jules the carpenter, in the little room that probably still reeked of the ointment on that suppurating face.

"From one prison to another," said Papa.

"Don't exaggerate, Staf!"

"Just as I was beginning to get used to it here, too."

"Staf, think of your comrades still in the Flandria."

"You're right, Constance," said Papa absently, tucking a pile of Lord Listers and Nick Carters under his arm.

"Louis, you mustn't tell anybody where I am, even if they pull out your tongue."

"How can I say anything if my tongue's been pulled out?"

The chief messenger and go-between was Aunt Angelique, Uncle Armand's pregnant wife, who was forced to listen to many offensive insinuations about the way in which her child, or half-child, had been conceived in prison. Each time she went scarlet and said, "It cost a lot of money."

She reported that Papa was playing hand after hand of *manille* with the carpenter, that he had fixed the proof press, that it was a bit awkward for Papa when he had to use the privy because the carpenter was in it most of the time, that Mama must try to find the libretto of *The Merry Peasant* among his papers, "still, he doesn't complain, Constance, it's not like it is with my Armand, dear, oh dear, what babies men can be! Armand does nothing but complain."

"That shows he has good reason to," said Meerke cuttingly.

"If you've committed no crime and you're being persecuted, then you're touchier about it than if you're guilty," said Aunt Violet.

"He was good to people, that was his only crime," said Mama.

Aunt Angelique rubbed her stomach against the edge of the table, the child could feel the movements. *"Hi, Lew,"* said the child and winked.

"Armand had a note from his old boss, Van Belleghem, all it said was: 'Armand, think of your children!' The prison governor called me in. 'Madame,' he said, 'is that some sort of secret code? Does it mean: Armand, don't forget the money or those gold bars that were hidden away? It's in your own best interest to tell us everything, or rather, to tell me everything, because he could really end up in hot water, his case would normally be coming up next month but it could easily be postponed for a year, so you'd better come clean with me, anything you tell me will remain strictly between the three of us.' I said, 'Sir, it doesn't mean anything to me, but I'll try to get it out of him.' And I couldn't sleep a wink, I kept thinking of those children and wondering if Armand, with that dissolute life he used to live, and that's not too strong a word, could be a father, running a household full of children somewhere behind my back. Menfolk are devious and underhanded creatures. But it turned out to be something quite different."

"It's what the fans behind the goal shout when Armand keeps goal for the prison team!" exclaimed Louis. " 'Think of your children!' "

"No, it's what they used to say when they were playing cards, he and Van Belleghem, over at Economic Affairs. They would say it to each other when they played whist."

"Postponed for a year!" said Meerke.

"See where it gets you doing things for other people!" said Aunt Violet.

"Ungrateful Belgium!" said Mama with, strangely enough, an echo of Grandpa's dead voice.

"Raising agricultural standards," said Aunt Violet as if to her former class. "Making sure every field in the country produces the maximum yield. Securing the grain imports. Preventing the Germans from requisitioning everything and carrying it off with them. How could he and his men see to all that without coming down hard on the black-marketeers? Once the Germans had left, everyone here had enough to eat, even if it wasn't a lot, but just look at Holland, where they had to eat the soles of their shoes."

" 'Small thanks for my pains,' says Armand. I say, 'Best forget it.' 'Not on your life!' he says. 'I'm going to spend the rest of my life getting even with the Belgian State, with all the means at my disposal.' "

"At his disposal," said Louis. "What can he possibly have at his disposal?"

"He was in the Administration, in Economic Affairs, he knows all the ropes down there. 'Just wait till I get my civic rights back and a little job with the government,' he says, 'then you'll see.' "

"We'll see, we'll see," said Louis, and Hector, flapping, said amen to that.

"Armand has always been sensitive," said Meerke. "He gets that from me. And I got it from my Uncle Theo."

The sundial pointed to noon, the sun was exactly in the south, the shadow of the arm fell in the direction of Holst, who was sitting on the terrace steps. Over his head, under the eaves, swallows were flitting to and fro.

"He's been pulling his wire exactly this morning," said Raf, "you can tell." And Louis did see it, recognized it, that guilty sitting and staring after the loss of one's soul, that all-pervasive loss in an immense forest of longing, so much larger and darker than the woods around the house of the vanished Madame Laura, the loved one wreathed in mourning laurel.

"They're at my heels," said Holst and let them in. The Bastegem Excelsior juniors had withdrawn, but the village policeman had warned him that he would have to appear before the Judge Advocate in the near future, the summons was on the way. The double-barreled shotgun stood behind the door, gleaming dependably. They drank wine from goblets decorated with laurel leaves in gold leaf.

"There are still cellars full of the stuff," said Holst. "Where is Konrad?"

"Perhaps he'll come," said Raf.

"Perhaps! Perhaps!"

"If he's promised, then he'll come."

"If he doesn't come, I've had it. Mertens and Morrens have lodged a complaint. That during the Dieppe landings I tied up an English soldier on one of those little French islands."

"You certainly did do that," said Raf.

"I don't deny it. It's in my dossier, and I've signed it. In Dieppe five infantrymen and one lance corporal, all Germans, were captured by the English. They were left lying on the ground for more than half an hour with their hands tied behind their backs, in just their shirts. They were tied to each other with ropes so that they couldn't put on their tunics. To a German soldier that's the worst thing you can do, it's against his sense of military honor. And that's why they started singing 'Denn wir fahren gegen Engeland,' and that's why the English got jittery and finished them off with bayonets. And that's why our superiors told us, 'Men, if you take an Englishman prisoner, we won't bother about the conventions anymore and we'll . . .' "

". . . slit his throat," said Louis. "An eye for an eye."

"No, no. 'Bind his hands and feet with rope.' And that's what I did."

"What were you doing there in Dieppe, Holst?"

Holst shrugged his shoulders, poured. Santenay, Domaine des Hautes Cornières. Almond flavor.

"Where's Konrad?"

Konrad was studying, said Raf, in Kappel in Switzerland, where Zwingli was killed. Studying so hard that he had sent Raf away after two weeks, he couldn't concentrate properly with two in the apartment.

"The question is, where has Madame Laura got to?" said Louis. His face was glowing from the Santenay, he could taste almonds and strawberries together, and, turning into a combination of Wallaert van Outryve, the Judge Advocate, and Lord Lister, he snapped, "Where?"

"She'll be sitting in a wardrobe somewhere here," said Raf.

"What?"

"Sitting?" said Holst.

"Or standing or lying. *Supposons,*" said Raf. (Thérèse to Uncle Omer!) "She opens the big, heavy wardrobe in her bedroom or some other room, she looks in the mirror inside the door, she checks that her wig is in place, and what does she see? She sees a spot on her slip, never mind right now what sort of spot. 'Oh no!' she cries, because in this state she can't possibly go see her protector and financier, Notary and Minister Baerens, so she takes off her slip, but because you, Holst, haven't washed any clothes for weeks, as is well known, as has been recorded, she starts looking in a pile of underwear in the depths of the wardrobe for another slip, the door slams shut behind her, locks, she can't get out, she bangs, she calls for two whole days . . ."

"And where was *I?*"

"That's something I still have to get to the bottom of."

"I thought everything had been recorded?" Holst's face had a crafty, watchful look.

"Perhaps you were at home?"

"Perhaps, perhaps!"

"You let her call, she lies there in her own excrement, the woodworms come out of the wardrobe, walk all over her clothes."

"And perish in her promised land," cried Louis, getting heated.

"She's never worn a wig," said Holst.

"Of course she has. She wore a wig and you wore a truss!"

The giant went over to the sink, picked up a small pan caked with burned beans and began scrubbing it vigorously with steel wool.

"We can still have a laugh now and then," said Raf. "Can't we? Don't take it like that, I'll see to it that Konrad gets here. *Allee,* Holst, don't be such a wet blanket. We can still have a laugh now and then."

"What's his face like now?" asked Holst grudgingly.

"It's a miracle it's all healed up so well and getting even better. Sometimes he looks just like Robert Taylor in *The Lady with the Chamomile.*"

"I'll have to come around one day and burn those old planks and the rest of the junk behind the hedge."

"No hurry," said Michèle.

"No. I still have a lot of other things to do."

"But if you can spare the time . . ."

"When?"

"Whenever you have the time."

Michèle was suntanned. She had been to the seaside with Thérèse, she said. To her mother-in-law's flat in Knokke, for her birthday. Little René had made a gnome out of clay, but it might as well have been a toadstool, in any case it was red with spots. Louis hardly dared look at Michèle's lips, the quarter-turned mirror image of that pouting second mouth, dripping with tears, under her pleated skirt. Nor at her pointed breasts.

"*Hollywood Canteen* is on in Ghent, with the Andrews Sisters," he said.

"I've seen it, oh, months ago."

"Do you think of me sometimes?"

"Not every day."

"When can I come and burn all that stuff?"

She had to think. Wednesday was impossible, her cleaner came then, the day after that was the Davidsfonds meeting, and over the weekend she was going back to Knokke, she'd promised.

"Next week sometime. At the end of next week."

"If I can," he said feebly.

She greeted Father Mertens, who passed them, frowning. "I must go home," said Michèle then, "I'm expecting a phone call." She jumped onto her bicycle, crushing the bouncy peach-plum to pulp against the saddle.

"*Au revoir, mon petit prince.*"

"*Au revoir.*" (*Maîtresse,* mattress.)

Louis got off the tram in the Corn Market and approached a postman. He did not understand the throaty, half-swallowed dialect, but the postman pointed, the Brothers Milbau Street was close by, to the left, "joost 'crost de Cadedral." He wandered past the statue of the Brothers van Eyck, the Castle of Gerard the Devil, the Cathedral where the Lamb of God of the picture postcards must be, and rang the doorbell as the church bells chimed. A pinched little man in spectacles who had just been to the toilet—because you could hear the flushing—offered him a damp hand.

"The notary is out of town," he said and walked ahead, through a passage papered in faded green silk at the time of the Empress Maria

Theresa, who had banned the Jesuit Order, or maybe at the time of General Belisarius, who had died a begger.

In the lawyer's office, full of chests of drawers and filing cabinets reaching to the ceiling, Vlieghe's father sat down behind the desk, clearly not his usual place. The desk was bare except for a marble inkstand with no ink in it and a blotting pad. Mussolini's desk was always bare, too, not much work gets done where these are lots of papers and files lying about. The carillon played: "Say, little nun, will you dance?" The little dark-green windowpanes cast an unreal light over Vlieghe's father, the man in the lawyer's chair.

"The notary has gone to Normandy," he said. "You look just as my son often described you. You look like a decent young man."

"More or less," said Louis.

"Sit down. I said in my letter to you . . ." (On the notary's writing paper. "Dear Sir, I should be obliged if you would call at the offices of Notary Montjoie between the hours of noon and two o'clock to meet me on a matter of a personal and important nature, Adhemar Vlieghe, Clerk."

"At first I thought I would notify you of Gerard's death by letter. But then I felt compelled to tell you in person, no matter how painful that would be for me. But you seem to be a decent young man, and that's why . . ."

"Death," said Louis.

"Yes," said the father. In his lifetime Vlieghe had never grown taller than this man, who had been a notary himself before the war, during the war.

"I would offer you coffee, but the kitchen is locked, the notary is away sailing in Normandy. Perhaps some lemonade from Gisèle's office . . ."

"No, thank you. He's dead?" (In the Youth Battalion, the *"Langemarck"* Grenadier Division on the Oder? As second gunner, manning an antiair-craft battery to the bitter end? When? All that time like a squashed fly, a squashed *vlieg*, Vlieghe. Other flesh-eating flies are feeding on him. I haven't thought of him in months. "Not every day." When the Germans and Ukrainians marched off in *Wehrmacht* uniform with their bedding and kitchen utensils on their gun carriages, I assumed he would be among them. If I were a girl, I would burst into tears. Handkerchief, snot, consolation.)

With difficulty the man opened a drawer in the desk that was stuck, took out a sheet of writing paper with Notary Montjoie's letterhead on it, and started mechanically to doodle a row of small flowers in the shape of cloverleaves.

"I delude myself that, despite everything, he had a quick and peaceful end." His Adam's-apple moved up and down over the shabby, too-wide collar, his spectacles misted over. "He asked me, the morning of the day he died, to give you a letter, I have it here." He leaned to one side and took out of his back pocket a light-blue envelope marked AIRMAIL in red letters. Louis saw his name written in bold capital letters. The Y had a perfectly rounded curl underneath, like a little meathook.

The man polished his spectacles with his handkerchief, there were ocher rings under the narrowed eyes. "All his teachers were agreed that he showed much promise."

"I knew nothing about it, nothing at all," said Louis. "If I'd known . . ."

"He was buried eleven days ago."

"I would certainly have come."

"Before his death?"

"Before and after." (Not: during.)

"We never know what to do for the best, we who bring up children. We only know when it's too late. If you are strict, it's no good. If you are easygoing, it's no good either. You think, If I can just limit the damage . . . He was your age."

"Say, little nun, will you dance?" The succulent plant under the painting of cows wading through the Leie, or maybe the Schelde, was getting either not enough water or too much. Water was trickling through the central-heating pipes, as through Gustav Vierbücher, the dwarf of Mecklenburg, who had difficulty peeing.

"He played his banjo right up to the very last day. And all I ever said was 'For Heaven's sake, stop it!' "

"How did he die? How? Why?"

"He committed suicide," said Vlieghe Senior, factually, like a policeman.

"The same age as you, Louis," he said quietly.

What does this seedy man want from me? Why does he talk to me as if to an equal, to someone who can talk, just as he is doing, with satanic coldness about him, Vlieghe, sandy-haired Vlieghe, whom I used to call "my love," how well I remember that.

The man stood up, went out. Meanwhile Vlieghe lay at the front door of the Institute, a smoking revolver in his hand. Sister Adam said, "He'll freeze lying here, come, Louis, help me." The two of them dragged the limp boy to Bernadette Soubirous's grotto. The Holy Virgin in her flaking blue cloak with the golden stars said, "Apostle Peter, you shall shed hot tears!"

Between the burning, wet slits of his eyes, Louis saw Vlieghe's father come back in with a bulging imitation-leather school briefcase, he pulled out some gray, wooly wadding that turned out to be a pullover with a row of Ar runes knitted around the neck, Ar is the sun. Aryan. *Arbeid,* work, the spoils of the sun. The Ar motto is "Honor the light."

Louis spread the pullover slowly over his knees.

"His mother knitted that pullover. She'll never get over this. She'll have to devote herself to little Ed now, luckily he's still too young to understand what happened to his brother."

"Say, little nun, will you dance?" How much longer? Is it never going to end?

"It's the priests' fault!" cried Mijnheer Vlieghe suddenly in a shrill voice. "That's why I wrote to you and asked you to come here. Because I don't want one more child to fall victim to those priests."

He drew a row of little flowers at top speed.

"Gerard went just once, not twice, to a woman of bad repute. Just once, not twice. And this woman gave him the disease the priests call the women's-disease."

"Is that why he . . . ?"

Mijnheer Vlieghe nodded.

"There are cures for that sort of thing, it's possible in such cases to intervene before it's too late, it's a disease like any other, but our boy, our boy can't have known that! Who knows what those priests insinuated? Softening of the brain, spinal consumption, who knows?"

Stunned, Louis walked along the Grass Quay past the fake-antique façades of a World's Fair, past the pseudo-Gothic Post Office. Stunned by the clanging of the trams, the car horns, the crowds of shoppers, and the nagging, slow voice of Vlieghe's father. Suddenly it occurred to him that the pullover he was clasping under his arm might well have come from that house of ill repute in which Vlieghe had been crucified by the Woman of Easy Virtue, no, more likely by the wife of a Black, one of the sisters, mothers, daughters of an imprisoned Black who, for revenge, infected judge advocates and police superintendents and, indirectly, that snake-in-the-grass Vlieghe, who now wants to hand on his inheritance to me, who still claws at me from out of his coffin in the mire, spreading his pestilence through this pullover, the wool with the Ar runes teeming with Mizzlers, wriggling, invisible, voracious bacilli. With a snarling little cry, Louis flung the pullover into the gutter, stepped on it, trampled on it with both feet, set off at a gallop, slowed down, calmed down beside the statue of Lieven Bauwens, industrialist and friend of Napoleon.

The slowly and cautiously uttered phrases of Vlieghe's father resurfaced. Away with them. He tore the airmail envelope open. The letter had no margin. Thrifty Vlieghe with the foxy-red hair.

"Friend Louis, I am addressing these words to you from the grave, you who abandoned me even while I was still alive. But I do not blame you for that, you were entitled to. During the minutes of life I have left, I cannot blame you for anything. Have you ever had any idea how much I loved you? You never heard me breathe a word of that, ever, because I believe that the person who is loved must feel and recognize that by himself. If not, *tant pis, mon chéri.* But now I must tell you how much I loved you, for when otherwise can I do it? There is no otherwise for me. Nor any other when. Very soon my body will start to heal. Or to die. A hard nut to crack, dear L., but I have faith. After all, I wanted to study to become a doctor, a surgeon. I can try my hand at it now. But I don't have faith enough yet, not perfect faith. You never can tell. In case my body should recover, you won't be getting this letter to read. In the other case, dot, dot, dot. In the other case I am no longer of this earth. It sounds silly and I have to laugh at it, although I don't have an ounce of humor, you said so yourself years ago in the refectory. But I won't ramble on any longer. I thought that the revival of Flanders, even under the German heel, would meet my ideal, but in my last minutes, dot, dot, dot, I no longer know. *Levet Scone,* dear comrade, your little fly, *Vliegje.* P.S. I am putting our amulet in my mouth so that I can bite on it if things get too bad. Do you still remember our amulet, Apostle Peter? May our amulet stand me in good stead so that I never have to send this letter, so that nobody will ever be any the wiser. Your Little Fly."

Louis walked on past the Castle of Gerard the Devil, past the building of the Bishopric, along the Leie, or the Schelde, or a canal, where a broken boat was moored. The shreds of the letter landed on the tarred planks. Too late. Never realized. I wrote to the dead Maurice, the dead Vlieghe writes to me. This senseless ruminating, this sorrow for something that never was, since I never knew that it was there. Now it is there.

The father's voice, laden with bad breath, groped, probed, returned like a tongue to a painful tooth. Sirens from a factory. But the overbearing, cloying voice full of tediously righteous indignation at the injustice done to him, rather than to his child, ground on and on. Vlieghe in the neo-Gothic little turreted building of our childhood preceded by one of the seven wise virgins dressed in nun's-habit with her scoop of glowing coals in front of her, walks through the imitation-marble corridors. He has always been there, I don't know how he ever managed to disengage himself from the anonymous herd of little ones, to be exposed as a Vlieghe with a name and sleepy-sandman-sand in a pair of amber eyes, with a running nose and soapsuds in his hair and then, even then, with a millstone around his neck.

And all this time the thick voice of the father, as far away as a badly tuned Radio London and as close as a breath, is saying that Gerard had taken a razor that belonged to his grandfather and had made a cut in his scrotum, he who had wanted to study medicine had wanted to make the testicles fall off, but it didn't work, he had soaked a cotton thread in iodine and tied it up, that contaminated part of the lowest part of his body, and then he had cut it through, and flushed the testicles down the toilet bowl, "where else? They were nowhere to be found, and then he just lay there to the end, Louis, the end, which turned out to be gentler than one would have imagined, because, according to our family doctor, bleeding to death causes a kind of euphoria, he was lying with his banjo in his arms, more I cannot tell you, Louis, but no less, either. And with a worn old lead knucklebone between his back teeth."

"I don't know if it's the same for you, but I don't recognize people anymore. During the war they were different. In what way? Well, how can I put it? A certain ideal. I'm not talking of for or against Hitler, of course. Just the idea of pulling together, helping one another out with margarine and coal nuts and now and then a little piece of sausage. If you could make a little profit as well, so much the better, of course, but the main thing was lending your fellow man a hand, but now, I don't know, take Pete the Pipe, all his life he was an honest plumber, always ready to help out whenever there was a leak, and polite: 'If there's anything else wrong, mademoiselle, you have only to say,' and now? He came to repair the leak in my toilet. He hadn't reached the gate before it started dripping again. I've been asking him for a whole week now, 'Pete, when may I expect to see you again?' And what does he say? 'Madame Violet' (when he knows perfectly well that it's 'Mademoiselle'), 'I can't cut myself into four!' "

"Oh, what a lovely little hat, Angelique!"

"It's a cloche. But it wasn't till I got back home that I found out it's only half-lined. The sneaky so-and-sos. Queen Elisabeth was wearing the same model in *De Volksgazet*. But hers, of course, was fully lined."

"The white goes well with your hair."

"It's more of an off-white."

"Shows the dirt pretty quickly, I suppose?"

"I clean it with acetone . . . But I wash my hands carefully every time before I put it on, anyway."

"You can clean it with dry bread, too. I always do that with my beige hat."

"Who would have believed it? That we should use bread on our hats!"

"The way Verbauwen is putting up these apartment houses one after the other! Mind you, it's easy enough if your brother's in the Cabinet. During the war it wouldn't have been like that. The Germans would have said, 'Verbauwen, let's just take a look at your books. No, not those ones, the ones you keep in that strongbox under your bed. What have we here? Madame Louise Schellekes, your brother's wife, a shareholder. *Allee*, off to labor camp with you for a few years!' "

"Yesterday I had to catch my tram, so I'm all in a rush when I buy my football pools coupon and *Het Volk*. I get home, I sit myself down by the stove, I open *Het Volk*, and damned if they haven't gone and fobbed me off with day-before-yesterday's paper. So this morning I go back. 'Oh, no, mijnheer,' he says, 'I can't do anything for you there. Anyone could finish reading the paper and bring it back next day.' "

"The Jews are regrouping again. They're going to turn nasty. Of course, they've got every right. How would you behave if it had happened to you? And on such a scale! And now the scales are tipping the other way, it's only right. They're going to get even with everyone who isn't Jewish, what would you do in their place? It's their turn to look after their own and to hell with everyone else, it's what you'd expect. There's no such thing as fairness in this world. That would be too good to be true."

"But did Madame Laura wear a wig or didn't she?"

"I never saw her close up."

"I did. And it was human hair."

"But a wig is made of human hair as well."

"In my opinion it was a wig. Because she was too lazy to go to the hairdresser's. You put a thing like that on, *ni vu, ni connu*, no one's the wiser, and you're all set, always neat and tidy."

"And Holst, that poor fellow, still alone the whole time in that house with its eighty-two doors."

"Are you going to vote?"

"You have to, as a Belgian. Or it's a two-hundred-franc fine."

"I'll be voting Socialist for the first time in my life. Because Van Acker has promised not to prosecute the boys who went to work in Germany.

I know perfectly well he's only saying it because it gets him a few hundred thousand votes extra, but it's the gesture that counts."

"I don't know who to vote for. You either have to vote for people you don't know from Adam, who claim they were good patriots in secret during the war, working with the underground, which means that the man-in-the-street has no way of checking up on it, or else you do know them from before '40 and they're the ones who took fright and scuttled off to London with shit in their pants. And if it isn't them, then it's their uncle or brother-in-law."

"That difference in color, that's just pulling the wool over the ordinary citizen's eyes. They all stick together. Trade unionists, deputies, shareholders, the army brass. To sell newspapers, they give them a color, but it's all been fixed beforehand. We shift a little to the left and then a little to the right, it's like a tango, but meantime we look after number one."

"It's marvelous how they all stick together through thick and thin, how they don't split up and feud with each other."

"Because they're all hand in glove. Just one big lump of shit stuck together. You're allowed to put so many fingers in the till, but try one finger more and I'll stick a knife in your back. Okay, now I'll shut my eyes while you put your fingers in the till.—Hey, you're stabbing me in the back anyway.—Ah, you should have known better than to turn your back on me."

"And the radio these days! They spit in the listener's face! During the war they'd put on a record softly, nicely, just right. Now they just throw the records on. They're scratched, they get stuck in a groove, they stop right in the middle of some nice bit . . ."

"Our King is still waiting to come home."

"He's waiting till the coast is clear, as the pirates used to say."

"He'll give his brother the Regent a kiss on both cheeks, left, right, so that the whole nation can see, and then he'll give him a good kick up the arse."

"He's got too much blood on his hands, the Regent has."

"And his hands were already pretty filthy, what with all their pawing of loose women in the bars of Ostende."

"That's right, he couldn't even hold a pen to sign a pardon."

"The man was scared of doing the wrong thing."

"Who? Charles Theodore Henri Antoine Meinard, that creep of a Count of Flanders? Too bone-idle, all right, too pie-eyed, more like it!"

"It's understandable. All his life the man's heard nothing but 'Oh,

Leopold, oh, Your Majesty, oh, Sire, oh, King Leopold the Third!' and 'Charles, who's that? Oh yes, the brother!' So now he's playing at being king himself, he wants to try playing master over life and death, too, it's understandable."

"Well, then, it's also understandable that the dead should rise from their graves and hold him to account. Otherwise there's no hope left. Otherwise there's nothing but an Antichrist reigning on this earth."

"I run into Goeminne. Or rather, he passes me in a brand-new Buick. I say, 'Business must be thriving, Maurice. A bricklayer in a car like that!' 'Excuse me,' he says, 'it's Maurice's Repair Company now!'

"We stop to chat and he tells me about a little terrace he had to repair at some house, the rain was getting through . . . Well, as he was working away with his blowtorch, he noticed that the people in the house had three or four paintings hanging in their bedroom and lots of Chinese pottery lying around, in short they were much better off than he'd thought. 'I climbed onto the roof,' he said, 'and gave the felt four or five slashes with my knife. I say to the lady of the house, "Madame," I say, "your roof is leaking, true enough, but that's because something is wrong with your guttering. "Oh," she says, "then that'll have to be repaired as well." I stick on a few patches costing fifty francs and she coughs up seven hundred and fifty. If they can afford paintings in their bedroom, they can afford to fork out.'

"I say, 'Goeminne, some people aren't worth the planks in their coffin.' He says, 'Are you talking about me?' I say, 'I'm talking in general. If the shoe fits.' "

"We're being squeezed between the Americans and the Russians. But try looking at it with a little detachment and you'll see they're just the same. Both crazy about technology, which is running away with them, and crazy about working things so that everyone's equal, never mind their roots."

"We ate enough roots during the war."

"And the Russians never had a Renaissance!"

Posters had been put up for a forthcoming folk festival. The shrimpers dragging their nets on horseback had been drawn by Dolf Zeebroeck, the streaked, doom-laden sky bearing the legend "Our fishermen, knights of the sea!" in Gothic letters.

Leevaert and his assistant Louis sat side by side on a bench, the beach at their feet. With subdued little cries and chugs, the fishing boats entered port from the milky sea. Behind their bench two women on roller skates passed by, arm in arm. The light on the waves: silver paper.

That day, Leevaert had already sold one set of Ruusbroeck's *Collected Works* in four volumes, one *Mechanic's Encyclopedia,* and three copies of *Jenny, a Destiny,* including two signed copies with inscriptions, which meant forty francs extra.

Louis had been lugging around half their stock of the heavy leather-bound presentation copies. He had promised to bring Aunt Violet fresh shrimps from Ostend, he wondered when he would have time to get them, they still had three addresses to call on, one of which was that of a named collaborator, Louis couldn't go there with hands smelling of shrimp, and he knew he couldn't resist opening the bag and having some. And it was getting dark.

The chatter on the dyke was mostly in French. The mailboat came in, lights already on. Leevaert stood up, did a couple of stretching-and-bending exercises. "Up and at 'em!"

"Mevrouw," said Leevaert, "we bring cordial regards from Doctor Raemdonk" (or Lawyer, Canon, Maître, or Professor), "who is paying his respects to you *par personne interposée"* (or, if the family in question was obviously of Flemish sympathies: "through your humble servant"). Then would follow compliments on the modern yet classical interior, in refined language with just a touch of coastal dialect. Meneer was usually not at home. "Louis, please show the volume on Expressionism to mevrouw. Just put the book on that étagère over there to see the effect. Mevrouw, the spine alone, in calf, costs one hundred and eighty francs." Or: *"The History of the West* by a team of scholars under the direction of Professor Weynants, you are familiar with the name, of course, from the University of Leuven. Sold out. Only a few volumes left, obtainable separately from antiquarian booksellers at scandalous prices. And tremendously interesting. It reads like a novel. And how often don't you ask yourself, Now, that Battle of Poelkapelle, it took place only a stone's-throw from here, when was it again? Who was the general killed there?"

Then it was really dark. Leevaert had been able to sell one more *Jenny, a Destiny.* The buyer had said, "Come on, then, put a signature on it," and "I'm only buying it to show my solidarity, you understand, I'll say no more."

Leevaert now set off resolutely in the direction of an avenue with small side streets full of red-lit bars. He came to a sudden halt under a dim streetlight in front of a gleaming black showcase containing photographs of women in underwear. Louis stopped a few feet away from him. Leevaert bent forward, almost licking the glass. Louis squirmed with shame. Sailors walked past singing "Heigh-ho, heigh-ho," the song of the Seven Dwarfs. The light in the showcase flashed on, the letters "L'Escale" in wine-red shone over Leevaert, who exclaimed, "Aha," put on his spectacles, and bent even farther forward.

"We don't open till ten, pal," said a heavily built man who wore his doorman cap like the kepi of a Black Brigade officer.

"Tell me, pal," said Leevaert, "didn't Chouchou used to work here, Mieke Lauwers?"

"That must have been before my time," said the doorman.

"True, I can't see her portrait here."

"You can't rely on the girls nowadays, meneer. But it's probably for the best. That way you get fresh flesh all the time."

The Orient Bar was a miniature mosque with little round windows that gave off a rosy glow behind an ornate wrought-iron trellis. Leevaert walked in as if entering a grocery. I'd never dare. *"Bonsoir, mon petit chou,"* said Leevaert and kissed the powdered cheek of a buxom platinum-blonde in an evening gown. Louis took her callused hand and kissed the palm.

"Olala, a man of the world," she cried. There was a piano on a platform, Marnix de Puydt lay sleeping with his forearm across the closed lid, his childish thick lips parted. The lights of passing cars flashed through the bar.

"The master sleeps," said the lady.

"Two *coupes,"* said Leevaert. "And for you, Margot?"

"I'll have a small Cointreau," said Margot.

"That's never hurt anybody," said Leevaert. Three businessmen were explaining to two Ostend girls dressed in Austrian or Tyrolean costumes that either Champs-Élysées, or Narcissus Five, or else that miracle filly Clopinette was sure to win tomorrow. The champagne sparkled. The sleeping De Puydt brought together his plump little mandarin's-feet in their pointed shoes, one pointed toe bobbing in time with his fingers, which strummed on the piano lid much as Hölderlin once did on a harpsichord without strings. One of the Ostend girls looked like Prince Valiant, with her cropped flaxen hair and a necklace of copper coins. She was sitting on the lap of the Champs-Élysées man, who was pinching, tickling, pawing, kissing. She said that the only thing keeping her mother alive was the hope of fresh mussels, they had been promised for next week. "Meanwhile, let's have a taste of your own little mussel," cried Champs-Élysées, she laughed, displaying a pink tongue, the coins twinkled. After the third *coupe* offered him by Margot,

Louis needed to pee urgently but didn't dare. He guessed that the little padded door beside the bar was the toilet, but nobody seemed to be using it.

De Puydt got up. "What would the hetaerae and the gentlemen care to hear? My repertoire is limited but eclectic."

" 'O, Fla-anders tha-at I lo-ove with all my hea-art,' " sang Louis.

"Mind your manners," hissed Leevaert.

"If that's what the boy likes," said Margot, putting her hand on Louis's crotch, where, fortunately, nothing was stirring. If I get up and run to that little door, I'll probably fall flat on my face. And if I fall against Prince Valiant, she won't have any panties on.

Margot asked if he wanted to be put up for the night, her apartment was nearby. And if he'd like to lodge with her for a while longer, all he'd have to do would be to run a few errands a day.

(My dead Grandpa said: "You are no *commerçant,* Louis.")

"I'll have to sleep on that," Louis said.

"Well, you can do that with me," said Margot.

"Margot," Louis said ponderously, "you're not serious. You're talking about board and lodging, but how much will I have in my hand come the end of the month?"

And the miracle came to pass. She stared at him nonplussed, momentarily completely bemused, then kissed him on the mouth and said, the marvel of the fiery tongues aflame above the heads of the chosen, "Oh, you. You little *commerçant.* "

"I shall now play for you," said De Puydt, "the *Requiem in C* by the youngest son in a version syncopated specially for you." He played and looked like Grandpa's father after his beard had been shaved off. Although there were no photographs of him. In that state. Mute. Morbid. Moribund, you look your best in photographs. "And now, to please Margot," said De Puydt after what seemed hours, after the bar, which had been packed with whores, pill-swallowers, vandals, heretics, and trolls of all sorts, had emptied, had fallen into a void of silence with at most a single woodworm burrowing about in Louis's temple, "now I shall play for her, by the selfsame youngest son, that renegade turned Roman Catholic out of greed, the profound *Salve Regina in E-flat.* "

It was profound. Profoundly nauseating. "Play something from *The Land of Smiles,* " shouted Louis.

"No," said Margot, "no, no, and no again." She smelled of the sea. And did still as they walked later along the shore, the four of them, arm in arm, tottering. "I'll show you what love is, little one, just you wait and see."

"Where may a person partake of some decent refreshment at this hour?" said Leevaert. The white-rippled sea, whitecaps.

"In the Banco."

"If they're feeling civil," said De Puydt.

In high spirits they reached the café, where the croupiers from the Casino were eating jellied calf's head in tomato sauce.

"People are getting fat again," said De Puydt. "Just look. As if nothing, absolutely nothing, had happened to us, as if we had imagined the whole thing. *Je voudrais que vous raisonassiez de ce que je vous dis là.*" His curly white head dropped forward and found his glass.

"Fat or not, they'll have to take me as I am," said Margot. "Don't you agree, sweetie?"

"The Russians are at the gate," said Leevaert. "Give me another Pale-Ale." Dirty-brown threads of onion soup hung from the corners of his mouth. The croupiers were playing poker in paradisiacal calm. The ashtrays were full to overflowing with Mizzlers.

"Aren't you glad to see me?" asked Louis.

"No," said De Puydt.

"Don't you recognize me, Mijnheer de Puydt?"

The man thrust out his chest, flung his locks back, drummed his fingers on the table, close to the edge, on black and white keys.

Margot said, "I'll wash your shirt tomorrow, I've got a washing machine," and tugged at the tip of Louis's collar. Cold sweat ran into his eyes. I have two one-eyed paladins. Maurice de Potter and Dirty Dick. Pieter de Coninck, doyen in 1300 of the weavers in Bruges, had two eyes. The reason he was painted as a one-eyed man is that during the copying or writing of the chronicles some stupid or nearsighted Italian monk confused him with another Pieter, Pieter Flotte. *Voilà.* And now you!

"That night and that rose full of flames in Haarbeke," said De Puydt, addressing himself exclusively to Louis.

"Yes," said Louis. "Yes."

"That night I was lying in my bed in Walle. My wife, who now weighs two hundred and twenty pounds, was lying next to me in my bed in my bedroom in Walle, I was busy reading Montaigne and *Woman's Realm,* and it came to me that what I really wanted was to be alone on this earth, that I had to be alone if I were to safeguard my wretched art, to save the stale little flame of my art, altogether alone, and then, Louis, I thought, If only this one at my side, if only all of them in this household of mine, would vanish from my sight and hearing, oh, if only they could all of them be blown up at one fell swoop, in one great act of liberation."

"All of them," said Louis, asked Louis.

570

"All of them, wife and child and maid and cat and goat, so that in the morning, alone, liberated, I would be able to listen to the beat of my heart, or to the sparrows."

"The children, as well," said Louis.

"As well," said De Puydt. "Above all. Above all the ceremony of the innocent. 'God in Heaven,' I said, I prayed, 'please let them both get blown up, in God's name, so that I may have just one moment's peace, so that just for once I can hear the flutings of the birds.'

"And He heard me that night and the rose opened up, the gigantic rose of fire, and at that very moment the bombers descended upon Haarbeke."

"Yes," said Louis.

"And my poor little mite in Haarbeke was blown up and burned up in his little bed, with his pajamas, his corn biscuits from Winterhulp, his Animal Atlas, his knucklebones, his marbles . . ."

Louis leaped up from the bench, pushed Margot's callused hand aside, tugged the inert De Puydt up by his locks, felt the hairs snap, and slapped De Puydt's cheek as hard as he could. The slap rebounded against the mirrored walls of the Banco.

"Hey, hey," said a croupier with narrow shoulders.

A fisherman in an orange pea jacket covered with scales, swathes of cigarette smoke around his head, came over, legs wide apart.

"Well, I never," said Margot. De Puydt felt his cheek, grimaced, stuck the tip of his tongue into his cheek, making an obscene bulge.

"He didn't mean it," cried Leevaert. "Truly." And sat down beside De Puydt, thigh by thigh.

"Forgive me," said Louis (the word *"pardon"* in French was trembling on his lips when it came to him in a flash that he had slapped a *Flemish* Mind).

"He didn't know what he was doing," cried Leevaert more loudly.

"I'm sorry," Louis said. De Puydt emptied Leevaert's Pale-Ale, his cheek red. The croupiers turned back to their card game.

"Aren't you ashamed of yourself?" said Margot. Louis nodded, nibbled at a piece of sausage. De Puydt said to the fisherman, "In my day, people would buy a round after a misunderstanding like that. Right?"

"Tournée générale," Louis called, but the owner did not hear him or did not want to hear him or did not take him seriously. De Puydt rubbed his cheek, then thrummed his chubby fingers on the table again, partita, chaconne. He said, "Louis Seynaeve."

"Yes."

"You cannot abide my calling to you from out of the depths."

"That's too deep for me," said Margot and went and sat down on the other side of De Puydt, licked his cheek. "I'll show you what love is tonight, Marnix, just you wait and see."

Unblinking, De Puydt continued to stare defiantly at Louis.

"I'll stand a round," said the fisherman at their table, "for everyone except that whippersnapper over there."

The whippersnapper said, "Well, Mijnheer de Puydt, what is it now? Spit it out."

"*Il faudrait que je cessasse de vivre,*" said the man, thrumming.

Louis and Aunt Violet compared the regulation yellow postcards they had received that morning from Holst, now in De Nieuwe Wandeling prison in Ghent. Louis's message read, "Don't believe everything they say. A. Holst," Aunt Violet's, "I am in De Nieuwe Wandeling. A. Holst." The two lines of writing were right at the top of both cards, the letters a shade more slanting on Aunt Violet's card. She said, "De Wandeling, I ask you, 'The Walk,' is that a name for a prison? It can only be to tease, the people there can't go for a walk."

"But they do, Aunt Violet. Every day, in a circle, hands behind their backs."

"He always liked me," said Aunt Violet.

"Everybody likes you," said Meerke, cross because she hadn't received any mail.

"I'm not saying he was an admirer. I mean just as a human being."

The populace of Bastegem had surmised that, for one dark reason or another, Holst had lost his highly placed protection and, wordlessly jubilant, wordily long-winded, had testified at the police inquiry that he had married above his station, just to be able to look down his nose at the village, a village that had always looked down on him.

Was he capable of doing harm to Madame Laura, his spouse?

"That, Your Honor, would be going too far, but there was that difference between them."

"Yet Madame Laura was of humble origins herself."

"But the money, Your Honor, that's what makes the difference."

While Holst was out on a duck shoot ("With whom? You don't go out shooting ducks by yourself." "He did, Your Honor"), someone had broken into the house with the many rooms.

"Who?"

"They do say, but then they say a lot of things, don't they, that it could have been the Bastegem Excelsior juniors."

"Which ones?"

"I wasn't there, Your Honor."

"Someone had smashed a pane in the scullery and tried to open the window but failed because Holst came back unexpectedly. Who was that?"

"Who indeed?"

"De Keyser, Gaston, the locksmith, has stated that he and a court official then opened the front door."

"If De Keyser says so, then presumably it's the truth."

"Who was this court official?"

"You should ask De Keyser that, not me."

"But De Keyser, Gaston, states that he does not know the name of the court official. And we don't know who it was, either."

"That's not our fault, Your Honor."

A little sea-green satin shoe had been found beside the railway track with traces of congealed blood on the heel. No one in Bastegem except Madame Laura would ever have dreamed of wearing a shoe like that. You could hardly stand up in it.

The court had also subjected the coconut mat at the entrance to the little castle to examination. More traces of blood.

Two objects in the house had been officially impounded, namely a large bread knife and a kitchen knife.

What else transpired? What other testimony was given?

That, while on a visit to the house of the victim, De Bock, Rafael, had noticed two deep gashes and a little lime on the skirting board, just opposite the cellar entrance, some eighteen inches from the partition wall.

That Goossens, Anton, village policeman, on his night rounds, had heard an altercation from the little castle and had clearly recognized the voice of Madame Laura, I mean, Vandenghinste, Laura.

That De Brauwere, Arthémise-Arlette, had heard from the accused's own mouth that Madame Laura would no longer make water in the grass as she had formerly so liked to do. Asked for an explanation in respect thereto, the accused had declared that that was just how it was, that's all. De Brauwere, Arthémise-Arlette, had conceded that this had taken place following considerable consumption in the little room next to the main bar of the Picardy inn, an establishment not known as a disorderly house but nevertheless of dubious repute. Read, agreed, and signed.

"If he can just get himself a good lawyer," said Meerke. "Because the evidence has to be stronger than that. There must be a body. He can't be accused without a body."

"You'll never make me believe he used a bread knife or a kitchen knife," said Mama. "He strangled her. With those big hands of his."

"Strangled her. Then cut her into little pieces. Then dropped her in the quicklime," Louis said.

"No," said Mama. "That's not his way. He's far too romantic."

Raf also received a postcard from prison. "Where is Konrad? Please."

The hereinbefore-identified De Brauwere, Arlette, addressing the examining magistrate at the judicial inquiry and the King's Deputy Prosecutor, declares that she wishes to speak in Flemish and states that she is anxious to hand over to the Court, in full, the sum of four thousand francs which Holst, André, spent on his last visit to the Picardy establishment, since she wants nothing to do with the proceeds of a murder.

There are two windows to the left of the front door that bear the inscription "Picardy." These windows have curtains that draw apart in the middle. The façade is painted red. At the appointed time two young ladies were sitting in the right-hand window, in full view of passers-by. The entrance door gives access to a small hallway from which a door to the left affords entry to the bar proper. At the far end of the hall, opposite the entrance, is a door that gives onto the stairwell. At the bottom of the stairwell is a door that gives onto a covered urinal. There is also another door giving onto the stairwell, that affords access to a second room abutting the bar proper.

The bar proper is divided from the second room, which is furnished as a lounge, by a wall with an archway that can be shut off by an opaque curtain. This curtain was drawn back when we entered. The first room, fitted out as the bar, is supplied with a counter, three small tables, and some eight stools or taborets.

The light in the room is poor, we noted an absence of light fixtures, the illumination is indirect. The second room has a window that gives onto a covered courtyard, and the indirect illumination notwithstanding, a somber light prevails. A divan stands in front of the window. In addition the room is furnished with three tables and four club chairs. The window is fitted with dark curtains and opaque hangings. There is no schedule of rates and charges on display.

When asked, the owner, Mevrouw de Lentdekker, Antoinette, declared that the hostelry had been named after a region in Italy, but that another factor had also been taken into consideration, viz., her meeting in Brussels in the year 1939 with Professor Auguste Picard, who had shown her a model of the metal sphere with which he had been exploring the ocean, the so-called *bathyscaphe*.

When asked, Merkès, Josiane, declared that during sexual intercourse the accused had once given a loud scream. Asked for an explanation, the response of the accused had been that he had killed his wife. At the time, Merkès, Josiane, had not taken him seriously, because she knew the accused very well from previous visits, during which she had always appreciated his shy and gentle nature.

We confronted Merkès, Josiane, with the accused. The latter repeated his statement in the presence of the young woman, whom he knows as the waitress at the Picardy, that he had not had sexual intercourse with her, because he had not been in the right and necessary mood for it and because he did not feel physically attracted to women of a different or of mixed race. However, Merkès, Josiane, is able to name certain physical peculiarities present on the accused's body and to draw them roughly on paper. Most striking is an appendectomy scar in the shape of a little semicircular meathook.

The accused then alleged that Merkès, Josiane, had been trying to lead him on that night and had used all sorts of wiles to draw attention to herself. As an example he mentioned that she had twice jumped over a club chair in such a manner as to display her private parts. He also claimed that the Picardy sold cigarettes without revenue stamps.

"Holst can't get himself a good lawyer, he hasn't got two francs to rub together."

"He can always sell the little castle."

"But, my poor lamb, it's still in her name."

"Or the furniture, in a pinch."

"But that's already been confiscated by Minister Baerens. He came on the scene pretty fast. All the invoices are in his name. Down to the bills for her shoes and aprons."

"Madame Laura didn't wear aprons, surely!"

"Yes, she did. When she came up from Brussels for two or three days, she liked nothing better than to scrub the floors and wax the parquet."

"To give her something else to think about," said Aunt Violet. "Father Mertens does that, too. When the weather's hot, he does the spring cleaning in his swimming trunks."

Raf testified that he knew that Madame Laura, her solemn promise to be faithful to Holst notwithstanding, had resumed intimate relations with Minister Baerens. The fact was, her erotic feelings were aroused exclusively by older men radiating a certain amount of social prestige or personal achievement. Their looks did not matter, so long as they were rich and powerful enough, in their fifties, wore three-piece tailor-made suits and gold wristwatches, and gave orders in a loud, self-assured voice. Baerens, red in the face and fat, an industrialist, lawyer, and government minister, fulfilled this ideal. In the beginning she had managed to keep her adulterous behavior a secret, then had denied it, claiming that she and Baerens kept company out of pure friendship. Whereupon Holst, out of his mind, had begun singing the folk song: "And for ten francs or so, just for ten francs or so, she would let her pussy show." Bursting into laughter, she had then owned up.

Raf testified that Holst had told him in the strictest of confidence how the crime had been committed.

"I bet Raf laid it on with a trowel," said Meerke.

"Everyone does that," said Mama.

Night falls over the sundial, the rhododendrons, the hedges. In the drawing room a woman pale as a wraith is lying on the sofa. She lifts her knee. There is a run in her silk stocking. The white flesh, pressed between garter, stocking, and panties, bulges. The woman looks to see if her cellulite is worse. From the woman wafts the smell of putrefaction, such as red-haired people are alleged to give off when it rains. An enormous man in forester's-clothes cannot keep his eyes off her. He leans against the chimney. The woman lifts up her knee and examines the broken tip of her satin shoe. The man picks up his double-barreled shotgun and wipes the barrels with an oily rag.

"Why has a gulf grown between us?" he asks. "Tell me that, Laura. Perhaps there is still something we can do about it."

"We could live together like brother and sister," she says.

"Holst and Madame Laura would never talk like that," said Mama. "Holst would never get his tongue around something like that."

"Why not?" asked Uncle Omer. He shone, he had just had a good wash in the scullery tub. He was wearing a freshly ironed pair of striped pajamas.

"If you ask me, Raf picked up that kind of talk from his parents," said Meerke.

"Well, Laura?"

The woman sticks her tongue out at him. The man is reminded that the boys at school used to do that, too, because he was always dressed in rags, couldn't or wouldn't talk, picked up and ate the sandwiches they threw away. He puts down his gun and strikes her on the temple with the side of his hand. She loses consciousness at once, her wig falls onto the carpet. With one of the lawyer's gray silk ties he binds her wrists to the central-heating pipe. Five minutes later she comes to as he is sprinkling her with water from a watering can. She tells him that none of this changes anything between them, that no matter what he does, her soul is free.

"God preserve her soul," muttered Aunt Berenice.

At that moment a badger ambles into the light of the small lantern on the patch of grass outside.

"What do you mean, a badger? Do you mean Notary Baerens had come to badger her?" asked Uncle Omer.

"No, no, a real badger that lives underground and sometimes comes out to the pond. He leaves his sett at night to find slugs," said Louis.

"A musteline animal," said Aunt Violet. "About thirty inches long. You hardly see them anymore."

Holst goes to the door, opens it very, very quietly, looks out at the badger, which stops and pricks up its ears, peers around myopically. Madame Laura screams for help. Holst lunges at her and stuffs the oily rag into her mouth. Quickly he says, "What am I to do with you? I don't know how to talk to you, I never learned how to, you knew that when you agreed to become my wife. What am I to do? Take classes to learn how to tell you what is in my heart? It's all my fault, I know, but can't you help me? Nod if you can. Nod!" Because he has been talking without stopping for breath, he now has the hiccups. He says quickly three times, again without stopping for breath, "Hiccup, hiccup, go away, don't come back till Saturday." He continues to hiccup.

"Is it because of the war that we can't say one blessed thing without immediately thinking the opposite? Or that we pick holes immediately in everything we think?

"What am I to do? Fuck you? And then? What will I have conveyed to you with that?"

He hiccups, goes to the table, takes an orange from the bowl of fruit he has brought for her, and eats it without drawing breath, peel and all.

"It could be so nice and easy for us living here. Maybe it is difficult for you to love anybody or anything other than yourself. But do I have to sit up and beg for you like a dog for the rest of my life? Here, in this cold church?"

Raf testified that the man then said that he felt pity for her because she was trying to retch, that he had been afraid that she, pale as she was, would perhaps get something wrong with her lungs again as had happened when she was fourteen, that he had taken the sour and sickly-smelling gag from between her teeth and begged for forgiveness, that she, as if vomiting it out, had cried that pardon was impossible, never, no pardon, let me go, you dog. And that he had said, "I will let you go, Laura, set you free," and had gone hiccuping into the kitchen, had taken the bread knife from the drawer, put it down again, picked up the serrated meat knife, and had gone back to face her curses.

Holst made a gesture indicating he would like to take off his corduroy jacket. He was given permission by the Deputy Prosecutor. He pointed out his wife's position by the central-heating radiator. He identified the meat knife he was shown as the one with which he had killed his wife. He allowed himself to be photographed with the meat knife in his hand. Then he demonstrated how he had cut the necktie, how he had picked his wife up under the arms and dragged her down the stairs. He suggested that he should change position slightly because he could tell from the lens that the camera wouldn't get all of him in the photograph.

The Deputy Prosecutor asked him if he was cold, because he was shivering all over. He answered in the negative. He was again handed the meat knife. He demonstrated where he had put his left hand at the moment he had made the various cuts. For most of the time it was under his wife's chin. Before leaving, the accused asked if he might take his scapular with him. His request was granted. Thereupon the electricity in the house was turned off, the spring lock of the front door was secured, and the front door was sealed.

Madame Laura is lying on her back, fully dressed. Her wig is lying approximately nineteen inches from the body. The head is pointing in the direction of Bastegem church steeple.

She is of average build, height five feet six inches. The fingernails are cyanotic. Presence of an ecchymosis on the lower left eyelid and at the level of the left zygomatic bone. The left earlobe shows contusions indicating incisions. The throat is completely cut across, in such a manner as to half-sever the head from the body. The sparsely hirsute scalp shows four contusions indicating incisions. The right half of the neck shows signs of at least four attempted incisions. The throat has been cut between the hyoid bone and the thyroid cartilage. The anterior wall of the esophagus is severed, as are the jugular veins and the branches of the carotid artery. The buccal cavity is free. The brain is contused. The lungs lie free in the chest. The bronchi contain mucus mixed with blood. The abdominal cavity is dry. The intestines are glossy. The spleen weighs one hundred grams. Both kidneys together weigh two hundred and twenty grams. The contusions on the left and right wrists indicate violent movements made while the wrists were bound. The left leg lies across a basket containing quinces. The right hand lies on a blood-soaked floorcloth, the left hand lies in a feeding bowl of a special shape made for long-haired dogs.

"See what happens, Omer, if you don't pay attention?" said Meerke severely.

"Leave Omer alone," said Aunt Violet.

"God preserve her soul," said Aunt Berenice.

"There is no God, and Mary is His mother," exclaimed Omer.

"Omer, you're going too far again," said Meerke.

"Don't say things like that, brother," said Aunt Berenice softly.

"Where are you going, Louis?"

"Upstairs, Mama."

"Isn't your story finished yet? When will we be able to read it?"

"There's still another ten pages to do."

"Two or three days more?"

"I've got to make a fair copy yet," said Louis sullenly.

Louis propped his bicycle against the shed wall, lifted off the basket with the pot of stew. Jules was reading the Farmer's Almanac for the year 1922, and asked, as always, "Which way did you come?"

"First up to Dr. Vandenabeele's house, then the little side road past Liekens's sister, then the lane to Klasteren, and then through the little copse by the chapel."

"You're lying again. Just like him."

"I didn't meet anybody, Jules, not a soul." He had caught a glimpse, briefly, of one of the juniors by the chapel, but the boy had probably just been poaching.

"Tell your mother to come and take your father away," said Jules, also for the umpteenth time.

"I'll tell her."

"I may be a little bit simple, but I'm not altogether stupid. I thought he was an educated man, but I was thoroughly mistaken about that. I'm listening to a sermon on the radio. He says, 'Jules, turn that off!' I say, 'Staf, religion is the only thing that can save us now.' 'Tell that to my judges,' he says!"

Papa devoured the stew there and then, too impatient to heat it up. "Too much kidney."

"Mama thought you liked that, lots of kidney."

"What does she know about what I like?" His right eye was lower than his left. I can do without a third one-eye.

Papa wiped his mouth with his sleeve and gave his instructions. To tell Mama he couldn't stand it here any longer. "But make it sound serious. Be a bit dramatic!"

Then to get Mama to sound out the Judge Advocate as to how things really stood with his house arrest, whether the whole matter couldn't finally be quietly dropped now. "She sees the Judge Advocate quite often, doesn't she? Two or three times a week at his office doesn't she? Surely he's ready to do anything he can for her by now isn't she? They're thick as thieves, aren't they? They go out together, don't they? Don't you take her side! She was seen with him in a *pâtisserie* in Maricolen Street!"

Then he wanted Louis to go to the library and take out *Through Wildest Kurdistan* and *Through the Land of the Skipetars* by Karl May.

And when he went to Walle next week, would he please ask Grandma for a pound of pickled herring and a photograph, quarto-size, of Grandpa. And would he also go to Grandpa's grave and do a little weeding, "because I'll bet it's a real wilderness over there by now."

"It stinks in here."

"But I opened the window this morning."

"You don't wash, Papa."

"Every day. Almost every day. Ask Jules. What is Mama doing?"

"She's waiting."

"For me to get back home?"

"Of course."

"But what does she do all day? Knit, sew? No, she's all thumbs. Gossiping, of course. About her husband. Drinking coffee, eating cake, and making a fool of her husband behind his back. Does she go out much at night?"

"Never."

"Yes, well, but then you go to bed early, how can you know what she gets up to at night? They say that The Goat, the sacristan, calls regularly these days at Villa Heliotrope on his bicycle at one o'clock in the morning. And that the radio is still on then."

With an ink-black fingertip he scraped a sliver of meat from the bottom of the pan. Sucked it up with an odd rapture. "But I mustn't complain. Certainly not, now I know that Churchill's been kicked out of office. And what did he say? That the English Socialists were like the Gestapo! He's in the shit now, Mr. W. C. of *Marlbrooghs'en va-t-en guerre!* The English aren't nearly as stupid as they look in their bowler hats!"

Aunt Berenice the Benevolent cast her eyes down while her mother spoke, as she had been taught to do at boarding school, or when she was at home, by Uncle-Adieu-Firmin, by the Mormons, or the Bogomils, or whoever they were. Aunt Berenice had never referred to it again, to her sect. Only to God. Her hands were red from scraping asparagus.

Mama was kneading the crumb of the loaf into little balls, each time the tiny oblique cuts made by her fingernails produced a small, round

Chinese face with an even smaller groove for a pouting mouth, and each time Mama then flattened it on the oilcloth patterned like Cordovan leather. In Bruges, in the golden age of the Flemish guilds and corporations, there had been four hundred artisans working with Cordovan leather. Or was it three hundred?

"It's for your own good, Berenice. It would be better for us all if you left. Least said, soonest mended," said Meerke.

"Then you ought to keep quiet yourself," said Louis.

"Oh, you, you're in the plot, too."

"The plot," said Aunt Berenice.

"Call it what you like."

"I've only done my duty," said Aunt Berenice, looking straight in front of her, it sounded like a rebel yell to her, she was startled by her own presumption and went and sat down beside Mama, ate up an almost flat little Chinaman.

"An act of charity," said Mama.

"Tending the sick," said Louis.

"Omer is none the better for it. On the contrary. But let's keep that under our hats."

"What can you have against her looking after her own brother?"

"Looking after him? Come on, Constance!"

"What can you have against her having a chat with her own brother for a few hours?"

"They don't chat for a few hours, Constance, they just sit there looking into each other's eyes without saying a word."

"We do chat," said Aunt Berenice with the smile of the damned.

"What about?"

"Everything."

"About God and His Bulgarian saints, I suppose?"

"That's a terrible thing to say, Mother."

"Berenice, you'll turn black with all your lies."

"Or I read to him from the paper. I pick the passages out first."

"And you've never sat on his lap, I suppose?"

Mama watched her sister blush, flinch, in her almost spotless white apron, and showed no compassion.

"He is unhappy," said Aunt Berenice.

"Because you turn his head."

"His head was turned when he arrived here," said Mama.

"Which way was it turned, Mama?"

"Louis, will you please stop trying to trip me up all the time! It's not because you read all those books . . . Oh, I'm sick to death of you!"

Aunt Berenice scraped the asparagus, not too much, not too little, but just right. It was the end of the asparagus season, the spears were already turning bitter. After boiling them, you had to put them in cold water.

"If you think it better that I leave, Mother, just say so."

Meerke did not reply. "What do you think, Constance?"

"That our mother has gone around the bend," said Mama firmly. Louis lit a match for her cigarette.

"I don't want any trouble," said Aunt Berenice. She started to tie up the asparagus. "I'll go and pack my suitcase."

"Oh no, you won't!" exclaimed Mama. "Pay no attention to her."

"Mother is right," said the Meek One. "I can see that I do sow discord here."

"For goodness' sake, Berenice, will you stop coming out with these biblical sayings of yours!"

She went on tying the asparagus. Mama looked at the calm fingers and said, "Just for once be a human being like the rest of us and stand up for yourself!"

Aunt Berenice turned away from her sister. From her steely gray-blue eyes, just like Mama's, sprang tears as from a little one's, small transparent pearls rolling down her cheeks. "He is so unhappy."

Uncle Omer only noticed her disappearance several hours later. He bellowed, kicked the turkey. He pulled up a whole bed of cauliflowers and stamped on them with both feet. All night long he called for her, until Mama went to him.

It snowed in Walle. The flakes were as thick as in Vienna that day behind Mozart's coffin.

It rained in Walle for months on end, bringing famine and infectious diseases. The corn rotted in the fields. Innocent children were killed with flails because they couldn't stop coughing.

It was a mysteriously scorching summer in Walle, the bombers flew low, it was so hot that the people refused to go down into the air raid shelters. Wheel rims, girders, half a locomotive lay in the burning *pâtisserie*. Soldiers used their rifle butts to drive people into flat-bottomed boats on the Leie. Then they shot holes in the boats. On the bank a priest who had refused to swear the oath of hatred against royalty was tied to the mouth of a cannon. Shrapnel and tattered pieces of the priest rained down on the water.

The sun was shining weakly over Walle when Louis passed the Church of Our Lady. A soft light lay over the Market Square. A French Republican officer staggered out of the church, his arms laden with golden chalices and salvers, the sacred vessels with the consecrated Host. On seeing this, the owner of the Café Patria ran after the Occupier in a rage and flung himself at him. Before the Frenchman could draw his sword, the Fleming had already run off toward the Upper Town cheered on by all the people of Walle, who then held a procession, shouting, "We want a Constitution!" That happened on the twenty-third of *Pluviôse,* in the third year of the French Republic. On the Market Square, facing the Town Hall, where the guillotine used to be erected in former times, Dirty Dick was standing in a truck, hands up.

A half-naked creature with swaying breasts who looked like Michèle and represented the Goddess of Reason was dancing on a platform next to the Belfry. "Filthy French rats, go back to your traps," screamed the populace.

The sun was shining weakly over Walle when Louis arrived at Grandma's house. Grandma didn't have any pickled herring. And she didn't want to come along to Grandpa's grave, either. "It would upset me too much." She pointed to the locket on her chest, where a white curl of Grandpa's lay on red velvet like a slender little meathook. "I was there only last week with three roses for the thirty-seven years of happiness I knew with him, there was no better man on earth."

"But Grandma, when he was alive . . ."

"Your grandfather had less pleasant sides to him, like everyone else, but the main thing is that he looked after his family to the very last."

"The main thing is that he's six feet under," said Aunt Hélène. "With the lid firmly on." She was fat, squeezed into a tailored suit, a lady-about-Walle who ate *éclairs* and *boules de Berlin* every afternoon at the Pâtisserie Mérécy.

"I'm going to go and buy a Sidney Bechet record," said Louis. "Do you want to come and help me choose?"

"No thanks, Louis," she said listlessly.

"Don't you like Sidney Bechet?"

"It's all the same to me," she said. "Do you want me to get anything, Mother?"

"But Hélène, I gave you the list!"

"I think she must be expecting," said Grandma after watching her pass by through the basement window. "And she hasn't exactly hit the jackpot with that dry stick of an Eric of hers. What on earth is the matter with my daughters? It really is too sad about Hélène, the child deserves better. What she sees in Eric I cannot imagine, but perhaps it's just that *extrêmes se touchent.* Anyway, last week she asks me over, I say to myself, Surely it can't be, but it was, it was ox tongue again with white sauce and mushrooms. And if it isn't ox tongue, then it's chicken with white sauce. And vanilla ice cream to finish with again."

"Vanilla is an aphrodisiac," said Louis. (Marnix de Puydt had refused to eat anything else for weeks after Aristotle's death. Because it had been the last thing his child had eaten.)

"Well, I must say I never noticed!" shrieked Grandma. She had a coughing fit from laughing so much, her jowls wobbled. Louis patted her gently on the back. She leaned back, and his hand got caught against the chair, in a panic he tugged it free. "All those years," she cried, "all that vanilla ice cream I ate and I never felt a thing! Be a pet and pour me a little glass of Grand Marnier, it isn't good for me, but who cares?"

They played two-handed *manille.* "*Manille* and *vanille,*" Grandma giggled. She won all the time, crowing triumphantly, insisting on immediate payment. Louis made coffee for her. Grandpa was hanging above her armchair in quarto format, in a scrolled gilt frame. I am among you. Grandma followed Louis's glance.

"A saint," she said. "Do you think of him sometimes? The way he could hold forth in that High Flemish of his! In his palmy days he'd go to Communion twice every day. At half-past five to the curate's Mass and at nine to High Mass. Hélène says it was just to show the people of Walle how God-fearing he was. I say, 'Child, it's the intention that counts.'"

The coffee wasn't to her liking. Oh, of course, he had forgotten to add a pinch of salt.

"You still have a lot to learn, my little Louis."

She ate fifteen almond biscuits.

"Nora and Leon don't talk to each other anymore. They put on a dumb show instead. It upsets Nora, she needs conversation. It's all Vervaecke's fault, the postman, you remember him, don't you? He still moans every day about failing his examination in the Great Seminary in Roeselare, and according to your Grandpa he made a point of marrying the sister of the woman he loved because, your Grandpa said, he didn't want to give in to his carnal desires, and that sister was as ugly as sin and sickly to boot, she kept spitting gall as green as that cucumber over there. Well, I say *was,* but she's still alive. If you can call that living."

"It was all Vervaecke's fault?" said Louis.

"Yes. That halfwit Vervaecke calls while Nora is out shopping in the Sarma. And he takes a bankbook out of his postman's bag. '*Tiens,*' says Leon, 'what's that?' 'Ah, that's your wife's savings book,' says that bonehead. So that's how Leon learned his wife was saving money behind his

584

back. Which is against the law, because the head of the family is the only one allowed to save."

"Maybe she's saving up for his funeral, in case something happens to him."

"Our Nora?" roared Grandma, but her flareup subsided immediately, a passing summer cloud. "No, it was for a new fireplace, four thousand francs' worth, slate, antique Flemish style. She'd seen it in some lawyer's house. 'I've been looking at my old fireplace now for twenty years,' she says, 'and that's too long.' And she wanted a new chandelier, too, with turned brown arms, cartwheel type, also in medieval style. 'A chandelier,' she says, 'you can look at for five or six years at the most.' "

"And it's because of that savings book that they haven't been speaking to each other?"

"Oh no, Louis, that's just the *hors d'oeuvre* of the whole story.

"You know that Leon makes beautiful landscapes and still lifes by sticking little strips of wood together in all different shapes and colors. He learned how to do that in Germany. First it was watercolors, now it's wood. The sky, say, in cherry wood, the Leie in mottled teak. Magnificent. Now, there's a lady up the road, I'll call her Madame X because you're a blabbermouth, and she orders a picture in wood collage from Leon and gives him a photograph to copy, a view of St. Bernard's Tower with a corner of Friars Street, because her parents used to run a children's clothing shop there. Leon, who wants to earn a bit on the side, makes it for her, and it turns out to be a masterpiece, the Dean himself wants one for his drawing room. *Bon.* Madame X, a good-looking woman by the way, says, 'Leon, please would you bring that masterpiece of yours around next Wednesday evening at nine o'clock, it's a surprise birthday present for my husband, and he'll be out playing cards just then. I'll leave the front door on the latch because I may be out in the garden.' "

"In the garden at nine o'clock at night, Grandma?"

"Wait, you haven't heard the rest yet."

"And that lady said, 'Bring that masterpiece of yours'? But she hadn't even seen it!"

"Look, who's telling the story, you or me? Just listen. Leon arrives, he finds the door on the latch, he goes inside, there's a light on in the hall. He calls, 'Is anybody in?' 'Oh, Leon,' she calls down from upstairs, 'do go into the drawing room and take a seat. There's cognac and Cointreau.'

"In the drawing room Leon looks around to see where his picture would look best. And then she comes in, in her peignoir. 'Martha,' says Leon, 'I've brought you my work of art.' 'Oh, just put it down over there on that chair,' she says. He puts it down on the chair, and she opens her peignoir and underneath, Louis, she is stark naked, and then she goes and lies down on the divan.

" 'But, but, but, but,' says Leon, 'I've come here with my picture and I really don't have time for that sort of thing!' 'No time,' she says, 'how can that be?' 'Martha,' says Leon, 'I must tell you straight out, I'd rather not get involved with anybody from the neighborhood, that sort of thing only ends in tears.' 'Oh,' she says, 'Leon, supposing I lived somewhere else, let's say in St. Ignatius's Lane, would it be all right then?' 'I'd have to think about it,' says Leon, and she, Madame X that is, starts to sob and to wail, 'Leon, Leon, Leon!' "

Face contorted, Grandma uttered a monstrous peacock screech, the drowsy street outside woke up.

" 'Leon, Leon, Leon. My husband hasn't come near me these past six weeks, he sleeps alone because he's about to take his exams as a construction engineer, and your wife Nora, my best friend, told me that you used to be the biggest womanizer in the district, and Leon, Leon, Leon, I didn't know what to do, I just thought to myself, If that's how the land lies, I can't do any better than to ask Leon.' "

She gave a deep sigh, his ponderous grandmother, her young-girl's-eyes glistening with the lewd truth, her lips in their web of puckered corners drawn up in a smirk at the strange antics of the human race. And in a kind of song to ward off death. A different song from Vlieghe's with his blood-stained banjo in his arms.

"I know who Madame X is, Grandma."

"You do?"

"Martha Kerskens, who used to live across the road from us and moved to the Zwevegem district."

"What put that idea into your head?"

"You said 'Martha' yourself."

"Martha? No, I never said the name."

"And her husband was studying engineering back then, too."

"No, it's someone else entirely," said Grandma. "Unless you heard it from Mona."

"I haven't seen Aunt Mona for ages."

"That's just as well. She's sitting on a whole pile of shares her father left her. But she won't let anyone touch them. 'I must carry out his last will and testament,' she says. 'I'd like nothing better than to bring them out right now and divide them among you and my brothers and my sisters, but what would be left over then after the lawyer's commission, the inheritance tax and this and that, not to mention the expenses? So I'd better keep them in my strongbox.' I say, 'Yes, you do that, Mona, and just keep on drawing the interest from the bank every month, too.' 'Just six months,' she says, 'then no more objections can be registered by anyone else who's after a slice of the cake.'

"Who she meant, of course, was Antoinette Passchiers. But what that actually means is I'm going to have to receive Mona here, under my own roof, for at least another six months."

Aunt Hélène came back with two bulging bags. Louis helped her to clean and cut up the vegetables, the turnips, the carrots, the celery, the white of the leeks, the green cabbage. Grandma peeled the potatoes. There was beef, scrag end of veal, shoulder of mutton, smelt, a pig's tail, and lean salted bacon. "Not the kind of hotchpotch your mother makes, Louis, that wishy-washy stuff from her part of the world. I don't call that stuff hotchpotch, I call it soup or *pot-au-feu*. When you stick a fork in a real hotchpotch it stands up. You should have come tomorrow instead, Louis, it'll be even better then. Just like us when we've put in a good night's sleep on all our troubles." Louis said he had to go, to visit the churchyard.

"That grave won't run away," said Grandma, chuckling. "Nor the fellow who's in it."

Suddenly she was enveloped in an air of deep mourning.

"Here I am preparing this huge hotchpotch, and who is it for? Tomorrow Hélène will take some around to Nora, that's all. She doesn't like it herself all that much, I wouldn't let Mona have any unless it had rat poison in it, Robert has given up eating meat, and that snob Monique thinks hotchpotch is only for the hoi polloi. And now you're running off as well, Louis. I'll just have to imagine that our Florent is sitting opposite me at the table tonight. And there he is lying over there in English soil. Every day when I climb out of my bed I look at the little picture on his obituary notice. 'Christian Soul, Come unto Jesus in His most Holy Sacrament, He is Your Sacrificial Lamb.'

"And every time something gets burned in the kitchen, I think of him, of our Florent."

Louis got out at Brussels South station, into the penetrating aroma of chocolate. The driver was reading *Le Soir* in the first taxi at the stand, the smallest car, but when he saw Louis the country bumpkin, he spoke to him in Brussels Flemish and made him sit in the front. Mortification appeases the gods, so Louis sat confined, knees drawn up, elbow jammed against the door. *"Born loser,"* said Jay-Dee. *"No,* Jay-Dee." Jay-Dee, who had also disappeared into the maze that was Europe. Or was back in

America by now. Married or about to get married to a psychiatrist, according to Gene. Should have left me *Harmonium.* The memory of the *blackbird* was fading already. Blackbird, bye-bye.

The driver kept up a steady mutter: ". . . oh no you don't, you haven't got the right of way, no, Mister Bus Driver, no, I really should have taken the Rue Agneessens, Madame wants to get past, out of the way, you silly old bag, the Arenberg and then the Rue Saint Jacques, Boulevard Jacqmain, *voilà,* that was pretty quick after all."

All the lights in the immense building were on at four o'clock, on a sunny day. A girl behind plate glass said that classified advertisements must be handed in at the next counter, but that it was closed. "A competition? What competition?"

"For the best story about the war or about something indirectly to do with the war, the closing date is the day after tomorrow, so I . . ."

"André, do you know anything about a competition?"

"You mean Miss Belgium?"

"For a story about the war."

"Or a short story," said Louis.

"A story?" Sprawled behind his desk, André telephoned, nodded six or seven times as he inspected Louis. "First floor."

"That's what I thought," said the girl.

With a thumping heart, Louis waited in a stuffy little room opposite the plaster bust of a Flemish Mind with beard and lavaliere, painted forest-green. A man in a bow tie said that he was the secretary of the jury, what could he do for Louis? "I've come to hand in my story." (My text, stapled, numbered, my life's work, heart's blood, my orphan. Mama paid a lot of money to an ex-captain of the Black Brigade to have it typed in triplicate. "What did you think of it?" "When I type, I don't read." "No, but what was your general impression?" "It's not my sort of thing.")

"The Sorrow, by Louis Seynaeve," the man read in a deep bass voice as if announcing a play on the radio. "But, my boy, what in the world were you thinking of? This is completely against the rules."

"The date . . ." (Mama has thrown away the little strip of paper, the newspaper clipping with the rules. But I remember the date. And the address of *Het Laatste Nieuws.* And that there had to be three typed copies.)

"Your name is on it! That's not allowed!"

"It's not my name," said Louis. "It's my brother's name."

"Can't your brother read the rules, then? Every entry has to be sent in by post. The postmark is proof of the date of delivery. *We're* not the ones who thought up the rules. And now you bring this in here with the author's name on it, your brother's name, when the only inscription should be a motto. We're not allowed to know the author's identity, otherwise we could be accused of bias. I've never heard of such a thing."

Louis's heart hammered, slammed against the hollow of his chest. I am going to have a heart attack.

"The author," he said, "couldn't read the rules, because he is dead."

The secretary indicated an old leather chair with copper studs. He sat down himself. "That does pose a problem."

"My brother died in a concentration camp," said Louis. "He was an intellectual working for the Underground, and he never tasted the fruits of his clandestine labors."

"Is this entry about his experiences?"

"His own experiences, yes, of course."

"*Het Laatste Nieuws* would certainly be interested in that."

"It doesn't deal directly with the concentration camp. It's rather . . ."

"Which concentration camp?"

". . . symbolic. Uh, Neuengamme." (I'll be struck down for that. Till the blood runs. Terminal cancer. Starting with the intestines. Then it spreads all over.)

"It's a good subject. The Belgian people are going to have to learn the facts. From the source."

"He handed me the text before he was taken away. In a cattle truck. 'Take good care of it, Louis,' he said."

"I thought *his* name was Louis."

"He asked me to adopt his name. So as to save his life's work after his death, to continue it. My real name is Maurice."

"We ought to be able to find a way around this. As secretary of the jury, I naturally do not have a vote myself. In a sense, therefore, I cannot be biased. I think I can take it upon myself to say that the manuscript arrived by post."

He weighed the envelope in the palm of his hand. "About twenty francs. Drop the envelope in the box around the corner right away, then it will get here tomorrow and be within the rules. No one will be the wiser. I would gladly pay for the stamps out of my own pocket. A Resistance fighter should have as much chance as everyone else, if not more so, but I also have to watch the household budget at the end of the month. I have three daughters, and that makes a hole in your pocket."

"Thank you, mijnheer."

"Presumably it's full of horrific details?"

"It's more about his youth."

"*The Sorrow,* that's a good title. On the other hand . . . It's a bit lacking in something. It's so . . . so . . . bald. Everyone has some sorrow. Why don't you call it *The Sorrow of the Fatherland?* I often write the titles for our house organ here, and . . ."

"I don't know if my brother would approve."

"Or just simply *The Sorrow of Belgium* . . . Has a nice ring to it. If you win the prize under that title, you can always think of me, just a small commission." It was a joke. It was no joke.

"I was thinking of giving the money to Louis's mother," said Louis. "She's saving up for a memorial tablet."

"Of course," said the secretary. "Good heavens! The motto. Think of a motto. To be repeated in the letter giving your *curriculum vitae.*"

"*Levet Scone,*" said Louis.

"Out of the question. Too Flamingant. This really isn't the moment for such medieval ideas. Gersaint van Koekelare, our chairman, wouldn't even give it a second glance. Not that he looks at any of the manuscripts. But he would vote against anything that smells of Flamingantism, even remotely, with his eyes shut. Not that he can see all that well with them open. But in case of a tie, he has a casting vote."

"*Kol nidrei,*" said Louis. The wailing wall in Jerusalem groaned from one end to the other.

"Is that Greek?"

"Hebrew."

"Of course, of course. The name Seynaeve had me confused. Seynaeve, Sneyssens, it sounds so Flemish. Of course. That also explains his work in the Resistance. You Jews were in the front line against the Nazis. To think that didn't occur to me right away! Do excuse me."

"You didn't notice this?" asked Louis and showed the man his battered West Flemish profile, the same as Papa's and Grandpa's.

"Now that you mention it. I mean, now that you're pointing it out. What was that motto again? Kool nitree? I'll have to remember that during the jury's deliberation."

Louis spelled it out, letter by letter, and felt nauseated by the boy who, years ago, had been humiliated in class by the claim of Daels, the Dutch teacher, that he hadn't written his composition about spring in the city himself, and who was now taking his vile revenge. But that didn't stop him from posting the envelope complete with motto, and the accompanying letter, complete with motto, in the box around the corner.

Uncle Omer was standing with legs wide apart against an apple tree and rubbing his belly against the trunk. Although no one else was at home, Louis ran over to his uncle.

"Don't do that, Uncle!"

"Why not?" (Why, why not, the stupidest of all questions.)

"Your mother will see you."

The jerking stopped. A hollow silence. Louis took the warm, trembling hand in his and led Uncle Omer toward the house. Uncle Omer imitated a biplane, with put-put-put noises and sweeping arms, then all of a sudden he uttered a yelping little cry, scampered into the garage, and locked the door. Uncle Armand came riding past the dahlias on his motorbike. He took off his goggles, their imprint remaining on his face. He put his finger to his lips, approached the garage on tiptoe, peered through the filthy little window with solicitous curiosity. Louis, by his side, saw that Uncle Omer had crawled under four or five English army blankets, leaving his legs sticking out. His bare calves under the rucked up trouser legs looked vulnerable, lily-white.

"Look at that," whispered Uncle Armand, "will you just look at that." He dusted the chalk from his shoulders and made for the scullery. Louis said that the women had gone to the dressmaker's. Uncle Armand looked in the kitchen dresser, a son alone in the maternal home, found some *speculaas*, ate a few with his long, yellowish teeth.

A monotonous wailing sounded from the garage, it lasted longer than usual, perhaps because Uncle Omer was waiting for the familiar accompaniment of Hector, who had been eaten, one half going to Papa.

"We'll have to find Uncle Omer a woman," said Uncle Armand. "Perhaps one of those three from the Sirocco. But I haven't got any money. I could take him to the Sirocco on the back of my bike, round about three o'clock, say, if there isn't much else going on. It would help calm him down."

"Or the opposite."

"You're right there, Louis. Anyway, I don't have the money."

Uncle Armand gave off creaking sounds. There was brown paper against his bare chest. He had caught something to do with his lungs in prison.

"The opposite," he said. "You're right. Why can we never get it into our heads that we'd all be better off pulling our wire or sticking our pricks in a milkbottle?"

Papa and Louis were pitching a small lead disc at a cork on which lay several one-franc coins. The coins flew upward, Papa gave a Tarzan yell. Mama called down from her bedroom window, "Finished yet, you big baby?"

"She means you," said Papa.

"Moron," said Louis. They went indoors.

"When I get back to Walle, I'll organize a whole recital evening of Flemish poems for the dead. Marnix de Puydt can play the piano accompaniment. In honor of my comrade Serruys, who has died from a sort of typhus from being interned in the Flandria. I just heard it this morning."

"Who was Serruys?"

"The man who used to play Wanten on the radio, an engineer. Pharmacist Paelinck will have to brush up his act and play Dalle again. Poems by Guido Gezelle, Cyriel Verschaeve, Rodenbach, and in between for a bit of comic relief, like in the old days, a few Wanten and Dalle jokes."

"But who's going to play Wanten?"

"Me, of course," said Papa. "I know that repertoire inside out. And I'm a quick learner."

"Come and eat," bellowed Aunt Violet.

"What about us going together to Argentina? The Byttebiers have a timber business over there. You earn more than enough as a simple warehouseman there to make a living. And life is very cheap. All that meat straight off the pampas."

"And what about Mama?"

"She could come, too," said Papa, hesitating. "If you insist."

Uncle Robert has stopped eating meat. He can't stand the sight or the smell of it any longer. And he isn't allowed to eat too many eggs or too much chocolate, either, on account of his liver, which is the hardest to repair of all human organs.

"A small cigar, Louis? Go on, you're wearing your knickerbockers, you'll be all right if you get the runs. They're strong little cigars, but they don't make you cough."

Lion of Flanders cigars, just the brand for the Blacks.

"Your Uncle Robert," says Aunt Mona, "doesn't know what to do with his money. Minister Gutt hasn't been able to lay his hands on it, Robert saw him coming and put all his money into houses and land. Under different names, of course. But the best thing is that, in strictest secrecy, he had a mirror fitted to the ceiling of his Louis XVI bedroom, you understand, Louis, to see what they're like together, you catch my drift. *Bon*, the first night they lie down, Robert and his dried-up herring of a Monique, and it's only then that it dawns on them that in point of fact they both wear spectacles and that while they're, while they're at it, you get my meaning, they'd have to keep their spectacles on if they wanted to see anything. I nearly wet myself!"

"Your Aunt Mona," says Uncle Robert, "may have diddled Father out of his last few cents, but I still feel sorry for her, seeing what she has coming with her Cecile. What, you don't know? Cecile is in the family way. Fifteen and knocked up by a *danseur,* sixteen years old. The youngest parents in all Belgium. Monique and I, we were in stitches, because it happened after a performance by the Flemish Ballet in the Municipal Theater, the boy comes from around Denderleeuw and he walked her back home, so to speak, necking and petting all the way until they got to the Gendarmerie, and that's where it happened, up against the Gendarmerie wall, standing up. I say, 'Mona, they couldn't have chosen a better place, because it's just across the street from the maternity clinic.' We split our sides, Monique and I did."

"There's just one thing that worries me," says Aunt Mona, "and that is if that child gets my narrow ankles and neck, I've had trouble from them all my life. But as for the rest, let Robert laugh all he wants."

"Oh, it's very modern, Mona. The young start early these days."

"And Romeo and Juliet, how old were they? Also fifteen."

"I'm going to rent out Father's room to the young couple, that way everyone will be satisfied. And anyone who isn't, well, they can just go take a running jump."

"We'll be hearing any day now that our Louis is also thinking of walking out with someone, eh, Louis?"

"Our Louis is not very keen on women," said Mama, silkily and bitterly, her long fingers with the scarlet-lacquered nails lying in her barren lap wherein once, perforce, I rocked and floated.

"You had just been born, Louis," said Aunt Violet, "I came to see your mother. I was seasick from the train journey. Your Mama had had an injection and was only just waking up, she opens her eyes and sees me, and she says, 'Good grief, Violet, what in the world is that you're wearing?' And I had bought that outfit specially to visit the maternity home, it was charleston-style with a short jacket, washable, it went well with my crushed velvet. 'But, Violet,' she cries, 'you don't have the figure for flounces.' And from that day to this I have never, ever worn flounces again."

"We had to take Uncle Omer back again to the Brothers of Charity. But they didn't have any room. He's in St. Bernard's Abbey now. It couldn't go on like that. The neighbors were complaining about that yowling for Berenice every night. And he would sit all day long, jabbing knitting needles into himself. He's allowed to work in the monastery garden. It's no ordinary abbey, St. Bernard's. The former Prime Minister of China is there as well. Yes, in a habit. No, not as a patient, of course not, a Prime Minister. He used to be married to a Belgian. Wasn't she a Countess Kervijn de Roozebeke? His name was Fu, or Tu, I can't remember anymore, and now he is Petrus-Celestinus, and the novices are very fond of him because he can tell them a lot about Oriental things. They have an entirely different sort of skull from ours. But a charming man. Yes, I talked to him in the parlor while Omer was being given a bath, because when there are visitors they always get a good scrub first. We talked about Church affairs. He knows everything there is to know about the Vatican, Fu. Or Tu. That's what you get with converts, they're much more fanatical than we are. We had a good laugh, too. Because he said that Pope Leo the Umpteenth used to preach all the time against the sin of gaming and he played chess himself for nights on end. And Pope Pius, I think it was Pius IX, was a first-rate billiards player."

"And for ten francs or so, she would let her pussy show." Bekka in the clay pits.

"Hey-baba-hey-ba-ba." Helen Humes on the American Forces Network. Cancer in her voice.

Papa wants to start a new, a brand-new, printing shop. In Leupegem. Mama is against it. "I'm not going to bury myself in Leupegem, Staf." "You'd prefer to stay in the Great Metropolis of Bastegem?" "My brothers and sisters are here." "And your mother." "What about my mother?" "A real shrew, that's what about her."
"Why?"
"Because."

Papa walks in, burnt by the Blankenberge sun. He had ab-so-lute-ly had to see the sea. His own little sea.
"I am burnt to a crisp, Constance."
"Put some margarine on."
"I've brought back some crab claws, couldn't be fresher."
"I'm not going to do any cooking tonight. And leave me alone. I'm listening to the radio."
"But they're cooked already. They're meant to be eaten cold, with mayonnaise." (Mayonnaise, which curdles with an almost inaudible hiss when the vapors flow out of her, from out of her pussy.)
(All right, then, with vinaigrette. Finely chopped parsley and chives.

594

Where are the scissors? In Dirty Dick's eye. They are as steady as a rock there, those scissors made of Solingen steel.)

Papa hits the crab claws with a hammer on the kitchen table. They shall yield up the last fibers of their flesh, the crabs, their last ounce of connective tissue.

"Staf, will you stop it, please!"

Because, oh dear, Mama's having trouble hearing the radio.

"Get some other station, Constance."

"I can't, Violet, not at this hour."

You will never hear the German woman on the radio stop for breath, gasp for breath, hiccup, never: *"Kreis Donaueschingen, Haus, Habermann, Hahlen, Heber, Heck, Oberleutnant Herbst, Heussler, Hieber, Hirsch . . .*

"In einer Nacht im Monat Januar des Jahres 1942, ich wiederhole. Am dritten September 1940 . . .

In the kitchen Papa laid the crab claws on a towel folded three times, put the towel on the kitchen floor, and hit it more softly, too softly for the shells but too loudly for her, who shouts, "Haven't you finished yet? Haven't you finished yet?"

At the M of Mahler, Maschler, Mattheus, she comes in with her own smell of the sea. And grumbles about the smell of the crabs.

And about her just-washed floor! And the shells! What are we going to do with the shells? (Smash them up, crush them like human bones after an overhasty cremation, after which the ashes are strewn like fertilizer over the fields around the toy factories.)

"Try some, Constance! They're as fresh as they come!"

"No, thank you."

Papa eats the crabmeat too quickly, in too much of a Seynaeve hurry, always dodging the reaper's scythe. And too much food, mouthful after mouthful, swallowing and grinding without pause, and the German woman on the radio does not pause, either, Mama alone is one long, interminable pause. And Papa, roly-poly with crabmeat, stands belching and puffing on the veranda.

"A simple little house. If need be with a thatched roof," he says. "In a parish like Leupegem you can still find that sort of thing. And do it up yourself. Evenings beside the Mechlin stove with a good book or listening to the blackbirds."

Aunt Violet switches over to the American Forces Network. It doesn't matter. The alphabet of war casualties will be continued tomorrow, same time.

Not a word about the maggots inside Madame Laura in that cellar of quinces. And yet weren't they audible? Little eggs, larvae. If it was hot in the quince cellar, it would only take them a day to hatch. The eggs are usually laid during the day, in the sunlight. The maggots gorge themselves greedily, making more haste than generations of Seynaeves.

The secretary of the jury says: "A contemptible maneuver, utterly contemptible. We are at a loss for words. There are spheres that one does not, that one never . . .

"In a word, the jury and I have found your mode of procedure unworthy. But, then, you are still young, and for that reason . . .

"Putting to one side the morality of it all, the slate will be considered wiped clean.

"When all is said and done, it concerns . . .

"It is, to be sure, interesting enough to . . .

"But too long, much, much too long, good heavens, it's a . . .

"One would call this a novel these days, yes, indeed.

"All the same, too convoluted for our ordinary . . .

"And too crude as well. Our average reader . . .

"You will be . . . Mijnheer Johan Vergijsen of *Mercurius* will . . . Yes, the journal *Mercurius.*"

Le jour de gloire est arrivé. I left to catch the train. The lover of bulls, Iwein-the-Cow, brandished a pitchfork and called "dirty Black" after me.

No juniors in sight at the station. *"Juniores,"* Morrens calls them.

And then the *omen.* Ominously the guard blew his whistle. He gave the signal to the engine driver to pull out just as Woman-in-Turban was still struggling to get off, was in the process of getting off, and she fell onto the gravel, then rose to her astonished fat knees by hoisting herself up on the suspenders of Stationmaster Bakels, who embraced her. Woman-in-Turban, recovering her composure, struck him. The guard lost his cap and complained that he had already waited the regulation time, that is to say fifty seconds.

Had myself shaved, for the first time in my early-to-ripen-early-to-rot life.

My nose was squeezed between strong fingers.

Jay-Dee: "If you want to take it easy for the rest of your life and never to have to shave, you've got to singe the first hairs of your beard." Had he been joking or not?

(Dalle, shrilly: "What is the height of patriotism, Wanten?"

Wanten, ponderously: "Search me."

Dalle, the Fury: "Plopping a yellow turd from a red backside on a black stone!")

("What is the height of Flemish nationalism?"

"Search me."

"Starving to death with a loaf of French bread under your arm.")

You could never tell with Jay-Dee whether it was a joke. Blue gangster's-cheeks. Gray cheeks that time Papa had offered his apologies.

Lathered up, I wanted to sneeze all the time but quelled my body with its rebellious glands. Dropped behind the lines by Harry the Hopeless Pilot, I was stuck in the mud of the Leie up to my nose. SS *Leibstandarte* tanks were rolling past. A sneeze would be fatal.

And so my body did not sneeze.

" 'Nkyew. A little further back. *Merci,* 'nkyew. A little to the side. 'Nkyew."

Gave the barber a twenty-five percent tip. He didn't bat an eye.

Johan Vergijsen of *Mercurius* was sipping port. "Did you ever read my *Waiting for Gwendolyn?* Or have a look at it?"

"Some time ago."

"Indeed. Some time ago? In nursery school, I take it."

"No. At College."

"*At* College? In the College library?"

"What I meant was, when I was going to College."

"Had you started writing by then?"

"Verse."

"Well. Well, well. A Flemish Rimbaud."

"Hands off Rimbaud!" The diners in the Canterbury restaurant, some with their napkins tied under their chins, others with giant lobsters printed on the lobster aprons stretched across their paunches, looked up quickly. A man like a military policeman, in a tailcoat with a golden chain around his neck, drew himself up, outraged. Johan Vergijsen, ambassador of the cultural journal *Mercurius,* looked as if he wanted to crawl under the table.

"At the Embassy," he said rapidly so as to stifle any fresh war cries, "I received a five-pound tin of caviar from Gromyko. In my capacity as President of the PEN Club." And to thwart any further uproar, he whispered, "I don't like caviar, but if you do, my apartment is a ten-minute walk away. No, I really don't like it, I'm the same with champagne, no, give me cider any day. Or take oysters, no, I'd rather have mussels every time.

"Now then, the *Mercurius* editorial board has decided, er, that is to say, the editorial board of *Mercurius* is proposing, to take your work. But forgive us our reservations. Can you read English? Yes? As I thought.

"Well, some of us have been of the opinion . . . *Not* yours truly, of

597

course. And *not* our chairman, because he has an incredibly sensitive nose . . .

"But so much is being published, dear boy, so very much! In particular for the troops, is it not? Those Signets, Zephyrs, Penguins, Coronets. It would be quite easy, wouldn't it, to lift a passage, indeed a whole book? The most erudite among us may be easily taken in.

"But I have a good nose for such things myself. And now that I've met you . . ."

Theo van Paemel's leg is nearly useless now. Festering osteomyelitis. "It's simple, Louis, a great deal of pus collects in the medullary cavity and under the periosteum, and the leg is kaput, done for, it's really quite simple.

"I can't go hunting anymore. Neither for beast nor for man. I'm not all that bothered. Things come and things go. I still have a few good years left. And it does me good to move from one sector or another. They've put me in Culture. Yes, Louis, adviser at the Ministry of Education, Cultural Division. I've always been one for the fine arts, you know me. And culture, that's a very broad concept.

"Incidentally, tell your father not to sneak into meetings of the Joost van den Vondel Circle any longer, there are more of our crowd there than he thinks. It's not the right time, now that Moscow is stirring."

Arrived at a bucolic little railway station. Waited.

Read the paper in the slow train. Read: "danger of gas," "gas filters," "the gas balance." Smelled gas. Tasted gas.

The yellow star-of-Bethlehem is a flower.

Waited ten minutes, during which a girl of sixteen or so jumped without pause across a ditch, left to right, right to left, each time landing with her two feet flat on the ground. Then Claessens came driving up in a 1939 white Mercedes with black leather seats.

"Claessens, Julien. I've come in place of Arnold Parmentier, he sends you his most cordial greetings. He is the most cordial man in the world, but when *Mercurius* is having one of its Days, Arnold takes off in a cloud of dust. Off to his sailing club. Then I have to do the honors. I've read the proof of your contribution. Very promising."

Mercurius and Omer Bossuyt have their Good Days and their Bad Days.

Diarrhea. Like a fifty-year-old, I climb the stone steps of the staircase leading to The Days of *Mercurius*. Parmentier's house, says Claessens as I clench my buttocks, conquer my heaving, am besieged by peasants in 1502.

A jovial mare, Mevrouw Parmentier, with the horsey face of one who rides horses every day. Johan Vergijsen at her side. La Parmentière whinnies.

"Extremely pleased to see new blood in *Mercurius.*" (Not *my* blood, *poupoule!*)

Shaking hands with Flemish Minds. Gut-gripes, iron will. During the *apéritif maison,* tribute to Arnold Parmentier, who every year places his house, his museum, his country estate, at the disposal of The Days of *Mercurius,* Parmentier the Maecenas, even in wartime leaping fearlessly into the breach of our culture, alas detained today for family reasons.

Everybody on the terrace for the group photograph, yes, the young Seynaeve, the Benjamin, right in front. Crouching!

The St. Meropius brass band sounds a fanfare. Three girls dressed as shrimpers sing, "Love daily brings me here to pine / To spread my net outside your door / My heart with yours to intertwine / Enraptured evermore."

Find the right place immediately down a corridor. Bliss. A lackey stands waiting outside the door, shows me to my place, to the left of Mevrouw Fernandel Parmentier.

Speech by someone with white handlebar mustache and white side-whiskers and measles, *Mercurius* in person, founder and chairman and author of *The Valley of the Displaced.* Concerning the inner resistance of the Flemish intelligentsia, the sacrifice of the many, the shame of the few. But the spirit had, as ever, proved victorious.

Total victory conjures up misfortune.

"No, Louis, wine is not drunk with asparagus. It spoils the . . ."

"Mevrouw."

"Yes, *cher auteur.*"

"Did we ever meet in the Picardy?"

"I don't believe . . . no . . . I know the Aisne fairly well . . . Chateau-Thierry, Soissons . . ."

"Mevrouw, did we meet at any time in the Picardy?"

"No."

"Then please don't call me by my first name."

". . ."

"And, mevrouw, one does drink wine with asparagus, but only *champagne nature.*"

The horse teeth extracted from the skulls by the two apprentice butchers in Uncle Robert's house following a sulfurous night in Walle had been restored to their niche in her equine face. She beckoned.

"Fernand. Fetch me the *Coteaux de Champagne de Moët,* quickly."

599

The lackey went and returned. The mount by my side neighed.

The Flemish Minds with texts published in *South and North*, *The Golden Lyre*, *Flemish Abundance*, *The Silver Flute*, and *Aurora* gaped, stared, whispered, swallowed.

"Mevrouw."

"Yes, Mijnheer Seynaeve."

He spoke and said, turning in his saddle, "May I make so bold as to compliment you on your exquisite dinner service?"

"Indeed you may. Certainly. It is. My husband. Made off with it, captured it I should say. When he was in the Piron Brigade, fighting to the bitter end against the *Volkssturm*. It's not complete, but even so. Perhaps. The most complete *Bückelburgerbauer* service in existence."

In the salon she never strayed from my side, even while floating, clutching at, flitting among the reddening-faced guests, the *connoisseurs*.

"The trouble, my dear fellow, is that our authors are downright ig-no-rant of the exact sciences. Thus I am convinced that the excellent Van-hool, my very good friend in the *Académie* and the author of per-fect ballads, doesn't even know what a prime number is."

"What is so particularly well done is Louis's anal phase."

"I, too, have a son who writes. He started even younger than you. I believe I have something of his in my wallet, from when he was twelve . . ."

"The use of commas is somewhat bizarre too, at times. A comma is surely for taking breath . . ."

"But when he was seventeen, he stopped. It caused me a lot of sorrow, the sorrow of Belgium, hahaha."

"And the hyperbole, my dear fellow! Altogether too lavish. And too far-fetched. I made a note, wait a minute, yes, on page 162, for instance, 'the spyglass of love,' on page three hundred and something 'The forest of longing'. Come now, I ask you."

"The comma, *la virgule*, is not derived from *virgo*, maiden, but from *virgula*, rod or staff."

"As you know, there are no prime numbers in Euclid."

"No, no, and no to your view of history. The ideal history of a people must also include its dreams. No."

"But, Karel, history is the memory of a people. You have only to distort that memory and . . ."

"I've had a cough now for a whole week. I took some syrup, and it did absolutely no good at all. That syrup of Paelinck's, which tastes of chartreuse."

"But Paelinck's syrup is a pick-me-up!"

"I had a good laugh when those youngsters got hold of that other one by the rear end, that part with the knucklebone. I did something similar myself once, I believe it was in '26, I was at the College then, and . . ."

"I was never *frightened* during the Occupation. Not even when I was mentioned under my full name in the *Brüsseler Zeitung.*"

"Marcel, are you coming to Siam? With the PEN Club? To see if it's true what they say about Chinese women? You're surely not going to bring your wife along again, are you?"

"I must say, I prefer to take my own chow along. I prefer to eat from a proper plate."

"That new fellow at the Ministry seems to be a hard worker. Van Haemel, Van Maele, Van Paemel, something like that."

"It's autobiographical, of course. You can tell. It's got the ring of truth. When I was at St. Armand's College, I, too, I freely admit, I, too, was attracted by . . ."

I spotted him in a Venetian rococo mirror. His head was half the size of mine.

I beckoned him. With a crooked forefinger like a little meathook. He was thickset, with light-brown hair, a fleshy nose, narrow mouth, and red-rimmed eyes. He came. I was drunk and not drunk at all.

"What are you looking at me like that for? Have I turned black?"

"No," he said petulantly.

"What are you doing here?"

"I have to be on hand for my uncle, in case he needs anything."

"Who is your uncle?"

"Julien Claessens."

"That stallion of Mary Mare Maria Parmentier's?"

My tongue was saturated, floundering.

"What will you do with the money?" he asked.

"What money?"

"The money *Mercurius* will pay you for publishing your novel."

"It's a short story."

"*Kaas* by Elsschot is shorter. And you get eighty francs a page."

He cleaned the plate. Cake, almond biscuits, ginger snaps, little pieces of nougat, pralines. Then the sugar crumbs around the copper coffee pot.

"It's unfair."

"What is?"

"That they'll never print anything of mine in *Mercurius*. And I'm a year older than you."

"Why wouldn't they print anything of yours?"

"Because I am a poet for our times."

I clapped my hands. The Parmentier Museum lowered its lights and muffled its sounds.

"Brothers! I have the honor of presenting a poet for our times."

He did not start, did not blush, did not mess his pants like someone I know. He turned to all sides and bowed. He brought out a large, very recently folded sheet of paper, and read with an unmodulated Kortrijk that which I now transcribe:

> *Blessed is the strangler of the nightingale, blessed are all*
> *female mammals, the coelenterates and the tributary rivers,*
> *the nits and Zwevegem.*
> *Blessed are the indispensable needs and the tides*
> *and the gas-filled skins and the amber flies.*
> *Blessed are they who have been weaned from the mire*
> *and they who do not know things as they are*
> *but only as they appear to be.*
> *Blessed is the plant and Tarzan who hangs from the plant.*
> *Blessed be I.*

He bowed to the scattered applause. He handed me the sheet of paper. "Don't lose it."

The Flemish Minds gabbled softly together, then one of them called out, "Blessed are the hawthorn and the rhino's horn."

Claessens, his uncle, said, without looking at his nephew, "Mijnheer Seynaeve, as soon as you'd like to be taken home, I'm at your disposal."

"You won't miss much," said the nephew. "They're all off to the family chapel and then to the parish hall to elect this year's Maid of Flanders."

"You have only to give me a nod as soon as you . . ." said the uncle, and I said, "Listen, you, up yours."

The nephew walked with me to the little country station.

"It was a fine poem. Bravo."

"I write three of those a day," he said.

"That's quick!"

"It's my technique. I take all the clues from a crossword puzzle and then jumble them together."

He said nothing more. So I said nothing, either. Together we sang *"Tout va très bien, ma-da-me la Marquise,"* the foxtrot by Ray Ventura and his Collegians. We heard the saxophone and the beat of the drum. We saw a gull that limped.

We'll see. We'll see. Anyhow.

glossary

"allee"	"come on," "come," "let's home" (from the French *allez*)
"angenehm"	"pleased to meet you," an old-fashioned phrase in German, no longer used in polite society
Black Brigades	Belgian collaborators with the Germans
Bluefoot	the *Blauwvoet,* the fulmar in English, a symbol of Flemish nationalism since the nineteenth century
"Brabançonne"	the Belgian national anthem.
"dedju"	short for *"nondedju"* (q.v.)
DEVLag	*Deutsch-Vlämische Arbeitsgemeinschaft,* German-Flemish Labor League, pro-German organization in favor of the integration of Flanders into a pan-German state.
Dinaso (Verdinaso)	*Verbond van Diets National Solidaristen,* the League of Dutch-Speaking National Solida-

	rists, a Flemish fascist movement, founded in 1931 by Joris van Severen
"Donnerwetter"	mild oath in German
Einsatzkommando	A detachment of the *Sicherheitspolizei* (the German Security Police) and the SS (q.v.), forming part of an *Einsatzgruppe,* a task force undertaking special missions in occupied territory
ERLA-*Werke*	*Ersatz Lager und Werke*, aircraft spare parts factory and store.
Feldmarschall	Field Marshal in the German Army
Feldwebel	Quartermaster-Sergeant, or Technical Sergeant, in the German Army
Flamingants	general term in Belgium for supporters of the Flemish movement
Flemish National League	synonymous with the VNV (q.v.)
Franskiljons	inhabitants of Flanders, who, despite their Flemish descent, support the use of French as the first language throughout Belgium.
"godverdomme"	a mild oath, equivalent to "goddam it"
Great Netherlands Bluefoot Troop	a Flemish fascist youth group
gueules cassées, les	"the smashed faces," French war veterans with severe facial injuries
Hauptsturmführer	an SS rank, equivalent to Captain
"houzee"	a nineteenth-century pseudoarchaic form of greeting, revived by Flemish fascists during World War II
Hulp Organization	see *Winterhulp*
kerlinne(ke)	junior female member of the *Nationale Jeugdstorm* (see under *Stormer*)
Kinderlandverschickung	organization for the evacuation of children to the (German) countryside
knaap (pl. *knapen*)	junior male member of the *Nationale Jeugdstorm* (see under *Stormer*)
Kommandantur	Command Headquarters
KSA	*Katholieke Studenten Actie*, the Catholic Students' Action movement
"nondedju"	a mild oath (from the French *"nom de Dieu"*)

NSDAP	*Nationalsozialistische Deutsche Arbeiterpartei,* the National Socialist German Workers' Party, the Nazis, founded in Germany in 1919; seized political control under Adolf Hitler in 1933
NSJV	*Nationaal Socialistische Jeugd Vlaanderen,* the National Socialist Youth of Flanders, a Nazi youth movement
NSKK	*Nationalsozialistisch Kraftfahrkorps,* the National Socialist Motor Corps.
Obergruppenführer	SS rank, equivalent to General
Oberleutnant	Lieutenant, or First Lieutenant, in the German Army
Oberst	Colonel in the German Army
Organisation Todt	a semimilitary German government agency set up in 1933 to construct strategic highways and military installations; named after its first chief
Ortsgruppenleiter	a Nazi Party official in charge of part of a town
Propaganda-Abteilung	Propaganda Department
Rex	Belgian Fascist party, founded by Léon Degrelle in 1935, and representing French-speaking Fascism in Belgium; the name came from Christus Rex (Christ the King); became allied with the VNV (q.v.), but lost its popularity, and most of its parliamentary seats, in 1939; Rexists collaborated with the Germans during the war
Scharführer	SS rank, equivalent to Staff Sergeant
Schein (pl. *Scheine*)	a special permit, issued by the Germans
"*Schild en Vriend*"	during the uprising against the French in Bruges in 1302 led by Pieter de Coninck, every man who could not correctly pronounce the Flemish password "*Schild en Vriend*" (Shield and Friend) was put to death; almost every Frenchman was killed
SD	*Sicherheitsdienst,* the SS Security Service formed in 1932, the intelligence organization of the German Nazi Party

Sondergericht	special disciplinary court under the jurisdiction of the SS and the German police
SS	*Schutzstaffel* (literally, the protection or guard detachment), the most powerful paramilitary formation of the German Nazi Party
Standartenführer	SS rank, equivalent to Colonel
Stormer (m.), *Stormster* (f.)	senior member of the *Nationale Jeugdstorm,* the National Youth "Strike Force," a Nazi youth movement in Belgium, affiliated to the NSJV (q.v.)
Untermensch	Nazi term of abuse, meaning "subhuman"
Untersturmführer	SS rank, equivalent to Second Lieutenant
"verdomme"	see *"godverdomme"*
VNV	*Vlaams Nationaal Verbond,* the Flemish National League, a right-wing party founded by Staf de Clercq in 1933, whose original aim was the unity of Flanders with the Netherlands, and later the federal organization of the Belgian State; the VNV collaborated with the Germans during the war
White Brigades	members of the Belgian resistance movement
Winterhulp	an organization (whose name means "Winter Help") founded in the Netherlands to aid the needy; used as a propaganda tool by the NSB (the *Nationaal-Socialistische Beweging,* the Dutch Nazi Party)